Praise for *Summ*

"Simmons writes like a hot-rodding an[...] mare with scares, suspense, and a swe[...] [...]gia. One of those rare must-read books . . . I am in awe of Dan Simmons."
—Stephen King

"An outstandingly eerie and truly horrifying tale, a page-turner of the first order."
—*Dallas Times Herald*

"Impressive . . . combines beautiful writing and suspense into a book for which Dan Simmons deserves the bestseller status of King and Koontz."
—*The Denver Post*

"One can only wonder what Simmons will do next, now that he's shown us he can do everything the best writers in horror and science fiction can do."
—*Philadelphia Inquirer*

"It stands with the best of King and Straub in the traditional modern horror genre. . . . *Summer of Night* is a powerful horror novel, graphic without explicitness, well-written without obvious stylistic tricks. . . . This is a writer who not only makes big promises, but keeps them."
—*Seattle Post-Intelligencer*

"If you like Stephen King's *It* and *The Body*, you will be enthralled by *Summer of Night*."
—*Rocky Mountain News*

"Blood-freezing scenarios . . . the true source of Simmons's terrifying vision lies in his uncanny ability to tap into that primal dread that every child knows and every adult denies; the monster under the bed, the darkness in the closet, the not-quite-human face at the window. . . . If you are easily frightened, don't buy this book."
—*Los Angeles Daily News*

"A superior read in the genre."
—*Kirkus Reviews*

"An outstandingly eerie horror story about a group of Midwestern boys stalked by an ancient evil."
—*Publishers Weekly*

"Simmons, winner of several prestigious awards for science fiction and horror, ranks with the best the genre has to offer. . . . The children are well drawn and affecting in their bravery."
—*Library Journal*

Also by Dan Simmons

Flashback
Black Hills
Drood
The Terror
A Winter Haunting
Children of the Night
Carrion Comfort
Song of Kali

Ilium
Olympos

Hyperion
The Fall of Hyperion
Endymion
The Rise of Endymion

Prayers to Broken Stones
Worlds Enough & Time
Lovedeath

Summer Sketches
Entropy's Bed at Midnight

Phases of Gravity
The Hollow Man
Fires of Eden

Darwin's Blade
The Crook Factory

Hardcase
Hard Freeze
Hard as Nails

DAN SIMMONS

Summer
of
Night

THOMAS DUNNE BOOKS
ST. MARTIN'S GRIFFIN
NEW YORK

This is a work of fiction. All of the characters, organizations, and events portrayed in this novel are either products of the author's imagination or are used fictitiously.

THOMAS DUNNE BOOKS.
An imprint of St. Martin's Press.

www.thomasdunnebooks.com
www.stmartins.com

Library of Congress Cataloging-in-Publication Data

Simmons, Dan.
  Summer of night / Dan Simmons.—1st ed.
      p. cm.
    ISBN 978-0-312-55067-7
  I. Title.
    PS3569.I47292S86 2011
    813'.54—dc22

                          2011013348

First published in the United States by Penguin Putnam

20 19

INTRODUCTION

Since *Summer of Night* was published in 1991, I've received more mail, e-mail, and comments on it than on any of my other novels (except perhaps for *Hyperion*). What fascinates me is that the preponderance of letters are from people around the world who are about my age, who remember a childhood from the era around the summer of 1960 when the novel is set, and who have been moved to say that their childhood memories of freedom are so similar to that of the kid-characters in my novel. And then they lament that their own children and grandchildren lack that freedom. But, I always wonder, how can someone who grew up in France or Russia or Japan or Israel—all sources of these letters of recognition—have had similar childhoods as my American kids in the rural summer of 1960?

Summer of Night, while on the surface a horror novel, is actually a celebration of the secrets and silences of childhood. But it's also a tale of a separate world of childhood that we've lost or may be on the verge of losing. Therein may lie one of the elements that seems to have made this novel accessible to so many people.

But what are some of the other common denominators that have allowed people from around the world to identify so strongly with Mike, Dale, Lawrence (Don't-Call-Me-Larry), Kevin, Harlen, Cordie, and the other kids from *Summer of Night*?

EE-AAW-KEE!

The secret and common element, I believe, is the freedom kids had to inhabit their own worlds in 1960 . . . a freedom for kids to be kids in an active physical universe separate from their parents and other adults but still in the real world, a rich kid-world that, I also sincerely believe, has all but disappeared in the 21st century.

Dale, Lawrence, Mike, Kevin, and Harlen waved good-bye to their mothers (if Jim Harlen's mother was around to wave good-bye to) after breakfast early in the summer morning and, more often than not, were out of sight and on their own until dinnertime or, sometimes, until after dark.

On page 29 of the original hardcover version of *Summer of Night,* I see those five members of the Bike Patrol setting off for their evening "patrol" of their little Illinois town of Elm Haven:

> "Come on," Mike said softly and stood on the pedals, leaning far forward over his handlebars and taking off in a shower of gravel.
>
> Dale and Lawrence and Kevin and Harlen followed.
>
> They rode south down First Avenue in the soft gray light, moving under elm shadow and emerging quickly into the open twilight. The low fields lay open to their left, the dark houses to their right.

Imagine a group of eleven-year-olds going out into the twilight today on bikes, staying out after dark. The TV would be blaring Amber Alerts. Helicopter searchlights would be stabbing down. The parents would be interviewed, blubbering, on the evening news.

Mike, Dale, Lawrence, Kevin, and Harlen might have been scolded when they came riding their bikes home at ten P.M. on a summer evening in Elm Haven—Kevin, with a fussy mother, perhaps scolded and interrogated the most; Harlen, whose mother would probably be out on a date, scolding not at all—but for most of the kids, it wouldn't be a serious scolding.

As the first paragraph of chapter three of *Summer of Night* told us:

> Few events in a human being's life—at least a male human being's life—are as free, as exuberant, as infinitely expansive and filled with potential as the first day of summer when one is an eleven-year-old boy. The summer lies ahead like a great banquet and the days are filled with rich, slow time in which to enjoy each course.

As an elementary-school teacher of eighteen years, I read the proclamations by so many school districts around the country that summer vacation should be abandoned, that kids should attend school year-round, and I feel sick to my stomach.

Of course the three-month summer vacation is an anachronism, something left over from when kids of all ages were unpaid labor for planting and harvest, branding and roundup, on their families' farms and ranches.

Of course kids tend to forget some of what they'd been taught the previous school year when they have more than two months off and return in late August or early September and have to be retaught some concepts.

So what? is my response. What kind of human being in his or her right mind would trade a great banquet of summer days filled with rich slow time in which to enjoy each course—of freedom—for remembering a few more of the multiplication tables?

And, as an elementary teacher of eighteen years, I can testify that those bits and pieces of pedagogical data lost over the summer can be recaptured in a few weeks of teaching the first month of the new school year. (And I can also testify that most of the lost stuff was not really worth learning in the first place.)

But there will always be Dale and Lawrence Stewart's waking-on-the-first-morning-of-summer sense that *"the barrier of the gray school year had been raised and color had been allowed to return to the world."*

Who in his right mind would trade that precious summer infusion of color and kid-freedom for a few lousy social-studies facts or lists of memorized spelling words?

THE CHICKENHOUSE RADIO

The kids in the Bike Patrol liked to gather in Mike O'Rourke's chickenhouse. In the novel, they did so on their first free morning of the summer of 1960.

The place no longer had chickens in it although their smell still remained. Someone had dragged in a sprung and spring-leaking old couch and some spavined armchairs. Someone else, probably Mr. O'Rourke, had stuck the empty shell of a huge old shortwave console radio from the 1930s in one corner of the chickenhouse. While some of the guys, including brilliant and overweight Duane McBride in from his farm, lounge around the chickenhouse on the first day of summer, Jim Harlen crawls behind and then into the shell of the console radio. He imitates the sound of the old radio warming up, static, then—

"He's going back! Back! Back against the right field wall of Comiskey Park! He's jumping for it! He's going up on the wall! He's . . ."

"Aw, nothin' here," muttered Duane. "I'll try the International Band. Dum-da-dee . . . here we are . . . Berlin."

"Ach du lieber der fershtugginer ball ist op und outta hier!" came Harlen's voice, changed instantly from the excited Chicago Dizzy-Deanish drawl to a throaty, Teutonic lashing of syllables. "Der Fuhrer ist nicht gehappy. Nein! Nein! Er is gerflugt und vertrunken und er veilige pisstoffen!"

"Nothing here," muttered Duane. "I'll try Paris."

When I read and hear these days about "online communities," I think of Mike, Dale, Lawrence (Don't-Call-Me-Larry), Duane McBride, Kevin, and their other friends in the Bike Patrol hanging out in Mike's chickenhouse before jumping on their bikes again and taking off for *some-where*. To me, "online communities" are just more texts, more blobs of electronic ink on a glass page, just one more glass teat that the kids and grown-ups of our era can stay home and suck on rather than emerge into the light and engage with the real world. Why do today's kids have so damned much to *say* and so damned little to *do*?

One answer may be that we've stolen most of the real world from them.

OUR THEFT OF OUR CHILDREN'S SPACE

The boys (and most of the girls) of Elm Haven in the summer of 1960 had a fun radius of action on their bikes:

All of their town of Elm Haven could be explored in about a mile of pedaling. The ride out east of town past the Lone Tree Tavern and down the hills and into the woods to Corpse Creek at the bottom of the hill and Calvary Cemetery at the top of the next hill was a little over a mile and a half of pedaling effort on the gravel road. Uncle Henry and Aunt Lena's farm beyond there was an easy two-mile bike ride, Duane McBride's house a half mile farther, the old quarry now called Billy Goat Hills in the woods another mile of walking behind Calvary Cemetery, the eternal mystery of Gypsy Lane another two miles or so beyond that in the thick woods.

Stone Creek, where they could swim in the deep area under the one-lane highway bridge—where the crawdads were—was about four miles out along the mostly gravel road. No problem. Jubilee State Park was about four or five miles beyond Stone Creek on the same road and a full day's bike trip including the time spent playing in that big state park and hiking to and threatening to jump from the high cliff called Lover's Leak (so named by the other boys because Harlen had once urinated from its heights).

In the morning, the parents didn't ask where the kids were headed and the kids didn't tell. It was a good policy.

So the effective unattended play range of these kids of Elm Haven on any given summer day (with good weather for cycling) was about ten miles out, twenty miles round-trip. That's changed a bit since 1960.

I've tried to find some good sociological evidence on just *how much* that range of a pre-teenager's roaming space has decreased in the past three or four decades, but even with the help of some far-more-savvy researchers from my friendly online forum, very little has turned up. One has to depend upon personal observation and other people's anecdotes, and that opinion is overwhelming in saying that kids are all but prisoners of their houses, yards, and parent-scheduled activities in the 21st century.

I am looking at an interesting study by Sanford Gaster—"Urban Children's Access to Their Neighborhood: Changes Over Three Generations"—published in *Environment and Behavior*, Vol. 23, January 1991.

As it says in the title, it's a study of the loss of "free roaming space" for American kids over three generations, but it's an urban study and it looks at the generations between 1915 and 1976, specifically in the suburban neighborhood of Inwood on the northern tip of Manhattan. Obviously anything having to do with kids in Manhattan doesn't seem to connect to the freedom of Mike, Kevin, Dale, Lawrence, Duane, Harlen, Cordie, and the other kids from 1960 in tiny little Elm Haven, Illinois (Pop. 650—Speed Electrically Timed).

But it does.

Inwood's earliest urban residents were Irish, German, and Russian immigrants. There were later influxes of Italians, Poles, Greeks, and Armenians. It was a working-class neighborhood, and a clean and decent one. The first African-American families arrived in the 1950s and by the time the study was done, large sections of Inwood were all-black so no research could be done on white kids there.

The kids in the 1920s and 1930s had it best in Inwood, in terms of sheer freedom, since their play sites included woods, construction sites, and the huge Inwood Hill Park. Then in the 1930s, the New Deal's Works Progress Administration changed the landscape forever by putting the Henry Hudson Parkway right through Inwood Hill Park, thus building a Great Wall of China right through the kids' woods and roaming ground. (In that same project, the Henry Hudson Bridge, with all its access ramps, was built there to link Inwood with the mainland: a dubious improvement from the local kids' point of view.)

During the same New Deal period, the wild still-accessible areas of Inwood Hill Park were "civilized" with benches, pathways, lighting, sports fields, game courts, and playgrounds replacing the woods and trails. By the mid-1960s, most of the unsupervised areas of Inwood Hill Park were the predatory domain of black youth gangs. The African-American community—parents and clergy—responded quickly and shifted their kids' activities to highly organized and supervised amusements: adult-run Little League, school programs, youth-center activities, etc.

Thus the African-American non-gang-member kids eight to thirteen were the first to be heavily supervised, their days of roaming free in woods and empty lots curtailed and then ended, and the white kids would follow that path to heavy adult supervision in all things by the 1970s. A 1920s "roaming radius" of three to five miles for kids in Inwood Hill Park all but disappeared as children's activity, largely out of parents' fear of gangs, drug dealers, and automobiles, continued to shrink to the house, the fenced yard, and the supervised playgrounds.

This was part of the study's conclusion:

> Over much of this century an interplay of forces in Inwood has worked to restrict children's unsupervised neighborhood activity. Most prominent were the erosion of the number and variety of places children can or may visit and the increasingly adult-directed nature of outdoor play. Neither crime, physical environment decay, nor automobile traffic are [sic] solely to blame.
>
> In the 1920's [sic], the rapid, almost relentless excavating, building, obliterating, and otherwise transforming of Inwood gave its children a universe of unsupervised play opportunities— pits, rocks, farms, swamps, woods, barns, mansions, and construction debris. In the 1940's [sic], with the building of Inwood largely complete, with the population at its peak, and with the New Deal landscape firmly in place, play environments became conventionalized and supervised—playgrounds, ballfields, and, in the 1950's [sic], housing projects.

Inwood's 1940s experience for kids was a mirror of the environment for my little brother and me in Des Moines in 1956–57. We had a private forest preserve behind our house, wild gulch "city woods" running two miles and more behind that, and those linking to an extensive forest preserve that was almost free of trails or improvements. More to the point, there was a myriad of new home construction going on around that gulch and, as any boy can tell you, "construction debris"—the abandoned holes, pits, hills of dirt, partially constructed houses, even the empty construction equipment in evenings and weekends, make for the perfect playground. We celebrated such spaces by doing everything from walking along narrow boards high on the open, floorless third floors of just-framed houses to having clod fights to taping my little brother (always the daredevil of the group) up in a big cardboard box and heaving him off the top of a thirty-foot heap of dirt to land in a twenty-foot-deep construction pit half-filled with water. (Houdini-like, my little brother always survived.)

When we eventually moved from Des Moines to the tiny little town of Brimfield in central Illinois (Pop. 650—Speed Electrically Timed), the town that was to be the template for "Elm Haven," our radius of free roaming increased dramatically, and not just because we were a couple of years older. We had to bike and hike farther—almost five miles—to get out to the abandoned gravel quarry in the woods (Billy Goat Hills) to tape my little brother Wayne up in a slightly larger box and throw him off a slightly higher hill (fifty feet tall) into a deeper (twenty-five-foot) quarry quite filled with water, but it was worth the effort. (He escaped the box. Eventually. But for a long time it was just a matter of bubbles coming up to the surface of the dark quarry, then a longer time with no bubbles, and I admit that I was thinking up a wide variety of explanations-to-curious-parents to explain my kid brother's demise. Most of the explanations involved gangs of gypsies who came out of the woods and taped Wayne up in their box and threw him in the quarry while the rest of us kids were tied up.) (It's hard being an older brother.)

My research friends have found a relative plethora of UK-based studies on kids' restrictions on play and roaming, and the conclusions of that research pretty much mirror the anecdotal evidence I have from friends and my own observations re: the relative disappearance of roaming freedom for kids eight to thirteen in the States.

One such article summarizing research in *The Observer*, Sunday, August 3, 2008, begins:

> It is a scene that epitomises childhood: young siblings racing towards a heavy oak tree, hauling themselves on to the lower branches and scrambling up as high as they can get. Yet millions of children are being deprived of such pleasure because their parents are nervous about exposing them to risk.
>
> A major study by Play England, part of the National Children's Bureau, found that half of all children have been stopped from climbing trees, 21% have been banned from playing conkers, and 17% have been told they cannot take part in games of tag or chase. Some parents are going to such extreme lengths to protect their children from danger that they have even said no to hide and seek.

Now, I don't know what the British game "conkers" consists of, but having been a kid—and having had access to balls and dirt clods—I can guess. The study goes on to include—

> The tendency to wrap children in cotton wool has transformed how they experience childhood. According to the research, 70% of adults had their biggest childhood adventures in outdoor spaces among trees, rivers, and woods, compared to 29% of children today. The majority of young people questioned said that their biggest adventures took place in playgrounds.

A kid's biggest adventures taking place on a friggin' *playground*!!??
Dale, Lawrence, Mike, Duane, Kevin, Harlen, and their friends would
have never stopped throwing up at such a statement. (Cordie Cooke
would have laughed heartily before throwing up.)

You'll note in *Summer of Night* that even on the huge center-of-town
playground that fully surrounded the giant, scary Old Central School,
their favorite playground toy was a giant new septic tank that had been
brought in and rolled up against the tallest slide (so tall it would be forbidden on all school playgrounds today) and the kids used that eight-foot-tall
tank to play king of the mountain and shove each other off it, only to run
up the giant slide and jump down on the slippery, treacherous curved
surface again to start the shoving match all over.

Well, it beats conkers.

The final UK article that my research friends have come up with is
titled "How Children Lost the Right to Roam in Four Generations,"
published in 2007, and it pretty much says it all both for England and
the United States, for kids suburban and even small-townish.

The longitudinal study looked at one family and the roaming ranges
of an eight-year-old, the youngest in my eight-to-twelve roaming-range
interest, from 1919 to 2007:

Great-grandfather George, age eight in 1919, was allowed to walk
six miles to go fishing outside of town. Most of that walk was through
heavy woods down railroad tracks, back roads, and trails.

Grandfather Jack, aged eight in 1950, was able to walk about a mile
on his own to the woods to play. *But he played alone or with friends of the
same age in the woods!* Jack, like the boys of Elm Haven in 1960, spent
most of his time outside and almost none in his house listening to radio or
watching TV. (At age eighty-eight when the report was written, he was
still a "keen walker.")

The mother, Vicky, when age eight in 1979, was allowed to walk
alone to the swimming pool in town, about half a mile away. But Vicky
adds, "I was able to go out quite freely—I'd ride my bike around the estate, play with friends in the park, and walk to the swimming pool and
school."

The son today, Ed, eight years old in 2007, was only allowed to walk
to the end of his street, about three hundred yards away.

Even that is more freedom than I've seen local kids granted. Until
he was older than twelve, the son of one of our neighbors wasn't allowed
out of the yard without adult supervision even though our "old part of
town," the historical old section, was comparatively safe and small-
town-feeling. When the boy finally started riding a bicycle, he did so
armored like a medieval knight—wearing not only helmet but some sort

of shin guards from a Rollerblade store. (How, one wonders, did Mike, Dale, Lawrence, Kevin, Harlen, and the other kids from Elm Haven survive without bike helmets? Adults didn't ride bikes then, so there were no good examples of spandex-wrapped grown-ups hunkered over $3,500 handlebars, their precious skulls encased in several hundred bucks' worth of helmet. The kids of Elm Haven—the kids of my generation—never wore bike helmets. Oddly enough, we knew of no kids dead or paralyzed with brain injuries. We all went over the handlebars sooner or later, but that meant scrapes and bruises, not a lifetime spent in the vegetable ward.)

Anyway, besides all kids in our neighborhood now always being as helmeted as a Nazi storm trooper if they get within fifteen paces of a bicycle, their bikes in the 21st century have ten-foot wands on them, each wand sporting an orange "Don't Run Over Me, Please!" pennant. Neighborhood boys aren't allowed to ride out of sight until they are fourteen, and then only to the end of the block and back. Even for that modest distance—something the kids of Elm Haven would have done without thought or worry on anyone's part when they were seven—mothers now watch their sons like a proverbial hawk.

As a sobering UK 2001 study by Gill Valentine and John McKendrick concluded:

> It is not the lack of play facilities that limits children's outdoor or unsupervised play, but parental anxieties about children's safety. Parents feel that children are more at risk today than they were as youngsters. In all the studies of parental anxieties, the two biggest fears voiced by parents are abduction by strangers and road traffic. Yet, despite the increasing levels of worry, in reality children have never been safer.

Wait! you say. That's in the UK. Here in America, the shrubberies are overflowing with child-kidnappers, pedophiles, crazy people, and ax-murderers!

Are they?

Statistically, American kids outside the killing zones of the inner cities—i.e., those in the American suburbs and small towns and rural areas—are about as safe now as they were in the 1940s, '50s, '60s, and on through the turn of this century and beyond. But we adults—we parents—don't *believe* the kids are safe outside of our direct sight and adult supervision (even though research also shows that a lot of those "pedophiles" end up in jobs giving "adult supervision" in schools, playgrounds, preschools, and organized athletic programs to kids who used to roam free and unpredatored).

But the twenty-four-hour TV news announces every Amber Alert in the nation. And the movies and TV cop shows are filled with stories of child abductions, murder, torture.

Adults override their common sense—much less the memories of their own times as free kids aged eleven and thereabouts, a time filled with freedom to roam and play with other kids—and err on the side of caution.

And they make their children prisoners.

And now those prisoners, like those in a mental asylum, are kept calm and in the house by the tranquilizing drugs of cell phones, computers, iPads, iPods, TVs, texting, and other glass teats.

But, I argue to this day, and the Bike Patrol kid-voices of Mike, Dale, Kevin, Lawrence, Duane, Harlen, Cordie and the others back me up, that if you adults steal the space and time of childhood, you steal childhood itself.

THE DEATH OF A KID CHARACTER

And yet . . .

And yet . . .

One of the kid-characters in *Summer of Night dies*. (I'm sorry if this is a spoiler, but I won't give any more clues as to *which* important kid-character.) (Other than it is a boy.)

The death of this character was very hard for me to write, and not only because it was a kid or because the death of any central character in a novel should bother the novelist, the character's creator. More than that, even though much has been written about the effect of the death of a child on parents, there are very few inquiries—sociological, psychological, or fictional—on the death of a child on that child's peers and friends. (One of the best *fictional* treatments I've encountered of this sort of trauma in kids at the loss of a young friend was in Weldon Hill's little-known novel, *The Long Summer of George Adams*.)

Also, this character who dies in *Summer of Night* deeply interested me, both in real life when I knew him and in the novel where I re-created him by blending him with another dear friend of mine. One of the two real-life friends upon which I based this character was murdered.

More than that, *Summer of Night* was as autobiographical as anything I've ever written, and while the characters are fictional, they engaged me deeply. I knew even when I was writing the novel in 1990 that those characters might well pop up in later stories and novellas and novels that I would write, even though I somewhat disagree with the practice of any writer spreading his characters across separate and disparate books.

Sure enough, one of the boy-characters (who, I discovered, had lost a leg in Vietnam less than a decade after the events in Elm Haven in the summer of 1960), ends up as a priest in Romania (and one of the two main characters) in my novel *Children of the Night*. I was pleased to see him and pleased to see that, despite his loss of part of one leg, he was still the same generous, bold, courageous character I'd known as a kid in *Summer of Night*. He showed up again a few years later as a much more minor character, post-priesthood, as an unnamed helicopter pilot in the Hawaiian Islands in my novel *Fires of Eden,* and I was fascinated to learn whom he'd married in the interim since *Children of the Night* and what he was up to.

The brave little white-trash girl from *Summer of Night,* Cordie Cooke, whom I never expected to see or hear from again, also shows up in *Fires of Eden,* and she has a central supporting-character role. After my initial astonishment at learning she was very wealthy, I heard the reason for that in the tale I was telling and understood completely. Cordie was never anything if not indomitable.

In my comic-suspense-thriller *Darwin's Blade,* 2000, another favorite boy kid-character from *Summer of Night* showed up in a primary supporting role. A skinny little-brother daredevil in the Elm Haven novel of 1960, this character was—in 2000—a six-foot-two, 230-pound accident investigator in California, running his own insurance investigation company with his wife. His sense of humor had stayed the same. (And he still hated being called "Larry.") Through him, we heard some of what had come of his older brother.

One member of Elm Haven's 1960 Bike Patrol shows up as the *central* character in my 2002 novel *A Winter Haunting.* That character, an English professor in Montana during some of the interim since his childhood, had just lost his wife and family in a deserved divorce and was suffering a massive nervous breakdown as he decided—disastrously or miraculously, whichever you choose—to return to a "haunted" farm near Elm Haven, one formerly belonging to a kid-friend of his, to write a novel.

Elm Haven and its stark surroundings in the winter of 2000 were radically different, it turns out, than they had been in the rich, warm-lighted summer of 1960. But then, this main character in *A Winter Haunting* remembered the events of 1960 differently than they had been laid out in *Summer of Night*. The supernatural elements were no longer supernatural. The unexplained and inexplicable were at last . . . mostly . . . explained.

My goal when writing *A Winter Haunting* was to create a fictional Mobius strip of the two novels—almost literally a twisted circular two-sided tale with, topologically speaking, *only one side*. Just as one can draw a pencil around *both sides* of a physical, three-dimensional Mobius strip without ever lifting the pencil from the paper, so the reader can read *A Winter Haunting* and *Summer of Night* as two separate tellings, two separate but equal (and strangely interdependent) realities, yet both based on a single series of events.

When readers tell me that they want to read both books and ask if they should start with *Summer of Night* or its "sequel," *A Winter Haunting,* I try to explain—not always successfully—that the second novel is not really a sequel and that it doesn't matter which book one reads first. Either way, the other novel will help illuminate the first one you read. (It doesn't matter where you set the point of the pencil down to trace a continuous line around a Mobius strip.)

But there is a "ghost" in *A Winter Haunting.* That ghost is the indelible memory of a boy-character with infinite promise who dies far too young, far too violently. Whichever explanation for the death the reader accepts, the death itself is irrevocable.

Or is it?

It turned out that I wasn't the only one who was upset when this central character died in *Summer of Night.* Much of the mail I've received from around the world since the publication of 1991 demands that I "bring the character back to life." (Whether I did that in *A Winter Haunting* will be up to the reader to decide.) Angry—or hurt and generous—letters and e-mails sent to me have had elaborate explanations of how this interesting (and vulnerable) character *isn't really dead* but has been carried away and cocooned under one of the farm fields outside of Elm Haven. (And so forth.)

Years ago, when an artist I knew was doing a huge 125-year anniversary wall-ceramic rendition of Central School where I taught for eleven years here in my Colorado town, people would ask her, "Who's the rather sad-looking boy looking out the second-story window of the school?"

It was my lost character from *Summer of Night,* and that was this artist's way of keeping him alive.

KIDS AS ECONOMIC TARGETS OF OPPORTUNITY

One huge difference between the kids of Elm Haven circa 1960 and the kids of today is that the great marketing and sales apparatus of American capitalism hadn't discovered the Elm Haven kids yet.

The most important and expensive things any of the Elm Haven kids owned were their bikes and—with only Kevin as an exception—these bikes were either handed down from older siblings or purchased used, very used, by the boys' parents. The boys loved their bikes and *needed* them (the bikes did, after all, grant them the freedom to roam the relatively vast distances they took for granted) and although the bikes lay out in front yards at night without fear of theft (except when villain Chuck Compton and his toady assistant-villain Archie, real names from my past, *did* steal them) the boys tended to treat their priceless vehicles rather carelessly. Most specifically, the boys of Elm Haven—except for Kevin—had the habit of dismounting their bikes at high speed and allowing them to career, riderless, across someone's yard until they finally fell over or crashed into Mike's chickenhouse.

The other *valuable thing* that each boy of Elm Haven had was his baseball glove. These mitts, old and re-restrung as they were, were invaluable since not only did most of the boys play on the small town's Little League team—traveling to nearby towns such as Kickapoo, Illinois, where dreaded pitcher Dave Ashley was on the mound—but they also played ball from early morning to late dusk for weeks on end out on the high-school ball field that was in the fields beyond Dale, Lawrence, and Kevin's backyards, out there on the north end of town where the endless farm fields began.

But other than those treasures—their bikes and baseball gloves— the boys of Elm Haven (other than Kevin Grumbacher, Chuck Sperling, and a few other "rich kids") owned very little that wasn't ragged or used or handed down or all three.

The boys wore their universal kid-uniform of jeans—rather stiff by today's standards, rolled up at the bottom—and T-shirts. The only logo on any of the T-shirts was the Boy Scout–logoed T-shirt that Dale Stewart liked to wear. Lawrence and Harlen liked to wear their old Cub Scout uniform shirts, washed and rewashed to soft thinness and so short, at least on Jim Harlen, that the cuffs of the faded blue shirt barely reached below his elbows.

The idea of wearing designer labels—other than the word *Levi* hidden somewhere on the jeans' buttons—would have struck both the boys of Elm Haven and their parents as absurd.

For summer footwear, the boys of Elm Haven wore Keds or high tops. Old ones. *Very* old ones. Socks and toes peeked out of almost all these shoes. Here the only exception was Duane McBride—who was an overweight bundle of exceptions—since Duane wore his ancient black high-top sneakers all the time. (And his faded corduroy pants and flannel shirts, even in the heat of summer.)

It should be noted that all the boys of Elm Haven, even the poorest like Mike O'Rourke, whose family had a pump-handle sink with water in the house but no other indoor plumbing and who had to go to the outhouse (next door to the chickenhouse, unfortunately for the Bike Patrol on hot summer days) even in the worst cold nights of winter, still separated their "school clothes" from their "play clothes." Most didn't wear jeans to school, although if they did, they still had a collared shirt that would be tucked in. Almost all had a pair of oxfords to wear to school—old and broken in, but, like the children themselves, capable of being shined to a gloss several times a year.

Only Duane McBride wore the same clothes and black sneakers every day.

The total wealth of one of the boys of Elm Haven's wardrobe on a summer day would probably have been around $4.50—and that when the jeans and T-shirt and Keds or high tops were *new*.

To decry commercialism is the ultimate cliché. (Although I like the way young Alvin Greenman, as Alfred, the slightly overweight young janitor in 1947's *Miracle on 34th Street* explains it to Edmund Gwenn (the *real* Santa Claus)—"*Yeah, there's a lot of bad 'isms' floatin' around this world, but one of the worst is commercialism. Make a buck, make a buck. Even in Brooklyn it's the same—don't care what Christmas stands for, just make a buck, make a buck.*")

That was 1947. Alfred—and Santa Claus—would drop their collective dentures if they saw the "commercialism" of the 21st century.

My mentor during my eighteen years as a public-school teacher (and beyond that) on important educational issues was the author, media and culture critic, and indefatigable humanist Neil Postman. Although Postman died in 2003, his observations on the effect technology and cultural change has had on us all—but especially upon children—are more relevant than ever. When I was completing my master's degree in education to become a teacher in 1971, Postman's seminal book was *Teaching as a Subversive Activity,* and those who didn't understand him thought that he was another sixties radical. Years later in 1979, amidst the chaos of those postsixties years, Postman wrote *Teaching as a Conserving Activity,* and those who didn't understand him thought that he was a Reagan conservative.

Neil Postman was far more than either of those mislabelings. He was a man who understood André Gide's all-but-forgotten statement—"*The only true education comes from what goes counter to you.*"

More importantly, Postman understood—and explained most eloquently—that "childhood" as we know it is a space, place, and concept that didn't really exist for adults (or children) until the late 18th century and which had been all but destroyed by the late 20th century. (As an artist and lover of art, I knew the first part of Postman's equation quite well—children simply weren't portrayed in the actual proportions of children in paintings and portraits through the centuries, at least until the 1800s. It wasn't just primitivism in art that made children always look like shrunken adults, all with the wrong proportions of head to torso, until the mid-eighteenth century. Painters, like everyone else, simply *thought of children as small adults* and rendered them that way.)

That era where childhood was finally respected as a distinct time of life unto itself and one with different rules—in other words, as a period when children shouldn't be subjected to the same shocks and demands and realities that burden adults—really came into existence after the invention of the printing press when men worked on the assumption that the information environment of children should be different—more restricted—than the information environment of adults.

That protective wall has been taken down. (Actually, I think of the end of childhood that I've witnessed in the last decades of the 20th century as the removal of the parents' bedroom door. Nothing that adults, including parents, do—including sex—or think or talk or argue or worry about is hidden from children any longer.)

Our reflexive habit is to celebrate all technological and cultural revolutions in recent decades, but this is one revolution we should pause and think about.

This revolution, heralded by almost all of us (including parents), is one that has killed the kid-dom childhood so celebrated by Dale, Lawrence (Don't-Call-Me-Larry), Mike, Kevin, Harlen, Cordie, Donna Lou, and the many other children of 1960 Elm Haven. Postman writes about this revolution that has made the eighteenth- and nineteenth-century versions of childhood as a separate and protected place problematic to the point of no longer being viable.

> I refer, of course, to the 'information revolution' which has made it impossible to keep secrets from the young—sexual secrets, political secrets, social secrets, historical secrets, medical secrets; that is to say, the full content of adult life, which must be kept at least partially hidden from the young if there is to be a category of life known as childhood. (*Postman*, Building a Bridge to the Eighteenth Century: How the Past Can Improve Our Future, p. 124)

Without separate secrets and silences, there can be no protective barrier between childhood and the roughest aspects of adulthood.

The kids of Elm Haven thought they were facing terrible supernatural foes—the evil and sentient Borgia Bell in the cupola of Old Central, the dead Doughboy who had come back to haunt and attack Memo, the unspeakable Rendering Truck—but they never seriously considered going to their parents or other adults for help (with the single exception of Mike's bringing in the young priest, which turned out to be a terrible idea).

The worlds between kid-life and adulthood were simply separate then. During the course of *Summer of Night*, each of the kid-characters is forced to face some terrible aspect of the adult world—raw sexuality, the death of a friend one's own age, violence, loneliness, drunkenness—but in each case the kids of Elm Haven summoned strength from each other and from the separate place and secrets and silences that were childhood itself.

Today, children of all ages have become the targets of advertising and commerce. Instead of Levis, middle-class kids expect to wear designer jeans. Instead of generic T-shirts (or a beloved Boy Scout T-shirt), kids today wear designer labels stenciled wide across shirts as if paying for the privilege to be a billboard for some corporation. Too many boys expect to wear different athletic shoes—basketball shoes, cross trainers, court shoes, running shoes—that go for $60 and up a pair, when the boy of 1960 did *every* sport in his Keds or high tops. Girls put "American Girl" dolls on their Christmas want lists—dolls that may cost $100 and more.

As Neil Postman wrote in 1999: "*The point is that childhood, if it can be said to exist at all, is now an economic category. There is very little the culture wants to do for children except to make them into consumers.*" It's only gotten worse in the decade and more since Postman wrote those sentences. (Since, as I mentioned, Postman died in 2003, he was mercifully spared the soul-sickening über-marketing Lolita-phenomenon known as "Hannah Montana" that debuted on the Disney Channel in 2006.)

For the most part, Mike, Kevin, Lawrence, Duane, Cordie, Donna Lou, Dale, Harlen, and the other kids of Elm Haven 1960 didn't really have any money to spend, other than the random nickels for a cold bottle of Coke from the red A&P machine on Main Street where Mike's mother worked or the occasional gumball from the dispenser in the Parkside Café during the Free Show in Bandstand Park. The great All-Seeing Eye of the Mordor-proliferating media and Madison Avenue with its army of orcs hadn't discovered them yet. Kids weren't yet "consumers."

They were still human beings.

THE SMARTEST KID NOT ON THE BLOCK

All through the year at the end of the day at Old Central School, teachers had the farm kids line up to go to their buses while the town kids stayed at their desks, fidgeting, waiting for the lines of farm kids to file out. Then the town kids were finally released.

Farm kids and town kids. It was a serious division. The town kids spent the summer playing with each other, riding their bikes together, forming the Bike Patrol, playing ball together. The farm kids . . . well, most of them had chores. If there were other farm kids close enough to walk to see through the ever-rising fields of corn, they hung out with these other kids, swimming in a cow-watering hole, tossing cobs high in the corn silo, shooting sparrows in the barn with their BB guns, but mostly farm kids had a more solitary life than town kids.

The exception was Duane McBride.

Duane McBride was an exception in most ways.

He was a farm kid who lived more than two miles out of Elm Haven but through the summer he hung out with Mike, Dale, Kevin, and the other Chickenhouse kids. Duane was a member of the Bike Patrol, but he didn't own a bike. The other boys were all lean—partly because of modest diet, mostly because of amazing amounts of daily outdoor exercise throughout the year—but Duane McBride was fat.

The other boys had little use for school because it (and their teachers) was boring. Duane had gone beyond Old Central School and beyond most schools.

Duane was mostly an autodidact and a brilliant one. With some guidance from his Uncle Art, Duane McBride had read most books, fiction and nonfiction, that would constitute a solid college curriculum. Mostly alone on the farm in winter, while his father was off drinking, Duane had learned five foreign spoken languages, his accent honed by old 78-rpm foreign-language records he'd found and checked out from the archives of the Oak Hill Public Library. He'd read the *Iliad* in Greek, the *Aeneid* in Latin, and Kant's *Prolegomena zu einer jeden künftigen Metaphysik* in Fraktur German. And he had done all this before he was twelve.

Duane McBride was different in another important way.

All the other kid-characters in *Summer of Night* were fictional distortions and composites of actual boys and girls I knew during my few years in the tiny town of Brimfield. Duane McBride was an amalgam of two young men I would meet much later, during my four years at Wabash College in Indiana.

One of those brilliant young men that went into creating Duane McBride was named Keith N————, a sophomore when I was a senior but many, many years ahead of me in his scholarship and general knowledge. Keith is alive and well and teaching Latin, Greek, Classics, film history, and a host of other subjects at a medium-size liberal arts university in Indiana. I've been asked at SF convention panels—"Dan, you've spent time with Stephen King, Dean Koontz, Harlan Ellison, Peter Straub, David Morrell, and so many other great writers. Who's the smartest person you've ever known?"

And each time I have to answer, "The smartest person I've ever known is probably a guy named Keith N————."

Sometimes I might doubt that, but recently Keith came to my daughter's wedding here in Colorado and as I watched and listened to him talking to other people—artists, sociologists, editors, housewives, airline pilots, linguists, film agents, doctors, drug counselors, university recruiters, video producers—*always with Keith knowing so much about the other person's field that it was as if they were talking with a fellow professional,* I realized that I was correct in feeling that he was almost certainly the first among so many highly intelligent people I know.

The other half of the amalgam that was the character of Duane McBride, his first name Duane, was a college friend who was murdered in real life just a couple of years after our graduation. As founder and editor-in-chief of the underground literary publication *The Satyr* during our senior year at Wabash, I published examples of both Duane's nonfiction and short fiction. It was brilliant. *He* was brilliant. And unhappy.

The details of my off-and-on friendship with that Duane (and our literary rivalry at college, a rivalry that existed only in Duane's mind), as well as details of his murder, as well as my frustrated efforts to establish a writing award in Duane's name at Wabash College, all appear in a "Writing Well" essay from the archives on my Web site—http://www.dansimmons. com/writing_welll/archive/2009_12.html.

And yes, I also dislike links in print materials. Unless you're reading this from a Kindle, it doesn't do you much good, I admit. But just to add insult to injury, the October and November "Message from Dan" essays on my same Web site were in the form of a two-part short story, set in Elm Haven, starring some of the boys of Elm Haven, and occurring—or at least beginning the narrative—during the televised Kennedy-Nixon debates on October 21, 1960.

BUT READER BE WARNED!

The events in these two ministories occur not just in October of 1960, after all the events of *Summer of Night,* but they also look decades into the futures of many of the main characters from the novel. You may not like that. Read these two free pieces of short fiction at your peril and only *after* you've read *Summer of Night*:

http://www.dansimmons.com/news/message/2008_10.html

http://www.dansimmons.com/news/message/2008_11.html

But briefly back to Duane McBride.

Part of my pleasure of creating and writing about Duane McBride was the simple fact that Duane was probably the only *genius* I've ever set in my fiction.

We use the word "genius" too casually—often just to denote an especially bright person. But my focus for my master's degree in education and further training at BOCES New York and beyond prepared me to work not only with seriously learning-disabled elementary students, but also with the very gifted.

And Duane McBride was that rarest of ava . . . the profoundly and globally gifted. In real life, you and I run about the same odds of bumping into an actual, functioning *genius* as we do coming across an extraterrestrial.

Everyone discounts IQ tests, but they remain the single best way to predict academic and professional success. After a century of measuring it, no one knows exactly what the "g-factor" is that is measured in an IQ test, but—at least in Western civilization based on books and learning— that g-factor may be the major determinant on our lives.

Most of us remember that one standard deviation in such testing is 15 points. Well, assuming that most of us score somewhere around the median IQ score of 100, we're all used to dealing with people who are a standard deviation—15 points or an IQ of around 85—*below* us. We even know how to conduct ourselves politely with those two standard deviations below the norm, IQs somewhere around 70, which is bordering on serious mental retardation.

A three-standard-deviation difference—trying to communicate with someone holding an IQ of 55 or below—is all but impossible. In some ways, these people are not really in the human intellectual community.

Well, the same goes for those human oddities smarter than us. We're often impressed with those people whose IQ is a standard deviation or so above our own. We often work for people with a gifted IQ of 130 or above, two standard deviations above the norm. Most of us, whether we know it or not, will meet at least one person who would score three standard deviations above the IQ norm. For better or worse, those individuals tend to change the world.

But Duane McBride?

Duane's IQ might have been set near 220 or so, more than seven standard deviations above the norm for intelligence, but unfortunately—or fortunately—IQ tests can't accurately test intelligences that high. They are literally off the scale. And, in many real ways, beyond our comprehension.

I'm interested that Mike, Dale, Lawrence, Kevin, and most of the other kids liked Duane McBride so much, even though he often said things the others didn't understand at the time. Dale Stewart, we know from *A Winter Haunting,* grew up to be a respected college professor and a writer, but he was always aware that, at his academic height, he didn't know as much about things as his friend Duane McBride had when Duane was eleven years old.

Jim Harlen was probably the most suspicious of Duane, but I've discovered in my "Election Night" stories and elsewhere that Harlen had a ferocious intelligence of his own, and it was a hurt and jealous one. It would follow its own dark path.

I literally loved the character of Duane McBride. I would have been fascinated to follow his adventures later in life, perhaps in politics, certainly in the intellectual realm. He was my Mycroft to the lesser Sherlock. He was Nero Wolfe, thinking and deducing circles around all the mere Sam Spades out there, and he had a touch of a Peter Ustinov *raconteur* thrown in. I would have loved to have been Duane McBride's friend, even if only to learn from him the way I learned from Keith N———— and the other real-life Duane.

But in the end I wasn't surprised to learn that Duane McBride had only one perfect friend and *confidante*—his elderly collie Wittgenstein.

THE FREE SHOW

Life doesn't often get the chance to imitate art imitating life. But not long ago it did for me.

A central metaphor and narrative focal point in *Summer of Night* is the "Free Show." The Free Show was the movie projected onto the side of the Parkside Café most Saturday nights in the summer in Elm Haven in 1960, just as such a Free Show had been part of my kid-life in Brimfield. For an actual photograph of the Free Show (nestled in with photos of the actual kids who were the templates for Mike O'Rourke, Kevin Grumbacher, Jim Harlen, Dale Stewart, Lawrence Stewart, and others) I refer you again to my Web site archives at: http://www.dansimmons.com/about/snapshots2.htm.

The last old 1960 snapshot on that page is of people on blankets and in pickup trucks, with kids on the bandstand, waiting for the actual Free Show to begin.

Well, cut to our new home, where we've lived since 2007. Not long after we arrived here, Karen and I—often with grown-daughter Jane's help—initiated the Simmons Summer Cinema Series (Movies Under the Stars!). Neighbors and friends show up on frequent Saturday nights through the summer to sit in our darkened backyard (darkened except for yellow bulbs along the nearby pergola where the popcorn, lemonade, and other treats are set out on a bench) and to watch old movies digitally projected onto a huge screen we labored to set up.

Most of the Summer Cinema Series guests probably know I'm a writer, but it's never pertinent to our backyard-movie conversations. More pertinent are the movie-trivia-contest e-mails I send out to those invited, asking the most detailed and outrageous questions about, say, *Singin' in the Rain*. (At the end of this summer's cinema series, a gentleman and lady who'd won several of these truly difficult contests presented Karen and me with an "Honorary Oscar" for contributing to continued interest in the motion-picture arts. The award was a heavy thing, and we found out that they'd purchased it through a place in Hollywood that was the only licensed vendor in the United States for such statuettes.)

On that last movie evening of this past summer—hard to imagine as I look out the window and watch the sun set here not long past four-thirty on this first day of December—I said that I'd explain why we did these films. I then brought out a copy of *Summer of Night* and read the following passage aloud to forty-some people settling into their lawn chairs in the dusk, the kids sprawling on sleeping bags on the late-summer-scented grass—

> The Free Show began at dusk, but people started arriving at Bandstand Park even while sunlight still lay along Main Street like a tawny cat slow to leave the warm pavement. Farm families backed their pickups and station wagons onto the parking-lot gravel along the Broad Avenue side of the park so as to have the best view when the movie was projected against the Parkside Café; then they picnicked on the grass or sat on the bandstand and chatted with townfolk they hadn't seen for a while. Most of the local residents began to arrive when the sun had finally set and the Avenue under its arch of elms seemed a dark tunnel opening onto the lighter width of Main Street and terminating at the bright promise of the park with its light and noise and laughter.
>
> The Free Show was a tradition dating back to the early days of World War II when the nearest picture show—Ewalts Palace in Oak Hill—had closed due to the Ewalts' son and only projectionist, Walt, enlisting in the Marine Corps. Peoria was the next nearest source of movie entertainment, but the forty-mile trip was too much for most people because of gas rationing. So the older Mr. Ashley-Montague had brought a projector out from Peoria each Saturday evening that summer of 1942 and shown the newsreels and war-bond ads, cartoons, and feature attractions there in Bandstand Park, the images cast twenty feet tall on the whitewashed canvas screen stretched against the Parkside Café.

. . .

Now, on the fourth evening of June in the summer of 1960, Mr. Ashley-Montague's long Lincoln pulled into the space always left open for it due west of the bandstand. Mr. Taylor and Mr. Sperling and other members of the City Council helped him carry the massive projector to its wooden platform on the bandstand, families settled onto their blankets and park benches, adventurous children were shooed from the lower tree branches and their hiding places in the crawlspace beneath the bandstand, parents in the back of pickup trucks adjusted their folding chairs and handed around bowls of popcorn, and the park settled into a pre-show hush as the sky darkened above the elms and the canvas rectangle on the wall of the Parkside Café came alive with light.

If this is your first time reading *Summer of Night,* I hope you enjoy the show. For those of you returning—welcome back to Elm Haven.

Dan Simmons
Colorado
Dec. 1, 2010

Note: I'd like to acknowledge Craig and Chris Wolf, James D. French, Brad Miller, William Coleman, and other members of my online forum for helping me find research data for my "kids' roaming range" comments.

These fascinating studies include:

Asthana A, "Kids Need the Adventure of 'Risky' Play," *The Observer,* Sunday 3 August, 2008;

Barnodo's, *Playing It Safe,* London: Barnado's, 1995;

Carver A, Timperio A, and Crawford D, "Playing it safe: The influence of neighbourhood safety on children's physical activity," Centre for Physical Activity and Nutrition Research, School of Exercise and Nutrition Sciences, Deakin University, Vic. 3125, Australia Received 31 August 2006; received in revised form 18 June 2007; accepted 19 June 2007;

Cunningham J, "Children's unsupervised play is not a luxury, but a crucial aspect of their development," Play Scotland annual conference 2001, article published 3 January 2002;

Derbyshire D, "How children lost the right to roam in four generations," *Daily Mail*, 15 June, 2007;

Ennew J, "Time for children or time for adults?" in J Qvortrup, M Bardy, G Sgritta, and H Wintersberger (eds), *Childhood Matters: Social Theory, Practice and Politics*, Aldershot: Avebury Press, 1994;

Gaster S, "Urban children's access to their neighborhoods: Changes over three generations," *Environment and Behaviour*, January 1991, 70–85;

Hillman M, Adams J, and Whitelegg J, *One False Move . . . A Study of Children's Independent Mobility*, London: Policy Studies Institute, 1990;

Skenazy L, *Free-Range Kids: How to Raise Safe, Self-Reliant Children (Without Going Nuts from Worry)*, Web site of the same name;

Wheway R and Millward A, *Child's Play: Facilitating Play on Housing Estates*, London: Chartered Institute of Housing, 1997.

The upshot of all of the above is that the current generation of parents are scared s***less for their kids, and they act on that fear by oversupervising, overworrying, overscheduling, and overdirecting their children's lives, stealing from that younger generation the space, time, secrets, and silences that are necessary for childhood to survive into the 21st century.

ONE

Old Central School still stood upright, holding its secrets and silences firmly within. Eighty-four years of chalkdust floated in the rare shafts of sunlight inside while the memories of more than eight decades of varnishings rose from the dark stairs and floors to tinge the trapped air with the mahogany scent of coffins. The walls of Old Central were so thick that they seemed to absorb sounds while the tall windows, their glass warped and distorted by age and gravity, tinted the air with a sepia tiredness.

Time moved more slowly in Old Central, if at all. Footsteps echoed along corridors and up stairwells, but the sound seemed muted and out of synch with any motion amidst the shadows.

The cornerstone of Old Central had been laid in 1876, the year that General Custer and his men had been slaughtered near the Little Bighorn River far to the west, the year that the first telephone had been exhibited at the nation's Centennial in Philadelphia far to the east. Old Central School was erected in Illinois, midway between the two events but far from any flow of history.

By the spring of 1960, Old Central School had come to resemble some of the ancient teachers who had taught in her: too old to continue but too proud to retire, held stiffly upright by habit and a simple refusal to bend. Barren herself, a fierce old spinster, Old Central borrowed other people's children over the decades.

Girls played with dolls in the shadows of her classrooms and corridors and later died in childbirth. Boys ran shouting through her hallways, sat in punishment through the growing darkness of winter afternoons in her silent rooms, and were buried in places never mentioned in their geography lessons: San Juan Hill, Belleau Wood, Okinawa, Omaha Beach, Pork Chop Hill, and Inchon.

Originally Old Central had been surrounded by pleasant young saplings, the closer elms throwing shade on the lower classrooms in the warm days of May and September. But over the years the closer trees died and the perimeter of giant elms which lined Old Central's city block like silent sentinels grew calcified and skeletal with age and

1

disease. A few were cut down and carted away but the majority remained, the shadows of their bare branches reaching across the playgrounds and playing fields like gnarled hands groping for Old Central
herself.

Visitors to the small town of Elm Haven who left the Hard Road
and wandered the two blocks necessary to see Old Central frequently
mistook the building for an oversized courthouse or some misplaced
county building bloated by hubris to absurd dimensions. After all, what
function in this decaying town of eighteen hundred people could demand this huge three-story building sitting in a block all its own? Then
the travelers would see the playground equipment and realize that they
were looking at a school. A bizarre school: its ornate bronze and copper
belfry gone green with verdigris atop its black, steep-pitched roof more
than fifty feet above the ground; its Richardsonian Romanesque stone
arches curling like serpents above twelve-foot-tall windows; its scatter-
ing of other round and oval stained-glass windows suggesting some absurd hybrid between cathedral and school; its Châteauesque, gabled
roof dormers peering out above third-story eaves; its odd volutes looking
like scrollworks turned to stone above recessed doors and blind-looking
windows; and, striking the viewer most disturbingly, its massive, misplaced, and somehow ominous *size*. Old Central, with its three rows of
windows rising four stories, its overhanging eaves and gabled dormers,
its hipped roof and scabrous belfry, seemed much too large a school for
such a modest town.

If the traveler had any knowledge of architecture at all, he or she
would stop on the quiet asphalt street, step out of the car, gape, and take
a picture.

But even as the picture was being snapped, an observant viewer
would notice that the tall windows were great, black holes—as if they
were designed to absorb light rather than admit or reflect it—and that the
Richardsonian Romanesque, Second Empire, or Italianate touches were
grafted onto a brutal and common style of architecture which might be
described as Midwestern School Gothic, and that the final sense was not
of a striking building, or even of a true architectural curiosity, but only of
an oversized and schizophrenic mass of brick and stone capped with a
belfry obviously designed by a madman.

A few visitors, ignoring or defying a growing feeling of unease,
might make local inquiries or even go so far as drive to Oak Hill, the
county seat, to look up records on Old Central. There they would find
that the school had been part of a master plan eighty-some years earlier
to build five great schools in the county—Northeast, Northwest, Cen-

tral, Southeast, and Southwest. Of these, Old Central had been the first and only school constructed.

Elm Haven in the 1870s had been larger than it was now in 1960, thanks largely to the railroad (now in disuse) and a major influx of immigrant settlers brought south from Chicago by ambitious city planners. From a county population of 28,000 in 1875, the area had dwindled to fewer than 12,000 in the 1960 census, most of them farmers. Elm Haven had boasted 4,300 people in 1875 and Judge Ashley, the millionaire behind the settlement plans and the building of Old Central, had predicted that the town would soon pass Peoria in population and someday rival Chicago.

The architect Judge Ashley had brought in from somewhere back east—one Solon Spencer Alden—had been a student of both Henry Hobson Richardson and R.M. Hunt and his resultant architectural nightmare reflected the darker elements of the coming Romanesque Revival without the sense of grandeur or public purpose those Romanesque buildings might offer.

Judge Ashley had insisted—and Elm Haven had agreed—that the school would be built to accommodate the later, larger generations of schoolchildren which would be drawn to Creve Coeur County. Thus the building had housed not only K–6 classrooms but the high-school classrooms on the third floor—used only until the Great War—and sections which were meant to be used as the city library and even serve as space for a college when the need arrived.

No college ever came to Creve Coeur County or Elm Haven. Judge Ashley's great home at the end of Broad Avenue burned to the ground after his son went bankrupt in the Recession of 1919. Old Central remained an elementary school through the years, serving fewer and fewer children as people left the area and consolidated schools were built in other sections of the county.

The high-school level on the third floor became redundant when the real high school opened in Oak Hill in 1920. Its furnished rooms were closed off to cobwebs and darkness. The city library was moved out of the arched Elementary section in 1939, and the upper mezzanine of shelves stood largely empty, staring down at the few remaining students who moved through the darkened halls and too-broad stairways and basement catacombs like refugees in some long-abandoned city from an incomprehensible past.

Finally, in the fall of 1959, the new city council and the Creve Coeur County School District decided that Old Central had outlived its usefulness, that the architectural monstrosity—even in its eviscerated state—was too difficult to heat and maintain, and that the final 134 Elm Haven students in grades K–6 would be moved to the new consolidated school near Oak Hill in the fall of 1960.

But in the spring of 1960, on the last day of school, only hours before she would be forced into final retirement, Old Central School still stood upright, holding its secrets and silences firmly within.

TWO

D ale Stewart sat in his sixth-grade classroom in Old Central and was quietly certain that the last day of school was the worst punishment grown-ups had ever devised for kids.

Time had slowed worse than when he was in a dentist's office waiting, worse than when he was in trouble with his mom and had to wait for his dad to come home before punishment could be meted out, worse than . . .

It was bad.

The clock on the wall above Old Double-Butt's blue-dyed head said that it was 2:43 P.M. The calendar on the wall informed him that it was Wednesday, June 1, 1960, the last day of school, the last day that Dale and the others would *ever* have to suffer the boredom of being locked in the belly of Old Central, but to all intents and purposes time seemed to have stopped so completely that Dale felt that he was an insect stuck in amber, like the spider in the yellowish rock Father Cavanaugh had loaned Mike.

There was *nothing* to do. Not even schoolwork. The sixth graders had turned in their rented textbooks by one-thirty that afternoon, Mrs. Doubbet checking off their books and meticulously inspecting each for any damage . . . although Dale failed to see how she could tell this year's damage from the years of outrage already suffered by the moldy text from previous renters . . . and when that was finished, the classroom bizarrely empty even down to the bare bulletin boards and well-scrubbed wooden desks, Old Double-Butt had lethargically suggested that they read, even though school library books had been due the previous Friday at peril of not receiving the final report card.

Dale would have brought one of his books from home to read—perhaps the Tarzan book he had left open on the kitchen table at noon when he went home for lunch, or perhaps one of the ACE double-novel science fiction books he was reading—but though Dale read several books a week, he never thought of *school* as a place to read. School was a place to do worksheets, to listen to the teacher, and to give answers so simple that a chimp could have gleaned them from the textbooks.

So Dale and the other twenty-six sixth graders sat in the summer heat and high humidity as a storm darkened the skies outside and the already dim air in Old Central grew darker and summer itself seemed to recede as the clock froze its hands and the musty thickness of Old Central's interior lay on them like a blanket.

Dale sat in the fourth desk in the second row from the right. From where he sat he could see out past the cloakroom entrance into the dark hallway and just catch a glimpse of the door to the fifth-grade class where his best friend, Mike O'Rourke, also waited for the end of the school year. Mike was the same age as Dale . . . was a month older actually . . . but had been forced to repeat fourth grade so that for the past two years the friends had been separated by the abyss of an entire grade. But Mike had taken his failure to pass fourth grade with the same aplomb he showed toward most situations—he joked about it, continued to be a leader on the playground and among Dale's band of friends, and showed no malice toward Mrs. Grossaint, the old crone of a teacher who had failed him . . . Dale was sure . . . out of sheer malice.

Inside the classroom were some of Dale's other close friends: Jim Harlen on the front desk of the first row where Mrs. Doubbet could keep an eye on him. Now Harlen lounged with his head on his hands, eyes flicking about the room in the dance of hyperactivity Dale also felt but tried not to show. Harlen saw Dale watching and made a face, his mouth as elastic as Silly Putty.

Old Double-Butt cleared her throat and Harlen slumped back into submission.

In the row closest to the windows were Chuck Sperling and Digger Taylor—buddies, leaders, class politicians. Jerks. Dale didn't see Chuck and Digger much outside of school, except during the Little League games and practices. Behind Digger sat Gerry Daysinger in a torn and gray t-shirt. Everyone wore t-shirts and jeans outside of school, but only the poorest kids like Gerry and Cordie Cooke's brothers wore them to school.

Behind Gerry sat Cordie Cooke, moonfaced and placid with an expression somehow beyond stupidity. Her fat, flat face was turned toward the windows, but her colorless eyes seemed to see nothing. She was chewing gum—she was always chewing gum—but for some reason Mrs. Doubbet never seemed to notice or reprimand the girl for it. If Harlen or one of the other class cutups had chewed gum with such regularity, Mrs. D. probably would have suspended them for it . . . but with Cordie Cooke it seemed a natural state. Dale did not know the word bovine, but an image of a cow chewing its cud often came to mind with Cordie.

Behind Cordie, in the last occupied desk of the window row, in almost shocking contrast, sat Michelle Staffney. Michelle was immaculate in a soft green shirt and pressed tan skirt. Her red hair caught the light and even from across the room Dale could see the freckles standing out against her pale, almost translucent skin.

Michelle looked up from her book as Dale stared and although she did not smile, the faintest hint of recognition was enough to get the eleven-year-old boy's heart pounding.

Not all of Dale's friends were in this room. Kevin Grumbacher was in fifth grade—legitimately, since he was nine months younger than Dale. Dale's brother, Lawrence, was in Mrs. Howe's third-grade class on the first floor.

Dale's friend Duane McBride *was* here. Duane—twice as heavy as the next-chubbiest kid in the class—filled his seat in the third desk in the center row. He was busy, as always, writing something in the worn spiral notebook he dragged around with him. Duane's unruly brown hair stuck up in tufts and he adjusted his glasses with an unconscious movement as he frowned at whatever he was writing and went back to work. Despite the temperature in the high eighties, Duane wore the same heavy flannel shirt and baggy corduroy trousers he had worn all winter. Dale could never remember having seen Duane in jeans or a t-shirt, despite the fact that the heavier boy was a farm kid . . . Dale and Mike and Kevin and Jim and most of the others were city kids . . . and Duane had to do chores.

Dale fidgeted. It was 2:49 P.M. The school day ended, for some abstruse reason involving bus schedules, at 3:15.

Dale stared at the portrait of George Washington on the front wall and wondered for the ten thousandth time that year why the school authorities would put up a print of an unfinished painting. He stared at the ceiling, fourteen feet above the floor, and at the ten-foot-high windows along the far wall. He looked at the boxes of books on the empty shelves and wondered what would happen to the texts. Would they be shipped to the consolidated school? Burned? Probably the latter since Dale couldn't imagine such ancient, moldy books in the brand-new school his parents had driven him by.

Two-fifty P.M. Twenty-five minutes before summer really began, before freedom reigned.

Dale stared at Old Double-Butt. The name did not come to mind with any malice or derision; she had *always* been Old Double-Butt. For thirty-eight years Mrs. Doubbet and Mrs. Duggan had shared the teaching of sixth grade—originally in adjoining classrooms and then, when the population of students had declined about the time Dale was born, sharing the same class—Mrs. Doubbet teaching reading and composition and social studies in the morning, Mrs. Duggan teaching math and science and spelling and penmanship in the afternoon.

The pair had been the Mutt and Jeff, the humorless Abbott and Costello of Old Central—Mrs. Duggan thin and tall and twitchy, Mrs. Doubbet short and fat and slow, their voices almost opposite in timbre and tone, their lives intertwined—living in adjacent old Victorian homes on Broad Avenue, attending the same church, taking courses in Peoria together, taking vacations in Florida together, two incomplete persons somehow joining their skills and deficiencies to create one well-rounded individual.

Then, in this final year of Old Central's domination, Mrs. Duggan had taken ill just before Thanksgiving. Cancer, Mrs. O'Rourke had told Dale's mother in a soft voice she thought the boys would not overhear. Mrs. Duggan had not returned to class after Christmas vacation but rather than have some interloper fill the afternoon hours, confirming the seriousness of Mrs. Duggan's illness, Mrs. Doubbet had taught the courses she despised, "just until Cora returns," while nursing her friend—first in the tall pink house along Broad, then in the hospital—until one morning even Old Double-Butt had not appeared, there was a sixth-grade substitute teacher for the first time in four decades, and word was whispered around the playground that Mrs. Duggan had died. It was the day before Valentine's Day.

The funeral was in Davenport and none of the students attended it. None would have attended if it had been held right here in Elm Haven. Mrs. Doubbet returned two days later.

Dale looked at the old lady and felt a stirring of something like pity. Mrs. Doubbet was still fat, but the weight hung on her now like an oversized coat. When she moved, the undersides of her fat arms wiggled and shook like crepe paper hanging from bone. Her eyes had darkened and sunk in their sockets until they looked bruised. Now the teacher sat staring at the window, her expression as hopeless and empty as Cordie Cooke's. Her blue hair looked tousled and yellowed at the roots, and her dress hung oddly as if she had misbuttoned something somewhere. There was a bad smell around her which reminded Dale of the smell around Mrs. Duggan right before Christmas.

Dale sighed and shifted in his seat. 2:52 P.M.

There was the slightest movement in the dark hall, a furtive shifting and pale glow there, and Dale recognized Tubby Cooke, Cordie's fat and idiot brother, moving across the landing. Tubby was staring in, trying to catch his sister's attention without being noticed by Old Double-Butt. It was no use. Cordie was hypnotized by the sky outside the window and wouldn't have noticed her brother if he had thrown a brick at her.

Dale nodded slightly, at Tubby. The big fourth grader in bib overalls flipped him the bird, held up something that might have been a bathroom pass, and disappeared in the shadows.

Dale shifted. Tubby occasionally played with him and his friends despite the fact that the Cookes lived in one of the tarpaper shacks up on cinderblocks out along the railroad tracks near the grain elevator. Tubby was fat and ugly and stupid and dirty and used more profanity than any fourth grader Dale had ever known, but that didn't necessarily disqualify him from being part of the group of city kids who called themselves the Bike Patrol. But usually Tubby didn't want any part of Dale or his friends.

Dale wondered fleetingly what the dope was up to and then looked back at the clock. It was still 2:52.

Bugs in amber.

Tubby Cooke gave up trying to wave at his sister and headed for the stairway before Old Double-Butt or one of the other teachers noticed him out on the landing. Tubby had a bathroom pass from Mrs. Grossaint, but that didn't mean that one of the old bags wouldn't order him back to his classroom if they caught him loitering in the halls.

Tubby shuffled down the wide stairs, noticing where the wood was actually worn into ruts where generations of kids' feet had passed, and hurried down to the landing beneath the circular window. The light coming through was red and sickly from the storm building up outside. Tubby moved under rows of empty shelves where the city library used to be on the landing and the narrow mezzanine surrounding this in-between floor, but he did not really see them. The shelves had been empty for as long as Tubby had gone to school there.

He was in a hurry. There was less than a half hour of school remaining and he wanted to get downstairs to the boys' bathroom before the day ended and they shut up this damn old place forever.

There was more light on the first floor and the hum of activity from the primary grades, one through three, made the space here seem more human, even with the dark stairwell opening overhead into the darkness of the upper floors. Tubby hurried across the center of the open space before a teacher saw him, passed through a door, and hurried down the stairs into the basement.

It was weird that the stupid school had no restrooms on the first or second floor. Only the basement had johns and there were too many down there . . . the primary and intermediate restrooms, the locked john off the hole-in-the-wall room labeled TEACHERS' LOUNGE, the little toilet off the boiler room where Van Syke took a leak when he had to, even rooms that may have been other bathrooms down the unused corridors that led away into darkness.

Tubby knew what other kids knew—that there were steps leading *down* from the basement—but, like the other kids, Tubby had never gone down there and had no plans to. There weren't even *lights,* for Godssake! No one but Van Syke and maybe Principal Roon knew what was down there.

Probably more bathrooms, thought Tubby.

He went to the intermediate boys' restroom, the one marked BOY'S. That sign had been like that for as long as anyone could remember— Tubby's old man told him it was that way when *he* went to school in Old Central—and the only reason either Tubby or his old man knew that the whatchamacallit, the apostrophe, was in the wrong place was that Old Lady Duggan in sixth grade bitched and moaned about the stupidity of it. She'd whined about it when Tubby's Old Man was a kid. Well, Old Lady Duggan was dead now—dead and rotting in the Calvary Cemetery out past the Black Tree Tavern where Tubby's Old Man hung out most days—and Tubby wondered why the old lady hadn't *changed* the god-damn word if it bugged her so much. She'd had about a hundred years to go down and repaint the sign. Tubby guessed that she *liked* bitching and moaning about it . . . that it made her feel smart and made other people, like Tubby and his old man, feel stupid.

Tubby hurried down the dark and winding hallway to the restroom marked BOY'S. The brick walls had been painted green and brown here decades ago, the low ceiling was festooned with pipes and sprinklers and cobwebs, and the feeling was like you were wandering through this long, narrow tunnel in some tomb or something. Sort of like the mummy movie Tubby'd seen when his older sister's boyfriend had sneaked him and Cor-die into the Peoria drive-in last summer by hiding them in the trunk. It'd been a good movie, but Tubby would've liked it more if he hadn't had to listen to all the slurping, sucking, gasping sounds from the back seat as his older sister Maureen made out with that pimply guy named Berk. Mau-reen was pregnant now, and living with Berk out beyond the dump near where Tubby lived, but he didn't think she and the Berk dope were mar-ried.

Cordie had stayed turned around in the front seat all through the double feature, watching horny Maureen and Berk rather than the neat movies.

Tubby paused now at the entrance to the BOY'S restroom, listening to see if he could hear anyone else down here. Sometimes Old Van Syke sort of sneaked up on kids down here, and if they were messing around like Tubby planned to do . . . or sometimes doing nothing at all . . . Van Syke would give them a slap on the side of the head or a mean pinch on the arm. He wouldn't hurt just any kids . . . not some rich snot like Dr. Staffney's daughter, whatshername, Michelle . . . just the kids like Tubby or Gerry Daysinger or somebody. Kids of parents who didn't give a shit or who were afraid of Van Syke.

Lots of kids were afraid of Van Syke. Tubby wondered if lots of the kids' parents were afraid of him, too. Tubby listened, heard nothing, and almost tiptoed into the restroom.

The room was long, low-ceilinged, and dim. There were no windows and only one light bulb worked. The urinals were ancient and looked like they were made out of some smooth stone or something. Water trickled in them all the time. The seven toilet stalls were battered and heavily carved upon . . . Tubby's name could be found cut into two of them and his Old Man's initials were in the end one . . . and all but one had lost their doors. But it was beyond the sinks and urinals, beyond the stalls, in the darkest area near the rear, stone wall, where Tubby had business.

The outside wall was stone. The opposite wall, the one which held the urinals, was scabby brick. But the inside wall . . . the one beyond the stalls . . . this wall was some sort of plaster, and here Tubby paused and grinned.

There was a hole in this wall, a hole starting six or eight inches above the stone cold floor (how could there be another basement *below* a stone floor?) and rising almost three feet. Tubby could see fresh plaster dust on the floor and rotten lathing sticking out like exposed ribs.

Other kids had been working on this since Tubby had been down that morning. That was OK. They could do some of the work as long as Tubby got to kick the final shit out of the thing.

Tubby crouched and peered into the hole. It was wide enough to stick his arm in now and he did, feeling a wall of brick or stone a couple of feet deeper in. There was space to his left and right and Tubby felt around, wondering why somebody'd put up this new wall when the old wall was still back there.

Tubby shrugged and started kicking. The noise was loud, plaster cracking, lathing tearing, bits of wall and clouds of dust flying every which way, but Tubby felt fairly certain that nobody would hear him. The stupid school had walls thicker than a fort's.

Van Syke haunted these basement rooms like he lived here . . . maybe he *does* live here, thought Tubby, nobody's ever seen him live any-where . . . *else* . . . but the weird custodian with his dirty hands and yel-low teeth had not been seen by the kids for days, and it was obvious that he didn't give a shit if some of the boys (*Boy's*, thought Tubby) kicked in a wall in the intermediate john. Why would Van Syke care? In a day or two, they'd be boarding up this big old shithouse of a school. Then they'd be tearing it down. Why would Van Syke care?

Tubby kicked away with a fury he seldom showed, putting all the frustration of five years of suffering, even in kindergarten, and being called a "slow student" in this rotten heap of a school. Five years as a "behavior problem" having to sit there, tucked up close to old bags like Mrs. Grossaint and Mrs. Howe and Mrs. Farris, his desk rammed up right next to theirs so they could "keep an eye on him" so that he had to smell their old-lady stink and listen to their old-lady voices and put up with their old-lady rules . . .

Tubby kicked at the wall, feeling it give quickly now as the hole enlarged, until suddenly plaster tumbled across his sneakers, a two-by-four collapsed, and he was staring into a real hole. A *big* hole. A fucking *cave*!

Tubby was fat for a fourth grader, but this hole was so big that he could almost fit in there. He *could* fit! A whole section of wall had come down so the hole was like a hatch in a submarine or something. Tubby turned sideways, forced his left arm and shoulder into the opening, his head still out of the hole, a big grin beginning to form on his face. He moved his left leg into the gap between the fake wall and the old one behind. It was a goddamn secret passage in here!

Tubby crouched and stepped into the hole, pulling his right leg in until only his head and part of his shoulders protruded. He crouched lower, grunting a bit as he settled back into the cool darkness.

Wouldn't Cordie or my old man shit if they came in and saw me now! Of course, Cordie wouldn't be coming into the BOY'S restroom. Or would she? Tubby knew that his older sister was pretty weird. A couple of years earlier, when she was in fourth grade herself, Cordie'd followed Chuck Sperling, the hotshot Little League baseball player, track star, and all-around-asshole, out to Spoon River when he was fishing alone, tracked him for half a morning, and then jumped him, knocked him down, sat on his stomach, and threatened to pound his head in with a rock if he didn't show her his dick.

According to Cordie, he'd pulled it out, crying and spitting blood, and showed her. Tubby was pretty sure that she hadn't told anybody else, and it was damn sure that *Sperling* wasn't going to tell anybody.

Tubby leaned back in his little cave, feeling the plaster dust in his crew cut, and grinned at the dimly lit restroom. He'd jump out and scare the shit out of the next kid who came in to take a leak.

Tubby waited a full two or three minutes but no one came. Once there was a scuffle or rattle way down the main basement corridor, but the sound of approaching sneakers didn't come and nobody showed. The only other noise was the constant trickle of water in the urinals and a soft gurgling in the overhead pipes, like the damned school was talking to itself.

It's like a secret passage in here, Tubby thought again, turning his head to the left to look down the narrow passageway between the two walls. It was dark and smelled like the ground under the front porch of his house where he'd hid from his ma and his Old Man and played when he was smaller. The same musty, rich, rotten smell.

Then, just as he was feeling a bit cramped and weird in the little space, Tubby saw a light at the far end of the passage. It was about where the end of the restroom and the outer wall might be . . . maybe a little farther. It wasn't really a light, he realized, but a kind of glow. Sort of like the soft, green light Tubby'd seen coming off some fungus stuff and rotting mushrooms in the woods at night when he and his Old Man went out coon hunting.

Tubby felt his neck grow cold. He started to step out of the hole, but then he realized what the light must be and he grinned. The GIRLS' (the sign painter had got that right) restroom next door must have an opening in it. Tubby imagined peeking out of whatever hole or crack in the laths was letting that light out of the girls' bathroom.

With a little luck he'd see some girl taking a leak. Maybe even Michelle Staffney or Darlene Hansen or one of those stuck-up sixth-grade bitches with their underpants down around their ankles and their secret parts showing.

Tubby felt his heart pounding, felt the blood stirring elsewhere in his body, and began shuffling sideways, away from the hole, deeper into the passage. It was a close fit.

Panting, blinking cobwebs and dust out of his eyes, smelling the under-the-porch richness of earth all around him, Tubby shuffled toward the glow and away from the light.

Dale and the others were lined up in the room, ready to receive their report cards and be dismissed, when the screaming started. At first it was so loud that Dale thought it was some strange, high-pitched thunder from the storm that was still darkening the sky beyond the windows. But it was too high, too shrill, and lasted too long to be part of the storm, even though it sounded like nothing human.

At first the noise seemed to come from above . . . from up the stairwell on the darkened high-school level . . . but then it seemed to echo from the walls, from downstairs, even from the pipes and metal radiator.

It went on and on. Dale and his brother, Lawrence, had been out at their Uncle Henry's and Aunt Lena's farm the previous autumn when a pig had been prepared for butchering, its throat cut as it hung upside down from the barn rafter above a tin basin set to catch the blood. This noise was a little like that: the same falsetto squeal and screech, like fingernails being dragged along a blackboard, followed by a deeper, fuller scream, ending in a gurgling noise. But then it began again. And again.

Mrs. Doubbet froze in the act of handing a report card to the first student in line—Joe Allen—and she turned toward the doorway and stared at it for a full moment after the terrible noise stopped, as if expecting the source of the scream to appear there. Dale thought that the old lady's expression combined terror with something else . . . anticipation?

A dark shape appeared in the gloom of the doorway and the class, still lined up alphabetically to receive their cards, took a collective breath.

It was Dr. Roon, the principal, his dark, pinstriped suit and slicked-back hair blending with the darkness on the landing behind him so that his thin face seemed to float there, disembodied and disapproving. Dale looked at the man's pink skin and thought, not for the first time: *Like the skin of a newborn rat.*

Dr. Roon cleared his throat and nodded toward Old Double-Butt, who stood precisely where she had been, report card still half-extended toward Joe Allen, her eyes wide, her skin so pale that the rouge and other makeup on her cheeks looked like colored chalkdust on white parchment.

Dr. Roon glanced at the clock. "It is . . . ah . . . three-fifteen. The class is ready for dismissal?"

Mrs. Doubbet managed a nod. Her right hand was clenched so tightly on Joe's card that Dale half-expected to hear a crack as her finger bones snapped.

"Ah . . . yes," said Dr. Roon and his eyes flicked over the twenty-seven students as if they were trespassers in his building. "Well, boys and girls, I thought I would just explain that the . . . ah . . . odd noise you just heard was, Mr. Van Syke informs me, merely the boiler being tested."

Jim Harlen turned around and for a second Dale was sure that he was going to make a funny face—a sure disaster for Dale, who was so tense that he was bound to break up in laughter. Dale desperately did not want to be kept after school. Harlen widened his eyes in an expression more skeptical than funny and turned back to face Dr. Roon.

". . . at any rate, I wanted to take this opportunity to wish you all a pleasant summer vacation," Roon was saying, "and to urge you all to remember the privilege you have had in receiving at least part of your education in Old Central School. While it is too early to tell what the final disposition of this fine old building will be, we can only hope that the school district, in its wisdom, will see fit to preserve it for future generations of scholars such as yourself."

Dale could see Cordie Cooke far up the line, still staring over her left shoulder at the windows and nonchalantly picking her nose.

Dr. Roon did not seem to notice. He cleared his throat as if preparing to give another speech, glanced again at the clock, and said only, "Very well. Mrs. Doubbet, if you would be so good as to distribute the children's fourth-quarter reports." The little man nodded, turned his back, and faded into the shadows.

Old Double-Butt blinked once, seemed to remember where she was, and handed Joe Allen his card. Joe didn't pause to look at it, but hurried to line up at the doorway. Other classes were already descending the stairs in lines; Dale always noticed that on the TV shows and movies about school, kids ran like crazy when they were dismissed or when a bell rang ending a period, but his experience in Old Central was that everyone traveled everywhere in lines, and these last seconds of the last minute of the last day in school were no exception.

The line was shuffling past Mrs. Doubbet, and Dale accepted his report card in its brown envelope, smelling a sour sweat-and-talcum smell around his teacher as he stepped past her to get in the other line. Then Pauline Zauer had her card, the lines at the door were formed—they didn't line up alphabetically for dismissal, but boys and girls, bus students in the front of each line, city kids behind—and Mrs. Doubbet stepped out in front of them, folded her arms as if to give one last comment or admonition, paused, and then silently gestured for them to follow Mrs. Shrives's fifth grade just disappearing down the stairway.

Joe Allen led the charge.

Outside, Dale breathed in the humid air, almost dancing in the light and sudden freedom. The school loomed behind him like a giant wall, but on the graveled drive and grassy playing fields, kids milled in excitement, gathered bikes from the bikestands, ran for the school buses where drivers shouted to hurry, and generally celebrated with noise and motion. Dale waved good-bye to Duane McBride, who was being shooed aboard a bus, and then caught sight of a cluster of third graders still gathered like quail near the bike stand. Dale's brother, Lawrence, galloped up the walk, showing his overbite grin below thick glasses and hanging on to his empty canvas bookbag as he left his third-grade buddies and ran up to join Dale.

"Free!" cried Dale and swung Lawrence around in the air.

Mike O'Rourke and Kevin Grumbacher and Jim Harlen made their way over. "Jeez," said Kevin, "did you hear that sound just as Mrs. Shrives was lining us up?"

"What do you think it was?" asked Lawrence as the group started out across the grassy baseball field.

Mike grinned. "I think it was Old Central getting some third grader." He rubbed his knuckles across Lawrence's crew cut.

Lawrence laughed and twisted away. "Naw, *really*?"

Jim Harlen bent over, offering his backside to the old school. "I think it was Old Double-Butt ripping a fart," he said and provided the sound effects.

"Hey," cried Dale, taking a kick at Jim Harlen's backside and nodding toward his little brother. "Watch it, Harlen."

Lawrence was already laughing and rolling on the grass.

The school buses roared away, heading down different streets. The schoolyard was emptying quickly, kids hurrying off under the tall elms as if in a rush to beat the storm.

Dale paused at the edge of the baseball field, just across the street from his house, and looked back at the black clouds piled up behind Old Central. It was humid and the air felt still and quiet the way it did before tornado warnings, but he could tell by looking that the storm front was almost past. A band of blue sky was visible above the trees to the south. As the group watched a breeze came up, the leaves stirred on the trees ringing the block, and the summer scent of new-mown grass and blossoms and foliage filled the air.

"Look," said Dale.

"Isn't that Cordie Cooke?" asked Mike.

"Yeah." The short figure stood alone outside the north entrance to the school, her arms folded, foot tapping. She looked dumpier and sillier than ever in the oversized housedress that almost dragged the gravel. Two of the smallest Cooke boys, the twins, who were in first grade, stood behind her, their bib overalls sagging. The Cookes lived far enough out of town to have the school bus take them home, but no bus went out toward the grain elevator and dump, so she and her three brothers walked out the railroad tracks. Now she was screaming something at the building.

Dr. Roon appeared at the door and shooed her away with a flick of his pink hand. White blurs in the tall windows above may have been the faces of teachers looking out. Mr. Van Syke's face floated behind the principal's in the dark doorway.

Roon called something else, turned his back, and closed the tall door. Cordie Cooke bent down, grabbed a rock from the gravel drive, and heaved it at the school. The rock bounced off the window of the main door.

"Jeez," breathed Kevin.

The door slammed open and Van Syke emerged just as Cordie

grabbed her two little brothers by the hand and took off down the drive and then down Depot Street toward the train tracks. She moved very fast for a fat girl. One of her kid brothers tripped as they crossed Third Avenue but Cordie just dragged him through the air until his feet found pavement again. Van Syke ran to the edge of the schoolground and stopped, his long fingers groping at air.

"Jeez," Kevin said again.

"Come on," said Dale. "Let's get out of here. My mom said she'd have lemonade for all of us after school."

With a whoop and a holler the band of boys left the school-grounds, loped under the elms, bounded across the crowned asphalt of Depot Street, and ran toward freedom and summer.

THREE

Few events in a human being's life—at least a male human being's life—are as free, as exuberant, as infinitely expansive and filled with potential as the first day of summer when one is an eleven-year-old boy. The summer lies ahead like a great banquet and the days are filled with rich, slow time in which to enjoy each course.

Awakening on that first delicious morning of summer, Dale Stewart had lain for a moment in that brief twilight of consciousness, already savoring the *difference* even before realizing what it was: no alarm clock or mother's shout to rouse him and his brother, Lawrence, no gray, cold fog pressing at the windows and no grayer, colder school awaiting them at eight-thirty, no loud chorus of adult voices telling them what to do, what workbook pages to turn to, what thoughts to think. No, this morning there were the sound of birds, the rich, warm air of summer coming through screens, the sound of a lawnmower down the street as some early-rising retired person began the daily yard chores, and—already visible through the curtains—the rich, warm benediction of sunlight falling across Dale's and Lawrence's beds as if the barrier of the gray school year had been raised and color had been allowed to return to the world.

Dale had rolled to one side and seen his brother's eyes open and staring above the glass-black eyes of his teddy bear. Then Lawrence had grinned that overbite-joyous grin of his, and the two boys were up, throwing their pajamas off in a rush, tugging on jeans and t-shirts waiting on nearby chairs, pulling on clean white socks and less-than-clean sneakers, and then were out, clattering down the stairs for a perfunctory breakfast, laughing with their mom over silly things, and then out again . . . onto their bikes, down the street, away, off into summer.

Three hours later the brothers were in Mike O'Rourke's chickenhouse, sprawled with their friends on the legless, sprung couch, torn chairs, and littered floor of their unofficial clubhouse. The others were there— Mike, Kevin, Jim Harlen, even Duane McBride in from his farm while his dad shopped at the co-op store—and all seemed stunned into incapacity by the bewildering array of choices facing them.

"We could ride out to Stone Creek or Hartley's Pond," said Kevin. "Go swimming."

"Uh-uh," said Mike. He was lying on the sofa with his legs over the back, his back in the sprung cushions, and his head on a catcher's mitt lying on the floor. He was shooting at a daddy longlegs on the ceiling with a rubber band that he would retrieve after each ricochet. So far he had been careful not to hit the insect, but it was shuttling back and forth in some agitation. Each time it got close to a concealing crack or two-by-four rafter, Mike would fire the rubber band and send it scuttling in the opposite direction. "I don't want to go swimming," said Mike. "Water moccasins will be all worked up because of the storm last night."

Dale and Lawrence exchanged glances. Mike was afraid of snakes; it was the only fear they knew their friend had.

"Play ball," said Kevin.

"Nah," said Harlen from where he lay on a sprung armchair reading a Superman comic. "I didn't bring my glove and I'd have to ride all the way home to get it." While the rest of the boys—with the exception of Duane—lived within a short block of each other, Jim Harlen lived on the far end of Depot Street, near the tracks that led out to the dump and the squalid shacks where Cordie Cooke lived. Harlen's house was all right, an old, white farmhouse which had been swallowed up by the town decades before, but a lot of his neighbors were weird. J.P. Congden, the crazy justice of the peace, lived only two houses away from Harlen, and J.P.'s son, C.J., was the meanest bully in town. The boys didn't like playing at Harlen's house, or even going up that way if they could help it, and they understood Jim Harlen's reluctance to go back that way to get his stuff.

"Head out to the woods," suggested Dale. "Maybe check out Gypsy Lane."

The other boys stirred restlessly. There was no obvious reason to veto the suggestion but lethargy had them firmly in its grip. Mike fired the rubber band and the daddy longlegs scurried away from the impact site.

"That'd take too long," said Kevin. "I've got to be home for dinner."

The other boys smiled but said nothing. They were all familiar with the voice of Kevin's mother when she opened the door and shouted "Ke-VIIIN!" in a rising falsetto. And they were familiar with the alacrity with which Kevin dropped whatever he was doing and ran for the white ranch house on the low hill next to Dale and Lawrence's older home.

"What do you want to do, Duane?" asked Mike. O'Rourke was the born leader, always polling everyone before deciding.

The big farm boy with his goofy haircut, baggy corduroy pants, and placid gaze was chewing on something—not gum—and his expression was almost retarded. Dale knew how misleading that dumb hick appearance was—all the boys sensed it—because Duane McBride was so smart that the others could only *guess* at his thought patterns. He was so smart that he didn't even have to show how smart he was in school, preferring to let the teachers writhe in frustration at the oversized boy's perfectly correct but terse answers, or scratch their heads at verbal responses tinged with an irony which bordered on impertinence. Duane didn't care about school. He cared about things the other boys didn't understand.

Duane stopped chewing and nodded toward the old RCA Victor floor-model radio that was in the corner. "I think I'd like to listen to the radio." He took three thumping steps toward the thing, squatted gracelessly in front of it, and began twiddling the dial.

Dale stared. The cabinet was huge, almost four feet tall, and impressive with its different dial bands—the top one saying NATIONAL and listing Mexico City at 49 Megahertz, Hong Kong, London, Madrid, Rio, and a list of others at 40 Mh, the sinister cities of Berlin, Tokyo, and Pittsburgh at 31 Mh, and Paris alone and mysterious far down the dial at 19 Mh—but the cabinet was empty. There were no works left at all.

Duane squatted and twiddled the dials carefully, head cocked, alert for the slightest sound.

Jim Harlen caught on first. He scooted behind the cabinet, pulling it back in the corner so no part of him showed.

Duane said, "I'll try the domestic band." He twiddled the middle dial between INTERNATIONAL and SPECIAL SERVICE. "This is labeled Chicago down here," he muttered to himself.

From inside the cabinet came a hum, as if of tubes warming up, then a rasp of static as Duane moved the dial. Short bursts of baritone were silenced as announcers were cut off in midsentence, snatches of rock and roll music exploded and were silenced, static, rasp, a ballgame—the Chicago White Sox!

"He's going back! Back! Back against the right field wall of Comiskey Park! He's jumping for it! He's going up on the wall! He's . . ."

"Aw, nothin' here," muttered Duane. "I'll try the International Band. Dum-da-dee . . . here we are . . . Berlin."

"Ach du lieber der fershlugginer ball ist op und outta hier!" came Harlen's voice, changed instantly from the excited Chicago Dizzy-Deanish drawl to a throaty, Teutonic lashing of syllables. "Der Fuhrer ist nicht ge-happy. Nein! Nein! Er ist gerflugt und vertunken und der veilige pisstof-fen!"

"Nothin' here," muttered Duane. "I'll try Paris."

But the falsetto and phony French from behind the cabinet was lost in the giggles and laughter in the chickenhouse: Mike O'Rourke's last shot with the rubber band went wild and the daddy longlegs escaped into a crack in the roof. Dale crawled toward the radio, ready to try some stations, while Lawrence rolled on the floor. Kevin crossed his arms and pursed his lips while Mike prodded him in the ribs with his sneaker.

The spell was broken. The boys could do anything they wanted to.

Hours later, after dinner, in the long, painfully sweet twilight of a summer's evening, Dale, Lawrence, Kevin, and Harlen slid their bikes to a stop at the corner near Mike's house. "Ee-aw-kee!" shouted Lawrence.

"Kee-aw-ee!" came the shouted response from the shadows under the elms and Mike rode out to meet them, sliding his rear tire in the loose gravel, spinning to face the same direction the others were facing.

This was the Bike Patrol, formed two years earlier by these five boys when the oldest were in fourth grade and the youngest still believed in Santa Claus. They didn't call it the Bike Patrol now because they were self-conscious about the name, too grown up to pretend they patrolled Elm Haven in order to help people in distress and to protect the inno-cent from evildoers, but they still *believed* in the Bike Patrol. Believed with the simple acquiescence to the reality of *now* which once left them lying awake on Christmas Eve with pulses racing and mouths dry.

They paused there a moment on the quiet street. First Avenue con-tinued past Mike's house out into countryside, north to the water tower a quarter of a mile, and then turning east until it disappeared in the eve-ning haze above the fields near the horizon where the woods and Gypsy Lane and the Black Tree Tavern waited out of sight.

The sky was a softly burnished shield of gray, fading now in the hour between sunset and dark, and the corn in the fields was low, not yet up to an eleven-year-old's knees. Dale looked out over the fields that stretched east past distance-softened horizons of trees and imagined Peoria there—thirty-eight miles away beyond the hills and valleys and stretches of tim-ber, lying in its own river valley and glowing with a thousand lights—but there was no glow there, only a quickly darkening horizon, and he could not really imagine the city. Instead he heard the soft rustle and whisper of the corn. There was no breeze. Perhaps it was the sound of the corn growing, thrusting its way up to become the wall that would soon surround Elm Haven and seal it off from the world.

"Come on," Mike said softly and stood on the pedals, leaning far forward over his handlebars and taking off in a shower of gravel.

Dale and Lawrence and Kevin and Harlen followed.

They rode south down First Avenue in the soft gray light, moving under elm shadow and emerging quickly into open twilight. The low fields lay open to their left, the dark houses to their right. Past School Street and the hint of Donna Lou Perry's house glowing a block to the west. Past Church Street and its long corridor of elms and oaks. And then they were at the Hard Road, Highway 151 A, and slowing out of habit before swinging right onto the empty but still-warm pavement of the two-lane main street.

They pedaled furiously, swinging up onto the sidewalk after the first block to let an old Buick roar past. They were riding west now, toward the glow in the sky, and the building fronts on the two blocks of Main Street gleamed in the fading light. A pickup truck pulled out of the diagonal parking in front of Carl's Tavern on the south side of the street and weaved toward them down the Hard Road. Dale recognized the driver of the old GM truck as Duane McBride's dad. The driver was drunk.

"Lights!" shouted all five boys as they pedaled past. The pickup continued on without headlights or taillights, making a wide turn up First Avenue behind them.

They jumped from the raised sidewalk to the empty Hard Road and continued west past Second Avenue and Third, past the bank and the A&P on their right, past the Parkside Cafe and Bandstand Park all dark and quiet under the elms to their left. It *felt* like Saturday night but it was only Thursday. No Free Show illuminated the night with its light and noise in the park. Not yet. But soon enough.

Mike hollered and swung left down Broad Avenue along the north end of the small park, past the tractor dealership and the small houses clustered there. It was getting dark in earnest now. Behind them, the tall streetlight flicked on along Main Street, illuminating the two blocks of downtown. Broad Avenue was a quickly darkening tunnel under the elms at their backs, an even darker tunnel in front of them.

"Touch the stairway!" shouted Mike.

"No!" yelled Kevin.

Mike always proposed it; Kevin always opposed it. They always did it.

Another block south, in a part of town the boys visited only during these twilight patrols. Past the long, dead-end street of new houses where Digger Taylor and Chuck Sperling lived. Past the official end of Broad Avenue. Up the private lane to the Ashley Mansion.

Weeds choked the rutted drive. Untended limbs hung low and thrust from the thickets on either side to slash at the unwary biker. It was full dark in this tunnel of a driveway.

As always, Dale put his head down and pedaled furiously to stay close to Mike. Lawrence was gasping to keep pace on his smaller bike but he kept up . . . just as he always did. Harlen and Kevin were nothing but the sound of wheels on gravel behind them.

They emerged into the open area near the ruins of the old house. A pillar caught gray light above the brambles and thickets. The stones of the charred foundation were black. Mike wheeled around the circular drive, swung right as if he were going to climb the weed-littered stone stairs to leap into the collapsed foundation, and then slapped the flat slab of porch stone as he continued on.

Dale did likewise. Lawrence swung and missed but did not go back. Kevin and Harlen pedaled past in a flurry of gravel.

Around the wide circle of overgrown drive, wheels crunching and slipping on ruts and gravel. Dale noticed how much darker it was with the summer growth shutting out the light. Behind him the Ashley Mansion became a dark jumble, a secret place of burned timbers and collapsed floors. He liked it best that way—mysterious and slightly ominous as it was now rather than merely sad and abandoned as it was in the light of day.

They emerged from the night-black lane, formed up five abreast on Broad Street, and coasted downhill past the new section and Bandstand Park. They caught their breath and pedaled quickly to cross the Hard Road between a semi headed west and a semi headed east. The westbound truck's headlights caught Harlen and Kevin in their glare and Dale looked back in time to see Jim give the trucker the finger.

An airhorn blasted behind them as they pedaled up Broad Avenue, bikes almost silent on the asphalt under the overarching elms, breathing in the scent of new-mown grass on the broad lawns which swept back away from the street to the big house. Gliding north past the post office and the small white library and the larger white building which was the Presbyterian Church where Dale and Lawrence went, farther north, another long block past tall houses where leaf shadow moved above and below streetlamps and where Mrs. Doubbet's old house showed a single light on the second floor and Mrs. Duggan's house showed no light at all.

They reached Depot Street and slid to a stop in the gravelly intersection, breathing softly. It was full night now. Bats darted above their heads. The sky cut pale patterns from the dark foliage above them. Dale squinted and saw the first star to the east.

"See you guys tomorrow," said Harlen and swung his bike west up Depot Street.

The others waited and watched until he was out of sight under the lower oaks and cottonwoods which darkened the street, until the sound of his pedaling was gone.

"Let's go," whispered Kevin. "My mom's going to be furious."

Mike grinned at Dale in the dim light and Dale could feel a lightness and energy in his arms and legs, an almost electrical charge of potential in his body. *Summer*. Dale punched his brother affectionately on the shoulder.

"Cut it out," said Lawrence.

Mike stood and pedaled east down Depot. There were no lights on this street and the last of the glow in the sky painted pale shapes on the road surface—shapes which were quickly erased by moving leaf shadows.

They rushed past Old Central without speaking, but each of them glanced to his right to look at it, the view somewhat obstructed by the dying elms, the mass of the old building blocking out the sky.

Kevin peeled off first, swinging left and crunching up his driveway. His mother was not in sight but the inner door was open—a sure sign that she had been calling him.

Mike slid to a stop at the intersection of Depot and Second Avenue, the schoolyard an entire block of darkness behind them.

"Tomorrow?" he said.

"Yeah," said Dale.

"Yeah," said Lawrence.

Mike nodded and was gone.

Dale and Lawrence put their bikes around back on the small open porch. They could see their mother moving around in the lighted kitchen. She was baking something and her face was flushed.

"Listen," said Lawrence, grabbing his older brother's hand.

Across the street, in the darkness around Old Central, there was a sibilant rush as of voices speaking hurriedly in an adjoining room.

"It's just a TV somewhere . . ." began Dale, but then he heard the sound of breaking glass, a shout quickly stifled.

They stood there another minute but a wind had come up and the leaves rustling in the broad oak over the drive drowned any further sound.

"Come on," said Dale, still holding his brother's hand.

They went into the light.

FOUR

Duane McBride waited in Bandstand Park until the Old Man got drunk enough to be thrown out of Carl's Tavern. It was past eight-thirty when the Old Man came staggering out, stood weaving on the curb, shook his fist and shouted curses at Dom Steagle, the owner of Carl's (there had been no Carl since 1943), and then tumbled into the pickup, cursing as he dropped his keys on the floor, cursing again as he found them, ground the starter, and flooded the engine. Duane hurried. He knew that the Old Man was drunk enough to forget that Duane had ridden with him when they had come into town almost ten hours earlier "to pick up a few things at the co-op."

"Duanie," said the Old Man, squinting at his son. "What the hell are you doing here?"

Duane said nothing, letting the Old Man's memory work.

"Oh, yeah," the Old Man said at last, "did you see your friends?"

"Yeah, Dad." Duane had left Dale and the others in late afternoon when they'd gone over to the city ballpark to play a pickup game. There had been a chance that the Old Man would stay sober enough to head home before Dom threw him out.

"Hop in, kiddo." The Old Man was enunciating with the precise care and south Boston accent that came out only when he was seriously drunk.

"No thanks, Dad. I'll ride in the back if that's OK."

The Old Man shrugged, ground the starter again, and got the heap started. Duane jumped into the back next to the tractor parts they'd picked up that morning. He stuck his notebook and pencil in his shirt pocket and crouched low on the metal truckbed, peering over the side, hoping that the Old Man wouldn't rack up this new GM junker the way he had the last two used trucks they'd owned.

Duane saw Dale and the others riding down Main in the dim light, but he didn't think they'd seen this vehicle before so he lay low in the truckbed while the Old Man weaved past. Duane heard the shouted "Lights!" but the Old Man ignored them or hadn't heard. The truck screeched around the corner on First Avenue and Duane sat up in time to see the old brick home on the east side—the Slave House the town kids called it although most didn't know why.

Duane knew why. It was the old Thompson place and it had been a way station on the Underground Railroad in the 1850s. Duane had become interested in the slave escape route when he was in third grade and had done some research in the city library over in Oak Hill. Besides the Thompson place, there had been two other Underground Railroad way stations in Creve Coeur County . . . one, an old frame farmhouse belonging to a Quaker family in the Spoon River valley toward Peoria, had burned down before the Second World War. But the other one had belonged to the family of a kid in Duane's third-grade class and one Saturday Duane had ridden his bike there—eight and a half miles each way—just to see the place. Duane had shown the kid and his family where the hidden room was behind the closet under the stairway. And then he had pedaled home. The Old Man hadn't been drinking that Saturday and Duane had avoided a beating.

They roared past Mike O'Rourke's place, out past the city ballpark north of town, and turned east at the water tower. Duane shifted around in the truckbed as they hit gravel. He hunkered down and closed his eyes as gravel flew and dust surrounded him, tickling his neck under his heavy plaid shirt, settling in his hair and between his teeth.

The Old Man didn't run off the road, although he almost missed the turnoff to County Road Six. The truck braked, skidded, tipped, righted itself, and then they were pulling into the crowded parking lot of the Black Tree Tavern.

"I'll be just a minute, Duanie." The Old Man slapped at Duane's arm. "Just stop in to say hi to the boys before we head home to work on the tractor."

"OK, Dad." Duane settled lower into the pickup bed, propped his head against the back of the cab, and pulled out his worn notebook and pencil. It was full dark now, the stars were visible beyond the trees behind the Black Tree, but enough yellow light spilled through the screen door to allow Duane to read if he squinted.

The notebook was thick, warped with sweat and smeared with dust, and the pages were almost filled with Duane's tiny script. There were almost fifty similar notebooks in the secret hiding place in his basement room at home.

Duane McBride had known that he wanted to be a writer since he was six years old. Duane's reading—he had read complete books since he was four years old—had always been another world for him. Not an escape, since he rarely sought escape . . . writers had to confront the world if they were going to observe it accurately . . . but another world nonetheless. One filled with powerful voices relaying even more powerful thoughts.

Duane would always love the Old Man for sharing books and the love of reading with him. Duane's mother had died before he was old enough to really know her, and the intervening years had been rough, what with the farm going to hell and the Old Man's drinking, the occasional beatings and even more occasional abandonments, but there were good times too—the normal flow of days when the Old Man was on the wagon, the easy cycle of hard work in the summers even if they couldn't keep up, the long evenings with the two of them talking to Uncle Art . . . three bachelors cooking steaks in the backyard and talking about everything under the stars, including the stars.

Duane's old man had dropped out of Harvard but gotten his master's in engineering at the University of Illinois before coming back to run his mother's farm. Uncle Art had been a traveler and poet—merchant marine one year, teaching at private schools in Panama or Uruguay or Orlando the next. Even when they drank too much, their talk was interesting to the third bachelor in the circle, young Duane, and he drank in information with the insatiable appetite of the terminally gifted.

No one in Elm Haven or in the Creve Coeur County school system thought of Duane McBride as gifted. The term simply did not exist in 1960 rural Illinois. He was fat. He was odd. The teachers often had described him—in written comments and the rare parent-teacher conferences—as unkempt, unmotivated, and inattentive. But not a discipline problem. Merely a disappointment. Duane did not apply himself.

When confronted by his teachers, Duane would apologize, smile, and amble on with whatever private thoughts and projects were possessing him at the time. School was not a problem, not even a hindrance really since he liked the *idea* of school . . . it was merely a distraction from his studies and his preparation for becoming a writer.

Or it would have been merely a distraction if there hadn't been something about Old Central that bothered him. Not the kids so much. Not even the principal and teachers, slow-witted and provincial as they seemed. There was something else.

Duane squinted in the dim light and flipped his notebook back a few pages to yesterday, the final day of school:

"Others don't seem to notice the smell here, or if they do, they don't talk about it: a smell of coldness, meat-locker taint, faint hint of corruption like the time the heifer died down behind the south pond and the Old Man and I didn't find it for a week.

"Light is odd in Old Central. Thick. The time the Old Man took me to the abandoned hotel in Davenport when he was going to salvage all that stuff and make a fortune. *Thick* light. Filtered through dust and thick drapes and memories of former glory. Same musty, hopeless smell, too. Remember shafts of light from a high window to the parquet floor in that abandoned ballroom—like the stained-glass windows above the stairways in Old Central?

"No. More a sense of . . . foreboding? Evil? Too melodramatic. A sense of *awareness* to both places. That and the sound of rats scurrying in the walls. Wonder why no one else talks about the sound of the rats in Old Central. Wouldn't think the county health people would be too thrilled with an elementary school with rats, rat droppings everywhere, rats running on top of the pipes down in the basement where the restrooms are. I remember when I was in second grade in Old Central and I went down there. . . ."

Duane skipped ahead to the notes he had made that afternoon in Bandstand Park.

"Dale, Lawrence (never Larry), Mike, Kevin, and Jim. How to describe peas in a pod?

"Dale, Lawrence, Mike, Kevin, and Jim. (How come everybody calls Jim 'Harlen'? You get the feeling even his mom does. Course *she's* not even a Harlen anymore. Took her old name back when she got divorced. Who else do I know in E.H. who got divorced? Nobody if you don't count Uncle Art's wife who I never met and who he probably doesn't even remember because she was Chinese and the marriage only lasted two days, twenty-two years before I was born.)

"Dale, Lawrence, Mike, Kevin, and Jim.

"How to compare peas in a pod? Haircuts:

"Dale's got the basic Elm Haven crew cut—old Friers does it in his spooky barbershop (barber pole = guild sign. Blood spiraling down. Maybe they were vampires in the Middle Ages). But Dale's crew cut is a little longer in front—hair almost long enough to make bangs. Dale doesn't pay attention to his hair. (Except that time his mom cut it when we were in third grade and left those chunks and gashes . . . little archipelago of bald spots . . . then Dale kept his Cub Scout cap on, even in class.)

"Lawrence's hair is shorter, stuck up in front with butch wax. Goes with his glasses and buck teeth. Make a skinny face skinnier. Wonder what haircuts'll look like in the future? Say, 1975? One thing's for sure—won't look like the science fiction movies where the actors've got today's look with shiny clothes and skullcaps on. Maybe long hair? Like in T. Jefferson's day? Or greased down and parted in the middle like the way the Old Man looks in his old Harvard photos? One thing's for sure, we'll all look back at our photos from now and think we look like geeks."

Duane paused, took his glasses off, and thought about the origins of the word "geek." He knew it meant the guy in the circus sideshow who bit the heads off chickens . . . Uncle Art had told him that and Art was reliable with words . . . but what was the etymology?

Duane cut his own hair. When he remembered. It was long on top . . . much longer than common for a boy in 1960 . . . but cut quite short over the ears. He did not comb it. Now it felt grimy—the dusty ride from Elm Haven. Duane opened the notebook again.

"Mike: same crewcut-type haircut, probably from his mom or one of his sisters since they don't have enough money for barber, but somehow it looks better on O'Rourke. Longer in front but not sticking up, not bangs either. Never noticed but Mike has eyelashes as long as a girl's. His eyes are strange—so gray-blue you notice them from far away. His sisters would probably kill to have eyes like that. But he's not sissified, effeminate (sp.?) . . . just handsome in a way. Sort of like Senator Kennedy only not like him at all, if that makes sense. (Don't like it when Mailer or somebody describes a character as looking like an actor or something. Lazy.)

"Kevin Grumbacher's hair sort of leaps straight up, like curry comb above a rabbit's face. Goes with his prominent Adam's apple and freckles and nervous grin and general air of anxious consternation. Always waiting for his mommy to call him home.

"Jim's hair—Harlen's hair—not really a crew cut, although it's short. Sort of a squarish face with a wisp of hair on top. Jim Harlen reminds me of that actor we saw in the Free Show last summer, in the movie *Mr. Roberts,* the fellow who played Ensign Pulver. Jack Lemmon. (Oops, here you go again. Just describe characters in your books as looking like movie stars; it'll help the casting when they sell to H'wood.) But Harlen *does* look like the Ensign Pulver guy. Same mouth. Same nervous, funny mannerisms. Same tense, sarcastic chatter. Same haircut? Who cares.

"O'Rourke's sort of calm, a leader, the way Henry Fonda was in that movie. Maybe Jim Harlen's just acting out his character from that film, too. Maybe we're all imitating characters we saw at the Free Show last summer and we don't know . . ."

Duane closed the notebook, took off his glasses, and rubbed his eyes. He was tired although he'd done no work that day. And hungry. He tried to remember what he'd fixed for breakfast, gave it up. When the others had scattered for lunch, Duane had stayed in the chickenhouse, making notes, thinking.

Duane was tired of thinking.

He jumped down from the pickup and walked to the edge of the woods. Fireflies winked against the blackness. Duane could hear the frogs and cicadas calling from around the creek in the ravine below him. The hillside behind Black Tree Tavern was littered with garbage and junk, black shapes against the blacker background, and Duane unzipped and urinated into the darkness, hearing the patter fall on something metallic below. Heavy laughter came through a lighted window and Duane could pick out the Old Man's voice, rising above the others, getting ready to hit them with the punch line to the story.

Duane loved the Old Man's stories, but not when he was drinking. The usually humorous tales turned mean and dark, edged with cynicism. Duane knew that the Old Man thought of himself as a failure. Failed Harvard man, failed engineer, failed farmer, failed inventor, failed get-rich-quick businessman, failed husband, failed father. Duane generally agreed with the Old Man's assessment although he thought that the jury might still be out on the last charge.

Duane went back to the pickup and climbed into the cab, keeping the door open to let the whiskey smell out. He knew that whatever bartender was working tonight would toss the Old Man out just before he got violent. And he knew that he'd get the Old Man into the back of the pickup so he wouldn't struggle or grab the wheel, and then he—Duane, eleven years old last March, a C student with an IQ of 160 + according to Uncle Art, who'd dragged him up to the U. of I. two winters ago to be tested for God knows what reason—then he would drive the Old Man home, put him to bed, make supper, and go out to the barn to see if the parts fit in the John Deere.

Later, much later, Duane was awakened by a whispering in his ear.

Even half asleep he knew that he was home—he'd driven the Old Man over the two hills, past the cemetery and Dale's Uncle Henry's place, then out County Six to the farm; he'd planted the Old Man snoring in his bed and set in the new distributor before coming in to cook some hamburger—but he was surprised that he'd gone to sleep with the radio receiver still whispering in his ear.

Duane slept in the basement, in a corner he'd partitioned off with a hanging quilt and some crates. It wasn't as pathetic as it sounded. The second floor was too cold and empty in the winter and the Old Man had given up sleeping in the bedroom he had shared with Duane's mother. So now the Old Man slept on the daybed in the parlor and Duane had his basement; it was warm down there near the furnace, even when the winds blew across stubbled fields in the cold belly of winter, there was a shower there and only a tub on the second floor, and Duane had brought down a bed, a dresser, his lab and darkroom stuff, his workbench, and his electronics.

Duane had listened to the radio late at night since he was three years old. The Old Man used to, but had given it up some years before.

Duane had crystal sets and store-bought receivers, Heath kits and rebuilt consoles, shortwave and even a new transistor model. Uncle Art had suggested that Duane get into ham radio, but Duane wasn't interested. He didn't want to send, he wanted to *listen*.

And listen he did, late at night in the shadows of his basement with antenna wire strung everywhere, running up conduits and out windows. Duane listened to Peoria stations, and Des Moines, and Chicago, and the big stations from Cleveland and Kansas City, of course, but he most enjoyed the distant stations, the whispers from North Carolina and Arkansas and Toledo and Toronto, and occasionally, when the ion layer was right and the sunspots quiet, the babble in Spanish or slow Alabama tones almost as foreign, or the call letters of a California station or a Quebec call-in show. Duane listened to sports, closing his eyes in the Illinois darkness and imagining the floodlit ballfields where the grass was as green as arterial blood was red, and he listened to music—he liked classical, loved Big Band, but lived for jazz—but most of all, Duane listened for the call-in talk shows where patient, unseen hosts waited for useless listeners to call in with their rambling but fervent comments.

Sometimes Duane imagined that he was the single crewman on a receding starship, already light-years from Earth, unable to turn around, doomed never to return, unable even to reach his destination in a human lifetime, but still connected by this expanding arc of electromagnetic radiation, rising now through the onionlike layers of old radio shows, traveling back in time as he traveled forward in space, listening to voices whose owners had long since died, moving back toward Marconi and then silence.

Someone was whispering his name.

Duane sat up in the darkness and realized that his earphones *were* still in place. He had been testing the new Heath kit before falling asleep.

The voice came again. It was probably feminine but seemed oddly sexless. The tone was made tenuous by distance but was as clear as the stars he had seen on his way in from the barn at midnight.

She . . . it . . . was calling his name.

"Duane . . . Duane . . . we're coming for you, my dear."

Duane sat up on his bed, clamped the earphones tighter. The voice didn't seem to be coming through the earphones. It seemed to be coming from under his bed, from the darkness above the heating pipes, from the cinderblock walls.

"We *will* come, Duane, my dear. We will come soon."

No one called Duane "my dear." Not even in jest. He had no idea if his mother had when she was alive. Duane ran his hand down the earphone cord, found the cold jack on his blankets where he had pulled it free after turning off the receiver.

"We will come soon, Duane, my dear," the voice whispered urgently in his ear. "Wait for us, my dear."

Duane leaned out into darkness, felt for the hanging cord, and tugged on the light.

The earphones were not plugged in. The receiver was off. None of his radios were on.

"Wait for us, my dear."

FIVE

Dale smelled Death before he saw it.

It was Friday, the third of June, their second day of summer, and the bunch of them had been playing ball since just after breakfast—by midafternoon they were caked with dust made muddy by their sweat—when Dale smelled Death coming.

"Je-zuz!" cried Jim Harlen from his place between first and second base. "What is *that*?"

Dale was just stepping up to the plate to bat, but now he stepped back and pointed.

The smell had come from the east, blowing with the breeze down the dirt road that connected the city ballpark to First Avenue. The smell was Death—corruption, the stench of recent roadkill, the bloated-to-bursting gasses of bacteria working in dead stomachs—and it was coming closer.

"Oh, *yechhh*," said Donna Lou Perry from the pitcher's mound. She kept the ball in her right hand, raised her baseball mitt to her mouth and nose, and turned to look the direction Dale was pointing.

The Rendering Truck turned slowly from First Avenue and rolled down the hundred yards of dirt road toward them. The truck's cab was scabrous red and the bed behind was shielded by solid wooden slats. Dale could see four legs protruding straight up—a cow perhaps, or a horse, it was hard to tell at this distance—the corpse obviously tossed in among others, the hoofs pointing skyward like a cartoon of a dead animal.

This was no cartoon.

"Aww, give us a *break*," said Mike from his catcher's position behind the plate. He lifted his t-shirt over his mouth and nose as the stench came on stronger.

Dale took another step away from the plate, his eyes watering and stomach churning. The Rendering Truck reached the end of the dirt road and pulled into the grassy parking lot behind the bleachers to their right. The air seemed to grow thick around them as the stench of dead things closed over Dale's face like a hand.

Kevin jogged in from third base. "Is that Van Syke?"

Lawrence came off the bench and stood next to Dale as they both squinted toward the truck, the bills of their wool baseball caps pulled low.

"I don't know," said Dale. "Can't see in the cab because of the stupid glare. But Van Syke usually drives it in the summer, doesn't he?"

Gerry Daysinger had been waiting on-deck behind Dale. Now he held his bat like a rifle and made a face. "Yeah, Van Syke drives it . . . most of the time."

Dale glanced at the shorter boy. All of them knew that Gerry's dad sometimes drove the Rendering Truck or mowed the cemetery . . . odd jobs around town that Van Syke usually took care of. No one had ever seen Mr. Van Syke with a *friend,* but Gerry's dad sometimes hung around with him.

As if reading their thoughts, Daysinger said, "It's Van Syke. My old man's up at Oak Hill today working on a construction job."

Donna Lou walked in from the mound, her mitt still over the lower part of her face. "What's he want?"

Mike O'Rourke shrugged. "I don't see any dead things around here, do you?"

"Just Harlen," said Gerry, flicking a clod of dirt at Jim as he loped in to join the group.

The Rendering Truck sat there, ten yards away, the windshield opaqued by glare and the thick layers of paint on the cab looking like caked blood. Through the slats on the side, Dale could catch a glimpse of hides gray and black, another hint of hoof near the tailgate, something large and brown and bloated just behind the cab. The four legs jutting skyward belonged to a cow. Dale pulled the bill of his cap lower and could see white bone showing through rotted hide. The air was thick with the buzzing of the flies that hung over the truck like a blue cloud.

"What's he *want?*" Donna Lou asked again. The sixth grader had hung around with the Bike Patrol boys for years—she was the best pitcher on their pickup teams—but this summer Dale had noticed how tall she'd grown . . . that and the curves under her t-shirt.

"Let's go ask him," said Mike. He tossed down his glove and started walking toward the opening in the backstop.

Dale felt his heart lurch. He didn't like Van Syke at the best of times. When he thought of him—even in the context of school with teachers and Dr. Roon within shouting distance—he had the image of long, spidery fingers with dirt under the nails, dirt-lined wrinkles on the back of a blister-reddened neck, and yellow teeth which were much too large. Like the teeth on the rats at the dump.

And the thought of walking closer to that truck—that smell—made Dale's insides quiver again.

Mike had reached the fence and was going through the narrow gap there.

"Hey, wait a minute!" called Harlen. "Look!"

A kid was riding down the dirt road and now the bike swerved into right field and crossed the dirt infield in a spray of clods. Dale saw that it was a girl's bike, and that the girl riding it was Sandra Whittaker, Donna Lou's friend.

"Oh, *peww*," said Sandy as she brought the bike to a sliding halt near the group of them. "What died?"

"Mike's dead cousins just drove up," said Harlen. "He was just going over to give them a hug."

Sandy gave Harlen a look and dismissed him with a flounce of her braids. "I've got news. Something *weird's* going on!"

"What?" said Lawrence and adjusted his glasses. The third grader's voice was tense.

"J.P. and Barney and everybody's over at Old Central. Cordie's there and her weird-looking mom. Roon's out there. Everybody. They're looking for Cordie's stupid brother."

"Tubby?" said Gerry Daysinger. He rubbed his runny nose with his hand and wiped it on his gray t-shirt. "I thought he ran away on Wednesday."

"Yeah," panted Sandy, talking to Donna Lou now, "but Cordie thinks he's still in the *school*! Weird, huh?"

"Let's go," said Harlen, running for the row of bikes near first base. The others followed, pulling handlebar grips away from the fence, tucking baseball gloves on their handlebars or onto bats thrown over their shoulders.

"Hey!" called Mike from the other side of the backstop. "What about Van Syke?"

"Give him a kiss for us," yelled Harlen and started pedaling down the dirt road.

Dale followed, Lawrence and Kevin right behind him. Dale pedaled hard, pretending to be excited about Sandy's news. Anything to get away from the stench of Death and the silent Rendering Truck.

Mike waited a minute while the others fled, dust rising behind them. Daysinger didn't have a bike but he rode on the front of Grumbacher's, Kevin's long legs rising and falling as he pedaled hard. Donna Lou glanced toward Mike and then got on her aqua and white bike, threw her mitt in the basket, and rode off with Sandy.

For a moment Mike was all alone on the ballfield. Just him and the terrible stench of dead things and the silent truck. Mike stood there, just behind the backstop, and glared at the truck. It was at least ninety degrees out today—the sun so fierce that it made the sweat run in rivulets down his dusty neck and cheeks. How could Van Syke stand it if he was in that cab with the windows closed?

Mike stood there as the gang of kids reached First Avenue and swung right onto the asphalt street. Sandy and Donna Lou were the last to turn out of sight behind the row of elms there.

Flies buzzed. Something in the back of the Rendering Truck shifted with a soft, liquid sound and the stench grew worse, became almost visible in the thickening air. Mike felt panic begin to rise in him the way it did late at night when he heard a scrabbling in his grandmother's room below him and thought it was her soul scratching to get free . . . or when he knelt too long at High Mass, half-hypnotized by the incense and litany and his own sleepiness, thinking of his sins and the terrible fires of hell and the slimy things waiting for him there. . . .

Mike took another five steps closer to the truck. Grasshoppers jumped away in the dry grass. There was a shadow just visible through the windshield glare.

Mike stopped and gave the truck and its occupants—living and dead—the finger. Then he turned slowly and walked back through the gap in the wood-and-wire backstop, willing himself not to run but waiting for the slam of the cab door and the rush of heavy footsteps.

There was only the sound of flies. Then, softly, unmistakably, there rose from the truckbed a soft mewling which grew to an infant's wail. Mike froze in the act of sliding his mitt onto his handlebars.

No mistake. A baby was crying back there in that crib of death filled with roadkill scraped off asphalt, dead dogs with their guts spilling out, bloated cattle and white-eyed horses, flattened piglets and the rotting offal of a dozen farms.

The crying rose in pitch and intensity, shifted to a wail which perfectly matched Mike's sudden stab of terror, and then fell off to a gurgling . . . as if whatever was there was feeding. Nursing.

Mike pushed his bike away from the fence with legs gone soft. He pedaled out past first base, turned onto the dirt road, and headed for First Avenue.

He did not stop.

He did not look back.

They saw the cars and commotion a block away. J.P. Congden's matte-black Chevy was parked in the school lot next to the constable's car and an old blue panel truck that Dale guessed belonged to Cordie Cooke's mom. Cordie was there, wearing the same shapeless dress she'd worn the entire last month of school, and the overweight, moonfaced woman next to her had to be her mother. Dr. Roon and Mrs. Doubbet stood at the base of the stairs at the north entrance as if blocking the way. The justice of the peace and the town constable—Barney—stood between the two groups like referees.

Dale and the others slid to a stop on the grassy field about twenty-five feet from the group of adults: not so close so they'd be shooed away, not so far away they couldn't hear. Dale looked up as Mike pedaled up and slid to a stop. His friend's face was pale.

"And I say that Terence never came home Wednesday!" shouted Mrs. Cooke. The woman's fat face was browned and wrinkled into folds which made Dale think of Mike's catcher's mitt. Her eyes had the same gray, washed-out, hopeless look that he recognized from his classmate Cordie.

"Terence?" whispered Jim Harlen and made a face.

"Yes, ma'am," said Barney, still standing between the fat woman and the principal and teacher. "Dr. Roon understands that. But they're sure he left the school. We need to find out where he went after school."

"Bullshit!" cried Mrs. Cooke. "My Cordelia says that she didn't see him crossin' the schoolyard . . . and my Terence wouldna left school without permission nohow. He's a good boy. And I woulda tanned his behind to the bone if he hadda."

Kevin turned toward Dale and raised an eyebrow. Dale didn't look away from the group of intense adults.

"Now, Mrs. Cooke," began the short, bald, mean little justice of the peace, "we all know that Tubby . . . uh . . . Terence had his mis-chevious ways about him and . . ."

Mrs. Cooke rounded on the little man. "Shut your face, J.P. Congden. Everybody knows your boy C.J. is the meanest little asshole who ever carried a switchblade. Don't you be tellin' me about my Terence's ways." She looked back at the skinny constable everyone in town called Barney and thrust a blunt finger toward Dr. Roon and Old Double-Butt. "Constable, these people is hidin' something."

Barney made a gesture with both hands, palms out. "Now, now, Mrs.

Cooke. You know they looked everywhere. Mrs. Doubbet *saw* Terence leaving school that afternoon before the children were dismissed . . ."

"An' I say bullshit to that!" shouted Cordie's mother. Cordie herself looked over her shoulder, saw the group of kids, and gave them a blank stare.

Mrs. Doubbet seemed to come out of her daze. "No one speaks to me like that. I have been an educator in this district for almost four decades and I . . ."

"I don't give a pig's ass how long you been teachin' . . ." began Mrs. Cooke.

"Ma, she's *lyin*'!" cried Cordie, tugging on her mother's shapeless dress. "I was lookin' out the window and I didn't see Tubby nowhere. Old Double-Butt wasn't even lookin'."

"Just a minute, young lady," began Dr. Roon. His long fingers played with the watch chain across his vest. "We understand you are upset by your brother's . . . ah . . . temporary absence, but we cannot allow such . . ."

"You tell me where my boy is!" cried Mrs. Cooke, pressing forward against the justice of the peace as if trying to get her small, fat hands on the principal.

"Hey! Hey!" cried J.P. Congden, taking a step back.

Barney stepped between the two again, spoke quickly and earnestly to Cordie's mother in tones the kids could not hear, and then said something softly to Dr. Roon.

"I agree that we should continue the discussion out of the . . . ah . . . public glare," came Dr. Roon's sepulchral tones.

Barney nodded, said something else, and the group went into Old Central. Cordie looked back over her shoulder once at Dale and the others but there was no hostility in her face now . . . only sadness and something which might have been fear.

"It would be better if . . . ah . . . *Mr.* Cooke could join us," Dr. Roon was saying as they went inside.

"He's been feelin' poorly all this week," Cordie's mother said in a tired monotone.

"He's been drunk as a junkyard skunk all this week," said Jim Harlen in a passable imitation of Mrs. Cooke's Okie twang. Harlen squinted at the sun and the now-empty parking lot. "Shit, it's getting late and I promised Mom I'd get the yard mowed. I think the fun's over here."

Lawrence pushed his glasses higher on his nose. "Where do you think Tubby went?"

Harlen leaned over the third grader, twisted his face into a terrible grimace, and raised fingers like claws. "Something *got* him, punko. And tonight it's gonna get *you*!" He leaned closer, saliva dribbling onto his chin.

"Knock it off," said Dale, stepping between Harlen and his brother.

"*Knock it off,*" Harlen parroted in falsetto. "Don't distoib my wittew brudder!" He minced and pirouetted, all wrists and fluttered fingers.

Dale said nothing.

"You'd better go if you're going to mow the yard," said Mike. There was an edge to his voice.

Harlen glanced at O'Rourke, hesitated, said, "Yeah. See ya, simps," and pedaled away down Depot Street.

"See. I toldya it was *weird*," said Sandy and rode away with Donna Lou. Donna shouted "Tomorrow!" back over her shoulder as they reached the line of sentinel elms on the southeast side of the schoolyard.

Dale waved.

Gerry Daysinger said, "Hell, nothing else's going to happen. I'm going home to get a soda pop." He ran off toward his frame-and-tarpaper house on cinderblocks across School Street.

"Ke-VIIINNN!" The shrill cry sounded like a Johnny Weissmuller Tarzan shout. Mrs. Grumbacher's head and shoulders were just visible at the front door.

Kevin wasted no time for farewells but spun his bike and was gone.

The shadow of Old Central spread almost to Second Avenue, pulling the color from the playing fields lying green where sunlight touched and shading the lower levels of three great elms.

J.P. Congden emerged a few minutes later, shouted something bullying at the kids, and then drove away in a shower of gravel.

"My dad says that he uses that Chevy to trick people into speeding," said Mike.

"How?" said Lawrence.

Mike sat down in the grass and plucked a blade of grass. "J.P. hides down in the dairy driveway on the hill where the Hard Road dips down to cross Spoon River. When people come along, he roars out and tries to race them. If they race, he puts his light on top of his car and arrests them for speeding. Drags them to his house and fines them twenty-five dollars. If they *don't* race . . ."

"Yeah?"

"He gets in front of them right before the bridge, slows down, and arrests them for passing within a hundred feet of the bridge when they finally go around."

Lawrence chewed on his grass and shook his head. "What a shitheel."

"Hey!" said Dale. "Watch your mouth. If Mom hears you talking like that . . ."

"Look," said Lawrence, jumping up and running over to a furrowed ridge in the soil. "What's this?"

The two boys ambled over to look. "Gopher," said Dale.

Mike shook his head. "Too big."

"They probably dug a ditch to lay in some new sewer pipe or some-thing and the hump's still here," said Dale. He pointed. "See. There's another ridge. They both run to the school."

Mike walked over to the other furrow, followed it until it disappeared under the sidewalk near the school, and chewed on his blade of grass. "Doesn't make much sense to put in new pipes."

"Why not?" said Lawrence.

Mike gestured toward the shaded side of the school. "They're tearing it *down*. A couple more days, once they get all the junk out, they'll be boarding up the windows. If they . . ." Mike stopped, squinted up toward the eaves, and backed away.

Dale walked over to join him. "What is it?"

Mike pointed. "Up there. See in the center window on the high-school floor?"

Dale shielded his eyes. "Uh-uh. What?"

"Somebody looking out," said Lawrence. "I saw a white face before it moved away."

"Not somebody," said Mike. "It was Van Syke."

Dale glanced over his shoulder, past his house, to the fields beyond. Tree shadow and distance kept him from seeing if the Rendering Truck was still out by the ballfield.

Eventually Mrs. Cooke, Cordie, Barney, and Old Double-Butt came out, said a few unheard words, and drove away in different directions. Only Dr. Roon's car remained and just before dark, just before Dale and Lawrence were called in for dinner, he too came out, locked the school door, and drove away in his hearselike Buick.

Dale kept watching from his front door until his mother ordered him to the table, but Van Syke did not emerge.

He checked after dinner. Evening light touched only the tops of the trees and the scabby green cupola. The rest was darkness.

SIX

Saturday morning, the first Saturday of summer, and Mike O'Rourke was up at dawn. He went into the darkened parlor to check on Memo—she hardly slept at all anymore—and when he saw the pale glint of skin and the blink of an eye in the tangle of comforters and shawls, was sure that she was still alive, he kissed her—smelling the faintest hint of the decay that had come from the Rendering Truck the day before, and then he went out to the kitchen. His father was already up and shaving over the cold-water tap there; he clocked in at seven A.M. at the Pabst brewery in Peoria and the city was more than an hour's drive away. Mike's dad was massive—six feet tall but well over three hundred pounds, most of it in a wide, round belly that kept him far from the sink even while he shaved. His red hair had receded until it was little more than an orange fuzz over his ears, but his forehead was sunburned from weekends working in the garden and broken capillaries in his cheeks and nose added to the general rosiness of his complexion. He shaved with the antique straight razor that had belonged to his grandfather, and he paused now—finger on one stretched cheek, blade poised—to nod at his son as Mike headed for the outhouse.

Mike had only recently come to realize that his was the only family in Elm Haven that still had to use an outhouse. There were other outhouses— Mrs. Moon had one behind her old frame house, Gerry Daysinger had one behind his toolshed—but those were just remnants, artifacts from an earlier age. The O'Rourkes *used* their outhouse. For years Mike's mother had been talking about putting in plumbing other than the pump over the sink, but Mike's dad always decided that it was too expensive since the city had no sewer system and septic tanks cost a fortune. Mike suspected that his father didn't *want* a bathroom inside: with Mike's four sisters and mother always talking, talking, talking in the tiny house, Mike's dad often said that the only place he found true peace and quiet was out back in the john.

Mike finished up, walked back along the flagstone walk that wound between his mother's flower garden and his father's vegetable garden, glanced up to see starlings whirling among high leaves catching the first light of dawn, went in through the small back porch, and washed his hands at the kitchen sink which his father had just vacated. Then he went to the junk cupboard, got out his writing tablet and school pencil, and sat at the table.

"Gonna be late for the papers," said his dad. He was standing at the counter, drinking coffee and looking out through the kitchen window at the garden. The wall clock said 5:08.

"No, I'm not," said Mike. The papers were dropped off at five-fifteen in front of the bank next to the A&P on Main Street where Mike's mother worked. He had never been late in picking them up.

"What're you writing there?" asked his dad. The coffee had seemed to focus him.

"Just some notes to Dale and the guys."

His father nodded, not really seeming to hear, and looked out at his garden again. "That rain the other day really helped the corn."

"See you, Dad." Mike folded the notes in his jean pockets, pulled on a baseball cap, gave his father a bop on the shoulder, and was out the door and on his ancient bike, pedaling down First at full speed.

As soon as Mike finished his morning paper route, he would pedal to St. Malachy's over on the west side of town near the railroad tracks, where he would serve as altar boy while Father Cavanaugh said Mass. Mike did this every day of the year. He had been an altar boy since he was seven, and although other kids came and went, Father C. said that none were as dependable as Mike . . . nor pronounced the Latin as carefully and reverently. The schedule was hard sometimes, especially in winter when the drifts were deep and he couldn't use his bike to get around town. Sometimes then he'd come running into St. Malachy's, tuck his surplice and cassock on without taking time to shrug out of his coat or get into his brown oxfords, say Mass with snow melting from the soles of his boots, and then, if only the usual seven-thirty congregation was there—Mrs. Moon, Mrs. Shaughnessy, Miss Ashbow, and Mr. Kane—Mike would, with Father C.'s permission, take off right after Communion so he could get to school before the last bell rang.

He was still late frequently. Mrs. Shrives wouldn't even talk to him anymore as he came in, merely glower and nod toward the principal's office. Mike would wait there for Dr. Roon to find time to scold him or give him a rap with the Enforcer, the paddle Roon kept in his lower lefthand drawer. The whippings didn't bother Mike anymore, but he hated to sit in the office and miss reading class and most of math.

Mike put the thought of school out of his mind as he sat on the high

sidewalk in front of the bank and waited for the truck carrying the Peoria morning paper. It was *summer*.

The thought of summer, the warmth-in-the-face, smell-of-warming-
pavement-and-moist-crops *reality* of it, filled Mike's spirit with energy and
seemed to expand his chest with air even as the truck arrived, even as he
unbundled the papers and folded them—sticking notes in some and setting those in the extra pocket of his delivery bag, even as he rode the morning streets, tossing papers, shouting good mornings to the women getting
their milk bottles and the men getting into their cars for the commute
elsewhere, and the reality of it, the lessened-gravity of summer, continued
to buoy him up even as he leaned his bike against the wall of St. Malachy's
and rushed into the cool shade-and-incense interior of his favorite place in
the world.

Dale woke late, after eight, and lay in bed a long moment. Light and leaf-
shadow from the giant elm outside filled the window. Warm air came
through the screens. Lawrence was gone already; Dale could hear the
cartoon sounds from the living room downstairs as his brother watched
Heckle and Jeckle and Ruff and Reddy.

Dale got up, made both his and Lawrence's beds, pulled on underwear, jeans, a t-shirt, clean socks and his sneakers, and went downstairs
to breakfast.

His mother had his favorite cereal and raisin toast ready. She was
chipper, chatting about what movies might be shown at the Free Show
that night. Dale's dad was still gone on a road trip—his sales territory
stretched across two states—but he'd be home late that night.

Lawrence called from the living room that Dale should hurry, that
he was missing Ruff and Reddy.

"That's a little kids' show!" Dale shouted back. "It doesn't interest
me." But he ate more quickly.

"Oh, this was in the paper this morning," said his mom. She set the
note next to his bowl.

Dale smiled at the sight of the cheap Big Chief Tablet paper, recognized Mike's careful writing and awful spelling:

EVERYBODY MEAT AT THE CAVE AT NINE THIRTY
—M

Dale scooped up the last of his Wheaties and wondered what was so important that they had to go all the way out there to meet. The Cave was
reserved for special events—secrets, emergency powwows, the special

Bike Patrol meetings back when they were young enough to care about such things.

"Now it's not *really* a cave, is it, Dale?" his mother said, a slight undertone of worry in her voice.

"Uh-uh, Mom. You know it's not. It's just that old culvert out beyond the Black Tree."

"All right, just as long as you remember that you promised to mow the yard before Mrs. Sebert come over to visit this afternoon."

Duane McBride's father didn't subscribe to the Peoria paper—he didn't read any newspaper except for *The New York Times,* and that only rarely—so Duane didn't receive one of Mike's notes. The phone rang around nine A.M. Duane waited: they were on a party line—one ring meant their closest neighbors, the Johnsons; two rings meant Duane's line; and three rings meant a call for Swede Olafson down the road. The phone rang twice, stopped, rang twice again.

"Duane," came Dale Stewart's voice. "I figured you'd be out doing your chores."

"Already did my chores," said Duane.

"Your dad home?"

"He went to Peoria to buy some things."

There was a silence. Duane knew that Dale knew that Duane's Old Man often didn't return from his Saturday "buying trips" until late Sunday night.

"Hey, we're getting together at the Cave at nine-thirty. Mike's got something to tell us."

"Who's 'we'?" Duane glanced down at his notebook. He'd been working on his character sketch since after breakfast. This particular piece had been in progress since April and the notebook was filled with scratch outs, substitutions, entire passages and pages X'ed out, notations scrawled in tiny margins. He knew that this exercise was going to be as far from perfect as all the rest.

"You know," said Dale, "Mike and Kevin and Harlen and maybe Daysinger. I don't know. I just got the note in the paper a while ago."

"How about Lawrence?" Duane looked out at the ocean of corn rising—almost knee-high now—on either side of the long gravel road to their house. His mother, when she was alive, had forbidden the planting of anything taller than beans in the front twenty acres. "It makes me feel too isolated when the corn gets tall," she'd told Uncle Art. "Too claustrophobic." So the Old Man had humored her and planted beans. But Duane couldn't remember a time when summer did not mean the slow secession of their farm home from the world around them. "Waist-high by the Fourth of July," went the old saying about corn, but usually the corn in this part of Illinois was shoulder-high to Duane by the Fourth of July. And beyond that point of the summer, it wasn't so much that the corn *grew* as the farmhouse *shrank*. Duane couldn't even see the county road at the end of the lane unless he went to the second floor to peer over the corn. And neither he nor his Old Man went up on the second floor anymore.

"What about Lawrence?" said Dale.

"Is he coming?"

"*Sure* he's coming. You know he always hangs around with us."

Duane smiled. "Just didn't want you to forget your little brother," he said.

There was an exasperated noise on the line. "Look, Duane, are you coming or not?"

Duane thought of the work he had to do around the farm that day. He'd be lucky to be finished by dark even if he started at once. "I'm pretty busy, Dale. You say you don't know what Mike has in mind?"

"Well, I'm not sure, but I think it has something to do with Old Central. Tubby Cooke missing. You know."

Duane paused. "I'll be there. Nine-thirty, huh? If I start walking now, I should get there about then."

"Jeez," said Dale, his voice tinny over the line, "haven't you got a bike *yet*?"

"If God had meant for me to have a bike," said Duane, "I would have been born with Schwinn as my last name. See you there." He hung up before Dale could reply.

Duane went downstairs to find his notebook with his word-sketch of Old Central in it, pulled on a cap with the word CAT on it, and went out to call his dog. Witt came at once. The name was pronounced "Vit" and was short for Wittgenstein, a philosopher that the Old Man and Uncle Art argued over incessantly. The old collie was almost blind now and moved with the slow-motion painfulness of arthritis, but he sensed that Duane was going somewhere and approached with the hopeful tail-wagging that showed he was ready to join the expedition.

"Uh-uh," said Duane, worried that the walk would be too much for his old friend in this heat. "You stay here today, Witt. Guard the spread. I'll be back by lunchtime."

The collie's cataract-clouded eyes managed to look both hurt and imploring. Duane patted him, led him back to the barn, and made sure his water bowl was full. "Keep the burglars and corn monsters at bay, Witt."

The collie surrendered with a canine sigh and settled onto the blanket on straw that served as his bed.

The day was hot as Duane ambled down the lane toward County Six. He rolled up the sleeves of his plaid flannel shirt and thought about Old Central and about Henry James. Duane had just read *The Turn of the Screw* and now he thought about the estate called Bly, about James's subtle suggestion that a place could resonate with such evil that it provided "ghosts" to haunt the children Miles and Flora.

The Old Man was an alcoholic and a failure, but he was also a thoughtful atheist and dedicated rationalist, and he had raised his son that way. As early as Duane could remember, he had viewed the universe as a complex mechanism following sensible laws: laws that were only partially and poorly understood by the feeble intellects of humankind, but laws nonetheless.

He flipped his notebook open and found the passage about Old Central. ". . . a sense of . . . foreboding? Evil? Too melodramatic. A sense of *awareness.* . . ." Duane sighed, ripped the page out, and stuck it in the pocket of his corduroy pants.

He reached County Six and turned south. Sunlight blazed off the white gravel of the road and burned against Duane's exposed forearms. Behind him, in the fields on either side of the lane to his home, insects rustled and stirred in the growing corn.

Dale, Lawrence, Kevin, and Jim Harlen rode to the Cave together. "Why do we have to meet so damn far away?" grumbled Harlen. His bike was smaller than the others', a seventeen-incher, and he had to pedal twice as hard to keep up.

They rode past O'Rourke's house under its large shade trees, north toward the water tower, then east on the wide gravel road, Kevin and Dale and Lawrence in the hard-packed left rut, Harlen on the right. There was no traffic, no wind, and no sound except for their breathing and the crunch of gravel under their tires. It was almost a mile to County Six. In the fields beyond and to the northeast of the junction, hills and heavy timber began. If they had stayed on the road from the water tower, they would have run into the hilly country between Elm Haven and the almost abandoned town called Jubilee College. County Six continued south for a mile and a half, connecting to Highway 151A, the Hard Road that ran through Elm Haven, but that shortcut was little more than dirt ruts through fields and was impassable during most of the winter and spring.

They turned north, passed the Black Tree Tavern, and roared down the first steep hill, almost standing on their brake pedals. The trees arched over the narrow road here, dappling it in deep shadow. The first time Dale had heard "The Legend of Sleepy Hollow" when Mrs. Grossaint, their fourth-grade teacher, had read it to the class, he had pictured this place with a covered bridge at the bottom.

There was no covered bridge, only rotting wooden railings on either side of the gravel road. The kids slid to a stop at the bottom and walked their bikes down a narrow trail through the weeds on the west side of the road. The weeds were waist-high or taller here, and covered with dust from cars that had passed. Barbed-wire fences separated the dark woods from the thick foliage along the roadside. They stowed their bikes under shrubs, making sure they were invisible from the road, and then followed the trail farther down, into the coolness of the creekside.

At the bottom, the trail was almost invisible as it led *under* the tall weeds and short trees, winding along the narrow stream. Dale led the others into the Cave.

It wasn't a cave. Not exactly. For some reason the county had laid a precast-cement culvert under the road here, rather than use the thirty-inch corrugated steel pipes found everywhere else. Perhaps they had expected spring floods; perhaps they had a cement culvert they hadn't known what to do with. For whatever reason, the thing was huge—six feet across—and there was a fourteen-inch groove in the base of it that let the stream trickle through so that the kids could recline on the curved base of the culvert and stretch their legs out without getting wet. It was cool in the Cave on the hottest of days, the entrances were almost covered over with vines and weeds, and the sound of cars passing on the roadbed ten feet above them just made the hiding place seem that much more concealed.

Beyond the far end of the Cave, a small drainage pond had formed. It was only seven or eight feet wide and perhaps half that deep in summer, but it had a certain surprising beauty about it, with the water dripping from the culvert like a miniature waterfall and the surface of the pond made almost black by deep shade from the trees.

Mike had named the stream that fed it Corpse Creek because the small pool so frequently held roadkill tossed from the road above. Dale could remember finding the bodies of possum, raccoon, cats, porcupine, and once the corpse of a large German shepherd in the pool. He recalled lying there at the edge of the Cave, elbows on cool cement, and staring at the dog through four feet of perfectly clear water: the German shepherd's black eyes had been open, staring back at Dale, and the only hint that the animal was dead—other than the fact it was lying on the bottom of a pond—was a small trail of what looked like white gravel coming from its open muzzle, as if it had vomited stones.

Mike was waiting for them in the Cave. A minute later, Duane Mc-
Bride joined them, huffing and panting as he came down the trail, his
face red under his cap. He blinked in the sudden darkness of the culvert.
"Ah, the Thanatopsis Clam and Chowder Society convening," he said,
still wheezing a bit.

"Huh?" said Jim Harlen.

"Never mind," said Duane. He sat down and mopped his face with
the tail of his flannel shirt.

Lawrence was poking at a large spiderweb with a stick he'd found.
He turned around as Mike began to speak.

"I've got an idea."

"Whoa, stop the presses," said Harlen. "New headline for tomorrow's
paper."

"Shut up," said Mike with no anger in his voice. "You guys were all
there yesterday at the school when Cordie and her mom came looking
for Tubby."

"I wasn't there," said Duane.

"Yeah." Mike nodded. "Dale, tell him what happened."

Dale described the confrontation between Mrs. Cooke and Dr. Roon
and J.P. Congden. "Old Double-Butt was there, too," he concluded. "She
said she saw Tubby leave. Cordie's ma said that was bullshit."

Duane raised an eyebrow.

"So what's your idea, O'Rourke?" asked Harlen. He was using twigs
and leaves to build a small dam in the groove in the bottom of the culvert. Water was already backing up and pooling on the cement.

Lawrence moved his sneakers before they got wet.

"You want us to go give Cordie a smooch so she's not unhappy anymore?" asked Harlen.

"Uh-uh," said Mike. "I want to find Tubby."

Kevin had been tossing pebbles into the pond. Now he stopped.
His freshly laundered t-shirt looked very white in the gloom. "How are
we supposed to do that if Congden and Barney can't? And why *should*
we?"

"The Bike Patrol should," said Mike. "That's the kind of thing we
wanted to do when we made up the club. And we *can* because we can go
places and see things that Barney and Congden can't."

"I don't get it," said Lawrence. "How do we find Tubby if he ran
away?"

Harlen leaned over and pretended to grab Lawrence's nose. "We
use you as a *bloodhound*, punk. We give you an old pair of Tubby's stinky
socks and you sniff him out. OK?"

"Shut up, Harlen," said Dale.

"Make me," said Jim Harlen, flicking some water toward Dale's face.

"Shut up *both* of you," said Mike. He went on as if he hadn't been interrupted. "What we do is, we follow Roon and Old Double-Butt and Van Syke and the others, find out if they did anything to Tubby."

Duane was playing cat's cradle with a string he'd found in his pocket. "Why would they do anything to Tubby Cooke?"

Mike shrugged. "I don't know. Maybe because they're creeps. Don't you think they're weirdos?"

Duane didn't smile. "I think a lot of people are weirdos, but that doesn't give them a motive to go around kidnapping fat kids."

"If it did," said Harlen, "you'd be a goner."

Duane smiled, but turned slightly toward the other boy. Harlen was a foot shorter than Duane and weighed about half as much. "Et tu, Brute?" Duane said.

"What's that mean?" asked Harlen, his eyes narrowing.

Duane went back to his cat's cradle. "That's what Caesar said when Brutus asked him if he'd eaten any Harlenburgers that day."

"Hey," said Dale, "let's get this decided. I have to get home to mow the yard."

"And I'm helping my father clean the milk truck's tank this afternoon," said Kevin. "Let's decide."

"Decide what?" said Harlen. "Whether we're following Roon and Double-Butt around to see if they killed and ate Tubby Cooke?"

"Yeah," said Mike. "Or if they know what happened to him and are covering it up for some reason."

"Do *you* want to follow Van Syke around?" Harlen asked Mike. "That guy's the only one of the Old Central weirdos nuts enough to kill a kid. And he'd kill us if he found us following him."

"I'll take Van Syke," said Mike. "Who wants Roon?"

"Me," said Kevin. "He never goes anywhere except the school and that room he rents, so it shouldn't be hard to follow him."

"How about Mrs. Doubbet?" asked Mike.

"Me!" said Harlen and Dale at the same time.

Mike pointed at Harlen. "You take her. But make sure she doesn't know you're following her."

"I'll blend in with the trees, man."

Lawrence knocked Harlen's dam apart with his stick. "Who do Dale and I get?"

"Somebody should check on Cordie and her family," said Mike. "Tubby might come back while we're farting around and we wouldn't know it."

"Aw," said Dale. "They live way out by the dump."

"You don't have to go every *hour*. Just check on them every day or two, keep your eye out for Cordie coming into town, that sort of thing."

"OK."

"What about Duane?" said Kevin.

Mike tossed a rock into the pond and looked at the bigger boy. "What do you want to do, Duano?"

Duane's string now resembled Lawrence's spiderweb in complexity. He sighed and collapsed the intricate arrangement. "What you guys really want to do is nuts, you know. You want to know if *Old Central* is behind this somehow. So I'll follow Old Central."

"Think you can keep up with it, lard bucket?" asked Harlen. He'd stepped to the edge of the culvert and was urinating into the dark pool.

"What do you mean you'll follow it?" asked Mike.

Duane rubbed his nose and adjusted his glasses. "I agree that something's strange about that school. I'll research it. Get some background information. Maybe I can dig up something on Roon and the others, too."

"Roon's a vampire," said Harlen, flicking away the last few drops and zipping up. "Van Syke's a werewolf."

"What's Old Double-Butt?" asked Lawrence.

"She's an old bitch who gives too much homework."

"Hey," said Mike. "Watch the anguagelay in front of the idkay."

"I'm no idkay," said Lawrence.

Mike said to Duane, "Where would you get this information?"

The bigger boy shrugged. "There's almost nothing in Elm Haven's pitiful excuse for a library, but I'll try to get over to Oak Hill."

Mike nodded. "OK, well, we can get back together in a couple of days to . . ." He stopped. One or two cars had roared overhead while they had been talking, gravel flying into the leaves and dust drifting down after each vehicle passed, but now there came a rumbling so deep that it sounded like a semitrailer was lumbering overhead. The truck stopped with a screech of brakes.

"Shhh!" whispered Mike and the six of them lay on their bellies in the culvert as if that might conceal them further. Harlen moved back from the opening.

Overhead, an engine idled roughly. There came the sound of a truck door opening just as a terrible stench drifted down and settled around them like invisible but poison gas.

"Oh, fuck," whispered Harlen. "The Rendering Truck."

"Shut up," hissed Mike. Jim obeyed.

Boots crunched on gravel above them. Then silence as Van Syke or whoever it was stood at the edge of the road directly above the pool.

Dale picked up Lawrence's dropped stick and held it like a skinny club. Mike's face seemed pale as cream. Kevin looked around at the others, his Adam's apple working. Duane folded his hands between his knees and waited.

Something heavy ripped through leaves and splashed into the pool, throwing water on Harlen.

"Shit!" cried Harlen and started to say more until Mike clamped a hand over his mouth.

More gravel crunched, then came the sound of weeds snapping as if Van Syke was starting down the hillside.

Another car's engine became audible as a car or pickup came down the hill from Calvary Cemetery. Then the sound of brakes and a horn honking.

"He can't get around," whispered Kevin.

Mike nodded. The crunch of weeds paused, receded. A truck door slammed again and the Rendering Truck moved uphill toward the Black Tree with a grinding of gears. The car behind it honked again. Within a minute it was quiet again and the stench had almost gone. Almost.

Mike stood up and moved to the edge of the culvert. "Holy shit," he whispered. Mike almost never cussed.

The others crowded to the lip of the culvert.

"What the hell is it?" whispered Kevin. He held his t-shirt up to his face to get away from the smell that seemed to rise from the dark water.

Dale looked over Kevin's shoulder. The ripples and disturbed mud were just settling down, the water was not quite clear, but he could make out the white flesh, bloated belly, thin arms, fingers, and the dead brown eyes staring up through the water.

"Oh, Jesus Christ, Jesus," gasped Harlen. "It's a baby. He threw a dead baby in there."

Duane took Dale's stick, got down on his stomach, reached his arm into the water, and poked at the dead thing, turning it over. Hair on the corpse's arms moved and fingers seemed to waggle. Duane brought the head almost to the surface.

The other boys backed away. Lawrence moved to the far end of the cave, whimpering slightly, close to tears.

"Not a baby," said Duane. "At least not a human baby. It's some sort of monkey. A rhesus monkey, I think. A macaque."

Harlen strained to see, but stepped no closer. "If it's a fucking *monkey*, where's its fur?"

"Hair," said Duane absently. He used another stick to turn the thing over. Its back broke the surface of the water, and they could plainly see the tail. It also was hairless. "I don't know what happened to its hair. Maybe it was sick. Maybe somebody boiled it off."

"Boiled it off," repeated Mike, staring at the pond with an expression of pure revulsion.

Duane let the thing go, and they all watched as it settled back to the bottom. Its fingers moved as if it were signaling them or waving farewell.

Harlen tapped the curved cement wall above him in a tense staccato. "Hey, Mikey, you still want to take Van Syke?"

Mike didn't turn around. "Yeah."

"Let's get out of here," said Kevin.

They scrambled out, smashed weeds in their hurry to get to their bikes, and milled around for a minute before pedaling uphill. The smell of the Rendering Truck still hung in the air here.

"What if it comes back?" whispered Harlen, saying what Dale was thinking.

"Dump the bikes in the weeds," said Mike. "Take off through the woods. Head for Dale's Uncle Henry's and Aunt Lena's."

"What if it comes back when we're on the road to town?" asked Lawrence. His voice was shaking.

"Into the cornfields," said Dale. He touched his little brother's shoulder. "Hey, Van Syke isn't after *us*. He was just dumping that dead monkey in the creek."

"Let's get going anyway," said Kevin and they mounted up, ready for the steep uphill slog.

"Wait a minute," said Dale. Duane McBride had just gotten up to the road. The heavy boy was red-faced and wheezing, his asthma audible. Dale turned his bike around. "You OK?"

Duane gestured with his hand. "Fine."

"You want us to go back to the farm with you?"

Duane grinned at them. "Then you going to stay and hold my hand until the Old Man gets home sometime after midnight? Or tomorrow?"

Dale hesitated. He was thinking that Duane should come home with him; that they should all stick together. Then he realized how silly the thought was.

"I'll get in touch with you guys when I find something out about Old Central," said Duane. He waved, turned, and began slogging up the first of the two steep hills that stood between him and the way home.

Dale waved and joined the others for the tiring pull up their own hill. Beyond the driveway to the Black Tree, the road was as flat as only Illinois roads could be. They pedaled hard and the water tower was within sight as soon as they turned off County Six onto the Jubilee College road.

No cars or trucks passed before they reached Elm Haven.

SEVEN

The Free Show began at dusk, but people started arriving at Bandstand Park even while sunlight still lay along Main Street like a tawny cat slow to leave the warm pavement. Farm families backed their pickups and station wagons onto the parking-lot gravel along the Broad Avenue side of the park so as to have the best view when the movie was projected against the Parkside Cafe; then they picnicked on the grass or sat on the bandstand and chatted with townfolk they hadn't seen for a while. Most of the local residents began to arrive when the sun had finally set and the bats were beginning to fly against the darkening shield of sky. Broad Avenue under its arch of elms seemed a dark tunnel opening onto the lighter width of Main Street and terminating at the bright promise of the park with its light and noise and laughter.

The Free Show was a tradition dating back to the early days of World War II when the nearest picture show—Ewalts Palace in Oak Hill—had closed due to the Ewalts' son and only projectionist, Walt, enlisting in the Marine Corps. Peoria was the next nearest source of movie entertainment, but the forty-mile trip was too much for most people because of gas rationing. So the older Mr. Ashley-Montague had brought a projector out from Peoria each Saturday evening that summer of 1942 and shown the newsreels and war-bond ads, cartoons and feature attractions there in Bandstand Park, the images cast twenty feet tall on the whitewashed canvas screen stretched against the Parkside Cafe.

The Ashley-Montagues had not actually lived in Elm Haven since the week their mansion had burned and the grandfather of the current Mr. Ashley-Montague had committed suicide in 1919, but male members of the family still visited occasionally, made donations to community causes, and generally watched over the small town like Old English squires protecting a village which had grown up on their estate. And, eighteen summers after the son of the last Elm Haven Ashley-Montague brought his first Saturday-night Free Show to town in June of 1942, *his* son carried on the tradition.

Now, on the fourth evening of June in the summer of 1960, Mr.

Ashley-Montague's long Lincoln pulled into the space always left open for it due west of the bandstand, Mr. Taylor and Mr. Sperling and other members of the City Council helped him carry the massive projector to its wooden platform on the bandstand, families settled onto their blankets and park benches, adventurous children were shooed from the lower tree branches and their hiding places in the crawl space beneath the bandstand, parents in the back of pickup trucks adjusted their folding chairs and handed around bowls of popcorn, and the park settled into a preshow hush as the sky darkened above the elms and the canvas rectangle on the wall of the Parkside Cafe came alive with light.

Dale and Lawrence left late, hoping their father would arrive home in time for the whole family to go to the Free Show. He didn't, but a little after eight-thirty he called from the state line to say that he was on his way and not to wait up. Dale's mom made popcorn for them, gave each boy his own brown bag of it and a dime to buy a soft drink at the Parkside, and told them to come home as soon as the picture was over.

They didn't take their bikes. Normally, neither boy would walk anywhere if he could help it, but walking to the Free Show was a tradition dating back to when Lawrence was too small to have a bike and Dale walked him to the park, holding his hand as they crossed the silent streets.

The streets were silent now. The glow in the evening sky had faded but not been replaced by stars; the gaps between the elms were dark as clouds moved in. The air was thick, rich with the scent of new-mown grass and blossoms. Crickets tuned up for the nightly symphony in the dark gardens and thick hedges, and an owl tested its voice in the dead cottonwood tree behind Mrs. Moon's house. Old Central was a dark mass in the center of its abandoned playgrounds and the boys hurried down Second Avenue past it, turning west on Church Street.

There were streetlights on each corner, but the long spaces between were dark beneath the trees. Dale wanted to run so as not to miss the cartoon, but Lawrence was afraid of tripping on the uneven sidewalk stones and spilling his popcorn, so the two hurried along in a fast walk, moving through leaf shadow as the trees stirred above them. The big old homes along Church Street were either dark or lighted only by the blue-and-white pulse of television light through bay windows and screen doors. A few cigarettes glowed on porches, but it was too dark to see the people there. On the corner of Third and Church, where Dr. Roon rented rooms on the second floor of Mrs. Samson's old boardinghouse, Dale and Lawrence ran across the street, trotted past the dark brick building holding the skating rink now closed for summer, and turned left onto Broad.

"It feels like Halloween," said Lawrence, his voice small. "Like there're people dressed up in the shadows where we can't see them. Like this is my trick-or-treat bag but nobody's home and . . ."

"Shut up," said Dale. He could hear the music from the Free Show now, bright and tinny: a Warner Brothers cartoon. The elm-covered tunnel of Broad was behind them, only a few lights showing in the big Victorian homes set far back from the street. First Presbyterian, the Stewart family's church, glowed pale and empty on the corner across from the post office.

"What's that?" whispered Lawrence, stopping and clutching his bag of popcorn.

"Nothing. What?" said Dale, stopping with his brother.

There was a rustling, sliding, screeching from the darkness in and above the elms.

"It's nothing," said Dale, tugging at Lawrence to get moving. "Birds." Lawrence still wouldn't move and Dale paused to listen again. "Bats."

Dale could see them now: dark shapes flitting across the paler gaps between the leaves, winged shadows visible against the white of First Prez as they darted to and fro. "Just *bats*." He tugged at Lawrence's hand.

His brother refused to move. "Listen," he whispered.

Dale considered slugging him, kicking him right in the seat of his Levi's, or grabbing him by one oversized ear and *dragging* him the last block to the Free Show. Instead, he listened.

Leaves rustling. The manic scales of a cartoon soundtrack dulled by distance and humid air. The leathery flap of wings. Voices.

Instead of the near-ultrasonic chirp of bats scanning the way ahead, the sound in the motion-filled darkness around them was the screech of small, sharp voices. Cries. Shrieks. Curses. Obscenities. Most of the sounds teetered on the brink of actually being words, the maddeningly audible but not-quite-distinct syllables of a shouted conversation in an adjoining room. But two of the sounds were quite clear.

Dale and Lawrence stood frozen on the sidewalk, clutching their bags of popcorn and staring upward, as bats shrieked their names in consonants that sounded like teeth scraping across blackboards. Far, far away, the amplified voice of Porky Pig said, "Th-th-th-that's all, folks!"

"Run!" whispered Dale.

Jim Harlen had orders not to go to the Free Show; his mother was gone— off to Peoria on another date—and while she said that he was old enough to stay home without a baby-sitter, he was not allowed to go out. Harlen made up his bed with his ventriloquist's dummy turned with its face to the wall and a bunched-up pair of jeans to extend the legs under the cover, just in case she got home before him and checked in on him. She wouldn't. She never got home before one or two o'clock in the morning.

Harlen grabbed a couple of Butterfingers from the cupboard for his movie snack, got his bike out of the shed, and tore off down Depot Street. He'd been watching *Gunsmoke* on TV, and it'd gotten dark sooner than he'd planned for. He didn't want to miss the cartoon.

The streets were empty. Harlen knew that anyone old enough to be able to drive but young enough not to be so stupid as to hang around to watch Lawrence Welk or the Free Show had left for Peoria or Galesburg hours ago. *He'd* sure as hell not hang around Elm Haven on a Saturday night when he got older.

Jim Harlen didn't plan on hanging around Elm Haven much longer in any event. Either his mother would marry one of those greasers she was dating—probably some garage mechanic who sank all his money into suits—and Harlen would be moving to Peoria, or else he'd run away in a year or two. Harlen envied Tubby Cooke. The fat kid had been about as bright as the 25-watt bulb Harlen's mom kept lit on the back porch, but he'd known enough to get the hell away from Elm Haven. Of course, Harlen didn't get *hit* the way Tubby probably did—based on how drunk his old man was most of the time and how stupid his ma looked—but Harlen had his own problems.

He *hated* his mother's taking her old name back, leaving him stranded with his father's last name when he wasn't even allowed to *mention* his dad in front of her. He *hated* her being gone every Friday and Saturday, all dressed up in the low-cut peasant blouses and sexy black dresses that made Harlen feel funny . . . sort of like his mom was one of those women in the magazines he kept hidden in the back of his closet. He *hated* it when she smoked, leaving the lipstick rings around the butts of the cigarettes in the ashtrays, making him imagine that same lipstick on the cheeks of greasers Harlen didn't even *know* . . . on their bodies. He *hated* it when she had too much to drink and tried to hide it, acting the perfect lady— but Harlen could always tell by the precise diction, the slow movements, and the way she got all sloppy and tried to hug him.

He *hated* his mother. If she hadn't been such a . . . Harlen's mind skittered around the word "whore" . . . if she'd just been a better wife, then his father wouldn't have had to start dating that secretary *he'd* run away with.

Harlen headed down Broad Avenue, pedaling hard and wiping his eyes with an angry swipe of his sleeve. Something white moving between the big old homes on the left side of the street made him glance, look again, and then bring his low bike into a sweeping, gravel-sliding stop.

Somebody was moving into the alley between wide yards. Harlen caught another glimpse of a short, wide body, pale arms, and pale dress before the figure was swallowed by the darkness in the alley. *Shit, it's Old Double-Butt.* The alley ran between her big old house and the boarded-up pink Victorian that had belonged to Mrs. Duggan.

What the hell is Old Double-Butt doing slinking down the alley? Harlen almost put it out of his mind and headed off toward the Free Show, but then he remembered he was supposed to be following the teacher.

That stuff's bull. O'Rourke's dipped in donkey shit if he thinks I'm going to follow this old dinosaur around town all the time. I didn't see him or any of the others out following their people around this afternoon. Mike's hot stuff at giving orders . . . all those other idiots love to do what he says . . . but I'm too big for that baby shit.

But what was Mrs. D. doing going down the alley after dark?

Taking out the garbage, stupid.

But the garbage pickup wasn't until Tuesday. And she hadn't been carrying anything. In fact, she'd been all dressed up . . . probably in that fancy pink dress she'd worn the last day before Christmas break. Not that the old battle-ax had given them a real party—just thirty minutes to pass around presents to the people whose name they'd drawn for Secret Santa.

Where the hell's she going?

Wouldn't O'Rourke be surprised if Jim Harlen was the only one in their piss-ant Bike Patrol who actually *found out* something about the people they were supposed to be following. Like maybe Old Double-Butt was doing it with Dr. Roon or creepy Van Syke while everybody was off at the Free Show.

The thought made Harlen sort of sick.

He pedaled across the street, dumped his bike behind the bushes on Mrs. Duggan's side of the alley, and peered around the shrubs. The pale form was just visible, already almost all the way down the alley to where it ran into Third Avenue.

Harlen crouched there a second, decided that the bike would make too much noise on the cinders and gravel, and started off on foot, moving from shadow to shadow, keeping near the high fences, avoiding garbage cans so as not to make noise. He thought of dogs barking and remembered that the only dog in a backyard along here would be Dexter, who belonged to the Gibsons, but Dexter was old and they treated him like a child. He'd probably be indoors watching Lawrence Welk with them.

Old Double-Butt crossed Third, passed the boardinghouse where Roon had his apartment on the third floor, and went across onto the playground on the south side of Old Central.

Shit, thought Harlen, *she's just going to get something in the school.* Then he remembered she couldn't. When he'd gotten back into town that afternoon from their dipshitty trip out to the Cave, he and Dale and the others had noticed that somebody'd boarded up the windows on the first floor of Old Central—probably to protect them from kids like Harlen who hated the place—and there were chains and padlocks on both the north and south doors.

Mrs. Doubbet—Harlen had seen her clearly in the light from the corner streetlight—disappeared in the shadow at the base of the fire escape, and Harlen hid behind a poplar across the street. Even from two blocks away he could hear music as the main feature started at the Free Show.

There came the sound of heels on metal stairs and Harlen caught a glimpse of pale arms as she climbed the fire escape to the second floor. A door up there scraped open.

She's got her own damn key.

Harlen tried to think of why Old Double-Butt would go into Old Central at night—on a Saturday—in the summer—*after* the school had been emptied for possible demolition.

Shit, she is making it with Dr. Roon.

Harlen tried to use his imagination to see Mrs. Doubbet stretched out across her oak desk while Dr. Roon slipped it to her. Harlen's imagination wasn't up to the task. After all, he hadn't actually *seen* anybody having sex . . . even the magazines in his closet just showed the girls alone, playing with their titties, acting like they were *ready* to have sex.

Harlen felt his heart pounding as he waited for a light to come on up there on the second floor. No light came on.

He moved around the school, staying close to the building so she wouldn't see him if she was peering out one of the windows.

No light.

Wait. There was a glow here on the northwest side, a slight phosphorescence coming through the high windows of the corner room. Mrs. Doubbet's old room. *Harlen's* room that past year.

How could he see what was going on? The doors downstairs were padlocked, the basement windows covered by metal grilles. Harlen considered climbing the fire escape and going through the door Old Double-Butt had just entered. Then he imagined meeting her on that fire escape or—worse yet—in the dark hallway upstairs, and then he abandoned that idea quickly.

Harlen stood there a moment, watching the glow move from window to window as if the old biddy were carrying a jar of fireflies around the classroom. From three blocks away came the sound of laughter; the movie must be a comedy tonight.

Harlen looked along the corner of the school. There was a trash

dumpster that would get him up on the narrow ledge six feet above the
sidewalk. A drainpipe with metal brackets would take him to the ledge
above the first-floor windows, to that stone molding along the corner of
the school. All he'd have to do was continue up the drainpipe between the
stone windowframe, shinnying where he could, getting his sneakers into
the grooves of that molding where he had to brace himself, and he'd be
up there on the ledge that went around the second floor a few feet under
the windows.

The ledge was about six inches wide—he'd stared out the classroom
window at it enough to know, even fed pigeons out the window with
junk from his pockets when he'd been kept in for recess. It wasn't wide
enough for him to stand on alone . . . walk around the school on or anything . . . but it was plenty wide to balance on while holding the drainpipe for support. He'd just have to scoot over about two feet and then lift
his head to peer in the window.

The window from which the faint glow gleamed, faded, grew again.

Harlen started to clamber up on the dumpster, and then paused to
look up. It was a *high* two stories . . . well over twenty feet. The ground
here was mostly flagstone sidewalk and gravel.

"Hey," whispered Harlen, "ef it. Let's see *you* do this, O'Rourke."

He began to climb.

Mike O'Rourke was taking care of his grandmother on the night of the
Free Show. His parents had gone out to the Knights of Columbus dance
at the Silverleaf Dance Emporium—an aging building set back under
silver leaf trees twelve miles down the Hard Road toward Peoria—and
Mike was left with his sisters and Memo. Technically, his oldest sister,
seventeen-year-old Mary, was left in charge, but Mary's date had shown
up ten minutes after Mr. and Mrs. O'Rourke left. Mary was not allowed
to date on evenings when her parents were out—and she was currently
grounded for a month due to recent infractions Mike didn't know about
and didn't care to know about—but when her pimply date showed up in
his '54 Chevy, she was out and away, swearing her sisters to secrecy and
threatening to kill Mike if he squealed. Mike shrugged; it was another bit
of blackmail he could use against Mary someday when he needed leverage.

Fifteen-year-old Margaret was then in charge, but ten minutes after
Mary left, three high-school boys and two of Peg's girlfriends—all too
young to drive—called from the backyard darkness and Peg was off to
the Free Show. Both girls knew that their parents didn't get home until
long after midnight on dance nights.

Officially, that left thirteen-year-old Bonnie in charge, but Bonnie

never took charge of anything. Mike sometimes thought that no girl had
ever been so misnamed. While all the rest of the O'Rourke children—
even Mike—had inherited beautiful eyes and an Irish grace to their features, Bonnie was overweight, with dull brown eyes and even duller brown
hair, a sallow complexion now mottled with the early ravages of acne,
and a bitter attitude that reflected her mother's worst side when sober
and her father's bitterness when drunk. Bonnie had stomped off to the
bedroom she shared with seven-year-old Kathleen, promptly locked the
younger girl out, and refused to open the door even when Kathleen
burst into tears.

Kathleen was the prettiest of the O'Rourke girls—red-haired, blue-
eyed, with a rose-and-freckle complexion and stunning smile that made
Mike's dad tell tales of the village girls in an Ireland he'd never visited.
Kathleen was beautiful. She was also borderline retarded and was still in
kindergarten at age seven. Sometimes Kathleen's struggle to understand
the simplest thing made Mike go off to the outhouse to fight back tears
in solitude. Every morning, as he helped Father Cavanaugh serve Mass,
Mike said a prayer that God would fix whatever was wrong with his
younger sister. But so far He hadn't, and Kathleen's slowness became more
and more apparent as playmates her age solved the riddles of reading
and simple arithmetic, leaving the bewildered child further and further
behind.

Now Mike calmed Kathleen, cooked stew for her dinner, tucked her
into Mary's bed under the low eaves, and went down to take care of Memo.

Mike had been nine when Memo had her first stroke. He remembered the confusion in the household as the old woman ceased to be the
verbal presence in the kitchen and suddenly became the dying woman in
the parlor. Memo was his mother's mother, and while Mike did not know
the word matriarch, he remembered the functional definition: the old
woman in the dotted apron, always in the kitchen or sewing in her parlor,
the problem-solver and decision-maker, the thickly accented Irish voice of
Mary Margaret Houlihan lilting up through the heating grille in Mike's
floor as she jollied his mother out of one of her cynical depressions, or
scolded his father out of another evening of drinking with his friends. It
had been Memo who had saved the family financially when John O'Rourke
had been laid off from Pabst for a year when Mike was six—he remembered overhearing the long conversations at the kitchen table as his father
protested, it was her life's savings, and Memo insisted—and it was Memo
who saved Mike and Kathleen physically when he was eight, Kathleen
four, and the mad dog had come down Depot Street. Mike had noticed
something strange about the animal and had hung back, calling to Kathleen not to go closer. But his sister loved dogs and could not comprehend

that one could hurt her; she had rushed toward the growling, foaming animal. Kathleen was within an arm's length, the dog was focusing its caked eyes and preparing to charge, and all Mike could do was cry in a high, shrill voice that didn't sound like his own even to him.

Then Memo had appeared, her polka-dotted apron flying, broom in her right hand, and her graying red hair loose from her kerchief. She had swept up Kathleen with one arm and swung the broom so hard that it had lifted the dog off all four feet and deposited it in the middle of the street. Memo had thrust Kathleen at Mike, ordered him to take her inside with a voice that was calm but incapable of being defied, and then turned just as the dog got to its feet and lunged again. Mike had looked over his shoulder as he ran, and he would never forget the sight of Memo standing there, legs apart, kerchief around her neck . . . waiting, waiting . . . Later, Constable Barney said that he'd never seen a dog killed by a broom—especially a mad dog—but that Mrs. Houlihan had almost taken the monster's head off.

That was the word Barney had used—monster. After that, Mike had known in his heart that whatever monsters might prowl the night, Memo was more than an equal match for them.

But then, less than a year later, Memo had been laid low. The first stroke had been massive—paralyzing her, cutting the cables to the muscles of that ever-animated face. Dr. Viskes said that it was a matter of weeks, perhaps days. But Memo survived that summer. Mike remembered how strange it had been to have the parlor—the center of Memo's inexhaustible activity—converted to a sick room for her. With the rest of the family, he had waited for the end.

She had survived that summer. By autumn, she was communicating her wants through a system of coded blinks. By Christmas, she was able to speak, although only the family understood the words. By Easter, she had somehow won enough of the battle with her body that she could use her right hand and was beginning to sit up in the living room. Three days after Easter, the second stroke hit her. A month later, the third.

For the past year and a half, Memo had been little more than a breathing corpse in the parlor, her face yellowed and slack, her wrists bent like the claws of a dead bird. She could not move, could not control her bodily functions, and had no way to communicate with the world except the blinks. But she lived on.

Mike went into the parlor just as it was getting dark outside in earnest. He lighted the kerosene lamp—their house had electricity but Memo had always preferred oil lamps in her room upstairs and they had continued the tradition—and went over to the high bed where she lay.

She was on her right side, facing him, just as she always was except when they turned her carefully each day to reduce the unavoidable bedsores. Her face was lined with a maze of wrinkles, the flesh looking yellowed, waxy . . . not human. The eyes stared blackly, blankly, bulging slightly with some terrible internal pressure or the sheer frustration of not being able to convey the thoughts which lay behind them. She was drooling, and Mike took one of the clean towels laid out at the foot of the bed and gently wiped her mouth.

He checked to make sure that she did not need to be changed—he was not supposed to join his sisters in this job, but he watched over Memo more than all of them combined, so the needs of his grandmother's bowels and bladder were no secret to him—found her clean and dry, and sat on the low chair to hold her hand.

"It was a pretty day out, Memo," he whispered. He didn't know why he whispered in her presence, but he noticed the others did, too. Even his mother. "It really feels like summer."

Mike looked around the room. Heavy drapes across the window. Tabletops littered with medicine bottles, while the other surfaces were covered by the tintypes and sepia photos of her life when she had been alive. How long had it been since she had been able to turn her eyes toward one of her pictures?

An old Victrola sat in the corner, and now Mike put on one of her favorite records—Caruso singing from *The Barber of Seville*. The high voice and higher scratches filled the room. Memo did not respond—not so much as a blink or twitch—but Mike thought that she could still hear it. He wiped saliva from her chin and the corner of her mouth, set her more comfortably on the pillow, and sat on the stool again, still holding her hand. It felt like something dry and dead. It had been Memo who had told Mike "The Monkey's Paw" one Halloween when he was little, scaring him so badly that he'd needed a night-light for six months.

What would happen, he wondered, *if I wished on Memo's hand?* Mike shook his head, banishing the unkind thought and saying a Hail Mary for penance.

"Mom and Dad are at the Silverleaf," he whispered, trying to sound bright. The singing around them was soft, more scratches than human voice. "Mary and Peg are off to the movies. Dale says that they're showing *The Time Machine* at the Free Show tonight. He says it's about a guy who goes into the future or something." Mike broke off and watched carefully as Memo seemed to move slightly: a slight, involuntary twitch of the hip, a stirring of the bedclothes. There was a soft sound as she broke wind.

Mike spoke quickly to cover his embarrassment. "Sort of a weird idea, huh, Memo? Going into the future? Dale says people'll be able to do it someday, but Kevin says it isn't possible. Kev says it isn't like going into space like the Russians did with Sputnik . . . remember when you and I watched that go over a couple of years ago? I said maybe they'd send a man next, and you said you wished you could go?

"Well, anyway, Kev says it isn't possible going up or back in time. He says it makes too many para—" Mike struggled for the word. He hated to appear stupid in front of Memo; she was the only one in the family who hadn't thought he was stupid when he flunked fourth grade. "Para—*Para-doxes.* Sort of like, what would happen if you went back in time and accidentally killed your grandfather . . ." Mike shut up when he realized what he was saying. His grandfather—Memo's husband—had been killed at the grain elevator thirty-two years before when a metal door had given way and dumped eleven tons of wheat on him while he was cleaning the main bin. Mike had heard his father tell other men that old Devin Houlihan had swum in the rising whirlpool of grain like a dog in a flood until he'd suffocated. An autopsy had shown his lungs filled solid with dust, like two bags packed with chaff.

Mike looked down at Memo's hand. He stroked the fingers, thinking back to one fall evening when he was six or seven and Memo had been rocking in this same parlor, talking to him while she sewed. "Michael, your grandfather went when Death came for him. The man in the dark robe just walked into that grain elevator and took my Devin by the hand. But he put up a fight—oh, my dear, he put up a fight! And that is just what I will do, Michael dearest, when the man in the dark robe tries to get in here. I won't let him in. Not without a fight. No, Michael, not without a fight."

Mike had imagined Death as a man in a dark robe after that, and had always imagined Memo swatting him the way she had swatted the mad dog. Now he lowered his face and looked in her eyes, as if mere proximity could make contact. He could see his own face reflected there, distorted by the lens of her pupils and the flickering of the kerosene lamp.

"I won't let him in, Memo," Mike whispered. He could see where his breath stirred the pale hairs on her cheek. "I won't let him in unless you tell me to."

Between the drapes and the wall, he could see darkness pressing against the windowpane. Upstairs, a board creaked as the old house settled. Outside, something scratched against the window.

The record ended, scraping along blank grooves now, rasping like claws on slate, but Mike continued to sit there, his face close to Memo's, his hand firm on hers.

The bats seemed a laughable thing, distant and already half-forgotten, as Dale Stewart sat next to his brother in Bandstand Park and watched *The*

Time Machine. Dale had heard this might be the movie—Mr. Ashley-Montague often brought films that closed a few days before in the theater he owned in Peoria—and Dale had been dying to see the movie since he'd read the Classic Comic the year before.

A breeze rustled the trees in the park as Rod Taylor saved Yvette Mimieux from drowning in the stream while apathetic Eloi watched without expression. Lawrence sat on his knees—as he always did when he got excited—and chewed on the last of his popcorn, occasionally taking a sip from the bottle of Dr Pepper they had bought in the Parkside Cafe. Lawrence's eyes were very wide as he watched Rod Taylor descend into the underground world of the Morlocks. He edged closer to his older brother.

"It's all right," whispered Dale. "They're afraid of light and the guy has matches."

On the screen, the Morlocks' eyes burned yellowly like the fireflies in the bushes on the south end of the park. Rod Taylor lit a match and the monsters backed away, shielding their eyes with their blue forearms. The leaves continued to rustle and Dale looked up, noticing that the stars had been occluded by clouds. He hoped that the Free Show wasn't going to be rained out.

Mr. Ashley-Montague brought two extension speakers in addition to the one built into the portable projector, but the sound was still tinnier than it would have been in a real theater. Now the shouts of Rod Taylor and the cries of the enraged Morlocks blended with the rustling of leaves in the rising wind and the leathery flap of wings as dark shapes darted through the trees above the park.

Lawrence shifted closer, getting grass stain on his Levi's and forgetting to munch his popcorn. He'd pulled off his ballcap and, as he often did when he was nervous, was chewing on the bill of it.

"It's OK," whispered Dale, gently tapping his little brother on the shoulder with his fist. "He gets Weena out of the caves."

The colored images continued to dance as the wind rose.

Duane was in the kitchen having a late snack when he heard the truck turn into the drive.

Normally, in the basement with his radio on, he wouldn't have heard the truck, but the screen door was open, the windows were up, and it was quiet except for the incessant summer sounds of crickets, tree frogs out near the pond, and the occasional bang of the metal self-feeding door on the hog trough.

The Old Man's home early, he thought and realized in the same instant that the engine noise hadn't been right. This was a bigger truck . . . or at least a bigger engine.

Duane crouched and peered out the screen. In a few weeks, the rising corn would obscure even this view of the drive to the house, but now he could still see the last hundred feet or so of the lane. No pickup appeared. The expected crunch of gravel was not audible.

Duane frowned, took a bite of liverwurst, and went out through the screen door, stepping out across the turnaround between the house and barn for a clear view down the drive. It happened that people turned around in their lane, but not often. And the sound had definitely been a truck engine; Uncle Art refused to drive pickups—said there was enough curse to living in the country without being stuck in the ugliest form of locomotion ever designed by Detroit—and the engine Duane had heard hadn't been Uncle Art's Cadillac.

Duane stood out in the warm darkness, eating his sandwich and looking down the lane. The sky was dark, a featureless ceiling of clouds, and the fields of low corn were silent in that silken hush before a storm. Fireflies winked along the ditches and against the blackness of the low crab-apple trees beside the driveway to County Six.

There was a large truck with its headlights off standing motionless near the entrance to the drive a hundred yards away. Duane could see no details, but the size of the thing formed a dark wedge where a lighter gap should be.

Duane paused a few seconds, finishing his sandwich and trying to decide if he knew anyone with a truck that size who would be visiting on a Saturday night. He didn't.

Somebody bringing the Old Man home drunk? It had happened before. But not this early.

Far to the south, there was a flicker of lightning, too far away for thunder to be heard. The brief illumination had not shown Duane any details of the truck, only that the dark shape was still there.

Something brushed against Duane's thigh.

"Shhh, Wittgenstein," he whispered, dropping to one knee and putting an arm around the old collie's neck. The dog was trembling and making a sound in its throat that was not quite a growl. "Shhh," whispered Duane, patting the dog's thin head, holding it. The shaking did not stop.

If they left the truck, they could be almost here by now, thought Duane. And then he thought, *Who?*

"Come on, Witt," he said softly. Leading the collie by the collar, he went back into the house, turned off all of the lights, went into the junk-strewn room the Old Man called his study, found the key in the desk, went into the dining room, and unlocked the gun cabinet. He hesitated only a second before leaving the over-and-under, the .30-06, and the 12-gauge in their places and taking out the 16-gauge pump.

In the kitchen, Wittgenstein whined. His claws scrabbled on linoleum. "Shhh, Witt," Duane said softly. "It's OK, boy." He checked the breech to make sure it was clear, pumped it, checked it again, held it up to check the empty magazine against the pale light coming through the curtains, and opened the lower drawer. The shells were there in their yellow box, and Duane crouched next to the dining room table as he loaded five of them and put three more in the pocket of his flannel shirt.

Wittgenstein barked. Duane left him in the kitchen, loosened the window screen in the dining room, stepped out into the darkness of the side yard, and moved slowly around the house.

The glow from the pole light illuminated the turnaround and the first ten yards of driveway. Duane crouched and waited. He realized that his heart was beating faster than usual and he took deep, slow breaths until it slowed to normal.

The crickets and other insect noises had stopped. The thousands of stalks of corn did not stir, the air was absolutely still, and lightning flickered to the south again. This time the thunder was audible, coming fifteen seconds later.

Duane waited, breathing shallowly through his mouth, his thumb on the safety. The shotgun smelled of oil. Wittgenstein had quit barking, but Duane could hear the nails on linoleum as the collie went from closed door to closed door in the kitchen.

Duane waited.

It was at least five minutes later that the truck engine ground, started, and the gravel crunched.

Duane moved quickly to the edge of the cornfield, stayed low, and went down the first row to where he could see the driveway.

Still no lights. The truck backed onto County Six, paused a moment, and then went south—toward the cemetery, the Black Tree Tavern, and Elm Haven.

Duane lifted his head from the corn and watched, but he saw no taillights as the sound receded down County Six. He dropped back into the corn and crouched there, breathing softly, keeping the 16-gauge across his knees and listening.

Twenty minutes later, the first drops of rain began to fall. Duane gave it another three or four minutes and then he came out of the corn, staying close to the fields so as not to be silhouetted against the sky, made a complete circuit of the house and barn—the sparrows in the barn were silent, the pigs in the side lot grunting and rooting normally—and went in through the kitchen door.

Wittgenstein wagged his tail like a puppy, peering myopically at Duane carrying the shotgun and going from boy to door, door to boy.

"Uh-uh," said Duane, ejecting the shells one by one and lining them up on the checkered tablecloth of the kitchen table, "we're not going hunting tonight, dimwit. But you *are* going to get a special meal . . . and then you're going to spend the night downstairs with me tonight." Duane went to the cupboard and Witt's tail beat a faster tattoo against the linoleum.

Outside, the rain had let up after the initial flurry, but wind rustled the corn and whipped at the crab-apple trees.

Jim Harlen found that it wasn't such easy climbing after all. Especially not with the wind coming up, blowing dust from the gravelled playground and school parking lot. Harlen paused halfway up the drainpipe to rub grit out of his eyes.

Well, at least the wind banging things around would cover any sound he might make shinnying up this stupid pipe.

Harlen was between the first and second floors, already almost twenty feet above the dumpster, before he realized just how stupid a move this was. What was he going to do if Van Syke or Roon or somebody came along? Probably Barney. Harlen tried to imagine what his mother would say when she came home from her date and found her only son down at J.P. Congden's detention shed, awaiting transport to the Oak Hill jail.

Harlen smiled slightly. That would get his mother's attention. He shinnied up the last few feet of drainpipe, found the second-story ledge with his right knee, and rested there, his cheek against brick. The wind tugged at his t-shirt. Ahead of him, he could see light shining *up* through elm leaves from the streetlight at the corner of School Street and Third Avenue. He was very high.

Harlen wasn't afraid of heights. He'd beaten O'Rourke and Stewart and all the rest of them when they were climbing the big oak tree behind Congden's garden last fall. He'd climbed so high, in fact, that the other guys had shouted at him to come down, but he'd insisted on stepping up one last branch . . . a branch so thin it didn't seem solid enough to hold a pigeon without breaking . . . and peering out from the top of the oak to the ocean of treetops that was Elm Haven. This was kid's stuff compared to that.

But Harlen glanced down and wished he hadn't. Except for the drainpipe and corner molding, there was nothing between him and the metal dumpster and concrete sidewalk twenty-five feet down.

He closed his eyes, concentrated on finding his balance on the narrow ledge, and opened them to look up at the window.

It wasn't two feet away . . . it was more like four. He'd have to let go of the goddamned pipe to get over to it.

And the glow was gone. He was almost sure. Harlen had this sudden image of Old Double-Butt coming around the corner of the school, looking up at him in the dark, and shouting, *"Jim Harlen! You get down here at once!"*

And then what? Was she going to flunk him out of the sixth grade he'd just graduated from? Revoke his summer?

Harlen smiled, took a breath, put all his weight on his knees, and inched along the ledge, spread-eagled against the brick wall, nothing but friction and four inches of ledge holding him up.

His right hand found the window ledge, and his fingers grasped the weird molding below the sill. He was steady. He was OK.

Harlen stayed in that position for a moment, head bowed, cheek against brick. All he had to do was lift his head to look in the room.

At that second, part of his mind told him not to. *Leave it alone. Go to the Free Show. Get home before Mom gets back.*

The wind rustled leaves below him and tossed more grit in his eyes. Harlen glanced back at the drainpipe. No problem getting back; shinnying down would be a lot easier than getting up. Harlen thought of Gerry Daysinger or one of the other guys calling him a pussy.

They don't have to know I was up here.

Then why'd you climb up here, asshole?

Harlen thought of telling O'Rourke and the others—of embroidering the story a little bit if it was just Old Double-Butt picking up her goddamned favorite chalk or something. He imagined the shock those pansies would show when he told them about his climb, about seeing Old Double-Butt and Roon doing it on her desk, right there in the classroom. . . .

Harlen lifted his head and peered in the window.

Mrs. Doubbet was not at her desk at the far end of the room, but was sitting at the small worktable at this end of the classroom—not three feet from Harlen. There were no lights on, but a pale phosphorescence filled the room with the sick light of rotting wood in a dark forest.

Mrs. Doubbet was not alone. The phosphorescence emanated from the shape next to her. This figure also sat at the small table, less than an arm's length from where Harlen pressed his face to the glass. He recognized her at once.

Mrs. Duggan, Mrs. Doubbet's ex-teaching partner, had always been thin. During the months when the cancer had ravaged her until she quit teaching just before Christmas, she had grown even thinner. Harlen remembered how her arms had seemed to be little more than bones wrapped in speckled flesh. No one in the class had seen Mrs. Duggan during the last weeks before her death in February—or at the funeral—but Sandy

Whittaker's mom had visited her at home and in the funeral home, and had told Sandy that the old lady had wasted away to nothing but skin and bones at the end.

Harlen recognized her at once.

He glanced once at Old Double-Butt—she was bent forward, smiling broadly, totally intent on her partner at the table—and then his gaze returned to Mrs. Duggan.

Sandy had said that Mrs. Duggan had been buried in her finest silk dress—the green one she had worn to the Christmas party on her last day of teaching. She was wearing the dress now. It had rotted through in several places, and the phosphorescence shone through.

The old lady's hair was still carefully combed back, held in place by tortoiseshell barrettes Harlen had noticed in class, but much of it had come out in patches, and areas of bare scalp glowed whitely. There were holes in the scalp, just as there had been holes in the silk dress.

From three feet away, Harlen could see Mrs. Duggan's hand on the table—the long fingers, the loose gold ring, the soft gleam of bone.

Mrs. Doubbet leaned closer to the corpse of her friend and said something. She looked puzzled, then glanced toward the window where Harlen crouched, his knees pressed against the ledge.

He realized in that last instant that he must be visible—that the glow would illuminate his face against the pane as easily as it illuminated the exposed tendons gleaming like spaghetti strands through the cracks in Mrs. Duggan's wrist, as easily as it outlined the dark colonies of mold under the translucent flesh. What was left of the flesh.

From the corner of his eye, Harlen realized that Old Double-Butt had turned to look at him, but he did not avert his gaze from the back of Mrs. Duggan's neck as the parchment-skin there folded and vertebrae visibly shifted like white stones moving beneath rotted cloth.

Mrs. Duggan turned and looked at him. From two feet away, the phosphorescent glare burned through the dark pool of deliquescence where her left eye had been. Teeth gleamed in a lipless smile as she leaned over as if to give Harlen a kiss through the windowpane. No breath fogged the glass.

Harlen stood and turned to run, not remembering that he was on a thin ledge twenty-five feet above stone and concrete. He would have run even if he had remembered.

He did not cry out as he fell.

EIGHT

Mike loved the ritual of the Mass. On this Sunday—as on all Sundays except special holy days—he helped Father Cavanaugh serve the regular seven-thirty Mass and then stayed to be head altar boy for the ten o'clock High Mass. The earlier service was the crowded one, of course, since most of the Catholics around Elm Haven put themselves through the extra half-hour of High Mass only when they had to.

Mike always kept a pair of brown oxfords in the room that Father Cavanaugh called the chancel; old Father Harrison hadn't minded his altar boys' tennis shoes showing under the surplice, but Father C. said that helping to prepare the Eucharist demanded that more respect be shown. Mike's dad had grumbled at the expense. Mike had never had a new pair of dress shoes before—his dad said that it was hard enough keeping the four girls in clothes—but in the end, his father couldn't argue with showing respect to God. Mike wore the oxfords no place except St. Malachy's, and then only when he was serving Mass.

Mike loved every aspect of the church service, and loved it more the more he did it. When he'd started as an altar boy almost four years earlier, Father Harrison had demanded little from the few boys willing to serve except that they show up on time. Like the others, Mike had walked through the motions and mumbled the Latin responses, not really paying attention to the translations on the laminated card on the step where he knelt, not really *thinking* about the miracle that was on the verge of occurring when he carried the small bottles of wine and water to the priest in the preparation for Communion. It had been a duty he agreed to because he was Catholic and this is what a good Catholic boy did . . . although the other Catholic boys around Elm Haven seemed to have excuses for *not* doing it.

But then, a little over a year ago, Father Harrison had retired—or had *been* retired; the old priest had been showing signs of age and alcoholism and his sermons were growing increasingly bizarre—and Father Cavanaugh's arrival had changed everything for Mike.

Father C. was, in many ways, an exact opposite of Father H., despite the fact that both men were priests. Father Harrison had been old and Irish, gray-haired and rosy-cheeked, ambling in his thinking, speech, and attitudes. The Mass seemed to have been a ritual that Father H. had performed so many times, with so few in attendance, that it appeared to have no more special significance to him than shaving would have. Father Harrison had really lived for the visitations and dinners where he was a guest—even a visitation to the sick or dying became an excuse for the old priest to sit, talk, have coffee, tell stories, and recall local people who were long dead. Mike had accompanied Father H. on some of these visitations— frequently the ill took Communion and Father H. thought that having an altar boy along added some sense of ceremony to the simple ritual. Mike was always bored out of his mind during these visits.

Father Cavanaugh, on the other hand, was young, dark-haired— Mike knew that the priest shaved twice a day and *still* had a five-o'-clock shadow showing through his dark skin—and incredibly intense. Father C. *cared* about the Mass—he called it Christ's invitation for us to join Him at the Last Supper—and he made the altar boys care. Or at least the ones who continued to serve.

Mike was one of the few who continued to serve on a regular basis. Father C. demanded a lot: the altar boy had to *understand* what he was saying, not merely mumble Latin phrases. Mike had gone to a special Wednesday-evening catechism class taught by Father C. for six months to learn both the rudiments of Latin and the historical context of the Mass itself. Then, the altar boys had to *participate*—really pay attention to what was going on. Father C. had a fierce temper and would turn it on any boy who was lackadaisical or remiss in his duties.

Father Harrison had loved to eat, and loved drinking even more— everyone in the parish, no, in the entire county, had known of the old priest's alcohol problem—but Father C. never drank except during Communion and seemed to view food as a necessary evil. He had some of the same attitude toward visitations; Father Harrison had talked about everything and everyone—he would sometimes spend an afternoon discussing crops and weather with retired farmers at the Parkside; but Father C. wanted to talk about God. Even his visitations to the sick and dying were like Jesuit commando raids, last-minute spiritual quizzes for those about to take the Ultimate Final Exam.

Father C.'s one vice, as far as Mike could tell, was smoking—the young priest chain-smoked, and when he wasn't smoking he seemed to be *wishing* he could—but that was all right with Mike. Both his parents smoked. All of his friends' parents smoked—except for Kevin Grumbacher's, and they were German and *weird*—and Father C.'s smoking just seemed to make him more intense.

On this first Sunday of true summer, Mike served both morning Masses, enjoying the coolness of the sanctuary and the hypnotic murmuring of the congregation as they mumbled their responses. Mike pronounced his carefully, precisely, neither too loud nor too low, articulating the Latin the way Father C. had taught him during those long evening lessons in the rectory.

"Agnus Dei, qui tollis peccata mundi . . . miserere nobis . . . Kyrie eleison, Kyrie eleison, Kyrie eleison. . . ."

Mike loved it. While part of him was totally involved in preparing the miracle of the Eucharist, another part wandered free . . . as if he truly could leave his body . . . being with Memo in her dark room, only now Memo could talk again and they would have conversations like when he was a little kid and she would tell him stories from the Old Country; or floating above the fields and forests out beyond Calvary Cemetery and the Cave, flying free like a raven with a human mind, looking down on treetops and streams, and the strip-mined hills the kids called Billy Goat Mountains, floating serenely above the faded wagon ruts of Gypsy Lane as the old road wound through woods and pasture. . . .

Then Communion was over—Mike always waited until the High Mass on Sunday to take Communion himself—the final prayers were said, responses given, the Eucharist was sealed in the tabernacle atop the altar, Father Cavanaugh blessed the congregation and led the procession from the sanctuary, and then Mike was in the little room they used to change, setting his cassock and surplice aside to be laundered by Father C.'s housekeeper, carefully placing his polished oxfords in the bottom of the cedar wardrobe.

Father Cavanaugh came in. He had changed out of his own black cassock into chinos, a blue work shirt, and a corduroy sport coat. It always shocked Mike to see the priest out of uniform.

"Good job, as always, Michael." For all of his informality in other ways, the priest had never called him Mike.

"Thanks, Father." Mike tried to think of something else to say— something to lengthen the moment alone with the only man he admired. "Not too many at the second Mass today."

Father C. had lit a cigarette and the small room filled with the smoky scent of it. The priest stood at the narrow window and stared out into the now-empty parking lot. "Hmmm? No, there seldom are." He turned to look at Mike. "Was your little friend there today, Michael?"

"Huh?" Mike knew few other Catholic boys his age.

"You know . . . Michelle whatshername . . . Staffney."

Mike blushed all the way to the base of his neck. He'd never mentioned Michelle to Father C. . . . never really mentioned her to *anyone* . . . but he always checked to see if she was in the congregation. She rarely was—she and her parents usually went all the way to St. Mary's cathedral in Peoria—but on those rare occasions when the redhead *was* there, Mike found it very hard to concentrate.

"I'm not even in the same class as Michelle Staffney," snorted Mike, trying to sound casual. He was thinking, *If that rat Donnie Elson told Father C. about her, I'll beat him to a pulp.*

Father Cavanaugh nodded and smiled. It was a gentle enough smile, no derision visible there, but Mike blushed again. He lowered his head as if concentrating fiercely on tying his sneakers.

"My mistake," said Father C. He stubbed out his cigarette in an ashtray on the bureau top, patted his pockets for another one. "You and your friends have plans for this afternoon?"

Mike shrugged. He had been planning to hang around with Dale and the others and then start his surveillance of Van Syke today. He blushed again, realizing how silly their little spy game was. "Uh-uh," he said. "Nothing going on."

"I thought I'd look in on Mrs. Clancy around five," said Father C. "I seem to remember that her husband stocked the pond on their farm before he passed away last spring. Thought she might not mind if we brought our fishing poles along and saw how well the fish were doing. Want to come along?"

Mike nodded, feeling joy rise in him like the picture of the Holy Spirit as a dove painted on the west wall of the sanctuary.

"Good. I'll pick you up in the Popemobile about four forty-five."

Mike nodded again. Father C. always talked about the parish car—a black Lincoln Town Car—as the Popemobile. At first Mike had been deeply shocked by the phrase, but then he realized that Father C. probably wouldn't make that joke around anyone else. He might even get in trouble if Mike repeated the phrase to someone—Mike had images of two cardinals from the Vatican suddenly appearing from a helicopter, grilling Father C. in the rectory, taking him away in leg irons—so the joke was actually a form of trust, a way of saying, "We're both men of the world, Michael my lad."

Mike waved good-bye and went out of the church into the sunlight of Sunday noon.

Duane worked most of the day, repairing the John Deere, spraying the weeds down along the ditch, moving the cows from the west pasture to the field between the barn and the cornfields, and finally walking the rows even though it was too early to weed.

The Old Man had come home around three A.M. Duane had kept one of the basement windows open even though it didn't have a screen, so he'd heard the car coming. The Old Man was drunk, but not falling-down drunk. He came in cussing and made a sandwich in the kitchen with even more cussing and shouting. Duane and Wittgenstein stayed in the basement, the old collie whining even while his tail beat on the cement floor.

When the Old Man wasn't hung over on Sunday mornings, he and Duane used to play chess until almost noon. There was no chess this Sunday.

It was midafternoon when Duane came in from walking the rows and found the Old Man in the wooden lawn chair under the poplar on the south lawn. A copy of *The New York Times* Sunday edition was spread out on the grass around him.

"Forgot I'd picked this up last night in Peoria," mumbled the Old Man. He rubbed his cheeks. He hadn't shaved for two days and the gray stubble looked almost silver in the light.

Duane dropped down on the grass and went through the stack looking for the Review of Books. "Last Sunday's paper?"

The Old Man grunted. "What the hell do you expect, *today's* paper?"

Duane shrugged and began reading the lead review. It was all about Shirer's *The Rise and Fall of the Third Reich* and other books that might tie in to the capture of Adolf Eichmann in Buenos Aires the week before.

The Old Man cleared his throat. "I didn't mean to . . . ah . . . to get home so late last night. Some sparrowfart professor from Bradley started arguing with me about Marx in a little pub down on Adams Street and I . . . well, everything go all right here?"

Duane nodded, not looking up.

"That soldier spend the night here or what?"

Duane lowered the book review section. "What soldier?"

The Old Man rubbed his cheek and neck again, obviously straining to sort fantasy from memory. "Uh . . . I remember giving some soldier a ride. Picking him up near the Spoon River bridge." He rubbed his cheek again. "I don't usually stop for hitchhikers . . . you know that . . . but it was starting to rain . . ." He stopped, looked back toward the house and barn as if the soldier might still be sitting in the pickup. "Yeah, I remember it more clearly now. He didn't say anything the whole trip. Just nodded when I asked him if he'd just gotten out of the service. The damnedest thing is, I knew something wasn't right at the time about the way he was dressed, but I was too . . . ah . . . too tired to notice what was wrong."

"What was wrong?" said Duane.

"His uniform. It wasn't a modern uniform. Not even an Eisenhower jacket. He was wearing heavy wool . . . brown wool, an old broad-brimmed campaign hat, and puttees."

"Puttees," said Duane. "You mean the leggings the doughboys wore back in World War One?"

"Yeah," said the Old Man. He chewed on the nail of his forefinger the way he did when he was considering a new invention or get-rich-quick scheme. "In fact, everything about that soldier was from the Great War . . . puttees, hobnailed boots, the old campaign hat, even a Sam Browne belt. He was real young but he couldn't have been a real soldier . . . must have been wearing his grandfather's uniform or been coming home from some sort of masquerade party." The Old Man focused on Duane. "Did he stay for breakfast?"

Duane shook his head. "He didn't come in with you last night. You must have dropped him off somewhere."

The Old Man concentrated a moment and then shook his head vigorously. "Uh-uh. I'm *sure* he was in the truck with me when I turned up the lane. I remember thinking that I'd sort of forgotten he was there, he was so quiet. I was going to give him a sandwich and let him sleep on the couch." The Old Man stared at Duane. His eyes were bloodshot. "I *know* he was still with me when I came up the lane, Duanie."

Duane nodded. "Well, I didn't hear him come in with you. Maybe he walked into town."

The Old Man squinted over the corn toward County Six. "In the middle of the night like that? Besides, I seem to remember him saying that he lived right around here somewhere."

"I thought you said he didn't talk."

The Old Man chewed his nail. "He didn't . . . I don't remember him talking at all . . . well, shit with it." He went back to reading the financial section.

Duane finished the review and then walked back to the house. Witt came out of the barn, obviously rested from one of his frequent naps and ready to go somewhere with Duane.

"Hey, boy," said Duane, "you see a doughboy from World War One wandering around in the barn?"

Witt whined slightly and cocked his head, not sure of what he was being asked. Duane rubbed him behind the ears. He walked over to the pickup and opened the door on the passenger side. The heated cab smelled of whiskey and old socks. There was a depression in the vinyl on the passenger seat, as if an invisible someone were sitting there now, but that had been there for as long as they'd owned the truck. Duane poked under the seat, checked the floorboards, and looked in the glove compartment. Lots of junk—rags, maps, some of the Old Man's paperbacks, several empty whiskey bottles, a church key, beer cans, and even a loaded shotgun shell—but no clues. No swagger stick or Spanish Mauser accidentally left behind, no diagram of trenches around the Somme or map of Belleau Wood.

Duane smiled at himself and went back out to the yard to read the paper and play with Witt.

It was evening before Mike and Father Cavanaugh ended their fishing expedition. Mrs. Clancy, who was dying of crotchetiness as much as old age, hadn't wanted anyone else in the house while Father C. heard her confession, so Mike had waited out by the pond, trying to skip rocks across it and wishing he hadn't skipped dinner. There were few things that would have gotten Mike excused from Sunday dinner, but helping Father C. turned out to be one of them. When the priest had said, "You've eaten already, haven't you?" to him, Mike had nodded. He would include that in his confession next time under the general category of *Several times I've not told the truth to adults, Father.* As Mike got older, he realized the real reason why priests couldn't marry—Who would want to live with someone you had to confess to regularly?

Father C. joined him by the pond by seven P.M.—he brought the fishing gear from the trunk of the Popemobile—and it seemed earlier with the June sun low but still above the trees. The two fished for over an hour, with only Mike catching something—a couple of sunfish which he threw back— but with conversation that was so rich that it made the boy a bit dizzy: the nature of the Trinity, what it was like growing up on Southside of Chicago when Father C. was younger, what street gangs were like, why everything else had to be created but God could just *be*, why old people came back to the Church—Father C. explained Pascal's Wager to Mike . . . or tried to— and a dozen other topics. Mike loved to talk about such things with the priest; talking with Dale and Duane and some of the other real brains among the kids could be fun—they had some weird ideas—but Father C. had *lived*. He was wise not only to the mysteries of Latin and the Church, but to the tough, cynical side of Chicago life that Mike had never imagined.

The tree shadows had crept across the grassy bank and were well out onto the pond when Father C. glanced at his watch and exclaimed, "Good heavens, Michael, look how late it is. Mrs. McCafferty will be worried." Mrs. McCafferty was the rectory housekeeper. She had tended to Father Harrison like a sister trying to keep a wayward brother out of trouble; she babied Father C. as if he were her son.

They stowed the gear and headed back to town. Driving south on County Six, a cloud of dust rising behind the Popemobile on the gravel road, Mike caught a glimpse of Duane McBride's home off to the right, then Dale's Uncle Henry's place on the left just before they descended

the first steep hill and climbed again to pass Calvary Cemetery. Mike saw
the graveyard empty and golden in the evening light, noticed the lack of
any cars in the grassy area along the road, and suddenly remembered that
he was supposed to have checked out Van Syke today. He asked Father C.
to stop and the priest steered the Popemobile onto the grass parking strip
between the road and the black wrought-iron fence.

"What is it?" asked Father C.

Mike thought fast. "I . . . uh . . . I promised Memo I'd check Grandpa's grave today. You know, see if the grass's been cut, if the flowers we left
last week are still there. You know, stuff like that." Another lie for Confession.

"I'll wait for you," said the priest.

Mike blushed and turned to look out at the cemetery so Father C.
wouldn't see the blush. He hoped the priest wouldn't hear the lie in his
voice. "Uh . . . I'd rather be alone for a while. I want to say some prayers."
*Good, Mike, that made a lot of sense. You want to say prayers so you tell a priest
to get lost. Is it a mortal sin to lie about praying?* "Besides, I may have to pull
some flowers in the woods and it'll be a while."

Father Cavanaugh looked west across the road, toward the sun that
hung like a red balloon low above the cornfields. "It's almost dark, Michael."

"I'll get home before dark. Honest."

"But it's at least a mile to town." The priest sounded dubious, as if
he suspected some mischief but couldn't figure out what it might be.

"It's no problem, Father. Us guys hike and bike it all the time. We
play in the woods out here a lot."

"You're not going into the woods after dark?"

"Naw," said Mike. "Just do what I promised Memo and walk home. I
like walking." He was thinking, *Could Father C. be afraid of the dark?* He
rejected the idea. For a second he considered not lying, telling the priest
about their hunch that something was wrong with Old Central—something
involving Tubby Cooke's disappearance—and all about how he was planning to check on the toolshed behind the cemetery where Van Syke was
rumored to sleep sometimes. Then he rejected that idea, too—he didn't
want Father Cavanaugh thinking he was a nut.

"You're sure?" said Father C. "Your folks will think you're with me."

"They know I promised Memo," said Mike, finding the lie easier now.
"I'll be home before dark."

Father Cavanaugh nodded and leaned over to open the door for
Mike. "All right, Michael. Thanks for the fishing companionship and
conversation. Tomorrow, early Mass?"

It was a rhetorical question. Mike served every early Mass. "Sure, tomorrow," he said, closing the heavy door and leaning forward to speak through the open window. "Thanks for . . ." He paused, not knowing what he was thanking the priest for. *Being a grown-up who talks to me?* "Thanks for loaning me the fishing pole."

"Any time," said Father C. "Next time we'll go down to Spoon River where there are real fish." He saluted with two fingers, backed the Popemobile out, and disappeared down the next hill to the south. Mike stood there a minute, blinking away dust and feeling the grasshoppers leap away from his legs in the low grass. Then he turned and looked at the cemetery. His shadow merged with the black and barbed lattice of the shadow of the iron fence. *Great. Jeez, what if Van Syke's here?*

He didn't think the part-time custodian, part-time cemetery handyman was there. The air was still, rich with the corn and dust smell of a humid June evening. And the place looked, sounded, and *felt* empty. He pulled back the knobbed bar on the pedestrian gate and walked inside, conscious of his shadow leaping ahead, conscious of the tall headstones throwing their own shadows, and especially conscious of the hushed silence after the hours of conversation.

He did stop by Grandpa's grave. It was about halfway back in the four-acre cemetery, three headstones left of the gravel-and-grass lane that bisected the rows of graves. The O'Rourkes were clustered in this area—his mother's people nearer the fence on the other side—and Grandpa's grave was the closest to the road. There was a wide grassy space here that Mike knew was reserved for his parents. And his sisters. And him.

The flowers were still there—wilted and dead but still there—from the previous Monday, Memorial Day, and so was the tiny American flag the American Legion had set there. They replaced the flags each Memorial Day, and part of Mike's sense of what season it was depended on how faded the flag was on Grandpa's grave: he had enlisted during World War I but had never gone overseas, merely spent fourteen months in a camp in Georgia. When Mike was very young, he had listened to Memo's stories of Grandpa's friends' adventures overseas in the Great War and received the definite impression from Memo that Grandpa's failure to see action was one of the few things the old man wished had turned out different in his life.

The colors of the flag were bright: blood red and crisp white above the green grass. The low, horizontal light made everything brighter and richer. Somewhere on Dale's Uncle Henry's farm one hill and a quarter of a mile away, a cow lowed and the sound was quite clear in the still air.

Mike bowed his head and said a prayer. Perhaps he wouldn't have to confess the little lies after all. Then he crossed himself and walked down the lane toward the rear of the cemetery and Van Syke's shed.

It wasn't really Van Syke's shed, merely the old toolshed that had been in the cemetery for years and years. It was set back near the rear fence, across a mowed strip of stubble far from the last row of graves—although, Mike thought, someday the cemetery would grow around it—and the thick sunlight lay across its west wall like butter spread on stone.

Mike noticed that the padlock was on the door and he strolled past as if he was headed for the woods and strip-mined hills far behind the cemetery—the kids' usual destination when they cut through here—and then turned back, stepping into the deep shadow on the west side of the little building. Grasshoppers leaped blindly from the stubble under his sneakers and brittle weeds cracked underfoot.

There was a window on this side—the only window the shed had— and it was tiny and neck-high on Mike. He went closer, shielded his eyes, and peered in.

Nothing. The window was too grimed and the interior too dark.

Whistling, hands in his pockets, Mike strolled around the building. He glanced over his shoulder several times to make sure that no one was coming down the lane. The road had been empty since Father C. had driven off. The cemetery was quiet. Beyond the road, the sun had gone down with the crimson, slow-motion elegance reserved for Illinois sunsets. But the empty sky was still burnished with June evening light, fading now toward true twilight and summer dark.

Mike inspected the lock. It was a solid Yale padlock, but the metal plate where the hook was attached to the doorframe was set into splinters and rot. Still whistling softly, Mike wiggled the plate back and forth until one—then two—of the three rusty screws were free of the frame. The last screw took some urging from Mike's pocketknife, but finally it came free. Mike glanced around, made sure there was a stone nearby to pound the screws back in when it was time to leave, and then he stepped into the shed.

It was dark. The air smelled of fresh soil and something more sour than that. Mike closed the door behind him—leaving a crack for light and so that he could hear if a car drove up to the front gate—and he stood there blinking a moment, letting his eyes adapt.

Van Syke wasn't there—that was the important thing Mike had checked on even before stepping in. Not much was there: a bunch of shovels and spades—standard equipment for a graveyard, he figured— some shelves with fertilizer and jars of dark liquid on them, some rusted and barbed iron bars, obviously part of the fence that had been removed for replacement, stacked in one corner, some attachments for the tractor that mowed the grounds, a couple of small crates—one which had a

lantern on it and looked as if it had been used as a table, some thick canvas straps which Mike puzzled over for a moment before he realized that
they were the straps that went under a coffin so it could be lowered into
the grave, and, directly under the grimed window, a low cot.

Mike checked out the cot. It smelled strongly of mildew and there
was a blanket thrown on it that didn't smell much better. But someone
had obviously used this as a bed recently—a Wednesday edition of the
Peoria Journal Star lay crumpled against the wall on it—and the blanket
lay half on the floor as if someone had thrown it off in a hurry.

Mike knelt next to the cot and moved the newspaper. Under it was a
magazine with slick, glossy pages mixed in with cheaper paper. Mike
lifted it, began to thumb through it, and then dropped it in a hurry.

The slick pages held glossy black and white photos of naked ladies.
Mike had seen naked ladies before—he had four sisters—and he had even
seen *magazines* with naked ladies in them: Gerry Daysinger had shown
him a nudist magazine once. But he had never seen photos like this.

The women lay with their legs open and their private parts showing.
The nudist pictures Mike had seen had been airbrushed—no pubic hair,
only a modest smoothness between the legs—but these photos showed
everything. Hair, the ladies' slits, the open lips down there . . . often held
open by the ladies themselves, lacquered nails tugging apart the opening
to their most secret parts. Other women were on their knees, rump to the
camera, so you could see their bum hole as well as the hairy parts. Others
were playing with their titties.

Mike felt his blush fade, but at the same second, as if the blood had to
flow *somewhere,* he felt his penis getting hard. He touched the magazine—
although not picking it up again—and flipped pages.

More women. More spread legs. Mike had never imagined that ladies would do such a thing in front of someone with a camera. What if
their families ever saw these pictures?

He felt his erection throbbing against his jeans. Mike had touched
himself before—even rubbed himself all the way to the climax that had
surprised him so much the first time it happened a year earlier—but Father Harrison had gone to great lengths to explain the consequences of
self-abuse, both spiritual and physical, and Mike had no intention of going insane or of getting the special type of acne that self-abusers always
suffered—thus letting the world know they were self-abusers. Besides,
Mike had confessed his particular sin the few times he'd done it, and
while it was one thing confessing something like that to Father Harrison
in the dark and getting bawled out for it, it would be quite another telling
Father Cavanaugh. Mike had realized that he would rather become an

atheist and go to hell than confess this sin to Father C. And if he *did* it and *didn't* confess . . . well, Father Harrison had described the punishment in hell that awaited sinners who were depraved.

Mike sighed, stuck the magazine back where he had found it, arranged the newspaper over it, and got to his feet. He'd jog down the hill and walk briskly up the next one; that should get rid of the bad thoughts and the hardness against the inside of his fly.

The blanket slipped off the cot as Mike rose and a raw smell filled the room.

Mike backed away and then came closer, lifting the blanket away.

A stench of raw earth . . . and something worse . . . rose from beneath the cot. Mike held his breath a second, and then he lifted the cot and set it against the packing crate.

There was a hole there. It was more than two feet across and perfectly round, as if it were an open manhole in a city street. But the edges were packed dirt. Mike got down on all fours and peered in.

The smell was very bad. Mike had gone to a slaughterhouse near Oak Hill once, and this stench was sort of like the room where they'd tossed the entrails and other bits and pieces they couldn't sell. The blood smell was the same. It mixed with the rich, raw earth scent to make a stench so strong that it made Mike dizzy. He teetered for a moment, eyes closed.

When he opened them, he caught a flicker of movement far down the hole as if something had just scurried from the light. Mike blinked. The edges of the hole were weird—raw red, although the soil around here wasn't clay, and striated, evenly ridged. It reminded Mike of something, although he couldn't think of what for a minute. Then he remembered.

Dale Stewart had a set of Compton's Pictured Encyclopedias. The boys liked to look at the section about the human body; there were transparent overlays there. One of the pictures was of just the digestive system, with cross sections and colored cutaways.

The sides of the hole looked like a section of human gut. Red and raw.

As Mike watched, the red ridges seemed to move slightly—contracting, then relaxing. The smell from the hole grew worse.

Mike crawled backward on all fours, breathing shallowly. There was a scraping, scrabbling sound from somewhere. *Rats outside . . . or something down there?*

Mike had a sudden image of this tunnel running into the cemetery, connecting to the graves there. He imagined Van Syke crawling head-first into this hole, disappearing down this raw gut into the deeper bowels of the earth . . . Van Syke slithering like a snake, sliding out of sight as he heard Mike's whistling a minute before.

Van Syke . . . or something worse?

Mike shivered. The filthy window suggested that it was already dark outside, although the crack in the door showed pale light.

Mike shoved the cot back in place, making sure the newspaper and magazine were as he had found them, and readjusted the blanket so it concealed the hole. It wouldn't take the blanket to hide it, he realized. *It's so dark in here, somebody might not notice the hole even if the cot weren't here if the smell didn't tip you off.*

Mike was still on his knees when he imagined a grub-white hand and arm sliding out from the blackness beneath the cot . . . sliding out and grabbing his wrist, gripping his ankle.

Mike's sexual excitement was completely gone. For a second he felt like he was going to throw up. He closed his eyes, opened his mouth to lessen the smell, and concentrated on saying a Hail Mary and an Our Father.

It didn't help.

He imagined that he heard stealthy footsteps in the grass stubble outside.

Mike flung the door open and threw himself outside, not caring if he ran into whoever it was, wanting only to be away from the hole . . . out of there.

The cemetery was empty. The sky was darker, one star hung in the east above the treeline there, the woods looked dark, but it was still summer twilight. A red-winged blackbird sat on a tall gravestone twenty yards away and seemed to stare at Mike.

He started to leave, walking quickly away, but then remembered the lock. He hesitated, realized that he was being an idiot, and then went back and began pounding in the screws. The last one had to be screwed in, and Mike noticed that his hand was shaking slightly as he used his penknife to do it.

If something comes out of that hole, how does it get out of the shed? Maybe it slithers through the window.

Shut up, stupid. The knife blade slipped and sliced his little finger. Mike ignored it, driving the screw the last quarter inch, oblivious of the drops of blood dripping onto the wooden frame.

There. It wasn't perfect. A close inspection would show where the latch frame had been pulled out and then readjusted. So what? Mike turned and walked down the lane.

There was still no traffic on County Six. Mike jogged down the hill, wishing the shadows here at the bottom were not so deep. It looked like night in the thick woods on either side.

The Black Tree Tavern was closed and dark—no alcohol could be served on Sunday—and it was strange to see the little building with no cars in front. Mike slowed to a walk when he got up the hill and past the Black Tree driveway. The woods continued to his left, Gypsy Lane was in there somewhere, but the country opened out to cornfields to his right and it was much lighter up here. Mike could see the junction with Jubilee College Road only a couple of hundred yards ahead, and once there, Elm Haven's water tower would be visible three quarters of a mile to the west.

Mike had slowed even more, silently cursing himself as a coward, when he heard gravel crunch behind him. It wasn't a car, but the soft tread of footsteps.

Still moving, he turned to walk backward, hands unconsciously raised to fists.

Another kid, he thought when he first saw the shadow separate itself from the darkness under the trees on the road at the top of the hill. He didn't recognize the kid, but saw the old-fashioned Boy Scout hat and uniform. The boy was about fifteen yards behind him.

Then Mike realized that it wasn't a kid. It was a guy in his twenties maybe, and the outfit wasn't a Boy Scout uniform but some sort of soldier suit like the uniforms Mike had seen in old photographs. The guy's face seemed waxy, smooth, and oddly featureless in the dim light.

"Hi!" yelled Mike and waved. He didn't know the soldier, but he was still relieved. When Mike had heard the footsteps behind him, he'd had a sudden image of Van Syke on the road with him.

The young soldier didn't wave back. Mike couldn't see his eyes, but it was almost as if the guy was blind. He wasn't running—just walking quickly in a sort of stiff, straight-legged march, but it was a fast enough march that the soldier had already closed some of the distance between them. He was ten yards away now and Mike could clearly see the brass buttons on the brown uniform, the weird khaki wrappings—like bandages—around his legs. The hobnailed boots made crunching noises on the gravel. Mike tried again to see the face, but the broad-brimmed hat cast deep shadows despite the dim light.

The young man was marching so quickly that Mike got the definite feeling that he was trying to catch up . . . was hurrying to close the distance.

The shit with this, thought Mike, vaguely aware that he would have to confess another bad word to Father C.

Mike turned and began running down Jubilee College Road toward the distant smudge of trees that was Elm Haven.

Dale's little brother Lawrence was afraid of the dark.

As far as Dale could tell, the eight-year-old wasn't afraid of anything else. He'd climb places that no one else—except perhaps Jim Harlen—

would even consider attempting. Lawrence was tough with that kind of quiet physical courage that sent him ripping into bullies half again as tall as him, his head down, fists pummeling even while he was taking a beating that would send an older kid fleeing in tears. Lawrence loved daredevil stunts—he would jump his bike from the highest ramp they could build, and when it came time in their backyard daredevil show for someone to lie down in front of the ramp while *others* jumped their bikes over him, Lawrence was the only one to volunteer. He played tackle football against mobs of kids bigger than him, and his idea of fun was to be taped up in a cardboard box and thrown off the strip-mined cliffs of Billy Goat Mountains. Sometimes Dale was sure that Lawrence's lack of fear would get him happily killed someday.

But he was afraid of the dark.

Lawrence was especially afraid of the dark in the hallway at the top of their stairs, and even more afraid of the dark in their bedroom.

The Stewarts' house—they had rented for the five years they had lived here since their move from Chicago—was old. The light switch at the bottom of the stairs controlled the bulbs on the small chandelier above the lower entrance hall, but left the landing above steeped in darkness. To get to the boys' room, one had to walk around the landing in that semidarkness. Worse, from Lawrence's point of view, was the fact that there was no wall switch in their room. To turn on the hanging light bulb in the center of the room, the boys had to walk into the darkness, feel around for the cord hanging in midair, and tug it on. Lawrence hated that part and begged Dale to go up to turn on the light for him.

Once, as they were falling asleep with the night-light on, Dale had asked him why he hated to do that . . . what exactly was he afraid of? It was *their room*. At first, Lawrence wouldn't answer, but finally he'd said sleepily, "Somebody might be in here. Waiting."

"Somebody?" Dale had whispered. "Who?"

"I dunno," Lawrence had sleepily whispered back, "somebody. Sometimes I think I'll come into the room and be feeling around for the light cord . . . you know, it's sorta hard to find . . . and instead of the cord, I'll feel this face."

Dale's neck had gone cold.

"You know," continued Lawrence, "some tall guy's face . . . only not quite a human face . . . and I'll be in here in the dark with my hand on his face . . . and his teeth'll be all slick and cool, and I'll feel his eyes wide open like a dead person's . . . and . . ."

"Shut up," Dale had whispered.

Even with the night-light on, Lawrence was afraid of things in the room. The house was old enough not to have closets—Dale's dad had said that people used big wardrobes for their clothes back then—but the previous owners or renters had added a closet to the boys' room. It was a crude thing—hardly more than a floor-to-ceiling box of painted pine boards in one corner—and Lawrence said that it reminded him of a coffin propped up there. It reminded Dale of a coffin, too, but he wouldn't admit it. Lawrence would never be the first to open the closet door, even in the daytime. Dale could only imagine what his brother thought might be waiting in there.

But mostly Lawrence was afraid of what might be under his bed.

The boys slept a few feet apart on small beds, identical down to the Roy Rogers blankets on them. But Lawrence was sure that something waited under his bed.

Lawrence would kneel to say his prayers if his mom was in the room, but when the two boys were alone, he was quick to get into his pajamas and jump onto the bed—not even come within grabbing distance of the darkness under it—and then he would go through a ritual of tucking his blankets in, securing everything so that nothing could drag him down, pull him under. If he was reading a comic or something and it fell on the floor, he would ask Dale to pick it up. If Dale didn't, the comic remained on the floor until morning.

Dale had reasoned with his brother for years. "Look, stupid," he'd said, "there's nothing under your bed but dust-balls."

"There could be a hole," Lawrence had whispered once.

"A hole?"

"Yeah, like a tunnel or something. With something in it waiting to get me." Lawrence's voice had been very tiny.

Dale had laughed. "Peabrain, we're on the second floor. There can't be a hole or tunnel on the second floor. Plus, it's solid wood." He'd leaned over and rapped the floor with his knuckles. "See, solid."

Lawrence had closed his eyes as if expecting a hand to reach out and grab Dale's wrist.

Dale had given up trying to convince Lawrence that there was nothing to be afraid of. Dale wasn't afraid of the dark upstairs—his fear was centered on the basement, specifically the coal bin where he had to go down to shovel coal every winter night—but he'd never told Lawrence or anyone about that anxiety. Dale loved summer because he didn't have to go down in the basement. But Lawrence was afraid of the dark all year round.

On this first Sunday night of summer vacation, Lawrence asked Dale to go upstairs to turn on the light for him and Dale had sighed, closed the Tarzan book he was reading, and gone up with his brother.

There were no faces in the dark. Nothing came out from under the bed. When Dale opened the closet door to hang up his brother's striped shirt, nothing leaped out or pulled him in. Lawrence got into his Zorro pajamas and Dale realized that even though it wasn't quite nine P.M., he was sleepy, too. He pulled on his own blue pajamas, tossed his dirty stuff in the hamper, and got into bed to read about Tarzan and the lost city of Opar.

They heard footsteps and their dad stood at the door. He had his reading glasses on and the dark frames made him look older and more serious than usual.

"Hi, Dad," said Lawrence from his bed. He'd just finished his ritual of tucking everything in tightly and making sure that there was nothing loose that might fall down and tempt the under-the-bed creatures.

"Hey, tigers. Hitting the sack early tonight, huh?"

"Going to read awhile," said Dale and suddenly knew that something was wrong. Their dad didn't usually come up to say goodnight, and this night there was a tightness around his eyes and mouth. "What's the matter, Dad?"

Their father came in, removed his glasses as if just remembering they were on, and sat on Lawrence's bed with his left hand bridging the gap to Dale's. "Did you guys hear the phone?"

"Uh-uh," said Dale.

"Yeah," said Lawrence.

"That was Mrs. Grumbacher . . ." began their dad. He played with his glasses, folding and refolding them. Then he stopped and put them in his pocket. "Mrs. Grumbacher called to say that she saw Miss Jensen over in Oak Hill today . . ."

"Miss Jensen," said Lawrence. "You mean Jim Harlen's mom?" Lawrence had never understood why Harlen's mom had a different last name . . . or why she could be a "miss" and still have a kid.

"Hush," said Dale.

"Yes," said their dad and patted Lawrence's leg under the blanket. "Jim's mom. She told Mrs. Grumbacher that Jim has had an accident."

Dale felt his heart lurch and then sink. He and Kevin had gone up to find Harlen that afternoon—Mike hadn't been around and they wanted enough guys to play ball—but Harlen's house had been dark and locked. They'd figured he'd gone out on some Sunday outing to see relatives or something.

"An accident," Dale repeated after a minute. "Is he dead?" Dale knew intuitively, certainly, that Harlen was dead.

Dale's dad blinked. "Dead? No, kiddo, Jim's not dead. But he was hurt pretty badly. He was still unconscious in the Oak Hill hospital today when Mrs. Grumbacher talked to his mom."

"What happened?" said Dale. His voice sounded dry, raspy.

Their dad rubbed his cheek. "They're not sure. It looks like Jim was climbing around the school . . ."

"Old Central!" breathed Dale.

"Yes, climbing around on the school across the street and he fell. Mrs. Moon found him this morning. She was looking for newspapers and cans in the dumpster they have over by the school . . . well, Jim had fallen in there either the night before or early that morning and was unconscious."

Dale licked his lips. "How bad hurt is he?"

Their father seemed to debate the answer for a second. He patted both boys' legs under their covers. "Mrs. Grumbacher says that Miss Jensen says he'll be all right. He's still unconscious—she says that he hit his head and there was a fairly serious concussion . . ."

"What's a concussion?" asked Lawrence, eyes wide.

"It's like bruising your brain or splitting your skull," whispered Dale. "Now be quiet and let Dad talk."

Their dad smiled slightly. "He's not quite in a coma, but he is still unconscious. The doctors say that that's normal with a serious head injury. I guess he's also got some broken ribs and a multiple fracture of one of his arms . . . Mrs. G. didn't say which one. Evidently Jim fell quite a ways and hit the rim of the dumpster. If there hadn't been some soft junk in there to break his fall . . . well . . ."

Lawrence piped up. "He woulda been like Mike's kitten that got squashed flat on the Hard Road last summer, huh, Dad?"

Dale punched his brother on the arm. Before his dad could snap at him, he said, "Can we go over to Oak Hill to visit him, Dad?"

Their father took his glasses out of his pocket. "Sure. I don't see why not. Of course, it'll be a few days at least. Jim has to regain consciousness and they have to make sure he'll be OK. If he were to get worse or not come to, they might have to transfer him to a hospital in Peoria . . ." He stood and patted Lawrence's leg a last time. "But we'll go to see him this week if he's feeling better. You guys don't read too long, OK?" He walked to the door.

"Dad?" said Lawrence. "How come Harlen's mom didn't know he was gone last night? How come nobody looked for him until this morning?"

Their dad's face showed anger for just a second. Not anger at Lawrence. "I don't know, kiddo. Maybe his mom thought he was home sleeping. Or maybe Jim went out and climbed onto the school this morning."

"Uh-uh," said Dale. "Harlen sleeps the latest of any kid I know. It was last night. I'd bet on it." Dale thought of the Free Show, of the lightning and first drops of rain that had sent everyone to cars or huddling under trees for several minutes while Rod Taylor fought the Morlocks, and of the second feature that got rained out. He and Lawrence had walked back with one of Mike's sisters and her dumb boyfriend.

What was Harlen doing climbing on Old Central?

"Dad," said Dale, "do you know where Harlen was climbing? Which part of the school?"

Their dad frowned. "Well, he fell into the dumpster that's near the parking lot, so I guess it was on the corner on this side. That's where your classroom was this year, wasn't it?"

"Yeah," said Dale. He was imagining the route Harlen would have climbed . . . the drainpipe probably, maybe the stone ridges on the corner, definitely the ledge outside the classroom. *Cripes, that's way up there. Why the hell would Harlen be way up there?*

His dad seemed to speak Dale's thoughts aloud. "Do either of you know why Jim might've tried to climb into his old room over there?"

Lawrence shook his head. He was hugging the ragged panda bear that he called "Teddy." Dale shook his head and said, "Uh-uh, Dad. It doesn't make any sense."

Their dad nodded. "I'll be traveling tomorrow night and Tuesday, but I'll call to check on you guys . . . and to see how your friend's doing . . . and we'll go visit Jim later in the week if you want to."

Both boys nodded.

Later, Dale tried to read, but the adventures of Tarzan in the lost city suddenly seemed pretty silly. When he finally got up to turn out the light, Lawrence extended his hand across the gap between their beds. Lawrence usually wanted to hold hands while falling asleep—it was the one risk he took with something grabbing him—but most times, Dale told him no. Tonight he held his little brother's hand.

The curtains on both windows were open. Leaf-shadow painted silhouettes on the screens. Dale could hear crickets and the rustle of leaves. He couldn't quite see Old Central from this angle, but he saw the pale glow of the single pole light near the north entrance.

Dale closed his eyes, but as soon as he tried to drift off to sleep he imagined Harlen lying there in that dumpster amidst the broken boards and other junk. He imagined Van Syke and Roon and the others gathered around the dumpster in the dark, looking down at the unconscious kid and smiling at each other with their rat's teeth and spidery eyes.

Dale snapped awake. Lawrence was asleep, still clutching Teddy and snoring softly. A thin line of moisture wet the pillow under his mouth.

Dale lay there silently, barely breathing. He did not let go of Lawrence's hand.

NINE

Duane McBride awoke before dawn on Monday morning and thought for a confused second that he had to get his chores done and meet the school bus at the end of the lane. Then he remembered that it was Monday—the first Monday of summer vacation—and that he'd never have to go to Old Central again. A weight lifted from his shoulders, and he went upstairs whistling.

There was a note from the Old Man: he'd left early to meet some friends for breakfast at the Parkside Cafe, but he would be home by early afternoon.

Duane did the morning chores. Finding the eggs in the henhouse reminded him of when he was a tiny little kid and terrified of the militant hens, but it was a good memory because it was one of the few he had of his mother—even if the memory was of little more than a polka-dotted apron and a warm voice.

After breakfast of two of the eggs, five strips of bacon, toast, hash browns, and a chocolate donut, Duane was ready to go outside again—the pump on the water tank in the back pasture needed cleaning and a new pulley—when the phone rang. It was Dale Stewart. Duane listened silently to the news about Jim Harlen. After Dale waited a second for a response that did not come, he went on to tell Duane that Mike O'Rourke wanted a meeting of everybody in his chickenhouse at ten o'clock that morning.

"Why not in *my* chickenhouse?" was Duane's response.

"Your chickenhouse has chickens in it. Besides, we'd all have to ride our bikes way out to your house."

"I don't have a bike," said Duane. "I'll have to walk all the way in. What about meeting in your secret hideout in the culvert?"

"The Cave?" said Dale. Duane could hear the hesitancy in the other eleven-year-old's voice. Duane didn't especially want to go back to the culvert today either.

"OK," he said. "I'll be there at ten o'clock." After Duane hung up, he sat in the kitchen for a moment, thinking of the chores he'd have to double up on that afternoon. Finally he shrugged, found a candy bar to give him energy on the trip, and went outside. Witt met him in the yard, tail wagging, and this time Duane didn't have it in his heart to leave the old dog behind. There was a high cloud cover that day that cut down on the heat a bit—it was in the low eighties—and he thought Witt might like the exercise.

Duane went back in the house, stuffed his pants pockets with dog biscuits, grabbed a second candy bar for lunch, and the two set off down the lane. Duane never thought about it, but from a distance the two made odd companions—Duane with his ambling, loose-jointed semiwaddle; Wittgenstein limping along arthritically, setting his paws carefully like a barefoot quadruped on hot gravel, and peering myopically at things he could smell but not quite see.

The shade at the bottom of the hills was a relief, but Duane was sweating freely under his plaid flannel shirt by the time he climbed the grade to the Black Tree Tavern. There were a few cars there already. His dad's pickup wasn't one of them, but Duane guessed that the "breakfast" had already moved from the Parkside Cafe to Carl's Tavern in town.

The overcast began to break up by the time the boy and dog had turned west on Jubilee College Road, and the distant water tower shimmered in heat waves. Duane glanced at the fields of corn on either side, comparing their growth to the fields at his own farm—these were a few inches taller—and checking out the yellow signs along the barbed-wire fence to see what the brand and hybrids were. The sunlight was a solid thing now, heavy on his face and shoulders, and Duane cursed himself for forgetting his cap. Witt poked along, occasionally sniffing out an interesting scent trail and careening off blindly into the dust-covered weeds in the ditch alongside the road. The fence would usually stop his investigations and the collie would come limping back to where Duane waited patiently.

Duane was less than a quarter of a mile from the water tower and the turn in the road into town when the truck came. He smelled it almost as soon as he heard it; it had to be the Rendering Truck. Witt raised his head, blindly trying to find the source of the scent and noise, and Duane caught him by the collar and pulled him over to the side of the gravel road. Duane hated it when trucks passed while he was walking here; the grit stayed in his eyes and mouth and hair for hours. If too many vehicles passed him, he might even have to take a bath one of these days.

Standing at the edge of the weeds, Duane noticed how fast the truck was coming. It had to be the Rendering Truck—how many trucks were there around here with peeling red paint on the cab and the high slats behind? The windshield was a mirror of sky glare. The thing was not only roaring along at fifty or sixty miles per hour, it wasn't moving to the center or left of the road as most vehicles would. Duane thought of flying gravel and he pulled Witt farther back, onto the verge of the shallow ditch itself.

The truck roared right, whipping weeds under its massive bumper and heading straight for Duane and the dog at fifty miles per hour.

Duane didn't take time to think. He bent, lifted Witt in a single motion, and leaped across the low ditch, almost colliding with the barbed-wire fence. He barely managed to hold on to the panicked and wiggling collie as the truck missed them by three feet, throwing dust, stubble, gravel, and junk from the side of the road into the air around them.

Duane could see the corpses of several cows, a horse, two hogs, and what looked to be a pale dog in the back as the Rendering Truck swerved back onto the gravel road and continued on in a cloud of dust.

"You son of a bitch!" he shouted, stepping out onto the gravel but still holding the terrified old dog in his aims. His hands were occupied, he couldn't shake a fist, so Duane spat after the truck. The gob of saliva was dust-colored.

The truck reached the water tower and turned left, the squealing of tires quite audible as it hit the asphalt there.

"Stupid bastard," muttered Duane. He almost never cursed, but he felt the need now. "Cretinous cowturd motherfucker." Witt was whining and wiggling in his arms, and Duane suddenly realized how heavy the old dog was and how hard Witt's heart was pounding. He could feel the throbs against his forearms. He stepped out onto the packed ruts in the road, set Witt down, and calmed him with long, slow strokes and gentle words.

"It's all right, Witt. It's OK, old friend," he crooned. "That dumb old stupid piss-ant preliterate asshole of a simple-minded custodian didn't hurt us, did he? No." The soothing tones were calming the dog, but his pulse was still visible against his ribs.

Actually, Duane hadn't seen Van Syke at the wheel—he was too busy lifting Witt and backing into barbed wire to check in the cab as the truck roared by—but he had no doubt that the crazy custodian-cum-dead-varmint collector was at the wheel. Well, everybody would know about this soon enough. It was one thing to scare a bunch of kids by dropping a dead monkey in the creek; it was something else to try to kill one of those kids.

Duane suddenly realized that Van Syke—or whoever it was—*had* tried to kill him. It hadn't been a prank. It hadn't been some sort of insane warning. The truck had *aimed* at them, and only the vehicle's speed and the certainty of turning over after hitting the low ditch at that speed had kept the driver from moving over the required thirty-six inches to get them. *Somebody would've come along and found my body in the weeds,* thought Duane. *And Witt's. They'd never have known who did it. Just some careless kid and a hit-and-run driver.* Duane remembered the barbed wire and felt his back. His hand came away red with blood. Worse than that, there were two large rips in his shirt that he would have to sew up.

Duane continued to pet Witt, but now the boy was shaking worse than the dog had been. With his free hand, Duane dug in his pocket, found a biscuit for Witt, and then got out the candy bar for himself.

The Rendering Truck roared around the corner by the water tower.

Duane stood and stared, the chunk of Butterfingers unchewed in his mouth. It was the Rendering Truck; he could clearly see the red cab and massive bumper ahead of the cloud of dust. It was going slower now, but was still traveling at least thirty miles per hour. Fast enough to turn Witt and him into instant roadkill when one considered the three tons above those wheels.

"Oh, shit," Duane whispered reverently. Witt whimpered and pulled at Duane's grip on his collar.

Duane dragged the dog to the left side of the road as if headed for the fields on the south side. The ditch was weed-filled but very low there, almost flat. No hindrance to a vehicle.

The Rendering Truck swerved right, filling Duane's side of the road. It had covered half the distance now and Duane could make out the silhouette of a driver in the cab. The man was tall but hunched forward, intent on driving . . . on *aiming.*

Duane grabbed Witt's collar and dragged the panicked collie across the road—his forelegs were locked and straight, gravel slid beneath his paws—and tugged him into the ditch.

The Rendering Truck cut left, coming off the road, bouncing across the ditch until its left wheels were almost scraping the fence. Weeds whipped under the front bumper and the dust cloud filled the air.

Duane glanced over his shoulder, hoping without hope that another car would come the other way, that some adult would intervene . . . that he would wake up.

The truck was less than a hundred feet away and seemed to be accelerating.

Duane realized that he couldn't get back across the road in time with Witt, and even if he could, the truck could get them while he was trying to climb the fence there.

Wittgenstein barked and jerked, snapping at Duane's wrist in his frenzy. For a fraction of a second, Duane considered letting the collie go—letting him fend for himself—but then he realized that Witt wouldn't have a chance. Even in the adrenaline of panic, the old dog's joints were too stiff, his eyesight too poor.

The truck was twenty yards away and closing. Its left front wheel struck a rotted fence post and snapped it out of the ground. The wire fence hummed like a shattered harp.

Duane bent, lifted Witt, and in one smooth move threw the dog as far over the fence and into the field as he could. Witt landed three rows of corn in, slid on his side, and scrambled to get his feet under him.

Duane had no more time to watch. He grabbed a skinny wooden post and heaved himself up. The entire fence wobbled and sagged. Barbed wire cut into Duane's left hand. His foot was too big for the square of wire he'd stuck it in and his sneaker was stuck.

The Rendering Truck filled the world with roar and dust and an oncoming wall of scabrous red metal. The driver was no longer visible as the windshield glinted blindingly. It was less than thirty feet away and bouncing on, ripping fence posts out of the ground as it came.

Duane left his sneaker where it was, pulled his foot free, heaved himself over—feeling the barbed wire rip at his belly—fell heavily into soft soil at the edge of the field, and rolled away across cornstalks even as he gasped for breath.

The truck missed him, snapping off the fence post he'd climbed and throwing wire and weeds and gravel into the air around him.

Duane got to his knees in the deep loam of the field. He was stunned. His flannel shirt was in tatters and blood from torn skin on his stomach dripped onto his corduroys. His hands were a mess.

The Rendering Truck bounced back onto the road. Duane could see the brake lights glowing like red eyes through the cloud of dust.

Duane turned to find Witt, saw him lying two rows over—still stunned—and then he looked back. The truck turned slowly, ponderously to its left, nosedown in the ditch. The rear wheels spun, throwing gravel like birdshot. Duane heard stones patter on the corn in the opposite field. The truck backed up, bounced into the low ditch across the road, moved its long hood in Duane's direction, and came on.

Staggering, weaving, Duane kicked aside cornstalks to get to Witt, lifted the listless dog, and waded off through the rows, moving deeper into the field. The corn was lower than his waist. Witt's tail dragged across tassels. There was nothing but this low corn for a mile to the north, and then only another fence and a few trees.

Duane kept moving, not looking back even when he heard the truck bounce across the ditch, heard the fence snap and tear a second time, heard the sound of cornstalks smashing under bumper and wheels.

It rained just a couple of days ago, Duane was thinking as he slogged on, moving at a glacial pace. Witt hung tired and heavy in his arms. Only the slight panting and movement of his ribs showed that he was alive. *Just a couple of days ago it rained. The top inch or so is dust, but beneath it . . . mud. Please, God. Let it be mud.*

The truck was in the field with him now. Duane heard the whir of the differential and the grating of gears. It was as if some huge, insane animal was coming after him. The smell of dead livestock was very strong.

Duane plunged on. He wondered if he should stop and face it— lunge aside at the last second like some nimble matador. Try to get behind the damn thing. Find a rock and throw it at the windshield.

He wasn't nimble. He couldn't dodge that way with Witt in his arms. He slogged on.

The truck was forty feet behind him, then twenty, then fifteen. Duane tried to run but could only manage a broad-strided walk. Corn whipped around him and pollen matted Witt's fur. He realized that a row he'd just crossed had been wide and wet, a crude irrigation ditch. He kept on moving.

Behind him, the roar of engine and wheels on dirt turned into a whine, then a scream.

Duane glanced back. The truck was at an odd angle, left rear wheels spinning wildly. Mud and torn vegetation flew in an arc behind it.

Duane kept on moving, kicking aside stalks that threatened to scrape at Witt's eyes. When he looked back again, the truck was a hundred feet behind him, still at an odd angle but rocking back and forth now. Stuck in the mud there.

Duane fixed his vision on the line of scattered fields to the north and kept on moving. Beyond that fence was Johnson's pasture . . . and beyond that, to the north and east, the woods that ran all the way to the Black Tree. There were hills there. And a deep gully along the stream.

Another ten rows and I'll look back.

He was pouring sweat now, and he felt it mixing with the blood and dirt as a terrible itch between his shoulder blades. Witt stirred once, moved his legs the way he had since he was a pup when he was dreaming about chasing rabbits or something, and then relaxed as if willing to let his master do all the work.

Eight rows. Nine. Duane kicked aside corn and glanced back.

The truck was free and moving again. But backwards. It was backing out of the field, bouncing and jolting. But definitely moving backwards.

Duane did not stop. He continued to lurch toward the fence—less than a hundred yards away now—even as he heard the whine of wheels and differential change pitch, heard the distant scrape of gravel as the truck accelerated.

There's no way in here. No way it can head me off. I can get all the way to our own back pasture if I stay in the woods, away from the roads and driveways.

Duane reached the fence, gently dropped Witt across it, and lost more skin climbing barbed wire before he allowed himself a second to rest.

He squatted next to his dog, wrists limp on his torn knees, panting loudly and listening to the roar of his own pulse in his ears. He raised his head and looked back.

The water tower was clearly visible. Another quarter of a mile south, he could see the dark trees of Elm Haven. The road was empty. There was no sound. Only a slowly settling cloud of dust and the ravaged fence far across the field told Duane that he hadn't dreamt it all.

He crouched next to Witt and petted his side. The collie did not stir. His eyes were glassy. Duane lowered his cheek to Witt's ribs, held his own breath so his mad breathing would not drown out sound.

There was no heartbeat. Witt's heart had probably stopped on him even before they'd crossed the first fence. Only the old collie's urge to stay by his master had kept him breathing and struggling as long as he had.

Duane touched his old friend's narrow head, patted the thin fur there, and tried to close Witt's eyes. The eyelids would not come down.

Duane knelt there. There was a great pain in his chest and throat which had nothing to do with cuts or bruises. The pain became a terrible swelling, almost an explosion of emotion, but he could not swallow it or bring it up as tears. It threatened to choke him as he gasped for air, raising his face to the now blue sky.

Kneeling there, pounding his bleeding hands against the soil, Duane promised Witt and the God he didn't believe in that someone would pay for this.

Mike O'Rourke and Kevin Grumbacher were the only ones who showed for the Bike Patrol meeting that Mike had called. Kevin was nervous, pacing the length of the chickenhouse and fiddling with a rubber band, but Mike just shrugged. He realized that Dale and the others had better things to do than come to a silly meeting on a summer morning.

"We'll skip it, Kev," he said from where he lay sprawled on the sprung couch. "I'll talk to the guys sometime when we're together."

Kevin paused in his pacing, started to say something, and then stayed silent as Dale and Lawrence burst through the small door.

It was obvious that something had excited Dale: his eyes were wild, his short hair in disarray. Lawrence was also agitated.

"What?" said Mike.

Dale gripped the doorframe and gasped for breath. "Duane just called . . . Van Syke tried to kill him."

Mike and Kevin stared.

"It's true," gasped Dale. "He called me just when the cops were getting there. He had to call Carl's Tavern to get his dad to come home, and then he called Barney, and he thought maybe Van Syke would come while he was waiting at home, but he didn't, so his dad got home but doesn't really believe him, but his dog is dead. . . . Van Syke didn't exactly kill him, but in a way he did, because . . ."

"Hold it," said Mike.

Dale stopped.

Mike stood up. "Start at the beginning. The way you tell stories when we go camping. First things first. Is Duane OK and how did Van Syke try to kill him?"

Dale threw himself on the couch that Mike had just vacated. Lawrence found a cushion on the floor. Kevin stood where he had stopped pacing, motionless except for the movement of his hands as he unconsciously formed intricate patterns with the rubber band.

"OK," said Dale and took another few seconds. "Duane just called. About half an hour ago, Van Syke . . . he *thinks* it was Van Syke but didn't really see him . . . somebody in Van Syke's Rendering Truck tried to run over him on Jubilee College Road. Not too far from the water tower."

"Jesus," Kevin said softly. Mike shot him a glance that silenced him.

Dale nodded, eyes slightly unfocused as he concentrated on what he was saying and as the real significance of it hit home. "Duane says that the truck tried to hit him on the road and then tore down the fence chasing him into the field. He says his dog died then . . . sort of scared to death."

"Witt?" said Lawrence. There was pain in the younger boy's voice. Every time he and Dale went out to Duane's place to visit, Lawrence would play for hours with the old collie.

Dale nodded again. "Duane had to cut across the Johnsons' fields and Corpse Creek and the woods there to get to his own place. And the weird thing is . . ."

"What?" Mike said softly.

"The weird thing is, Duane said he carried his dog all the way home. He didn't leave him there in the field where he died to go back for him later."

Lawrence nodded as if he understood perfectly.

"Is that all he said?" urged Mike. "Did he say *why* Van Syke might have gone after him?"

Dale shook his head. "He said he wasn't doing anything except walking in here. I called him to tell him about the meeting. He said that the truck wasn't fooling around . . . it wasn't like when J.P. Congden or one of those assho—" Dale glanced at his younger brother. "It wasn't

like when one of those other old jerks sort of pretends to swerve his
pickup to scare you. Duane said that whoever was driving the Rendering
Truck was really trying to kill him and Witt."

Mike nodded, apparently lost in thought.

Dale combed his cowlick down with his fingers. "He had to hang up
because Barney was just getting there."

Kevin collapsed the cat's cradle between his fingers. "And he was
calling you from his home?"

"Yeah."

Kevin looked at Mike. "Does this have anything to do with what
you wanted us to talk about?"

The tallest boy snapped out of his reverie. "Maybe." He glanced toward the yard where their bikes were lying everywhere. "Let's get going."

"Where?" asked Lawrence. He'd been chewing on the bill of his
wool baseball cap—a common habit of his when nervous or distracted.

Mike smiled slightly. "Where do you think Duane's going to take
Barney and his dad? If the truck chased him *into* the field, there's going
to be a lot of wheel tracks and stuff."

All four boys ran for their bikes.

Barney was there. His green Pontiac with the faded gilt letters spelling
CONSABLE on the door was parked by the side of the road, as were Duane's
dad's pickup and J.P. Congden's black Chevy. Duane and his dad were
standing in the gap where the fence had been torn down, Duane speaking
softly and occasionally pointing to the deep ruts in the field. Barney was
nodding and taking notes in a small spiral notebook. J.P. was smoking a
cigar and glowering as if Duane were the suspect in all this.

Dale and the other kids spun their bikes to a stop thirty feet from
the group in the field. Congden turned away from Duane's explanation,
spat into the weeds, and shouted at the boys to go away. Mike and the
others nodded and stayed where they were.

Duane's father was talking. ". . . and I want you to get out there and
arrest him, Howard." Barney's real name was Howard Sills. "Goddamned idiot tried to kill my boy."

Barney nodded and made a note. "Actually, Martin, we don't have
any evidence that it was Karl Van Syke . . ."

Mike glanced at Dale, Kevin, and Lawrence, and they returned the
look. They'd never heard Van Syke's first name before.

". . . and your son said that he didn't get a clear look," Barney finished quickly, rushing to finish before Mr. McBride exploded again.

Duane's dad was getting red in the face, nearing that instant of explosion, when J.P. Congden shifted his cigar from one side of his mouth to the other and said, "Wasn't Karl."

Barney shifted his cap and raised an eyebrow in the justice of the peace's direction. From thirty feet away, Dale thought, *Barney doesn't really look like Barney on the show.* Sheriff Howard Sills was short and balding, and had a hint of Don Knotts's poor posture and wide-eyed stare, but really he didn't resemble the deputy on *The Andy Griffith Show.* But everyone called him Barney.

"How do you know it wasn't Karl?" Barney asked the fat man.

Congden shifted the cigar again and squinted at Duane and his dad as if the two were the kind of white trash with whom a justice of the peace shouldn't waste his time. "I know 'cause I was with Karl all morning," he said. He removed the cigar, spat again, and grinned. His teeth were approximately the color of the stogie. "Karl and me was down at Spoon River, doin' a little fishin' below the highway bridge."

Barney nodded. "Van Syke usually drives the Rendering Truck," he said, his voice flat. "I checked with Billy Daysinger and he said he hasn't driven it since last summer."

Congden shrugged and spat again. "Karl told me this mornin' that somebody stole the truck last night from where it was parked near the tallow plant."

Mike O'Rourke glanced at the other boys. The tallow plant was an ancient, rotting structure north of the abandoned grain elevators on the way to the dump. It was the place where all the dead livestock and roadkill had been brought before it also had been abandoned. The smell lingered and sometimes it drifted all the way to Harlen's house on the northwest edge of the town.

Barney scratched his small chin. "Why didn't you report it, J.P.? You or Karl?"

Congden shrugged, obviously bored by all this. *What little hair he still has sticks out behind his ears like wet weasel's fur,* thought Dale, *and the top of his head doesn't sunburn, it just glows in the sunlight like the belly of a carp.*

"Like I said, we was busy," said the township's justice of the peace. "Besides, I just figured that some of these goddamned kids just took it as some sort of prank. How do we know that these little shits didn't do it?" He gestured toward the group of boys on their bikes.

Barney looked up at them impassively.

Congden raised his voice while jerking a thumb in Duane's direction. "And who says this kid wasn't part of it? Foolin' around with his friends? Wastin' our time so it looks like they wasn't the ones who

fucked up and lost control, tearin' down Summerson's fence and everything . . ."

Duane's father stepped forward over torn strands of barbed wire.
His face was mottled, more purple than red now. "Goddamn you, Congden, you lying piece of capitalist dogshit. You know my boy . . . none of
these boys . . . had anything to do with this. Someone tried to *kill* Duane,
tried to run over him right here, and for all I know you're covering up for
that miserable excuse of Australopithecine subhumanity named Van
Syke because the two of *you* stole the truck. It's no worse than the stealing you do with the so-called 'speeders' you drag into court to keep you
in beer money, you stupid . . ."

Barney stepped between the two men and laid a hand on Mr. Mc-
Bride's shoulder. The grip must have been more firm than it looked because Duane's dad grew pale, quit talking, and turned away.

"Aw, fuck him," said the justice of the peace and strode back to his
car.

"Tell Karl to come see me," Barney said.

Congden didn't even nod as he slammed the door of the black
Chevy and turned the key in the ignition. The specially tuned engine
roared into life and the justice of the peace threw gravel twenty feet behind him as he roared back toward town. The boys had to move their
bikes hurriedly into the ditch or get run over as Congden passed.

Mr. McBride talked for a few minutes, gesturing toward the field,
shouting occasionally, and finally settling down to an agitated murmur as
Barney took notes. Through all this, Duane had stood back a few feet in
the field, arms crossed, eyes impassive behind the thick lenses of his
glasses. When Duane's dad and the sheriff walked back to the road to talk,
the boys dropped their bikes into the dusty weeds and hurried through
the gap in the fence.

"You OK?" asked Dale. He wanted to touch the bigger boy, put his
arm on Duane's shoulder, but protocol didn't allow it.

Duane nodded.

"Did he really kill Witt?" asked Lawrence. The eight-year-old's voice
was unsteady.

Duane nodded again. "Witt's heart stopped," he clarified. "He was
old."

"But somebody tried to run you over?" asked Kevin.

Duane nodded.

Duane's dad was calling for him. Duane uncrossed his arms and
said softly to the boys, "Something's going on. I'll talk to you later today
if I can get in." He waddled through the break in the fence and joined
his father. Barney spoke to him a moment, finally laying a hand on his

shoulder. The boys could hear, "Sorry about the dog, boy." Then Barney seemed to be cautioning Duane's dad about something. Finally the constable got in his Pontiac and left, pulling away slowly down the gravel road so as not to leave a cloud of dust for the others.

Duane and his dad stood there a moment, looking out at the field, and then they got in their truck, made a U-turn with several swings back and forth, and drove back out Jubilee College Road toward County Six. Duane didn't wave.

The four boys stood in the field a moment, kicking at the deep, muddy ruts and the swath of crushed cornstalks. They looked around as if the ghost of Duane's collie might come running through the waist-high corn.

"Hey," Kevin said at last, looking around. The fields were still. The sky was cloudy again. There was no movement, no sound. "What if the Rendering Truck comes back?"

They were on their bikes in eight seconds and pedaling toward town with spurts of gravel marking their wake. Dale held back so that Lawrence could keep up, but the eight-year-old's seventeen-inch bike was almost a blur as it passed Dale's larger bike, then Kevin's, and finally Mike's old red clunker.

They were safely under the unstirring elms and oaks of Elm Haven before they slowed, panting and leaning backward, arms dangling, hands off the handlebars as they coasted down Depot Street past Dale's house and Old Central. They let their bikes crash on the hill alongside the driveway to Kevin's house and they rolled on the cool grass there, still catching their breaths, their short hair matted and moist.

"Hey," gasped Lawrence when he could talk, "what's a capitalist?"

TEN

The attempt on Duane McBride's life was the topic of earnest discussion for half an hour or more, but after a while the boys lost interest and went off to play ball. Mike deferred his Bike Patrol meeting until after the game or when Duane finally came into town, whichever came first.

The city ballfield was in the field behind Kevin's and Dale's homes, and to get there most of the kids in town climbed the Stewarts' fence where the thick wooden post had a diagonal wooden crossbrace on this side. That turned the Stewarts' driveway and the west side of their long yard into a public thoroughfare for kids—which was fine with Dale and

Lawrence—and the result was that their home was a constant meeting place for kids from around town. It also didn't hurt that Dale's mom was one of the few who didn't mind mobs of boys there—in fact, she went so far as to provide sandwiches and lemonade and other treats for the packs of kids.

On this day the pickup game started slow—Kevin and Dale versus Mike and Lawrence for the first hour, with the pitcher's-hands-out rule in effect—but by lunchtime they'd been joined by Gerry Daysinger and Bob McKown, Donna Lou Perry and Sandy Whittaker—Sandy could bat all right but threw like a girl, but she was Donna Lou's friend and both teams wanted Donna Lou—and then some of the guys from the ritzier end of town showed up: Chuck Sperling, Digger Taylor, Bill and Barry Fussner, and Tom Castanatti. Other kids heard the noise or caught a glimpse of the crowd and by early afternoon they were on their third game and playing with regulation-size teams and bench-sitters rotating in.

Chuck Sperling wanted to be captain—he always wanted to be captain; his dad managed Elm Haven's only Little League team so that Chuck could be captain as well as pitcher, even though Chuck threw a little less well than Sandy Whittaker—but today he was shouted down. Mike was first captain when they chose up for the fourth game, and Castanatti—a chunky, quiet kid who had the best bat in town (he was a good batter, but mainly he owned the best *bat*, a beautiful white-ash Louisville Slugger that his dad had got from a friend on the Chicago White Sox team), was the second to choose.

Mike chose Donna Lou first and nobody minded. She'd been the best pitcher in town for as long as anybody could remember, and if the Little League had allowed girls, most of the guys on the team—or at least the guys who weren't afraid of Chuck Sperling's father—would have petitioned him to let her pitch so they could win a few games.

The team selection more or less shook down to the north end of town—Dale's end, the poor end—playing the south end, and while the dress code was the same, jeans and white t-shirts, the difference could be seen in mitts: Sperling and the others from the south end played with new, relatively huge, and rather stiff baseball gloves, while Mike and the others were fielding with hand-me-down mitts their fathers had used. The old mitts didn't really have pockets as such—they looked more like *gloves* than the tapered, pocketed leather wonders Sperling and Taylor wore—and it hurt to catch fastballs, but the boys didn't mind. It was part of the game, just like the bruises and scrapes that went with a day on the diamond. None of the boys ever played softball except when Mrs. Doubbet or some other old crone insisted at school, and then they switched to the forbidden hardball as soon as the teacher wandered away.

But now teachers were the last thing on their mind as Mrs. Stewart came out with a hamper of baloney and peanut-butter-and-jelly sandwiches and a cooler of Kool-Aid; the guys called a brief seventh-inning stretch even though it was only the second inning, and then they went back to work. The sky stayed gray but the heat had returned, rising into the nineties and building to a solid wall of moist discomfort. The kids ignored it. They shouted and played, batted and fielded, jogged into the benches and back out to the field, argued about whose turn it was to rotate in or who had held what position too long, but generally got along better than most Little League teams. There was good-natured heckling—especially when Sperling insisted on pitching and gave up five runs in the fourth inning—and a lot of joking, but mostly the boys and two girls took their baseball seriously and played it with the Zen-poem perfection of wordless concentration.

It was the rich southside against the lower-middle-class northside—although none of the kids thought of it that way—and the northside kicked butt. Castanatti hit well and got four of his team's six runs in the first game, but Donna Lou shut down most of the other batters and Mike, Dale, and Gerry Daysinger had a good day, scoring at least four runs each. At the end of their second nine-inning game, Mike's team had won 15–6 and 21–4. Then they shuffled players and started the third game.

It probably wouldn't have happened if Digger Taylor, McKown and a couple of the others hadn't ended up playing on Donna Lou's team this time around. It was three innings in, she had pitched twenty-one straight innings, and her arm was as strong as ever when she struck out Chuck Sperling for about the millionth time and Mike's team trotted in to the bench. Lawrence was the first one up, so the others leaned back against the wire of the backstop and stuck their legs out: ten clones in faded jeans and white t-shirts. Sandy had gotten tired of playing and had wandered off when Becky Cramer and a couple of her friends had come by: Donna Lou was the only girl left.

"It's a shame we can't tell the teams apart," said Digger Taylor.

Mike mopped muddy sweat from his brow with his t-shirt. "Whaddya mean?"

Taylor shrugged. "I mean it's too bad we all gotta look alike. Both teams, I mean."

Kevin cleared his throat and spat in that rather prissy way he had. "You think we need uniforms or something?" The idea was silly. Even the town Little League team only had unnumbered t-shirts with the official logo printed on it, and the logo faded away after about a dozen washings.

"Naw," said Taylor. "I was just thinking shirts and skins."

"Hey, yeah," said Bob McKown, a kid who lived in a grungy tarpaper house near Daysinger's grungy tarpaper house, "I'm too hot anyway." He peeled off his t-shirt. "Hey, Larry!" he shouted to Lawrence. "We're skins now! Get outta your t-shirt or get out in the field!"

Lawrence glared at the older boy for calling him by the forbidden name, but he peeled out of his size-seven Fruit of the Loom and stepped up to bat. His skinny little spine poked against the pale flesh of his back like miniature stegosaurus scales.

"Yeah, hot!" hooted one of the Fussner twins and both of them tugged off their shirts. They had identical little potbellies.

McKown slapped his bare chest and turned to Kevin sitting next to him. "You gonna skin down or join the other side?"

Kevin shrugged and pulled off his shirt, folding it next to him on the bench. There were pale freckles on his sunken chest.

Daysinger was next, and he made a production out of sailing his shirt over the backstop. It struck on the top, twelve feet up, and the kids in the field roared. A ten-year-old named Michael Shoop—a troublemaker in school and a total klutz on the field—was sitting next in line and he wadded his gray shirt up and managed to land it next to Daysinger's on the top of the fence. It was the first good throw Dale had seen the kid make all day.

Mike O'Rourke was next. He looked slightly disgusted, but he pulled off his shirt. His skin was tanned, the muscles well-defined beneath the skin.

Dale Stewart was next. He'd already pulled off his wool cap and reached for the bottom of his shirt before he realized who was next. He paused for a second. Donna Lou was the last one on the bench. She wasn't looking at him; she didn't seem to be looking at anything. She was wearing dirty sneakers, faded jeans, and a white t-shirt. Even though the shirt was looser than most of the rest of theirs, Dale realized that he could see the curves through it. Donna Lou's body had developed over the winter— the previous summer her t-shirt had been as tight and flat as anyone else's on the team—and while they weren't exactly mountains yet, her breasts were suddenly noticeable.

Dale hesitated a second. He didn't exactly know *why* he was hesitating—Donna Lou's t-shirt was Donna Lou's problem, wasn't it?— but he also felt that something wasn't quite right. He'd played ball with Mike and Kevin and Harlen and Lawrence and *her* all these years, not with these other jerks on the bench and in the field now.

"Whatcha afraid of?" Chuck Sperling called in from where he'd been demoted to first base. "Got something to hide, Stewart?"

"Yeah, come on!" called Digger Taylor from the far end of the bench. "We're *skins*, Stewart."

"Shut up," said Dale. But he could feel the blush hot on his cheeks and behind his ears. Partially to conceal it, he pulled off his shirt. The air was hot but his skin felt cold and clammy. He turned and looked at Donna Lou Perry.

She'd finally turned to look at the others. Lawrence had struck out and now stopped near the head of the bench. He was all ribs and pow-dered dust, his wrists and neck comically darker than his torso, as he paused with the bat on his shoulder and frowned at the sudden silence. No one got up to step into the on-deck circle. No one in the field made a noise. The bench was silent, all heads were turned toward Donna Lou. They sat there—Taylor, Kevin, Bill and Barry, McKown, Daysinger, Mi-chael Shoop, Mike, and Dale—nine sets of jeans and sneakers and bare upper bodies.

"Come on," said Digger Taylor softly. There was something strange about his voice. "We're skins, Perry. Get it off."

Donna Lou stared at him.

"Yeah," said Daysinger. He nudged Bob McKown with his elbow. "Come on, Donna Lou. You with the team or not?"

A gust of wind came in from center field and lifted a streamer of dust past Castanatti on the pitcher's mound. He didn't move. No one in the field spoke.

"Come on," said Michael Shoop in that insect whine of his, "hurry up and get it off before they call delay of game."

No one corrected him by pointing out that he was mixing up football rules with baseball. No one said anything. Dale was so close to Donna Lou that his elbow was almost touching hers—had been absently touch-ing hers a second before—and now he looked into eyes that he suddenly realized were blue and filling with tears. She didn't say anything either, just sat there, her old first baseman's–type mitt still on her right hand, her left hand—her pitching hand—curled into a weak fist in the center of it.

"Come on, Perry. Hurry it up," Digger said. There was a new, older, meaner tone in his voice now. "Take it off. We don't care what you have. We're skins now. You're either with us or off the team."

Donna Lou sat there for another ten seconds of silence so deep that Dale could hear the corn rustling in the fields north of them. Some-where far above, a hawk made a soft cry. Dale could see the freckles on the bridge of Donna Lou's small nose, the sweat on her forehead in the shadow of her blue wool cap, and her eyes—very blue and very bright now—as she looked at him, at Mike, at Kevin. Dale knew that there was a question or plea in that look, but he didn't know what it was.

Digger Taylor started to say something else, but shut his mouth as the girl rose.

Donna Lou stood there a second, then walked over to get her baseball and bat from where they lay near the fence. Then she walked away. She didn't look back.

"Shit," said Chuck Sperling from first base. He gave his friend Taylor a smirking look.

"Yeah," laughed Digger. "Thought we were gonna see some itty bitty titty today." Michael Shoop and the Fussner twins laughed.

Lawrence looked around, frowning, not quite understanding. "Is the game over?"

Next to Dale, Mike stood and pulled on his shirt. "Yeah," he said, his voice sounding tired and disgusted. "It's over." He got his own mitt, bat, and ball, and walked off toward the fence behind Dale's house.

Dale sat there, feeling . . . strange . . . sort of a combination of excitement and sadness and an odd feeling of having had the wind knocked out of him. At the same time he felt as if something important had happened that he had missed—something that had gone by him as surely as it had Lawrence—but it left an autumny, end-of-things feel to it, much like when the Old Settlers fair was over in August and had moved on, leaving nothing ahead but the dreaded resumption of school. He felt a little like laughing and a lot like crying, and he had no idea why he felt either emotion.

"Pussy!" Digger Taylor shouted after Mike.

Mike didn't look back. He tossed his stuff across the fence, grabbed the post, easily vaulted the high fence, picked up his gear, and crossed the yard to disappear into the elm shadows near Dale's driveway.

Dale sat there, waiting for a break between innings before he'd tell Lawrence that they had to get home, even though it wasn't dinnertime yet. The sky seemed to be a darker, featureless gray, hiding the horizon in haze and leeching light from the afternoon.

The game went on.

It was evening before Duane came.

Dale had eaten dinner and was lying around on his bed upstairs, reading an old Scrooge McDuck comic as the light softened through the screens, only half aware of the evening coming on and the rich scent of new-mown grass on the breeze, when Mike called from the front lawn.

"Eeawkee!"

Dale rolled off his bed and cupped his hands to his mouth. "Keeawee!" He rattled down the stairway, crashed through the front door, and jumped the four steps from the porch.

Mike stood with his hands in his pockets. "Duane's in the chicken-house."

Mike hadn't bothered with his bike so Dale left his lying in the side yard. Both boys jogged east down Depot Street.

"Where's Lawrence?" asked Mike as he ran. He wasn't breathing hard.

"Went on a walk with Mrs. Moon and Mom."

Mike nodded. Mrs. Moon was eighty-six, but still enjoyed her evening walks. Most people in the neighborhood took turns walking with her when her daughter—Miss Moon, the librarian—wasn't able to.

Mike's backyard was a mass of shadows from the big oaks and elms along the street and the apple trees behind the house. Fireflies were winking along the edge of Mr. O'Rourke's half-acre of garden. The chickenhouse glowed white in the gloom, its door a black rectangle. Dale stepped in ahead of Mike and let his eyes adapt to the dimness.

Duane was there, standing next to the empty console radio. Kevin lay on the couch, his t-shirt a startling white. Dale glanced around for Harlen before remembering that their friend was in the hospital.

Dale bent over to catch his breath while Mike stepped into the center of the room. "It's good that Lawrence isn't here," said Mike. "What Duane has to say is sort of spooky."

"You OK?" Dale asked the overweight boy. "How'd you get to come into town?"

"The Old Man came in to go to Carl's," said Duane and adjusted his glasses. He seemed even more distracted than usual. "It really happened," he added. "The Rendering Truck really tried to kill me today." His voice was as soft and unexcited as ever, but Dale thought he heard the slightest undertone of tension.

"I'm sorry about Witt," said Dale. "So's Lawrence."

Duane nodded again.

"Tell them about the soldier," said Mike.

Duane told them about his father's return late Saturday night— early Sunday morning actually—and about the young man in the odd uniform who had hitched a ride.

Kevin put his hands behind his head. "So? What's weird about that?"

Mike told them about the same guy following him down Jubilee College Road the evening before. "It was sort of spooky," he finished. "I began running . . . I usually run pretty good . . . but somehow this guy almost kept up just by walking. Finally, I got fifty or sixty feet ahead of him, but when I turned by the water tower I couldn't see him anymore."

"Was it dark?" asked Dale.

"About like now. Not so dark I couldn't see him a minute before. I even walked back to where the road turns, but it was empty all the way back the way I'd come."

Kevin began humming the theme music from that new TV show called *The Twilight Zone*.

Dale sat in the sprung easy chair under the narrow window. "The guy could've hidden in the fields. Laid down in the corn."

"Yeah," said Mike, "but why? What was he doing?" He told about the hole he'd seen in the toolshed behind Calvary Cemetery.

Kevin sat up. "Jeez, O'Rourke, you actually *broke in*?"

"Yeah. But that's not the point."

Kevin whistled. "It'll be the point if Congden or Barney finds out."

Mike stuck his hands in his pockets again. He seemed as distracted as Duane and far more out of sorts. "Barney's OK, but I think Congden's a real creepo. You saw him today with Duane's dad. I think the guy was lying about Van Syke."

Dale leaned forward. "Lying? Why?"

"Because he's with them," said Mike. "Or helping them."

"With who?" said Kevin.

Mike went to the door and looked out with his hands still jammed deep in his pockets. The darkness outside was just enough lighter than the darkness inside to silhouette him in the doorway. "With them," he said. "Dr. Roon. Van Syke. Probably Old Double-Butt. Whoever's doing this stuff."

"And the soldier guy," said Dale.

Duane cleared his throat. "The uniform's consistent with what doughboys wore back during the First World War."

"What's a doughboy?" asked Mike.

Both Dale and Duane began to explain. Duane nodded and Dale finished the explanation.

"And when was that war?" asked Mike, although he knew from Memo's stories.

Duane told him.

Mike swiveled in the doorway and slapped the doorframe. "Great. What's a guy dressed like a World War One soldier doing wandering around here?"

"Maybe he's taking a stroll near where he resides," said Kevin in his mocking tone.

"And where's that?" asked Dale.

"The cemetery."

Kevin had meant it as a joke, but it was too dark and the death of Duane's dog had been too recent. No one spoke for a while.

Mike broke the silence. "Anybody hear anything about Harlen?"

"Yeah," said Kevin. "Ma was up in Oak Hill this afternoon and saw his ma there. She was eating dinner in the drugstore just across the square from the hospital, and she told Ma that Harlen's still unconscious. His arm's all busted up. Multiple compound fractures."

"Is that bad?" asked Dale, realizing as he spoke how stupid the question sounded.

Mike nodded. He had more Scout badges in First Aid than anybody else Dale knew. "Compound fractures mean it's broken more than once. Bone probably came through the skin, too."

"Oh, yech," said Kevin. Dale felt a little sick at the thought.

"The concussion's probably the most serious thing," continued Mike. "If Harlen's still out, it's probably pretty bad."

There was another silence. A mouse or shrew made scurrying sounds beneath the floorboards. The room was dark enough now that Dale could see only the other boys' outlines—Kevin's shirt glowing the brightest, Duane's dark flannel only a shadow amidst shadows—and now there were more fireflies visible beyond the door and windows, glowing like embers in the dark. Like eyes.

"I'm going up to Oak Hill tomorrow," Duane said at last. "I'll check in on Jim and let you guys know how he is."

Kevin's t-shirt moved in the gloom. "Maybe we could all go."

"Uh-uh," came Duane's voice. "You guys have stuff to do around here, remember? Have you followed Roon yet?" The question was directed at Kev in the darkness.

Grumbacher grunted. "I've been busy."

"Yes," said Duane. "We all have. But I think we'd better do the things we agreed to do at the cave on Saturday. Something weird's going on."

"Maybe Harlen saw something," said Dale. "They found him in the garbage bin behind Old Central. Maybe he was following Old Double-Butt or something."

"Maybe," agreed Duane. "I'll try to find out tomorrow. In the meantime, it would help if someone else checked out Mrs. Doubbet until Jim's back."

"I will," said Dale, surprised to hear himself volunteer.

Mike's shadow at the doorway said, "I didn't find Van Syke at the cemetery, but I'll get him tomorrow."

"Be careful," said Duane. "I didn't see him for sure in that truck, but I somehow was sure that it was him driving."

The boys clamored for more details of the near disaster. Duane summarized it as briefly as he could. "I've got to get going," he said finally. "I don't want the Old Man drinking too much at Carl's."

The other three shifted in embarrassment, glad for the darkness. "Can I tell Lawrence this stuff?" Dale asked.

"Yeah," said Mike. "But don't scare him to death."

Dale nodded. The meeting was over, everybody was expected some-where else, but nobody seemed to want to leave. One of the O'Rourke cats came in, leaped onto Dale's lap, and curled up, purring.

Kevin sighed. "None of this shit makes sense." Kevin almost never swore.

The others said nothing, just staying there another moment, to-gether in the darkness. Silence was their agreement.

That night, Mike O'Rourke lay awake counting fireflies out his window. Sleep was like a tunnel, and he had no intention of going in.

Something moved on the front lawn, under the linden tree. Mike leaned forward, set his nose against the screen, and tried to see between the leaves and the eaves of the small front porch.

Someone had moved out of the deep shadows under the tree near Memo's window and stepped out onto the road. Mike listened for foot-steps on asphalt or the crunch of the gravel on the roadside, but there was no sound except for the silken rub of corn tassels.

He had only caught a glimpse, but Mike had seen the round shadow of the top of a hat. Too perfectly round to be a cowboy hat. More like a Boy Scout hat.

Or the campaign hat Duane had described on the soldier he'd called a doughboy.

Mike lay by the window, heart still pounding, holding sleep off like an enemy that had to be kept at bay.

ELEVEN

Duane McBride left for the library as soon as morning chores were done on Tuesday. The Old Man was awake and sober and in the foul mood which that combination usually brought. Duane went into the Old Man's workshop to tell him he was leaving.

"Chores done?" grunted his father. He was tinkering with the newest model of his "learning machine." The Old Man's workroom had once been the family dining room, but since Duane and his father ate only in the kitchen—when they ate together at all, which was rarely—the Old Man had turned the dining room into his workshop. Half a dozen doors on sawhorses served as massive tables, and most of these were littered with variations on the learning machine or other prototypes.

The Old Man was a real inventor; he had five patents approved, although only one of these—the automatic mailbox alarm—had ever made any money for him. Most of his devices were as impractical as the learning machine over which he now fussed: a massive metal box with cranks, viewing panel, buttons, punch-card slots, and assorted lights. The thing was supposed to revolutionize education. When properly programmed with scrolls of the appropriate reading/questioning material and the required student-response punch cards, the machine could provide hours of instructional choices and private tutoring. The problem—as Duane had pointed out repeatedly—was that each learning machine would cost almost a thousand dollars with the necessary printed stuff, and it was *mechanical.*

Duane had long argued that computers would someday do this stuff, but his father disliked electronics as much as Duane loved it. *You know how big a computer would have to be to carry out the simplest autonomous teaching task?* his father would demand. *As Big as Texas,* Duane would respond. *With the hourly total flow of Niagara Falls required to cool it.* But then he would add, *But that's with vacuum tubes, Pop. They're doing exciting things with transistors and resistors now.*

The Old Man would grunt and go back to work on a new learning-machine prototype. Duane had to admit they were fun—he'd run through an entire high-school political science course on one when he was eight— but they were clunky and forbidding. Only one had been sold—almost four years earlier, to the Brimfield School District, and Uncle Art knew a purchasing guy there. Meanwhile, prototypes continued to clutter the workshop tables and end up taking space in the hallways and empty bedrooms upstairs.

Duane figured that as a hobby, the perpetual-motion learning-machine project wasn't as harmful as the full-serve twenty-four-hour-a-day rural shopping center the Old Man had tried to run back in the mid-fifties. There had been two stores in the "shopping center," a hardware store and the Old Man's multipurpose OmniMart, which sold mainly bread and milk, but the Old Man had been the entire delivery force, taking calls at home in the middle of the night and driving down gravel and dirt backroads at all hours, delivering a loaf of bread at four A.M. to some old lady over in Knox County only to discover that she wanted it put on the OmniMart Instant Credit Plan. Uncle Art—who'd run the hardware store—was as glad as Duane to see that vision die. To this day, the Old Man insisted that he'd been right about "shopping centers"—just look at Sherwood Center now growing up in Peoria, nine stores!—but that he'd been ahead of his time. The Old Man predicted that someday shopping centers would be huge, indoor affairs—dozens of specialty stores under a single glassed roof like the gallerias he'd seen in Italy after the war. Most people would listen and ask *Why?* with a puzzled expression, but Duane and Uncle Art had learned to nod and keep quiet.

"Chores done?" repeated the Old Man.

Duane shook himself out of his contemplation of the learning machines. "Yeah. Thought I'd go into the library."

The Old Man looked up and let his close-work glasses slip down on his nose. "Library? Why today? Didn't you go Saturday?"

"Yeah, but I forgot to see if they had a small-motor repair manual."

The Old Man frowned. The pump on the old windmill needed repair. "I thought you already knew all about that stuff."

Duane shrugged. "That motor's *old*. It was put in before the rural electrification around here. I'd better have a manual if I'm going to do anything but change the belts and brushes."

The Old Man's gaze lost focus and Duane could imagine what he was thinking: he'd been spooked by the truck trying to kill his boy the day before—when they'd buried Witt in the afternoon, Duane had thought he'd seen tears in the Old Man's eyes . . . but the wind was blowing and it might've just been blowing sand irritating them—but on the other hand, the Old Man couldn't keep Duane penned up at home all summer or drive him around all the time.

"Can you get there without taking the road in?"

"Yeah, easy," said Duane. "I'll just cut back through the south pasture and walk the edge of Johnson's fields."

The Old Man looked back at the web of gears and pulleys he was adjusting. "All right. Just be home for supper, understand?"

Duane nodded, went to the kitchen, made himself a couple of baloney sandwiches and stuck them in a greasy sack, filled a Thermos with coffee and hung it on his belt by the cup handle, checked to make sure he had his notebook and pen in his pocket, and ambled out. He'd made four steps toward the barn to say good-bye to Witt before he remembered. Duane adjusted his glasses and went through the gate, heading for the south pasture just as he'd told the Old Man.

And he would use the Johnson fields to get as far west as the railroad tracks. He hadn't lied to his father. But he hadn't exactly told the truth, either: the library he was heading for wasn't the tiny one in Elm Haven, a little more than two miles away . . . it was the library in Oak Hill, more than eight miles along the backroads and easily more than ten the way Duane was planning to go.

Duane settled down into his distance-gobbling waddle, the Thermos batting against his left leg with every other step, his black sneakers scaring grasshoppers into flight in the high weeds. The sun was out today and the morning was the hottest of the summer so far. Duane opened the top two buttons of his flannel shirt and considered whistling a tune as he walked.

He decided not to.

The best way to get to Oak Hill from Duane's house would have been to go north on County Six until it ran into the unnumbered gravel road north of the Barminton farm, head west until that road intercepted State Highway 626, better known as Oak Hill Road, and then take that the final four and half miles into town. But that meant roads.

Duane crossed his first road north of Elm Haven—moving quickly across the gravel road that ran south to become First Avenue—and then cut through the forest of metal grain-storage silos arrayed north of the town's playing fields. A row of pines that ran west from the water tower obscured the view for Duane, so he couldn't check to see if his friends were playing ball that day.

West of there, he ambled north again to avoid the town and the upper reaches of Broad Avenue.

He did have to follow a narrow lane through the bushes to the railroad tracks after Catton Road ended, but he couldn't imagine the Rendering Truck forcing its way through the branches and shrubs here. He realized then that he was only a few hundred yards from the tallow plant—the place from which Congden had said the truck had been "stolen"—but the woods were so thick here that Duane couldn't even see the tin roof of the place.

The railroad embankment was a relief after all the underbrush, and Duane slowed his pace enough to unhitch his Thermos and pour himself a cup of coffee. He did not stop, but sipped as he walked, putting up with coffee spilled on his shirt and pants. Well, the pants were about the same color as the stains.

He smelled the dump before he saw it, and just at that second he saw the squalid huddle of shacks just outside the south entrance to the dump. Cordie Cooke lived in one of those homes—if you could call that collection of tarpaper and tin on cinderblocks *home*—but Duane wasn't sure which one. Something moved in the shrubbery on the west side of the tracks, but although Duane looked over his shoulder, he caught no glimpse of the animal.

He ambled on, passing the heaps of the county dump—the mountains of garbage clearly visible through and above the trees—and then crossing the low trestle over what, three miles east of here, would become Corpse Creek. He was in luck: the wind was blowing from the north, so once he left the dump behind, he left it behind.

From the dump, it was a simple seven-mile walk through the fields and forests of Creve Coeur County and Duane made it in a little over two hours.

Oak Hill was more than three times as large as Elm Haven, boasting almost 5,500 people. It had a small hospital as well as a library bigger than a chicken coop, a small factory on its outskirts, a county courthouse, a block of suburbs—everything.

Duane came down off the tracks as the railroad embankment curved east to miss the town. He didn't mind walking the tree-lined streets of Oak Hill, although every time a car or truck turned a corner behind him, he glanced over his shoulder quickly and was peripherally aware of porches within running distance.

He paused on the courthouse lawn in the shade of an oak and a bronze cannon to eat his baloney sandwiches and finish his coffee. He was hot—it was at least in the nineties today—but his flannel shirt wasn't sticking to him. Finished, he tucked the Thermos on his belt and crossed to the hospital on the south side of the square.

The lady's name on the green badge was Miss Alnutt, her desk was planted firmly in the middle of the only corridor leading to the wards, and she was implacable. "You can't come in," she said in her maiden-aunt rasp. The talcum-powder and old-skin scent of her wafted to Duane on the slight breeze from the overhead fan. "You're too young."

Duane nodded. "Yes, ma'am. But Jimmy's my only cousin and his mama said I could come see him."

Miss Alnutt jerked her head in what might have been dismissal. "You're too young. No one under sixteen is allowed in the patients' wing. No exceptions." She peered at him through the half-lenses perched on her nose. "Besides, no extraneous food or drink is allowed in the patients' rooms."

Duane glanced down at his Thermos and quickly unhooked it from his belt. "Yes, ma'am. I could leave this here. I only want to see him for a minute or two—I promise I'll just look in on him and come right back."

Miss Alnutt made a flicking motion with her veined wrist and turned her attention back to the cards in her small file box. Duane had noticed the room number when he'd first asked about Harlen. Now he said, "Thank you, ma'am," and turned to trudge back through the lobby.

The only pay phone was down the corridor to the public restrooms. The only phone he had seen in the lobby was at the admissions desk, twenty paces beyond his corridor and around the corner. He'd brought fifty cents in change, just in case. He only needed a nickel. The number was in the tattered phone book.

They didn't page her. One of the nurses from the lobby came around, whispered to Miss Alnutt, and walked with her as the older lady rushed to the front desk. It was, after all, an important call.

Duane strolled by the empty desk, turned into the patients' ward, and for the second time that day, resisted the impulse to whistle.

After breakfast, Dale Stewart borrowed his dad's binoculars and headed down Depot Street to the depot and then out the railroad tracks to Cordie's. He didn't really want to go—that whole side of town gave him the willies because of Congden's house, and the woods out by the dump were worse—but after the talk in the chickenhouse the night before, Dale sort of felt it was his duty. But what Cordie and Tubby Cooke had to do with some jerk scaring Duane with the Rendering Truck, Dale had no idea.

J.P. Congden's shabby house was on the same block as Harlen's home, but the black Chevy wasn't where it was usually parked in the yard and nothing stirred in the weedy backyard. Dale wasn't so much afraid of the justice of the peace—although the old fart had scared him well enough yesterday—but he was afraid of J.P's juvenile-delinquent son, C.J. *Every* kid in town was afraid of C.J.

C.J. Congden had finally dropped out of school the previous year—sixteen years old and still in eighth grade, who could blame him?—and most of the boys in Elm Haven felt like giving a victory party that day. Congden was like some cartoon stereotype of what a small-town bully should be: duck's-ass haircut, zits that looked like some sort of tropical disease was eating his sallow face, greasy t-shirt with a cigarette pack rolled up in the sleeve, tall, lean, but well-muscled with big, mean hands, grimy jeans slung so low that guys watching him walk half-expected his dick to pop out above the beltline, heavy engineer boots with metal taps that kicked up sparks on the cement as he scuffed along, a can of snuff in his back pocket and a folded knife in his front pocket . . . Dale once remarked to Kevin that C.J. Congden must have some Manual for Bullies that he referred to.

But Dale didn't make jokes about C.J. where they might be overheard or repeated. When the Stewarts had first moved to Elm Haven from Peoria four years earlier—Dale just entering third grade and Lawrence going into first—Dale had made the mistake of catching C.J.'s attention. Congden was twelve years old and still a fifth grader then, but he roamed the small kids' playground like a shark among schools of rainbow fish.

After the second schoolyard beating, Dale had gone to his dad for help. His dad told him that all bullies were cowards, that if you stood up to them, they backed down. The next day, Dale stood up to C.J.

Dale had lost two of his baby teeth that day and had several of the permanent ones loosened. His nose bled on and off for three days, and he still carried the scar on his hip where C.J. had kicked him after he'd fallen down and curled up. Dale hadn't felt quite the same about his father's advice since that week.

Dale tried bribery. Congden took the Twinkies and lunch money and beat the shit out of Dale anyway. Dale tried being a follower, even going so far as to try to slouch around the playground as part of the bully's entourage of toadies. Congden kicked the hell out of him at least once a week on general principles.

What made matters worse, was that Congden's one legitimate sidekick—Archie Kreck—was in Dale's class. Archie would have been the town bully himself if Congden hadn't existed: he affected the same wardrobe, had cleats on his boots, was short and stocky and mean, looked a bit like Mickey Rooney's evil twin, and had a glass eye.

No one knew how Archie had lost his real eye . . . word on the playground was that C.J. Congden had dug it out with a penknife as part of some bizarre initiation when Archie was only six or seven . . . but the glass eye, his left, was used to good effect. Sometimes when Mrs. Howe was droning on in a geography lesson, Archie would pop out the eye, set it in the pencil trough at the front of his desk, and pretend to doze off while his eye kept watch.

Dale had laughed the first time he'd seen this, but Archie had waited after the principal was through with him and jumped Dale on the way to the boys' (or BOY'S as it was marked in Old Central) john. Archie had held Dale's face in the urinal for five flushes while urging him to laugh again. After school that day, Archie and C.J. were *both* waiting at the edge of the playground. Dale had never run so fast—scooting down the alley behind Mrs. Moon's house, crashing through Mike's chickenhouse, cutting back through Grayson's garden, and then sprinting across the street to his own house, slamming through the front door two seconds in front of the two human Dobermans in engineer boots.

They'd caught up to him two days later and kicked the shit out of him. Despite what fathers say and mothers don't understand, there's no escaping bullies. And these two were world class.

Dale was pleased to be past the Congden place: C.J. didn't have his own car, and his old man wouldn't let him drive the souped-up Chevy, but Dale had seen him driving a lot of his "friends'" cars. It was wonderful when the town bully began driving; it got him off the streets.

Harlen's house was three doors down, just a hundred yards from the old depot. Dale slid his bike to a stop by the front stoop and rapped on the door, but the house looked closed and silent and no one came to the door. Still glancing down the street to make sure that C.J. and Archie didn't suddenly show up, Dale walked his bike down the street. His dad's leather binocular case bounced against his chest as he walked.

There were two ways to get to Cordie Cooke's house: push the bike over the railroad embankment and through the weeds to the gravel road that ran back to the dump; or leave his bike somewhere and walk the tracks.

Dale didn't like to leave his bike in this part of town—once Lawrence's bike had ended up missing for two weeks until Harlen found it in the orchard behind Congden's house—but he also remembered Duane's game of tag with the truck.

Dale stowed the bike in the weeds behind the depot, pulling branches to camouflage it completely, and—scanning with the binoculars to make sure that C.J. wasn't lurking around somewhere—moved cautiously down the west side of the embankment until he was out past the grain elevator. Then he picked up a branch and walked the right rail, whistling and hitting pebbles into the fields. He wasn't worried about trains: the line was rarely used—sometimes weeks went by between freights, according to Harlen, who lived close to the tracks.

Beyond Catton Road, the trees disappeared except for the cottonwoods by the stream and occasional patches of timber between the fields. Dale began wondering what he was going to do. What if someone caught him peeking at the Cookes' house with binoculars? Wasn't there a law against doing that? What if Cordie's drunken father caught him . . . or he ran into one of the other creepos that lived out by the dump? What if the binoculars got broken?

Dale tossed the stick into the weeds and walked along, one hand on the leather case.

This is nuts.

He saw the roof of the tallow plant off to the left, but no red Rendering Truck came charging out of the bushes to squash him. Then he smelled the dump and saw Cordie's place through the trees.

Dale got off the embankment and slipped down through marshy grass, staying where the trees were thickest. It was almost a hundred yards to the house itself, so he felt fairly safe here in the woods. No one could see him from the dump road or from the tracks behind him. It'd be hard to sneak up on him because of all the dry sticks lying around. He settled back in an enclosed area between two trees and a thick bush, focused the binoculars on Cordie's house, and waited.

Cordie's house was a mess. It was so small that it was hard to believe that four adults—a couple of her uncles lived there—and a bunch of kids could inhabit the place. The house made Daysinger's shack and Congden's rattrap look like palaces.

Three old homes lay in the hollow near the gate to the dump. Cordie's place was the worst, and they were all awful. All the houses were set on cinderblocks, but her place looked like it'd fallen off in the back and actually slanted like some boat beached after a storm. Grass grew thick and green along the edge of the woods and beside the stream thirty yards behind the house, but the yard was packed dirt relieved only by deep mud puddles. Junk was strewn everywhere.

Like most guys, Dale liked junk. If the dump didn't have so many mean rats and neighbors like the Cookes and the Congdens, he and the other boys would be out here playing, digging, exploring, and retrieving all the time. As it was, the Bike Patrol spent more time checking out things being thrown away along the town's alleys and streets on pickup day than in any other activity. Junk was neat. People threw away the neatest things. Once Dale and Lawrence had found an actual tank helmet—some sort of cushioned thing with real leather and German writing on the inside—and Lawrence had used it in his one-against-ten football games ever since. Another time, Dale and Mike had found a great sink that they'd carried all the way back to Mike's chickenhouse before Mr. O'Rourke screamed at them to take it back.

Junk was neat.

But not this junk. Behind Cordie's house there were rusted springs, broken toilets—although Dale was sure that Cordie'd said once that they had an outhouse—car windshields with shards of broken glass slanting up through chokeweeds, rusted auto parts that looked like the organs of some monster robot, hundreds of rusty old cans with their sharp lids raised like buzzsaw blades, broken tricycles that looked like they'd been smashed by a truck driving back and forth over them, discarded dolls with mold on their pink plastic flesh and dead eyes staring skyward. Dale spent at least ten minutes inspecting the junkyard behind Cordie's house before lowering the glasses and rubbing his eyes. *What the heck do they do with all that crap?*

Spying was boring business, Dale discovered. Within a half an hour his legs felt cramped, bugs were crawling on him, the heat was making his head hurt, and all he'd seen was Cordie's mother out back pulling wash off the line—the sheets looked gray and spotted—and shouting at the two grimy little Cooke kids who sat splashing each other in the deepest mud puddle, while picking their noses and wiping it on their shorts.

No sign of Cordie. No sign of whatever he was looking for. What *was* he looking for? Hell, let Mike come out and do this if he wanted to check out Cordie Cooke.

Dale was about ready to call it a day when he heard footsteps on the cinders along the railroad embankment. He crouched down, shielding the glasses so sun wouldn't glint off the lenses, and tried to catch a glimpse of who it was. He saw corduroy pants through the leaves, legs walking in a familiar waddle.

What the heck is Duane doing over here?

Dale ran to a different position, making noise in the underbrush as he did so, but the railbed curved out of sight a hundred feet north, and by the time Dale got where he could see something, there wasn't anything left to see.

He started walking back to his observation post, but a movement of gray in the trees ahead of him made him take cover and use the glasses.

Cordie was striding purposefully through the woods, heading for the tracks. She was carrying a double-barreled shotgun.

Dale felt his knees go sort of weak. What if she'd seen him? Cordie was crazy—that wasn't an insult, just a fact. The year before, in fifth grade, there was a new music teacher she didn't like—Mr. Aleo from Chicago—and Cordie sent him a letter saying that she was going to sic her dogs on him and have them tear his arms and legs and other stuff off. She'd read the letter to the class on the playground before going in to give it to him.

It was the line about the "other stuff" being torn off that probably had gotten her suspended. Mr. Aleo gave up on Elm Haven and went back to Evansville before the school year was over.

Cordie was crazy. Fact. If she'd seen Dale, she could easily be hunting him with murder on her mind.

Dale flattened himself in the weeds, trying not to breathe, trying not even to *think,* since he had a theory that crazy people were telepathic.

Cordie did not look right or left as she strode through the woods, climbed the embankment about fifty feet south of where Dale had come down, and began walking toward town. The gun was bigger than she was and she carried it over one shoulder like some midget soldier.

Dale waited until she was out of sight, and then he began to follow, being careful not to show himself. They were halfway back to town, between the tallow plant and the abandoned grain elevator, and Cordie was still a couple of hundred feet ahead—never looking back, never looking from side to side, marching from railroad tie to railroad tie like a windup toy in a grungy gray dress—when suddenly he came around a turn and she was gone.

Dale hesitated, scanned the railbed and woodline ahead with the glasses, and cautiously poked his head up to see if she'd gone into the woods on the east side of the tracks.

A familiar voice behind him said, "Hey, it's the fucking Stewart kid. You lost, punk?"

Dale turned slowly, still holding his dad's binoculars.

C.J. and Archie were both there, not ten feet behind him. He'd been so careful not to let Cordie see or hear him that he'd never checked his tail.

Archie was shirtless, a red bandanna tied around his forehead. Greasy hair stuck out above it. His fat face was flushed and the glass eye glinted in the late-morning light. C.J. was standing with one foot up on the rail, the other boot on the cinder right-of-way. The pose made Dale think of some sort of acned white hunter on safari. It was perfect right down to the rifle C.J. held in the crook of his arm.

Jesus Christ, thought Dale. His legs suddenly were so weak that he didn't think he could run if he got the chance. *What is this, National Gun Day?* He imagined saying that aloud, as dumb as it sounded. He imagined C.J. and Archie laughing, maybe one of them clapping him on the back, and then the two of them turning around and heading back to the dump to shoot rats.

"What the fuck are you smiling at, punk?" snapped C.J. Congden, only son of Elm Haven's justice of the peace.

He raised the rifle and pointed it directly at Dale's face from ten feet away. There was a click of a safety being slid off, or maybe the hammer being lifted.

Dale tried to close his eyes but couldn't even manage that. He realized that he was shielding the binoculars so that the bullet wouldn't smash them when it passed through his chest. He felt the urge to hide behind something so strongly it was like the need to urinate when you just couldn't stand it any longer . . . but the only thing to hide behind was himself.

Dale's right leg began vibrating slightly. His heart was pounding so wildly that it seemed to have ruined his hearing; C.J. was saying something, but no sound came through.

Congden took two steps and set the muzzle against Dale Stewart's throat.

Duane McBride found Jim Harlen's room easily enough. It was a double room, but the curtain was pulled back and the second bed was empty. Rich June light filled the window and painted a white rectangle on the tile floor.

Harlen was sleeping. Duane checked the empty corridor and pulled the door shut just as the squeak of a nurse's shoes approached the corner.

Duane stepped closer and hesitated. He hadn't been sure what to expect—Harlen in an oxygen tent, perhaps, features distorted by clear plastic, all but surrounded by tall oxygen bottles the way Duane's grand-dad had looked just before he'd died two years ago—but Jim was sleeping peacefully enough under a starched sheet and a thin blanket, with only the thick cast on his left arm and the white crown of bandages around his head testifying to his injuries. Duane stood there until the squeak of shoes in the corridor went past, and then he stepped closer to the bed.

Harlen opened his eyes quickly, like an owl waking up, and said, "Hey, McBride."

Duane almost jumped backward. He blinked and said, "Hey, Harlen. You OK?"

Harlen tried to smile and Duane noticed how thin and bloodless the other boy's lips looked. "Yeah, I'm OK," Harlan said. "I woke up here with this terrible damn headache and my arm all torn and smashed to shit. Other than that, I'm great."

Duane nodded. "We thought you were . . ." He paused, not wanting to say "in a coma."

"Dead?" said Harlen.

Duane shook his head. "Unconscious."

Harlen's eyes fluttered as if he were sliding back into a coma. He opened them wide and frowned as if trying to focus. "I guess I was. Unconscious, I mean. I woke up a few hours ago with this stinking lousy headache to find my mom sitting on the edge of the bed. I thought it was Sunday morning for a while. Shit, I didn't even know where I was for a few minutes." He looked around as if he still was not sure where he was.

"Where's your mother now, Jim?"

"She went across the square to get lunch and call her boss." Harlen spoke slowly, as if each word hurt.

"You OK, then?" Duane asked again.

"Yeah, I think so. This morning there were a bunch of doctors in here, shining lights in my eyes and making me count to fifty and every-thing. They even asked me if I could tell 'em who I was."

"Could you?"

"Sure. I said I was Dwight Goddamn Eisenhower." Harlen smiled through the pain.

Duane nodded. He didn't have much time. "Jim, do you remember how you got hurt? What happened?"

Harlen stared up at him for a very long moment, and Duane noticed how wide the pupils of the boy's eyes were. Harlen's lips were trembling now as if he were trying to keep the smile in place. "No," he said at last.

"You can't remember being at Old Central?"

Harlen closed his eyes and his voice was almost a whine. "I don't remember friggin' *anything*," he said. "At least anything after our stupid half-assed meeting out at the Cave."

"The Cave," repeated Duane. "You mean Saturday at the culvert."

"Yeah."

"Do you remember Saturday afternoon? *After* the Cave?"

Harlen's eyes flickered open and there was anger there. "I just *said* I didn't, fatso."

Duane nodded. "You were in the dumpster at Old Central when they found you on Sunday morning . . ."

"Yeah, Mom told me. She started cryin' when she told me, like it was her fault."

"But you don't know how you got there?" Duane heard the intercom paging some doctor in the hall outside.

"Uh-uh. I don't remember anything about Saturday night. For all I know, you and O'Rourke and a bunch of other shits dragged me out of bed, hit me with a board, and dumped me there."

Duane looked at the massive cast on Harlen's arm. "Kevin's mom says that your mom says that your bike was up on Broad Avenue, near Old Double-Butt's house."

"Yeah? She didn't tell me that." Harlen's voice sounded flat, listless, and devoid of curiosity.

Duane ran his fingers along the soft border of the blanket. "Do you think you might've left it there because you were following Mrs. Doubbet somewhere? To the school?"

Harlen raised his left hand to cover his eyes again. His fingernails had been chewed to the quick. "Look, McBride, I said I didn't goddamn *know*. So leave me alone, OK? You're not even supposed to be in here, are you?"

Duane patted Harlen's shoulder through the crinkly hospital gown. "We all wanted to know how you were," he said. "Mike and Dale and the other guys want to come see you when you feel better."

"Yeah, yeah." Harlen's voice was muffled with the palm of his hand over his lower face. His fingers tapped at the bandages.

"They'll be glad to hear you're OK." Duane glanced toward the hall, where there were more footsteps: hospital people coming back on duty after lunch maybe. "Anything we can bring you?"

"Michelle Staffney naked," said Harlen, his hand still over his face.

"Right," said Duane and moved to the door. The hall was empty for the moment. "We'll catch you later, Fried P'tater." That phrase had been a big deal among the boys when they were all in fourth grade.

Harlen sighed. "McBride?"

SUMMER OF NIGHT   119

"Yeah."

"You can do one thing." The intercom squawked on in the hall. Outside the window, someone fired up a lawnmower. Duane waited. "Turn on the light," said Harlen. "Would you?"

Duane squinted in the bright sunlight already filling the room, but he switched on the light. The additional brightness wasn't noticeable in the glare.

"Thanks," said Harlen.

"Can you see all right, Jim?" Duane's voice was soft.

"Yeah. I can see." Harlen lowered his hand and stared at Duane with an unreadable expression. "It's just that . . . well . . . if I go back to sleep, I don't want to wake up in the dark. You know?"

Duane nodded, waited a moment, thought of nothing else to say, waved toward Harlen, and slipped out, heading for the side exit.

Dale Stewart stared down the rifle barrel at C.J. Congden's pimply face and thought, *Jesus, I'm going to die.* It was a new idea and it seemed to freeze the scene around him into a single block of impressions: Congden, Archie Kreck, the sunshine warm on Dale's face, the shadowed leaves and blue sky above and behind C.J., the heat reflected from the cinders and rails, the blue steel of the rifle barrel and the slight but somehow giddying scent of oil that rose from the weapon—all this combined to seal the moment in time as surely as Mike's block of amber had captured a spider from a million years ago.

"I asked you a fucking question, you stupid fuckface," rasped C.J.

Dale seemed to hear Congden's voice from very, very far away. His pulse was still pounding loudly in his ears. Although it took most of his concentration just to avoid surrendering to the dizziness that was assailing him, Dale managed an answer. "Huh?"

Congden sneered. "I *said,* what the fuck are you smiling at?" He raised the stock of the rifle to his shoulder, never allowing the barrel to lose contact with the base of Dale's throat.

"I'm not smiling." Dale heard the quaver in his own voice and realized that he should be ashamed of it, but it was a distant thing. His heart seemed to be trying to tear itself out of his chest. The earth felt like it was tilting slightly, so Dale had to concentrate on keeping his balance.

"The fuck you ain't!" shouted Archie Kreck. The second-string bully's face was turned slightly in profile and Dale could see that his glass eye was slightly larger than his real one.

"Shut up," C.J. said absently. He raised the barrel so that the pressure left Dale's throat—he could feel the pain now from where the muzzle had pressed and knew there was a red ring there—and aimed it directly at the younger boy's face. "You're *still* grinnin', fuckface. How'd you like it if I blew a hole in that stupid grin?"

Dale shook his head, but he couldn't stop grinning. He could feel the smile, a rictus he could not control. His right leg was shaking visibly now and his bladder felt very full. He concentrated on keeping his balance and not wetting his pants.

The muzzle of the rifle was ten inches in front of his face. Dale could not believe how large it was. The black opening seemed to fill the sky and dim the sunlight; Dale recognized it as a .22 caliber rifle, the kind one broke at the breech to load a single cartridge at a time—good for shooting rats at the dump, which is where these two rats probably had been headed—and his imagination allowed him to see the .22 shell at the base of that barrel, awaiting only the drop of the hammer to send the lead slug through Dale's teeth and tongue, the roof of his mouth, his brains. He tried to remember what damage a .22 slug would do to an animal's brains, but all he could remember from his dad's teaching during preparation for their hunting together was that a .22-long could travel a mile.

Dale fought back the urge to ask C.J. if the rifle was loaded with a .22-long cartridge.

"Wouldja like that, fuckhead?" C.J. asked again, sighting down the barrel as if to pick exactly which tooth he would fire through.

Dale shook his head again. His arms were at his side and he thought it might be a good idea to raise them, but they didn't seem to want to move.

"Shoot him! Shoot him, C.J.!" Archie's voice was cracking with either excitement or puberty or both. "Kill the little fucker."

"Shut up," said Congden. He squinted at Dale. "You're that Stewart fuck, aren't you?"

Dale nodded. His fear of C.J. over the years and his anger and frustration after the beatings had put him in such an intimate relationship with the bully that the thought of Congden not knowing his name seemed incredible.

C.J. squinted at him again. "You gonna tell me what the fuck you were doin' spying on us an' grinning at us, or you want me to pull this trigger?"

The question was too complicated for Dale at this moment and he shook his head again. It seemed that the most important part to respond to was the question about whether he wanted the trigger pulled. He did not.

"OK, then, fuckface, you called it," said C.J., evidently taking Dale's gesture as a refusal to talk. He pulled the hammer back on the single-shot rifle with an audible click and lowered his cheek to the stock.

Dale's breathing simply stopped. His chest was frozen. He wanted to raise his hands in front of his face, but he saw the image of the bullet passing through his palms before smashing into his mouth. Dale realized for the first time what death was: it was not walking any farther on the railroad tracks, not eating dinner tonight or seeing his mom or watching *Sea Hunt* on TV. It wasn't even being allowed to mow the lawn next Saturday or help his dad rake the leaves come fall.

It was having no choice at all except lying dead here on the cinders beside the railroad track, letting the birds pluck your eyes like berries and the ants stroll across your tongue. It was *no choices, no decisions, no future at all*. It was like being grounded for all eternity.

"Bye-bye," said Congden.

"You pull it, I'll blow *your* fuckin' melon to bits," came a voice from behind Dale.

Congden and Archie jumped as if someone had startled them in a dark room. C.J. glanced to his left but didn't lower the rifle.

Still not breathing, Dale found that he could move his head a little bit to the right to see who was there.

Cordie Cooke had come out of the woods and was standing with one foot still in weeds and the other on the cinders of the railbed. The double-barreled shotgun was raised, stock firmly against her small shoulder, and both barrels were aimed at C.J. Congden.

"Cooke, you little cunt . . ." began Archie Kreck in his high, broken voice.

"Shut up," said C.J. The bigger boy's voice was calm enough. "What do you think you're doing, Cordie?"

"I'm aimin' my daddy's twelve-gauge at your zitty face, moron." Cordie's voice was as thin and scratchy as ever—skinny chalk on old slate—but it was absolutely steady.

"Put the gun down, stupid," said C.J. "This doesn't have nothing to do with you."

"You put yours down," said Cordie. "Lay it on down and walk away your ownself."

C.J. glanced at her again as if judging how long it would take to swing the barrel in her direction. At that second, grateful to Cordie as he was for the intervention, Dale fervently hoped C.J. *would* aim it at her. Anything was better than having that muzzle aimed at your own face.

"What's it to you if I shoot this little fuck?" C.J. asked in a conversational tone. The muzzle was still ten inches in front of Dale.

"Put it on down, Congden." Cordie's voice sounded much as it did in class to Dale, on those rare occasions when she spoke: soft, out of it, vaguely bored. "Lay it on down and back away. You can come get it again when I'm gone. I ain't gonna touch it."

"I'm gonna shoot him and then shoot *you,* you little cunt," snapped C.J. He was angry now. The pustules and rivulets of acne on his skinny face grew livid, then red again.

"It's a single-shot Remington, Congden," said Cordie.

Dale glanced at her again. Her finger was curled around both triggers of the ancient shotgun. The thing looked huge and heavy, the barrels tinged with what might have been rust, the wood stock splintered with age. But Dale had no doubt but that it was loaded. He wondered idly if the spread pattern of the buckshot would hit him when it took C.J.'s head off.

"Then I'll shoot you first," snarled C.J. But he didn't swing the barrel in her direction.

Dale saw the muscles tensing in the punk's bare upper arms, and he realized that Congden was as frozen with fear as he was.

"Get her, Archie," commanded C.J.

Kreck hesitated, his head swiveling as he used his good eye to take in the situation, and then he nodded, reached into his droopy jeans to pull out a knife, clicked the five-inch blade open, and began to shuffle across the rails toward Cordie.

"He comes across the second rail, you're dog food," she said to Congden.

"*Stop!*" shouted C.J. It was a general command, almost a scream, but Archie was the one who stopped. He looked to his leader for further directions.

"Back off, goddamn you to hell you stupid fuck," C.J. said to his best friend.

Archie backed off to the far side of the first rail.

Dale realized that he was breathing again. Time was moving again—slower than usual, but definitely moving—and he wondered what he should do. He'd watched about a million cowboy shows where Sugarfoot or Bronco Lane or somebody had a gun on them, sort of like this, and they wrestled it away from the bad guy. It'd be easy enough to do: the barrel was still ten inches from Dale's face and all Congden's attention was on Cordie now. All he had to do was grab it and twist.

Dale realized that he could more easily walk on air than make a move at this moment.

"Come on," said Cordie in her tired monotone. "Make up your stupid mind, Congden. My finger's getting tired."

The muscles on C.J.'s cheek spasmed. Dale could see sweat dripping from the bully's nose and chin.

"You know I'll get your ass, don't you, Cordie? You know I'll lay for you and do somethin' *real* bad, don't you? Ain't no getting away with this, you know."

Cordie seemed to shrug, although the barrels didn't waver. "You do anything to me that doesn't kill me, C.J., *you* know I'll come after you with Daddy's twelve-gauge. I sicced the dogs on Mr. Aleo last year. I ain't gonna mind killing you."

Dale knew about the episode with the music teacher and the dogs. Everyone in town knew about it. Cordie had been suspended for ten weeks. When she came back to school, Mr. Aleo had left for Chicago.

"Fuck you," said C.J. And he laid the rifle down slowly, setting it on the wooden ties with great care. He backed away. "And you, Stewart, Fuckface Stewart, don't think I'll forget *you*." C.J. backed away from the rifle and nodded toward Archie. Knife still brandished, Archie joined him and the two walked backward down the railbed, turned when they got to the weeds, and moved quickly into the trees.

Dale stood there a second, staring at the rifle at his feet as if it would suddenly float into the air and threaten him again. When it didn't, he felt the earth lurch back into its usual gravity field. He almost fell, found his balance, staggered a few feet, and sat on the rail. His knees were shaking.

Cordie waited until C.J. and Archie had disappeared completely in the small woods, and then she shifted so that the shotgun was pointed toward Dale. Not *at* him exactly, but in his general direction.

Dale didn't notice. He was too busy staring at Cordie with a perception made acute by great quantities of adrenaline. She was short and pudgy; her dress was the same shapeless, dirty gray thing she'd worn to school so often; she wore filthy sneakers with her right big toe poking through; her nails and elbows were dirty, her hair hung down in limp, oily strands, and her face was flat, doughy, and moon-shaped, with her tiny eyes, thin lips, and blob of a nose pushed together in the center as if designed for a much thinner face.

At that second, she was the most beautiful thing Dale had ever seen.

"What the hell were you doin' followin' me, Stewart?"

Dale found that his voice was still shaky, but he tried to answer. "I wasn't . . ."

"Don't give me that cowflop," she said and the shotgun twitched a bit more in his direction. "I seen you with your little spyglasses there, peekin' at my house. Then you come sneakin' along behind me like I couldn't see and hear you plain as day. *Answer* me."

Dale was too wrung out to try a lie. "I was following you because . . . some of us are trying to find Tubby."

"Whaddya you want with Tubby?" When Cordie squinted, it was as if she had no eyes at all.

Dale realized that his pulse was no longer filling most of his hearing. "We don't want anything with him. We just want to . . . find him. See if he's OK."

Cordie broke the breech of the shotgun and cradled it in her pudgy right arm. "An' you think I done somethin' with him?"

Dale shook his head. "Uh-uh. I just wanted to see what was going on out at your place."

"Why do you give a damn about Tubby?"

I don't, thought Dale. He said, "I just think something's going on. Dr. Roon and Mrs. Doubbet and those guys aren't telling the truth."

Cordie spat and hit the rail. "You said 'we.' Who else is messin' around with you tryin' to find Tubby?"

Dale glanced at the shotgun. He was more certain now than ever that Cordie Cooke was as crazy as a loon. "Just some friends."

"Hmmmph," snorted Cordie. "Must be O'Rourke and Grumbacher and Harlen and those other pansies you hang around with."

Dale blinked. He'd had no idea that Cordie had ever noticed who he hung around with.

The girl walked toward him, lifted the Remington, broke the breech, extracted a .22 cartridge, tossed it into the woods, and laid the weapon in the weeds. "Come on," she said, "let's get goin' before those two piss-ants get each other's courage goin'."

Dale got to his feet and hurried to keep up with her as she strode toward town. Fifty yards down the tracks, she went down into the trees and headed for the fields beyond.

"If you're huntin' for Tubby," she said, not looking at Dale, "how come you're out at my house where's the one place he *ain't?*"

Dale shrugged. "Do you know where he is?"

Cordie glanced at him with disgust. "If I knew where he was, you think I'd be *huntin'* for him like I am?"

Dale took a breath. "Do you have any idea what happened to him?"

"Yeah."

Dale waited twenty strides, but she said nothing else. "What?" he prompted.

"Somebody or somethin' at that goddamn school killed him."

Dale felt his breath lurch from him again. For all the Bike Patrol's interest in finding Tubby, none of them had thought the boy was dead. Run away probably. Kidnapped maybe. Dale had never really thought of his classmate being *dead.* With the memory of the muzzle still fresh in his mind and viscera, the word had taken on new meaning. He said nothing.

They reached Catton Road near where another lane ran south to become Broad Avenue.

"You better be gettin'," said Cordie. "Don't you nor none of your Boy Scout buddies get in my way in findin' my brother, hear?"

Dale nodded. He glanced at the shotgun. "You going into town with that?"

Cordie treated that question with the silent disgust she obviously thought it deserved.

"What're you going to do with it?" Dale asked.

"Find Van Syke or one of them other shits. Get'em to tell me where Tubby is."

Dale swallowed. "They'll throw you in jail."

Cordie shrugged, pulled a few strands of stringy hair out of her eyes, turned, and headed toward town.

Dale stood there staring. The little figure in the gray sack dress was almost in the shade of the elms at the head of Broad Avenue when he suddenly yelled. "Hey, thanks!"

Cordie Cooke did not stop or look back.

TWELVE

After seeing Jim Harlen, Duane sat in the shade on the courtyard square for several minutes, drinking coffee from his Thermos and thinking. He didn't know Jim well enough to know if he was telling the truth about not remembering what had happened on Saturday night. If he wasn't telling the truth, why the lie? Duane sipped coffee and considered possibilities:

(A) Something had scared Harlen so badly that he wouldn't . . . or couldn't . . . talk about it.

(B) Someone had told him not to talk and backed it up with sufficient threat to make Harlen obey.

(C) Harlen was protecting someone.

Duane finished his coffee, screwed the lid on the Thermos, and decided that the last possibility was the least likely. The first choice seemed the most likely, although there was nothing but a feeling Duane had to suggest that Jim Harlen *had* been lying. Any head injury serious enough to leave someone unconscious for more than twenty-four hours certainly could leave that person without memory of the injury.

Duane decided that it would be safest to assume that Jim did *not* remember what happened. Perhaps later.

He crossed the square to the library and hesitated before going in. What did he expect to find here that would help O'Rourke and company find out anything about Tubby, Van Syke, Harlen's injury, Duane's own close call, or anything else? Why the library? Why look at the history of Old Central when it was obviously some individual bit of insanity—or probably just Van Syke's perversity—that was behind these seemingly random events?

Duane knew why he was going to the library. He'd grown up searching out things there—answering the many private mysteries that arose in the mind of a kid too smart for his own good. The library was a no-questions-asked, private source of information. There had to be many intellectual puzzles that could *not* be solved by a visit—or many visits—to a good library, but Duane McBride hadn't found one yet.

Besides, he realized, this whole tempest-in-a-teacup mystery had begun because of his and the other kids' bad feeling about Old Central. It was something that had bothered Duane and the others long before Tubby Cooke disappeared. This research was overdue.

Duane sighed, set his Thermos behind a bush alongside the library steps, and went inside.

It took more hours than Duane had expected, but eventually he found most of what he wanted.

Oak Hill Library had only one microfiche machine and few things actually on microfiche. For the history of Elm Haven—and of Old Central in particular—he had to go back into the stacks for the locally published and bound books kept there by the Creve Coeur County Historical Society. Duane knew that the Historical Society actually had been one man—Dr. Paul Priestmann, former professor at Bradley University and a local historian who had died less than a year earlier—but the ladies who had collected money to publish Dr. Priestmann's books, the last volume posthumously Duane discovered, kept the Society alive even if only in name.

Old Central had a prominent part in the history of Elm Haven—and in Creve Coeur County, Duane discovered—and it took half of his notebook to record the pertinent parts. Every time Duane visited this library, he wished that it had one of the new Xerox copying machines that businesses were beginning to use. It would make the job of copying information from reference books one couldn't check out ever so much easier.

Duane looked at the pages of old photographs Dr. Priestmann had set in to illustrate the construction of Old Central . . . just Central School in 1876 . . . and then more pages, the photos sepia tinted and frozen in the formality of early, slow photography, showing the opening ceremonies in the late summer of 1876, the Old Settlers' Picnic held on the school grounds in August of that year, the first class to enter Central—29 students who must have been lost in that huge building—and ceremonies at Elm Haven's train depot as the bell arrived earlier that summer.

The large-print caption under the last photo read: *Mr. and Mrs. Ashley and Mayor Wilson Greet Borgia Bell for New School.* And the subcaption went on: *Historic bell to be crowning achievement for Elm Haven's citadel of learning and pride of County.*

Duane paused. The belfry on Old Central had been boarded and sealed for as long as he could remember. He had never heard any mention of a bell, much less of something called a Borgia Bell.

Duane leaned close to the page. In the old photograph, the bell was still in its crate on the flatcar, the bell itself partially in shadow, but obviously huge: it stood almost twice as tall as the two men on the flatcar who stood shaking hands in the center of the picture—the better-dressed man with mustaches and a well-dressed woman hovering near his side probably Mr. Ashley; the shorter, bearded and bowler-hatted man perhaps Mayor Wilson. The base of the bell looked to be eight or nine feet wide. Although the ancient photo was of too poor a quality to give much detail—a carriage on the far side of the tracks seemed to be hitched to two phantom horses because the time exposure was too slow to capture their movements—Duane used his glasses as a magnifying glass to make out metal scrollwork or some sort of inscriptions running in a band around the bell about two-thirds of the way up.

He sat back and tried to imagine how much a bell ten or twelve feet tall and eight feet wide might weigh. He couldn't do the math, but the mere thought of it hanging on rotted timbers above his and the other kids' heads over the past years made the flesh on his neck go cold. *Surely it couldn't still be there.*

For the next few hours, Duane pored through the Historical Society books and spent a dusty hour in the "archives"—a long, narrow room off the room where Mrs. Frazier and the other library employees ate their lunch—going through the tall books holding old copies of the *Oak Hill Sentinel Times-Call,* the local paper that Duane's Old Man invariably referred to as the *Sentimental Times-Crawl.*

Newspaper articles from the summer of 1876 were the most informative, going on in their overwrought, hyperbolic Victorian style about the "Borgia Bell" and its place in history. Evidently Mr. and Mrs. Ashley had discovered the artifact in a warehouse on the outskirts of Rome during their honeymoon-cum-Grand Tour of the Continent, verified its authenticity via local and imported historians, and then purchased the thing for six hundred dollars to be the *pièce de résistance* for the school the Ashley family had been so instrumental in building.

Duane scribbled quickly, filling one notebook and going into his spare. The story of the Borgia Bell's shipment from Rome to Elm Haven took up at least five newspaper articles and several pages of Dr. Priestmann's book: the bell seemed—at least in the lurid prose of the Victorian correspondents—to bring bad luck to everyone and everything associated with it. After the Ashleys purchased the bell and set sail for the States, the warehouse the thing had been stored in burned to the ground, killing three local people who apparently had been living in the old structure. Most of the unnamed and uncatalogued artifacts in the warehouse were destroyed, but the Borgia Bell had been found sooty but intact. The freighter carrying the bell to New York—a British ship, the *H.M.S. Erebus*—almost foundered during an off-season storm near the Canary Islands: the damaged freighter was towed to harbor and its cargo transferred, but not before five crewmen drowned, another was killed during a sudden shifting of cargo in the hold, and the captain was disgraced.

No disasters seemed to accompany the bell's month-long storage in New York, but some confusion in labeling almost left the thing lost there. Some of the Ashley family's New York lawyers tracked down the missing piece of history, had a major reception for the bell at New York's Natural History Museum, where attendees included Mark Twain, P.T. Barnum, and the original John D. Rockefeller, and then loaded it aboard a freight train bound for Peoria. There the spell of bad luck seemed to reassert itself: the train derailed near Johnstown, Pennsylvania, and its replacement was involved in a trestle collapse just outside of Richmond, Indiana. The press accounts were unclear, but apparently no one was killed in either accident.

The bell finally arrived in Elm Haven on July 14, 1876, and was ensconced in its reinforced belfry several weeks later—that summer's Old Settlers' Fair used the bell as its centerpiece and there were numerous dedications, including one which involved bringing in Peoria- and Chicago-based historians and grandees on specially laid-on railroad cars.

Evidently the thing was in the belfry in time for the beginning of school on the third of September that year, for a news tintype of the opening day of Creve Coeur County schools showed an Old Central in a town strangely devoid of trees, under the caption: *Historic Bell Rings Local School Children to New Era of Learning.*

Duane sat back in the archives room, mopped sweat from his face with the tail of his flannel shirt, closed the stiff-boarded newspaper volume, and wished that the excuse he had given Mrs. Frazier for his work in here had been true—that he *had* been planning to do a paper on Old Central and its bell.

But no one seemed to remember that the bell was there. After another hour and a half's research, Duane had come up with only three other references to the bell—and none of them referred to it any longer as the Borgia Bell. Dr. Priestmann's book reprinted early captions calling the thing the Borgia Bell, but nowhere did the local historian himself refer to it as such. The closest reference Duane could find was a paragraph mentioning—"the massive bell, reported to date from the Fifteenth Century and quite possibly being that old, which Mr. Charles Catton Ashley and his wife purchased for the county during their tour of Europe in the winter of 1875."

It was only after reading through four volumes of the Historical Society's books that Duane realized that there was a volume missing. The 1875–1885 volume was intact, but it was mostly photographs and highlights. Dr. Priestmann had written a more detailed and scholarly account of the other years of the decade under the general heading *Monographs, Documentation, and Primary Sources,* with the dates indicated in brackets: 1876 simply was not there.

Duane went downstairs to talk to Mrs. Frazier. "Excuse me, ma'am, but could you tell me where the Historical Society keeps its other papers these days?"

The librarian smiled and lowered her glasses on their beaded chain. "Yes, dear. You must know that Dr. Priestmann passed away . . ."

Duane nodded and looked attentive.

"Well, since neither Mrs. Cadberry nor Mrs. Esterhazy . . . our ladies who were responsible for the fund-raisers to support the Society . . . since neither of them wished or were able to continue Dr. Priestmann's research, they donated his papers and other volumes."

Duane nodded again. "To Bradley?" It made sense that the old scholar's papers would go to the university from which he had graduated and at which he had spent so many years teaching.

Mrs. Frazier looked surprised. "Why, no, dear. The papers went to the family who had really supported Dr. Priestmann's research for all those years. I believe it had been arranged previously."

"The family . . ." began Duane.

"The Ashley-Montague family," said Mrs. Frazier. "Certainly being from Elm Haven . . . or living *near* there . . . certainly you've heard of the Ashley-Montagues."

Duane nodded, thanked her, made sure all of the books were reshelved properly and that his notebooks were in his pockets, went outside to retrieve his Thermos, and was shocked at how late it had grown. Evening shadows stretched from the trees and lay across the courthouse grounds and the main street. A few cars moved down the highway, their tires hissing on the cooling concrete and making galloping sounds on the tarpatched joints in the pavement, but the downtown itself was emptying out toward evening.

Duane considered going back to the hospital to talk to Jim again, but it was around dinnertime and he guessed that Harlen's mother would be there. Besides, it was still a two-to three-hour walk home the long way, and the Old Man might worry if Duane were out after dark.

Whistling, thinking about the Borgia Bell hanging dark as a forgotten secret in the boarded-up belfry of Old Central, Duane headed for the railroad tracks and home.

Mike gave up.

He'd tried hard on Monday afternoon and again all day Tuesday to find Karl Van Syke in order to follow him around, but the man wasn't to be found. Mike tried hanging around Old Central, saw Dr. Roon show up shortly after eight-thirty on Tuesday morning, and watched until a bunch of workmen with a cherry picker—but no Van Syke—showed up an hour later to start putting boards over the second- and third-floor windows. Mike continued to hang around the door of the school until Roon chased him away in midmorning.

Mike checked the places one might usually see Van Syke. Carl's Tavern downtown had three or four of the usual drunks hanging around—including Duane McBride's dad, Mike was sorry to see—but no Van Syke. Mike used the phone in the A&P to call the Black Tree Tavern, but the bartender said that he hadn't seen Van Syke in weeks and who was this calling? Mike hung up fast. He walked up to Depot Street, checked out J.P. Congden's house because he knew Van Syke and the fat justice of the peace hung out together a lot, but the black Chevy wasn't there and the house looked empty.

Mike considered hiking out the tracks to hang around the old tallow plant, but he felt sure that Van Syke wouldn't be there. For a while, he just lay in the tall grass out by the ball diamond, chewing on a stalk of grass and watching the little bit of traffic that went out First Avenue past the water tower; mostly farmers' dusty pickups and big old cars. No Rendering Truck with Van Syke at the wheel.

Mike sighed and rolled over on his back, squinting at the sky. He knew he should hike out to Calvary Cemetery and check out the shed there, but he couldn't. It was that simple. The memory of the shed, the soldier, and the figure in the yard last night lay across Mike's chest like a heavy weight.

He rolled over and watched Kevin Grumbacher's dad's chrome-silver dairy truck coming in from Jubilee College Road. It wasn't noon yet and Mr. Grumbacher was almost done with his day's work collecting milk from all the county's dairy farms. Mike knew that the truck would head off for the Cahill Dairy twelve miles east, right at the head of the Spoon River Valley, and then Mr. G. would be finished for the day except to come home, rinse the truck, and fill it with fuel again from the gas pump he had on the west side of their house.

By rolling on his left side, Mike could see the Grumbachers' new house under the elms next to Dale's big old Victorian house. Mr. G. had bought Mrs. Carmichael's old abandoned place on Depot Street about five years ago, just before Dale's family had moved to Elm Haven, and the Grumbachers had razed the old house and put up the only new ranchhouse-style home in the old section of town. Mr. Grumbacher himself had used a bulldozer to raise the level of the soil so the low home sat higher than the windows on the east side of Dale's house.

Mike always felt funny the few times he'd been in Kev's home. It was air conditioned—the only air-conditioned place Mike had ever been except for Ewalts' movie theater over in Oak Hill—and it smelled funny. Stale, but not really stale. It was as if the cool scent of the concrete-and-pine two-by-fours and fresh carpet still filled the house even after four years of the people living there. Of course, it never really *looked* to Mike that people actually lived there: the Grumbachers' living room had plastic runners on the floor and a crinkly plastic on the expensive couch and chairs, the kitchen was bright and spotless—it held the first dishwashing machine and eating counter Mike had ever seen in a home—and the dining room looked like Mrs. G. polished the long cherry table every morning.

The few times Mike and the other kids were allowed to play in Kevin's house, they went straight to the basement . . . or what Kev called the "wreck room" for some reason. There was a Ping-Pong table there, and a TV—Kev said they had two more television sets upstairs—and an elaborate electric-train layout filling half the back room. Mike would have loved to play with the trains, but Kev wasn't allowed to touch the controls unless his dad was there, and Mr. G. slept most afternoons. There was also a long galvanized steel water trough in the back room—the metal as bright and clean as everything else in the house—which Kevin said his dad had put in so the two of them could play with motorized boats the two made in their spare time. But Mike, Dale, and the other kids were only allowed to watch the boats, not touch them or handle the neat radio-control devices.

The gang didn't spend much time in Kev's house.

Mike got to his feet and started walking toward Dale's back fence.

He knew he was thinking of dumb things, trying not to think about the soldier.

Dale and Kevin were lying on the grassy incline between the Grumbachers' and Stewarts' driveways, waiting for Lawrence to fly a balsawood glider. Then both of the older boys would fire away with gravel from Dale's driveway, trying to knock the plane out of the sky. Lawrence had to launch and duck fast before the missiles flew.

Mike grabbed some gravel and flopped down on his back next to the two. The trick seemed to be to hit the thing without raising your head from the grass. Lawrence launched and ducked. Rocks flew. The glider looped once, flew toward the big oak tree that sent branches over Dale's bedroom upstairs, and then landed in the driveway untouched. All three grabbed more ammunition while Lawrence retrieved the plane and straightened the wing and tail.

"Gettin' rocks in your side yard," Mike said to Dale. "Going to be tough when you mow."

"I promised Mom we'd pick them up when we're through," said Dale, cocking his arm in anticipation.

Lawrence launched a high one. They all missed on the first ground-to-air attack, each boy unselfconsciously making gun or missile sounds as he threw. Mike hit it with his second throw, smashing the right wing and sending the glider into a spin into the grass. All three of the others made jet-out-of-control and crashing-and-burning sounds. Lawrence slid out the broken wing and ran to a stack of replacement parts by the old stump.

"I can't find Van Syke," Mike said, feeling as if he were in Confession.

Kev was piling launch-sized stones next to himself in the grass. His parents would never let him throw rocks in *his* yard. "That's OK," he said. "I found Roon this morning, but he isn't doing anything except supervising the windows getting boarded up."

Mike looked. Old Central looked different with all three levels boarded up—four levels if you counted the basement windows, and Mike could just make out that they had removed the screens, boarded those windows, and set the screens back. The school looked weird . . . blind in a strange way. Now only the tiny dormer windows set in the steep roof had glass panes, and few kids Mike knew could throw that high to hit them. The belfry had always been boarded up.

"Maybe this following people around isn't such a great idea," Mike said. Lawrence was putting masking tape around parts of the next plane . . . "armoring it," he said.

"I know it wasn't a good idea for me this morning," said Dale. The other two boys quit playing with their ammunition while Dale explained most of what had happened out on the tracks this morning.

"Jeez," whistled Kevin. "Criminitly."

"What'd Cordie do next?" asked Mike, trying to imagine having a rifle pointed at him. C.J. Congden had picked on Mike a couple a times in the lower grades, but Mike had always fought back so hard, so fast, and so fiercely that the town's two punks tended to leave him alone. Mike glanced at the school. "Did she come in and shoot Dr. Roon?"

"If she did, we haven't heard it," said Dale.

"Maybe she used a silencer," said Mike.

Kev made a face. "Idiot. Shotguns can't have silencers."

"I was kidding, Grump-backer."

"Groom-bokker," Kevin corrected with automatic sullenness. He didn't like it when people fooled with his name. Everyone in town said Grum-backer.

"Whatever," said Mike with a sudden grin. He gently tossed a rock at Dale's knee. "So what happened next?"

"Nothing," said Dale. Something in his voice suggested that he was sorry he'd told the others. "I'm keeping a watch out for C.J."

"You didn't tell your mom?"

"Uh-uh. How'm I supposed to explain why I had Dad's binoculars to spy on Cordie Cooke's house? Huh?"

Mike made a face and nodded. Being a Peeping Tom was one thing; doing it at Cordie Cooke's house was worse than weird. "If he comes after you," he said to Dale, "I'll help. Congden's mean but stupid. Archie Kreck's even stupider. Get on Archie's blind side in a fight and it's no contest."

Dale nodded but looked gloomy. Mike knew that his friend wasn't very good in fights. It was one of the reasons Mike liked him. Dale muttered something.

"What?" said Mike. Lawrence was saying something at the same time from the end of the driveway.

"I said I didn't even go back for my bike," Dale said a second time.

Mike recognized the tone of voice as the one he used for his most serious sins during Confession. "Where is it?"

"I hid it behind the old depot."

Mike nodded. To retrieve the bike, Dale would have to go back through Congden's neighborhood. "I'll get it," he said.

Dale looked at him with what looked like a mixture of relief, embarrassment, and anger. The anger, Mike figured, was at feeling so relieved. "Why? Why should you get it? It's my bike."

Mike shrugged, discovered that he was still carrying some of the

grass from the field, and chewed on the bottom part of it. "It doesn't make
any difference to me. But I'm going up that way to church later, and it
makes sense that I get it. Think . . . Congden isn't looking for *me*. Besides,
if I'd had a rifle aimed at my face once today, I wouldn't go looking for
another chance. Uh-uh, I'll get it after lunch when I'm up there running
an errand for Father C." Mike thought, *Another lie. Do I confess this one?*
He didn't think so.

This time, Dale's expression showed so much pure relief that he had
to look down as if he were counting his pile of stones to hide it. "OK," he
said faintly. And even more faintly, "Thanks."

Lawrence was standing twenty feet away, "armored" plane poised.
"Are you jerks ready or are you gonna keep talking all day?"

"Ready," said Dale.

"Launch!" cried Kevin.

"Duck!" yelled Mike.

The missiles flew.

The Old Man wasn't home when Duane got there just before sunset, so
he walked back out through the fields to Wittgenstein's grave.

Witt had always carried his after-dinner and gift bones out to this
flat, grassy area in the east pasture, burying them in the soft soil at the
top of the hill above the creek. So that's where Duane had buried Witt.

Beyond the pasture and cornfields to the west, the sun hung on the
horizon in the thick-aired, full-bellied Illinois sunset that Duane could
not imagine living without. The air around him was blue-gray with the
end of day and sound traveled with the slow ease of thought. Duane
could hear the soft shuffle and wheeze of the cows coming in from the far
reaches of pasture even though they were still out of sight over the hill to
the north. Smoke hung thick in the air from where old Mr. Johnson had
been burning weeds along his fence more than a mile to the south, and
the evening tasted of dust and tiredness and the sweet incense of that
smoke.

Duane sat next to Witt's small grave while the sun set and the evening allowed itself to go gently into night. Venus appeared first, blazing
above the eastern horizon like one of the UFOs that Duane used to sit in
this field at night and watch for with Witt lying patiently at his side.
Then the other stars moved into the sky, each quite visible this far from
any scattered light. The air began to cool off slowly, reluctantly, the humidity still causing Duane's shirt to cling to his ample torso, but eventually the day's heat dissipated and the heaped soil under Duane's hand
cooled to the touch. He patted the grave a final time and ambled slowly
back to the house, aware again of how different it was to walk alone

through the high grass rather than keeping one's pace slow to accommodate an aging and half-blind collie.

The Borgia Bell. He'd wanted to talk to the Old Man about it, but his father wouldn't be in any mood to talk if he'd been at Carl's or the Black Tree all afternoon.

Duane made dinner for himself, frying pork chops in the large skillet, cutting up potatoes and onions with a practiced hand while turning his radio, and listened for a while to WHO from Des Moines. The news on the hour was the usual stuff—Nationalist China was still complaining in the U.N. about Red China's shelling of Quemoy the previous week, but no one in the U.N. seemed to want another Korea; Broadway shows were still shut down by an Actors Equity strike; Senator John Kennedy's people were saying that the once and future candidate was going to give a major foreign-policy speech in Washington the next week, but Ike seemed to be stealing the limelight from all potential candidates by planning a major trip to the Far East; the U.S. was demanding that Gary Powers be returned by the Russians while Argentina was demanding that Israel return the kidnapped Adolf Eichmann. The sports included an announcement of a ban on homemade scaffolds at the Indianapolis 500 of the kind that had collapsed during this year's Memorial Day race, killing a couple of people and injuring almost a hundred more. There was talk of the upcoming rematch between Floyd Patterson and Ingemar Johansson.

Duane turned the volume up and listened as he ate alone at the long table. He liked boxing. He'd like to write a story about it someday. Something about Negroes maybe . . . Negroes finding equality through fighting in the ring. Duane had listened to the Old Man and Uncle Art talk about Jackie Johnson years ago, and the memory had stuck in his mind like the plot of a favorite novel. *It could be a good novel,* Duane thought, *if I knew how to write it.* And knew enough about boxing and Negroes and Jackie Johnson and life and *everything* to write it.

The Borgia Bell. Duane finished his dinner, washed the dishes and coffee cup along with the Old Man's breakfast dishes, put them back in the cupboard and walked through the house.

It was dark except for the kitchen light and the old place seemed creakier and eerier than usual. The upstairs, with the Old Man's bedroom deserted, Duane's old room unused, seemed a heavy presence above him. *The Borgia Bell, hanging up there in Old Central above us all these years?* Duane shook his head and turned on a light in the dining room.

The learning machines sat there in all their dusty glory. Other inventions littered the worktables and floor. The only one that was plugged in or working was the phone-answering device the Old Man had built a couple of winters ago out of pique at missing calls: a simple combination of telephone parts and a small reel-to-reel tape recorder, the device plugged into the phone socket, gave a recorded message, and invited the caller to leave a message.

Almost everybody who called—except Uncle Art—hung up in anger or confusion at having a machine answer the phone, but sometimes the Old Man could tell who was calling by recorded curses or mutters. Besides, Duane's father liked the irritation it caused. Even to the phone company. Ma Bell people had been out to the farm twice, threatening to shut off the McBrides' service if Mr. McBride didn't quit breaking the law by tampering with the phone company's equipment and hookups, not to mention violating federal regulations by tape-recording people's conversations without their permission.

The Old Man had pointed out that these were *his* conversations, that the people were calling *him*, that FCC regulations demanded that the person *know* they were being taped—which he said right on *his* tape—and, when it came right down to it, Ma Bell was a motherfucking capitalist monopoly and it could go stick its threats and equipment up its corporate ass.

But the threats had kept the Old Man from ever trying to market his answering devices—what he called his "telephonic Jeeves." Duane was just happy they still had a phone.

Duane had refined the Old Man's device in recent months so that a light blinked when there were recorded messages. He'd actually wanted to fix it up so that different-colored lights would glow at the recognition of different voices on the tape—green for Uncle Art, blue for Dale or one of the other kids, flashing red for the phone company guy, and so forth—but while the problem of voice recognition hadn't been too hard to solve . . . Duane had hooked up a rebuilt tone generator to an ID-circuit based on old tape recordings of callers, then made a simple schematic for a feedback loop to the battery of who's-calling lights . . . the parts had been too expensive, so he'd quit at having a light blink once for each call on the tape.

The light was off. No messages. There seldom were.

Duane went to the screen door and looked out toward the pole light near the barn. The light threw the driveway turnaround and outbuildings into arc-lamp glare, but made the fields beyond seem even darker. The crickets and tree frogs were very loud tonight.

Duane stood at the door a minute, thinking about how he could get Uncle Art to drive him to Bradley University the next day. Before going back into the dining room to call, however, he did something he'd never done before. He put the hook latch on the screen door and made sure that the rarely used front door was locked.

It would mean that he'd have to stay up until the Old Man got home to let him in, but that was OK. They never locked their doors—not even during those rare times when Duane and the Old Man joined Uncle Art for a weekend in Peoria or Chicago. It just wasn't something they thought of doing.

But Duane didn't want the door unlocked tonight.

He tapped the tiny hook set into the light wood, realized that he could open it himself from the outside with one serious tug or a kick at the screens, smiled at his own foolishness, and went back to call Uncle Art.

Mike's small bedroom was above what had been the parlor but was now Memo's room. The upstairs had no direct heat, merely broad metal grilles that allowed the warm air to rise into the upper rooms. The grille was right beside Mike's bed and he could see the faint glow on his own ceiling of the small kerosene lantern they let burn all night in Memo's room as a nightlight. Mike's mother checked on Memo several times each night, and the dim light made it easier. Mike knew that if he got down on his knees and peered through the grille, he could see the dull bundle of bedclothes that were Memo. He wouldn't do that; it would be too much like spying.

But sometimes Mike was sure that he heard Memo's thoughts and dreams come up through the grille. They weren't words or images, but rose to him like half-heard sighs, alternate drafts of warm love or the cold breezes of anxiety. Mike often lay awake in his low-ceilinged room and wondered if Memo died at night when he was here, would he sense her soul rising past him through the grille, pausing to enfold him in its warmth the way her body used to each night when he was little and she stopped by to tuck him in and check on him, the flame of her small kerosene lamp flickering and making a soft hissing in its glass chimney?

Mike lay there and watched the faint leaf shadows stirring on the steeply pitched ceiling. He had no desire for sleep. All afternoon he had been yawning and gritty-eyed from the previous night's lost sleep, but now that darkness and deep night were here, he was afraid to close his eyes. He lay there and tried to stay awake—imagining conversations with Father C., dreaming of the days when his mother still smiled at him and hugged him—when her voice was less sharp to everyone and her tongue dripped Irish sarcasm but not so much bitterness, and finally just dreaming of Michelle Staffney, imagining her red hair—as soft and pretty as his sister Kathleen's but framing intelligent eyes and an expressive mouth rather than his sister's slow gaze and slack features.

Mike was on the verge of drifting off to sleep when he felt a cold breeze brush past him. He snapped awake.

The room was hot even with the small window open. All the day's heat had risen into the upstairs and there was no cross-ventilation to dispel it. But the breeze that had wafted past Mike had been as cold as the drafts that blew through the small room on January nights; and it had carried a cold-meat and frozen-blood smell which Mike associated with the refrigerated lockers where they kept the sides of beef down at the A&P.

Mike rolled out of bed and onto his knees by the grille. The lamplight down there was flickering wildly, as if a windstorm were blowing in the small room. The cold enveloped Mike as surely as if chill hands were seizing his wrists and ankles and throat. He expected to see his mother rush into the room, robe clutched shut and hair awry, checking to see what was wrong—but the house lay still and silent except for the sawing of his father's snores in the back room where his parents slept.

The cold faltered, seemed to withdraw through the grate, and then rose with the force of a January wind through open windows. The kerosene lamp flickered a final time and went out. Mike seemed to hear a moan from the corner of blackness where Memo lay.

Mike jumped to his feet, grabbed a Louisville Slugger from the corner, and flew down the steep staircase, his bare feet making almost no noise on the wooden steps.

Memo's door was always left open a crack. Now it was closed tightly.

Half-expecting the door to be bolted on the inside—an impossibility if Memo were alone—Mike crouched a few seconds outside the room, fingers flat on the door like a fireman feeling for the heat of flames behind the wood—although it was the cold he half-sensed through his fingertips—and then he swung the door wide and went in quickly, baseball bat off his shoulder and ready to be swung.

There was enough light to see that the room seemed empty except for the dark bundle that was Memo and the usual clutter of her framed photographs on every surface, the medicine bottles, the hospital tray table they had bought, the additional useless clutter of her rocking chair, Grandpa's favorite chair sitting in the corner, the old Philco radio that still worked . . . all the usual stuff.

But even as he stood there on the balls of his feet, baseball bat poised, Mike felt certain that he and Memo were not alone. The cold air blew and rippled soundlessly around him, a whirlpool of chill, foul-smelling air. Mike had once cleaned out a freezer full of chicken and ground beef at Mrs. Moon's after the electricity had been off for ten days. This smelled like that, only colder and more repellant.

Mike lifted the bat even as the wind blew in his face, whirled around him: cold fingernails rasped at his stomach and back where the pajamas did not cover; a sensation like cold lips brushed the back of his neck;

there came a foul breath on his cheeks as if some invisible face were inches from his, exhaling the rot of the grave into his face.

Mike cursed and swung the bat at darkness. The wind whipped around him; he could almost hear its black roar like someone hissing in his ears. The loose papers in the room were not disturbed. There was no external sound except for the faintest rustle of corn in the fields across the street.

Mike choked back a second curse but swung the bat again with both hands, standing in the middle of the room in a stance part batter's, part prizefighter's. The dark wind seemed to retreat to the far corner; Mike took a step toward it, glanced over his shoulder and saw Memo's face pale in the heap of black bedclothes, and stepped back instead so that whatever it was couldn't get around him. To her.

He crouched in front of Memo, feeling her dry breath on his back now—knowing that she was still alive at least—trying to keep the coldness from her with the heat of his own body.

There was a final rustle and curling of breeze, almost like a soft laugh, and the cold rushed out of the open window like black water pouring out a drain.

Suddenly the lamp flickered on, its hissing flame and dancing shadows of gold light startling Mike onto his feet and causing his heart to leap somewhere near his throat. He stood there with the bat hefted, still waiting.

The cold was gone. The open window admitted only warm June breezes and the sudden resumption of cricket sounds, leaf stirrings.

Mike turned and crouched next to Memo. Her eyes were wide open and the irises looked all black and moist in the light. Mike leaned forward, was reassured by her rapid exhalations, and touched her cheek with his free hand.

"Are you all right, Memo?" Sometimes she seemed to understand and blinked her answers—one blink for yes, two for no. More often these days, there was no response.

One blink. Yes.

Mike felt his heart resume its wild pounding. It had been a long time since Memo'd talked to him . . . even in this crude code.

He felt his mouth go completely dry. He uncleaved his tongue from the roof of his mouth and forced the words. "Did you feel that?"

One blink.

"Was something here?"

One blink.

"Was it . . . real?"

One blink.

Mike took a deep breath. It was like talking to a mummy except for the blinks, and even those seemed illusory in the half-light. He would have given anything he had or would ever earn in his lifetime if Memo could've talked to him at that second. Even if just for a minute.

He cleared a throat suddenly filled with emotion. "Was it something bad?"

One blink.

"Was it like . . . a ghost?"

Two blinks. No.

Mike looked into her stare. Between answers, she did not blink at all. It was like interviewing a corpse.

Mike shook his head to get rid of the traitorous thought.

"Was it . . . was it Death?"

One blink. Yes.

When she had answered him, her eyes closed, Mike leaned forward to make sure she was still breathing, and then touched her cheek with his palm again. "It's all right, Memo," he whispered next to her ear. "I'm here. It won't come back tonight. Go to sleep."

He crouched next to her until her choppy, ragged breathing seemed to slow and regulate somewhat. Then he got Grandpa's chair and dragged it close to the bed—even though the rocker would have been infinitely easier to move, he wanted Grandpa's chair—and then he sat in it, the baseball bat still on his shoulder, the chair and him between Memo and the window.

Earlier that evening, a block and a half west of Mike's house, Lawrence and Dale made ready for bed.

They had watched *Sea Hunt* with Lloyd Bridges at nine-thirty—their one exception to the nine P.M. bedtime rule—and then gone upstairs, Dale first to enter the darkened room and feel around for the light cord. Even though it was ten o'clock, a faint glow of the near-solstice twilight still came through the windows.

Lying in twin beds separated by only eighteen inches, Dale and his little brother lay whispering for a few moments.

"How come you aren't scared of the dark?" Lawrence asked quietly. He was lying with his panda bear in the crook of his arm. The bear, whom Lawrence insisted on calling Teddy despite Dale's insistence that it was a *panda* and not a teddy bear, had been won at the monkey-race attraction at Chicago's Riverview Park years before and looked the worse for wear: one eye loose, the left ear almost chewed through, the fur balding around the middle where it had been rubbed off by six years of hugs, and the black string of the mouth unraveling to give Teddy a lopsided, smirking appearance.

"Scared of the dark?" said Dale. "It's not dark in here. The night-light's on."

"You know what I mean."

Dale knew what his brother meant. And he knew how hard it was for Lawrence to admit his fear. During the day, the eight-year-old was afraid of nothing. At night he usually asked for Dale to hold his hand so he could get to sleep. "I don't know," said Dale. "I'm older. You're not afraid of the dark when you're older."

Lawrence lay in silence for a minute. Downstairs, their mother's footsteps were barely audible going from the kitchen through the dining room. The footsteps stopped as they reached the carpet of the living room. Their dad was not home from his sales trip yet. "But you used to be scared," said Lawrence, not quite making it a question.

Not as chicken as you, scaredy-cat was the first reply that came to Dale. But it wasn't the time for teasing. "Yeah," he whispered. "A little bit. Sometimes."

"Of the dark?"

"Yeah."

"Of coming in to find the light cord?"

"When I was little in the apartment in Chicago, my room—our room—didn't have a light cord. It had a switch on the wall."

Lawrence raised Teddy to his cheek. "I wished we lived there now."

"Naw," whispered Dale, putting his hands behind his head and watching the leaf shadows move on the ceiling. "This house is a million times neater. And Elm Haven's a lot more fun than Chicago. We had to go to Garfield Park when we wanted to play, and some grown-up had to go with us."

"I sort of remember," whispered Lawrence, who was only four when they moved. The insistency came back into his voice. "But you *were* afraid of the dark?"

"Yeah." Dale actually couldn't remember being afraid of the dark in their apartment, but he didn't want Lawrence to feel like a total sissy.

"And of the closet?"

"We had a real closet then," said Dale. He glanced over at the corner closet made of yellow-painted pine.

"But you were afraid of it?"

"I don't know. I don't remember. Why are you afraid of this one?"

Lawrence didn't answer at once. He seemed to hunker deeper in the bedclothes. "Something makes noises in it," he whispered after a while.

"This old house has mice, stupid. You know Mom and Dad are always setting traps." It was Dale's job to dump the traps and he hated it. Frequently at night he could hear the scurrying in the walls even up here on the second floor.

"It's not mice." There was no doubt in Lawrence's voice, although he sounded sleepy.

"How do you know?" Despite himself, Dale felt a chill at what his brother had just said. "How do you know it's not mice? What you think it is, some sort of monster?"

"Not mice," whispered Lawrence, on the verge of sleep. "Same thing that's under the bed sometimes."

"There's nothing under the bed," snapped Dale, tired of the conversation. "Except dustballs."

Instead of continuing the conversation, Lawrence extended his hand across the short space between the beds. "Please?" His voice was dreamy, slurred with sleep. Lawrence's sleeve was halfway up his forearm because his favorite Roy Rogers pajamas were too small for him but he refused to wear anything else.

Sometimes Dale refused to hold his brother's hand—after all, they were both way too old for that—but this night it was all right. Dale realized that he needed the reassurance himself.

"G'night," he whispered, expecting no answer. "Pleasant dreams."

"Glad you're not afraid of stuff," Lawrence whispered back. His voice was from another place, filtered by the veil of sleep.

Dale lay with his left hand holding Lawrence's, feeling how small his brother's fingers still seemed. When he closed his eyes, he saw the muzzle of C.J. Congden's .22 pointed at his face and he lurched awake, his heart pounding.

Dale knew that there were still darknesses he was afraid of. Only these were *real* fears, *real* threats. During the coming weeks he'd have to be extra careful to stay away from C.J. and Archie.

At that moment, Dale realized that the game they'd been playing hunting for Tubby Cooke and following Roon and the others around was finished. At least as far as he was concerned it was over. It was silly and it was going to get someone hurt.

There weren't any mysteries in Elm Haven—no Nancy Drew or Joe Hardy adventures with secret passages and clever clues—just a bunch of assholes like C.J. and his old man who could really hurt you if you got in their way. Jim Harlen had probably *already* broken his arm and stuff because of their stupid sneaking around. Dale had gotten the feeling that afternoon that Mike and Kevin were tired of the whole thing, too.

Much later, Lawrence sighed and rolled over in his sleep, still clutching Teddy but releasing Dale's hand. Dale rolled over on his right side, beginning to drift off. Beyond the screens on the two windows, leaves rustled on the big oak and crickets played their mindless tunes in the grass. The last of the evening glow was long gone from the window, but a few fireflies sent signals against the blackness of branches.

As Dale dozed off, he thought he could hear his mother ironing in the kitchen downstairs. For a while there was no sound in the room except for the regular breathing of the two boys. Outside, an owl or a dove made swallowing sounds. Then closer, in the closet in the corner, something scrabbled and clawed, paused, and then scratched a final time before falling into silence.

THIRTEEN

Duane McBride had convinced his Uncle Art that Wednesday would be a good day to drive in to the university library—Art had spent most of his money over the years on books but still liked to visit a "decent library" now and then—so the two left shortly after eight that morning.

What Uncle Art hadn't spent on books he'd put into his car—a year old Cadillac—and Duane could only marvel at the battleship-sized grandeur of the thing. It had every option known to Detroit technology, including an automatic headlight dimmer with a ray-gun-shaped sensor rising from the dash like something Duane's Old Man would have designed. Uncle Art drove with three fingers on the bottom of the wheel, his heavy body comfortable in the cushions.

Duane liked his uncle. Art had one of those florid, rounded faces that combined with the kind of mouth which always seemed to be on the verge of a smile so as to give people the idea that he was amused by something just said or about to be said. Usually, with Uncle Art, that was true.

Art McBride was an ironist. Where Duane's father had fallen into bitterness and disappointment in his failure to get ahead, Uncle Art had cultivated an ironic resignation which he leavened with humor. Duane's Old Man tended to see conspiracies and cabals—in the government, in the telephone company, in the Veterans Administration, in the more prominent families in Elm Haven—while Uncle Art felt that most individuals and all bureaucracies were too cretinous to manage a conspiracy.

Each brother had failed in his own way. Duane's father had watched his businesses fail due to poor planning, terrible timing, and management techniques which never included efficiency amongst all the manic energy he poured into them. Added to that, the Old Man invariably would insult whatever individual or organization was indispensable to the success of the venture. Uncle Art, on the other hand, had gone into business only a few times—had made and spent his profits on his three wives, all deceased—and had decided that business simply wasn't for him. Art worked at the Caterpillar plant near Peoria when he needed money. Although he had degrees in engineering and business administration, he preferred the assembly line.

Duane had decided that a tendency toward ironic resignation and the ability to handle responsibility didn't necessarily go together too well.

"What bit of esoterica are you seeking in the Bradley library?" asked Uncle Art.

Duane pushed his glasses up on his nose with his middle finger. "Oh, just some stuff I wanted to know and couldn't find in Oak Hill."

"Did you try the Elm Haven library? Finest depository of knowledge since the Library of Alexandria."

Duane smiled. The one-room "library" on Broad Avenue was an old joke between them. It held about four hundred books. Uncle Art's library ran to over three thousand volumes. Duane would have searched there for information on the Borgia Bell, but he knew the library well enough to know that Art had very little on the Borgia era.

"Did I say *de*pository of knowledge?" continued Uncle Art. "I should have said *sup*pository. Good thing for you, keed, that I'm currently laid off."

"Yes," said Duane. Uncle Art spent a good part of the year laid off as demand for assembly-line workers waxed and waned. Art didn't seem to mind.

"Seriously, what're you hunting for?" Uncle Art turned off the air conditioning and touched a button to lower the window. Warm, humid air rushed in. Art ran a hand through his short hair; he had lustrous white hair, wavy and full, Duane remembered from the few times Uncle Art allowed it to get long. Usually he wore it in a crew cut as he did now. Duane remembered when he was little, when Art was returning from one of his year-long trips after the death of his third wife, and the four-year-old had confused his then-bearded uncle with Santa Claus.

Duane sighed. "I'm hunting for some stuff on the Borgias."

Uncle Art blinked interest. "Borgias? As in Lucrezia, Rodrigo, Cesare . . . that bunch?"

"Yeah," said Duane, sitting up taller in the cushions. "You know much about them? Or did you ever hear about some bell they had?"

"Uh-uh. Don't know much about the Borgias. Just the usual stuff about poisoning, incest, what bad popes they made. I'm more interested in the Medicis. Now *there's* a family worth reading about."

Duane nodded. They'd been heading southeast down the Hard Road—now merely thought of as the state highway—from Elm Haven, and were now descending into the valley of the Spoon River. The cliffs were about a mile apart, the hillsides so thick with trees that they overhung the road here, then opened out into rich bottomland with soil so black from frequent floods that the corn grew a foot higher here than in the fields around Elm Haven. The only structures in sight were a few corncribs and the metal highway bridge crossing the river itself. On the bridge, a narrow catwalk ran out to a corrugated steel, silo-shaped tower—no more than four feet in diameter—which dropped to its own concrete pilings thirty feet below. Duane knew that it held only a cramped spiral stairway down to a highway department storage area down at the river's level.

"Remember when you and Dad used to threaten to leave me in there if I didn't quit asking questions during the ride to Peoria?" said Duane, gesturing toward the corrugated metal tower. "You guys used to say it was a prison tower for blabby kids. You said you'd pick me up on the way home."

Uncle Art nodded and lit a cigarette from the car lighter. His blue eyes squinted toward where mirages rippled on the narrow road ahead. "Still applies, kiddo. One more question and you're gonna spend more time in a prison tower than Thomas More."

"Thomas who?" said Duane. He was feeding Uncle Art the straight line. They were both big Thomas More fans.

"Now *there's* a man!" began Uncle Art and launched into one of his monologues.

They reached Highway 150 and turned east toward the tiny town of Kickapoo and then Peoria. Duane settled back into the Cadillac's deep cushions and thought about the Borgia Bell.

Dale, Mike, Kevin, and Lawrence had left town just after breakfast that morning, headed east for the wooded hills behind Calvary Cemetery. They drove their bikes through the cemetery itself—Mike glancing toward the padlocked door of the storage shed but saying nothing to the other kids—and left them by the back fence. They crossed the pasture into the thick woods and a quarter of a mile later came to the strip-mined quarry they called Billy Goat Mountains. Here they climbed and shouted and threw dirt clods for an hour, before stripping off their clothes and swimming in the one shallow pool there.

Gerry Daysinger, Bob McKown, Bill and Barry Fussner, Chuck Sperling, Digger Taylor, and a couple more guys arrived about ten o'clock, just as Dale and the others were getting back into their clothes. The Fussner twins started shouting and the rest of the invaders began throwing dirt clods—Mike, Dale, and the others had been careful to circle around to the east side of the quarry before swimming—and both sides exchanged insults and clods across the water before the newcomers broke into two groups and began running around the weed-choked edges of the cliffs.

"They're trying to flank us," said Mike, zipping up his jeans.

Kevin threw a dirt clod that fell ten yards short of the north cliff. Daysinger screamed something nasty and kept running along the edge, occasionally stopping to pull a rock out of the ground and throw it their way.

Dale hurried Lawrence into his sneakers. He threw a clod . . . not a rock . . . and had the pleasure of watching Chuck Sperling have to duck.

Dirt clods and rocks were raining around them now, splashing in the shallow pool and kicking holes in the dunes of dirt behind them. The invaders had reached the far side of the quarry and were closing in from the north and south. But the woods started twenty feet beyond the quarry and went on for miles.

"Remember," said Mike, "if they get you they've got to actually hold you down before you're captured. You break away, you can keep going."

"Yeah," said Kevin, glancing toward the woods. "Let's go, huh?"

Mike grabbed the other boy's t-shirt. "But if they *do* get you, you don't tell them where the camps are or what the call signs are. Right?"

Kevin made a disgusted face. Jim Harlen had ratted them out once—they still couldn't use what had been Camp Five because of that—but none of the others had ever talked, even though it'd meant a fistfight once between Dale and Digger Taylor.

The attackers were close enough now to believe that their pincers movement might work. Clods whisked through the air and crashed into underbrush. Lawrence took aim, reared back, and fired a clod that hit Gerry Daysinger hard enough—even at thirty paces—to cause the older boy to sit down hard and let loose with a string of curses.

"Camp *Three*!" shouted Mike, telling them where to try to meet up in thirty minutes after they lost the attackers. *"Go!"*

They went, Dale trying to keep Lawrence with him as they crashed through the underbrush into the dense woods, Kevin and Mike turning south toward Gypsy Lane and the ravine where Corpse Creek ran under the slate cliffs, Dale and his brother running hard toward the creek that

ran north of the cemetery and the hidden pond that lay along the southern edge of their Uncle Henry's and Aunt Lena's property.

Behind them, the Fussner twins, McKown, and the others shouted
and bayed like fox hounds on a hunt. But the forest had a lot of new
growth here, saplings and shrubs and weeds and thickets and batches of
poison ivy, and everyone was too busy running and hunting or running
and eluding to take time to throw clods.

Running hard, occasionally tugging at Lawrence as they took a
sharp turn off some old trail or up a hill, Dale tried to keep ahead of the
pursuers while keeping a map in his mind, figuring out how to double
back to Camp Three without running right into the band behind them.

The hills echoed to the shouts of capture and aggression.

The library at Bradley University wasn't the best—the school specialized in education, engineering, and business, after all—but Duane knew
his way around it and soon found some information on the subject. He
moved from card catalog to microfilm and back to stacks while Uncle
Art sat in one of the easy chairs in the main lounge and caught up on
two months' reading of various journals and papers.

There really wasn't that much prime stuff on the Borgias, and less
about any bell. Duane had to skim through all the surface stuff before getting his first clue. It was a minor note in a long passage about the corona-
tion of popes:

> It was a shock to the Italians and a surprise to even his Span-
> ish kinsmen when His Excellency Don Alonso y Borja, Arch-
> bishop of Valencia, Cardinal of Quattro Coronati, was elected
> Pope at the age of seventy-seven in the Conclave of 1455. Few
> disputed that the Cardinal's primary qualifications were his
> advanced age and obvious illness; the conclave had need for
> a caretaker pope and no one doubted that Borgia, as the Ital-
> ians had civilized his rough Spanish name, would be just
> that.
>
> As Pope Calixtus III, Borgia seemed to find renewed en-
> ergy in his position and proceeded to consolidate Papal powers
> and to launch a new Crusade, the last as it turned out, against
> the Turks holding Constantinople.
>
> To celebrate his papacy and the ascendancy of the House
> of Borgia, Calixtus commissioned a great bell to be cast from
> metal mined in the fabled hills of Aragon. The bell was even-
> tually cast. Legend has it that the iron was culled from the

famous Coronati Star Stone, possibly a meteorite but certainly a source of the highest quality material for Valencia and Toledo metalsmiths for some generations past. It was displayed in Valencia in 1457 and was sent to Rome in a stately procession which tarried for further exhibition in every major city in the kingdoms of Aragon and Castile. Tarried for too long, as it turned out.

Calixtus's triumphant bell arrived in Rome on August 7, 1458. The eighty-year-old Pope did not appreciate it; he had died in his shuttered rooms late the night before.

Duane searched the index and skimmed the rest of this particular book, but there was no further mention of Calixtus's bell. He made a quick trip to the card catalog and returned with notes to find books that mentioned Pope Calixtus's nephew, Rodrigo.

There was ample information on Rodrigo. Duane scribbled quickly, glad that he'd brought along several of his small notebooks.

The twenty-seven-year-old Cardinal Rodrigo Borgia had been the prime mover in the ensuing Conclave of 1458. Not even remotely a candidate for pope himself, the younger Borgia had cleverly brokered the election of the next pontiff by engineering support for Bishop Aeneas Silvius Piccolomini, who emerged from the conclave as Pope Pius II. Pius did not forget the young cardinal's help in his time of need, and the former Piccolomini made sure that the next few years were fruitful for young Rodrigo Borgia.

But no mention of a bell. Duane speed-read two books and skimmed a third before he found the next clue.

It was a history written by Piccolomini himself. Pope Pius II appeared to have been a born chronicler, more historian than theologian. His notes of the Conclave of 1458—notes forbidden by rules and tradition—showed in great detail how he had urged Rodrigo Borgia to support him and how important that support had been. Then, in a passage covering Palm Sunday of 1462, four years later, Pius described a magnificent procession given in honor of the arrival of the head of St. Andrew in Rome. Duane smiled at that; a celebration for the arrival of a head.

The passage was chatty enough:

> All the cardinals who lived along the route had decorated their houses magnificently . . . but all were outstripped in expense and effort and ingenuity by Rodrigo, the vice-chancellor. His

huge, towering house, which he had built on the site of the old mint, was covered with rich and wonderful tapestries, and besides this he had raised a lofty canopy from which were suspended many and various marvels. Above the canopy, framed by elaborate and decorative woodwork, hung the great bell commissioned by the vice-chancellor's brother, Our predecessor. Despite its newness, the bell was said to have been the talisman and source of power for the House of Borgia.

The procession stopped before the vice-chancellor's fortress, a place of sweet songs and sounds, or a great palace gleaming with gold such as they say Nero's palace was. Rodrigo had decorated not only his own house for Our celebration but also those nearby, so that the square all about them seemed a kind of park full of the most riotous celebration. We offered to bless Rodrigo's home and grounds and bell, but the vice-chancellor attested that the bell had been consecrated in its own way two years before when the palace had been built. Bemused, we moved on with Our priceless relic through the reverent and celebrating streets.

Duane shook his head, pushed his glasses higher, and smiled. The thought that this bell was sitting, forgotten, in the boarded-up belfry of Old Central was beyond belief.

He checked his notes, wandered the stacks, pulled several more books from the shelves, and returned to his study carrel.

There was more.

Camp Three was on a hillside a quarter of a mile northeast of the cemetery. The woods were thick there, branches coming to within four feet of the ground in many places, and the shrubbery made walking hard going except on the few trails cattle and hunters had cut through the thickets. Camp Three looked like just another solid thicket of shrubs from every angle: a ring of bushes with multiple trunks the thickness of a boy's wrist, a tangle of branches overhead almost joining with the canopy of leaves from the trees. But if one got on one's knees at just the right spot and crawled through the maze of brambles and stems at just the right angle, the entrance to a truly wonderful place appeared.

Dale and Lawrence arrived first, panting and looking over their shoulders, hearing the shouts from McKown and the others only a hundred yards behind them. They made sure no one was in sight, dropped to all fours on the grassy hillside, and crawled into Camp Three.

The interior was as solid and secure as some domed hut, eight feet across in an almost perfect circle, the wall of shrubs allowing a few peep-holes but providing complete invisibility from searching eyes outside. Some quirk of the slope settling—perhaps due to the stockadelike ring of shrubs itself—had provided an almost level floor of soil here where the rest of the hillside was rather steep. A low, soft grass grew within this ring, providing a surface as smooth as a putting green.

Dale once had lain in Camp Three during a solid summer rainstorm and had remained as dry as if he were home in his own room. One snowy winter he and Lawrence and Mike had postholed their way through the woods and found Camp Three after some effort—the shrubs and woods here looked quite different without their foliage—and had crawled in to find the interior almost free of snow, the surrounding stockade of wooden stems as concealing as ever.

Now he and his brother lay there gasping as silently as possible, lis-tening to the excited shouts of McKown and the others as they crashed their way through the woods.

"They went this way!" came Chuck Sperling's voice. He was on the old trail that ran within twenty feet of Camp Three.

Suddenly there was a rustling and snapping right outside, Dale and Lawrence raised the sticks they'd been carrying like spears, and Mike O'Rourke slid through the low tunnel opening. Mike's face was flushed, his blue eyes were bright, and he'd been scratched by a branch so that a thin line of blood marked his left temple. He was grinning widely.

"Where'd they . . ." began Lawrence.

Mike covered the smaller boy's mouth with his palm and shook his head. "Right outside," he whispered. All three boys threw themselves flat on the grass, their faces next to the stems of the shrubs.

"*Damn* it," came Digger Taylor's voice from less than five feet up-hill, "I *saw* O'Rourke come this way."

"Barry!" It was Chuck Sperling's voice screaming from just outside the thicket. "You see 'em down there?"

"Uh-uh," came the fat Fussner twin's shout. "Nobody came down the trail this way."

"Shit," said Digger. "I *saw* him. And those Stewart dipshits were running this way, too."

In Camp Three, Lawrence made a fist and started to stand. Dale pulled his brother down, even though one could stand in the circle and still not be seen. Dale motioned for silence, but had to grin at how red Lawrence's face was getting. That deep flush was a sure sign that his brother was ready to put his head down and charge somebody. Dale had seen it often enough.

"Maybe they went back up the hill towards the cemetery or doubled back to the strip-mined place." It was Gerry Daysinger's voice, not fifteen feet from the Camp.

"Hunt around here first," commanded Sperling in that snotty tone he used in Little League because his dad was the coach.

Mike, Dale, and Lawrence held their sticks like rifles as they listened to the crashing and thrashing along the hillside as the other kids literally beat the bushes, hunting behind fallen logs and smashing through shrubs. Somebody actually bashed a stick against the south side of Camp Three, but it was like hitting a solid wall. Unless one knew the zigs and zags on the east side, crawling through the final hole smaller than a sewer pipe, you'd never find your way in.

Or so the three boys in Camp Three fervently hoped.

Shouts came from far up the trail.

"They got Kev," Lawrence whispered. Dale nodded and hushed his brother again.

The sound of boots and sneakers receded up the trail. There were more shouts. Mike sat up and brushed grass and thistles off his striped polo shirt.

"You think Kev'll give us away?" asked Dale.

Mike grinned. "Not Camp Three. He might show 'em Camp Five or the Cave. But not Camp Three."

"They already know where Camp Five is from last summer," said Lawrence, finally whispering now that he no longer had to. "And we're not using the Cave."

Mike just grinned.

They sprawled there for another half hour, tired from the couple of hours of running through the hills and the postadrenaline letdown from the chase. They compared close calls, commiserated over Kevin's demise—he'd be a prisoner if he didn't "join them" to help in the chase—and dug stuff out of their pockets to eat. None had brought a pack of real rations, but Mike had stuffed an apple in the pocket of his jeans, Dale had an almond Hershey bar that had melted and been sat on repeatedly, and Lawrence had a Pez dispenser with some of the candies left. They ate their lunch with gusto and then lay staring at the tiny fragments of sunlight and sky visible through the almost solid roof of branches.

They were discussing leaving to set up a clod ambush near the quarry when Mike suddenly said, "Shhh!" He pointed uphill.

Dale lay on his stomach and put his face against the stalks of the shrubs, trying to find one of the few angles that would give him a view of the trail.

There were boots out there. A man's boots, brown and large. For a second Dale thought that the guy was wearing muddy bandages and then he realized that those were the leggings that Duane had said soldiers used to wear. What had Duane called those things? *Puttees.* There was some guy standing six feet from Camp Three, wearing clunky boots and puttees. Dale could just see a hint of brown wool pantleg blousing out above the bandagelike wrappings.

"What . . ." whispered Lawrence, straining to see.

Dale turned and put his hand over his brother's mouth. Lawrence struggled free and punched him, but stayed silent for a change.

When Dale looked back the boots were gone. Mike tapped him on the shoulder and jerked his head toward the east wall of the circle.

Footsteps crunched leaves and twigs right outside the secret entrance.

Duane was finding out more about the Borgias than he really wanted to know.

He was skimming and speed-reading in the way he often did when trying to cram an inordinate amount of information into his brain in the shortest possible time. It was a strange sensation; Duane compared it to the effect when one of his home-built crystal radio sets was poorly tuned, pulling in several stations at once. This kind of speed-learning tired Duane out and made him a bit dizzy, but he had little choice. Uncle Art wasn't going to spend all day here in the library.

The first thing Duane learned was that almost everything he knew about the Borgias from "common knowledge" was wrong or badly distorted. He paused a minute, chewing on the stem of his glasses and looking at nothing, recognizing that this initial fact of the unreliability of general knowledge had been consistent with most of the serious learning he'd done on his own over the past few years. Nothing was as simple as stupid people assumed it to be. Duane wondered if this was a basic law of the universe. If so, it made him tired to think of all the years ahead of him trying to unlearn before he could begin learning. He looked around at the basement stacks, thousands of books upon thousands of books, and felt dispirited that he would never read even all these books . . . never encounter all the conflicting opinions, facts, and viewpoints just in this basement. . . . much less everything in the libraries of Princeton, Yale, Harvard, and all the other schools he wanted to visit and absorb.

Duane shook himself out of it, pushed his glasses into place, and reviewed the notes he'd taken.

First, Lucrezia Borgia seemed to be more a victim of bad press than the guilty party in all the legends he'd been aware of: no poison ring wiping out lovers and dinner guests, no banquets with bodies stacked like

cordwood by the time dessert was served. No, Lucrezia came across as
the victim of spiteful historians. Duane looked at some of the volumes
stacked on his study table: Guicciardini's *History of Italy*, Machiavelli's
The Prince and his *Discourses* and extracts from *The History of Florence
and the Affairs of Italy*, Piccolomini/Pius's chatty *Commentaries*, Gregoro-
vius's volume on Lucrezia, Burchard's *Liber Notarum* with its notes on
the day-to-day trivia of the papal court during the period.

But nothing more about the bell.

Then, on a hunch, Duane checked original sources on Benvenuto
Cellini, one of the Old Man's favorite historical personages, even though
Duane knew that the feisty artist had been born in 1500, eight years af-
ter Rodrigo Borgia became Pope Alexander VI.

At one point, Cellini wrote about his imprisonment in Castel Sant'
Angelo, the huge, hulking mass of stone Hadrian had built as a family
tomb fourteen hundred years earlier. Pope Alexander—Rodrigo Borgia—
had ordered the immense sepulcher fortified and modified as a place of
residence. Rooms and shafts in stone which had known only corpses,
darkness, and decay for well over a thousand years had become the home
and fortress of the Borgia pope.

Cellini *had* written about it:

> I was imprisoned in a gloomy dungeon below the level of a
> garden which swam with water and was full of spiders and
> venomous worms. They flung me a wretched mattress of
> coarse hemp, gave me no supper and locked four doors upon
> me. . . . For one hour and a half each day I got a little glim-
> mering of light which penetrated that unhappy cavern
> through a very narrow aperture. The rest of the day and
> night I abode in darkness. And this was one of the less terrible
> of cells. From my fellow unfortunates, I learned of the doomed
> souls who spent their last days in the foulest of Pits, those
> deeper dungeons set at the bottom of the airshaft to the in-
> famous Bell of the evil Borgia Pope. The word was spread
> throughout Rome and the provinces that this bell had been
> cast of unholy metal, consecrated with foul deeds, and hung
> even now as a manifest sign of the pact between the former
> pope and the Devil himself. Each of us in our cells, crouch-
> ing in rancid water and eating our foul scraps, knew that the
> tolling of that bell would announce the end of the world.
> There were, I confess, times that I would have welcomed that
> knell.

Duane scribbled notes. Curiouser and curiouser. There was no later mention of the bell in Cellini's autobiography or notes, but an earlier passage about the artist Pinturicchio—evidently a contemporary of the Borgia pope rather than Cellini himself—seemed relevant:

On the command and behest of his Pope . . .

Duane checked to make sure that this was Alexander, aka Rodrigo Borgia. It was.

On the command and behest of his Pope, this deaf and under-sized little artist . . .

Duane skimmed to make sure Cellini was talking about Pinturicchio, Borgia's artist. He was.

. . . mean in person and appearance as he was, set about painting the murals which filled the Torre Borgia with such bizarre effect, culminating in the Room of the Seven Mysteries in the dismal Borgia Apartments.

Duane called time-out from Cellini's passage to crosscheck the Torre Borgia. A guide to Vatican structures said that it was the massive tower Pope Alexander VI had ordered added on to the Vatican palace. A previous addition by Pope Sixtus had been a dark and drafty warehouse called the Sistine Chapel. Pope Innocent had opted for a lovely summer house in the far reaches of the Vatican gardens. Borgia built a tower. A note in an 1886 architectural tome mentioned that the Borgia Torre had been designed with a massive belfry at the apex of the columnar fortress, but no one other than the Pope and his illegitimate children were allowed to ascend that high in the tower through the maze of locked doors and passages.

Duane returned to Cellini's notes:

Pinturicchio, upon his Pontiff's command, descended into the Dead City beneath the City for his inspiration and models for the Borgia Apartment murals. There lay not the Christian Catacombs with their sanctified bones, but the random excavations of Heathen Rome in all its decayed glory.

It was said that Pinturicchio led apprentices and curious colleagues on these subterranean expeditions: imagine then the torchlight through these tunnels filled with the rubble of the Caesars, entry into chambers, corridors, entire dwellings, entire streets of the Roman dead, lying like forgotten arteries beneath the weed-choked lanes of our living but lessened city . . . imagine the exclamations when Pinturicchio, after braving the giant rats and hordes of bats which fed on offal and darkness there, raised his torch to illuminate the pagan decorations set there by men dead fifteen centuries and more.

This little man and ungodly artist brought these designs and heathen images to the apartments of the Borgia Pope in his Tower. Within the most private of the Corrupt Pope's secret chambers, these pagan images prevailed—covering walls, arches, ceilings, and even the massive iron bell which was said to be the Borgia talisman high in the Torre.

To this day, the lost paintings are called, by the ignorant, grotesques, because they were found and copied from the unholy subterranean caverns, or grotte, in the darkness beneath Rome.

Uncle Art leaned over Duane's shoulder and said, "Ready to go yet?" The boy jumped, reset his glasses on his nose, and managed a smile.
"Just about."
While Uncle Art wandered restlessly in the nearby stacks, Duane flipped through the final volumes. He found only one more mention of the bell, and again it related to the art of the wizened muralist named Pinturicchio:

But in the chamber which led from the Room of the Seven Mysteries to the locked staircase ascending to the belltower where only the Borgias might tread, the painter had reproduced the essence of those buried and forgotten murals which he had studied by the light of torches while water dripped from broken stone. Here, in what later would be called the Room of the Saints because of the seven great murals there, Pinturicchio had fulfilled his commission by filling every space between the paintings, every arch, nook, and column, with hundreds—some experts say thousands—of images of bulls.

The mystery is not that bulls should appear in his work or this hidden place; the bull was the emblem of the Borgia family; the benevolent ox had long been the metaphor for the papal procession.

But these bulls, as repeated almost endlessly in the dark hallways and grottos and entrance to the forbidden stairway above the Room of the Seven Mysteries, were neither of these emblems.

These were not the noble Borgia symbol, nor the peaceful ox. Reproduced countless times in these apartments was the stylized but unmistakable figure of the sacrificial bull of Osiris, the Egyptian god who ruled over the kingdom of the dead.

Duane closed the book and took off his glasses.

"Ready yet?" asked Uncle Art.

Duane nodded.

"Let's try that McDonald's drive-in place on War Memorial Drive," said his uncle. "Their hamburgers have gone up to a quarter, but they're pretty good."

Duane nodded, still thinking, and followed Uncle Art out of the basement and into the light.

The footsteps outside of Camp Three had stopped. Not receded, not gone away, merely . . . stopped. Mike, Dale, and Lawrence crouched by the low entrance and waited, barely breathing in their effort not to make noise. The sounds of the woods were quite distinct: a squirrel scolding someone or something far up the hill toward Dale's Uncle Henry's property; an occasional shout from Chuck Sperling's gang, farther away now, probably south of the quarry; the screech of crows in the treetops up the other hill toward Calvary Cemetery. But no sound from where the unseen soldier waited just outside the ring of bushes.

Dale slithered back to his previous vantage point, but there was nothing in view.

Suddenly there came a flurry of noise outside, footsteps pounding on the trail. Leaves rustled and the bushes on the east side of Camp Three shook as someone began forcing his way through the convoluted opening. Dale jumped back to one side of the gap and raised his stick. Mike did the same on the other side of the opening. Lawrence crouched with his club ready.

Branches bent upward, leaves shook, and Kevin Grumbacher crawled into the grassy circle.

Dale and Mike looked at each other, lowered their sticks, and let out a breath.

Kevin grinned at them. "What were you going to do, brain me?"

"We thought you were *them*," said Lawrence, lowering his stick with an expression of regret. Lawrence *liked* scuffles.

Dale blinked and then realized that the others hadn't seen the man's boots with the puttees. Mike and Lawrence probably thought that the noise out there had been Sperling's bunch.

"You alone?" asked Mike, crouching to check in the tunnel of branches.

"Sure I'm alone. I wouldn't come back here unless I was alone."

Lawrence scowled at the older boy. "You didn't tell them about the Camp, did you?"

Kevin gave Dale's brother a disgusted look and spoke to Mike. "They said I could be on their side if I told where the hiding places were. I wouldn't. So that dipstick Fussner tied my arms behind my back with some clothesline and they dragged me around with them like I was a slave or something." Kev held out his arms to show the red welts on his wrists and upper arms.

"How'd you get away?" asked Dale.

Kevin grinned again, his large teeth, bristly crew cut, and bobbing Adam's apple giving an amusing picture of self-satisfaction. "When they started chasing you guys this way, Fussner couldn't keep up while dragging me along. The dope tied me to a tree and ran up the trail to see which way they'd gone. I still had my fingers free so I just backed up to the tree and untied the rope."

"Stay here," whispered Mike and slipped through the opening without touching a branch. The other three sat in silence for several minutes, Kev rubbing his wrists, Lawrence eating some Milk Duds he'd brought along. Dale waited for a shout, a scuffle . . . some signs of the guy he'd seen through the bushes.

Mike slipped back in. "They're gone from around here. I heard their voices way out by County Six. It sounds like Sperling and Digger are going home."

"Yeah," said Kevin. "They were getting bored. Said they had better things to do at home. Daysinger wanted them to stay. The Fussners wanted to stick with Sperling."

Mike nodded. "Daysinger and McKown will hang around, wait for us to come out so they can ambush us." He used his stick to draw a map on a patch of bare soil near the entrance. "If I know Gerry, he'll head back to the quarry where there are lots of clods so he can see us if we head back that way from Dale's uncle's pasture or the woods and Gypsy Lane down here. He and Bob will probably hide out in the high ground here. . . ." He had scribbled in the paths, the quarry ponds, and now drew a mound on the west side of the gravel pits. "There's that sort of low place on the top of the biggest hill, remember?"

"We camped there a couple of summers ago," said Dale.

Lawrence shook his head. "I don't remember that."

Dale poked him. "You were too little to go with us on an overnight." He looked back at Mike. "Go on."

Mike poked lines in the dirt, showing a path from Camp Three, over the hill, across the woods and pasture behind the cemetery, and up the back of the gravel-pit mountain where he figured Daysinger and McKown would be waiting. "They'll be looking these three directions," he said, drawing arrows south, east, and west. "But if we use those pine trees on the south slope for cover, we'll be able to climb right up on 'em without them seeing us."

Kevin frowned at the map. "The last fifty feet or so will be in the open. That hilltop's just dirt up there."

"Right," said Mike, still grinning. "We have to be extra quiet. But remember, the gaps in their little fort up there look the other way. As long as we don't make noise, we'll be up above them and behind them before they know we're anywhere near."

Dale felt his excitement growing. "And we can pick up clods as we climb. There'll be plenty of ammunition."

Kevin was still frowning. "If they catch us in the open, we're dead. I mean, they've been throwing *rocks*."

"If it comes to that," said Mike, "we can throw rocks, too." He looked at them. "Who's for it?"

"I am!" Lawrence's vote was almost a shout. His face was bright with anticipation.

"Yeah," said Dale, still studying the map and thinking about how Mike had come up with this complicated plan with almost no hesitation. Every foot of the route he'd drawn between Camp Three and the dirt hill used maximum concealment. Dale had hiked these woods for years, but he wouldn't have thought to use the low ditch across the field behind the cemetery for cover. "Yeah," he said again. "Let's do it."

Kevin shrugged. "As long as they don't take me prisoner again."

Mike grinned at them, made a fist, and ducked down through the opening. The others followed as quietly as they could.

"You seem preoccupied, kiddo," Uncle Art said on the way home. They were just descending into the Spoon River valley. The sky was cloudless and the June heat seemed to have intensified after they had spent so many hours in the air-conditioned, dehumidified library. Uncle Art had the windows down with the air rushing in, even though the Caddy's air conditioner was rambling at the same time. He glanced over at Duane. "Anything I could help with?"

Duane hesitated. It didn't seem right telling Uncle Art somehow. But why not? All he was doing was trying to find some background information on Old Central. They hummed over the Spoon River bridge. Duane glanced at the dark water below, winding away to the north under overhanging branches, and then looked back at his uncle. *Why not?*

Duane told him about the newspaper articles. About the Borgia Bell. About the Cellini stuff he'd found in the library. When he was finished, he felt oddly tired and embarrassed, almost as if he'd exposed something shameful about himself. But he felt relieved at the same time.

Uncle Art whistled and said nothing for a moment, tapping his fingers on the steering wheel. His blue eyes seemed to be focused on something other than the Hard Road. They reached the dirt road running north to County Six and Uncle Art turned right, slowing so the Cadillac didn't throw stones against the undercarriage or bump too fiercely on the ruts. "Do you think that bell could still be there?" he asked at last. "Still be in the school?"

Duane adjusted his glasses. "I don't know. I've never heard of it, have you?"

Uncle Art shook his head. "Not in the years I've lived around here. Of course, that's just been since just after the war. It was your momma's people who had roots here. All the same, I would've heard *something* if such a bell were general knowledge." They reached the junction of County Six and Jubilee College Road and Uncle Art paused. His home was three miles east on the gravel Jubilee College Road, but he had to bring Duane home. Ahead and to their left, the Black Tree Tavern was just visible under the elms and oaks. A few pickups were there already, although it was just early afternoon. Duane looked away before he could tell if the Old Man's truck was among them.

"I'll tell you what, kiddo," said Uncle Art. "I'll ask around about the bell in town . . . check with some of the other old farts I know . . . and I'll look in my library to see if there's anything on the legend of the damned thing. OK?"

Duane brightened up. "You think you might have something on it?"

Uncle Art shrugged. "The thing sounds like it's more myth than metal. I've always had an interest in the supernatural stuff—I like to debunk it. So I'll check my reference books, Crowley, stuff like that. Fair enough?"

"Great!" said Duane. It was like a weight off his shoulders.

He glanced before they descended the first hill. The Old Man's truck wasn't at the Black Tree! It might be a good day after all. Past the cemetery and Duane caught a glimpse of a stack of bikes near the fence at the rear: it might be Dale and those guys and if he got out now, he might find them in the woods. Duane shook his head. He'd taken enough time out of his chores.

The Old Man was home and sober and working in their vegetable garden that took up three-quarters of an acre. His face was sunburned and his hands looked blistered, but he was in a good mood and Uncle Art stayed for a beer while Duane sipped an RC Cola and listened to the banter. Uncle Art didn't mention the bell.

After his uncle left, Duane rolled up the sleeves of his flannel shirt and went out to weed and hoe and work the rows with the Old Man. They worked in companionable silence for an hour or two and then went in to wash up for supper, the Old Man wandering in to tinker with one of his new machines while Duane cooked the hamburger and rice and boiled the coffee.

They talked about politics during supper, the Old Man describing his work for Adlai Stevenson in the previous elections. "I don't know about Kennedy," he said. "He's sure to get the nomination, but I've never trusted millionaires. It'd be good if a Catholic got elected, though. Break down some of the discrimination in the country." He told Duane about Alfred E. Smith's unsuccessful 1928 campaign.

Duane had read about it, but he listened and nodded, happy just to be listening to the Old Man when he was sober and not angry at somebody.

"So the chances of a Catholic getting elected are pretty slim," the Old Man concluded. He sat a moment, nodded as if concluding that there were no weaknesses in his analysis, and stood to clear the table, rinsing the dishes under the tap and setting them aside for washing.

Duane glanced outside. It was after five, still early, but the shade of the poplar behind the house was moving across the window. He asked the question he'd been dreading all afternoon, trying to keep his voice light and casual. "You going out tonight?"

The Old Man paused in the act of filling the sink. The steam had fogged his glasses. He took them off and wiped them on a shirttail, as if contemplating the question. "Guess not," he said at last. "I've got some things to do in the workroom and I thought we might finish that game of chess we've let gather dust."

Duane nodded. "I'd better get to my chores," he said, finishing his coffee and setting the cup on the counter. He was out in the barn, feed bucket in his hand, before he allowed himself to smile.

The surprise attack was a complete success.

Although the last thirty feet or so had been pretty hairy—crawling up the dirt slope on their bellies with absolutely no cover if McKown or Day-singer looked over their ramparts—Mike and Kev and Lawrence and Dale had made it, despite a muffled case of nervous giggles on Lawrence's part, and when they came over the top, they caught Gerry and Bob staring the other way with the ammo dump of dirt clods piled six feet behind them.

Mike threw first and caught Bob McKown in the back, just above the beltline. Then the six boys were in close combat, pelting each other with clods, trying to shield their faces while throwing, then grappling and wrestling around the lip of the cone-shaped hill. Kevin and Daysinger and Dale had tumbled over first, sliding down thirty feet of crumbling slope. Kevin got up first and ran for the ramparts and the ammo, but McKown pelted him with clods until Mike tackled the shorter boy from behind and it was their turn to roll down the slope in a cloud of dust.

For fifteen minutes or so it was King of the Hill, with the holders of the high ground being wrestled down the hill and then scrambling to reclaim it, usually in a hail of clods. After being deposed, Daysinger and McKown retreated to the edge of the quarry pond, throwing from long distance, but the King of the Hill fever caused internecine warfare to break out among Mike's troop, and pretty soon it was every man for himself.

Dale took a clod hit in the solar plexus that had him sitting and gasping for three minutes, the action whirling obliviously around him. Then Mike hit a half-buried rock during a tumble down the slope and cut his brow; the cut wasn't deep, but the amount of blood was impressive. Daysinger poked his head over the summit just long enough to catch a clod in the mouth at short range. He retreated, cursing loudly, to the bottom of the hill and walked around with both hands over his mouth for a minute or two until he was sure he hadn't lost any teeth. Then he brushed dirt off his cut lower lip and charged again, his chin mottled with mud and blood. Kevin was right behind his former leader when Mike wound up to throw a clod, and Kev got a fist right in the forehead. Action paused for a moment as the other boys on the summit watched curiously, but Grumbacher used the event to comic effect as he crossed his eyes, staggered in ever-smaller circles until his legs buckled, and slid backwards down the slope, legs as stiff as a corpse's. The other kids laughed and applauded by pelting him with clods.

It was Lawrence who refined the game to its essence.

For one blazing, ascendant minute, he was the only one on the summit as the wrestling clumps of older boys all found themselves deposed. Lawrence stood on the mounded rampart, held his arms high over his head, and shouted, "I'm King!"

There was a moment of respectful silence followed by three salvos of clods. At least six or seven hit home. Lawrence had turned his face away at the last second, but his grimy clothes actually puffed dust as he was hit, the impact stitching across his back and legs like machine-gun rounds, knocking the eight-year-old's baseball cap flying.

"Hey!" shouted Dale, waving the others to a cease-fire. Lawrence was frozen in the posture he'd been hit in, and Dale knew that if he started crying he was *really* hurt.

Lawrence pirouetted slowly, gracefully, dust still rising on him and around him from the impact of clods, and then he fell forward.

Actually he didn't *fall* forward; he threw himself into the air with the dying-swan grace of a cowboy stuntman, completed a full loop in the air before hitting the slope, and then jackknifed upward again in another dying tumble. His limbs were flung wide, boneless, limp with death. The other kids stepped back as the flying, tumbling body bounced by them, rolled out onto the flat by the edge of the pond, and came to a stop with one arm draped over the water.

"Wow," said Kevin. The others shouted their approval.

Lawrence got up, brushed dust from his clothes and crew cut, and gave a low bow.

From that point on and for the next couple of hours, as afternoon softened into evening in the woods, the boys died. They took turns standing on the summit while the others threw clods. After being hit, the dying commenced.

Kevin's was undeniably comic, if stiffly so. He was like a geriatric actor who had to lie down after being shot. Usually he held his cap in place as he slid down. Daysinger and McKown were the best screamers, tumbling to their doom with a maximum of groans, shouts, and grunts. Mike was oddly graceful as he fell, and held the pose the longest at the bottom. Even a second flurry of clods couldn't make him stir until he wanted to. Dale won approval by performing the first facefirst death dive, losing skin off his nose as he plowed a path with his head down the steep slope.

But it was Lawrence who retained the crown. His final *coup de grâce* consisted of staggering backwards out of sight for half a minute—the other five began grumbling, wondering where the brat was—until suddenly he came over the summit not running, but leaping at full speed. Dale actually gasped, feeling his heart leap into his throat as his little brother jumped straight out into space thirty feet above him. His first thought was, *Jesus, he's gonna die.* His immediate second thought was, *Mom's going to kill me.*

Lawrence didn't die. Not quite. The leap was wild and strong and far enough to carry him into the quarry pond—he missed the hard-packed ledge by three inches—and the resulting splash threw water on McKown and Kevin.

This end of the pond was the shallowest—barely five feet at this point—and Dale had images of his kid brother drowning with his pointy little head stuck in the mud at the bottom. Dale tugged off his t-shirt with some thought of leaping in to save him, part of his mind already gagging at the thought of giving mouth-to-mouth resuscitation to the little creep, when Lawrence bobbed to the surface, showing his overbite in a wide grin.

This time the applause was real.

Everyone had to try what Kev called The Death Leap. When Dale executed it he did so after three false starts and only because there was no turning back with the others watching from below. The pond was *so far away*. Even with a sixth grader's long legs, it took a hell of a fast run up the back slope and across the summit and just the right push off the rampart to have a chance of clearing the hard bank below. Dale would never have tried it—none of the other older kids would have—if they hadn't seen it was possible. Dale found a grudging admiration for his kid brother growing in the back of his mind even as he surprised himself by actually leaping on the fourth try.

For a few seconds Dale Stewart was flying, seeming to hover twenty-five feet above his friends' heads, still even with the summit of their little mountain, the pond an impossible distance away across muddy flats baked brick-hard by the sun. Then gravity remembered him and he was falling, arms and legs flailing as if he were trying to pedal air . . . sure that he would make it. . . . then absolutely positive that he would *not* make it . . . and then he had made it, by inches, and the green and tepid water of the quarry pond was around him and over him and filling his nose; he used bent legs to push himself off the weedy bottom, and then he was in air and light again, screaming from sheer exhilaration while the other kids shouted and applauded.

Kevin was the last to go—keeping the others waiting for ten minutes while he hemmed and hawed and tested the wind, tied his laces over and over, and built up the ramp a bit before finally shooting off the summit like a cannonball, his jump the farthest of them all, hitting the water four feet from the bank with his legs together and his fingers clamped over his nostrils. Kev had been the only one with sense enough to take off his jeans and t-shirt, wearing only his Jockey shorts and tennis shoes for the plunge.

He bobbed to the surface grinning. The others applauded and shouted and tossed his jeans and shirt and socks into the pond. Kevin emerged grumbling in German and barely watched as Lawrence made his sixth leap, doing a full somersault this time before hitting the water.

Already wet, the kids hiked around the quarry on squishy tennis shoes and went swimming in earnest, diving into the deeper side of the pond from the eight-foot cliffs there. This wasn't their usual swimming area—the presence of too many water moccasins and parental concerns about the "bottomless quarry" usually made them wait for someone to drive them to Hartley's Pond up Oak Hill Road—so the early-evening dip was just that much more delicious.

Afterward, they dried out on the bank for an hour or so—Dale actually dozing off and waking with a start—and then they shuffled teams to play hide-and-seek in the woods again. Mike smiled at the pack of kids with their clothes dried into strange wrinkles. "Who's with me?"

It turned out Lawrence and McKown were with him. Dale and Gerry and Kev gave them a five-minute head start—timed by counting to three-hundred Boy Scout—before heading into the woods to find them. Dale knew by silent assent that Mike or Lawrence wouldn't use one of their secret camps.

They chased each other through the trees and pastures for another hour and a half or so, changing teams as the mood suited them, pausing to drink from the water bottle McKown had brought along and refilled from the pond—although the greenish color didn't appeal to Kevin—and ending by just hiking together, wandering back on the south side of the quarry on the first half mile of Gypsy Lane.

Their bikes were where they'd left them by the back fence. The sun was a bulbous red orb hanging just above Old Man Johnson's cornfields to the west. The air was thick with evening haze, pollen, dust, and humidity, but somehow the sky looked endless and translucent as the blue prepared to deepen toward twilight.

"Last one past the Black Tree's a homo," said Gerry Daysinger and got a head start, pedaling on the hard-packed rut of the gravel road as it dipped into the shaded dimness at the bottom of the hill.

The others shouted and tried to catch up, roaring down the hill and through the darkness there at high speed, feeling the cooler air above the creek as it whipped through their crew cuts, then standing and pedaling hard to get up the slope. If a car had come over the rise by the Black Tree Tavern, the boys would have had to steer into the deeper gravel outside the ruts, making skinned knees and torn clothing a near certainty. They didn't care. They drove hard, their shouts dying as they saved their breath for the final twenty yards, all of them panting and gasping as they reached the flat near the tavern driveway.

Mike won. He glanced back and grinned before he put his head down and continued the race toward Jubilee College Road several hundred yards ahead.

They relaxed as they turned west toward Elm Haven, the six riding abreast in two groups of three, Lawrence being the first to take his hands off the handlebars and lean back with arms folded, still pedaling. Then all six of them rode with arms folded, gliding along between the rising walls of corn.

Dale didn't even glance sideways as he passed the place where the fence had been repaired after Duane McBride's near-accident. Wheel tracks still tore up the ditch there and the corn was smashed for yards beyond the fence, but Dale didn't look—he was looking west toward where the sun now crowned the low line of trees that was Elm Haven.

Dale was tired, achey from about a dozen bruises and strained muscles, scratched on his arms and legs, itchy from his now-stiff jeans, dehydrated to the point of cracked lips and a headache, and starved because he hadn't eaten any real food since breakfast thirteen hours earlier. He felt wonderful.

The whole sense of bad dreams, and encroaching darkness he'd felt since school had let out, had seemed to lift today. The terror of C.J. and the rifle had faded. Dale was glad that he and Mike and the others had silently decided to drop all this Tubby and Old Central business.

Summer felt the way it should.

The six kids grabbed the handlebars as they came off the gravel onto the cooling but still-soft asphalt at the head of First Avenue. Dale could see the trees in front of Mike's house at the intersection way down the road, could glimpse the back of his own house across the wide fields and ballfield of City Park.

McKown and Daysinger waved and pedaled ahead, eager to get to wherever they were going. Dale and Kev and Mike and Lawrence coasted the last fifty yards to the relative darkness under the first of Elm Haven's tall old trees.

Dale felt happy as they waved good-bye to Mike and pedaled easily down Depot Street for home. This was the way summer should be. This was the way it was *going* to be.

Dale had never been so wrong.

FOURTEEN

Duane's Old Man was sober for the rest of the week. It wasn't exactly a record, but it made Duane's first full week of summer vacation a lot happier.

On Thursday, the ninth of June and the day after the trip to Bradley U's library, Uncle Art had called and left the message that he was hunting for Duane's bell, don't worry, he'd find out something about it. Later that evening he called back and spoke to Duane in person, telling him that he'd called Elm Haven's mayor—Ross Catton—but neither the mayor nor anyone else Art had contacted remembered anything about a bell. He'd even asked Miss Moon, the librarian, who'd asked her mother and then called back. Miss Moon said that her mother would only shake her head no, but had grown very agitated at the question. Of course, she added, a lot of things made her mother agitated these days.

That same evening, the Old Man came home from a run into the A&P—Duane had been holding his breath to see if the A&P was the real destination—but the Old Man came in sober, and while they were storing the flour and canned goods, he said, "Oh, I heard from Mrs. O'Rourke that one of your classmates got arrested yesterday."

Duane stopped in mid-motion, a heavy can of lima beans in his right hand. With his free hand he pushed his glasses up. "Oh?"

The Old Man nodded, licking his lips and scratching at his cheek the way he tended to do when he was sober and hurting a bit. "Yes, someone named Cordie. Mrs. O'Rourke said that she was a year ahead of her son Mike." He looked up at Duane. "That puts her in your class, right?"

Duane nodded.

"Anyway," continued the Old Man, "she wasn't exactly arrested. Barney caught her walking around town with a loaded shotgun. He took it away from her and brought her home. She wouldn't say what she was doing except it had something to do with her brother Tubby." He scratched his cheek and seemed surprised to find that he'd shaved that day. "Isn't Tubby the kid who ran away a couple of weeks ago?"

"Yeah." Duane resumed unloading the box of canned goods.

"Have any idea why his sister's stalking around town with a shotgun?"

166

Duane paused again. "Who was she stalking?"

The Old Man shrugged. "Nellie O'Rourke said that the principal . . . whatshisname . . . Mr. Roon called Barney with a complaint. Said that the little girl was hanging around the school and outside his rented room with a gun. Now why would a kid do that?"

Duane nodded. Realizing that the Old Man was curious and obviously determined to stand there staring until he heard *some* comment from his son, Duane finished setting the cans on the cupboard shelves, turned from where he was standing on a chair near the counter, and said, "Cordie's all right, but she's a little crazy."

The Old Man stood there a minute, nodded as if accepting the answer, and went into his workroom.

On Friday, Duane hiked back to Oak Hill, leaving right at sunrise so that he could get home by midmorning. He wanted to check the books and newspapers there against the notes he'd taken at Bradley, but there was nothing new. *The New York Times* article about the 1876 party for the bell was interesting . . . external proof that the thing really existed outside of Elm Haven . . . but he couldn't find any other references to it. He tried getting the Ashley-Montagues' phone number from the librarian there, saying that he couldn't finish his school paper without seeing the Historical Society books that had been willed to the family, but Mrs. Frazier said that she had no idea of what their number was—rich families were always unlisted, which Duane had found out was the truth at least with *this* rich family—and then she took a playful swat at Duane's head and said, "It's not healthy to be doing school things in the summer anyway. Now go on with you, get out in the sunlight, get into something cooler and go play. Honestly, your mother should still be dressing you . . . imagine, with the temperature in the nineties today."

"Yes, ma'am," Duane had said, and adjusted his glasses and left. He was home in time to help the Old Man load four of the pigs and take them over to the Oak Hill market. Duane sighed as he watched the landscape of his four-hour hike repeated in ten minutes of driving. Next time, he'd check out the Old Man's schedule before heading off on foot.

On Saturday, the second Free Show of the summer featured *Hercules,* an older movie that Mr. Ashley-Montague obviously had held over from one of the three-feature Peoria drive-in bills. Duane rarely went to the Free Show for the same reason he and the Old Man owned a television set but never turned it on—primarily because they found books and radio shows more pleasing to the imagination than movies and TV shows.

But Duane liked Italian muscleman movies. There was something about the dubbing that he loved: the actors' mouths moving like mad for two minutes and then a few syllables coming from the soundtrack. Also, Duane had read somewhere that one old guy in a Rome studio did all of the sound effects for these films—footsteps, sword fights, horses' hooves, volcanoes erupting, *everything*—and that idea delighted him.

But that wasn't the reason he found himself walking into town on Saturday evening. Duane wanted to talk to Mr. Ashley-Montague, and this was the only place he knew he could catch him.

Duane would have asked his father for a ride, but the Old Man had started tinkering with one of his learning machines after dinner, and Duane didn't want to tempt the Fates by suggesting a ride into town past Carl's Tavern.

The Old Man didn't glance up from his soldering when Duane told him where he was going. "Fine," he said, his face obscured by the wraiths of smoke rising from the circuit board, "but don't be walking home after dark."

"OK," said Duane, wondering how the Old Man thought he *was* going to get home.

It turned out he didn't have to walk the entire way. He'd just passed Dale Stewart's Uncle Henry's house when a pickup pulled out of the drive carrying both Uncle Henry and Aunt Lena.

"Where you goin', boy?" Uncle Henry knew Duane's name but called every male under forty "boy."

"Into town, sir."

"Goin' to the Free Show?"

"Yessir."

"Hop in, boy."

Aunt Lena held open the door of the old International truck while Duane clambered in. It was a tight fit.

"I'll be happy to ride in back," offered Duane, aware that he was taking up half of the upholstered bench.

"Nonsense," said Uncle Henry. "Makes it cozier. Hang on!" The truck began the roller-coaster dip of the first hill, rattling through the darkness at the bottom and climbing toward the summit of the Calvary Cemetery hill.

"Stay to the right, Henry," said Aunt Lena. Duane imagined that the old lady said that every time they had come this way—which is every time that they went to town or almost anywhere else—and how many times would that be over sixty years? A million?

Uncle Henry nodded attentively and stayed right where he was, in the middle of the road. He wasn't going to relinquish the ruts to anybody. It was lighter up here, although the sun had set twenty minutes earlier. The truck rattled more loudly on the washboard ruts near the top and then roared into the darkness below the trees above Corpse Creek. Fireflies blinked against the blackness of the woods on either side. The weeds along the roadside were covered with a day's worth of dust and looked like some sort of albino mutations. Duane was glad that somebody had offered him a ride.

Heading toward the water tower, Duane glanced sideways at Henry and Lena Nyquist. They were in their mid-seventies—Duane knew that they were really Dale's great-uncle and aunt, related on Dale's mother's side—but *everyone* in Creve Coeur County called them Uncle Henry and Aunt Lena. They were an attractive couple, carrying as they did that Scandinavian dispensation from the worst of the ravaging effects of old age. Aunt Lena's hair was white, but full and long, and her face held a certain rosy-cheeked firmness amidst the wrinkles. Her eyes were very bright. Uncle Henry had lost some of his hair, but a shock still hung down over his forehead and added to an expression that could only be described as that of a mischievous boy who suspects that he might soon be caught by the authorities. Duane knew from his father that Uncle Henry was an old-style gentleman who, nonetheless, liked to swap bawdy stories over a beer.

"Isn't that there where you almost got run over?" said Uncle Henry, gesturing toward a patch of field where the scars were still visible.

"Yessir," said Duane.

"Keep both hands on the wheel, Henry," said Aunt Lena.

"They caught the fellow who done it?"

Duane took a breath. "No, sir."

Uncle Henry snorted. "I'd lay five to one odds that it was that no-good Karl Van Syke. Son of a . . ." The old man caught his wife's admonitory glance. "Son of a gun never was worth hiring for *anything*, much less as school custodian and caretaker out to the cemetery. Why, we can see over there through the winter and much of the spring, and that . . . that fellow Van Syke isn't *never* there. The place would go to weed and ruin if it wasn't for the helpers who come out from St. Malachy's every month."

Duane nodded, not wanting to say anything.

"Hush, Henry," Aunt Lena said softly. "Young Duane doesn't want to hear your blather about Mr. Van Syke." She turned toward Duane and touched his cheek with her rough, wrinkled hand. "We were sorry to hear about your dog, Duane. I remember helping your daddy choose him from 'Vira Whittaker's dog's litter before you were born. The puppy was a gift for your mother."

Duane nodded and looked away toward the city ballpark passing on their right, studying it earnestly, as if he had never seen it before.

Main Street was crowded. Cars were already slanting in on the diagonal parking, families moving toward Bandstand Park with their hampers and blankets. A group of men sat on the high curb outside of Carl's, holding bottles of Pabst in their reddened hands and talking loudly. Uncle Henry had to park all the way down by the A&P because of the crowd. The old man grumbled that he hated sitting on the folding chairs they'd brought along; he preferred staying in the truck and pretending it was a drive-in.

Duane thanked them and hurried toward the park. It was already too late to get much time alone with Mr. Ashley-Montague before the movie started, but he wanted to catch him for at least a minute.

Dale and Lawrence hadn't planned on going to the Free Show, but their father was home—he'd taken the Saturday off, which was a rarity—*Gunsmoke* and all the evening shows were reruns, and both parents wanted to go to the movies. They brought a blanket and a big bag of popcorn and walked downtown through the soft twilight. Dale noticed a few bats flitting above the trees, but they were only bats; the previous week's fright seemed a bad and distant dream.

There was a larger than usual crowd at the show. The grassy areas east of the bandstand and right in front of the screen were almost filled with blankets, so Lawrence ran ahead to claim a place near an old oak. Dale looked for Mike but remembered that he was watching his grandmother tonight, as he did most Saturdays. Kevin and his folks never came to the Free Show: they had a color television, one of only two in town. Chuck Sperling's family had the other one.

It was in that hush after real darkness had fallen and before the first cartoon began that Dale saw Duane McBride climbing the steps to the bandstand. Dale muttered something to his folks and ran across the park, jumping over extended legs and at least one teenage couple sprawled full length on their blanket. Leaping to the top step of the bandstand, which was usually reserved just for Mr. Ashley-Montague and whoever he brought along to act as projectionist, Dale started to say hello to Duane but saw that the bigger boy was talking to the millionaire by the projector. Dale leaned against the railing, said nothing, and listened.

". . . and what use would you have for such a book . . . if it existed," Mr. Ashley-Montague was saying. Next to him, a young man in a bow tie had finished plugging in the extension speakers and was threading the short reel of the cartoon. Duane was a broad silhouette next to the town's benefactor.

"As I said, I'm doing a paper on the history of Old Central School."

Mr. Ashley-Montague said, "School is out for the summer, son," and turned toward his assistant. He nodded and the screen on the side of Parkside Cafe leaped alight. The crowd on the lawn and in their trucks and cars shouted the countdown as the leader flicked down from ten to one. A Tom and Jerry cartoon began. The assistant focused the picture and adjusted the sound level.

"Please, sir," said Duane McBride, taking a step closer to the millionaire. "I promise I'll return the books safely. I just need them to complete my research."

Mr. Ashley-Montague sat on the lawn chair his assistant had set out for him. Dale had never been this close to the man before; he'd always thought of Mr. A.-M. as a young man, but in the light from the side of the projector and reflected from the screen, he could see that the millionaire was at least forty years old. Maybe older. His bow tie and sort of prissy way of dressing made him look older. Tonight he was wearing some kind of white linen suit that almost glowed in the dusk.

"Research," chuckled Mr. Ashley-Montague. "How old are you, son? Fourteen?"

"Twelve in three weeks," said Duane. Dale hadn't known that his friend's birthday was in July.

"Twelve," said Mr. Ashley-Montague. "Twelve-year-olds do not *do* research, my friend. Look up whatever you need for your school report in the library."

"I've used the library, sir," said Duane. Despite the use of "sir," Dale could hear no real deference in Duane's voice. It was as if one adult were talking to another. "It didn't have the necessary data. The Oak Hill librarian said that the rest of the county Historical Society materials had been willed to you. It would seem to me that the Historical Society documents are still for public use . . . and all I ask is a few hours to look over the material that relates to Old Central."

Mr. Ashley-Montague crossed his arms and watched the screen where Tom was clobbering Jerry. Or maybe it was Jerry clobbering Tom . . . Dale could never keep the cat's and mouse's names straight. Finally the seated man said, "And what, precisely, is the nature of your report?"

Duane seemed to take a breath. "The Porsha bell," he said at last. Or Dale *thought* he heard him say. At that second an explosion of noise from the Tom and Jerry cartoon almost drowned out the words.

Mr. Ashley-Montague shot up out of the chair, grabbed Duane's upper arms, released them, and stepped back as if embarrassed. "There's no such thing," Dale heard the man say under the machine-gun sounds from the speaker.

Duane said something that *was* lost as a giant firecracker under the cat exploded. Even Mr. Ashley-Montague had to lean forward to hear Duane.

". . . there *was* a bell," the millionaire was saying when Dale could hear again, "but it was removed years ago. Decades ago. Before the First World War, I believe. It was a fraud, of course. My grandfather was . . . taken, I believe the word is. Conned. Defrauded."

"Well, that's the kind of stuff I need to end my report," said Duane. "Otherwise, I'd have to hand in an essay saying the present whereabouts of the bell is a mystery."

Mr. Ashley-Montague walked back and forth beside the projector. The cartoon was over and his assistant was rushing to cue up the short subject—a *20th Century* newsreel about the spread of Communism, narrated by Walter Cronkite. Dale glanced up to see the dark-haired reporter sitting at a desk. The short subject was in black and white . . . Dale had seen it at school last year in a special presentation. Suddenly a map of Europe and Asia began to turn black as the Communist threat spread. Arrows plunged into Eastern Europe, China, and other places Dale couldn't quite name.

"There's no mystery," snapped Mr. Ashley-Montague. "I remember now. Grandfather's bell was taken down and stored sometime after the turn of the century. It couldn't even be rung, I believe, due to cracks in it. It was taken out of storage, melted down, and the metal used for military purposes early in the Great War." He stopped, turned his back, and sat down again as if the conversation were at an end.

"That'd be great if I could quote that from the book and maybe photograph a couple of the old pictures for my report," said Duane.

The millionaire sighed as if in response to the spreading ocean of Communist domination on the screen. Walter Cronkite's voice boomed as loud as the Tom and Jerry cartoon. "Young man, there *is* no book. What Doctor Priestmann willed to me amounted to a mass of unrelated, uncollated, and unmarked materials. Several cartonsful, if I remember correctly. I assure you I did not keep them."

"Could you tell me where you donated them . . ." began Duane.

"I did *not* donate them!" said Mr. Ashley-Montague, his voice rising almost to a shout. "I burned them. I supported the good professor's researches, but *I* had no use for them. I assure you, there is no mystery volume which will conclude your report. Quote *me*, young man. The bell was a mistake . . . one of many white elephants grandfather brought back from his honeymoon tour of Europe . . . it was removed from Old Central sometime around the turn of the century, stored in a warehouse . . . somewhere in Chicago, I believe . . . and melted down for bullets or somesuch in 1917 when we entered the war. Now, *that is all*."

The *20th Century* piece had ended, the assistant was hurriedly putting on the large first reel of *Hercules,* and several heads turned to look up at the bandstand as Mr. Ashley-Montague's voice boomed through the relative silence.

"If I could just . . ." began Duane.

"There is no 'just,'" hissed the millionaire. "There is no more conversation, young man. There is no *bell.* Now *that is all*." He gestured toward the bandstand steps with what Dale thought was a rather feminine swish of his wrist. Another gesture brought the assistant over—the movie now starting with a shouted leader countdown from the crowd—and Duane was staring at a six-foot-tall man with his sleeves rolled up. The assistant could have been a butler, a bodyguard, or a flunky from one of Mr. A.-M.'s movie theaters for all Dale knew.

Duane seemed to shrug and turn away, ambling down the stairs at a much slower speed than Dale would have used if an adult had shouted at *him.* Realizing that he was inconspicuous in the back corner of the bandstand while hidden by darkness, Dale nonetheless vaulted the railing and landed in the grass four feet below, almost stumbling onto Uncle Henry and Aunt Lena as he landed.

He ran to catch up to Duane, but the heavier boy had left the park and was strolling down Broad Avenue, his hands in his pockets, whistling a tune and evidently heading for the ruins of the old Ashley place two blocks south. Dale was no longer afraid of the night—that nonsense was *past*—but he didn't really want to go walking in that darkness under the old elms down there. Besides, the music and dubbed dialogue was swelling behind him and he wanted to watch *Hercules.*

Dale turned back to the park, figuring that if he didn't talk to Duane later that night then . . . well . . . he'd talk to him sometime in the next few days. There was no hurry. It was summer.

Duane walked west on Broad Avenue, too agitated to pay attention to the Hercules movie. Leaf-shadow lay heavy on the street. Streetlights along lanes running to the south were obscured by branches and leaves. To the north there was a single row of small homes, their undecorated lawns sprawling into one another and devolving into weeds where the train tracks curved a bit south and then swept off into the cornfields where the road ended. Only the old Ashley-Montague place, what people still called the Ashley Mansion, lay down that final dark lane.

Duane stared at the curved driveway, now turned into a tunnel by overhanging branches and untended shrubbery. Little remained of the place except the charred remnants of two columns and three chimneys, a few blackened timbers tumbled into the rat-infested cellar. Duane knew that Dale and the other kids often made a game of riding down that lane, sweeping past the front porch, leaning far out to touch the columns or porch steps without dismounting or slowing. But it was very dark—not even fireflies illuminated the brambled depths of the circular drive. The noise and light and crowds of the Free Show were two blocks behind and made more distant by intervening trees.

Duane was not afraid of the dark. Not really. But he had no interest in walking down that lane tonight. Whistling, he turned south along a gravel path to intersect the new streets where Chuck Sperling lived.

Behind him, in the darkness where the driveway was most overgrown, something stirred, moved branches, and scuttled around the periphery of a fountain long forgotten amidst the weed and ruin.

FIFTEEN

Sunday, the twelfth of June, was warm and hazy with cloud cover that turned the sky into an inverted gray bowl. It was eighty degrees by eight A.M, into the nineties by noon. The Old Man was up early and out in the fields, so Duane put off reading *The New York Times* until after some work was done.

He was walking the rows of beans back behind the barn, pulling the stalks of pioneer corn invading there, when he saw the car turn into the long drive. At first he thought it was Uncle Art, but then he realized that it was a smaller white car. Then he saw the red bubble on top.

Duane came out of the fields, mopping his face with the tail of his open shirt. It wasn't Barney's constable car; the green letters on the driver's side door read CREVE COEUR COUNTY SHERIFF. A man with a lean, tanned face with eyes hidden by reflecting aviator's sunglasses said, "Mr. McBride here, son?"

Duane nodded, walked to the edge of the beanfield, put two fingers in his mouth, and whistled loudly. He could see the distant silhouette of his father pause, look up, and begin walking in. Duane half expected Wittgenstein to come hobbling from the barn.

The sheriff was out of his car now: a big man, Duane noticed, at least six foot four. Perhaps more. He'd put on his broad-brimmed county mountie hat now and the full effect of the man's height, lantern jaw, sunglasses, gun belt, and leather boots made Duane think of a recruiting poster. The effect was only slightly marred by the half-moons of perspiration soaked through the khaki shirt under the arms.

"Something wrong?" asked Duane, wondering if Mr. Ashley-Montague had somehow sicced this cop on him. The millionaire had been visibly upset the night before, and hadn't been at the Free Show when Duane returned to get a ride home with Uncle Henry and Aunt Lena.

The sheriff nodded. "Afraid there is, son."

Duane stood there, sweat dripping from his own chin, until the Old Man strode down the last thirty feet of row.

"Mr. McBride?" said the sheriff.

The Old Man nodded and made a swipe at his sweaty face with a kerchief, leaving a muddy streak in gray stubble. "That's right. Now if this is about that goddamn telephone thing, I *told* Ma Bell . . ."

"No, sir. There's been an accident."

The Old Man froze as if he'd been slapped. Duane watched his father's face, seeing the second of hesitation and then the impact of certainty there. Only one person alive would carry the Old Man's name on an In Case of Emergency card in his billfold.

"Art," said the Old Man. It was not a question. "Is he dead?"

"Yessir." The sheriff adjusted his sunglasses at almost the same instant that Duane touched his middle finger to the bridge of his own glasses.

"How?" The Old Man's eyes seemed to be focused on something in the fields behind the sheriff. Or on nothing.

"Car accident. 'Bout an hour ago."

"Where?" The Old Man was nodding slightly, as if receiving expected news. Duane was familiar with the nod from when they listened to news on the radio or when the Old Man was talking about corruption in politics.

"Jubilee College Road," said the sheriff, his voice firm but not as flat as the Old Man's. "Stone Creek Bridge. About two miles from . . ."

"I know where the bridge is," the Old Man interrupted. "Art and I used to swim there." His eyes gained some focus and he turned toward Duane as if he were going to say something, do something. Instead, he turned back to the sheriff. "Where is he?"

"They were removing the body when I left," said the sheriff. "I'll take you there if you like."

The Old Man nodded and got into the passenger seat of the sheriff's car. Duane rushed to jump in the back.

This isn't real, he thought as they roared past Uncle Henry's and Aunt Lena's, hit the first hill doing at least seventy, and roared up past the cemetery. Duane's head almost banged the ceiling as they dove down into the woods again. *He's going to kill us, too.* The speeding sheriff's car threw dust and gravel thirty feet into the woods. All along the roadside as they climbed toward the Black Tree, trees, weeds, shrubs, and branches were gray-white, as if they were covered with powdered chalk. Duane knew that it was just dust from previous vehicles, but the gray foliage and the gray sky made him think of Hades, of the shades of the dead waiting there in gray nothingness, of the scene Uncle Art had read to him when he was very little about Odysseus descending into Hades and braving those gray mists to meet the shade of his dead mother and former allies.

The sheriff didn't slow for the stop sign at the intersection of County Six and Jubilee College Road, but turned in a controlled broadside onto the harder-packed gravel. Duane realized that the light above them was flashing, although there was no siren sound. He wondered what the rush was. Ahead of him, the Old Man's back was perfectly straight, head forward, moving only to the turns of the car.

They roared the two miles east. Duane looked across fields to his left to see where the long stretch of woods began where Gypsy Lane lay hidden. Then there were cornfields on either side except for the patches of timber at the bottom of the hills.

Duane counted dips, knowing that the fourth small valley held Stone Creek.

They dipped the fourth time, braked hard, and the sheriff pulled to the left side of the road, parking faced toward oncoming traffic. There was no traffic. The bottomland and sparsely wooded hillside were silent with a Sunday-morning hush.

Duane noticed the other vehicles parked along the shoulder near the concrete bridge: a tow truck, J.P. Congden's ugly black Chevy, a dark station wagon he didn't recognize, another wrecker from Ernie's Texaco station on the east end of Elm Haven. *No ambulance! No sign of Uncle Art's car! Maybe it was a mistake.*

Duane noticed the damage to the bridge railing first. The old concrete had been set forty or fifty years earlier with balustrade-like gaps beneath the three-foot-high shelf. Now a four-foot chunk of that concrete had been broken off on the east end. Duane could see rusted iron reinforcement bars trailing from the concrete like some weird sculptured hand pointing down the embankment.

Duane stood next to the Old Man and looked over the railing. Ernie from Ernie's Texaco was down there, along with three or four other men including the rat-faced justice of the peace. So was Uncle Art's Cadillac.

Duane saw at once what had happened. Art had been forced far enough right while barreling across the single-lane bridge that the concrete railing had struck the *left* front of the big car, smashing the engine back through the driver's side and sending the Caddy spinning out over Stone Creek like a twisted toy. Then two tons of automobile had hit the trees on the other side, shearing off the saplings and a ten-inch oak, before being bashed around by the larger elm on the hillside. Duane could see the deep gash there, the three-foot scar in the bark, still bleeding sap. He wondered idly if the elm would live.

After having the right rear door and quarter panel caved in by the second impact, the Caddy had rolled uphill thirty or forty feet, taking out shrubs and small trees and bounding over a boulder—the windshield had popped out at this point and lay shattered just beyond the rock—before gravity and/or collision with another large tree had sent the wreck rolling back down the hillside into the creek.

It lay there now, upside down. The left front wheel was missing, but the other three seemed strangely exposed, almost indecent. Duane noticed that there was plenty of tread left; Uncle Art worried about worn tires. The exposed undercarriage looked clean and new except where part of the transaxle had been torn away.

One door of the Caddy was open and bent almost in half. The passenger compartment was not submerged, although it lay in a foot or so of water. Bits and pieces of metal, chrome, and glass glinted across the hillside despite the lack of bright sunlight. Duane saw other things: an argyle sock lying on the grass, a pack of cigarettes near the boulder, road maps fluttering in the bushes.

"They took the body away, Bob," called Ernie, barely glancing up from where he was attaching a cable to the front axle. "Donnie and Mr. Mercer rode in with the . . . oh, hello there, Mr. McBride." Ernie looked back at his work.

The Old Man licked his lips and spoke to the sheriff without turning his head. "Was he dead when you got here?"

Duane saw the woods and ridgeline reflected in the sheriff's glasses. "Yessir. He was dead when Mr. Carter drove by and saw something down the hill 'bout half an hour before I got here. Mr. Mercer . . . he's the county coroner, you know . . . he said that Mr. McBr—ah, your brother . . . died instantly upon impact."

J.P. Congden came puffing up the slope, stood wheezing whiskey fumes on them, and hitched up his baggy overalls. "Real sorry about your . . ."

The Old Man ignored the justice of the peace and started down the steep slope, sliding where the hillside was muddy, hanging on to branches to get to the bottom. Duane followed. The sheriff picked his way down cautiously, careful not to get burrs or mud on his pressed brown slacks.

The Old Man crouched at the edge of the stream, staring into the wrecked Caddy. The roof had been caved in and water rose to the upside-down dashboard. Duane saw that the ray-gun automatic-dimming device had been torn free. The passenger's side was relatively unbattered, even the collapsed roof had spared it, but the seat-bench on the driver's had been driven back through the *backseat* cushions. There was no steering wheel, but the shaft still hung there, dripping into the water two feet below. In front, where the driver would have been, a mass of twisted engine metal and torn firewall filled the space like the corpse of a murdered robot.

The sheriff hitched up his pants and crouched, keeping his shined boots out of the mud and murky water. He cleared his throat. "After he lost control, your brother hit the guardrail on the bridge and . . . ah . . . as you can see, the impact must have killed him right off."

The Old Man gave the same nod as before. He was squatting with his feet and ankles in the stream and his wrists on his knees. He looked down at his own fingers and stared at them as if they were alien things. "Where is he?"

"Mr. Mercer took him into Taylor Funeral Home," said the sheriff. "He has . . . uh . . . a few things to finish up, then you can make arrangements with Mr. Taylor."

The Old Man shook his head gently. "Art never wanted a funeral. And definitely not at Taylor's."

The sheriff adjusted his glasses. "Mr. McBride, was your brother a drinking man?"

The Old Man turned and looked at the sheriff for the first time. "Not on Sunday morning he wasn't." His voice held the perfectly flat, calm tone that Duane knew threatened fury.

"Yessir," said the sheriff. They all had to back out of the way as Ernie began cranking up the cable with the winch on the wrecker. The front of the Caddy rose, dripped water from the windows, and began turning slowly toward the embankment. "Well, maybe he had a heart attack or a bee got into the car. Lotta people lose control because of insects in the car with 'em. You'd be surprised how many people . . ."

"How fast was he going?" asked Duane. He was amazed to hear his own voice.

The Old Man and the sheriff both turned to stare at him. Duane noted how pale and fat he looked in the sheriff's glasses.

"We figure about seventy-five or eighty," said the sheriff. "I've only looked at the skid marks, not paced 'em off. But he was moving."

"My brother didn't like to speed," said the Old Man, his face close to the sheriff's. "He had a real thing about obeying the law. I always told him it was foolish."

The sheriff stood face to face with the Old Man for a moment and then glanced up at the broken bridge. "Yeah, well, he was speeding this morning. That's why we have to do some tests to see if he was drinking."

"Look out!" shouted Ernie, and the three of them backed away as the Caddy rose vertically from the water. Duane saw a crawdad tumble out with the dirty water and soaked maps. He remembered hunting for crawdads here with Dale and Mike and the town kids a couple of summers ago.

"Could someone have forced him off the road?" asked Duane.

The sheriff stared at him for a long moment. "No sign of that, son. And no one reported the accident."

The Old Man snorted.

Duane walked closer to the Caddy, now twisting so that they could see the driver's side. He pointed to a red gash just visible on the mangled driver's side door. "Couldn't this paint be left by the vehicle that forced Uncle Art's car into the bridge railing?"

The sheriff stepped closer, bringing his sunglasses right up to the dripping wreck. "Looks old to me, son. But we'll look into it." He stepped back, set his hands on his gun belt, and chuckled. "Not many vehicles could force a Caddy this size off the road if it didn't want to go."

"Something the size of the Rendering Truck could," said Duane. He looked up the bank and saw J.P. Congden staring down at him.

"Y'all need to get out of there while we crank this goddamn thing up!" shouted Ernie.

"Come on," said the Old Man. These were the first words he'd spoken to Duane since the sheriff had come. The two started up the steep bank, feet sliding. Then the Old Man did something he had not done for five years. He took Duane's hand in his own.

The farm seemed different when they returned. The overcast was breaking up a bit and a rich light fell across the fields. The house and barn seemed freshly painted, the old pickup in the drive magically renewed. Duane stood by the kitchen door and thought while the Old Man listened to a few last words from the sheriff. When the car left it brought Duane up out of a numb reverie.

"I'm going into town," said the Old Man. "Wait here until I get back."

Duane started walking toward the pickup. "I'm going, too."

His father stopped him with a gentle hand on his shoulder. "No, Duanie. I'm going into Taylor's before that damn vulture can start cosmeticizing Art. And I have questions to ask."

Duane started to protest and then noticed his father's eyes and realized that the man wanted to be alone, *needed* to be alone, even if for the few minutes it took to drive into town. Duane nodded and went back to sit on the stoop.

He thought about finishing walking the rows, but decided against it. He realized with a pang of guilt that he felt hungry. Even though there was a burning in his throat, much worse than with Witt, and his chest seemed ready to explode from a great pressure building there, Duane was hungry. He shook his head and ambled into the house.

Munching on a liverwurst, cheese, bacon, and lettuce sandwich, he wandered through the Old Man's workroom, wondering where he'd left *The New York Times* even as a major part of his mind ran replays of the tortured Cadillac, the scattered chrome and glass, and the streak of red paint on the driver's door.

The green light was blinking on the Old Man's phone-answering device. Absently, still munching and thinking, Duane rewound the small reel-to-reel tape and pushed play.

"Darren? Duane? Damn it, why don't you disconnect that damn machine and answer your phone?" said Uncle Art.

Duane froze in midbite and punched the playback to Stop. His heart seemed to pause, then pound once—loudly—then lurch with a great ache. Duane swallowed with difficulty, took a breath, and pushed the Rewind and Play buttons.

". . . and answer your phone? Duane, this call's for you. I found what you're looking for. The bell thing. It was in my library the whole time. Duane, it's astounding. It really is. Incredible, but unsettling. I've asked about ten of my older friends in Elm Haven, but none of them can remember a bell. It doesn't matter . . . what this book says is . . . well, I'll show you myself. It's . . . uh . . . about nine-twenty now. I'll be there before ten-thirty. See you, kiddo."

Duane played the tape twice more, then turned off the machine, felt behind him, found a chair, and sat down heavily. The pressure in his chest was too strong to resist now, and he let it out, the tears running down his cheeks, an occasional silent sob shaking him. Once in a while he would remove his glasses, rub his eyes with the back of his hand, and take another bite of sandwich. It was a long time before he got up and went back into the kitchen.

There was no answer at the listed number for the sheriff's office, but Duane finally got in touch with the man at his home. Duane had forgotten it was Sunday.

"Book?" said the sheriff. "Uh-uh, I didn't see any book. Is it important, son?"

"Yes," said Duane. And added, "To me."

"Well, I didn't see it at the accident site. Of course the whole area hasn't been cleaned up yet. And it could have been in that mess . . . it could've been in the car."

"Where's the car now? Ernie's?"

"Yeah. Ernie's or J.P. Congden's place."

"Congden?" Duane tossed the crust of his bread into the garbage. "Why would it be at Mr. Congden's place?"

Duane heard the sheriff let out a breath that might have been a soft sound of disgust. "Well, J.P. hears about road accidents on his police band radio, then he does a deal with Ernie sometimes. J.P. pays Ernie for the wreck and sells it to the auto salvage yard over at Oak Hill. At least that's what we think he does with them."

Like most of the kids in town, Duane had heard adults talking about the rumors that the justice of the peace dealt in stolen cars. Duane wondered if parts from these wrecks would be useful in such a racket. He said, "Do you know where it went today?"

"Nope," said the sheriff. "Probably down to Ernie's lot, though, since he had to get the wrecker back. He's the only one on duty on Sunday and his wife hates pumpin' gas. But don't worry, son, any personal possessions we find'll be given to you and your dad. You are next of kin, aren't you?"

"Yes," said Duane, thinking about what an ancient and honorable word "kin" was. He remembered reading Chaucer—Uncle Art's copy— where the word was *cyn*. Uncle Art was kin. "Yes," he said again, softly.

"Well, don't you worry, son. Any book or anything else that was in the car will come to you folks. I'll go to Ernie's in the morning and check on it myself. Meanwhile, I may need to check some things for the report I'm writing. You and your dad be home tonight?"

"Yes."

The house seemed empty after the conversation ended. Duane heard the ticking of the big clock over the stove and the cattle lowing far out in the west pasture. The clouds had moved in again. Despite the heat, there was no real sunlight whatsoever.

Dale Stewart heard about Duane's uncle's death late that afternoon from his mom, who'd been talking to Mrs. Grumbacher who had heard it from Mrs. Sperling who was good friends with Mrs. Taylor. He and Lawrence were making a model Spad when their mother told them, her voice soft. Lawrence's eyes had filled and he'd said, "Gosh, poor Duane. First his dog and now his uncle."

Dale had punched his brother hard on the shoulder then; he wasn't sure why.

It had taken him awhile to work up the courage, but then he went to the phone in the hall and called Duane's number, letting the party-line phone ring twice the way he was supposed to. There was a click and that weird recording machine came on and said in Duane's emotionless voice, "Hi. We can't answer the phone right now, but whatever you say will be taped and we'll get back to you. Please count to three and speak."

Dale counted to three and hung up, face burning. He'd have enough trouble talking to poor Duane right now; expressing his condolences to a tape recorder was beyond him. Dale left Lawrence working on the model, his brother's tongue sticking out and eyes almost crossed with concentration, and rode down the street to Mike's.

"Eeawkee!" Dale let out the shout, hopped off the bike, and let it glide a few yards on its own before crashing onto the grass.

"Keeawee." Mike's answering shout came from the giant maple that overhung the street.

Dale jogged back, climbed the few remaining rungs to the lower treehouse fifteen feet up, and then continued climbing through branches toward the higher, secret platform thirty feet higher. Mike sat with his back to a bole of one of the diverging trunks, his legs dangling over the three-board platform. Dale pulled himself up and sat back against the other trunk. He looked down, but the ground was lost behind leaves and he knew that they were invisible from the ground. "Hey," he said, "I just heard . . ."

"Yeah," said Mike. He was chewing on a long piece of grass. "I heard a little while ago, too. I was going to come over to talk to you after a while. You know Duane better."

Dale nodded. He and Duane had become friends through discovering a common interest in books and rocketry in fourth grade. But Dale had dreamed of rockets; Duane had *built* them. Dale's reading was precocious—he'd read *Treasure Island* and the real *Robinson Crusoe* by fourth grade—but Duane's reading list was beyond belief. Still, the two *had* stayed friends, spending recesses together, seeing each other a few times over the summer. Dale thought that he might be the only person whom Duane had told about his ambition to become a writer. "There's no answer," said Dale. He made an awkward gesture. "I called."

Mike studied the piece of grass he was chewing and dropped it into the layer of leaves fifteen feet below. "Yeah. My mom called this afternoon, too. Got that machine. She's going out there later with a bunch of ladies bringing food. Your mom'll probably go."

Dale nodded again. A death in Elm Haven or the outlying farms meant a battalion of women descending like Valkyries bringing food. *Duane told me about Valkyries.* Dale couldn't quite remember what

Valkyries did, but he remembered that they came down when someone died. He said, "I've only met his uncle a couple of times. He seemed real nice. Smart, but nice. Not touchy like Duane's dad."

"Duane's dad is an alcoholic," said Mike. His voice said that it wasn't a judgment or criticism, merely a statement of fact.

Dale shrugged. "His uncle has . . . had white hair and used to wear a white beard. I talked to him once when I was out at the farm playing and he was . . . funny."

Mike plucked a leaf and began stripping it. "I heard Mrs. Somerset tell my mom that Mrs. Taylor said that he was torn apart when a steering wheel thingie went through him. She said Mr. Taylor said that no way could they have an open coffin. She said that Duane's dad came in and threatened to rip Mr. Taylor a new asshole if he touched his brother's body. Mr. McBride's brother's body, I mean."

Dale found a leaf for himself. He nodded. He'd never heard the phrase "rip him a new asshole" before and he had to fight to keep from smiling. It was a good phrase. Then he remembered what they were talking about and any threat of a smile fled.

"Father Cavanaugh went over to the funeral home," Mike was saying. "Nobody knew what religion Mr. McBride—the uncle Mr. McBride—was, so Father C. gave him Extreme Unction just in case."

"What's extreme . . . whatever?" asked Dale. He finished with the leaf and started on another. Some girls skipped by far below, never guessing that people were talking softly forty feet above them.

"The Last Rites," said Mike.

Dale nodded, although he understood no better than before. Catholics had lots of weird things that they assumed everybody knew about. Dale had watched in fourth grade when Gerry Daysinger had made fun of Mike's rosary—Gerry had stuck it around his own neck and danced around with it, accusing Mike of carrying a necklace around. Mike hadn't said anything, he'd merely pounded Daysinger's face in, sat on his chest, and carefully removed the rosary. No one had teased Mike about it since.

"Father C. was there when Duane's dad came in," continued Mike, "but he didn't want to talk or anything. He just told Mr. Taylor to keep his ghoul's hands off his brother and told him where to send the body for cremation."

"Cremation," whispered Dale.

"That's when they burn you instead of bury you."

"I know that, stupid," snapped Dale. "I was just . . . surprised." And relieved, he realized. In the past fifteen minutes part of his mind had been imagining going down to Taylor's to the funeral, having to see the body during the visitation, sitting with Duane. But cremation . . .

that meant no funeral, didn't it? "When's it going to be?" he asked. "The cremation?" It was such an adult and final word.

Mike shrugged. "You want to go out and see him?"

"See who?" asked Dale. He knew that Digger Taylor sometimes snuck his friends into the coffin room before the viewing, showing them corpses. Chuck Sperling once bragged that he and Digger had seen Mrs. Duggan when she was laid out naked in the embalming room.

"Who? Duane, of course," said Mike. "Who else do you think we ought to go see, dipstick?"

Dale grunted, crumbled the last of the leaf, and tried to brush sap from his hand. He squinted up at the sky through the thinning canopy above them. "It'll be dark pretty soon."

"No, it's not. We've got another couple of hours. The days are longer this week than any time in the whole year, dopehead. It's just cloudy this evening."

Dale thought about the long pedal out to Duane's house. He remembered Duane talking about the time the Rendering Truck had tried to run him down. They'd be on the same road. He thought of having to talk to Mr. McBride and whatever other grown-ups were out there. What could be harder to do than visit someone after a death?

"OK," he said. "Let's go."

They climbed down, grabbed their bikes, and headed out of town. The sky in the east was almost black, as if a storm were coming. The air was dead calm. Halfway to County Six, a truck became visible ahead of them as a cloud of dust. Dale and Mike pulled far to the right, almost into the ditch, to let it pass.

It was Duane and his dad going the other way in their pickup. The truck did not stop.

Duane saw his two friends on their bikes and guessed that they were probably headed out to the farm to see him, and he glanced over his shoulder in time to see them stopped and standing, staring after the truck for the few seconds before the cloud of dust enveloped them. The Old Man hadn't even noticed Mike and Dale. Duane said nothing.

It hadn't been easy convincing the Old Man that the book was important enough to go hunting for tonight. Duane had played the tape.

"What the hell is all this about?" the Old Man had asked. He'd been in a murderous depression since he'd returned from Taylor's.

Duane hesitated only a second. He could tell the Old Man everything, just as he'd explained it to Uncle Art. But the time seemed all wrong. The stuff about a Borgia Bell seemed idle nonsense in the face of the reality of loss the Old Man and he were feeling. Duane explained that he and Uncle Art had been researching this bell . . . an artifact one of the Ashley-Montagues had brought back from Europe and which seemed to have been forgotten by everyone. Duane made it sound like a lark, one of the uncountable projects he had shared with Uncle Art, like the times they had gone buggo on astronomy and built their own telescopes, or the autumn they had tried to build every device Leonardo da Vinci had designed. That kind of thing.

The Old Man understood but he didn't see the urgency in driving into town to stare at the wreck of the Cadillac again that night. Duane knew that the Old Man's temporary sobriety was tearing at him like steel pins. He also knew that if he let the Old Man get out of his sight into Carl's or the Black Tree, it would be days before he saw him again. The taverns were officially closed on Sunday but certain patrons found their way in the back door easily enough.

"Maybe I could go check for the book and you could pick up a bottle of wine or something," Duane said. "You know, have a toast tonight in Uncle Art's memory."

The Old Man glared at him, but slowly relaxed his features. He rarely settled on a compromise himself, but he knew a good one when he heard it. Duane knew that the Old Man had been warring between the necessity to stay sober until the arrangements for Uncle Art were concluded, and the absolute requirement to tie one on.

"OK," said the Old Man. "We'll take a look and I'll pick up something to bring home. You can lift a toast to him, too."

Duane nodded. The one thing in life that he was terrified of . . . until now . . . was liquor. He was afraid that the disease ran in the family and that one drink would send him over the edge, creating the craving in him that had driven the Old Man for thirty some years. But he had nodded and they had left for town after staring at a dinner neither one of them touched.

Ernie's Texaco was closed. It usually shut down at four P.M. on Sunday and today was no exception. There were three wrecks around back, but no Caddy. Duane told the Old Man what the sheriff had said about Congden.

The Old Man turned away but not before Duane heard a muttered "goddamn thieving capitalist sonofabitch."

Old Central was in shadows as they rolled up Second Avenue past it and turned down Depot Street. Duane saw Dale Stewart's parents sitting on their long porch and saw their posture change as they recognized him. They continued west on Depot past Broad.

Congden's black Chevy wasn't in the yard or parked on the muddy ruts that might have been a driveway around the side of the shabby house.

The Old Man pounded at the door but there was no response except for the frenzied barking of what sounded like a very large dog. Duane followed the Old Man around back, across a weedy lot filled with springs, beer cans, an old washing machine, and an assortment of rusted *things* out behind a small shed.

There were eight cars there. Two were up on blocks and looked as if they might be rebuilt someday; the others were sprawled in the high weeds like metal corpses. Uncle Art's Cadillac was the closest to the shed.

"Don't get into it," said the Old Man. There was something strange about his voice. "If you see the book in there, I'll get it out."

On its wheels again, the damage was even more obvious. The roof was smashed down almost to the level of the doors. Even from the passenger side where they stood, it was obvious that the heavy car had been twisted on its own axis by the collision with the bridge. The hood was gone, and Congden or someone had already spread engine parts across the grass. Duane walked around to the driver's side.

"Dad."

The Old Man came around and stared with him. Both the driver's and left-rear doors were missing.

"They were there when they fished the car out," said Duane. "I pointed the red paint out to the sheriff."

"I remember." The Old Man found a metal tie-rod and started poking through the waist-high weeds as if he would find the doors there.

Duane crouched and peered in, then went around back to look in through the opening where the rear window had been. He pried open a back door on the right side and leaned into what was left of the backseat.

Twisted metal. Torn upholstery. Springs. Fabric and insulation from the roof hanging like stalactites. Broken glass. The smell of blood, gasoline, and transmission fluid. No book.

The Old Man came back through the woods. "No sign of the doors. Find what you were after?"

Duane shook his head. "We've got to go back to the accident site."

"No." Duane heard a tone in his father's voice that said there would be no discussion. "Not tonight."

Duane turned, feeling a deep depression drop on his shoulders, something even heavier than the sharp-edged grief he already felt. He started back around the shed, thinking about the evening ahead with the Old Man and a bottle. The trade had been for nothing.

His hands were in his pockets when he came around the corner of the shed. The dog was on him before he could pull his hands free.

At first Duane didn't know it was a dog. It was just something huge and black and growling with a sound unlike anything Duane had ever heard. Then the thing jumped, teeth gleamed at eye level, and Duane fell back across springs and broken glass, the mass of the dog's body going over him and twisting, growling, lunging to get at him.

In that second, lying on the littered ground, hands free now but scraped and empty, Duane knew again what it meant to face death. Time seemed to freeze and he was frozen in it. Only the huge dog could move—move so fast that it was little more than a black blur—and it moved toward Duane, towering over him, nothing but teeth and flying saliva as it opened its huge mouth to rip at Duane McBride's throat.

The Old Man stepped between the dog and his fallen son and swung. The tie rod caught the Doberman in the ribs and flung it ten feet back toward the house. The animal let out a screech that sounded like stripped gears.

"Get up," panted the Old Man, crouching between Duane and the dog, which already had scrambled to its feet. Duane didn't know whether his father was talking to him or the Doberman.

Duane was on his knees when the animal lunged again. This time the thing had to go through the Old Man to get to the boy and it showed every intention of doing so, leaping with a growl that made Duane's bowels go loose.

The Old Man pirouetted, gripped the tie rod in both hands, let the dog fly by him, and swung the metal bar upward. Duane thought he looked like a batter hitting pop flies to a distant outfield.

The bar caught the Doberman under the jaw, snapped his head back in an impossible position, and caused the animal's body to do a perfect backflip before it crashed into the shed wall and slid down.

He got to his feet and staggered away from the animal, but the Doberman wasn't getting up this time. The Old Man walked over and kicked the beast under the jaw and the thing's head hobbled like something attached by loose string. Its eyes were wide and already clouding with death.

"Gosh," said Duane, feeling that if he didn't try to make a joke he'd just lie down again and start bawling, "Mr. Congden's going to be surprised."

"Fuck Congden," said the Old Man, but there was no passion in his voice. He sounded almost relaxed for the first time since the sheriff's car had pulled up the drive eight hours earlier. "Stay close."

Still holding the tie rod, the Old Man led the way around the house on blocks and went up to pound on the front door. It was still locked. No one answered the knocking.

"Hear that?" The Old Man stood tapping the metal rod.

Duane shook his head.

"Neither do I."

Duane understood then. Either the dog inside was suddenly deaf or it was the same one lying dead in the backyard. Someone had let it out.

The Old Man walked to the curb and looked up and down Depot Street. It was almost dark under the trees. A rumble from the east promised a storm. "Come on, Duanie," said the Old Man. "We'll find your book tomorrow."

They were almost to the water tower and Duane had almost stopped shaking when he remembered. "Your bottle," he said, hating himself for reminding the Old Man but figuring that he deserved it.

"Fuck the bottle." The Old Man looked at Duane and smiled very slightly. "We'll toast Art with Pepsi. That's what you and he used to drink all the time, isn't it? We'll toast him and tell tales about him and hold a real wake. Then we'll get to bed early so we can get going tomorrow and fix some things that need fixing. OK?"

Duane nodded.

Jim Harlen came home from the hospital on Sunday, exactly one week after he'd been hospitalized. His left arm was in a clumsy cast, his head and ribs were still bandaged, he had raccoon eyes where the blood had drained, and he was still on medication for the pain. But his doctor and mother decided that it was time for him to go home.

Harlen did not want to go home.

He did not quite remember the accident. He remembered more than he admitted: sneaking off to the Free Show that Saturday, following Old Double-Butt, even deciding to climb the school to get a peek inside. But of the actual fall—or what caused it—Harlen could not remember. Each night in the hospital he awoke from nightmares, panting, heart and head pounding, grasping the metal rail of the bed for support. Those first nights his mother had been there; after a while he learned to ring for the nurse, just to have a grown-up in the room. The nurses—especially Mrs. Carpenter, the old one—humored him and stayed in the room, sometimes stroking his short hair, until he fell asleep again.

Harlen didn't remember the dreams that sent him screaming up from sleep, but he remembered the *feeling* that they gave him, and that was enough to make him sick and goosefleshy. He had the same feeling about going home.

A friend of his mother's whom Harlen had never met drove them home, Harlen stretched out in the rear of the man's station wagon. He felt foolish and awkward in the cast, and had to lift his head from the pillows just to see the landscape go by. Each mile of the fifteen-minute trip from Oak Hill to Elm Haven seemed to absorb light, as if the car were moving into a zone of darkness.

"Looks like it might rain," said his mother's boyfriend. "Heaven knows the crops need it."

Harlen grunted. Whoever this dipshit was—Harlen had already forgotten the name his mother twittered at him during the introduction, so carefree and casual, as if this guy was an old family friend whom Harlen should know and love—whoever he was, he was no farmer. The clean and waxed station wagon, a Woody, and the man's soft hands and tweedy, citified suit proved that. This bozo probably didn't know or care whether the crops needed rain or manure.

They arrived home about six—his mother was supposed to pick him up at two but was hours late—and Bozo made a big production of helping Harlen up to his room, as if it had been his legs broken rather than his arm. Harlen had to admit that the exercise of climbing the stairs made him dizzy. He sat in his own bed, looking around at his room—seeming very strange and alien—and tried to blink away his headache while his mother ran downstairs for the medication. Harlen could hear hushed conversation and then a long silence. He imagined the kiss, imagined Bozo getting the old tongue in there and his mother bending her right leg up and back, long-heeled shoe dangling the way it always did when she gave her bozos their goodnight kiss while Harlen watched from the window in his room.

A sick yellow light coming through the window filled the room with a sulfurous tint. He realized suddenly why his room seemed so weird: his mother had cleaned it up. Cleaned up the piles of clothes, the heaps of comics, the toy soldiers and broken models, the dusty junk under his bed, even the heap of old *Boy's Life* that had sat stacked in the corner for years. With a rush of warm guilt, Harlen wondered whether she'd cleaned deep enough in his closet to find the nudie magazines. He started to get up to check, but the dizziness and headache pulled him back to the pillow. Fuck it. To add to the chorus of pain, his arm kicked in with its evening bone-deep ache. They had put a *steel pin in it* for Chrissakes. Harlen closed his eyes and tried to imagine a steel nail the size of a railroad spike driven through his splintered humerus.

Nothin' humorous about my humerus, thought Jim Harlen and realized that he was perilously close to tears. *Where the fuck is she? Or maybe, where is she fucking?*

His mother came into the room, all atwitter with good spirits and pleasure at having her little Jimmy home. Harlen saw how thick the makeup was on her cheeks. And her perfume wasn't the soft flowery scent of the nurses who checked on him at night; she smelled like some musky night-burrowing animal. A mink maybe, or a weasel in heat.

"Now take your pills and I'll get busy making dinner," she chirped.

She gave him the bottle of pills rather than the little cup the nurses used to dole out prescribed doses. Harlen swallowed three of the co-deine pills rather than the one he was supposed to take. *Fuck this pain stuff.* His mother was too busy flitting around the room, fluffing pillows and unpacking his hospital suitcase, to notice. If she was going to make a big deal out of the dirty magazines, Harlen realized, she was saving it for another day.

That was fine with him. She could go down and burn whatever din-ner she was planning—she cooked about twice a year and it was always a disaster—Harlen already felt the numbing buzz of the medication and was ready to drift into that nice, warm, wall-less space where he'd spent so much time the first few days in the hospital, when they'd given him the stronger stuff for the pain.

He asked his mother something.

"What, dear?" She paused in hanging up his robe and Harlen real-ized that his voice had sounded pretty slurry. He tried again:

"My friends come over?"

"Your friends? Why yes, dear, they're very worried and said to wish you their best."

"Who?"

"Pardon, dear?"

"Who?" snapped Harlen, and then worked to control his voice. "Who came over?"

"Why, you said that nice farm boy . . . whatshisname, Donald, came to the hospital last week . . ."

"Duane," said Harlen. "And he's not a friend. He's some farm kid with straw behind his ears. I mean, who came over to the house?"

His mother frowned and fluttered her fingers the way she did when she was flustered. Harlen thought that the bright-red nail polish made her white fingers look like they ended in bloody stumps. The idea amused him somehow. "Who?" he said. "O'Rourke? Stewart? Daysinger? Grum-bacher?"

His mother sighed. "I can't remember your little friends' names, Jimmy, but I did hear from them. At least from their mothers. They're all very worried. That nice lady who works at the A and P was especially concerned."

"Mrs. O'Rourke," sighed Harlen. "But Mike or the guys haven't come by?"

She folded up his hospital pajamas under her arm, as if cleaning them was a priority. As if his dirty pajamas and underwear hadn't laid around on this very floor for weeks before he went into the hospital. "I'm sure they have, darling, but I've been . . . well, busy, naturally, what with spending so much time in the hospital and having to look after . . . other things."

Harlen tried to roll over on his right side; the cast was an awkward protuberance on his left arm, bent at the elbow but heavy and stiff. He felt the codeine beginning to carry him away. Maybe he could con her into leaving the whole fucking bottle so he could take care of the pain himself. The doctors didn't care if you hurt; it was no skin off *their* noses if you woke up in the night scared and hurting so bad that you wanted to piss your pajama bottoms. Even the nice nurses who smelled so good didn't really give a shit; they'd come when called all right, but then they squeaked their shoes down the tile hall, went off duty, and went to screw some guy at home.

His mother kissed him and he smelled Bozo's cologne on her. He pulled his face away before her cigarette breath and Bozo's spoor made him sick.

"You sleep well now, dear." She tucked him in like he was a baby, except the cast didn't fit under the blankets and she had to sort of poke the covers around it like a Christmas-tree skirt. Harlen was floating on the sudden release from pain, the numbness that made him feel more alive than he had been all week.

It wasn't dark yet. Harlen allowed himself to fall asleep when it was daytime . . . it was the goddamn dark he hated. He could nap a bit before he woke to his silent sentinel duty. Trying to be alert in case *it* came.

In case *what* came?

The medication seemed to free his mind, as if the barriers to what had happened—what he *saw*—were ready to come down. The curtains ready to open.

Harlen tried to roll over, came up against the cast, and moaned fitfully, feeling the pain as some detached thing, like a small but persistent dog pulling at his sleeve. He wouldn't let the barriers come down, the curtains open. Whatever it was that woke him every night, sweating, heart pounding, *he didn't want it to come back.*

Fuck O'Rourke and Stewart and Daysinger and the rest. Fuck them all. They weren't real friends anyway. Who needed them? Harlen hated this whole fucking town with its fat, fucking people and its fucking stupid kids.

And the school.

Jim Harlen fell into a fitful doze. The sulfur yellow light shifted to red on his wallpaper before fading to darkness as the storm growled its approach.

Several blocks east on Depot Street, Dale and Lawrence sat on the porch railing an hour after nightfall and watched the heat lightning illuminating the dark sky. Their parents relaxed in their wicker porch chairs. Every time the silent lightning flashed, Old Central would be revealed through the screen of elms across the street, its brick and stone walls painted an electric blue by the strobe. The air was still, the wind in front of the storm having not yet arrived.

"Doesn't feel quite like tornado weather," said Dale's dad.

Their mother sipped her lemonade and said nothing. The air was thick, heavy with the approach of storm. Each time the silent lightning illuminated the school and playground and Second Avenue stretching south toward the Hard Road, she flinched slightly.

Dale was fascinated by the sudden explosions of light and by the strange color they imparted to the grass, homes, trees, and asphalt of the streets. It was as if they were watching their black-and-white Sylvania Halolight TV and suddenly it had begun transmitting, at least intermittently, in color.

The lightning rippled around the eastern and southern horizons, flickering above the treetops like a fierce aurora borealis. Dale remembered stories his Uncle Henry had told about artillery barrages in the First World War. Dale's dad had served in Europe in the more recent war, but never spoke about it.

"Look," said Lawrence softly and pointed toward the schoolyard.

Dale bent closer to follow his brother's pointing arm. When the heat lightning flashed, he saw the furrow across the playground ball diamond. There had been a few such furrows visible there since school had let out, as if someone had been laying pipe. But neither Dale nor anyone else in the family had seen men working in the schoolyard during the day. And why would they lay pipe to a school that was going to be torn down any day?

"Come on," whispered Dale, and he and his brother jumped from the railing to the stone steps, from the steps to the front lawn.

"Don't go far!" called their mom. "It's going to rain."

"We won't," Dale called over his shoulder. They jogged across Depot Street, jumping the low, grassy ditches on each side which substituted for storm sewers in town, and ran beneath the outstretched branches of the giant sentinel elm across the street from their house.

Dale looked around, realizing for the first time what a solid barrier the giant elms made. While it was simple to walk between them onto the playground, the effect was a bit like passing through a fortress wall into the courtyard of a castle.

And Old Central looked every bit the brooding castle this night. Lightning flickered and was reflected from the unboarded windows on the high dormers. The stone and brick looked oddly greenish in the light. The arched entranceway shielded only darkness.

"There," said Lawrence. He had stopped six feet from the mole-burrowish furrow which cut right across the playground. It was as if someone had laid a pipeline from the school—Dale could see where the mound touched brick near a basement window—straight through second base toward the pitcher's mound. But they had stopped halfway across the playground.

Dale turned and looked down the direction the furrow would take if it were extended farther. He was staring at his own front porch thirty yards away.

Lawrence let out a shout and jumped back. Dale wheeled.

In the brief explosion of light from the sky, Dale watched as the ground buckled, sods of dirt were pushed up—grass still intact—and the long line of mounded earth extended another four feet, then stopped less than a yard from his sneakers.

Mike O'Rourke was feeding Memo while the lightning pulsed beyond the curtain. Feeding the old lady was not pleasant: her throat and digestive system worked after a fashion, otherwise they couldn't take care of her at home and she would have been in an Oak Hill nursing home. But she could only eat strained baby foods and her mouth had to be opened and closed before and after each mouthful. Swallowing appeared to be more an act of choking it down than anything else. Invariably, much of the food ended up on his grandmother's chin and the wide bib they tied around her neck.

But Mike went through the process patiently, speaking to her of small things—delivering the Sunday papers, the coming rain, his sisters' exploits—during the long intervals between spoonsful.

Suddenly, between bites, Memo's eyes became very wide and she began blinking quickly, trying to communicate something. Mike often wished that she and the family had learned Morse code before her stroke; but why would they have thought they needed it? Now it would have come in handy as the old woman blinked, paused, blinked repeatedly, paused again.

"What is it, Memo?" whispered Mike, bending closer and cleaning her chin with a napkin. He glanced over his shoulder, half expecting to see a dark shape at the window. Instead there was only the darkness between the curtains, then a sudden ripple of heat lightning which revealed the leaves of the linden tree and the fields across the street. "It's OK," Mike said softly and offered another spoonful of strained carrots.

It obviously wasn't OK. Memo's blinking became more agitated and the muscles of her throat worked so rapidly that Mike feared she was going to regurgitate the evening meal. He bent closer to make sure that she wasn't choking, but it seemed she was breathing all right. The blinking became a frenzied staccato. Mike wondered if she were having another stroke, if she were actually dying this time. But he did not call his parents. Something about the pre-storm stillness outside had invaded his motions and emotions, freezing him in his chair as he bent toward Memo with spoon extended.

The blinking stopped and Memo's eyes grew very wide. At the same instant something scratched against the floorboards of the old house—Mike knew that there was nothing but a low crawlspace there—the scratching audible under the floor of the kitchen on the southwest corner of the house and then moving, scurrying, quicker than a cat or dog would run, across the kitchen, across the corner of the living room and the bit of hallway, under the floor of the parlor—of Memo's room—under Mike's feet and the massive brass bed where the old lady lay.

Mike looked down beneath his still-extended arm, between his sneakers on the frayed rug. The scratching was as loud as if someone on a railed dolly had slid under the house with a long knife or metal rod, clawing at every cross brace and stud under the old floorboards. Now it became a pounding, a chipping away, as if that same blade were being used to hack away at the boards between Mike's sneakers.

He stared down, open-mouthed, waiting for whatever it was to rip its way through the floorboards, imagining bladed fingers emerging and seizing his leg. One glance told him that Memo had quit staring and had closed her eyes as tightly as they could shut.

Suddenly, immediately, the clawing stopping. Mike found his voice. "Mom! Dad! Peg!" He was shouting, not quite screaming. His hand holding the spoon was still extended, but shaking now.

His father came in from the bathroom just across the hall, suspenders hanging loose, his massive belly and undershirt far out over the waistband of his trousers. His mother came in from their room, belting her old robe. A clatter on the stairs announced not Peg but Mary, leaning on the door-frame and peering into the parlor.

There was a cluster of questions snapped at him. "What in the hell are you screaming about?" his father repeated when there was a pause.

Mike looked from face to face. "You didn't hear it?"

"Hear what?" asked his mother in her voice that was always harsher than she meant it to be.

Mike looked down at the carpet between his sneakers. He could *feel* whatever it was down there. Waiting. He glanced back at Memo. Her eyes were still shut tightly, her body rigid.

"A sound," said Mike, hearing how lame his voice sounded. "A terrible sound from underneath the house."

His father shook his head and lifted a towel to dry his jowls. "I didn't hear anything in the bathroom. Must be one of those godda—" He glanced at his frowning wife. "One of those darned cats again. Or maybe another skunk. I'll go out with a flashlight and broom and shoo it away."

"No!" cried Mike, much louder than he had meant to. Mary made a face and his parents looked at him quizzically. "I mean, it's going to rain," he said. "Let's wait till tomorrow, when it's light. And I'll go in there and get it out."

"Watch for the black widow spiders," said Mary with a shudder and pounded back up the stairs. Mike could hear rock-and-roll music from her radio.

His father went back into the bathroom. Mike's mother came in, patted Memo's head, felt her cheek, and said, "It looks as if Mother has drifted off to sleep. I'll wait here to feed her when she wakes up if you want to go up and get ready for bed."

Mike swallowed and lowered his shaking arm, bracing it on a knee that wasn't that steady. He could *feel* something down there, separated just by three-quarters of an inch of wood and a forty-year-old carpet. He could feel it down there in the dark, waiting for him to leave.

"No," he said to his mother. "I'll stay and finish it." He gave her a smile. She touched his head and went back into her room.

Mike waited. After a moment, Memo opened her eyes. Outside, the heat lightning flashed silently.

SIXTEEN

It did not rain on Sunday night, nor on Monday, although the day was gray and thick with humidity. Duane's father had set Wednesday for Uncle Art's cremation in Peoria and there were details to be taken care of, people to notify. At least three people—an old army buddy of Uncle Art's, a cousin he had known well, and an ex-wife—insisted on coming, so there was to be a short memorial service after all. The Old

Man arranged it for three o'clock in Peoria at the only mortuary which did cremations.

The Old Man tried to call J.P. Congden through much of Monday, but the man was never home. Duane stood in the doorway and eavesdropped that afternoon when Constable Barney drove up with a complaint.

"Well, Darren," Barney had said to the Old Man, "J.P.'s telling everybody that you killed his dog."

The Old Man had shown his teeth. "The goddamn dog was attacking my boy. It was a big stupid Doberman with a microscopic little brain about the size of Congden's dick."

Barney shuffled his hat in his hands, running his fingers along the slick sweatband. "J.P. says that the dog was *inside* his house. That he found its body in the house. That somebody broke in and killed it."

The Old Man spat in the dust. "Goddamn it, you know that's as much of a lie as most of J.P. Congden's traffic arrests. That dog *was* inside when we knocked. Then when my boy and I came back around the shed after looking at Art's Cadillac . . . which by all rights shouldn't be there, you know. It's illegal for a third party to buy a wrecked vehicle before the accident's completely investigated. Anyway, the dog jumped Duane *after* we went into the backyard, which means that piss-ant Congden let it out knowing that it would attack us."

Barney looked the Old Man in the eye. "You don't have any evidence of that, do you?"

The Old Man laughed. "Why did he send you after me? Does Congden have evidence that I was the one who killed that Doberman?"

"He said that the neighbors saw you."

"Bullshit. Mrs. Dumont lives next to Congden and she's blind. The only other folks on that block that'd know me is Miz Jensen, and she's up in Oak Hill with her boy, Jimmy. Besides, I had a legal right to be on that property. Congden illegally impounded my brother's car and then tore the doors off it so the true nature of his accident wouldn't be revealed."

Barney set his hat on his head and tugged at the bill of it. "What are you talking about, Darren?"

"I'm talking about two missing doors on the driver's side of that Cadillac that hold evidence of the accident. Red paint. Red paint like the paint on the truck that tried to run my boy down a week ago today."

Barney removed a notebook from his pocket, wrote in it with a stubby pencil, and looked up. "Did you notify Sheriff Conway?"

"You're goddamned right I called him," said the Old Man. He was agitated, rubbing his cheeks. He had shaved that morning and the absence of stubble there seemed to disconcert him. "He said he'd 'look into it.' I told him he'd damn well better look into it, that I was going to file charges against him as well as Congden if they didn't carry out a thorough investigation."

"So you think there was a second vehicle?"

The Old Man glanced back at Duane standing in the doorway. "I *know* that my brother didn't drive that Cadillac into the bridge at seventy miles an hour on his own," he said to Constable Barney. "Art was a damned fool about obeying speed limits, even out on shitty roads like Jubilee College Road. No, somebody ran him off the road."

Barney walked back to his car. "I'll call Conway and tell him I'm checking into it as well."

Behind the screen door, Duane blinked. The town constable had no part in investigating deaths on county highways. What he was doing was a favor, pure and simple.

"Meanwhile," said the constable, "I'll tell our justice of the peace that his neighbors must have been mistaken. Perhaps the dog died of natural causes. The mean sonofabitch has gone after me a few times." He extended his hand to the Old Man. "I'm damned sorry about Art, Darren."

Surprised, the Old Man shook the constable's hand. Duane stepped out and stood next to his father while they watched the car recede down the long drive. Duane thought that if he turned to look at his father right then, he would find tears in the Old Man's eyes for the first time since the accident. He did not turn to look.

That evening they went to Uncle Art's home to get a suit to take into the Peoria mortuary the next morning.

"Damn fool thing," muttered the Old Man as they drove the four miles in the pickup. "They're not going to show him off, just incinerate him and the coffin. Art might as well be nude for all it matters to him or us."

Duane recognized the grumbling as the sign of another day without alcohol as much as grief or general bad temper. The Old Man was nearing a record for the past couple of years.

This trip was what Duane had been waiting for. He hadn't wanted to make a big deal out of searching for signs of whatever book Uncle Art had found and was bringing over to share when he was killed, but he knew the Old Man would have to go over there before the funeral.

It was dark when they arrived. Uncle Art lived in a small white farmhouse set back several hundred yards from the road. He leased the house from the family who still farmed the surrounding fields—set in beans this summer—and only the vegetable garden behind the house was Uncle

Art's handiwork. The Old Man looked at the garden a moment before they went in the back door, and Duane knew that he was thinking about how they'd have to come over and tend it. In a few weeks they'd be eating the tomatoes that Uncle Art loved so much.

The house wasn't locked. Duane blinked and adjusted his glasses as he entered, feeling the grief and sense of loss strike him anew. He realized that it was the scent of Uncle Art's pipe tobacco in the still, trapped air. In that second Duane realized how temporary life was, how fleeting any person's presence was: a few books, the scent of tobacco that a person would never enjoy again, a few clothes that would be used by others, the inevitable snapshots, legal papers, and correspondence that would mean so much less to someone else. A human being on this world, Duane realized with a shock of recognition approaching vertigo, made no more permanent impression than does a hand thrust in water. Remove the hand, and water rushes in to fill the void as if nothing had ever been there.

"I'll be just a minute," said the Old Man, almost whispering for a reason neither understood but both obeyed. "You can stay in here." They had walked through the kitchen into the darker "study."

Duane snapped on a light and nodded. The Old Man disappeared into the bedroom. Duane heard the closet door being opened.

Uncle Art's house was small: only a kitchen, a "study" converted from the unused dining room, a living room barely big enough to hold a BarcaLounger, many bookshelves, two armchairs on either side of a table with a chessboard—Duane recognized the game he and Uncle Art had been playing three weekends earlier—and a large console television set. The small bedroom was the last room. The front door opened onto a small cement porch that looked out on about two acres of yard. No visitors ever entered or left by the front door, but Duane knew that Uncle Art had enjoyed sitting on the front porch in the evening, smoking his pipe and looking out north over the fields. One could hear traffic on Jubilee College Road easily enough, but the cars were not visible because of the hillside.

Duane shook himself out of his reverie and tried to concentrate. Uncle Art once had mentioned that he kept a journal—had kept one every year since 1941. Duane thought that whatever book he had mentioned on the phone was gone—taken by Congden or whoever—but there might be some mention of it.

He clicked on the lamp on Art's cluttered desk. The dining room had been the biggest room in the house, and the "study" was floor-to-ceiling bookcases holding mostly hardcover editions and more low shelves in the center of the room on either side of the huge door Art had used as his desk.

The desk held bills, the telephone, stacks of correspondence which Duane only flicked through, clippings of chess columns from Chicago and New York papers, magazines, cartoons from *The New Yorker,* a framed photograph of Art's second wife, another frame holding a drawing by da Vinci of a helicopter-like machine, a jar of marbles, another jar of red licorice—Duane had raided that jar for as long as he could remember—and scraps of paper holding old shopping lists, lists of fellow union members from the Caterpillar plant, lists of Nobel Prize winners, and a myriad of other things. No journal.

The desk had no drawers. Duane looked around the room. He could hear the Old Man going through drawers in the bedroom, probably finding underwear and socks. It would only take another minute.

Where would Uncle Art keep a journal? Duane wondered if it was in the bedroom. No, Art wouldn't write in bed. He'd fill his daily entry here, at his work desk. Only there was no book here. No drawers.

Books. Duane sat in the old captain's chair, feeling how the varnish had been worn away by his uncle's arms. *He would write in the journal every day. Probably every evening, sitting here.* Duane extended his left hand. *Uncle Art was left-handed.*

One of the low bookshelves near the left trestle-base of the big door of a desk was within reach. It was actually a double shelf, with books facing outward and others—more than a dozen untitled volumes—facing inward, almost invisible in the darkness under the desk. Duane pulled one of the books out: leatherbound; heavy, quality paper; about five hundred pages. There was no printing within, only a tight script written with an old-fashioned pen. The script filled each page and was not only illegible, it was unreadable. Literally.

Duane spread the volume open and leaned closer under the lamp, adjusting his glasses as he did so. The entries were not in English. The tightly scrawled pages looked as if they had been written in some hybrid of Hindi or Arabic, a solid wall of scribbles, loops, arabesques, and squiggles. There were no separate words; the lines were one inseparable, indecipherable tangle of unknown symbols. But at the top of each column of text there were numbers, and these were uncoded. Duane looked at the top of this page and read 19.3.57.

Duane knew that Uncle Art had often said that Europe's—and most of the world's—way of writing the date with the day, then the month, then the year, made more sense than the American way. "Littlest to biggest," he'd said to his nephew when Duane was six. "Makes a hell of a lot more sense that way." Duane had always agreed. He was looking at his uncle's journal entry for March 19, 1957.

He set the book back, pulled out the one set farthest to the left. The one easiest to reach. The first page of scribbles read 1.1.60. The last page, unfinished, lay under a heading of 11.6.60. Uncle Art had not made an entry on Sunday morning, but he had written in his journal on Saturday evening.

"All set?" The Old Man was standing in the doorway, holding a suit still in the dry cleaner's cellophane, with Uncle Art's old gym bag in the other hand. He stepped into the circle of light near the desk and nodded at the book which Duane had instinctively closed. "Is that what Art was bringing you?"

Duane hesitated only a second. "I think so."

"Bring it along then." The Old Man went out through the kitchen.

Duane turned out the light, stood thinking about the other eighteen years of personal thoughts held in the volumes under the desk, and wondered if he was doing the wrong thing. Obviously the journals were in some sort of personal code. But Duane was good at breaking codes. If he broke this code, he would be reading things that Uncle Art had not meant for his eyes, or *any* eyes, to see.

But he wanted me to know what he found. He sounded excited about it. Serious, but excited. And perhaps a little scared.

Duane took a breath and lifted the heavy book, sensing his uncle's presence all around him now in the smell of tobacco, the familiar mustiness of the hundreds and hundreds of books, the scent of leather on the cover, even the slight, pleasant scent of his uncle's perspiration—the clean smell of a workingman's sweat.

It was very dark in the room now. The sense of Uncle Art's presence was a bit unnerving, as if the ghost of the man were standing there behind Duane, urging him to take the book, urging him to sit down there now, turn on the light, and read it with the spirit leaning over him. Duane half expected a cold touch of a hand on his neck.

Walking, not hurrying, Duane went out through the kitchen to join his father in the truck.

Dale and Lawrence had played ball all day despite the threatening clouds and cloying humidity, and by dinnertime they were saturated with dirt that had turned to mud where their sweat had run in rivulets. Their mother saw them coming out the kitchen window and made them stand in the back stairway and strip to their Jockey shorts before she'd let them enter. Dale got the job of carrying the clothes down to the back room of the basement where the washing machine sat.

Dale hated the basement. It was the one part of their big old house that made him nervous. It was OK in the summer when he almost never had to come down here, but in the winter it was his job to come down every evening after dinner and shovel coal into the hopper.

The stairs to the basement were each at least two feet high, made for someone with a greater-than-human stride. The huge concrete stairs wound to the left as they went down between the outside and kitchen walls, and the effect was that the basement seemed much farther down than it should be. *Dungeon stairs,* Lawrence called them.

The naked bulb at the top of the stairs shed almost no light down here where the corridor ran back to the furnace. There was another light beyond the furnace, but it had to be turned on by a hanging cord, as did the one in the coal bin. Dale glanced to his right at the opening to the coal bin as he passed it. It was not a door, really, just a four-foot opening in the wall, stepping up to the higher level of the bin. From floor to ceiling, it was only five feet in the little room and Dale knew how hard it was for his father to crouch in there and shovel coal. The hopper, door now closed, angled from the corridor to the bin so that one shoveled *down* into its waiting maw. Behind the hopper, seeming to fill the end of the short corridor where Dale now stood, was the ancient furnace itself: a huge and scabrous hulk of metal with its tentacles of pipe running every which direction.

What Dale hated most about the coal bin on those winter nights when he had to shovel down here wasn't the work—although he had calluses on his hands through the winter—or the coal-dust taste that lingered in the back of his mouth even after he brushed his teeth; no, it was the crawlspace at the back of the bin.

The far wall ran about three feet from the cement floor and ended just a couple of feet below the ceiling, revealing a dirt and stone floor, waterpipes, and a glimpse of cobwebs. Dale knew that the space ran under much of the room that his father used as an office when he was home and continued on under the huge front porch. He could hear mice and larger rodents scurrying in there when he was shoveling coal, and one cold night he had turned quickly to see small, red eyes staring out at him.

Dale's parents often complimented him on how diligently he filled the hopper, how quickly he worked. For Dale, those twenty or so minutes every winter night were the worst part of his day, and he was willing to work at breakneck speed just to get the damned hopper filled and to get out. He loved it when the coal bin had just been filled and he had only to stand near the hopper and shovel. Later in the month, when the coal was reduced to a low heap in the far corner, he had to walk the width of the bin, lift the load, carry it nine feet across the room, and dump it in, *with his back to the crawlspace.*

Not shoveling coal was one of the reasons Dale loved summer. One glance now told him that there was only a tiny heap of black anthracite in the far corner. Light from the top of the stairs barely cast a glow in the bin; the crawlspace was utter blackness.

Dale found the first light cord, blinked in the sudden glare, went around the mass of furnace into the second room—used for nothing but holding the furnace, passed through the third room where his dad had a workbench with only a smattering of tools, and curved right again into the far room where his mother kept the washer and dryer.

His father had said that it was a bitch to get those machines down here, and that if and when they moved, the washer and dryer stayed. Dale believed him; he remembered his dad, the delivery guys from Sears, Mr. Somerset, and two other neighbor men wrestling with those machines for well over an hour. This back room had no windows—none of the basement rooms did—and the light cord dangled in the center. Near the south wall, a circular pit with a three-foot diameter seemed to drop into darkness. It was the huge sump pump that kept water out of a downstairs set too deep for the local water table. Still, the basement had flooded four times in the four and half years they'd lived here, and Dale's dad once had to wade back here in water over two feet deep to fix the pump.

Dale tossed the filthy clothes onto the top of the washing machine, tugged the light out as he passed, and moved quickly—back room to workroom, workroom to furnace room, furnace room to corridor—not looking into the coal bin this time—then the ten giant steps up and around to the top step. It was so cool and damp in the basement that it came as a shock to feel the clammy air through the back screen door and to see the soft twilight above Grumbacher's house to the west.

Dale padded quickly through the kitchen, embarrassed to be wearing just his underpants. Lawrence was already splashing in the tub and making submarine attack noises. Luckily, Dale's mom was out on the front porch, so he half-skated down the hallway in his bare feet, ran up the stairs, circled the landing, and went into his room to get his robe before his mom came back in. He lay on his bed with the little reading lamp on, skimming through an old copy of *Astounding Science Fiction* until it was his turn to take a bath.

Once alone downstairs, in his quiet and lighted corner of the basement, it took Duane McBride less than five minutes to crack the code.

Uncle Art's journal looked as if it had been kept in Hindi, but it was simple English. There weren't even any transpositions. Of course, it

helped that Duane had shared his uncle's fascination with Leonardo da
Vinci.

The Renaissance genius had kept his own diary in a simple code:
writing reversed so that it could be read in a mirror. Duane brought a
hand mirror over to his worktable and there was the entry in English,
running from right to left. Uncle Art had run the words together so
that the code would not be too obvious; he'd also connected the letters
at the top, which gave the line of print its oddly Arabic or Vedic look.
Instead of periods, he'd used a symbol which looked like a reversed
capital F with two dots before it. A reversed F with one dot was a
comma.

Duane saw that the page and passage he'd opened to dealt with problems at work, a union foreman who was under suspicion of skimming
union funds, and a dialogue reproducing a political argument between
Art and his brother. Duane glanced at the passage, remembered the argument in question—the Old Man had been quite drunk and calling for the
violent overthrow of the government—and then he hurried on to the final
entry:

11.6.60

Found the passage on the bell Duane's been hunting for! It was in
the *Apocrypha: Additions to the Book of the Law* by Aleister Crowley. I should have realized that it would be Crowley, that self-
appointed mage of our age, who would know something about all
this.

Spent a couple of hours tonight out on the porch, thinking. At
first I was going to keep this to myself, but little Duane's worked
hard on researching this local mystery, and I decided that he has a
right to know. Tomorrow I'll take the book over and share the whole
section on "familiars" with him. The Borgia section makes for weird
reading.

A couple of the pertinent sections:

"Where the Medicis favored the traditional animal familiars for
their bridge to the World of Magick, it is said that the Borgia family
during those most productive centuries of the Renaissance (from the
point of view of practicing the Art) chose an inanimate object as their
talisman.

"Legend had it that the great Stele of Revealing, the iron Egyptian obelisk in the Shrine of Osiris, had been stolen from its rightful
place in the Fifth or Sixth Century (Christian Reckoning) and had
long been the source of power for the Borja family of Valencia,
Spain.

"In 1455, when a member of that ancient family of sorcerers became pope, a great irony since his political rise had occurred due to the Dark Powers in this pre-Christian symbol, his first act was to commission the construction of a great bell. There is little doubt that this bell—brought to Rome about the time of this Borja pope's death—was the Stele of Revealing, melted down and recast into a more palatable form for the masses of Christians awaiting its arrival.

"This bell was said to be much more than another magical object of the form found in almost every Moorish or Spanish royal household in those days: the Borjas looked upon it as the 'All devourer, All begetter.' In the Egyptian, the Stele of Revealing was known as the 'crown of death' and its transmogrification had been foretold in the *Book of the Abyss*.

"And unlike organic familiars, which act merely as medium, the Stele, even in its incarnation as a bell, demanded its own sacrifice. Legend says that Don Alonso y Borja offered a newly born granddaughter to the bell before going to Rome for the Conclave of 1455 which—against all odds—elected him Pope. But Don Alonso, now known as Pope Calixtus III, either lacked the stomach to continue the schedule of sacrifices or believed that the Stele's power had been profitably spent by his mere accession to power. For whatever reason, the sacrifices were discontinued. Pope Calixtus died. The bell was installed in the palace tower of Don Alonso's nephew, Rodrigo y Borja, Cardinal of Rome, successor to the Archbishopry of Valencia, and the first true heir to the Borgia dynasty.

"But, legend tells, the Stele, or bell as it was now disguised, had not finished with its own demands."

After his bath, Dale Stewart went up to his bedroom. Lawrence was in his own bed. Or rather, he was *on* it, sitting cross-legged in the center of the bed. There was something odd about his expression.

"What's the matter?" said Dale.

Lawrence was so pale that his freckles stood out. "I . . . I don't know. I came in to turn the light on and . . . well, I heard something."

Dale shook his head. He remembered the time a couple of years before when they'd been alone watching TV while their mother went shopping. It was a winter afternoon and they'd watched *The Mummy's Revenge* on the Saturday afternoon Creature Feature. As soon as it was over, Lawrence had "heard" something in the kitchen . . . the same slow, sliding step that the lame mummy had made in the movie. Dale had joined his little brother in panic then; they'd loosened the storm window and jumped into the front yard as the "steps" came closer. Their mother had come home to find them standing on the front porch in their socks and t-shirts, shivering.

Well, Dale was eleven now, not eight. "What'd you hear?" he asked.

Lawrence looked around. "I dunno. I didn't exactly *hear* it . . . I sort of *felt* it. Like someone else was in the room."

Dale sighed. He tossed some dirty socks in the hamper and tugged off the overhead light.

The closet door was open a bit. Dale pushed it shut as he walked toward his own bed.

The door did not click shut.

Thinking a slipper or something was in the way, Dale paused and pushed harder.

The door pushed back. Something inside the closet was pushing to get out.

In his basement, Duane mopped his face with a bandanna. It was usually cool down here even on the hottest days of summer, but he found that he was sweating freely. The book lay open on his "study desk" made out of a door on trestles. Duane had been copying pertinent information into his notebook as quickly as he could, but now he laid aside his pencil and just read.

His uncle's backward script almost made sense without the mirror now, but Duane still held the book up to the glass:

> The Stele of Revealing, now cast in its disguise as a bell, had been partially activated by the sacrifice of the first Borgia pope's granddaughter. But according to the Book of Ottaviano, the Borgias feared the Stele's power and were not prepared for the Apocalypse which, according to legend and lore, went with the Stele's full awakening. As recorded in *The Book of the Law,* the Stele of Revealing offered great power to those who served it. But at the same time, when the proper sacrifices were completed, the talisman became the Knell of the Final Days: a harbinger of the final Apocalypse which would follow that Quickening of the Stele by sixty years, six months, and six days.
>
> Rodrigo, the next pope of the Borgia dynasty, had the Bell taken to the tower he had added to the Vatican complex. There, in the Torre Borgia, Alexander—as Rodrigo Borgia

called himself as pope—was said to have kept the Stele from its Quickening by the mystical murals of a half-deranged dwarf of an artist named Pinturicchio. These "grotesques"—designs taken from the grottos beneath Rome—served to contain the Stele's evil while allowing the family to benefit from the talisman's power.

Or so Pope Alexander thought.

In both *The Book of the Law* and Ottaviano's secret books, there are hints that the Stele began to dominate the lives of the Borgias. Years later, Alexander had the Bell moved to the massive and impenetrable *Castel Sant' Angelo,* but even burying the artifact in that sepulcher of stone and bones did not lessen the thing's power over the human beings who had attempted to control it.

Ottaviano's shortened account tells of the madness that gripped both the Borgias and Rome during those decades: the murders and intrigues terrible even by the brutal standards of the day, accounts of demons roving the catacombs beneath Rome, of things less than human moving through *Castel Sant' Angelo* and the streets of the city, and tales of the domination of the Stele of Revealing as it worked towards its own quickening.

From this point, after the terrible death of Ottaviano, the legend of the Stele moves into darkness. The destruction of the House of Borgia is record. It is said that a generation later, when the first Medici pope ascended to the Throne of Saint Peter's, his first papal command was to have the Bell removed from Rome, melted down, and the accursed metal buried in sanctified ground far from the Vatican.

Today, no clue to the whereabouts or fate of the Stele of Revealing has survived. The legend of the Stele's power as "All devourer, all begetter" continues in necromancy to this day.

Duane set Uncle Art's book aside. He could hear the Old Man fumbling around upstairs in the kitchen. Then there was a mumbling, the slam of the screen door, and Duane heard the pickup start with a grind and move down the driveway. The Old Man's fast from booze was over. Duane hadn't heard whether the Old Man was heading toward Carl's or the Black Tree, but he knew that it would be hours before his father would return.

Duane sat in the circle of lamp light a few minutes, looking at the book and the notes he had taken. Then he went up to lock the screen door.

The closet door was slowly opening.

Dale leaned into it, stopped the slow opening with a four-inch gap showing into darkness, and turned to look at Lawrence. His brother was staring at him with wide eyes.

"Help," whispered Dale. There was renewed effort from the other side and the door opened another inch as Dale's socks slid on the bare wood floor.

"Mom!" screamed Lawrence as he jumped from his bed and ran to Dale's side. Together the two boys put their shoulders against the door, forcing it two inches closer to being shut. "Mom!" They were shouting in unison now.

The door stopped, pressure built on the yellow-painted boards, and it began opening again.

Dale and Lawrence stared at each other, their cheeks against the rough boards, *feeling* the terrible force being transmitted through the wood.

The door opened another three inches. There was no noise of any sort from the interior of the closet; here on the outside, though, both boys were puffing and gasping, Dale's socks and Lawrence's bare feet scrabbling on the floor.

The door opened another few inches. There was a gap a foot wide now, and from it a cold breeze seemed to be blowing.

"Jesus . . . can't . . . hold it," gasped Dale. His left thigh was braced against their old dresser, but he couldn't get enough leverage to move the door back. Whatever was in there had at least the strength of a grown-up.

The door opened another two inches.

"Mom!" screamed Lawrence. "Mom, help! Mom!"

There was some sort of reply from the front porch, but Dale realized that they could never hold the door long enough for their mother to arrive. "Run!" he gasped.

Lawrence looked at him, his terrified face only inches away, and let go. He ran, but not out of the room. With two steps and a huge bound, Lawrence leaped for his bed.

Without Lawrence's help, Dale couldn't hold the door. The pressure was unrelenting. He went with it, jumping onto the top of the four-foot-high dresser, pulling his legs up. The dresser lamp and some books crashed to the floor.

The door smashed open against Dale's knees. Lawrence screamed.

Dale heard his mother's footsteps on the stairs, her voice calling a question, but before he could open his own mouth to shout back a response, there was a wave of cold air as if they had opened a door to a meat locker, and then something came out of the closet.

It was very low and long—at least four feet long—and as insubstantial as a shadow, but much darker. It was a blackness, sliding along the floor like some frenzied insect that had just been freed from a jar. Dale could see leglike filaments whipping wildly. He lifted his feet onto the dresser top. A framed photograph crashed to the floor.

"Mom!" He and Lawrence had screamed in unison again.

The black thing moved across the floor in a blur. Dale thought that it was like a cockroach, if cockroaches were four feet long, a few inches high, and made out of black smoke. Dark appendages whipped and scrabbled on floorboards.

"Mom!"

The thing rushed under Lawrence's bed.

Lawrence made no noise as he leaped to Dale's bed, on his feet now, bouncing like a trampoline acrobat.

Their mother stood in the doorway, looking from one screaming boy to another.

"It's a thing . . . from the closet . . . went under . . ."

"Under the bed . . . black thing . . . *big*!"

Their mom ran to the hall closet, returned with a broom. "Out," she said. She tugged on the overhead light.

Dale hesitated only a second before hopping down, getting behind his mother, running to the doorway. Lawrence bounced from Dale's bed to his bed to the doorway. Both boys skidded into the hallway and went crashing into the banister. Dale peeked in the room.

His mom was down on all fours, lifting the dust ruffle under Lawrence's bed.

"Mom! No!" shouted Dale and rushed in to try to pull her back.

She dropped the broom and took her oldest son by the upper arms. "Dale . . . *Dale* . . . now stop. *Stop.* There's nothing there. Look."

Between gasps quickly turning to sobs, Dale peeked. There was nothing under the bed.

"It probably went under Dale's," said Lawrence from the doorway.

With Dale still clinging, their mom went around and lifted the dust ruffles from Dale's bed. Dale's heart almost stopped when she went down on all fours, the broom in front of her.

"See," she said, rising and brushing at her skirt and knees. "There's nothing there. Now what do you *think* you saw?"

Both boys gabbled at once. Dale listened to his own voice and realized what their description sounded like: something big, black, shadowy, low. It had pushed the closet door open and run under the bed like a giant bug.

Uh-huh.

"Maybe it's back in the closet," suggested Lawrence, barely holding back tears and gasping for breath.

Their mother looked at them a long second but went over and pushed the closet door wider. Dale cringed back toward the doorway to the hall as his mom shifted clothes on the rack, kicked tennis shoes aside, and glanced around the edges of the doorframe. The closet was not deep. It was empty.

She folded her arms and waited. The boys stayed in the doorway, glancing over their shoulders at the landing and the dark openings to their parents' room and the extra room as if the shadow would come scrabbling across the hardwood floors after them.

"You guys have been scaring each other, haven't you?" she asked.

Both boys denied it and began babbling, describing the thing again, Dale showing how they had tried to hold the closet door shut.

"And this bug pushed it open?" Their mom had a slight smile.

Dale sighed. Lawrence looked up at him as if to say, *Somehow it's still under my bed. We just can't see it.*

"Mom," said Dale as calmly as he could, his voice conversational, reasonable, "can we sleep in your room tonight? In our sleeping bags?"

She hesitated a second. Dale guessed that she was remembering the time they locked themselves out because of the "mummy" . . . or perhaps the time last summer when they'd sat out in the fields near the ball diamond at night trying to telepathically contact alien spaceships . . . and had come home terrified when a plane's lights had gone over.

"All right," she said. "You get your sleeping bags and the foldup cot. I have to go out and tell Mrs. Somerset that my big boys interrupted our conversation with screams because of a shadowy bug."

She went downstairs with both her sons within arm's length. They waited until she came back inside before they went upstairs again, having her wait at the doorway to the extra room while they scrounged around for the sleeping bags and the cot.

She refused to leave even the hall light on all night. Both boys held their breath when she went into their room to tug off the overhead light, but she returned all right, leaving the broom by the headboard like a weapon. Dale thought of the pump-action shotgun his father kept in the closet next to his own Savage over-and-under there. The shells were in the bottom drawer of the cedar chest.

Dale had his cot so close to the edge of the bed that there was no gap there at all. Long after their mother had fallen asleep, Dale could feel his brother's wakefulness, intense and watchful as his own.

When Lawrence's hand crept out from under the blankets onto Dale's cot, Dale didn't push it away. He made sure it was indeed his brother's hand and wrist . . . not something from the darkness below the bed . . . and then he held it tightly until he finally fell asleep.

SEVENTEEN

On Wednesday, June fifteenth, after he'd done his paper route and before he went to St. Malachy's to help Father C. say Mass, Mike went under the house.

The morning light was rich, the sun already high enough to build shadows under the elms and peach trees in the yard, when Mike pried off the metal access panel to the crawlspace. Everybody else he knew had basements. *Well,* he thought, *everybody else I know has indoor plumbing, too.*

He'd brought his Boy Scout flashlight and now he shone it into the low space. Cobwebs. Dirt floor. Pipes, the dark wood two-by-fours under the floor. More cobwebs. The space was barely eighteen inches high and it smelled of old cat urine and fresh soil.

There were more spiderwebs than cobwebs. Mike tried to avoid the solid, massy, milky webs he knew meant black widows as he crawled and wiggled toward the front of the house. He had to pass under his parents' room and the short hall to get there. The darkness seemed to stretch on forever, the faint light from the opening behind him fading. In a sudden panic, Mike wriggled around until he could see the rectangle of sunlight, making sure that he could find his way out. The opening looked very far away. Mike continued forward.

When he figured that he had to be under the parlor—he could see the stone foundation three yards ahead—Mike stopped, turned on his side, and panted. His right arm was touching a wooden cross brace under the floor; his left hand was tangled in spiderwebs. Dust rose around him, getting in his hair and making him blink. The powdery stuff floated in the narrow flashlight beam.

Geez, I'm going to be in great shape to help Father C. serve Mass, he thought.

Mike wiggled left, the flashlight beam finding the north wall fifteen feet away. The stone looked black. What the hell—What the heck was he looking for? Mike squirmed and began moving in a circle, checking the dirt for signs of its being disturbed.

It was hard to tell. The stone and dirt floor had been gouged by weather and pawed by generations of the O'Rourke cats as well as other animals seeking shelter here. A few dried cat turds littered the area.

It was a cat or skunk, thought Mike with a mental sigh of relief. Then he saw the hole.

At first it was just another shadow, but its blackness did not diminish with the flashlight beam playing across it. Mike wondered if it was a circle of dark plastic, some tarp or something his dad had left down here. He wiggled four feet closer and stopped.

It was a hole, perfectly round, perhaps twenty inches across. Mike could have gone down it headfirst if he'd wanted to. He did not want to.

He could smell it. Mike blinked away his revulsion and moved his head closer. The stench came out of the tunnel like a breeze from a charnel house.

Mike lifted a stone and tossed it into the hole. No noise.

Panting slightly, his heart pounding so loudly he was sure that Memo could hear it through the floor, he raised his flashlight to the two-by-fours, thrust it forward, and tried to shine a light down the hole.

At first he thought the walls of the tunnel were red clay, but then he saw the ribbed walls, like blood-red cartilage, like the inside of some creature's gut. *Like the tunnel in the cemetery shed.*

Mike backed away, kicking up a cloud of dust in his retreat, plowing through spiderwebs and cat turds in his panicked flight. For an instant, turning, he lost the rectangle of light and was sure that something had sealed the entrance.

No, there it is.

Mike crawled on his elbows and knees, batting his head against two-by-fours, feeling the webs on his face and not caring. The flashlight was half under his body now, illuminating nothing. Mike thought that he saw more tunnel openings a few yards to his left, under the kitchen, but he didn't crawl that way to find out.

A shape moved into the crawlspace opening, blocking the light. Mike could see two arms, legs with what might be puttees.

He rolled onto his side, lifting the iron bar. The shape crawled half into the opening, blocking the light.

"Mikey?" It was his sister Kathleen's voice, soft, pure, innocent in its slow way. "Mikey, Mom says that you have to get going if you're going to get to church."

Mike half-collapsed in the moist dirt. His right arm was shaking. "OK, Kathy, move back out so I can get through."

The shadow unblocked the entrance.

Heart actually aching from its exertion, Mike clambered through and out. He sealed the panel, pounding the nails through the top of the tin rectangle.

"Gee, you're a mess, Mikey," said Kathleen, smiling at him.

Mike looked down. He was covered with gray dust and cobwebs. His elbows were bleeding. He could taste the mud on his face. Impulsively, he hugged his sister. She hugged him back, apparently not caring at all if she got dirty, too.

More than forty people showed up for the "private" memorial service at Peoria's Howell Mortuary. Duane thought that the Old Man seemed almost disappointed by the turnout, as if he had wanted to keep his brother's final services to himself. But the notice in the Peoria paper and the few phone calls the Old Man had made brought people from as far away as Chicago and Boston. Several of Uncle Art's co-workers at the Caterpillar plant showed up, and one of them wept openly during the brief service.

There was no minister present—Uncle Art had held fast to the family tradition of being militantly agnostic—but short eulogies were given by several people: the co-worker who had cried and who cried again during his talk, their cousin Carol who had flown in from Chicago and who had to return that evening, and an attractive, middle-aged woman from Peoria named Delores Stephens whom the Old Man had introduced as "a friend of Uncle Art's." Duane wondered how long she and Uncle Art had been lovers.

Finally the Old Man had spoken: Duane found it a powerfully moving eulogy—there was no talk of an afterlife or rewards for a life well spent, only the grieved tones of a brother's loss leavened by a description of a personality bowing to no false icons but dedicated to treating other people decently and well. The Old Man ended by reading Shakespeare—Uncle Art's favorite writer—and although Duane expected "And flights of angels bear thee to thy rest . . ." knowing that Uncle Art would have appreciated the irony, what he heard was a song. The Old Man's voice threatened to break several times, but he kept going, his voice strengthening by the strange ending:

> *Fear no more the heat o' the sun,*
> *Nor the furious winter's rages;*
> *Thou thy worldly task hast done,*
> *Home art gone, and ta'en thy wages:*
> *Golden lads and girls all must,*
> *As chimney-sweepers, come to dust.*

Fear no more the frown o' the great;
    Thou art past the tyrant's stroke;
Care no more to clothe and eat;
    To thee the reed is as the oak;
The scepter, learning, physic, must
All follow this, and come to dust.

Fear no more the lightning flash,
    Nor the all-dreaded thunder stone;
Fear not slander, censure rash;
    Thou hast finished joy and moan;
All lovers young, all lovers must
Consign to thee, and come to dust.

No exerciser harm thee!
Nor no witchcraft charm thee!
Ghost unlaid forbear thee!
Quiet consummation have;
And renowned be thy grave!

There were sobs in the chapel. The Old Man had recited the verse without notes or book, and now he lowered his head and returned to his seat.

Someone in the curtain-covered alcove began playing an organ. Slowly, in small clusters or singly, the small group dispersed. Cousin Carol and a few others waited, chatting with the Old Man, patting Duane on the head. The buttoned collar and tie felt alien to him; he imagined Uncle Art stepping into the chapel and saying, "For heaven's sakes, kiddo, take off that silly thing. Ties are for accountants and politicians."

Finally, only Duane and the Old Man remained. Together they went down into the basement of the mortuary, where the powerful crematory furnace was, to watch as Uncle Art was consigned to the flames.

Mike waited until Father C. had invited him over to the rectory to eat their usual post-Communion breakfast of coffee and bagels before talking about the thing in the crawlspace.

Mike had never seen a bagel before Father Cavanaugh started serving them to the few reliable altar boys three years earlier. Now he was an expert, spreading lox or cream cheese with abandon. It had taken awhile to convince the priest that it was all right for an eleven-year-old to drink coffee; like calling the diocese car the Popemobile, it was a secret the two kept between them.

Mike munched on the bagel and wondered how to phrase his question: *Father C., I'm having a little problem with a sort of dead soldier tunneling under my house and trying to get at my grandma. Does the Church have anything that might help?*

Finally he said, "Father, do you believe in Evil?"

"Evil?" said the dark priest, looking up from his paper. "You mean evil in the abstract?"

"I don't know what that means," said Mike. He often felt stupid around Father C.

"Evil as an entity or force separate from the works of man?" asked the priest. "Or do you mean evil like this?" He held up a photo in the paper.

Mike looked. It was a picture of some guy named Eichmann who was a prisoner in a place called Israel. Mike didn't know anything about that. "I guess I mean the separate kind," he said.

Father Cavanaugh folded the paper. "Ahh, the ancient question of evil incarnate. Well, you know the Church's teachings."

Mike blushed but shook his head.

"Tut, tut," said the priest, obviously teasing now. "You're going to have to resume your catechism lessons, Michael."

Mike nodded. "Yeah, but what *does* the Church say about evil?"

Father Cavanaugh removed a pack of Marlboros from the pocket of his work shirt, shook a cigarette free, and lit up. He picked a bit of tobacco off his tongue. His voice turned serious. "Well, you know that the Church recognizes the existence of evil as an independent force . . ." He glanced at Mike's incomprehending stare. "Satan, for instance. The devil."

"Oh, yeah." Mike remembered the smell coming up out of the tunnels. *Satan.* Suddenly the whole thing seemed a little silly.

"Aquinas and other theologians have dealt with the problem of evil for centuries, trying to understand how it can be a separate force while the dominion of the Trinity can be the all-powerful, unchallenged force Scripture says that it is. The answers are mostly unsatisfactory, but certainly the dogma of the Church tells us to believe that evil has its own dominion, its own agents . . . Are you following this, Michael?"

"Yeah, sort of." Mike wasn't quite sure. "So there can be . . . evil powers sort of like angels?"

Father Cavanaugh sighed. "Well, we're getting into some medieval mind-sets here, aren't we, Michael? But, yes, essentially, that's what the tradition of the Church teaches."

"What kind of evil powers, Father?"

The priest tapped his long fingers against his cheek. "What kind? Well, we'd have demons, of course. And incubi. And succubi. And Dante categorizes whole families and species of demons, wonderful creatures with names like Draghignazzo—which would mean 'like a large dragon,' and Barbariccia, 'the curly-bearded one,' and Graffiacane, 'he who scratches dogs,' and . . ."

"Who's Dante?" interrupted Mike, excited at the prospect of some-one living around here who would be an expert in such things.

Father C. sighed again and stubbed his cigarette out. "I forgot that we were depending upon the educational system here in the seventh cir-cle of desolation. Dante, Michael, is a poet who lived and died some six centuries ago. I'm afraid I digressed from the substance of our discus-sion."

Mike finished his coffee, brought the mug to the sink, and carefully washed it. "Do these things . . . these demons . . . do they hurt *people*?"

Father Cavanaugh frowned at him. "We're talking about the intel-lectual creations of people who lived in an ignorant time, Michael. When people were ill, they blamed it on demons. Their only medicine was at-taching leeches . . ."

"Bloodsuckers?" Mike was shocked.

"Yes. Demons were blamed for illness, mental retardation . . ." He paused, possibly remembering that his altar boy's sister was retarded. "Apoplexy, bad weather, mental illness . . . anything that they couldn't explain. And there was very little that they *could* explain."

Mike turned back to the table. "But do you think these things ex-isted . . . exist? Do they still go after people?"

Father Cavanaugh folded his arms. "I think the Church has given us some wonderful theology, Michael. But think of the Church as a gi-ant steam shovel searching the river bottom for gold. It brings up a lot of gold, but there has to be some muck and refuse from all that scooping."

Mike frowned. He hated it when Father C. got into comparisons like that. The priest called them metaphors; Mike called it dodging the question. "Do they exist?"

Father Cavanaugh opened his hands, palms up. "Possibly not in the literal sense, Michael. Certainly in the figurative."

"If they *did* exist," persisted Mike, "would Church stuff stop them the way it does vampires in the movies?"

The priest smiled slightly. "Church stuff?"

"You know . . . crosses, the Host, Holy Water . . . stuff like that."

Father C. raised his dark eyebrows as if he were being teased. Mike, waiting for the answer, did not notice.

"Of course," said the priest. "If all that . . . Church stuff . . . works on vampires, it would have to work on demons. Wouldn't it?"

Mike nodded. He decided that he'd learned enough for now; Father

C. would think he was daffy if he started talking about the Soldier after all this stuff about demons and vampires. Father C. invited Mike to a "bachelor dinner" at the rectory on Friday, something he did about once a month, but Mike had to decline. Dale had invited him out to Uncle Henry's farm on Friday to search for the Bootleggers' Cave they'd been hunting for since he'd first met the Stewart family. Mike suspected that there was no Bootleggers' Cave, but he always enjoyed playing in Uncle Henry's fields. Plus, dinner at Dale's Uncle Henry's always meant great food—even if Mike couldn't eat the steak on Friday—with lots of vegetables fresh from the garden.

Mike said his good-byes, found his bike, and pedaled like mad for home, wanting to get the yard mowed and all the other household chores done by early afternoon so he could play. Passing Old Central, he remembered that Jim Harlen had been home for several days and realized with a pang of guilt that he and the other guys hadn't stopped by to see him yet. That thought led to the memory that today was Duane's uncle's funeral in Peoria.

The thought of death made Mike think of Memo, possibly home alone this time of day, except for Kathleen of course.

Mike pedaled faster, past the school, toward home.

Dale called Duane McBride on Wednesday evening, but the conversation was short and painful. Duane sounded tired beyond imagining and Dale's expressions of sympathy embarrassed them both. Dale told the other boy about Friday night's get-together at Uncle Henry's and pressed him until Duane said that he would try to be there. Dale went up to bed depressed.

"Do you think the thing's still under the bed?" whispered Lawrence an hour later. They'd left the night-light on.

"We checked," Dale whispered back. "You saw nothing's there." Lawrence had insisted on holding hands. Dale had compromised by allowing his little brother to hang on to the sleeve of his pajamas.

"But we *saw* it . . ."

"Mom says we saw a shadow or something."

Lawrence made a rude sound. "Was it a shadow that pushed against the door?"

Dale felt a chill. He remembered the insistent, unrelenting pressure of the closet door pushing against him. Whatever had been in there had refused to stay closed in. "Whatever it is," he whispered, hearing the edge in his own voice, "it's gone now."

"No, it isn't." Lawrence's voice was barely audible.

"How do you know?"

"I just do."

"Well, then, where is it?"

"Waiting."

"Where?" Dale looked across the short gap of the bed and saw his brother staring at him. Without his glasses, Lawrence's eyes looked very large and dark.

"It's still under the bed," his brother whispered sleepily. He closed his eyes. Dale allowed him to hold his hand rather than his sleeve. "It's waiting," mumbled Lawrence, drifting off to sleep.

Dale looked at the ten-inch gap they'd left when they shoved their beds closer. They'd wanted to push the beds together, but their mother said it was too hard to vacuum when they were that way. Ten inches was easy enough to reach across, small enough that nothing huge could come up at them.

But an arm could. A hand with claws. Maybe a head on a long neck.

Dale shivered again. This was silly. Mom was right, they'd imagined this thing the way they'd imagined the mummy's footsteps a couple of years ago. Or the UFO coming to get them.

But we didn't see those other things.

Dale closed his eyes. But a final thought before drifting off brought him awake again, blinking, staring down into the dark between the beds below where his exposed hand still touched Lawrence's.

Damn. If our beds are this close, then it can get under mine *without me seeing. It could raise those black legs on both sides of our beds and get both of us at once.*

Lawrence was snoring softly, drooling a bit onto his Roy Rogers pillowcase. Dale stared at the far wall, counting the spars and masts on the ships repeated in the wallpaper there. He tried not to breathe too loudly. The better to listen. The better to hear something if it made a sound before it struck.

EIGHTEEN

On Thursday the Old Man had to go back to Uncle Art's house to dig out some legal papers and Duane went along despite his father's unease at having him there.

The Old Man was edgy and irritable, obviously on the verge of falling off the wagon in a serious way. Duane knew that he had held on this long out of love for his brother and a real need not to disgrace himself in front of the family.

Part of the Old Man's anxiety had come from his indecisiveness about what to do with Uncle Art's ashes. He had been appalled when the mortuary people had given him the heavy decorative urn which had ridden back from Peoria with them like a silent and unwanted passenger.

After dinner on Wednesday evening, before Dale Stewart called, Duane had gone in to peek inside the urn. The Old Man had come into the room at that moment, lighting his pipe.

"Those white chunks that look like bits of broken chalk are bone," the Old Man had said, puffing the pipe alight.

Duane had resealed the lid.

"You'd think that when they put a body in a furnace approaching the temperature of the surface of the sun," his father said, "that there'd be nothing left but ash and memories. But bones are persistent things."

Duane had sat on a seldom-used chair near the fireplace. Suddenly his legs had felt both heavy and weak at the same time. "Memories are persistent things, too," he'd said, wondering aloud why he'd chosen a cliché.

The Old Man had grunted. "I don't have the damnedest idea where to spread those. Barbaric custom when you think about it."

Duane had glanced at the urn. "I think you're supposed to scatter them at some place important to the person's life," he said softly. "Some place they were happy."

The Old Man grunted again. "You know that Art left a will, Duanie. But he damn well didn't tell me where to toss his ashes. Some place where he was happy. . . ." He fell into musing, puffing at the pipe.

Duane said, "The main reading room of the Bradley Library would be a good place."

The Old Man guffawed. "That'd make Art laugh, too." He removed the pipe and stared away for a moment. "Any other ideas?"

"He used to love fishing along the Spoon." Duane felt the scalding peristalsis of grief seize his throat and heart again. He went into the kitchen for a glass of water. When he returned, the Old Man's pipe had gone out and he was cleaning it, tapping ashes into the fireplace. *Ashes.*

"You're right," the Old Man said suddenly. "That was probably the place he most enjoyed. He and I used to fish there even before Art moved down from Chicago. He used to take you there all the time, didn't he?"

Duane nodded, using a sip of the water as an excuse not to talk. Just then the phone had rung with Dale's call and when Duane returned, the Old Man had gone into his workroom to putter around with the Mark V learning machine.

They'd gone to the river just after sunrise, when the fish were rising to the surface to feed with great ripples, making Duane wish he'd brought his pole. There was no real ceremony; the Old Man had held on to the vase for a moment, as if suddenly reluctant to release the contents, and then as sunlight first illuminated the cypress and willows above them, he'd sprinkled the ashes, tapping the bottom of the vase until the final remnants had dropped away.

There *were* bones, making small splashes that attracted catfish and at least one bass that Duane could see in the shallow water near the shore. The ashes stayed together at first, forming a gray film that followed the currents and whirled around the snags that Duane knew so well from fishing here over the years. Then the faster current downstream toward the bridge caught them and the line of gray was torn apart, whirled under, and mixed with the waters of the river.

Duane tossed a rock in, remembering the times he'd done that when he was bored as a little kid. Probably scaring all the fish away that Uncle Art had been trying to catch. His uncle had never complained.

Then he had brushed his hands and followed the trail up the steep bank toward the car, noticing as he climbed how thin his father had grown over recent weeks and how sunburned and lined the back of his neck was. With his new growth of gray stubble, the Old Man finally looked *old* to Duane.

Uncle Art's house had lost the smell of the man and now merely smelled musty and unused.

As the Old Man went through the drawers and file cabinet, Duane surreptitiously checked old note pads and went through the wastebasket. Like Duane himself, Uncle Art had been a compulsive note-taker, reminder-writer, and record-keeper.

Bingo. The crumpled paper in the wastebasket had been lying beneath a cigar wrapper and some other junk. It had probably been written on Saturday night, the night before the accident.

> 1) The damned Borgia Bell or Stele of Revealing or whatever it is survived after all. Mention of it in the Medici section of *The Book of the Law.*
>
> 2) Sixty years, six months, six days. Assuming that the absurd and impossible has become reality, that the events Duane's talking about are because the thing has been "activated" after all these centuries, then the sacrifice would have been made around the turn of the century. Sometime after New Year in 1900. Check in town. Find people who would remember. Don't talk to Duane until there are some answers.
>
> 3) Crowley says the Bell, the Stele, *used* people. And summoned "agents from the Dark World," whatever the hell that's supposed to mean. Recheck the accounts of "things in the streets of Rome" in the time of the Borgia pope and the Medici section.
>
> 4) Get in touch with Ashley-Montague. Make him talk.

Duane took a breath, folded the paper into the pocket of his flannel shirt, and went out onto the porch. The grass of the lawn was growing wild. Insects hopped. Somewhere along the edge of the treeline, cicadas made a loud buzzing that made Duane a bit dizzy. He sat in the metal chair, lifted his legs to the low railing, and stared out at nothing, thinking. It wasn't until the Old Man came out onto the porch and paused with his hand still on the screen door that Duane realized what he looked like in this chair, this posture . . . *who* he must have looked like.

The Old Man had found the papers. They took care closing the house up, knowing that it might be weeks or even months until they came to clean it out before the auction.

Duane didn't look back as they bumped down the lane.

Duane chose Mrs. Moon.

The librarian's mother was in her eighties, had lived in Elm Haven all of her life, and had resided across the street from Old Central on the southeast corner of Depot and Second since she was a young woman. Duane knew her only slightly, mostly from seeing her with Miss Moon on their walks when he was visiting town.

Miss Moon, he knew well. Duane had been four when Uncle Art had taken him into town to get a library card.

Miss Moon had frowned slightly, shaken her head, and peered at the chubby little boy in front of her desk. "We have very few picture books, Mr. McBride. We prefer that the parents of . . . ah . . . pre-readers use their own cards when checking out books for the little ones."

Uncle Art had said nothing. Pulling the nearest volume off the shelf, he had handed it to four-year-old Duane. "Read," he'd said.

"Chapter One . . . I am born," read Duane. "Whether I shall turn out to be the hero of my own life, or whether that station will be held by anybody else, these pages must show. To begin my life with the beginning of my life, I record that I was born (as I have been informed and believe) on a Friday, at twelve o'clock at night. It was remarked that the clock began to . . ."

"OK," Uncle Art had said and returned the book to its shelf.

Miss Moon had frowned and fussed with the chain of her glasses, but she'd written out a lending card to Duane McBride. For years that card had been Duane's prize possession, despite the fact that Miss Moon always treated him with a chilliness bordering on resentment. Finally she had defined her role as one of limiting the number of books the overweight little boy could check out, remonstrating firmly with him when he returned something late—not, as it turned out, because he had tarried in reading it, but almost always because he had devoured the stack of books during the first few days after returning to the farm, then waited weeks for the Old Man to find time to drive him into town again.

When, in second grade, Duane had gone on a Nancy Drew mystery binge, alternating the female detective's adventures with C.S. Forester and everything by Robert Louis Stevenson, Miss Moon had pointed out that the Nancy Drews were *girls' books*—her term—and she asked pointedly whether Duane had a sister.

Duane had grinned at her, adjusted his glasses, and said, "Nope," checking out his limit of five books, all Nancy Drews. When that series was finished, he'd discovered Edgar Rice Burroughs and spent a delirious summer traversing the steppes of Barsoom, the jungles of Venus, and— most eagerly—swinging from the "middle terrace" of Lord Greystoke's jungle. Duane wasn't quite sure what the middle terrace was, but he'd tried to simulate it in the low oaks down by the creek, Witt watching him with a cocked head and puzzled eyes while Duane swung from limb to limb and ate lunch in the branches.

The following summer, Duane was reading Jane Austen but Miss Moon said nothing this time about *girls' books*.

Duane hiked into town just after he finished his morning chores. The Old Man had been tilling less and less acreage every year, leasing out most of the three hundred and forty acres to Mr. Johnson, so there wasn't too much to do. Duane still watched over the livestock, made sure they had water in the back pasture, but they were much less of a problem now that they were out of the barn. The dreaded manure-hauling had been completed in May, so Duane didn't have to worry about that.

This morning he had finished the maintenance work on the six-row cultivator; the hydraulic lift on the rear gangs was lowering too quickly, so Duane had adjusted the portable hydraulic-lift cylinder and oiled and tightened the implement setting frame. All the while Duane had been working on the cultivator, the big combine with the cornpicker-husker had been hovering over him in the barn. The Old Man had driven the thing into the central maintenance area to fiddle with the picker unit; he was always trying to improve the things, always modifying, adapting, and converting something on the farm machinery until they barely resembled the factory units. With the cornpicker, Duane noticed, the Old Man was doing something with the cornhead attachments. The shields were off each of the eight-row units and Duane could look in and see the bright steel of the snapping rolls, conveyors, and gather chains.

Most of the farmers in the area dragged cornpicker units behind their tractors or bought a self-propelled one, but the Old Man had bought an old full-size combine and attached the eight-row cornhead to it. It meant fast work in high-yield years, but mostly it meant lots of maintenance keeping the old combine running and "modifying" the threshing, husking, shelling, and cleaning parts of the huge machine.

Sometimes Duane thought that the Old Man only stayed in farming to tinker with the machinery.

That morning Duane had finished with the cultivator and turned to look at the combine looming behind him, snapping rolls reaching toward him like augered sword blades in the circle of light from overhead, and he'd considered doing some of the obvious modification himself as a surprise for his father. Then he'd decided not to spoil the Old Man's fun. Besides, he had more animals to feed and rows to hoe in the garden before breakfast, and he wanted to get into town before ten.

Duane would have liked to have waited for a ride—he still didn't like walking that last mile and a half down Jubilee College Road—but he knew

the Old Man had held off all week to start his serious binge on Friday
night at Carl's or the Black Tree, and Duane didn't want to ride with him
then.

So he walked. The day was bright and clear and stiflingly hot. Duane
unbuttoned the top three buttons on his plaid shirt, seeing where the
darkly tanned skin ended in a sharp V and his pale flesh began.

He paused by Mike O'Rourke's house on the edge of town. Mike
wasn't home but one of his older sisters said that it was all right for Duane
to get a drink from the backyard pump. Duane drank deeply, tasting the
iron and other elements in the water, and then splashed his head and forearms liberally.

When he tapped on Mrs. Moon's screen door, the old lady hobbled
toward the light with her two canes and retinue of cats.

"Do I know you, young man?" Duane thought that Mrs. Moon's
voice sounded like a parody of an old lady's voice—high, quivery, sliding
the scale of inflection.

"Yes'm. I'm Duane McBride. I've been over a few times with Dale
Stewart and Michael O'Rourke when they came over to take you for a
walk."

"Who did you say?"

Duane sighed and repeated everything in a louder voice.

"I'm not ready for my walk. I haven't eaten supper yet." Mrs. Moon
sounded querulous and a bit doubtful. The mob of cats brushed around
her canes and rubbed up against swollen legs wrapped in flesh-colored
tape. Duane thought of the Soldier with his puttees.

"No, ma'am," he said. "I just wanted to ask you some questions about
something."

"Questions?" She took a step back into the dimness of her parlor. The
old house was small, white-frame, and smelled as if it had been home to
uncounted generations of cats that never went outside.

"Yes'm. Just a couple."

"What about?" She peered myopically at him and Duane realized
that he must be only a rounded shadow filling her doorway. He took a
step back . . . the clever salesman's move, showing deference and a lack
of threat.

"Just about . . . the old days," he said. "I'm writing a school paper
about what life was like in Elm Haven around the turn of the century. I
wondered if you'd be so kind as to give me some . . . well, some atmosphere."

"Some what?"

"Some details," said Duane. "Please?"

The old woman hesitated, turned with a stiff movement of both canes, and receded with her retinue of cats, leaving him standing there alone. Duane hesitated.

"Well," came her voice from the darkness, "don't just stand there. Come on in. I'll put on tea for us."

Duane sat and sipped tea and munched cookies and asked questions and listened to tales of Mrs. Moon's childhood and her father and Elm Haven in the good old days. Mrs. Moon nibbled at cookies as she spoke and slowly but surely a small litter of crumbs had grown up on her lap. The cats took turns leaping onto the couch to eat the crumbs as she petted them absently.

"And what about the bell?" he asked at last, having gotten a pretty good sounding on how reliable the elderly lady's memory was.

"Bell?" Mrs. Moon paused in her munching. A cat stretched upward as if it were going to steal the morsel from her fingers.

"You were mentioning some of the special things about the town," prompted Duane. "What about the big bell in the school belfry? Do you remember that being talked about?"

Mrs. Moon looked flustered for a moment. "Bell? When was there a bell there?"

Duane sighed. This whole mystery was nonsense. "In eighteen seventy-six," he said softly. "Mr. Ashley brought it back from Europe . . ."

Mrs. Moon giggled. Her dentures were a bit loose and she used her tongue to adjust them. "You silly boy. I was *born* in eighteen seventy-six. How could I remember something from the year I was born?"

Duane blinked. He thought of this wrinkled and slightly senile lady as a wrinkled baby, pink and fresh and greeting the world in the year Custer's men were slaughtered. He thought of the changes she had lived through—horseless carriages appearing, the telephone, the First World War, the rise of America as a world power, Sputnik—all viewed from beneath the elms of Depot Street.

He said, "So you don't remember anything about a bell?" He was putting away his pencil and notebook.

"Why of course I remember the bell," she said, reaching for another of her daughter's cookies. "It was a beautiful bell. Mr. Ashley's father brought it from Europe on one of his voyages. When I went to school in Central, the bell used to ring every day at eight-fifteen and again at three."

Duane stared. He was aware that his hand was shaking slightly as he brought the notebook back out and began writing. This was the *first* confirmation—outside of books—that the Borgia Bell existed.

"Do you remember anything special about the bell?"

"Oh my, dear, everything about the school and the bell were special in those days. One of us . . . one of the younger children . . . was selected to pull the rope every Friday at the start of classes. I remember I was chosen once. Oh, yes, it was a beautiful bell. . . ."

"Do you remember what happened to it?'

"Well, yes. I mean, I'm not certain . . ." A strange look passed over Mrs. Moon's face and she absently set her cookie on her lap. Two cats devoured it as she raised trembling fingers to her lips. "Mr. Moon . . . my Orville, I mean, not Father . . . Mr. Moon was not involved in what happened. Not in any way." She reached over and stabbed at Duane's notebook with a bony finger. "You write that down, now. Neither Orville nor Father were there when . . . when that terrible thing happened."

"Yes, ma'am," said Duane, pencil stopped. "What *did* happen?"

Both of Mrs. Moon's hands were fluttering now. The cats jumped from her lap. "Why, the terrible thing. You know, that awful thing we don't want to talk about. Why would you want to write about *that*? You seem like a nice young boy."

"Yes'm," said Duane, almost holding his breath. "But I was told to write about *everything*. I certainly would appreciate the help. What terrible thing are we talking about? Something about the bell?"

Mrs. Moon seemed to forget he was in the room with her. She stared into the shadows where her cats were a mere whisper of movement. "Why, no . . ." she began, voice little more than a cracked whisper. Duane could hear a truck pass on the street outside, but Mrs. Moon did not blink. "Not the bell," she said. "Although they hanged him from it, didn't they?"

"Hanged who?" Duane was whispering now.

Mrs. Moon turned her face back in his direction but her eyes still seemed blind. "Why, that terrible man, of course. The one who killed and . . ." She made a noise and Duane realized that there were tears on Mrs. Moon's cheeks. One of them found its way down the gully of wrinkles to the corner of her mouth. "The one who killed and ate that little girl," she finished, voice stronger.

Duane stopped scribbling and stared.

"You write this down, now," commanded the old lady and stabbed a finger in his direction again. Her gaze had returned from wherever it had been and now it was burning into Duane. "It's *time* this was written down. Take it all down. Just be sure to include in your report that neither Orville nor Mr. Moon were there . . . why, they weren't even in the *county* when this terrible thing happened. Now you write this down now!"

And, as she talked in a voice which sounded to Duane like old parchment crinkling in a long-unopened book, he wrote it all down.

NINETEEN

Dale went over in person to invite Harlen to Friday's outing at Uncle Henry's and he realized how lonely their friend had been. Harlen's mother, Miss Jensen, had doubts as to whether Jimmy was well enough to go for such a long outing, but Dale had brought a note inviting her along as well and she gave in to Harlen's pleas.

Dale's dad got home about two and they all left for the farm at three-thirty, Harlen in his bulky cast riding in the backseat of the station wagon with his mom and Kev while Mike and Dale and Lawrence crammed into the back. They were in a great mood and sang as they roared up and down the hills past the cemetery.

Uncle Henry and Aunt Lena had set up chairs in the shady part of the yard and there was much greeting and chatter, while Biff, Uncle Henry's big German shepherd, danced around in an ecstasy of welcome. The grown-ups settled into the broad-boarded Adirondack chairs while the boys grabbed shovels from the barn and headed for the back pasture. They walked more slowly than usual, opening gates for Harlen rather than clambering over fences, but the injured boy kept up well enough.

Finally, in the rearmost pasture before the woods began, down along the creek that ran from the south, they found their excavation marks from previous summers and began digging for the Bootleggers' Cave.

The Bootleggers' Cave had started out as a legend, had been refined as a story Uncle Henry told them years before, and now was gospel to the boys. It seems that in the 1920s, during Prohibition and before Uncle Henry had bought the farm, the previous owner had allowed bootleggers from the next county to use an old cave in the back forty to hide their hooch. The cave became a central warehouse. A dirt road was put in. The cave was expanded, the entrance shored up, and an actual speakeasy was created underground.

"A lot of them big-time gangsters used to stop by here when they was passing through from Chicago," Uncle Henry had told them. "I have it on a stack of Bibles that John Dillinger was here once, and that three of Al Capone's boys came down to rub out Mickey Shaughnessy . . . but Mickey heard they was a-coming and lit out for his sister's place over on Spoon River. So the three Capone boys just shot the place up with Tommy guns and stole some of the booze."

The ending of the tale was the most enticing part. Legend had it that the Bootleggers' Cave had been raided by revenuers shortly before Prohibition ended. Rather than remove the goods, the federal men had just dynamited the entrance, collapsing the cave on the warehouse of liquor, the speakeasy with its tables and mahogany bar and player piano, even on three trucks and a Model A that had been parked in the warehouse section. Then they had obliterated the road so no one would ever find the cave again.

Dale and the boys were sure that the cave hadn't collapsed, only the entrance to it. Probably only six or eight feet of digging separated that archaeological find from the outside world. If they could find the right part of the hillside to dig . . .

Over the years, Uncle Henry had been a lot of help, showing the boys old tire tracks and rusting metal that he said had been left near the entrance, pointing out declivities in the hillside that were probably the entrance or at least the emergency exits, and generally remembering new details of the story when the boys' interest flagged after long days of digging and searching in the hot sun.

"Henry," Aunt Lena said once, her voice unaccustomably sharp with warning, "quit filling those children's heads with tall tales."

Uncle Henry had straightened up, shifted the wad of chewing tobacco to his other cheek, and said, "Aren't tall tales, Mother. That cave's out there somewhere."

It had been all the promise the kids needed. Over the years, Uncle Henry's easternmost pasture—used just for grazing the bull when he had one—began to look like the hillsides around Sutter's Creek circa 1849 as Dale and Lawrence and friends poked into every dip and shallow and grassy overhang, certain that *this* time they would find the entrance. Dale had often dreamed about how that last shovelful would feel as they broke through—the dark cave opening before them, perhaps with a gas lamp still burning in there, the odor of bathtub gin wafting out on a current of air that had been stilled for thirty years.

Duane arrived about six o'clock—his father dropping him off on his way to the Black Tree—and he passed half an hour talking to the adults on the shaded lawn before heading back through the barnyard to the back pastures. No one noticed it, but he had dressed up for the occasion in his newest tan corduroy trousers and a red flannel shirt that his Uncle Art had given him for Christmas.

In the last pasture, he found a circle of dirty and tired boys huddled around a hole dug three feet into the hillside. The slope below them was littered with large rocks they had pried out.

"Hi." Duane sat on one of the larger rocks. "Think you found it this time?" The shadows were growing longer and this part of the hillside was in shade. The stream was little more than a trickle twenty feet below, just beyond the flattened area that Dale had always been sure was the "bootleggers' road."

Dale mopped his forehead and left a trail of mud. "We thought so. Look . . . we found this old rotted wood in there behind that big rock."

Duane nodded. "An old log, huh?"

"No!" Lawrence said angrily. His t-shirt was a mess. "It's one of the log things over the cave entrance."

"Pilings," said Mike.

Duane nodded and nudged the log with his black sneaker. There were stubs of branches on it. "Hmm-hm."

"I told them they were full of shit," said Jim Harlen happily enough. He shifted so that his cast was more comfortable. It was obvious that his arm still hurt him, and there was a bandage wrapped around his head that reminded Duane of Crane's *Red Badge of Courage*. He tried to imagine Jim Harlen as Henry Fleming.

"You been digging, too?" asked Duane.

Harlen snorted. "I never did. My job's to sell the booze when we find it."

"Think it'll still be good?" Duane's voice was innocent.

"Hey, it ages, doesn't it?" said Harlen. "Wine and that stuff's worth more money after a while, right?"

Mike O'Rourke grinned. "We're not sure gin's the same way. What do you think, Duane?"

Duane picked up a twig and drew designs in the mound of fresh dirt they'd excavated. The hole was deep enough that when Lawrence poked his head in, only his legs from the knees down stayed in the open air. Duane noticed that it wasn't really a tunnel, though—there seemed no chance of a cave-in—merely a gouge in the hillside. The most recent of many.

"My guess is that you'd make more money selling the old cars that're in there," he said, joining in the game. After all, what harm was there in imagining this well-stocked cavern just a few yards away through soft soil? Was it any more fanciful than the "research" he'd been doing for two weeks?

Only now Duane knew that there was nothing fanciful about his research. He touched his shirt pocket, then remembered that he'd left his notebook at home with the others in their hiding place.

"Yeah," said Dale, "or make a fortune just giving tours of the place. Uncle Henry says that we can fix it up with electric lights and keep it just the way it was."

"Neat," said Duane. "Oh, your mom said to tell you to come on up to the house to get cleaned up. They've got the steaks on the grill."

The boys hesitated, pulled between their fading fixation and growing hunger. Hunger won.

They walked back at Harlen's pace, shovels over their shoulders like rifles, talking and laughing. The dairy cattle ambling back to the barn looked at the group quizzically and gave them a wide berth. The six boys were still a hundred yards away from the last fence when they smelled the aroma of sizzling steak on the evening breeze.

They ate on the stone patio on the east side of the house as shadows swallowed the golden light on the lawn. Smoke rose from the barbecue pit Uncle Henry had built beyond the pump near the wooden fence. Despite Mike's protests that the corn and salad and rolls and dessert would be more than enough dinner, Aunt Lena had pan-fried two catfish for him, breading them until they were extra crispy. Along with the fish and steak, the boys received two huge baskets of onion rings to go along with the vegetables that had been picked from the garden an hour earlier. The milk was ice cold and creamy, separated and stored in Uncle Henry's dairy barn that day.

They ate as the heat of the day dissipated. A breeze had come up to give relief from the humidity and rustle the branches above the lawn. The endless cornfields on the west side of the road and to the north seemed to sigh in some silken language.

The kids sat somewhat apart, perched on stone steps and flower planters—Aunt Lena had landscaped three acres of yard with flowers at all strategic spots—while the grown-ups sat in their circle, plates on their laps and on the broad arms of their wooden chairs. Uncle Henry had brought out a keg of his homemade beer and the mugs had been precooled in the freezer in the garage.

The voices were a medley so common to Dale's ear that he could not imagine a time when all or some of them would not be there as background: Kev's rising chuckle and excited tones, Harlen's drawled sarcasms that sent them sprawling with laughter, Mike's soft asides, Lawrence speaking high and shrill, as if he had to speak quickly to be heard at all, and Duane's rare comments. The grown-ups' tones were equally familiar: Uncle Henry's rasp as he told about the 1928 Pierce Arrow hood ornament that he'd found in the back pasture just last month—a sure sign that some gangster had driven back to the Bootleggers' Cave and come to a bad end; Aunt Lena's husky laugh—simply the most sensual and unique human sound Dale had ever heard; his mother's and father's voices, familiar as the breeze that touched the trees, his dad now more relaxed than usual and telling humorous stories of life on the road; Harlen's mom's somehow adolescent giggle, rushing, excited, as if she had already had too much to drink or, like Lawrence, felt that she had to hurry to be heard.

Their knives made pale red patterns on the paper plates. Everyone went back for seconds, most for thirds. The huge bowl of salad dwindled; the foil-wrapped ears of corn on the barbecue were snatched up; Uncle Henry laughed and bantered even as he put more steaks on the grill and stood there beaming at everyone in his Come 'N' Get It apron, long fork in hand.

After dinner, the boys took their desserts of homemade rhubarb pie and chocolate cake—none chose just one—up to the deck.

Uncle Henry and Aunt Lena had added on to their house over the years, never completing the remodeling, merely moving on to the next project: Dale remembered a four-room white frame house when he had come down from Chicago for his grandmother's funeral when he was six. Now the house itself was brick, with four bedrooms on the first level and a finished basement. Uncle Henry had added the garage the first year the Stewarts had moved to Elm Haven; Dale remembered playing in the framed skeleton of it as Uncle Henry raised cinderblocks to the right height. Now the garage was huge—holding three cars and another vehicle—built on the south side of the low hill the house was on so that one walked from the garage directly into the basement workroom, while above it, connected to the large guest room and larger master bedroom, was the deck.

The kids loved the deck in the evening, and they knew that sooner or later the adults would stir themselves from the stone patio and come up here. As large as a tennis court (although none in the group but Dale and Duane had ever seen a tennis court), set on several levels of built-up platforms, catwalks, and steps, the deck commanded a view west to the road and Mr. Johnson's fields; south it looked out over the driveway, the swimming pond Uncle Henry had built, the woods, and even offered glimpses of Calvary Cemetery when the trees began to thin in the autumn; to the east one looked down at the barn and barnyard from the level of the hayloft, and Dale always imagined himself a medieval knight, watching from the ramparts and seeing the maze of pigpens, feedlots, chutes, chicken coops, and barnyards as the battlements in his fortress world.

There were more Adirondack chairs on the deck—massive, strangely comfortable constructs of wooden planks turned out in Uncle Henry's basement workshop every winter—but the kids always opted for the hammocks. There were three on the southernmost platform: two on metal stands and one hooked to wooden posts which held the security lights overlooking the driveway fifteen feet below. The first ones there—Lawrence, Kev, and Mike—piled into that hammock and swung perilously over the railing. Mothers hated to watch them in that hammock, fathers raised their voices in warning, but so far no one had fallen out . . . although Uncle Henry swore that he had dozed off in that hammock one summer evening, awakened to Ben—the biggest rooster—the next morning, taken one step toward what he thought was the bathroom, and had ended up on bags of Purina chow stacked in the back of the pickup parked below.

They piled in their hammocks and rocked, and talked, and completely forgot that they were going back down to work some more on the Bootleggers' Cave. It was too dark anyway. The sky still held some pale blue, but several stars were visible and the line of trees south of the pond had faded from separate trunks to a black silhouette. Lightning bugs began to blink against that dark background. From around the pond and farther down the hill, frogs and tree frogs began their sad chorus. Swallows fluttered unseen in the barn and somewhere in the deeper woods an owl hooted.

The coming of night seemed to quiet the adults' conversation on the back patio to a friendly hum, and even the kids' babble began to slow and then stop altogether for a while so there was nothing but the creak of the hammock cords and the night sounds down the hill as the sky opened with stars.

Uncle Henry had turned off the automatic security lights and had not turned on the deck lamps, so Dale could imagine that they were on the poop deck of a pirate ship under tropical night skies. The rows of corn across the road made a soft sound much like the whisper of a ship's wake. Dale wished he had a sextant. He could feel the heat of the day's sun and exerted energies as a sunburn glow on his cheeks and neck, aches in his upper arms and lower legs.

"Look," Mike said softly, "a satellite."

All of them craned back in their hammocks. The sky had darkened perceptibly in the last half hour, the Milky Way was easily discernible here so far from city lights, and something *was* moving between the stars. An ember too high and fast and faint to be an aircraft.

"Probably *Echo*," said Kevin, using his professorial voice. He told them all about the huge reflecting balloon that the U.S. was going to orbit to bounce radio waves around the curve of the earth.

"I don't think they've launched *Echo* yet," said Duane in that diffident way he spoke even when he was the only one who knew the facts. "I think it's scheduled to go up in August."

"What is it then?" said Kevin.

Duane moved his glasses up his nose and looked skyward. "If it's a satellite, it's probably *Tiros*. *Echo* will be really bright . . . as bright as one of those stars. I'm looking forward to seeing it."

"Let's come back to Uncle Henry's place in August," said Dale. "We'll have an *Echo*-watching party and do some digging on the Bootleggers' Cave."

There was a chorus of assent. Then Lawrence said, "Look! It's fading away."

The satellite's glow was dying. They watched it track in silence for a moment. Then Mike said, "I wonder if we'll ever get people up there."

"The Russians are working at it," said Duane from the depths of the hammock he had to himself. Dale and Harlen sat opposite him.

"Hah . . . the Russians!" snorted Kevin. "We'll beat them by a mile."

The dark bulk that was Duane shifted, tapping sneakers against the deck. "I dunno. They surprised us with Sputnik. Remember?"

Dale remembered. He remembered standing out in the backyard on an October evening three years before—he'd been taking the garbage out and his dad and mom had come out when they'd heard on the radio when the Russian satellite was supposed to pass over. Lawrence, only a little first grader then, had been asleep upstairs. Together the three of them had watched up through the almost-bare branches until that tiny light had moved among the stars. "Unbelievable," Dale's dad had whispered, although whether he meant that it was unbelievable that mankind had finally put something into space, or unbelievable that it was the *Russians* who had done it, Dale never knew.

They watched the skies for a while. It was Duane who broke the silence. "You guys've been checking out Van Syke and Roon and the rest of those people, haven't you?"

Mike and Kevin and Dale exchanged glances. Dale was amazed to find that he felt guilty, as if he'd been slacking off or had broken a promise. "Well, we started to but . . ."

"That's OK," said Duane. "It was sort of silly. But I've got some stuff I want to talk about. Can we get together tomorrow . . . in the daylight?"

"How about the Cave?" said Harlen.

The others hooted him down.

"I'm not going back *there*," said Kev. "How about Mike's chickenhouse?"

Mike nodded. Duane said OK.

"Ten o'clock?" said Dale. The cartoons he and Lawrence liked to watch on Saturday mornings—Heckle and Jeckle, Ruff and Reddy—would be over by then.

"Let's make it later," said Duane. "I've got some chores in the morning. How about one o'clock. After lunch?"

Everyone agreed to be there except Harlen. "I've got some better stuff to do," he said.

"I'll bet," said Kevin. "Like having Michelle Staffney autograph your cast?"

This time the grown-ups did have to come over to join them before the laughter and punching stopped.

Duane enjoyed the rest of the evening. He was glad he'd put off talking about the research on the Borgia Bell—especially Mrs. Moon's revelations—since the kids and grown-ups started talking about stars and space travel and what it would be like to live out there, and the hours had passed with them chatting and staring at the night sky. Dale had told his father their idea for an *Echo*-watching party in August when the large satellite would be visible, and Uncle Henry and Aunt Lena had endorsed the idea immediately. Kevin promised to bring a telescope and Duane heard himself offering to bring his homemade one.

The party began to break up about eleven and Duane had prepared to walk home—he knew the Old Man wouldn't be home until the early-morning hours—but Dale's dad had insisted on them driving him the mile and a half. It had been a crowded station wagon that dropped Duane off outside his kitchen door.

"It looks pretty dark," Mrs. Stewart had said. "You think your father went to bed already?"

"Probably," said Duane. He kicked himself mentally for not remembering to leave a light on.

Mr. Stewart waited until Duane turned on the kitchen light and waved to them from the window. He watched as the red taillights receded down the drive.

Knowing that he was being paranoid, Duane checked the first floor and locked the back door before going down to his basement. He got out of his good clothes and took a shower in the corner downstairs, but rather than pulling on his pajamas, Duane tugged on old corduroys, slippers, and a patched but clean flannel shirt. He was tired, the long day lay on him like a weight, but his mind was very active and he thought he'd work on his writing for a while. With the door locked, he'd have to wait up for the Old Man anyway. He tuned the radio to WHO in Des Moines and went to work.

Or tried to work. His word sketches and notes looked childish and empty to him now. He wondered if he should try to write a complete story. No, he wasn't ready. His time line did not permit him to attempt a complete story until next year at the earliest. Duane looked at his notebooks full of character sketches, exercises in describing action, exercises in which he imitated various writers' styles—Hemingway, Mailer, Capote, Irwin Shaw—his heroes. He sighed and put it all away in his hiding place and lay back on his bed, slippers on the iron footboard. He'd outgrown his bed during the previous winter so now he had to sleep diagonally, feet against the wall, or curl his legs. He hadn't told the Old Man yet. They couldn't afford to buy a bed right now. Duane knew that there was an extra, unused bed on the second floor—but it had been his father's and mother's bed when she was alive. Duane didn't want to ask for it.

He stared at the ceiling and thought about Mrs. Moon, and the Bell, and the literally incredible web of fact, fancy, suggestion, and inference it all added up to. Uncle Art had seen the outline of it. If he'd known about the events of January 1900, what would he have thought then? Duane wondered if he should keep it from the other kids.

No, they've earned the right to know. Whatever's happening is happening to them as well.

Duane was on the verge of dozing off when he heard the Old Man's pickup coming up the drive.

Sleepily, Duane shuffled upstairs, walked through the dark kitchen, and unlatched the screen. He was halfway down the basement stairs before he realized that he could still hear the pickup's engine; the sound with the missing cylinder was unmistakable. Duane walked back up and went to the door.

The pickup was parked in the middle of the lot, its driver's-side door open, headlights still burning. The cab light was on and Duane could see the truck was empty.

Suddenly there was a roar from the barn that made Duane take a half-step back into the kitchen. He watched as the combine came rumbling out of the big south doors, its thirty-foot cornhead pushing ahead of it like a bulldozer blade with sharp extensions. Duane saw the gleam of the pole light reflecting on snapping rolls and chains and realized that the Old Man hadn't replaced the red metal shields on the eight units.

But he *had* opened the gate to the south fields, Duane noticed, as the huge machine roared across the barnyard and into the corn. He caught the briefest glimpse of his father as a silhouette in the open cab—the Old Man hated glassed-in booths and used one of the older, open combines—and then the machine was out in the corn.

Duane groaned. The Old Man had come home drunk and racked up the truck before, but he'd never wrecked a piece of farm machinery. A new combine or picker unit for the tractor would cost a bloody fortune.

Duane ran out through the barn lot in his slippers, trying to shout over the roar of the machine. It was useless. The combine cut into the first row of corn in the field and began eating its way south. The corn was only about twenty inches high and there were no ears yet, but the harvesting mechanism on the cornhead didn't know that; Duane groaned again as he saw the tender young stalks bend and snap off, the eight gatherer points guiding them to chains that fed them to the long metal snapper rolls. The lugged chains there dragged the stalks between the rolls and would have pinched off ears had there been any.

The air filled with dust and a spray of cornstalks as the combine swerved right, then left, and then lumbered straight ahead into the field, carving a thirty-foot-wide path through the crop. Duane ran through the open gate and followed, shouting and waving his arms. The Old Man never looked back.

The huge machine was almost two hundred yards out into the field when it suddenly clanked to a stop. The engine died away. Duane paused, gasping to catch his breath, imagining the Old Man bent over the steering wheel and weeping with whatever frustration had driven him to this.

Duane took a breath and jogged toward the now-silent combine.

The driving lights mounted high on the cab were off, the door was open, but the interior light was broken and the cab was empty. Duane approached slowly, feeling the sharp stalks under his slippers; he pulled himself up onto the small platform on the left side of the cab.

Nothing.

Duane looked out at the field. The corn was little more than knee-high, but it spread away to the dark borders more than half a mile away in each direction except back to the barn. The row of devastation behind the combine was visible enough even in the meager starlight. The pole light in the barnyard seemed as distant as the stars overhead.

Duane's heart had been pounding during the run and now it accelerated again. He leaned over the metal railing of the platform and looked down, half-expecting to see a man-shaped indentation in the crop where the Old Man had tumbled off. Nothing.

The corn grew very close together, the rows no longer visible as the leaves from the stalks overlapped. Another few weeks, Duane knew, and the field would be shoulder-high, a monolith of corn.

But he should be able to see the Old Man now. He stepped onto the front of the platform, peering out over the cornhead and around the right side of the combine as far as he could manage.

"Dad?" His voice seemed very small. Duane called again.

No answer. Not even a rustle of stalks to tell him which way the Old Man had walked.

There was a noise from the barnyard and Duane stepped to the rear of the platform to watch as the pickup truck became visible in the barnyard. It backed out of sight behind the house, reappeared in front of the house, and backed down the driveway. Its lights were still off, door still open. It looked like a movie being run in reverse. Duane started to shout but realized how useless that was; he watched in silence as the truck reached the end of the long drive, then disappeared down County Six with its lights still off.

It wasn't the Old Man. The thought struck him like cold water being poured down his back.

Duane stepped into the cab, sat on the high seat. He'd drive the goddamn thing back to the house.

There was no key. Duane closed his eyes, tried to remember all the modifications the Old Man had made to the ignition system of this thing. He tried the starter anyway. Nothing. The combine wouldn't start without the key the Old Man kept on a nail in the barn.

Duane flicked a toggle to turn on the bright running lights; he'd drain the battery quickly, but those lights would light up two hundred feet of the field as if it were daylight.

Nothing. Duane remembered; the key had to be on.

He stepped out onto the platform, feeling the sweat on his face, taking slow, deep breaths to calm down. The corn that had looked so short a few hours ago now seemed tall enough to hide anything. Only the thirty-foot-wide path of beaten stubble winding behind the combine offered a clear path back to the barn.

Duane was not ready to walk that way yet.

He stepped onto a metal ledge behind the cab, pulled himself up onto the empty grain tank. The metal cover groaned a bit under his weight. Duane leaned, found a handhold, and pulled himself onto the roof of the cab. From twelve feet above everything, the field was a black mass stretching out to the edge of the world. The west pasture was half a mile to his right, the black line of Mr. Johnson's stretch of timber straight ahead several hundred yards. To his left, the corn stretched a quarter of a mile to the road where he'd heard the pickup disappear. Duane could see the pole lights of Uncle Henry's farm a mile or so to the southeast.

A slight wind came up and Duane shivered, buttoning the top few buttons of his shirt. *I'll stay here. They'll expect me to walk back, but I'll stay here.* He wondered who the "they" were even as he thought it.

Suddenly there was the slightest whisper of motion in the corn and Duane leaned forward to watch as something moved . . . *glided* . . . through the low stalks. There was no other word for what he saw: something long and large slid through the corn with little more than a silky rustling. It was about fifteen yards out and only the slight motion of the stalks marked its wake.

If he had been at sea, Duane thought, he would have thought a dolphin was swimming alongside the ship, occasionally breaking the water with a smooth glistening of its back.

Starlight *did* glisten as something slid above the level of the cornstalks and then below, but the wet sheen Duane saw seemed to be a glint of starlight on scales rather than flesh.

Any thought that it was the Old Man out there, stumbling around in the low corn, disappeared as he watched the wake of the thing, sliding counterclockwise in a huge circle, moving faster than a man could walk. Duane had the sense of a giant serpent moving through the field, a thing with a body as thick through as Duane's own. Something that was many yards long.

Duane made a noise like a swallowed laugh. This was nuts.

The thing in the corn had circled a fourth of the circumference of its way around the combine when it reached the bare area where the machine had harvested its swath.

The wake veered as smoothly as a fish reaching the end of play on a line, turned back, began swinging around to the south along the same invisible line. Duane heard a noise and shifted to the opposite edge of the roof. Something equally large and silent was sliding through the corn on the west side of the machine. As he watched, Duane realized that the circling motion moved in a foot or so each time the things reached the end of their circuit.

Ah, shit, breathed Duane in the precise tone of a prayer. He was definitely staying with the combine. If he had started walking back when it made sense to, those things would have been sliding alongside him by now.

This is insane. He curbed that line of thinking. It *was* insane . . . impossible . . . but it was happening. Duane felt the cool metal of the combine roof under his palms and forearms, smelled the cool air and scent of moist earth, and knew that however impossible it was, it was real. He had to deal with what was happening and not slide into denial.

Starlight gleamed on something long and slippery as the serpent-slug things wound back and forth in their tireless circling. Duane thought of a lamprey he'd caught once in Spoon River when he was fishing with Uncle Art. The thing had been all mouth, circles of teeth descending into a reddened gut, just waiting until it could latch on to something and drain its vital fluids. Duane had had nightmares for a month. He watched as the things passed each other in their sentinel-slide, only the slightest rustle and hint of motion revealing their location.

I'll stay here until morning. Then what? Duane knew that it wasn't midnight yet. What would he do if he lasted the five hours until morning? Perhaps the things would go away in the daylight. If not, he could stand and on the roof, use his shirt as a flag, and wave toward traffic on County Six. Someone would see him.

Duane stepped from the cab to the grain tank, peering down behind the combine. Nothing was close. If the swirl of motion came closer to the machine, he'd be back up onto the roof in a second.

There was a noise from the driveway so far away, the sound of a truck driving, still no headlights.

It was the Old Man! He's coming back.

Duane realized that the engine sound was wrong at the same instant he caught a glimpse of the truck under the barnyard pole light.

Red. High sides. Scabrous cab.

The Rendering Truck crossed the barnyard and drove carefully through the gate into the field.

Duane jumped to the cab roof and had to sit to let the sudden nausea pass. *Ah, goddammit.*

The Rendering Truck pulled a hundred yards into the field, following the corridor of trampled corn, and then stopped, first pulling across the cleared strip diagonally as if to block his way. It was still almost a hundred yards away, but Duane could smell the dead things in the back of the truck as a breeze came to him from the northeast.

Stay there, stay there, he mentally commanded the truck.

It stayed where it was, but against the distant glow of the pole light, Duane could see movement in the back. Pale forms climbed down from the high sides, jumped down from the rear of the truck. They began shambling toward the combine.

Fuck. Duane pounded the roof with his fists. When the forms came between him and the distant light, he could see they were human-shaped. But they moved strangely . . . almost lurching. There were one, two . . . he counted six.

Duane swung down into the cab, pawed behind the seat for the toolbox the Old Man kept there. He stuck a nine-inch screwdriver in his belt, pulled out the largest and heaviest tool there—a fourteen-inch wrench. Hefting it, he stepped back out onto the platform.

The sliding things were circling closer, less than ten yards from the combine. The six figures were moving their way up the harvested path. Duane could only see four of them now, but it was very dark without the light behind them. They were less than twenty yards away.

"Help!" screamed Duane. "Help me!" He screamed in the general direction of Uncle Henry's house more than a mile away. "Please, help!"

He stopped. His heart was pounding so fiercely that he was sure it would rip its way out of his chest if he didn't calm down.

Hide in the grain tank. No. It took too long to pull up the access panel and it was no hiding place.

Hot-wire this thing. His heart lurched with hope. He went down on one knee and fumbled under the small switch panel. There was a tangle of wiring running into the steering column, all of it modified and recircuited by the Old Man. Without a light, there was no way that Duane could see the color of the insulation to guess which wires ran to the ignition circuits and which just supplied fans or lights or somesuch. He pulled four free at random, chewed off the insulation on the ends, and began splicing quickly. The first combination did nothing. Nor did the second. He looked up from the third and leaned outside at the sound of footsteps.

The human shapes were less than twenty feet from the back of the combine.

The closest two seemed to be men . . . the tallest might have been Van Syke. The third shape looked like a woman in rags or a shroud; tatters trailed behind her. Duane blinked as he realized that the starlight on her cheekbone seemed to be glinting on exposed bone.

Three other figures had moved into the knee-high corn. The closest one was shorter and wore a campaign hat that threw his features into shadow.

Duane sighed and stepped out onto the platform, hefting the wrench. Six of them. At least.

He stepped over the railing and jumped to the long corn-head, teetering on the narrow support bar. Eight of the picker units gleamed coldly, the long snapping rolls and gathering chains dipping to the ground, their snouts embedded in the stalks where the machine had quit feeding.

Metal stairs echoed behind him as someone stepped up onto the platform. A shadow came around the right side of the combine, still a few yards out. The stench from the Rendering Truck was stronger than ever.

Duane had been waiting until the sliding things in the corn had passed each other and were at the farthest point in their circuits. *Now.*

He jumped out over the cornpicker heads, snapped off stalks as he hit soft soil and rolled, and then was up, running, feeling the screwdriver where it had gouged his belly, making sure the wrench was still in his hand.

Cornstalks crackled to his right and left as the lamprey-things reversed course and plowed toward him. Behind him, there were footsteps on metal, more crunching as corn bent.

Duane ran as hard as he could, faster than he could have imagined he was capable of. The line of trees of Mr. Johnson's woods was straight ahead; he could see the fireflies winking there like eyes glowing.

Something passed him to his right, a wake of bending corn curling in front of him. Duane staggered, tried to stop, almost fell on it.

Once he and the Old Man had helped Uncle Art carry a roll of carpet into a friend's new house. The tube of carpet must have been thirty-five feet long, three feet tall when it was rolled. It weighed a ton. The thing in the corn ahead of Duane was longer than that.

Duane teetered as the thing turned toward him. It had stayed beneath the level of the cornstalks only because most of it was in the moist soil, burrowing like some gigantic grub. The front of it surfaced now and starlight glinted on teeth.

Just like the lamprey.

The thing lunged toward Duane like a guard dog on the attack. He pirouetted like a matador, brought the wrench down hard enough to smash a skull.

The thing did not have a skull. The wrench bounced off thick, moist hide. *It's like clubbing an underground cable,* was Duane's splinter of a thought as the maw of the thing burrowed under the soil again, the back arched like a sea serpent's, and starlight glinted on it. Duane thought of a catfish's slimy skin.

There were rapid footsteps and the sound of breaking stalks a dozen paces behind.

The Soldier. Pale hands coming up and forward.

Duane swiveled gracefully and threw the heavy wrench. The man in the uniform made no attempt to duck. The campaign hat flew off and there was a dull, sickening sound as the wrench struck bone.

The form did not pause or stagger. The arms were extended, fingers wriggling like grubs. Someone else—a tall, dark figure, was moving to Duane's right. A third figure ran farther out to cut Duane off. There was more motion in the shadows.

Duane pulled the screwdriver from his belt and crouched, shifted left, trying to stay low in the corn. He swiveled as there was a movement below and behind him, jumped to his right.

Not fast enough. The slug thing had emerged, brushed against Duane's left leg, then dived into the soil again.

Duane rolled through corn, struggling to get to his feet even as he felt a tingling in his left leg as if someone had applied an electric current to it. Staggering, screwdriver still held like a knife, he balanced on his right leg and looked down.

Something had taken a hand-sized bite out of the calf of his left leg. There was a ragged hole in his corduroy pants, a more ragged hole in his calf. Duane swallowed as he realized he could see exposed muscle tissue there. The blood looked black in the starlight.

Hopping on one leg, Duane pulled his bandanna from his pocket and wrapped it tightly around his leg, below the knee. He'd think about it later.

He began hobbling toward the dark line of woods so far away. A sudden turmoil in the cornstalks ahead made him turn left, toward the county road.

Three figures were waiting. Duane saw the dim light gleaming on teeth. The shortest figure—the Soldier—moved forward as if he were standing on a wheeled platform that was being pulled by a cable; stiffly upright, legs hardly moving, the thing glided in a rush straight at Duane.

Duane didn't try to run. As the white fingers reached for his throat, Duane made a noise part grunt and part snarl, lowered his head, and drove the screwdriver into the man's khaki-shirted belly. The tool went in as easily as a blade would penetrate a rotten muskmelon, ramming home to the hilt and skewering something soft and yielding inside.

Duane gasped and staggered back. The dark figure was still standing. Both of its hands were locked on Duane's left arm. Duane tried to pull free, could not. He slashed at the hand with the screwdriver blade.

Something heavy hit the back of Duane's neck and he went down, kicking, blood from his left leg saturating his trousers now and splattering his shirt. His glasses went flying into the night. He'd lost both his slippers and his feet were caked with mud as he kicked wildly at the forms closing around him. Something long and moist glided past his face, submerged itself in the soil. He tried to stab at it but realized that the screwdriver had been forced out of his hand. There were many fingers grasping and pulling at his arms now.

There were at least four holding him down. A bony hand was spread across his face, forcing his cheek into the mud. Duane bit at the hand, chewed flesh that tasted like chicken that had been lying in the sun for a week, spit it out, and felt his teeth gnawing bone. The hand did not relent. He caught a glimpse of an old woman's face eaten with leprosy and rot.

This is a nightmare, he prayed, even as he knew it was not. Something—not the serpent thing—was chewing at his good leg, growling like a maddened dog.

Witt, he thought, feeling hopelessness finally rising him like flood water, *help me.*

Somebody crouched near his head and put a heavy boot on his face, driving him deeper into the loam. A shattered cornstalk gouged his scalp. There was a noise like a great cat coughing up a furball.

Another noise. The world was roaring and circling around him now, but even as Duane teetered on the edge of consciousness, recognizing in some removed, clinical part of his mind that it was as much from shock and fear as from the loss of blood, he recognized part of that roar.

The combine had been started up. It was moving toward him in the darkness. He could hear the cornstalks being severed, chewed, dragged into the unshielded maw of the snapping rolls. The air was full of the stench of decay warring with the scent of fresh-harvested stalks.

Duane struggled to rise, kicked, bit, tried to free either hand so as to gouge or claw at the shapes and dark weights holding him down. The boot on his face pressed with renewed pressure. Duane felt his cheekbone snap but did not pause in his maddened struggles to rise, to fight these things, to get to his feet.

There was a sudden movement, a shifting of the stench around him, a glimpse of the stars, and then the noise and the mass of the combine filled the entire world.

The instant the boot left his temple, Duane lifted his face from the mud. There was a great tearing at his legs, an irresistible force lifted him and turned him, pulled him toward the vortex he could feel through every fiber of his body, but for that split second, that briefest of instants, he was free—he could see the stars—and he lifted his face toward them even as he was spun away into the darkness roaring below and around him.

In Elm Haven, Mike O'Rourke had fallen asleep in Memo's room, sitting in the upholstered chair by the window, a baseball bat across his knees. He awoke at a sudden sound.

On the south end of town, Jim Harlen spun up out of his nightmare of the face at the window. The room was dark. His arm hurt from the bone outward and there was a terrible taste in his mouth. He realized that it was a distant but powerful sound that had awakened him.

Kevin Grumbacher had been dreaming when something brought him up in bed and gasping for air in the sterile darkness of his room. Some sound had awakened him. Kevin listened, hearing only the loud hum of the central air conditioner through the vents. Then it came. And again.

Dale came awake with a start, precisely the way he did when he was falling asleep and dreamed that he was falling. His heart pounded as if something terrible was happening. He blinked at the shadowed room, peered toward the night-light. He could feel stirrings in the bed nearby and felt Lawrence's warm fingers tugging at his pajama sleeve, asking what was wrong.

Dale pushed back the covers, wondering what had frightened him awake even as he blinked at the darkness.

Then it came again. A terrible sound, deep, echoing in the confines of Dale's brain. He glanced at Lawrence, saw his brother covering his ears and looking at him with wide eyes.

He hears it, too.

It sounded again. A bell . . . louder, deeper, more terribly resonant than any church bell in Elm Haven. The first strike had wakened him. The second echoed away in the humid darkness. Then the third made Dale wince, cover his own ears, and hunker down in the bedclothes as if he could hide from the sound. He expected his mother and father to run into the room, shouts from the neighbors, but there was no noise but the bell, no response but his brother and he cowering from the awful noise.

The great bell seemed to be in the room with them as it struck four, struck again, and went on—relentlessly—striking the hour toward midnight.

TWENTY

Dale was playing baseball with the guys on Saturday morning when he heard the news. Chuck Sperling and some of his friends had just ridden up on their expensive bikes.

"Hey, your friend Duane is dead," Sperling called to Dale where he stood on the pitcher's mound.

Dale stared at him.

"You're nuts," said Dale at last, feeling how dry his mouth had suddenly become. Then he realized what they were talking about. "You mean Duane's uncle, right?"

"Uh-uh," said Sperling. "Uh-uh, I'm not talking about his *uncle.* That was last Monday, right? I'm talking about Duane McBride. He's dead as a roadkill."

Dale opened his mouth but found nothing to say. He tried to spit. His mouth was too dry. "You're a fucking liar," he managed.

"Uh-uh," said Digger Taylor, the undertaker's son. "He's not lying."

Dale blinked and looked back at Sperling as if the tall boy was the only one who could stop the joke.

"No shit," said Sperling, tossing the ball into the air and catching it. "They called Digger's dad out to McBride's farm this morning. The fat kid fell into a combine . . . a combine for Chrissakes. It took 'em more than an hour to get his body out of the gears and stuff. Torn to shit. Your dad says it'll never be an open-coffin funeral, isn't that right, Digger?"

Digger said nothing. He was looking directly at Dale with his pale gray eyes showing nothing. Chuck Sperling continued to toss the ball to himself.

"Take it back." Dale had dropped his mitt and ball and was walking slowly toward the taller boy.

Sperling freed his hand and frowned. "What the hell's wrong with you, Stewart? I thought you'd wanna know that . . ."

"Take it back," whispered Dale, but he did not wait for a response. He launched himself at Chuck Sperling, charging with his head down. Sperling got his arms up and bounced a rabbit chop off the top of Dale's head as Dale got inside the other boy's reach and started swinging. He punched Sperling hard in the gut, heard the wind go out of him, and got in three or four hard punches to the ribs, landing one right above the heart.

Sperling exhaled deeply and sagged back against the wire backstop. When his arms came down, Dale started punching him in the face. The second blow sent blood flying from Sperling's nose, the third crunched teeth, but Dale didn't feel the pain of his knuckles being ripped raw. Sperling began to fold up, whimpering and covering his face with his forearms, his hands on the top of his head.

Dale kicked him in the side, twice, very hard. When Sperling's arms came down, Dale got him by the throat and dragged him up against the wire. His left hand was choking him while his right was free and punching again, hitting him in the ear, the forehead, the mouth . . .

There were shouts very far away. Hands pulled and tore at Dale's t-shirt. He ignored them. Sperling swung wildly, slapping at Dale's face with his open palms. Dale blinked and hit the taller boy in the left eye as hard as he could.

Suddenly Dale felt a terrible pain in the kidneys, a hand grabbed under his chin and pulled him back, and he was torn away.

Digger Taylor moved between him and Sperling. Dale shouted something and stalled to charge through the short boy. Digger dropped his shoulder and punched Dale once, very hard, just above the solar plexus.

Dale went down into the dust, gasping and retching. He rolled up against the wire and tried to pull himself up. His lungs couldn't get any air and it felt as if his heart had stopped.

Lawrence came screaming off the old bench along the fence, launching himself six feet into the air and landing on Digger's back. Digger flipped the eight-year-old into the wire.

Lawrence bounced off and landed on his feet as if the fence were a vertical trampoline. His head was down and his arms were a blur as he waded into Taylor. Digger backed away, trying to hold Lawrence's head down and away. Both of them tripped over the wailing Chuck Sperling and went down in a heap, Lawrence still swinging and flinging dirt. Barry

Fussner walked in, pranced around the edge of the melee, and tried an effeminate kick at Lawrence's head.

"Hey!" cried Kevin, stepping closer for the first time. He shoved Fussner away. Barry tried kicking Kevin, but Kev grabbed the heavy boy's foot and flipped him into the dirt behind the plate. Bill Fussner shouted something and pranced forward, backing away as Kevin turned to face him. Bob McKown and Gerry Daysinger shouted general encouragement. Tom Castanatti had stayed where he was in the field.

Digger grabbed Lawrence by the t-shirt and swung him into the air, tossing him over the long bench. He picked Sperling up and began backing toward their two bikes. Lawrence leapt to his feet, fists clenched.

Dale staggered away from the fence, still unable to get a breath but not letting that stop him, and raised his fists. He took three steps toward Taylor and Sperling, knowing that this time he wasn't going to go down until they killed him or Sperling took the lie back.

Heavy hands fell on Dale's shoulders from behind. He tried to shrug them off, couldn't, cursed something and kicked backward, turning to fight off this hindrance so he could get at Sperling.

"Dale! Stop it, Dale!" His father loomed over him, holding him with one arm around his middle now.

Dale squirmed for a second, but then he looked up at his dad, saw his father's eyes, and knew. He sagged to his knees in the dirt and only his father's arm around him kept him from falling forward.

Digger Taylor and Chuck Sperling rode off, Sperling's bike wobbling as the boy tried to ride while doubled over and weeping. The Fussners loped along behind. Lawrence was standing at the edge of the parking lot, throwing rocks after them until his father ordered him to stop.

Dale never remembered the walk back to the house. Perhaps he leaned on his father's arm. Perhaps he walked alone. He remembered that he did not cry. Not then. Not yet.

Mike was getting ready to serve as altar boy at an old lady's funeral Mass when he heard about Duane. He'd just pulled his surplice over his cassock when Rusty Ramirez, the only other altar boy to show up that day, said, "Jeez, didja hear about the kid who got killed on a farm this morning?"

Mike froze. Somehow he knew at once what farm, what kid. But he said, "Was it Duane McBride?"

Ramirez told him. "They said he fell into some farm machinery. Maybe early this morning. My dad's on the volunteer fire department and they called them all out there. Couldn't do nothing for the kid . . . he was dead . . . but it took 'em a whole bunch of time to get him out of the machine an' all."

Mike sat down on the nearest bench. His legs and arms felt like water. The corners of his vision went sort of dark, so he lowered his head, his elbows on his knees. "You sure that it was Duane McBride?" he asked.

"Oh, yeah. My dad knows his dad. He saw him at the Black Tree just last night. My dad says that the kid musta been drivin' this combine rigged for huskin' corn, you know? Like he was crazy or something. Pickin' in June. An' somehow he fell out and got in the picker part . . . you know where the grinders and stuff are? Dad wouldn't tell me everything, but he said they couldn't get the kid out in one piece and when they tried to pull the arm . . ."

"That's enough!" snapped Father Cavanaugh from the doorway. "Rusty, go out and get the wine and water ready. *Now*." When the boy left, the priest came over to Mike and put his hand gently on his shoulder. Mike's vision was fine now, but for some reason he was shivering. He gripped his thighs tightly to stop the shaking, but he couldn't.

"You knew him, Michael?"

Mike nodded.

"A close friend?"

Mike took in a breath. He shrugged, then nodded. The shaking seemed to have moved into his bones now.

"Was he Catholic?" asked Father C.

Mike lowered his head again. His first response was to say, *Who the fuck cares?* "No," he said. "I don't think so. He never came to church here. I don't think he or his dad belong to any church."

Father C. made a soft noise. "It doesn't matter. I'll go out to visit him right after this service."

"You can't go out there to see Mr. McBride, Father," Rusty said from the doorway. He had the small bottles of wine and water in his hands. "The cops've got the kid's dad over to Oak Hill. They think maybe he murdered him."

"That's enough, Rusty," Father C. said in a deeper tone than Mike had ever heard him use. Then, amazingly, the priest said, "Now get your ass out there and wait for Michael and me."

Rusty's jaw dropped, he stared wide-eyed at Father C. for a second, and then he scurried out to the altar. Mike could hear the mourners for Mrs. Sarranza's funeral beginning to file in.

"We'll think of your friend Duane as we say Mass and ask for God's mercy," Father Cavanaugh said softly, touching Mike's shoulder a final time. "Ready?"

Mike nodded, lifted the tall crucifix that lay ready against the wall, and followed the priest out to the altar in solemn procession.

* * *

Late that afternoon, Dale's father came upstairs to talk to him. Dale was lying on his bed, listening to the shouts and cries of younger children playing in the schoolyard across the street. The happy noises sounded very far away.

"How you doing, tiger?"

"Fine."

"Lawrence is eating some dinner. Sure you won't join us?"

"No. Thanks."

His dad cleared his throat and sat on Lawrence's bed. Dale was lying on his back, his fingers laced on his forehead, staring at the tiny cracks in the ceiling. He listened when his dad sat down, half expecting to hear a stirring under the bed. There was only the outside noise, drifting through the screens like the heavy air. The day was gray and thick with humidity.

"I called Constable Sills again," said his dad. "I finally got through."

Dale waited.

"It's true about the accident," said his dad. His voice sounded hoarse, strained. "There was some terrible accident with the machine they used to harvest corn. Duane . . . well, Barney thinks that it probably happened very quickly. In all probability, Duane didn't suffer. . . ."

Dale flinched slightly, concentrated on finding a pattern in the cracks above him.

"The police were out there all morning," continued his dad, evidently understanding that no matter how terrible these facts were, they were what Dale needed now. "They're going to continue the investigation, but they're pretty sure it was an accident."

"What about his father?" rasped Dale.

"What?"

"Duane's father. Didn't the police arrest him?"

Dale's dad scratched his upper lip. "Who told you that?"

"Mike stopped by. He heard it from some kid. They said that Duane's dad had been arrested for murder."

His father shook his head. "Darren McBride was questioned according to the constable. He was . . . out drinking until late last night and couldn't account for his actions early this morning. But both Mr. Taylor's and the coroner's report . . . Dale, you don't want to hear this . . ."

"Yes," demanded Dale.

"Well, I guess they have ways of telling how long it's been since . . . since someone's passed away. At first they thought the accident had happened this morning, after Mr. McBride had gone home and . . . gone to sleep . . ."

"Passed out," said Dale.

"Yes. Well, at first they'd thought the accident had happened this morning, but then the coroner was sure that it occurred last night, sometime around midnight. Mr. McBride had been at the Black Tree until long after midnight. There were witnesses. Also, Barney says that the man is beside himself . . . hardly rational. . . ."

Dale nodded again. Midnight was correct. He remembered the peal of the bell toward twelve. The bell that did not exist in Elm Haven. He said, "I want to go out there."

His father leaned forward. Dale could smell the soap and tobacco scent of his hands and forearms. "Out to the farm?"

Dale nodded. He thought he could see a pattern in the cracks now. A pattern like a large question mark made of zigzag lines.

"I don't think it would be a good idea today," his dad said softly. "I'll call later. See how Mr. McBride's holding up. See if there'll be a memorial service or funeral. Then we'll take some food out. Perhaps tomorrow . . ."

"I'm going," said Dale.

His father thought that he meant to the funeral. He nodded, touched his son on the head, and went downstairs.

Dale lay there thinking for some time. He must have dozed because when he opened his eyes again, the room was gray with fading light, the children's cries had been replaced by crickets and night sounds, and darkness had crept from the corners. Dale lay perfectly still, hardly breathing, waiting for a sound from under Lawrence's bed, for the peal of a bell, for something. . . .

When the rain came, opening up as fiercely and quickly as a turned tap, Dale sat by the window and watched the leaves outlined against silent lightning, heard the gurgle of water in the pipes and the pattering of rain on leaves and the cinder driveway as the downpour lessened. A flash illuminated Depot Street wet and black in the night, the belfry of Old Central rising above the sentinel elms across the street.

The breeze coming in through the screen was chilly now. Dale shivered slightly but did not get back under the covers. Not yet. He had to think.

He and Mike went out after each had gone to their respective churches the next day. Dale had found Reverend Miller's sermon a distant drone; later, driving home, his mother had commented on how thoughtful the Reverend's comments about the McBride tragedy had been, but Dale hadn't heard them.

He told his mom that he was going over to Mike's chickenhouse; he didn't know what Mike told his family, if anything. Dale didn't have to eeawkee—Mike was waiting under the big elm where they'd first met. Mike was wearing a rubber poncho that the *Peoria Journal-Star* had given him for his delivery route.

"You're going to get soaked," said Mike when Dale slid to a stop on the sidewalk.

Dale peered up through the branches. It was still raining hard; he hadn't really noticed, although he realized he'd pulled on a windbreaker. The bill of his wool ballcap was already dripping. He shrugged. "Let's go."

Rain pattered on the knee-high corn as they pedaled out past the water tower, east on Jubilee College Road, north again on County Six. They hid their bikes in the high weeds on the hill to Uncle Henry's house. The rain was coming down harder now and Mike fussed about the bike getting wet.

"Come on," whispered Dale.

They climbed the fence and went into Mr. Johnson's woods. They could see the cemetery on the next hill behind them, the black iron fence giving off a wintry feeling outlined as it was against a gray sky. The woods dripped and Dale felt his tennis shoes getting more soaked as he and Mike climbed up through wet umbrella plants and knee-high weeds. The hillside was slippery and on the steeper parts they had to grab trees or weeds to pull themselves up.

They came out into the narrow pasture abutting the south side of the McBride farm and Mike led the way west, toward the back field. Duane's farm was just visible across almost a mile of low corn. The sky was a mottled variety of grays that seemed to lie low as a ceiling above them. They paused at the fence.

"I think this is breaking a law," whispered Mike.

Dale shrugged.

"Not just trespassing," said Mike. He adjusted the hood of his poncho and water slooshed off. "Messing up a crime scene or something."

"They said it was an accident." Dale found himself whispering even though no one was within a mile of them. "How can there be a crime scene if it was an accident?"

"You know what I mean." Mike pulled his hood off and stared out over the field. There was no sign of a combine. No sign of anything at all. The McBride barn was far away and it looked like any other barn.

"Are we going to do it or not?" asked Dale.

"Yeah." Mike tugged his hood back on and they clambered over the fence.

They moved across the field in a crouch. The road was several hundred yards away, but they felt exposed in the low corn. Dale felt like he was playing soldiers, running forward in a burst of speed, crouching low and gesturing Mike on. In that manner they crossed the field.

They were more than halfway across when they saw the swath of cleared corn. It was like someone had taken a lawnmower to the field, gouging out a drunken path of stubble through the green shoots. Then they saw the yellow tape.

They crossed the last twenty yards in a low shuffle that got their knees and hands muddy.

"God," whispered Mike.

The yellow tape said POLICE SCENE—DO NOT CROSS, the message repeated indefinitely, and the plastic stretched in a rough rectangle at least fifty feet on a side. Within that rectangle, the swath of harvested corn suddenly ended and there was an area that had been trampled by many feet.

Dale paused a second where the tape draped over the cornstalk, and then he crossed it, moving quickly to the cleared area. Mike followed.

"God," Mike whispered again.

Dale didn't know what he expected; the combine still to be there maybe, a human outline chalked on the ground like in the TV shows he watched. There was only the trampled corn . . . he could see where the big machine had turned around, where the wheels had left deep gouges in the dirt now turned to mud. It looked like the field where they held the Old Settlers' carnival each August, trampled by thousands of feet. Dale saw cigarettes lying in the wet and trampled cornstalks, a Red Pouch Tobacco bag, scraps of paper, some plastic wrappers. It was hard to tell exactly where the combine had been . . . where the accident had happened.

"Here," called Mike.

Dale moved over, staying low in case Mr. McBride or anyone at the farm was looking this way. He couldn't see the pickup in the barnyard or drive, but the house and barn shielded much of the view.

"What?" he said.

Mike pointed. Some of the trampled corn here looked as if the stalks had been sprayed a deep reddish-brown. Some of the color had faded because of the rain, but the undersides of the corn were still marked.

Dale crouched, touched a plant, brought his fingers up. There was a faint rusty residue there in the seconds before the rain washed it from his fingers.

Duane's blood? The thought was unsupportable. He got up and began moving around the circle of ravaged plants, seeing the turmoil everywhere, remembering overhearing his father telling his mother that Barney said that the state troopers and the volunteer firemen had stomped up the scene so much that the Oak Hill police hadn't been able to reconstruct much. *Reconstruct,* mused Dale. *Strange word for figuring out the way something or someone is destroyed.*

"What are we looking for?" whispered Mike from twenty feet away. "There's just a lot of crap lying around."

"Keep looking," Dale whispered. "We'll know when we find it." He stepped out into the corn, beyond the police line, crouching as he moved down the row.

Another five minutes and he found it, less than ten yards from the ravaged area. It was hard to see beneath the leaves of growing corn, but his sneaker had twisted in something and he'd bent to investigate. Mike ran over when he waved. The two crouched on hands and knees, the rain pattering on cornstalks next to their ears.

"A hole," whispered Dale. He measured it with his two hands. Not quite a foot across, but the earth looked bunched and strange around it. He put his hand into it but Mike quickly grabbed it and pulled it back.

"Don't."

"Why?" said Dale. "I just wanted to see if it was wider on the inside. It is. Feel."

Mike shook his head.

"The sides feel funny, too," said Dale. "Sort of stiff. And the hole has ridges along the side." He raised his head. There was no movement from the McBride farm, but he had the distinct impression that they were being watched. "Let's see if there are any more."

They found six more. The biggest was more than eighteen inches across, the smallest hardly larger than a gopher hole. There was no pattern to them, although most of them were closer to the farm, on either side of the harvested swath.

Dale wanted to sneak up on the barn and look in to see if the combine was there.

"Why the hell . . . why do you want to do that?" Mike whispered, pulling his friend down lower. They were too close. The boys could read the numbers on the tags in the ears of the few cows behind the barn.

"I just want to . . . I need to . . ." Dale took a breath.

The sound of a door slamming sent both boys flopping into the mud between the rows. Lying there, hearing a truck engine starting up, Dale realized that it had almost stopped raining. The air was still bleeding a fine mist, but the downpour had stopped.

"It's gone down the drive," whispered Mike. "But I think somebody's still there. Let's head back to the woods."

"One peek in the barn," Dale whispered back and began to rise.

Mike tugged him down. "I've seen those things before."

Dale crouched and blinked at Mike's ponchoed figure. "What things?"

"The holes. Those tunnels."

"Where?"

Mike turned back and began moving away from the farm. "Come on back with me and I'll tell you." He was gone, moving down the next row in a low crouch.

Dale hesitated. He was only a hundred feet or so from the barn. The feeling that he was being watched—observed—was still strong, but so was the desire to see the machine. There was little or no morbid curiosity in the desire; the thought of seeing the blades or gears or whatever that had actually killed his friend made him sick, but he had to *know* . . . to begin to understand.

The rain had started up again. Dale looked toward the south, caught the slightest glimpse of Mike's poncho moving above the corn, and then he turned and followed.

There'd be time.

TWENTY-ONE

It rained on and off for three weeks. Each morning the sky would be a rapidly shifting war between sunlight and clouds, but by ten A.M. the drizzle would begin and by lunchtime the rain would fall from lowering skies.

The Free Show was canceled for June 25 and July 2, although the skies were clear and the evening gentle on that second Saturday. The next morning the rain returned. Around Elm Haven, the hungry Illinois earth seemed to drink the moisture and ask for more. The black earth turned blacker. In most of America, farmers spoke of corn being "knee-high by the Fourth of July"; in central Illinois the rule always had been "waist-high by the Fourth of July," but this summer the corn was closer to shoulder-high by the Fourth.

The Fourth fell on a Monday, and although the adults seemed to enjoy the rare three-day holiday, their pleasure was ruined a bit by the rain that canceled the town parade and the evening's fireworks. Elm Haven had no city budget for a formal fireworks show, but a century of tradition had people bring their own Roman candles, skyrockets, and firecrackers to the school grounds. A few showed up this summer, but the wind had risen that evening, the nightly storm had blown in early, and the would-be revelers abandoned the effort after matches would not light and fuses failed.

Dale and Lawrence watched the lightning storm that had replaced a fireworks show from the safety of their front porch. Explosions of white light ran along the southwestern horizon, silhouetting trees, outlining gabled rooftops, and illuminating the looming mass that was Old Central. In the dark lulls between flashes, the school still seemed to glow from some inner light, a soft fungal phosphorescence that painted the grounds a blue-green and seemed to build a haze of static electricity around the ancient elms that surrounded the block. One of those elms exploded and died as Dale and Lawrence watched on the evening of July the Fourth; whether struck by lightning or simply torn asunder by the wind, they did not know. The sound was deafening even from sixty yards away. Half the tree remained standing, a jagged, broken tooth of a thing, while the leafy, living part of it fell onto the schoolyard with a lumberjack crash.

Dale and Lawrence went in after the storm had passed. They'd set off a few firecrackers from the porch, swung sparklers and lighted glow-worms on the stone steps, but the wind was cold and their hearts weren't really in it.

Around the town, in the hush which followed the storm, the millions of acres of corn grew taller, forming a solid mass of greenery that turned the county roads into corridors between high walls, hid the horizon from sight, and seemed to leech substance from the next day's sunlight until the brightest spot around was no brighter than the deep shadow under the elms of town.

Dale's family brought food to Mr. McBride. Half the families in town had. Dale rode along as they drove out the familiar but strangely unfamiliar county road, past the cemetery and Uncle Henry's, and turned down the long lane. The corn seemed taller here than in any of the adjacent fields, the driveway a veritable tunnel.

The first two times they tried, no one answered the door despite the fact that Mr. McBride's pickup was in the yard. The third time he opened the door, accepted the casseroles and pie with a mumbled litany of thanks, and mumbled something else when Dale's mother and father offered their regrets. Dale had always thought of Duane's dad as an older man than any of the other parents, but he was shocked at McBride's appearance: his remaining strands of hair seemed to have turned gray in the past month, his eyes were deep-set and bloodshot, the left one almost closed as if from a stroke, his face looked more like the bust of a cracked and poorly glued figurine than a man with wrinkles, and the gray stubble ran down his cheeks onto his neck and into his dirty undershirt.

Dale's parents spoke in low, sad undertones to each other during the long ride back. No one knew for sure what arrangements had been made for Duane's funeral or memorial service. Word in town was that Mr. Taylor had released the body to a mortuary in Peoria—the same one that had arranged Duane's uncle's cremation. Word was that the boy was also cremated, in a private service.

No one knew what Mr. McBride had done with the ashes.

At night, when he was drifting off to sleep, Dale thought of his friend now existing only as a handful of ashes and the thought brought him sitting up in bed, heart pounding with some deep realization that the universe was *wrong*.

At times, when mowing the yard between rainstorms or doing something else that freed his subconscious, Dale imagined that Duane McBride was still alive, that he had faked his own death and was hiding out somewhere like that comic strip character The Spirit, or like Mickey Mouse in the comic adventures when he was trying to find the Phantom Blot. At those times, Dale half-expected to get a phone call from Duane, his friend's calm voice saying, "Meet me in the Cave. I've got some information."

Dale wondered what information Duane *had* been prepared to share at the meeting in the chickenhouse. The meeting that never happened. He couldn't imagine how Duane could've found out much about Tubby or the school, restricted as he was to his farm and a library. But over the four years Dale had known him, he'd learned never to underestimate Duane.

After Mike's revelation about the tunnel he'd found in the cemetery and the similar tunnels under his home, the boys had seen less and less of each other. Each of them had seemed to withdraw into his own circle of family and daily chores, as if there would be safety from the encroaching darkness there.

Lawrence feared the dark more than ever before. He wept now sometimes in his sleep and insisted on a forty-watt bulb in the lamp on the dresser rather than the weak night-light. Their mother often came in and turned off the brighter light after Lawrence had fallen asleep, but several times the eight-year-old had awakened screaming.

Before their dad left on an eight-day selling trip through Indiana and northern Kentucky, their mother brought Lawrence and Dale to the local doctor to discuss their fears and the wild accusation Dale had made at dinner one night that grown-ups had murdered Duane and Tubby Cooke. The doctor was named Viskes, was a Hungarian refugee who had been in the country only eighteen months, and still had problems with English. All the kids in town called him Dr. Vicious because he was too cheap to buy new hypodermic needles and just kept sterilizing the old ones until the shots were pure agony.

Dr. Viskes prescribed hard work and fresh air to cure the children's nonsense. Dale overheard Dr. Vicious tell his mom that it was a shame about the McBride boy and his uncle, but that accidents tend to happen in twos.

Accidents happen in threes, thought Dale.

The other kids got together occasionally. For five days after the Fourth, Kev and Mike and Dale and Lawrence played almost nonstop Monopoly on the Stewarts' long front porch while the showers fell. They would leave the game out overnight, stones weighting their stacks of money and cards; when someone went broke, they changed the rules so that person could wander the board as a "bum" until the bank floated a loan or some old property brought in rent. With the rules changed, the game had no chance of being finished and they played on—meeting after breakfast and playing until mothers called them home for supper.

Dale dreamed Monopoly for two nights and was glad of it.

On the fifth day, the Grumbachers' stupid Labrador, Brandy, snuffled his way onto the porch while the boys were eating dinner and scattered the money and chewed up four of the cards. They ended the game by silent assent and for two days they did not see each other again.

On July 10, a Sunday which did not feel like a Sunday because Dale's dad was at the home office in Chicago, the basement flooded.

Things would never be the same again.

For two days Dale's mom put up with the flooding, moving things from the floor onto the workbench and trying to keep the sump pump working. The basement had flooded twice before during their four years in the house, but both times their father had been able to stop the backup at a couple of inches. This time the water kept rising.

On Tuesday morning the sump pump went out. By lunchtime the electricity went out in the house.

Dale came down from his room when his mother called. The giant basement stairs led down to solid darkness. His mom stood on the next-to-last step, her skirt soaked, a bandanna wrapped around her head. She looked close to tears.

Dale stared. The water had risen over the first step. It was at least two feet deep, probably more. It lapped at the step his mother was standing on like a dark sea.

"Oh, Dale, it's just so *damn* frustrating. . . ."

Dale looked at her. He didn't think he'd ever heard her curse before.

"I'm sorry, honey, but I haven't been able to get the pump to work and it's up to the level of the washing machine and I have to go way back to the back room to put a new fuse in and . . . damn, I wish your father were here."

"I'll do it, Mom." Dale was amazed to hear himself say it. He hated the goddamn basement at the best of times.

Something floated near the step. It might have been a tangle of dust in the water, but it looked like the back of a drowned rat.

"Go get your oldest jeans on," said his mother. "And bring your Boy Scout flashlight."

Dale went upstairs to change clothes in a half-daze. The sense of removal and retreat he'd been feeling since Duane's death now folded on him like a thick wrapping of insulation. He looked down at his hands as if they belonged to someone else. *Into the basement? In the dark?* He changed clothes, pulled on his holiest pair of old sneakers, rolled up his pant-legs, grabbed his flashlight from the extra room, tested it, and pounded down the stairs.

His mother handed him the fuse. "It's right above the dryer back in the . . ."

"I know where it is." The water hadn't risen visibly in the past few minutes, but it was already overrunning the second step. The short corridor toward the furnace room looked like the unlighted entrance to some flooded crypt.

"Just don't stand in the water when you put it in. Get up on the bench next to the dryer. Make sure your hands are dry and that the switch is on Off and . . ."

"Yeah, Mom." He stepped off before he lost his nerve and ran back up the stairs and out the back door.

The water came above his knees and was icy cold. His toes began to ache and cramp almost immediately.

"The whole drainage system has backed up . . ." he heard his mother say as he moved down the narrow corridor, shining his light on the cinderblock walls. The beam was dim; he should've changed the batteries.

The opening to the coal bin was a black rectangle to his right, the bottom of it just above the waterline. Black water milled around the hopper and there were dark lumps floating there that looked like human turds. *Coal,* thought Dale and shined the dim light on the tentacled monster of the furnace itself.

The water level wasn't quite to the grate yet. Dale had no idea what would happen if the furnace flooded.

A sound to his right made him wheel, splashing backward into the wall and shining his light into the coal bin.

It was dry in there but something had rustled up near the ceiling on the far side, where the unfinished area began. Dale saw small pinpricks of reflected light in that darkness. *Just the pipes. Just the insulation. Not eyes. Not eyes.*

He turned left around the furnace. The water seemed deeper here, even though he knew it couldn't be. *Maybe it could be. Maybe each room slants down a little bit. Maybe the back room is completely underwater.*

"Are you there yet?" came his mother's voice, distorted by stone and water and the curves of walls.

"Almost," he yelled, although he was less than halfway back.

There were no windows in this basement; it was too low. Dale's light skittered across the oily water and illuminated only a fraction of the furnace room—pipes, something floating—a piece of wood—more pipes, a soaked piece of paper washed up against the wall, the door to the workroom.

The workroom was a wide, black space. The water soaked higher into Dale's jeans until it was almost to his crotch. He'd have to be careful in the last room because the sump pump was built over a hole at least eighteen inches wide, a small well that pumped water into a jerry-rigged drainage system.

Just like the tunnels Mike saw. The tunnels at Duane's farm.

Dale realized that the flashlight beam was shaking. He steadied his right hand with his left, stepped deeper into the workroom, noted that his father's tools were high and dry although they'd forgotten a small wooden toolbox in the corner which was now floating under the bench. Lawrence had made that toolbox last winter.

"I can call Mr. Grumbacher!" called his mother. Her voice sounded light-years away, a faint recording played in a distant room.

"No," said Dale. He thought he said it; he might only have whispered it.

The basement rooms were linked in almost an S-shape, with the stairs being at the base of the S, the furnace room at the middle, the workroom just before the top curve, and the laundry room tucked back at the end of the curve, reaching back toward the coal bin and the unfinished crawl space.

Dale shone his light into the laundry room.

It seemed larger than it had been when the lights worked. The darkness created the illusion that the far wall had been removed and that only blackness stretched away there . . . under the house, under the yards, across the street and schoolyard to the school itself.

Dale found the sump pump, its motor just above the waterline on its clumsy tripod of pipes. He gave it a wide berth as he circled to the south wall and the washer and dryer and laundry bench.

It was wonderful to crawl up onto the bench and to lift his legs out of the water. He was shaking from the cold now, the flashlight beam whipping over the cobwebby rafters and maze of pipes above him, but at least the worst was over. With the new fuse in, the lights would come, the sump pump would begin working, and he could walk back without just the flashlight.

He fumbled in his pocket with numb fingers, almost dropped the fuse into the water, and lifted it carefully in both hands. Holding the flashlight under his chin, Dale made sure the power lever was Off and then opened the access plate.

It was immediately obvious which fuse had blown. The third one. Always the third one. His mother shouted something unintelligible from a great distance, but Dale was too busy to respond; if he moved his jaw to talk, the flashlight would have fallen. He set the new fuse in place and threw the switch.

Light. The far wall *was* there. A stack of laundry still sat in a basket near the edge of the table. An assortment of junk he and his mother had tossed on top of the dryer and washer to keep dry resolved itself from ominous shadows to simple stacks of old magazines, an iron, a baseball Lawrence had lost . . . just junk.

His mother called again. Dale heard clapping.

"Got it!" he shouted uselessly. He stuck the Boy Scout flashlight on his belt, rolled his soaked pantlegs a little higher, and jumped down into the water. The ripples moved across the room like the wake of a shark.

Dale smiled at his own fears and started walking back, already imagining the story he'd tell his dad about all this. He was almost to the door of the workroom when he heard the audible click behind him.

The lights went out. Goosebumps broke out over every inch of Dale's body.

Someone had thrown the power switch to Off. That click had been unmistakable.

His mother called, but it was the most distant and useless of sounds. Dale was breathing through his mouth, trying to ignore the roar of his pulse in his ears, trying to *hear*.

The water stirred a few feet from him. First he heard it and then he felt the ripples washing against his bare legs.

Dale backed up until he slammed into a wall. Cobwebs tangled in his hair and tickled his forehead but he ignored them as he fumbled on his belt for the flashlight. *Don't drop it Please God don't drop it Please.*

He thumbed it on. Nothing. The darkness was absolute.

There was a sliding, liquid noise five feet in front of him, as of an alligator sliding off the bank into dark water.

Dale banged the base of the flashlight, pounded it on his upper thigh. A weak, filmy light illuminated rafters. He held the flashlight in front of him like a weapon, sweeping the dying beam back and forth.

The distant dryer. Washer. Bench. Blackness of the far wall. The silent sump pump. Fuse box. Handle Off.

Dale panted through his mouth. He felt suddenly dizzy and wanted to close his eyes, but he was afraid that he would lose his balance and fall. Into the water. Into the dark water all around. Into the water where things waited.

Stop it goddammit! Stop it! The thought was so loud that for a moment he was sure that it was his mother shouting. *Stop it! Calm down, you damn sissy.* He took in short breaths and continued to command himself out of his panic. It helped a little.

The switch wasn't set all the way. It fell down.

How? I pushed it all the way up.

No, you didn't. Go fix it.

The flashlight beam died. Dale pounded it back into life. There were stirrings and ripples all across the room now. It was as if entire generations of spiders had come awake and lowered themselves from the rafters. The light flickered around the room, touching everything, illuminating nothing. There was more shadow than substance everywhere. *Spider legs.*

Dale cursed himself for being a coward and took a step forward. Water milled around him. He took another step, tapping the flashlight every time the beam threatened to go out. The water was above his waist now. *Impossible.* But it was. *Watch out for the sump-pump hole.* He moved left to stay nearer the wall.

He was turned around now, not sure of which direction he was going. The flashlight beam was too weak to reach the walls or the washer or dryer. He was afraid he was walking to the back of the room where the wall did not meet the ceiling and sharp little eyes stared out of the crawlspace even when there *were* lights and . . . *Stop it!*

Dale stopped. He pounded the base of the L-shaped Boy Scout flashlight and for a second the beam was strong and straight. The bench was ten paces to his left. He *had* gone the wrong way. Another three paces would have taken him to the sump-pump hole. Dale turned and began wading toward the bench.

The flashlight went off. Before Dale could bang it against his leg, something else touched his leg. Something long and cold. It seemed to be nuzzling against him like the snout of an old dog.

Dale did not scream. He thought of floating newspaper and floating toolboxes and he worked hard not to think of other things. The cold sliding against his leg lessened, returned, grew stronger. He did not scream. He pounded the flashlight, flicked the sliding switch, and tightened the lens. A weak glow trickled out, more like the spluttering of a tiny candle than a flashlight beam.

Dale bent over and aimed the dying beam at the surface of the water.

Tubby Cooke's body floated inches under the surface. Dale recognized him at once even though he was naked and his flesh was pure white—the white of rotting mushrooms—and terribly bloated. Even the face was bloated to twice or three times the size of a human face, like a pastry that had risen until the white dough was ready to explode from internal pressures. The mouth was open wide under the water—there were no bubbles— and the gums had blackened and pulled far back from the teeth so each molar and incisor stood far out like yellowed fangs. The body floated gently there just under the surface, as if it had been there for weeks and would always be there. One hand floated near enough to the surface that Dale could see pure-white fingers swollen to the size of albino sausages. They seemed to waggle slightly as a gentle current touched them.

Then, eighteen inches away from Dale's face, the Tubby-thing opened its eyes.

TWENTY-TWO

I n those three weeks of rain and gloom, Mike learned who and what the Soldier was and how to fight it.

The death of Duane McBride had bothered Mike deeply, even though he hadn't considered himself a close friend the way Dale had. Mike realized that after he had flunked fourth grade—mostly because reading was so difficult for him, the letters in words seemed to rearrange themselves in random patterns even as he concentrated on making sense of them—after he had flunked, he'd come to think of himself as the total opposite of Duane McBride. Duane read and wrote more easily and fluently than any adult Mike had ever known with the possible exception of Father Cavanaugh, while Mike could barely sound his way through the newspaper he delivered every day. He'd never resented that difference—it wasn't Duane's fault that he was brilliant. Mike respected it with the same equanimity that he respected gifted athletes or born storytellers like Dale Stewart, but the abyss between two kids about the same age had been infinitely larger than the grade level that separated them. Mike had envied Duane McBride the infinite number of doors that were open to him: not doors of privilege—Mike knew that the McBrides were almost as poor as the O'Rourkes—but doors of perception and comprehension that Mike barely glimpsed through conversation with Father C. He suspected that Duane had lived in those lofty realms of thought, listening to the voices of men long dead rising from books the way he'd once said he listened to late-night radio shows in his basement.

Mike felt a terrible sense of . . . not just loss, although loss there was, but of *imbalance.* It was as if he and Duane McBride had been on a see-saw together since they were tiny kids in Mrs. Blackwood's kindergarten, and now the corresponding weight was gone, the balance destroyed.

Only the stupid kid remained.

The rain did not keep the Soldier away. Nor the scrapings under the floor.

Mike wasn't a fool; he told his dad that some weird guy was watching the house. He even told him about the tunnels in the crawlspace.

Mr. O'Rourke was too fat to fit under the house these days, but he sent Mike back with a rope to plumb the depths of the tunnels and poison to sprinkle on various forms of bait, as if some giant possum had taken up residence there. Mike went back under the house with his heart in his throat, but there was no reason for the fear. The holes were gone.

His dad believed him about the weird guy in the army uniform—Mike had never lied to him as far as either one of them could remember—but he thought it was some teenage punk hanging around one of the girls. What could Mike say to that—it was something *else,* some thing that wanted Memo? Maybe it *was* some soldier that Peg or Mary had met in Peoria and who was hanging around. The older girls denied it—none of them knew any soldiers except for Buzz Whittaker, who had gone into the army eight months earlier. But Buzz Whittaker was stationed in Kaiserslautern, Germany, as his mother proudly told everyone, showing off his semiliterate letters and occasional color postcards.

It wasn't Buzz Whittaker. Mike knew Buzz, and the Soldier did not have his face. Strictly speaking, the Soldier didn't have a face at all.

Mike had heard a noise late on the Fourth—sensed it really—and had padded downstairs, bat in hand, expecting to find Memo curled in her fetal position on the bed, the lamp burning, with moths batting at the window, trying to reach the flame. He did, but the Soldier was also at the window, his face pressed against the glass.

Mike simply stood and stared.

It was raining hard outside, the inside window was closed except for a small gap at the bottom through which came the fresh smell of the moist fields across the road, but the Soldier had pressed up against the screen until it had bent inward to touch glass. Mike could see the campaign hat with water pouring from the brim, the wet khaki of the shirt illuminated by Memo's lamp only two feet away, the Sam Browne belt and brass buckles.

Water doesn't pour off a ghost's hat.

The Soldier's face was pressed against the window: not against the outside screen, but against the *glass*. Mouth agape, baseball bat hanging limply, Mike stepped between Memo and the apparition. He was less than three feet from the form at the window.

The last time Mike had seen the Soldier, his thought had been that the young man's face was shiny, greasy, less a face than a sketch of a face in soft wax. Now that soft wax face had flowed *through* the mesh of the screen and was flattening against the glass, flowing and widening against the glass like the fleshy pseudopod of some flesh-colored snail.

As Mike watched, the Soldier raised his hands and set them flat against the fine-mesh screen. His fingers and palms flowed through the screen like a candle melting in high speed. They re-formed against the glass and spread into waxy fingers, a shiny palm. The hand flowed out of the khaki sleeve like a slow-moving fountain of wax, the hand moving down the window glass. Mike raised his eyes to watch the face try to take shape, the eyes floating in the mess like raisins in a fleshy pudding. The hands slid lower.

Toward the opening.

Mike screamed then, shouting for his father, his mother. He stepped forward and slammed the baseball bat down on the top of the window sash, slamming the window shut just as ten melted streams of fingers were reaching the crack there. The arms and hands—melted more than a yard long by now—flowed sideways like fleshy tentacles, hunting for a gap.

Mike heard his mother's voice, his father rising with a groan of bed-springs. Peg shouted down the stairs and Kathleen began crying. His father growled something and there came the sound of his bare feet in the hall.

The Soldier's fingers and face flowed away from the pane, back through the screen, re-forming into the simulacrum of a human form with the speed of a movie run in fast reverse. Mike shouted again, dropped the bat, and leaned forward to slam the window tighter, knocking the kerosene lamp off the table as he did so. The chimney shattered but the lamp landed on its base and Mike knelt to catch it before it spilled fuel all over the carpet and ignited it.

In that second, his father appeared at the door and the shape at the window disappeared, arms at its sides, going straight down as if it were standing on a freight elevator.

"What the hell!" shouted Jonathan O'Rourke. His wife rushed in to see to Memo, who lay there blinking wildly in the flickering light.

"Did you see him?" shouted Mike, lifting the lamp with its open flame. He held it dangerously near the ancient curtains. "Did you see him?"

His father glared at the broken lamp, the disarrayed table, the slammed window, and the ball bat on the floor. "Goddammit, this has gone far enough." He ripped the curtains aside so roughly that the rod came off and the entire assembly fell behind the table. The tall rectangle of window showed only night and rain dripping from the eaves. "There's no one out there, damn it."

Mike looked to his mother. "He was trying to get in."

His father pushed the window up. The fresh breeze was pleasant after the stink of kerosene and fear in the room. His father's heavy hand slapped the sill. "The damned *latch* is on the screen. How could he get in?" He stared at Mike as though his son was losing his mind. "Was this . . . this soldier trying to tear the screen off? I would've heard it!"

Now that the electric lights were on, Mike shut off the lamp and set it on the table with shaking hands. "No, he was coming *through* . . ." He stopped, hearing how lame it sounded.

His mother came over and touched his shoulders, felt his forehead. "You're hot, dear. You have a fever."

Mike did feel feverish. The room seemed to tilt and resettle around him and his heart would not slow down. He looked at his father as steadily as he could. "Dad, I heard something and came down. He was . . . leaning hard against the screen. It was bending in, almost ready to give way. I swear I'm not lying."

Mr. O'Rourke looked at his son a minute, turned without a word, and came back a minute later with his trousers pulled over his pajama bottoms and his work boots on. "Stay here," he said softly.

"Dad!" shouted Mike, grabbing him by the arm. He handed him the baseball bat.

Mike's mother patted Memo's hair, hushed the girls back upstairs, and changed Memo's pillowcases while they waited. There was a shadow of movement outside. Mike flinched away from the window. His father stood there, a flashlight in his hand, the bottom of the window almost to his chest. Mike blinked; he'd seen most of the Soldier's body, yet his father was much taller than the Soldier had been when Mike had seen him on Jubilee College Road. How was it that his dad seemed to be standing so much lower? Could the Soldier have been standing on something out there? That would explain the way he had descended vertically. . . .

His father disappeared, was gone another five minutes, and came in the kitchen door with a great stamping of his feet. Mike went out to meet him in the hallway.

His dad's pajama tops and trousers were soaked through, the boots smeared with mud. What little red hair he had left was now plastered over his ears. Beads of water glistened on his forehead and bald spot. He reached out a huge hand and pulled Mike into the kitchen. "There were no footprints," he said softly, obviously not wanting Mike's mother or sisters to overhear. "Everything's mud, Mike. It's been raining for days. But no footprints under the window. It's flowerbed for ten feet along that side of the house, but no footprints anywhere. And none in the yard."

Mike felt his eyes scalding the way they used to when he was little and had allowed himself to cry. His chest hurt. "I *saw* him" was all he could say through the constriction in his throat.

His dad looked at him for a long moment. "And you're the only one who's seen him. Outside Memo's window. That's the only place?"

"And once following me on County Six and the Jubilee Road," he said, instantly wishing he'd told his father earlier or not said anything now.

His dad's stare lengthened.

"He could've been on a ladder or something," Mike managed, hearing how desperate he sounded even to himself.

His father slowly shook his head. "No marks. Not a ladder. Nothing." His big hand came forward, palm covering Mike's forehead. "You are hot."

Mike felt the shivering in him again and recognized the onset of flu. "But I didn't imagine the Soldier. I swear. I *saw* him."

Mr. O'Rourke had a broad, friendly face, heavy jowls, the remnants of a thousand childhood freckles that he had passed on to all of his children— much to the dismay of three of his four daughters. Now his jowls shook slightly as he nodded. "I believe you saw something. I also think you're getting sick from staying up nights to catch this Peeping Tom. . . ."

Mike wanted to protest. This was no Peeping Tom. But he knew it was better to keep his mouth shut right now.

". . . you get up to bed, let your mother take your temperature," his father was saying. "I'll move the cot downstairs to Memo's room and sleep in there for a while. I don't go on nights again at the brewery until a week from yesterday." He set the baseball bat aside, went to the locked pantry, fumbled the key from the crack over the sill, and brought out Memo's "squirrel gun"—a short-barreled shotgun with a pistol grip. "And if that . . . soldier . . . comes around again, he'll get more than a Louisville Slugger."

Mike wanted to say something but he felt actually dizzy from relief and the fever that he felt now as a pounding in his ears and a general lightheadedness. He hugged his father and turned away before tears came.

His mother stepped into the room, frowning but gentle as she hustled him upstairs to bed.

Mike was in bed for four days. At times the fever was so bad that he found himself awakening from dreams only to find that the awakening was a dream. He did not dream about the Soldier, or Duane McBride, or any of the things that had been haunting him: mostly he dreamt about St. Malachy's and saying Mass with Father Cavanaugh. Only in his fever dreams, it was he—Mike—who was the priest, and Father C. was a little kid in an oversized cassock and surplice who kept screwing up his responses despite the laminated card with printed lines lying right there on the altar step where the boy/man knelt. Mike dreamt that he was consecrating the Eucharist, lifting the Host high in the most sacred moment a Catholic could experience, much less actually perform. . . .

The strange part of the dream was that St. Malachy's was now a vast cavern and there was no congregation. Only dark shapes that moved just beyond the circle of light generated by the altar candles. And, in his dream, Mike knew that the altar boy Father C. was messing up his Latin responses because he was afraid of that dark and the things in it. But as long as the dream-priest Michael O'Brian O'Rourke was holding the Eucharist high, as long as he was whispering the sacred and magical words of the High Mass, he would be safe enough.

Beyond the cone of light, large things circled and waited.

Jim Harlen was thinking that this was the summer that wasn't.

First he breaks his goddamn arm and busts his skull open and loses his memory of how he did it—*the face is just a dream, only a nightmare*—and then when he finally gets well enough to get out and about, one of the guys he knows gets killed in some dumbass farm accident and the others seemed to have retreated to their houses like turtles pulling in their dumbshit heads. And, of course, there was the rain. Weeks of rain.

The first few weeks he was home, his ma stayed home every night, rushed to get him things when he was hungry and thirsty, and sat and watched TV with him. It was almost like the old days, minus his dad, of course. Harlen had been nervous as hell when the Stewarts had invited his ma to go with them out to Dale's Uncle Henry's place—Ma had the habit of drinking too much, laughing too loud, and generally making a drunken asshole of herself—but the evening had turned out pretty well, actually. Harlen hadn't talked a whole lot, but he'd sort of enjoyed being with his buddies and listening, even when the McBride kid was talking about interstellar travel and time-space continuums and a bunch of stuff that Harlen had no fix on whatsoever. Still, it'd been a pretty good night . . . Duane McBride's getting killed excepted.

Harlen's accident and long stay in the hospital had given him a different outlook on death; it was something he'd heard and smelled and come close to . . . the old guy in the next room who wasn't there the morning after all the nurses and doctors had rushed in there with a cart . . . and he had no intention of coming close to it again for another sixty or seventy years, thank you. McBride's death had rattled him, he admitted it to himself, but that kind of shit is what happened when you lived on a farm and screwed around with tractors and plows and shit like that.

Harlen's ma didn't spend every evening with him anymore. She snapped at him now when he didn't make his bed or pick up his breakfast dishes. He still complained of headaches, but the heavy cast had come off and even with the sling—which Harlen thought was sort of romantic, it should knock Michelle Staffney right out of her lacey pants if he got invited to her birthday party on the fourteenth—even with the sling, the lighter cast didn't create quite that much sympathy in his mother. Or perhaps she'd used up all the sympathy she could spare. Occasionally she'd be sweet and talk to him in that soft, slightly apologetic voice she'd used during the week or so after the accident, but more and more now she just snapped or reverted to the silence that had lain between them for so long.

Many weekend nights now, she wasn't there at all.

At first she'd paid Mona Shepard to come over and watch him. Actually it was Harlen who watched Mona, always trying to get a glimpse of the sixteen-year-old's tits or a shot up her skirt. Mona teased him sometimes . . . like leaving the bathroom door open a little bit when she was taking a leak and then shouting at him when he tiptoed up to it. But mostly she ignored him—Ma might as well have been home—and frequently she made him go to bed early so she could call one of her limpdick boyfriends over. Harlen hated the sounds he heard coming up from the living room; he hated his reaction to them. He wondered if O'Rourke was right and you went blind if you did it enough. Anyway, he'd threatened Mona that he was going to tell his ma all about the little panting sessions on the divan, so she stayed away. Ma was pissed that Mona was always busy and there was hardly anyone else to call this summer—the O'Rourke girls used to baby-sit, but they were too busy panting in the backseats of cars this summer.

So Harlen stayed home alone a lot.

Sometimes he went out, riding his bike—although he was forbidden by the doctor to do so until the second cast came off. It wasn't hard riding one-handed. Hell, he'd ridden *no*-handed enough times, and so had

everybody else in that sissy Bike Patrol club they used to have. Only it
was a little trickier with a cast.

He'd ridden down to the Free Show on the ninth of July, expecting
to see a repeat of *Somebody Up There Likes Me,* a boxing movie that Mr.
A.-M. had shown a few summers ago; everybody'd liked it so much that
he brought it back every summer. Only instead of the movie, Harlen
found Bandstand Park empty except for a couple of hick farm families
who—like him—hadn't got the word that the thing'd been canceled for
the third Saturday in a row because of rotten weather.

But the weather wasn't rotten. The almost nightly storms had held
off this night, the sunlight was low and rich across long yards where the
grass was growing as you watched it. Harlen hated the fact that the yards
were so damned big around here, almost fields although they were all
tidily mowed. There were almost no fences and it was hard to tell where
one yard ran into the next. He wasn't sure why he hated it, but he knew
that yards weren't supposed to be like that; they didn't look that way in
the TV shows he liked . . . *Naked City,* for example. There weren't any
yards at all in the *Naked City.* Eight million stories, but no damn yards.

Harlen had ridden his bike around town that night, oblivious of
night falling until the bats came and started screeching against the sky.
By habit, he'd stayed away from the school—it was one of the reasons he
didn't go up to see Stewart and those dickheads more often—but he
found that even pedaling down Main or Broad in the dark made him nervous.

He turned left on Church Street to avoid Mrs. Doubbet's place—not
sure why he did it even as he did so—and pedaled fast through the dark
stretches down there where the houses were smaller and the streetlights
few and farther between. There were bright lights around O'Rourke's
dinky little church and the priest place next to it, and Harlen tarried
there on the corner a minute before turning up West End Drive, the narrow and poorly lighted lane that led up to his house and the old depot.

He was moving fast, pedaling hard, confident that nobody could
catch him in the dark sections between pole lights—*unless they stuck an
arm in the spokes and sent you hurtling, then moved in on you*—that no one
could catch him. He shook his head as he pedaled, the moist air a breeze
in his short hair, trying to get rid of the bad thoughts. *Goddamn her. She
won't be home until one or two, if then. I'll watch the late show again. No,
dammit. It's the Creature Feature on Channel 19. Can't watch that.*

Harlen decided he'd play the radio real loud, maybe get into Ma's
stash of bottles in the bottom of the buffet again. He found if he measured them real carefully and filled them up to the mark with water
when he was done, she'd never notice. She'd probably never notice

anyway because she was always putting new bottles in there or slurping from the old ones when she was tipsy. He'd listen to the radio, playing the rock-and-roll stuff real loud, and have a few drinks mixed with Coke the way he liked it.

He passed the depot at full speed—the place had always given him the willies, even when he was little—and skidded around the broad corner onto Depot Street. He could see the long three blocks down the street— they'd be at least seven or eight city blocks in a real city, he knew, it was just here they were longer because they didn't have enough streets—all the way down the tunnel of branches and leaf-shadow and half-hidden lights and porches to where Stewart and old Grumpy-backer lived.

And the school.

He shook his head and wheeled into the drive, sliding to a stop by the garage and sticking his bike under the overhang.

Ma wasn't home; the Rambler was still gone. All the lights were on, just like he'd left them. Harlen started for the back door.

Something moved in front of the light in his room upstairs.

Harlen paused, one hand still on the doorknob. Ma *was* home. The goddamn car'd broken down again, or one of her new boyfriends had given her a lift because she'd had too much to drink. Christ, he was going to catch hell for being out of the house after dark. He'd tell her that Dale and his little Father-Knows-Best family had come by to take him to the Free Show. She'd never know that it'd been canceled.

The shadow moved in front of the light again.

What the hell's she doing poking around my room? With a sudden flush of guilt he thought of the new magazines he'd bought from Archie Kreck and hidden under the floorboard. She'd found and thrown out all his old ones while he was in the hospital, although she hadn't yelled at him about it for more than two weeks after he came home.

Blushing, cold with the thought of the confrontation—especially if she was tipsy—Harlen took three steps back toward the garage, trying to think of something. *Maybe they're Mona's. Yeah, or one of her boyfriends'. She put them there. If she denies it, I'll tell Ma about the condom I found floating in the toilet the last time she was over to baby-sit.*

He took a breath. It wasn't perfect, but it was better than nothing. He glanced up, trying to see if she was going through his closet.

It wasn't Ma.

The woman in his room crossed the lighted rectangle of window again. He caught a glimpse of a rotted-looking sweater, humped back, tendrils of white hair gleaming on a too-small head.

Harlen moved blindly away from the back door, backed into his bike. It fell and hit the garage door with a resounding racket.

The shadow eclipsed his light again. A face pressed against the window and looked down at him.

The face . . . looking at him . . . turning and looking at him.

Harlen fell to his knees, vomited on the gravel of the pavement, wiped his mouth with his sleeve, and was up and on his bike, pedaling like mad, away from the house before the shadow even left the window. He did not look back as he roared down Depot Street, swerving wildly as if someone were shooting at him, trying to stay close to the few streetlights. C.J. Congden, Archie Kreck, and a few of their punk friends were sitting on the hoods of some cars parked on the dirt lawn of J.P.'s place and they screamed something nasty at him over the blare of their car radios.

Harlen didn't pause or look back. He skidded to a stop at the wide intersection of Depot and Broad. Old Central was straight ahead. Double-Butt's and Mrs. Duggan's place was to the right.

The face at the window. Holes where the eyes should be. Maggots under the tongue. Teeth glistening.

In my room!

Harlen hung over the handlebars, panting, trying not to throw up again. Down Depot Street a block, where the school lights still glowed through the elms there, the black silhouette of a truck turned left from Third and came his way.

The Rendering Truck. He could smell it.

Harlen pedaled north on Broad. The trees were huge here, overhanging even the thirty-foot-wide street, the shadows deep. But there were more porch lights and streetlights.

He could hear the truck approaching the intersection behind him, grinding up through gears. Harlen clattered up onto the sidewalk, bounced across tilted paving stones there, and swerved down a driveway. There were barns back here, garages, and endless yards all interconnected without fences. He thought he was passing Dr. Staffney's place when a dog ahead of him went wild, barking and tugging at a clothesline leash, teeth gleaming in the yellow light from the back porch.

Harlen swerved left, skidded into the cinder-paved alley that ran behind the barns and garages, continued north. He could hear the truck coming up Broad even over the wild sound of all the dogs going crazy on the block. He had no idea where he was going.

He'd think of something.

Dale Stewart dropped his flashlight and ran through the thigh-deep water, screaming for his mother, striking a wall in the darkness and bouncing backward, stunned, losing his balance. He fell into black iciness up to his neck and screamed again when something under the water nudged his bare arm. He struggled to his feet and waded ahead, not sure of which way he was going in the almost absolute darkness of the basement.

What if I'm heading back toward the back room? Back toward the sump-pump hole?

He didn't care. He couldn't stand there in the midnight blackness, water swirling around his legs like cold oil, and *wait* for the damned thing to find him. He imagined the Tubby-thing opening that dead mouth wider, those long exposed teeth sinking into his leg under the water.

Dale quit imagining and concentrated on running, crashing into something that might have been his dad's workbench in the second room or maybe the laundry bench in the back room. He spun to his left, went to all fours again in water suddenly warm as urine or blood, and then staggered forward, seeing—*thinking that he saw*—a rectangle of somewhat lesser darkness that might have been the door from the workroom to the furnace room.

He crashed into something hollow and echoing, cutting his forehead but not caring. *The furnace! Go right, around it. Find the corridor past the coal bin.* . . . He shouted again, hearing his mother's answering screams mixing with his own cries in the echoing maze. There was the sound of something sliding through the water behind him and he turned to see it, could see nothing, staggered backward again, struck something harder than the furnace or hopper, and went face forward into the water . . . tasting the sewage-and-black-soil foulness of it mixing with the salt-sweetness of blood in his mouth.

Arms closed around him, hands forced him deeper and then lifted him.

Dale kicked and clawed and thrashed at the force. His face went under again and then was pulled against wet wool.

"Dale! Dale, stop it! Stop it! Calm down . . . it's Mom. Dale!" She did not slap him but the words had the same effect. He went limp, trying not to whimper but thinking of the dark water all around. *It'll trap us both. It'll cut us off and pull us down.*

His mother was helping him slosh through the corridor, the water somehow much shallower here. He could see the weak light now from the winding staircase. His mother hugged him tighter to her as his shaking began in earnest.

"It's all right," she said, although she was shaking too as they climbed the oversized stairs. "It's OK," she whispered as they went out—not into the kitchen but through the outside door—out into rich afternoon sunlight, staggering away from the house like two survivors of an accident trying to put distance between themselves and the wreckage.

They collapsed onto the lawn under the small apple tree, both of them wet and shaking, Dale blinking and half-blinded by the light. The heat and sunlight and color seemed unreal, a dream after the nightmare reality of the darkness and dead thing under the water. . . . he shut his eyes and concentrated on not shaking.

Mr. Grumbacher had been mowing his yard on the riding mower, and Dale heard the engine die, heard the man shout—asking if anything was wrong—and then came the long strides across the grass. Dale tried to explain without sounding insane.

"Some . . . some . . . something under the w-w-water," he said, furious that his teeth were chattering so. "Someth-thing tried to g-gr-grab me." His mother was hugging him, reassuring him, making jokes, her voice on the verge of tears. Mr. Grumbacher looked down—he was tall and was wearing the same gray uniform he wore each day to drive the milk truck; it made him look official somehow—and then he was gone and Dale's mother hugged him again and told him it was all right, and then Mr. Grumbacher was back, Kevin standing in the door of their ranch house and looking curiously across the broad lawn at them sprawled under the apple tree, and there was a blanket around Dale's shoulders and his mother's, and then Mr. Grumbacher was going through their door, down into the basement. . . .

"Don't!" screamed Dale in spite of himself. He tried to smile. "Please don't go down there."

Mr. Grumbacher glanced back at Kevin, still staring from the doorway. He motioned him back, tapped a long five-cell flashlight in his hand, and closed the screen door. The basement stairs descended from an enclosed little anteroom on the alley side of the kitchen; it kept the cold out in winter; they hung their extra coats on nails on the landing. *It was waiting for them down there. Mr. Grumbacher wouldn't have a chance.*

Dale shivered a moment and then got up, shrugging off the blanket. His mother grabbed his wrist but he squirmed out of her grip. "I've got to show him where it was . . . got to warn him about . . ."

The screen door opened. Kevin's dad came out, his neatly pressed gray work pants wet to the knee, his work boots making squeegee sounds on the flagstone. He clicked off the long flashlight that was in his left hand; he was carrying something else in his right. Something long, and white, and wet.

"Is it dead?" asked his mother. It was a foolish question. The corpse was bloated to twice its normal size.

Mr. Grumbacher nodded. "Probably didn't drown," he said in that soft but decisive voice Dale had heard directed at Kevin so many times.

"May have eaten poison or something. Maybe it came in with the backwash when the drainpipes backed up."

"Is it one of Mrs. Moon's?" asked his mother, stepping closer. Dale could feel her body shivering now.

Mr. Grumbacher shrugged and laid the corpse on the grass near the driveway. Dale heard it squish slightly and a bit of water drained out from between sharp teeth. He stepped closer, prodding it with the toe of his sneaker.

"Dale!" said his mother.

He pulled his foot back. "This isn't wh-what I saw," he said, trying to keep from shivering, trying to keep from sounding wild. "It wasn't a cat. This is a c-cat." He prodded the bloated thing again.

Mr. Grumbacher showed one of his small, tight smiles. "It's the only thing down there other than a floating toolbox and some little junk. The power's back on. The pump's beginning to work."

Dale glanced at the house. The switch had been down . . . *off.*

Kevin came down the hill and stood holding his elbows the way he did when he was a little nervous. He looked at Dale's pale face, soaked clothes, and wet hair, licked his lips as if he was going to say something sarcastic, caught the look from his father, and just nodded at Dale. He also poked at the dead cat with his sneaker. More water gurgled out.

"I think it is one of Mrs. Moon's," said Dale's mother, as if that settled things.

Mr. Grumbacher slapped Dale on the back. "Don't blame you for getting a little spooked. Stepping on Puss here in the dark, with a foot of water like that, well . . . it'd scare anyone, son."

Dale wanted to pull away and tell Grump-backer that he wasn't his son and that the dead cat wasn't what spooked him. Instead he managed to nod. He still tasted the bitter, sour flatness of the water he'd swallowed. *Tubby's still down there.*

"Let's go up and change clothes," his mom said at last. "We can talk about it later."

Dale nodded, took a step toward the screen door, and stopped. "Can we go in the front way?" he asked.

Jim Harlen pedaled through the dark, hearing the dogs going crazy up and down the block and listening hard for the sound of the Rendering Truck. It seemed to be staying at the intersection of Depot and Broad. *Cutting me off.*

The alley that he was racing blindly along went north and south between the barns, garages, and long yards behind the homes of Broad and

Fifth. The yards were so deep, the houses so surrounded by shrubs and foliage, the alley itself so bedecked in foliage made thick by the recent monsoon rains, that Harlen knew that there must be a hundred dark places to hide up ahead: barn lofts, open garages, that patch of black trees, the Miller orchard to the left up ahead, the empty houses up on Catton Drive. . . .

That's just what they want me to do.

Harlen skidded his bike to a stop on the black cinders of the alley. The dogs stopped barking. Even the moisture in the air seemed to hang suspended, a slight fog misting the air between the distant back-porch lights and Harlen, waiting for his decision.

Harlen decided. His momma didn't raise no fools.

He cut across a backyard, pedaling hard through a vegetable garden, tires flinging mud behind him, leaving the dark protection of the alley and swishing right by a startled Labrador that swung around in such surprise that it almost hanged itself on its rope before remembering to bark.

Harlen ducked quickly, seeing the wire clothesline a second and a half before it decapitated him, leaned left to avoid the pole—almost dumping his bike because of his slinged left arm being off balance—caught himself, skidded down the Staffneys' long driveway—giving the black mass of their old barn a wide berth—and skidded to a halt on their front walk four feet from the gas pole-lamp they kept burning there.

Half a long block away, the dark shape of a truck with high sides revved its engine and began moving in Harlen's direction under the tunnel of branches spanning the street. It had no lights.

Jim Harlen leaped off his bike, jumped the five steps to land on the Staffneys' porch, and leaned on the doorbell.

The truck picked up speed. It was less than two hundred feet away, pulling to this side of the wide street. The Staffney house was sixty or seventy feet away from the curb, with elms, a long yard, and a bunch of flowerbeds separating it from the street, but Harlen wouldn't have been happy with anything less than tank traps and moats between him and the truck. He banged on the door with his good fist while ringing the bell with the elbow of his cast.

The door swung wide. Michelle Staffney was there in her nightgown, the light behind her shining through the thin cotton and creating a nimbus around her long red hair. Ordinarily, Jim Harlen would have lingered to enjoy the view, but now he pushed past her into the well-lighted entry hall.

"Jimmy, what do you . . . hey!" managed the redhead before he had pushed past her. She shut the door and scowled at him.

Harlen paused under the chandelier, looking around. He'd just been in Michelle's home three times—once each year during her July fourteenth birthday party that seemed to be such a big deal for her and her folks—but he remembered the big rooms, high ceilings, and tall windows. Way too many windows. Harlen was wondering if they had a bathroom or something on the first floor with no windows and lots of strong locks when Dr. Staffney said from the stairway, "Can we help you, young man?"

Harlen put on his best lost-waif-on-the-verge-of-tears face—it didn't require much acting, he found—and cried, "My mom's gone and nobody's supposed to be home but I came home from the Free Show—they didn't have it because of the rain I guess—and there was some strange lady on the second floor and people were chasing me and a truck was after me, and I wonder . . . could you help me? Please?"

Michelle Staffney stared at him with her pretty blue eyes wide and her head cocked to one side as if he'd come in and taken a leak on her floor. Dr. Staffney was standing there in his suit pants and vest and tie and stuff; he looked at Harlen, put on his glasses, took them off, and came down the staircase. "Say that again," he said.

Harlen said it again, sticking to the high points. Some strange woman was in his house. *He didn't mention that she was dead and still moving around.* Some guys in a truck had come after him. *Never mind for now that it was the Rendering Truck.* His mother had to go out on an important errand to Peoria. *Probably to get laid, but no need to fill them in on that right now.* He was frightened. *No shit.*

Mrs. Staffney came in from the dining room. Harlen had heard from C.J. Congden or Archie Kreck or one of those guys that if you wanted to see how a girl would look in a few years—bazooms and all—check out her mom. Michelle Staffney had a lot to look forward to.

Michelle's mom fussed around Harlen—she said that she remembered him from all the birthday parties, but Harlen knew that there'd been too many kids there and he'd just been invited because everyone else in the class had been—and she insisted that he come into the kitchen for a cup of cocoa while Dr. Staffney called the constable.

The doctor looked a little confused, if not downright skeptical, but he checked out the door—naturally the truck wasn't in sight, Harlen peeked out behind him—and then went to the phone to call Barney. Mrs. Staffney insisted that they lock all the doors while they waited. Harlen was all for that; he wouldn't have minded shutting all those big windows either, but as rich as these folks were, they didn't have air conditioning in the huge house, and it would probably get very warm very quickly with-

out the screens open. Harlen contented himself with feeling secure while
Mrs. S. bustled around the kitchen warming up some leftover pot roast
for him—he'd said he hadn't had dinner, although he'd warmed up the
spaghetti Ma had left in the Tupperware—and while Dr. S. questioned
him for about the fourth time and while Michelle just stared at him with
a wide-eyed look that could have meant anything from hero worship at
his bravery in escaping to pure contempt for what an asshole he was being.

Harlen didn't really care at that moment.

The old lady in his room. *Her face at the window, looking down.* He'd
thought at first that it was Old Double-Butt, but then something had told
him that it was Mrs. Duggan. The other one. The dead one. *The dream.
The face at the window. Falling.*

Harlen shivered and Mrs. S. brought him some cake. Dr. Staffney
kept asking how frequently did his mother run these errands and leave
him alone in the house? Was she aware that there were statutes about
leaving children unattended?

Harlen tried to answer but it was difficult; he had a mouth full of
cake and he didn't want to look gross in front of Michelle.

Barney arrived only about thirty-five minutes after he was called:
probably a new town record, Harlen figured.

He told his story again, with a bit less sincere panic this time but in a
more well-oiled manner. When he got to the part about the face in the
window and the truck on the street, his voice quavered realistically
enough. Actually, he was thinking about how close he had come to riding
up the alley and hiding in one of those dark barns or empty houses on
Catton Drive, wondering what might have been waiting *there*.

There were real tears in his eyes when he finished describing the situation to the constable, but he blinked them back. No way was he going to
cry in front of Michelle Staffney. He just wished she hadn't run upstairs to
get into a flannel robe when her mother was fixing the hot chocolate. As it
was, the sexy bit of peekaboo when he came in was already mixing with
the memory of pure terror and the physical surge from the adrenaline that
had preceded it.

Constable Barney drove him home. Dr. Staffney came along and sat
in the car with him while Barney searched the house. The place was just
as Harlen had left it—lights blazing, door unlocked—but Barney had
gone to the back door and knocked—*knocked!*—before going in. Harlen
would have gone in low and fast with his revolver out and aimed, just like
the cops on *Naked City*. Barney didn't even *have* a revolver, or at least not
with him.

Harlen answered questions from Dr. S. about his ma's weekend travel habits while all the time he was waiting for a scream from inside the house.

Barney came out and waved them in. "No sign of any forcible entry," he said as they went up the back steps. Harlen realized that the constable was talking to the doctor, not him. "The place looks like it's been tossed about a bit. As if someone were looking for something." He turned to Harlen. "Is that the case, son, or is it always like this?"

Harlen looked around the kitchen and dining room with fresh eyes. The pans on the burner filled with old grease. The stack of dirty dishes in the sink, on the counter, even on the table. The stack of old magazines, boxes and crap on the floor. The overflowing garbage bags. The living room wasn't much better. Harlen knew that there was a couch under all those papers and TV dinner trays and clothes and stuff, but he could see why maybe the cop and doctor couldn't be sure.

He shrugged. "Ma's not the neatest person." He hated the way his voice sounded when he said that. As if he had to apologize to these two assholes.

"Do you see anything missing, Jimmy?" asked Barney as if he'd just remembered his name. Harlen hated being called Jimmy more than anything except being hit in the face. *Except when Michelle said it tonight.* He shook his head and walked from room to room in the small downstairs, unobtrusively trying to straighten a few things as he passed. "Uh-uh," he said. "I don't think there's anything missing. But I'm not sure." *What the fuck would they steal? Ma's electric back warmer? Our old TV dinners? My nudie magazines?* Harlen suddenly blushed at the thought of Barney or the FBI or somebody doing a real search and finding those under the loose floorboard of his closet.

"The old lady was upstairs, not down here," he said a bit more belligerently than he'd meant to.

"I looked upstairs," said the constable. He looked at Dr. S. "A lot of mess, but no sign of theft or overt vandalism."

The three of them went upstairs, Harlen feeling shittier by the minute. He could imagine the prissy doctor telling his prissy wife and kid all about the mess he'd seen. He'd probably go home to wake Michelle up to tell her to keep away from this slob of a Harlen kid. *She'd said Jimmy.*

"Anything missing?" asked Barney from the hallway while Harlen peered into his ma's room, then his. Goddammit, at least *she* could've made her goddamn bed or picked up the fucking Kleenex or magazines or something. . . .

"Uh-uh," he said, hearing how stupid he sounded. *The boy's a slob and retarded to boot,* he imagined the well-dressed doctor telling Mrs. S.

and Michelle at breakfast the next morning. "I don't think so," he added. Then, with real urgency in his voice, "Did you check the closets?"

"First thing," said Barney. "But we'll look again together."

Harlen hung back while the constable and the doctor peered in the closets. *They're humoring me. Then, when they're gone, that rotting corpse is going to come lurching up out of somewhere and bite my heart out.*

As if reading his mind, Barney said, "I'll wait until your mom gets home, son."

"So will I," said the doctor. He exchanged glances with the cop. "Jim, do you know when she might be back?"

"Uh-uh." Harlen bit his underlip. If he grunted those two syllables once more, he was going to find his dad's old revolver and blow his brains out right in front of these two. *The gun. Didn't he leave it with Ma so she could protect herself?* Gears started turning.

"You get into your PJs, son," said the constable. For the life of him, Harlen couldn't remember Barney's real name. "Do you have any coffee?"

"Some instant," said Harlen. He'd almost said *Uh-huh.* "On the counter. In the kitchen. Downstairs." *Schmuck, we just all walked through the kitchen.*

"You get ready for bed," the constable said again. He went downstairs with the doctor.

It was a small house. He could hear them easily enough. He and his ma couldn't fart without the other person hearing it; Harlen sometimes wondered if that's why his dad had taken off with the Bimbo. But tonight the house wasn't small enough. He went out on the small landing.

"Did you check under the beds . . . sir?" he called down.

Barney came to the foot of the stairs. "Sure did. And in the corners. No one's up there. No one's down here. Doc just looked around the yard. I'll check the garage in a minute. You don't have a basement, do you, son?"

"Uh-uh," said Harlen. *Damn.*

Barney nodded and went back in the kitchen. Harlen heard Michelle's dad say something about the health department.

Harlen went in without closing the door, kicked his tennis shoes in the corner, tossed his socks on the floor, snaked out of his jeans and t-shirt. Then he went over and picked up his socks and pants and tossed them into the closet, out of sight, without getting too close. *She stood right over there. By the window. She went back and forth.*

He sat on the edge of the bed. His alarm clock said 10:48. Early. These guys would be here another four or five hours if it was a typical Saturday night. Would they really stay? Harlen was going to run along behind the constable's car when they left if they didn't. No way was he staying here alone tonight.

Where the fuck does she keep the gun? It wasn't a big gun, but it was blue-steel and deadly looking. There'd been a white-and-blue box of shells. His dad had told him never to touch the gun or bullets; they'd used to be in Dad's drawer, but Ma had hidden it when he'd gone away with the Bimbo. *Where?* Probably illegal. Barney would find it and throw both of them in jail.

The back door banged. Harlen was pulling on his pajamas and he jumped at the sound. He heard their voices.

There were footsteps and Barney's voice came up the stairs much more loudly. "Care for some hot chocolate before you turn in, son?"

Harlen's stomach was gurgling from about a gallon of the stuff that Mrs. Staffney had forced on him. "Yeah!" he yelled back. "Be right down." He lifted his pillow to pull his pajama tops out from where he kept them there.

There was some sort of gray, snotty crap on them. Harlen frowned at his hands, wiped them on his pajama bottoms, pulled back the spread on his bed.

The sheet looked like it had been smeared with several gallons of something resembling a cross between snot and semen. The stuff glistened in the light from the desk lamp and overhead bulb. It was like the bed had been sandwich bread and someone had ladled on tons of gray jam—thick, slick mucousy stuff that caught the light, soaked the sheets, and was already drying into little curds and ridges. It smelled like someone had left a wet towel in a dirt hole to mildew for about three years, then had a bunch of dogs piss on it.

Harlen staggered back, dropped the pajama tops, and leaned against the doorframe. He felt like he was going to throw up. The wooden floor seemed to pitch like the deck of a small ship on a rough sea. Harlen went out to lean on the wobbly railing.

"Sir? Constable?"

"Yeah, son?" Barney was calling from the kitchen. Harlen could smell the instant coffee and milk heating.

Harlen looked back into the room, half expecting to see the sheets clean—or at least the kind of grimy clean they had been this morning—sort of like in the movies where guys have hallucinations or see mirages.

The gray mucus gleamed almost white in the light.

"Yes?" said Barney, coming to the bottom of the stairs. The man's forehead was wrinkled as if he cared. His dark eyes looked . . . what?

Worried? Caring maybe.

"Nothing," said Harlen. "I'll be right down for the cocoa." He went into the room, stripped the bed while trying not to touch the crap, tossed the whole mess and his pajamas—tops and bottoms—into the corner of the closet, found some pajamas in the bottom drawer of his dresser that were too little for him but clean, checked his ratty old robe, went in to wash his hands, and then went downstairs to join them.

Even later, Jim Harlen couldn't say why he had chosen not to show the two men this hard evidence that someone or something had been in his home. Perhaps he knew at that moment that he would have to handle this himself. Or perhaps it was just that some things were too embarrassing to share . . . that showing them the bed would be too much like pulling the magazines out of their hiding place and bragging about them.

She was *here*. It *was here*.

The hot chocolate was pretty good. Dr. Staffney had cleaned off the kitchen table and the three men sat there and talked until about twelve-thirty, when Harlen's mother came through the back door.

Harlen went upstairs then, found an extra blanket in the closet and pulled it up over him without worrying about sheets. He went right to sleep, smiling slightly at the sound of angry voices from downstairs.

It was a lot like when Dad used to live there.

TWENTY-THREE

During the worst part of his fever, Mike dreamed that he was talking to Duane McBride.

Duane didn't look dead. He wasn't all torn to shreds the way everyone in town said he'd been. He didn't lurch around like a zombie or anything; he was just the Duane that Mike had known all those years— heavy, slow-moving, corduroy pants and plaid flannel shirt. Even in the dream, Duane would take time to adjust his black-rimmed glasses every once in a while.

They were in some place that was unknown to Mike but quite famil-iar: a rolling pasture with high, rich grass. Mike wasn't sure what he was doing there, but he saw Duane and joined him on a rock near the edge of a cliff. The cliff was higher than anything Mike had seen in real life, higher even than Starved Rock State Park, where his family had gone when he was six. The view stretched on forever. There were cities down there, and a wide river with slow-moving barges on it. Duane wasn't even looking at the view; he was writing in his notebook. He looked up when Mike sat next to him.

"Sorry you're sick," said Duane and adjusted his glasses. He put his notebook away.

Mike nodded. He wasn't sure whether to say what he wanted to say, but he said it anyway. "Sorry you got killed."

Duane shrugged.

Mike bit his lip. He had to ask. "Did it hurt? Getting killed, I mean."

Duane was eating an apple now. He paused to swallow. "Sure it hurt."

"Sorry." Mike couldn't think of anything else to say. There was a puppy playing with a chew-toy over on the other side of Duane's rock, but Mike noticed with the kind of calm acceptance that's so much a part of dreams that it wasn't a dog, it was some sort of little dinosaur. The chew-toy was a green gorilla.

"You're having a real problem with that soldier," said Duane. He offered a bite of the apple to Mike.

Mike shook his head. "Yeah."

"The other guys are having problems, too, you know."

"Yeah?" said Mike. There was an airplane that was part bird blocking the sun. It soared out over the valley. "What other guys?"

"You know, the other guys."

That explained it to Mike. He was talking about Dale and Harlen. Maybe Kev.

"If you guys try to keep fighting this thing by yourselves," said Duane, adjusting his glasses and finally looking out at the view, "you're going to end up like me."

"What can we do?" asked Mike. He was vaguely aware that a dog was barking somewhere . . . a real dog . . . and there were sounds in the background that reminded him more of his house in the afternoon than this place.

Duane didn't look at him. "Find out about who these guys are. Start with the Soldier."

Mike stood up and walked to the edge of the cliff. He couldn't see anything down there now; it was all fog or clouds or something. "How do I do that?"

Duane sighed. "Well, who is it after?"

Mike didn't even think it was strange that Duane had said "it" rather than "he." The Soldier *was* an it. "It's after Memo."

Duane nodded and adjusted his glasses with an impatient move of his finger. "Well then, ask Memo."

"OK," agreed Mike. "But what about figuring out all the rest of the junk. I mean, we're not as smart as you were."

Duane hadn't moved, but somehow he was sitting much farther

away now. The same rock, but far off. And they weren't on a hilltop any longer, but on a city street. It was dark, sort of cold . . . a winter day maybe. Duane's rock was really a bench. It looked like he was waiting for a bus. He was frowning at Mike, looking almost angry. "You can always ask me," said Duane. When he saw that Mike didn't understand that, he added, "Plus, you *are* smart."

Mike started to protest, to tell Duane how he didn't understand half of what the bigger boy was talking about usually and read about one book a year, but he noticed that Duane was getting on his bus. Only it wasn't a bus, it was some sort of gigantic farm machine with windows on the side, a little wheelhouse on top like those Mike had seen in pictures of riverboats, and a paddle wheel on front made of what looked like revolving razor blades.

Duane leaned out one of the windows. "You're smart," he called down to Mike. "Smarter than you think. Plus you've got a real advantage."

"What's that?" shouted Mike, running to keep up with the bus/machine now. He couldn't tell which of the heads and waving arms belonged to Duane McBride.

"You're *alive*," came Duane's voice. The street was empty.

Mike woke up. He was still hot and he ached all over, but his pajamas and sheets were soaked through with sweat. It felt like early afternoon. Reflected sunlight and a slow stirring of air came through the screens. It must be a hundred degrees up here, even with the hall fan turning. Mike could hear his mother or one of his sisters vacuuming downstairs.

Mike was dying for a drink of water, but he felt too weak to get up right then and he knew they couldn't hear him downstairs over the sound of the Hoover. He contented himself with rolling closer to the window so a bit of breeze found him. He could see the grass on the front yard near the birdbath his grandfather had given them years before.

Ask Memo.

OK, as soon as he felt well enough to get into his jeans and get downstairs, he'd do it.

All the next day, Sunday the tenth, Harlen's ma was mad at *him*, as if *he'd* yelled at her instead of Barney and Dr. Staffney. The house was full of the kind of silent tension that Harlen remembered from the fights Ma and his dad used to have: an hour or two of yelling and three weeks of cold silence. Harlen didn't give a shit. If it'd keep her home, keep her between him and the face at the window, he'd call the constable over every other night to give her a good yelling-at.

"It's not as if I *abandon* you," she'd snapped at him when he was heating some soup for his lunch. It was the first time she'd spoken to him all day. "God knows I spend enough hours working my fingers to the bone taking care of you, taking care of the house . . ."

Harlen glanced toward the living room. The only empty surfaces were the ones he or the two men had cleared off the night before. Barney had washed the dishes the night before and the clean counter looked alien to Harlen.

"Don't you *dare* take that tone with me, young man," Ma snapped.

Harlen stared at her. He hadn't said a word.

"You know what I mean. These two . . . intruders . . . come in here and *presume* to lecture *me* on watching out for my child. Reckless *abandonment* he calls it." Her voice was shaking. She paused to light a cigarette and her hands were shaking as well. She fanned the match out, exhaled smoke, and stood tapping her lacquered nails on the counter. Harlen stared at the ring of lipstick on the cigarette. He hated that—the lipstick on cigarette butts around the house—more than anything else. It drove him crazy and he had no idea why.

"After all," she continued, in control of her voice now, "you are eleven years old. Almost a young man. Why, when I was eleven, I was taking care of three younger children in the family and working part time at the One-Fifty-One Diner over in Princeville."

Harlen nodded. He'd heard the story.

His mother inhaled smoke, and turned away, the fingers of her left hand still tapping out a fast tattoo on the counter, the cigarette jutting aggressively in the other hand the way only women held it. "The *nerve* of those idiots."

Harlen poured his tomato soup into a bowl, found a spoon, and hunkered over it, letting it cool. "Ma, they were only here because that crazy lady was in the house. They were worried she'd come back."

She did not turn back toward him. Her back had the same rigid look he'd seen turned toward his father so many times.

He tried the soup. It was too hot. "Really, Ma," he said. "They didn't mean anything. They only . . ."

"Don't tell *me* what they meant, James Richard," she snapped, finally turning toward him, one arm crossed in front of her, the other arm vertical, smoke still rising. "I understand an insult when I hear it. What *they* didn't understand is that you almost certainly *imagined* seeing someone through the window. *They* didn't understand that Doctor Armitage at the hospital said that you had a very serious blow to the head . . . a subdural hemmy . . . hemo . . ."

"Subdural hematoma," said Harlen. The soup was cool enough now.

"A *very* serious concussion," she finished and took a drag. "Dr. Armitage warned me that you might experience some whatchamacallims . . . hallucinations. I mean, it's not as if you saw somebody you *knew*, right? Somebody real?"

There are real people in the world who I don't know, Harlen was tempted to reply. He didn't. One day of this cold shoulder was enough. "Uh-uh," he said.

Ma nodded as if the point was made. She turned to stare out the kitchen window as she finished her cigarette. "I'd like to know where those high and mighty gentlemen were when I was spending twenty-four hours a day at your bedside at the hospital," she muttered.

Harlen concentrated on finishing his soup. He went to the fridge but the only milk carton had been there a long, long time and he had no intention of opening it. He filled a jelly glass with water from the tap. "You're right, Ma. But I was glad to see you when you came home."

The sudden rigidness of her back told him not to pursue that topic. "Weren't you going over to Adelle's Salon today to get your hair done?"

"If I do, I suppose you'll have that cop back here filing charges that I'm an unfit mother," she said, her voice carrying a freight of sarcasm he hadn't heard since Dad left. The smoke rose above her stack of dark hair and caught the sunlight in a pale halo.

"Ma," he said, "it's daytime. I'm not afraid of anything in the daytime. She's not gonna come back in the daytime." Actually, Harlen knew that only the first of those three statements was definitely true. The second was a lie. The third . . . he didn't know.

Ma touched her hair, stubbed the cigarette out in the sink. "All right. I'll be back in about an hour, maybe a little more. You got Adelle's number."

"Yeah."

He rinsed the soup bowl out and stacked it with the breakfast dishes. The Nash made its usual loud noises as it disappeared down Depot Street. Harlen waited two more minutes—Ma often forgot something and came rushing back in hunting for it—but when it was certain that she was gone, he went slowly upstairs, into her room. His heart was beating like crazy.

That morning, while Ma was sleeping, he'd rinsed the sheets and pillowcases out in the tub, then thrown them onto the washing machine in the utility room. The pajamas he'd tossed into the garbage can along the side of the garbage. No way was he going to sleep in those again.

Now he went through his Ma's dresser drawers, poking under the silken underwear, feeling an excitement like the first time he'd bought one of those magazines from C.J. and brought it home. It was hot in the room. The thick sunlight lay over the tangled sheets and spread of Ma's bed; he could smell her perfume thick and heavy. The Sunday papers lay scattered where she'd left them on the bed.

The gun wasn't in the dresser. Harlen checked in the nightstand next to her bed, shoving aside the empty cigarette packs and an almost-full package of Trojans. Rings, ballpoint pens that didn't work, matches from different supper clubs and nightclubs, pieces of paper and napkins with guys' names scribbled on them, some sort of mechanical muscle-relaxer thing, a paperback. No gun.

Harlen sat on the bed and looked around the room. The closet just had her dresses and shoes and crud . . . wait. He pulled over a chair so he could reach to the back of the only shelf, feeling around behind hatboxes and folded sweaters. His hand fell on cold metal. He pulled out a framed photo. His dad was smiling, one arm around Ma and the other around a grinning, dumb four-year-old that Harlen vaguely recognized as himself. One of the kid's front teeth was missing but he didn't seem to care. The three of them were standing in front of a picnic table; Harlen recognized Bandstand Park downtown. Maybe it was before a Free Show.

He tossed the picture onto the bed and felt under the last old sweater up there. A curved handle. Metal trigger guard.

He lowered it slowly in both hands, taking care to keep his finger away from the trigger. The thing was surprisingly heavy for its size. The metal parts were a dark blue steel; the barrel was surprisingly short, maybe two inches. The stock was a nice knurled wood, checked. It looked a lot like a toy .38 Harlen had played with when he was little, a year or two ago, and his guess was that this was a real .38. What had his dad called it when he was showing Ma how to hold it years ago? A belly gun. Harlen wasn't sure whether that was because it was small enough to carry around in your belt—if you were a man, of course—or if it was meant to be shot into somebody's belly.

He hopped down, found a catch that slid aside so that he could peer into the cylinder . . . he sure as hell wasn't going to turn it around so the muzzle was aimed at his face. The one hole was empty. It took another minute before he found out how to move the cylinder around freely; all the holes were empty. Harlen cursed, stuck the pistol in his belt—feeling the cold steel warm against the skin of his belly—and searched the rest of the shelf for bullets. Nothing. Ma probably threw them all out. He straightened the shelf up, put the chair back, took the gun out, and stood there holding it.

What the hell good was this thing if he didn't have bullets?

He looked under Ma's bed again, checked the whole room out, even emptied the junk in her cedar blanket chest. No bullets. He was sure that they'd been in a box.

Harlen checked one last time that he hadn't left any telltale signs of his search—it was hard to tell in the messy room—and then went downstairs.

Where the hell can I buy some bullets? Do they sell them to kids? Could I just go into Meyers' Hardware or Jensen's A&P and ask for some .38-caliber bullets? Harlen didn't think the A&P carried them and Mr. Meyers didn't like him; he'd almost refused to sell him nails when he was working on his treehouse last summer . . . no way was he going to sell him bullets.

Harlen had one last idea. His ma kept a lot of booze in the liquor cabinet, but she always had a bottle hidden away on the last shelf of the kitchen, way up on top. Like someone was going to steal the other stuff and she needed some hidden away. There were other bottles and crap up there.

Harlen stood on the counter, the snub-nosed revolver in his bandaged left hand while he searched. There were two bottles of vodka hidden away there. Some sort of jar filled with rice, another with what looked like peas. The third jar had a metallic glint to it. Harlen lifted it out into the light.

The bullets were all tumbled loose into the bottom of the canning jar. The lid was sealed. Harlen counted at least thirty or more. He found a knife, cut the seal, levered the lid open, and dumped the cartridges onto the counter. He was more excited than when he'd brought home C.J.'s dirty magazines for the first time. It took Harlen only a few seconds to figure out how to load the empty chambers, then spin the cylinder to make sure it was fully loaded. He filled the pockets of his jeans with the other bullets, put the jar back where it'd been, and went out back, climbing the fence and heading into the orchard, hunting for someplace to practice.

And for something to practice on.

Memo was awake. Sometimes her eyes were open but she was not really aware. This was not one of those times. Mike crouched by her bedside. His mother was home—it was Sunday on the tenth of July, the first Sunday Mass Mike had missed serving at in almost three years—and the vacuum was running, upstairs in his room now. Mike leaned close to the bed, seeing Memo's brown eyes following him. One of her hands was curved on the coverlet like a claw, the fingers gnarled, the back of her hand routed with veins.

"Can you hear me, Memo?" He was whispering, his mouth not too far from her ear. He leaned back and watched her eyes.

Blink. Yes. The code had been once for yes, twice for no, three times for "I don't know" or "I don't understand." It's how they communicated the most simple things to her: when it was time to change her linen or clothing, time to use the bedpan—things like that.

"Memo," whispered Mike, his lips still parched from the four days of fever, "did you see the soldier at the window?"

Blink. Yes.

"Have you seen him before?"

Yes.

"Are you afraid of him?"

Yes.

"Do you think he's here to hurt us?"

Yes.

"Do you still think he's Death?"

Blink. Blink. Blink. I don't know.

Mike took a breath. The weight of his fever dreams hung on him like chains. "Do you . . . did you recognize him?"

Yes.

"Is he someone you know?"

Yes.

"Is he someone Mom and Dad would know?"

No.

"Would I know him?"

No.

"But you do?"

Memo closed her eyes for a long time, as if in pain or exasperation. Mike felt like an idiot, but he didn't know what else to ask. She blinked once. *Yes.* She definitely knew him.

"Someone who is . . . who is alive now?"

No.

Mike was not surprised. "Someone you know is dead then?"

Yes.

"But a real person? I mean someone who used to be alive?"

Yes.

"Do you . . . do you think it's a ghost, Memo?"

Three blinks. A pause. Then one.

"Is this somebody you and Grampa knew?"

Pause. *Yes.*

"A friend?"

She did not blink at all. Her dark eyes burned at Mike, demanding that he ask the right questions.

"A friend of Grampa's?"

No.

"An enemy of Grampa's?"

She hesitated. Blinked once. Her mouth and chin were moist with saliva. Mike used the linen handkerchief on the night table to dry it. "So he was an enemy of Grampa's and yours?"

No.

Mike was sure that she had blinked twice, but he didn't understand why. She'd just said . . .

"An enemy of Grampa's," he whispered. The vacuum had quit running upstairs, but he could hear his mother humming as she dusted in the girls' rooms. "An enemy of Grampa's but not of yours?"

Yes.

"This soldier was your friend?"

Yes.

Mike rocked on his heels. Fine, now what? How could he find out *who* this person had been, why he was haunting Memo?

"Do you know why he's come back, Memo?"

No.

"But you're scared of him?" It was a stupid question, Mike knew.

Yes. Pause. *Yes.* Pause. *Yes.*

"Were you scared of him when . . . when he was alive?"

Yes.

"Is there a way I can find out who he was?"

Yes. Yes.

Mike stood and paced in the small space. A car went by on First Avenue beyond the screen. The scent of flowers and new-mown grass came in the window. Mike realized with a guilty start that his father must have mowed the yard while he was sick. He crouched next to Memo again. "Memo, can I go through your stuff? Do you mind if I look at your stuff?" Mike realized that he'd phrased it so she couldn't answer. She looked at him, waiting.

"Do I have your permission?" he whispered.

Yes.

Memo's trunk was in the corner. All of the kids were under strict orders not to get into it: the things there were their grandmother's most prized and private possessions and Mike's mom kept them as if the old lady would have use for them someday.

Mike dug down through clothes until he came to the package of letters, most of them from his grandfather during his sales trips through the state.

"In here, Memo?"

No.

There was a box of photos, most of them sepia tinted. Mike held them up.

Yes.

He thumbed through them quickly, aware that his mom was finishing with the girls' rooms and had only his room to go. He was supposed to be resting in the living room while she aired the room out and changed linen.

There must have been a hundred pictures in the box: oval portraits of known relatives and unknown faces, Brownie snapshots of their grampa when he was young, tall, and strong—Grampa in front of his Pierce Arrow, Grampa posing proudly with two other men in front of the cigar store they had owned briefly—and disastrously—in Oak Hill, Grampa and Memo in Chicago at the World's Fair, pictures of the family, pictures of picnics and holidays and idle moments on the porch, a photo of an infant, dressed in a white gown and apparently sleeping on a silken pillow—Mike realized with a shock that it was his dad's twin brother who had died as a baby—the photo was taken *after* the baby died. What a terrible custom.

Mike thumbed through the pictures faster. Photos of Memo as an older lady now—Grampa pitching horseshoes, a family picture when Mike was a baby, the older girls smiling into the camera, more old pictures . . .

Mike actually gasped. He dropped the rest of the photos into the box and held the one cardboard-framed picture at arm's length, as if it were diseased. The soldier stared out proudly. The same khaki uniform, the same leggings—whatever the hell Duane had called them, the same campaign hat and Sam Browne belt and . . . it was the same soldier. Only here the face wasn't sketched in on wax, it was a human face: small eyes narrowed at the camera, a thin-lipped smile, a hint of greased-back hair over large ears, a small chin, predominant nose. Mike turned the photo over. In his grandmother's perfect Palmer script, the legend said—*William Campbell Phillips: Nov. 9, 1917.*

Mike held the picture up.

Yes.

"This is it then? It's really him?"

Yes.

"Is there anything else in the trunk, Memo? Anything else to tell me about him?" Mike couldn't believe there was. He wanted to get things closed up before his mom came down.

Yes.

He blinked his surprise. He held up the box of photos.

No.

What else? Nothing but a small, leather notebook. He lifted it, opened it to a page halfway through. The entry was in his grandmother's hand. The date read January 1918.

"A diary," he breathed.

Yes. Yes. The old lady closed her eyes and did not open them.

Mike slammed the trunk shut, kept the photo and the diary, and moved quickly to her bedside, lowering his face until his cheek was almost touching her mouth. A soft dry breath moved through her lips.

He touched her hair once, gently, and then hid the diary and photo in his shirt and went out to the couch to "rest."

Jim Harlen found out that his father's phrase "belly gun" probably meant that you had to stick the damn thing in someone's belly to hit anything. The little gun couldn't hit shit.

He'd gone about two hundred feet into the small orchard behind his house and the Congdens', found a tree that looked like a good target, stepped off about twenty paces, raised his good arm straight and steady, and squeezed the trigger.

Nothing happened. Or rather, the hammer rose a bit and fell back. Harlen wondered if there was some sort of safety on the damn thing . . . no, there weren't any switches or doodads except for the one that had given him access to the cylinder. It was just harder to pull the trigger than he'd thought. Plus the damn cast was sort of throwing him off balance.

He crouched a bit and used the crook of his thumb to pull the hammer back until it clicked and cocked. Readjusting his hand on the grip, Harlen aimed the thing at the tree—wishing all the time it had a better sight than the little nub of metal at the end of the tiny barrel—and squeezed again.

The blast almost made him drop the gun. It was a fairly *small* pistol; he'd expected the sound and recoil to be small . . . sort of like the .22 rifle Congden let him fire every once in a while. It wasn't.

The loud *crack* had made Harlen's ears ring. Dogs started barking in the yards along Fifth Avenue. Harlen smelled what he thought was gunpowder—although it didn't smell a lot like the gunpowder stink of the firecrackers he'd fired off a week earlier—and his wrist carried the memory of energy expended. He walked over to see where the bullet had struck.

Nothing. He hadn't touched the tree. Eighteen inches across and he'd missed the whole damn thing. Harlen stepped off fifteen paces this time, took care cocking the damn thing, took greater care aiming, held his breath, and squeezed off another shot.

The pistol roared and leapt in his hand. The dogs went nuts again. Harlen ran up to the tree, expecting to see a hole dead center. Nothing. He looked around on the ground as if there might be a visible bullet hole there.

"Fuck this," he whispered. He walked back ten short steps, took careful aim, and fired again. This time, he found, he'd just nicked the bark on the right side, about four feet higher than he'd aimed. *From ten fucking feet away!* The dogs were going crazy and somewhere beyond the trees a screen door slammed open.

Harlen cut west to the tracks and headed north, away from town, out past the empty grain elevators almost to the tallow factory. There was a swampy tangle of trees and shrubs west of the tracks there and he figured he could use the embankment as a backstop. He hadn't thought of that before and felt a cold flush as he wondered if one of the bullets had traveled all the way across Catton's road into the pasture—and maybe one of the dairy cows—there. *Surprise, Bossie!*

Safely hidden in the thickets half a mile south of the dump, Harlen reloaded, found some bottles and cans along the dirt road heading out to the dump, set them as targets against the weedy embankment, braced the grip against his thigh as he reloaded, and began practicing.

The gun didn't shoot worth shit. Oh, it fired all right . . . Harlen's wrist ached and his ears were echoing . . . but the bullets didn't go where he aimed them. It looked so easy when Hugh O'Brian as Wyatt Earp shot somebody from fifty or sixty feet away—and that was to *wing* them. Harlen's favorite hero had been the Texas Ranger Hoby Gilman in *Trackdown*, starring Robert Culp. Hoby had a real neat pistol and Harlen had enjoyed the shows right up to the time *Trackdown* had gone off the air the year before.

Maybe it was the short barrel on his dad's stupid gun. Whatever it was, Harlen found that he had to be ten feet away from something to hit it, and then it took three or four shots just to get the damn beer can or whatever. He did get better at cocking it, although he had the feeling that you were supposed to pull the trigger and let the hammer rise and fall on its own. He managed to do that, but it took enough strength that it screwed up his aim even more.

Well, if I use this cocksucker on someone, I'll have to wait until I can set it against their chest or head or whatever so I don't miss.

Harlen had fired twelve of the bullets and was loading six more when he heard a slight sound behind him. He whirled with the pistol half-raised, but the cylinder loading-gate thing was still open and only two cartridges stayed in it. The others dropped to the grass.

Cordie Cooke stepped out of the trees behind him. She was carrying a double-barreled shotgun that was as tall as she was, but it was broken open at the breech the way Harlen had seen men carrying the guns out hunting. She looked at him with her piggy little eyes scrunched up.

Jesus, thought Harlen, *I'd forgotten how ugly she is.* Cordie's face reminded him of a cream pie that someone had stuck eyes, skinny lips, and a lumpy potato of a nose in. Her hair was hacked just below her ears, and hung down over her eyes in greasy strands. She wore the same shapeless bag of a dress Harlen remembered from class, although it looked sweatier and dirtier now, gray socks that'd once been white, and lumpy brown shoes. Her little snaggly teeth were about the same tone of gray as her socks.

"Hey, Cordie," he said, lowering the pistol to his side and trying to look casual. "What's happening?"

She continued squinting at him. It was hard to tell if her eyes were even open under those bangs. She took three steps toward him. "Dropped your bullets," she said in that nasal monotone that Harlen had imitated more than a few times to make the other kids laugh.

He twitched a smile at her and crouched to pick them up. He could only find two.

"One's behind your left foot," she said. "T'other one's *under* your left foot."

Harlen found them, stuck them in his pocket rather than finish loading now, closed the loading gate, and stuck the pistol in the waistband of his jeans.

"Better watch it," drawled Cordie. "You'll shoot your weenie off."

Harlen felt a flush rise from his neck to his cheeks. He adjusted his sling and frowned at the girl. "What the hell do you want?"

She shrugged, moving the massive shotgun from one arm to the other. "Jes' curious who was bangin' away over here. Thought maybe that C.J.'d got a bigger gun."

Harlen remembered Dale Stewart's story about his confrontation with Congden. "That why you're carrying around that cannon?" he asked as sarcastically as he could.

"Uh-uh. I ain't afraid of C.J. It's them others I gotta watch for."

"What others?"

She squinted more narrowly at him. "That piece of dog-poop Roon. Van Syke. Them what took Tubby."

"You think they kidnapped Tubby?"

The girl turned her flat face toward the sun and the railroad embankment. "They didn't kidnap him none. They kilt him."

"Killed him?" Harlen felt his insides contracting. "How do you know?"

She shrugged and set the shotgun on a stump. Her arms looked like skinny, pale pipes. She picked at a scab on her wrist. "I see him."

Harlen gaped. "You *saw* your brother's body? Where?"

"My window."

The face at the window. No, that was the old lady . . . Mrs. Duggan. "You're lying," he said.

Cordie looked at him with eyes the color of old dishwater. "I don't lie."

"You saw him out your window? Of your house?"

"What other window do I have, dipshit?"

Harlen considered shoving her flat face in. He glanced at the shotgun and hesitated. "Why didn't the police come get him?"

"'Cause he wouldn't have been there when they got there. And we ain't got a phone to call."

"Wouldn't have been there?" It was a hot day. The sun was out. Harlen's t-shirt was plastered to his back and his arm was sweating freely under his cast; it itched. But he shivered right then.

Cordie stepped closer until she could whisper and be heard. "He wouldn't have been there 'cause he was moving around. He was at my window, 'n' then he went under the house. Where the dogs usually stay, but they won't go there no more."

"But you said he was . . ."

"Dead, yeah," said Cordie. "I thought maybe they just took him, but when I seen him, I knew he was dead." She walked over and looked at his row of bottles and cans. Only two of the cans had holes in them and all of the bottles were intact. She shook her head. "My ma, she seen him, too, only she thinks he's a ghost. She thinks he just wants to come home."

"Does he?" Harlen was amazed to hear that his voice was a hoarse whisper.

"Naw." Cordie walked closer, stood staring at him through her bangs. Harlen could smell the dirty-towel scent of her. "It ain't really Tubby. Tubby's dead. It's just his body that they're usin' somehow. He's tryin' to get *me*. 'Cause of what I did to Roon."

"What'd you do to Dr. Roon?" asked Harlen. The .38 was a cold weight against his stomach. While the shotgun was open, he'd seen that there were two brass circles showing. Cordie was carrying it around loaded. And she was crazy. He wondered if he could get the pistol out in time if she snapped the shotgun shut and started to aim it at him.

"I shot him," Cordie said in the same flat tones. "Didn't kill him though. Wish't I had."

"You shot Dr. Roon? Our principal?"

"Yep." Suddenly she reached over, tugged up his t-shirt, and pulled out the pistol. Harlen was too surprised to stop her. "Goddamn, where'd you get this little thing?" She held it close, almost sniffing the cylinder.

"My dad . . ." managed Harlen.

"I had me an uncle'd had one of these. Little snub-nosed thing ain't worth shit over twenty feet or so," she said, still holding the shotgun in the crook of her left arm and pivoting to aim the pistol at the row of bottles. "Kapow," she said. She handed it back, butt first. "I wasn't kiddin' about not puttin' it in your pants like that," she said. "My uncle, he almost blew his weenie off once't when he stuck it in there when he was drunk and it was still cocked. Keep it in your back pocket and tug your shirt down."

Harlen did so. It was bulky and clumsy, but he could get at it quickly if he had to. "Why'd you shoot at Dr. Roon?"

"A few days ago," she said. "Right after the night Tubby come after me. I knew Roon'd sicced him on me."

"Not *when*," said Harlen. "Why."

Cordie shook her head as if he were the slowest thing in the world. "'Cause he killed my brother and sent that body-thing after me," she said patiently. "Something damn strange is goin' on this summer. Mama knows it. Pap does, too, but he ain't hanging around to pay attention."

"You didn't kill him?" said Harlen. The woods were suddenly dark and ominous around them.

"Kill who?"

"Roon."

"Naw." She sighed. "I was too goddamn far away. Pellets just tore the shit out of the side of his old Plymouth and hurt him a mite in the arm. Maybe I got him some in the ass, too, but I ain't sure."

"Where?"

"In the arm and the ass," she repeated, exasperated.

"No, I mean whereabouts did you shoot at him? In town?"

Cordie sat on the embankment. Her underpants were visible between skinny, pale thighs. Harlen had never thought he'd see a girl's underpants—on a girl—without being interested in the sight. He wasn't interested now. They were as gray as her socks. "If I shot him in town, shithead, don't you think I'd be in jail or somethin'?"

Harlen nodded.

"Uh-uh. I shot at him when he was out to the tallow factory. Just got out of his goddamn car. I woulda got closer, but the woods stop about forty feet from the front door. He hopped . . . that's why I think I got him in the ass, I could see where the linin' on the arm of his suit was tore up . . . and then he jumped in that truck and took off with Van Syke. I think they seen me though."

"What truck?" asked Harlen. He knew.

"You know what truck," sighed Cordie. "The goddamn Renderin' Truck." She grabbed Harlen by the wrist and tugged hard. He went to his knees next to her on the railroad embankment. Somewhere in the woods a woodpecker started up. Harlen could hear a car or track on Catton Road a quarter of a mile to the southeast.

"Look," said Cordie, still hanging on to his wrist, "it don't take much in the way of brains to know that you seen something in Old Central. That's why you fell an' busted yourself up. And maybe you seen somethin' else, too."

Harlen shook his head but she ignored him.

"They killed your friend, too," she said. "Duane. I don't know how they done it, but I know it was them." She looked away then and a strange, vague look came over her face. "It's funny, I been in Duane McBride's class since we was all in kindergarten together, but I don't know if he ever said anything to me. I always thought he was real nice though. Always thinkin', but I didn't hold that against him. I useta imagine that maybe him and me would go for a walk someday, just talkin' about stuff and . . ." Her eyes focused and she looked down at Harlen's wrist. Released it. "Listen, you're not out here shootin' your daddy's gun 'cause you're tired of beatin' your weenie and you need some fresh air. You're scared shitless. An' I know what scared you."

Harlen took a deep breath. "OK," he said, voice rasping. "What do we do about it?"

Cordie Cooke nodded as if it was about time. "We get your buddies," she said. "All of them what's seen some of this stuff. We get 'em together and we go after Roon and the others—the dead ones and live ones. All of them that're after us."

"And then what?" Harlen was leaning so close that he could see the fine hairs on Cordie's upper lip.

"Then we kill the live ones," said Cordie and smiled, showing her gray teeth. "Kill the live ones, and the dead ones . . . well, we'll think of something." Suddenly she reached over and put her hand on Harlen's crotch, squeezing him through his jeans.

He jumped. No girl had ever done that. Now that one had, he seriously considered shooting her to get her to let go.

"You wanta take that out of there?" she whispered, her voice a caricature of seduction. "Want both of us to take our clothes off? Ain't nobody around."

Harlen licked his lips. "Not now," he managed. "Maybe later."

Cordie sighed, shrugged, stood, and hefted the shotgun. She clicked the breech shut. "Hokay-dokay. What 'ya say we go into town and find some of your buddies and get this show on the road?"

"Now?" *Kill the live ones* echoed in Harlen's brain. He remembered Barney's kind eyes from the night before and wondered how kind they'd be when he and the state troopers came to handcuff him for shooting the school principal, custodian, and God knows who else.

"Sure now," said Cordie. "What the hell's the use in waitin'? It's gonna be dark before too long, then *they'll* come out again."

"All right," Harlen heard himself say. He got up, dusted his jeans off, adjusted his father's revolver in his hip pocket, and followed Cordie down the train tracks toward town.

TWENTY-FOUR

Mike had to go to the cemetery. There was no way in hell that he was going by himself, so he convinced his mother that they were overdue in bringing flowers to Grampa's grave. His dad started the night shift the next day, so it seemed like a good Sunday to visit the cemetery as a family.

He'd felt like a sneak reading Memo's diaries, hiding them under the quilt when his mother checked in on him. But it had been Memo's idea, hadn't it?

The journal was leatherbound and thick, keeping at least three years of Memo's almost daily entries, running from December of 1916 through the end of 1919. It told Mike what he wanted to know.

The photograph had said *William Campbell Phillips,* and he was mentioned as early as the summer of 1916. Evidently Phillips had been a schoolmate of Memo's . . . more than that, a childhood sweetheart. Mike had paused then, finding it strange to think of Memo as a schoolgirl.

Phillips had graduated from high school the same year Memo had, 1904, but when Memo went off to business school in Chicago—where, Mike knew from family stories, she'd met Grampa in an Automat on Madison Street—William Campbell Phillips evidently had gone to Jubilee College down the road and had been trained as a teacher. He was a teacher at Old Central, as far as Mike could tell from the entries in perfect Palmer script, when Memo had returned from Chicago in 1910 as a wife and mother.

But, according to the circumspect notes in Memo's diary in 1916,

Phillips had not ceased showing signs of his affections. Several times he had stopped by the house with gifts while Grampa was off working at the grain elevator. Evidently he had sent letters, and although the diary did not mention the contents, Mike could guess. Memo burned them.

One entry fascinated Mike:

JULY 29, 1917—

Ran into that vile Mr. Phillips while at the Bazaar with Katrina and Eloise today. I remember William Campbell as a quiet and gentle boy, rarely speaking, always watching the world with those deep, dark eyes of his, but there has been a change. Katrina commented on it. Mothers have spoken to the principal about Mr. Phillips' temper. He canes the children at the slightest provocation. I am glad that little John will not be in his grade for some years yet.

The gentleman's advances are quite upsetting. Today he insisted on enjoining me in conversation despite my obvious reluctance. I told Mr. Phillips years ago that there could be no social intercourse between us while he continued to show such inappropriate behavior. It does not help.

Ryan thinks that it is a joke. Evidently the men of the town feel that William Campbell is still a mommy's boy and no threat to anyone. Of course, I have never told Ryan about the letters I burned.

And Mike found an interesting note in late October of that same year:

OCT. 27,

With the menfolk beginning to relax after the hard work of the harvest, talk of the town has turned to Mr. Phillips, the schoolteacher, enlisting to fight the Hun.

At first it seemed a joke since the gentleman is almost thirty, but he returned to his mother's house from Peoria yesterday already in uniform. Katrina says that he looked quite handsome, but she also added that rumors abound that Mr. Phillips had to leave town because he was about to be dismissed from his position. Ever since the parents of that Catton child wrote to the School Board about Mr. Phillips' excessive use of force, of actual beatings in the classroom— Tommy Catton was hospitalized at Oak Hill for several days, although Mr. P. contended that the boy fell down the stairs after having been detained after class—ever since then, other parents have been complaining.

Well, for whatever reason, it is an honorable choice he has made.

Ryan says that he would go in a minute if it were not for John and Katherine and Ryan Jr.

And on November 9, 1917:

> Mr. Phillips stopped here today. I cannot write about what ensued, but I will be forever grateful that the iceman stopped by a few minutes after the teacher arrived. Otherwise . . .
>
> He insists that he will return for me. The man is a cad, recognizing none of the sanctity of my marriage vows, nor the sacred trust I hold as a parent to my three little ones.
>
> Everyone speaks of how handsome the man looks in his uniform, but I found him pathetic—a child in a baggy costume.
>
> I hope he never comes back.

And the final mention of him on April 27, 1918:

> Much of the town turned out for the funeral of Mr. William Campbell Phillips today. I could not attend because of my headache.
>
> Ryan says that the Army was prepared to bury him alongside the other men who had fallen in battle, in an American cemetery in France, but that his mother insisted that the government send his body home.
>
> His last letter to me arrived after we had heard of his death. I made the mistake of reading it, out of sentiment, I suppose. He had written it while recovering in the French hospital, not knowing that the influenza would finish what the German bullets had begun. In the letter, he said that his resolve had sharpened in the trenches, that nothing would stop him from returning to claim me. Those were his words—"claim me."
>
> But something did stop him.
>
> My headache is very bad this afternoon. I must rest. I will not mention this sad, obsessive person again.

Grampa's grave was near the front of Calvary Cemetery, to the left of the pedestrian gate and about three rows back. All of the O'Rourkes and Reillys were there and there was more space to the north where Mike's parents, and he and his sisters, would someday lie.

They set the flowers in place and said their usual silent prayers. Then, while the others busied themselves with plucking weeds and tidying up the area, Mike quickly walked the rows.

He didn't have to look at all the headstones; many he knew, but the biggest help were the tiny American flags the Scouts had put there on Memorial Day. They were faded now, the colors bleached by the heavy rains and bright sunlight, but most of the flags were still in evidence, marking the veterans' graves. There were a lot of veterans.

Phillips was far toward the back, on the opposite side of the cemetery. The memorial read: WILLIAM CAMPBELL PHILLIPS, AUGUST 9, 1888—MARCH 3, 1918 HE DIED SO THAT DEMOCRACY MIGHT LIVE.

The ground above the grave was freshly churned, as if someone had been digging there recently and had tossed the soil back in haphazardly. There were several circular depressions nearby, some almost eighteen inches across, where the concave earth had seemed to sag.

Mike's parents were calling to him from the parking strip of grass beyond the black fence. He ran to join them.

Father C. was glad to see him. "Rusty can't get the Latin right even when he reads it," said the priest. "Here, have another cookie."

Mike's appetite still hadn't returned, but he took the cookie. "I need help, Father," he said between bites. "Your help."

"Anything, Michael," said the priest. "Anything at all."

Mike took a deep breath and began, telling the whole story. He'd resolved to do it during the lucid periods of his fever, but now that he'd started, it sounded even crazier than he'd thought. But he kept going.

When he finished there was a brief silence. Father Cavanaugh looked at him with hooded eyes. The priest's five-o'clock shadow was in evidence.

"Michael, you're serious about this? You wouldn't be pulling my leg, would you?"

Mike stared.

"No, I guess you wouldn't." Father C. let out a long sigh. "So you think that you've seen this soldier's ghost . . ."

"Uh-uh," Mike began vehemently. "That is, I don't think it's a ghost. I could see where it bent the screen in. It was . . . solid."

Father C. nodded, still watching Mike carefully. "But it could hardly be *the* William Campbell . . . whatever . . ."

"Phillips."

"William Campbell Phillips, yes. It could hardly be him after forty-two years . . . so we're talking about a ghost or some sort of spiritual manifestation, correct?"

It was Mike's turn to nod.

"And you want me to do what, Michael?"

"An exorcism, Father. I've read about them in *True* and . . ."

The priest shook his head. "Michael, Michael . . . exorcisms were a product of the Middle Ages, a form of folk magic done to drive demons out of people when everyone thought that everything from illness to bedsores was caused by demons. You don't think this . . . this apparition you saw when you were suffering from fever was a demon, do you?"

Mike didn't correct Father C. about when he saw the Soldier. "I don't know," he said truthfully. "All I know is that it's after Memo and that I think you can do something about it. Will you go with me to the cemetery?"

Father Cavanaugh frowned. "Calvary Cemetery is sanctified ground, Michael. There's little I could do there that has not already been done. The dead there lie peacefully."

"But an exorcism . . ."

"An exorcism is meant to drive spirits out of a body or place they are possessing," interrupted the priest. "You're not suggesting that the spirit of this soldier has inhabited either your grandmother or your home, are you?"

Mike hesitated. "No . . ."

"And exorcisms are used against demonic forces, not the spirits of the departed. You know that we say prayers for our dead, don't you, Michael? We don't subscribe to the primitive tribal beliefs that the souls of the dead are malevolent . . . things to be avoided."

Mike shook his head, confused. "But will you come out to the cemetery with me, Father?" He did not know why it was so important, but he knew that it was.

"Of course. We can go right now."

Mike glanced toward the rectory windows. It was almost dark. "No, I meant tomorrow, Father."

"Tomorrow I have to leave right after early Mass to meet a Jesuit friend in Peoria," said the priest. "I'll be gone until very late. Tuesday and Wednesday I'll be back on retreat at St. Mary's. Can it wait until Thursday?"

Mike chewed his lip. "Let's go now," he said. There was still some light. "Can you bring something?"

Father Cavanaugh hesitated in the act of pulling on his windbreaker. "What do you mean?"

"You know, a crucifix. Better yet, a Host from the altar. Something in case it's there."

The older man shook his head. "The death of your friend has bothered you, hasn't it, Michael? Are we living a vampire movie now? Would you have me remove the Body of Our Lord from its sanctuary for a game?"

"Some holy water then," said Mike. He pulled a plastic water bottle from his pocket. "I brought this."

"Very well," sighed Father C. "You get our liquid ammunition while I get the Popemobile out of the garage. We'll have to hurry if we're going to get out there before the vampires arise for the night." He chuckled, but Mike didn't hear it. He was already out the door and running for St. Malachy's, water bottle in hand.

Dale's mother had called Dr. Viskes the day before, on Saturday. The Hungarian refugee had given Dale a hurried physical, noting the chattering teeth and the subdued symptoms of terror, announced that he was "not a child zykologist," prescribed warm soup and no more comic books or Saturday monster movies for the boy, and gone off mumbling to himself.

Dale's mom had been upset, calling friends to find the name of an Oak Hill or Peoria doctor who *was* a child psychologist, calling Chicago twice to leave messages at her husband's hotel, but Dale had calmed her down. "I'm sorry, Mom," he'd said while sitting up in bed, restraining shivers and fighting to control his voice. It helped that it was daylight. "I've just always been scared of the basement," he said. "When the lights went out again and I felt that cat under the water . . . well . . ." He managed to look ashamed and chagrined and sane again. Only the last part was difficult.

His mother calmed down, bringing him enough hot soup to drown the dead cat all over again. Kevin came over, but was told that Dale was resting. Lawrence came back from visiting his friend, waited until their mother was back downstairs, and whispered, "Did you *really* see something?"

Dale hesitated a second. Lawrence had his fair share of annoying kid-brother habits, but telling secrets wasn't one of them. "Yeah," he said.

"What was it?" whispered Lawrence, coming closer to Dale's bed but not getting his legs too near his own bed. He didn't trust the dark under there even in the daytime.

"Tubby Cooke," whispered Dale, feeling the terror well up in him like nausea just from saying the words. "He was dead . . . but his eyes opened." As soon as Dale said it, he was glad that he hadn't been that specific with his mom or Mr. Grumbacher. He'd probably be sitting in a padded cell somewhere by now if he had.

Lawrence just nodded. Dale realized with a shock that his brother believed him immediately, implicitly, and without reservation. "It probably won't come back till tonight," said Lawrence. "We'll get Mom to leave *all* the lights on."

Dale let out a long breath. He just wished everything could be solved as simply as Lawrence thought it could: leave the lights on.

They'd left the lights on Saturday night. And taken turns sleeping and standing watch . . . lying watch, rather, for Dale lay reading Superman comics and watching the shadowed corners. Once, sometime around three, there came the slightest of sounds from beneath Lawrence's bed . . . the faintest rustle as of a kitten stirring from its nap . . . and Dale sat up and gripped the tennis racket he'd brought to bed with him.

But the scratching was not repeated. Toward dawn, when the spaces between the black leaves beyond the screens began to be lighter than the leaves themselves, Dale allowed himself to sleep. His mother came in to rouse them for church around eight, but finding both boys so dead tired, she allowed them to go back to bed.

It was Sunday evening after supper . . . the same hour that Mike O'Rourke was riding out Jubilee College Road with Father C. to the cemetery . . . and Dale and Lawrence were in the backyard, using the last of the evening light to play catch, when they heard a quiet *Eeawkee* from the front yard.

Jim Harlen was there with Cordie Cooke. The pair of them struck Dale as so odd, so infinitely mismatched—he had never even seen them *speak* to one another in class—that he would have laughed if it had not been for Harlen's grim countenance, the black sling and cast on his left arm, and the shotgun the Cooke girl was carrying.

"Jeez," whispered Lawrence, pointing toward the gun, "you're going to get in real trouble carrying that around."

"You all shut up your face," Cordie said flatly.

Lawrence changed colors, clenched his fists, and took a step toward the girl, but Dale stepped in close and hugged his brother into immobility and silence. "What?" he said to the two.

"Things are happening," whispered Harlen. He looked up and frowned as Kevin Grumbacher came down the small hill from his driveway.

Kev looked at Cordie, did a slow double-take at the shotgun, raised both eyebrows almost to the line of his crew cut, and folded his arms. He waited.

"Kev's one of us," said Dale.

"Things are happening," Harlen whispered again. "Let's get O'Rourke and talk."

Dale nodded and let go of Lawrence, warning him with a look not to start anything. They got their bikes from the side yard. Kev coasted downhill to join them. Cordie had no bike, so the four mounted boys walked theirs down the sidewalk at her pace. Dale wished they'd hurry up before some grown-up drove by, saw the shotgun, and slammed to a halt.

There were no cars. Depot was an empty tunnel, brightest to the west. Third and Second avenues were abandoned to the Hard Road and no traffic moved there, either. The streets were Sunday-empty. Through the leaves, they could see clouds still catching fire from the last rays of sunlight, but it was almost dark here under the elms. The rows of corn at the east end of Depot Street were taller than their heads and had become a solid, dark-green wall with the loss of the day's light.

Mike didn't respond to their *Eeawkees* despite the fact that his bike was propped against the back porch. Lights had come on in the O'Rourke house, and as they watched from behind the pear trees out back, Mr. O'Rourke came out dressed in his gray work clothes, started up their car, and headed south down First toward the Hard Road.

Whispering, moving softly, the five of them moved into the concealment of the chickenhouse to wait for Mike's return.

Riding in the Popemobile with Father C. between the high rows of corn bordering Jubilee County Road, Mike had the feeling *Watch out, here comes my big brother.* He'd never had a big brother to shield him from bullies or pull him out of scrapes—too often Mike had served that purpose for younger kids—and it felt good now to hand the problem over to someone else.

Mike's fear of making a fool of himself in front of Father C. was balanced—and then some—by his fear for Memo, and his fear *of* whatever was sending the Soldier to her window at night. Mike touched the small plastic water bottle in his pants pocket as they turned onto County Six and drove past the dark and empty Black Tree Tavern, closed on Sunday evening.

It was dark at the bottom of the hill—the woods were black, the foliage on either side of the road thick and dust-covered. Mike was thankful that he wasn't in the Cave beneath the road. It was better in the relative open at the top of the hill: the sun had set, but high cirrus clouds glowed coral and pink. Granite headstones caught the reflected light from above and glowed warmly. There were no shadows.

Father Cavanaugh paused as they clicked the black gate shut behind them. He pointed to the bronze-green statue of Christ far to the rear of the long cemetery. "You see, Michael, this place is one of peace. *He* watches over the dead with as much care as he watches over the living."

Mike nodded, although the thought that went through his head at that second was of Duane McBride alone on his farm, facing whatever he had faced. *But Duane wasn't Catholic* part of his mind insisted. Mike knew that meant nothing. "This way, Father."

He led the way right through the long rows of graves. A breeze had come up and moved leaves on the few trees along the fenceline and the tiny veterans' flags amidst the headstones. The Soldier's grave was as he had left it earlier, the soil still tossed around as if worried at by shovels.

Father Cavanaugh rubbed his chin. "Does the condition of the grave bother you, Michael?"

"Well . . . yeah."

"It's nothing," said the priest. "Sometimes the older graves have a habit of settling and the groundsmen fill them with a bit of dirt from beyond the fence. See, there's been grass seed sprinkled here. In two weeks the grass will cover it again."

Mike chewed on a fingernail. "Karl Van Syke's a groundskeeper here," he said softly.

"Yes?"

Mike shook his head. "Can you bless the grave, Father?"

Father C. frowned slightly. "An exorcism, Michael?" He smiled easily. "I'm afraid it's not that easy, my friend. Only a few priests even know how to do an exorcism . . . it's an almost-abandoned ritual, thank God . . . and even they must receive permission from an archbishop or the Vatican itself before proceeding."

Mike shrugged. "Just a blessing," he said.

The priest sighed. The wind moving around them was cooler now, as if blowing in ahead of some unseen storm. The light had paled to the point where color was fading from the world: the headstones gray, the long sweep of grass a monochrome pale, the line of trees growing black as the last sunlight drained away. Even the clouds had lost their roseate glow. A star burned above the eastern horizon.

"I suppose a blessing is overdue for this poor soldier," Father Cavanaugh said.

Mike reached for the holy water, but the priest had already moved his right hand, three fingers raised, thumb and little finger touching in what Mike always thought was the most powerful of motions.

"In nomine Patris, et Filii, et Spiritus Sancti," said the priest, "Amen."

Mike handed him the water bottle with some sense of urgency. Father C. shook his head and smiled, but sprinkled a few drops on the grave and made the sign of the cross again. Belatedly, so did Mike.

"Satisfied?" asked Father Cavanaugh.

Mike stared intently at the grave. No growls from beneath the sod. No wisps of smoke where the droplets of holy water had landed. He wondered if he'd been an idiot.

They walked slowly back toward the car, Father C. talking softly about the burial customs of ages past.

"Father," said Mike, grabbing the sleeve of the priest's windbreaker and stopping. He pointed.

It was only a few rows in from the fence. The evergreens were some sort of juniper—thick branches, prickly needles, rising only fifteen feet or so. They were as old as the turn-of-the-century headstones there. The three trees grew in a rough triangle, creating a dark space between them.

The Soldier stood just within the cusp of branches. The last of the twilight showed his campaign hat, the brass on his Sam Browne belt, the muddy wrappings of puttees.

Something in Mike soared with exultation even as his heart rate accelerated. *He's real! Father C. sees him! He's real!*

Father Cavanaugh did see him. The priest's body grew rigid for a moment, then relaxed. He glanced at Mike, smiled slightly. "So, Michael," he whispered. "I should have known that whoever was doing the teasing, it wasn't you."

The Soldier did not move. His face was shadow under the broad-brimmed hat.

Father Cavanaugh took three steps toward him, moving his arm away as Mike tried to pull him back. Mike did not follow him.

"Son," said the priest, "come out of there." His voice was soft, persuasive, as if coaxing a kitten from a tree. "Come out and talk to us."

There was no movement from the shadows. The Soldier might have been a monument made of gray stone.

"Son, let's talk a moment," said Father Cavanaugh. He took another two steps toward the shadows, stopping perhaps five feet from the silent figure.

"Father," Mike whispered urgently.

Father Cavanaugh glanced over his shoulder and smiled. "Whatever game's being played, Michael, I think we can . . ."

The Soldier did not so much leap as seem to be catapulted out of the ring of trees. It made a sound that reminded Mike of the mad dog that Memo had fought off years ago.

Father C. was a foot taller than the Soldier, but the khaki-clad figure hit him high, arms and legs scrabbling like a big cat on loose shale, and the two of them went down in a heap, rolling, the priest too surprised to make any sound but a grunt, the Soldier's growling coming from deep in its chest. They rolled across the close-cut grass until they slammed up against an ancient headstone, the Soldier straddling Father C., its long fingers around the priest's throat.

Father Cavanaugh's eyes were wide, his mouth wider as he finally tried to cry out. Nothing but a gargling sound emerged. The Soldier's hat was still on, but the brim had been shoved back on his head now and Mike could see the smooth-wax face and eyes like white marbles. The Soldier's mouth opened—no, not opened, it grew round like a hole being carved in clay—and Mike could see teeth in there, too many teeth, an entire ring of short, white teeth surrounding the inside of the round, lip-less ring of a mouth.

"Michael!" gasped Father C. He was obviously straining with all of his considerable strength just to keep the Soldier's incredibly long fingers from choking him into unconsciousness. Father C. writhed and wriggled, but the smaller figure stayed planted across his midsection, khaki-clad knees seeming to grip the grass. "Michael!"

Mike unfroze, ran across the ten feet separating him from the struggling pair, and began pounding on the Soldier's narrow back. It was not like striking flesh, more like touching a bag of writhing eels. The thing's back twisted and squirmed under the shirt fabric. Mike swung at the Soldier's head, knocking the hat flying behind a tombstone. The top of the Soldier's skull was hairless, pink-white. He hit the thing on the head again.

The Soldier freed a hand from Father C.'s throat, slashed backward. Mike's t-shirt ripped and he found himself flung six feet into the darkness under the juniper trees.

He rolled, got to his knees, and ripped a heavy branch from the nearest trunk.

The Soldier was lowering its face toward Father C.'s neck and chest. The Soldier's cheeks seemed to bulge, as if a wad of chewing tobacco were forcing its way forward, the mouth itself elongating as if a set of dentures were wedged in front of its gums.

Father Cavanaugh had his left hand free now and his large fist struck at the Soldier's face and chest. Mike could see marks appear in the thing's cheeks and brow, a sculptor's angry fist making indentations in clay. The marks filled in within seconds. The Soldier's face flowed and reshaped itself, the white-marble eyes moving in flesh, fixing on the priest with no hint of blindness.

The thing's mouth rippled, grew longer, became a sort of flesh-rimmed funnel extending even as Mike stared and Father Cavanaugh screamed. The obscene proboscis was five inches long now—eight—as it lowered toward Father C.'s throat.

Mike ran forward, planted his feet as if he were stepping to the plate, and swung the heavy branch in a roundhouse swing, catching the Soldier above and behind the ear. The sound echoed across the cemetery and into the tree.

For an instant, Mike thought that he had literally knocked the creature's head off. The Soldier's skull and jaw flew sideways at an impossible angle, hanging from an elongated strand of neck, resting on the thing's right shoulder. No spine could have withstood that angle.

White eyes slid through flesh still writhing like flesh-colored liquid mud and focused on Mike. The Soldier's left arm shot up, quicker than a snake, grasped the branch, and wrested it from Mike's grasp. It crumpled the three-inch-thick bough like someone snapping a matchstick.

The Soldier's head righted itself, re-formed, the lamprey snout grew longer, lowered toward Father Cavanaugh's struggling form.

"My God!" cried Father C. The sound was choked off as the Soldier vomited on him. Mike stepped back, eyes widening in horror, as he saw that the torrent dropping from the elongated jaws was a brown and writhing mass of maggots.

The slugs fell on Father C.'s face, neck, and chest. They pattered against the priest's closed eyelids and tumbled into the open collar of his shirt. A few fell into his open mouth.

Father Cavanaugh spluttered and whimpered, trying to spit the live maggots onto the grass, trying to pull his head to one side. But the Soldier leaned closer, face still lengthening, and held the priest's face in impossibly long fingers, like a lover steadying his loved one for a long-awaited kiss. Maggots continued to stream from his full cheeks and open funnel of a mouth.

Mike stepped forward and stopped, heart freezing with a new level of horror as he saw some of those brown maggots wriggling on Father C.'s chest and *then burrowing under flesh.* Disappearing into Father Cavanaugh. Others burrowed into the priest's cheek and straining neck.

Mike screamed, reached for the broken branch, and then remembered the plastic bottle in his pocket.

He grabbed the bunched fabric of the Soldier's collar, felt the rough wool and the malleable substance beneath, and emptied the bottle down the length of the thing's back, expecting no more result than there had been when the grave had been blessed.

There was more of a reaction.

The holy water made a sound like acid burning through meat. A line of holes appeared in the khaki fabric, stitching across the back of the Soldier's uniform like machine-gun bullets. The Soldier made a sound like a large animal dropped in scalding water, more hiss and gurgle than scream, and it arched backward, bending impossibly far, the back of its waxy head almost touching the heels of its combat boots. Boneless arms twisted and flailed like tentacles, the fingers ten inches long and bladed now.

Mike jumped back and flung the last of the contents of the bottle onto the thing's front.

There was the stench of sulfur, the front of the Soldier's tunic burst into green flame, and the creature rolled away at an impossible speed, writhing in postures impossible for a human skeleton to assume. Father Cavanaugh rolled free and lay retching against a headstone.

Mike stepped forward, realized that he had used the last of his holy water, and stopped five feet from the circle of junipers as the Soldier scrabbled into the darkness there, laid its face and forearms against the bare soil, and *burrowed*—sliding into the black dirt and dead needles there as easily as the maggots had burrowed into Father C.'s flesh.

The Soldier was gone, out of sight in twenty seconds. Mike stepped closer, saw the raw-ridged tunnel there, smelled the sewage and decayed meat stench, and blinked as the tunnel folded in on itself and collapsed, becoming merely another depression of fresh-turned soil. He turned back to Father C.

The priest had reached his knees but was bent across the headstone, head down, vomiting repeatedly until there was nothing left to vomit. There was no sign of the slugs except for red marks on the priest's cheeks and chest—he had evidently ripped open his own shirt to find them. Between dry retches and gasps for air, the priest was whispering, "Oh, Jesus, Jesus, Jesus, Jesus." It was a litany.

Mike took a breath, stepped closer, and put his arm around the man.

Father Cavanaugh was weeping now. He allowed Mike to help him to his feet; he leaned on Mike as they staggered toward the gate of the cemetery.

It was quite dark now. The Popemobile was a dark shape beyond the black iron. Every breeze rustled leaves and the corn across the way and made Mike think of the sound of things sliding across the grass behind him, tunneling *under* the soil they walked on. He tried to get Father C. to hurry.

It was difficult to stay in contact with the priest—Mike imagined the brown-black slugs sliding through flesh from the other man to him—but Father C. could not stand alone.

They made the gate, the parking area. He tumbled Father Cavanaugh behind the steering wheel, ran around to get in, and leaned across the moaning man to lock the power doors and windows. Father C. had left the key in the ignition and now Mike turned it. The Popemobile started and Mike immediately switched on the lights, illuminating headstones and the clump of junipers thirty feet away. The tall cross at the back of the cemetery was beyond the reach of the lights.

The priest whispered something between labored gasps for air.

"What?" said Mike, having trouble breathing himself. *Are those dark shapes moving in the cemetery?* It was hard to tell.

"You'll . . . have to . . . drive," gasped Father Cavanaugh. He slumped sideways, blocking the seat.

Mike counted to three, unlocked the doors, and ran around to the driver's side, shoving the priest's moaning body aside as he set himself behind the wheel and locked the doors again. Something *had* been moving out there, near the storage shed at the back of the cemetery.

Mike had driven his dad's car a few times, and Father C. had let him steer the Popemobile down a grassy lane once when they were on a pastoral visit. Mike could hardly see over the Lincoln town car's high dashboard and hood, but his feet could reach the pedals. He thanked God that it was an automatic transmission.

Mike got the thing into gear, backed out onto County Six without looking for traffic, almost ran it into the ditch on the other side, and stalled it when he stopped too quickly. He smelled gasoline when he restarted it, but it roared to life quickly enough.

Shadows among the headstones, moving toward the gate.

Mike peeled out, throwing gravel thirty feet behind him as he roared down the steep hill, still accelerating over the Cave and up past the Black Tree, seeing only the darkness of the woods in his peripheral vision, almost not making the turn onto Jubilee Road, finally slowing as he realized that he was approaching the town water tower at seventy-eight miles per hour.

He crept through the dark streets of Elm Haven, sure that Barney or someone would see him and stop him, half wishing that they would. Father Cavanaugh lay silent and shivering on the front seat.

Mike shut off the engine and almost wept when he parked under the pole light alongside the rectory. He went around the other side to help Father C. out.

The priest was pale and feverish, eyes almost rolled up in his head under fluttering eyelids. The marks on his chest and cheeks looked like ringworm scars. They were livid in the harsh overhead light.

Mike stood shouting at the rectory door, praying that Mrs. McCafferty—the priest's housekeeper—was still waiting dinner on Father C. The porch lights came on and the short woman stepped out, face flushed, apron still on.

"Good heavens," she exclaimed, rough hands rising toward her face. "What on earth . . ." She glowered at Mike as if the boy had assaulted her young priest.

"He got sick," was all that Mike could say.

Mrs. McCafferty looked at Father C.'s appearance, nodded once, and helped Mike get him up the stairs to his bedroom. Mike thought it was strange that this lady helped undress the priest, pulling on an old-fashioned nightshirt as the priest sat moaning on the edge of the bed, but then he figured that she was like a mother to Father C.

Finally the priest was under the clean sheets, moaning slightly, face filmed with sweat. Mrs. McCafferty had already taken his temperature—a hundred and three—and was mopping his face with damp washcloths. "What are these marks?" she asked, finger almost touching one of the ringworm crescents.

Mike shrugged, not trusting himself to talk. When she had been out of the room, he'd tugged up his shirt and checked his own chest, looking in the dresser mirror to make sure that there were no marks on his own face and neck. *They burrowed right into him.* The adrenaline rush of the battle was fading now, and Mike felt the nausea and slight vertigo of its aftermath.

"I'll call the doctor," said Mrs. McCafferty. "Not that Viskes fellow, but Doctor Staffney."

Mike nodded. Dr. Staffney did not have a local practice—he was an orthopedic surgeon based at St. Francis Hospital in Peoria—but he was Catholic, sort of—Mike noticed him at Mass about twice a year—and Mrs. McM. didn't trust the Protestant Hungarian doctor.

"You'll stay," she said. It was not a question. She expected Mike to hang around to tell the doctor anything he could. *The maggots burrowing under flesh.*

Mike shook his head. He wanted to, but it was dark and his dad had to work the night shift starting tonight. *Memo's home alone except for Mom and the girls.* He shook his head again.

Mrs. McCafferty started to reprimand him, but he touched Father C.'s hand—it was cold and clammy—and ran down the stairs and out into the night on shaky legs.

He was half a block away before he thought of something. Panting, close to tears, he jogged back to the rectory, went past it, and let himself in the side door of St. Malachy's. He picked up a clean linen altar cloth from the dressing room and went into the darkened sanctuary.

The interior of the church was warm and silent, smelling of incense from Masses long past, the red lights from the votive candles giving a soft illumination to the Stations of the Cross on the walls. Mike filled his plastic bottle from the font of holy water at the front entrance, genuflected, and approached the altar again.

He knelt there for a moment, knowing in his heart that what he was about to do had to be a mortal sin. He was not allowed to touch the Host with his hands even if it fell during Communion and Mike missed it with the small bronze plate he held beneath the communicant's chin. Only Father Cavanaugh—an ordained priest—was allowed to touch the wafer of bread once it was consecrated as the literal Body of Christ.

Mike said a silent Act of Contrition, climbed the steps, and removed a consecrated Eucharist from its closed and curtained alcove in the small sanctuary atop the altar. He genuflected again, said a short prayer, wrapped the Host in the clean linen, and put it in his pocket.

He ran all the way home.

Mike was headed for the back door when he heard a movement in the darkness behind the outhouse, near the chickenhouse. He paused,

heart pounding but emotions oddly numb. He took out the bottle of holy
water and thumbed off the lid, holding it high.

There was movement in the darkness of the chickenhouse.

"Come on, goddamn you," whispered Mike, stepping closer. "Come
on if you're coming."

"Hey, O'Rourke," came Jim Harlen's voice. "What the hell kept
you?" A lighter flared and Mike could see the faces of Harlen, Kev, Dale,
Lawrence, and Cordie Cooke. Even the girl's improbable presence did
not surprise him. He stepped into the darkened shed.

Harlen's lighter flicked off and would not relight. Mike let his eyes
adjust to the dark.

"You're not going to believe what's been happening," began Dale
Stewart, voice taut.

Mike smiled, knowing they couldn't see the smile in the dark. "Try
me," he whispered.

TWENTY-FIVE

The boys left for Duane's farm in the morning. They were all on
bikes and there was some nervousness about the ride, but Mike
suggested a strategy if the Rendering Truck appeared: half go
into the fields on the north side of the road, half on the south. It had been
Harlen who said, "Duane was in a field. They got him."

No one had a better idea.

It had been Dale's idea to go out to Duane's farm. They'd talked for
over an hour in the chickenhouse on Sunday night, each person telling a
story. The rule was that nobody keep any secrets if it had to do with the
weird goings-on this summer. Each story seemed stranger than the last,
ending with Mike's, but nobody challenged anybody else or called anyone crazy.

"Okey-dokey," Cordie Cooke had said at last, "we heard what everybody had to say. Some goddamn somebody's killed my brother and your
friend an's tryin' to kill the rest of us. Whatta we do?"

There'd been general babble at that point. It was Kevin who said,
"How come you guys didn't tell the grown-ups?"

"I did!" said Dale. "I told your dad there was something awful in
the basement."

"He found a dead cat."

"Yeah, but that's not what I *saw* . . ."

"I believe you," said Kevin, "but why didn't you tell him and your mom that it was Tubby Cooke. His body, I mean. Sorry, Cordie."

"I seen him, too," said Cordie.

"So why didn't you tell?" Kev asked Dale. "Or you, Jim. Why didn't you show Barney and Dr. Staffney the evidence?"

Harlen hesitated. "I guess I thought they'd think I was nuts, and put me away somewhere. It didn't make any sense. When I said it was just an intruder, they paid attention."

"Yeah," said Dale. "Look, I just got a little crazy in the basement and my mom was ready to send me to a child psychologist in Oak Hill. Think of what she'd've done if I'd . . ."

"I told my ma," Cordie said softly.

There was a silence in the dark shed while everyone waited.

"She believed me," said Cordie. " 'Course, the next night, she saw Tubby's corpse alurchin' around the yard, too."

"What'd she do about it?" asked Mike.

Cordie had shrugged. "What *could* she do about it? She told my old man, but he hit her and told her to shut up. She keeps the little kids inside at night and bars the door. What else can she do? She thinks it's Tubby's spirit tryin' to come home. Ma growed up in the south and heard a lot of them nigger stories about spooks."

Dale winced at the word "nigger." No one said anything for a minute. Finally Harlen said, "Look, O'Rourke, you told someone. See what good that did."

Mike had sighed. "At least Father C. knows what's going on."

"Yeah, if he doesn't die of worms in his insides," said Harlen.

"Shut up." Mike had paced back and forth. "I know what you guys mean. My dad believed me when I said there was some guy peeping in our window. If I told him it was an old boyfriend of Memo's, coming back from the cemetery, my dad'd think I was nuts. He'd never believe me."

"We need proof," said Lawrence.

Everyone looked at him in the darkness. Lawrence hadn't spoken since he described the thing from the closet that had run under his bed.

"What do we know?" said Kevin in that little-professor voice of his.

"We know you're a dipshit," volunteered Harlen.

"No, shut up, he's right," said Mike. "Let's think. Who are we fighting?"

"Your soldier," said Dale. "Unless you killed it with your sacred water."

"Holy water," said Mike. "Uh-uh, it wasn't dead . . . I mean destroyed . . . I could tell that. He's still out there somewhere." Mike stood and looked through the window toward the house.

"It's OK," Dale said softly. "Your mom and sisters are still up. Your grandma's all right."

Mike nodded. "The Soldier," he said, as if ticking off a list.

"Roon," said Cordie. "That piss-ant."

"Are we sure Roon's in on it?" asked Harlen from the dark mass of the couch.

"Yep," said Cordie. There was no arguing with that tone of voice.

"The Soldier and Roon," said Mike. "Who else?"

"Van Syke," said Dale. "Duane was fairly sure it'd been Van Syke who tried to run him down on the road."

"Maybe it was him who finally got him at home," said Harlen.

Dale made a pained sound from where he sat against the old console radio.

"Roon, the Soldier, Van Syke," said Mike.

"Old Double-Butt and Mrs. Duggan," Harlen said in a strained voice.

"Duggan's like Tubby sort of," said Kevin. "It may be some *thing* that's being used. We don't know about Mrs. Doubbet."

"I *saw* them," snapped Harlen. "Together."

Mike paced back and forth. "All right. Old Double-Butt's either one of them or with them."

"What's the difference?" asked Kevin from the back corner.

"Shut up," said Mike, still pacing. "We've got the Soldier, Van Syke, Roon, the Duggan thing, Mrs. Doubbet . . . who're we forgetting?"

"Terence," said Cordie. Her voice was so soft they could hardly hear her.

"Who?" asked five voices.

"Terence Mulready Cooke," she said. "Tubby."

"Oh, yeah," said Mike. He ticked off the names again, adding Tubby. "That's at least six of them. Who else?"

"Congden," said Dale.

Mike stopped pacing. "J.P. or his kid C.J.?"

Dale shrugged. "Maybe both."

"I don't think so," said Harlen. "At least with C.J. He's too stupid. His old man hangs around Van Syke, but I don't think he's part of whatever's going on."

"We'll put J.P. on the list," said Mike, "until we know. All right, that's at least seven of them. Some of them are human. Some of them are . . ."

"Dead," furnished Dale. "Things they're using somehow."

"Oh, Jesus Christ," whispered Harlen.

"What?"

"What if they have Duane McBride come back like Tubby? What if his corpse comes scratching at our windows like Tubby's did?"

"Can't," said Dale. He could barely speak. "His dad cremated the remains."

"You sure?" asked Kevin.

"Yeah."

Mike moved to the center of the circle and crouched there. "So what do we do?" he whispered.

Dale broke the silence. "I think Duane had figured something out. That's why he wanted to meet with us that Saturday."

Harlen cleared his throat. "But he's . . ."

"Yes," said Dale. "But you remember how Duane was always writing stuff down?"

Mike snapped his fingers. "His notebooks! But how're we going to get them?"

"Let's go now," said Cordie. "It's not even ten yet."

There was a chorus of reasons no one could go that night. All of them valid—Mike had to stay with Memo, Harlen's mother would skin him if he didn't get home soon, after he had made *her* stay home, Kevin was out after curfew as it was, and Dale was still on the sick list at home. No one mentioned the real reason they couldn't go then. It was dark.

"Chickenshits," said Cordie.

"We'll go early tomorrow," said Dale. "Eight at the latest."

"All of us?" said Harlen.

"Why not. They might think twice about jumping us if we're all together. The things are always trying to get us alone. Look at what happened to Duane."

"Yeah," said Harlen. "Or maybe they're just waiting for us to get together in one lump."

Mike ended the debate. "We'll go together in the morning. But only one of us will go up to the house. The rest of us will stand watch and help if we need to."

Cordie cleared her throat and spat on the wood floor. "There's one other thing," she said.

"What's that?"

"I mean, really, one other thing. At least one."

"What the fuck are you talking about, Cooke?" asked Harlen.

Cordie shifted in the sprung armchair. The barrels of the shotgun shifted with her until they were pointed in Jim Harlen's general direction. "Don't go giving me none of your profane mouth," she said to him. "What

I mean is I seen somethin' else. Somethin' movin' in the ground near the house."

"The Soldier disappeared in the ground," said Mike.

"Uh-uh. This'n was big . . . longer'n any person . . . sorta like a snake or somethin'."

The kids looked at each other in the dim light.

"Under the ground?" said Harlen.

"Yep."

"The holes . . ." Dale said to no one in particular. The idea of something else, something they hadn't seen yet, made him sick to his stomach.

"Maybe it's like the thing that went under my bed," suggested Lawrence.

Dale had heard the conversation from a distance at that point, as if he were eavesdropping on talk in an insane asylum. And he was one of the inmates.

"It's settled," said Mike. "We meet tomorrow at eight to go to Duane's house and see if he left any notes that could help us."

No one had wanted to go home alone in the dark. They'd left in clusters, hanging together as long as they could until one by one they'd run for porch lights and the light behind screen doors. In the end, only Cordie Cooke had gone off in the darkness alone.

Mike pedaled to keep up with the group. As early as it was, the day was very hot, the sky cloudless, and small mirages and heat ripples were rising from the long gravel road ahead of them. And Mike was tired.

He'd been up with Memo much of the night, sneaking down after his mother was asleep. He'd sprinkled some of the holy water on the window frame, although he had no idea if that would help. Did the effect wear off when the water dried up? At any rate, there'd been no visitor in the night, and only one time that Mike had startled himself awake at what might have been a sound from beneath the house and might as easily have been the house settling. The chorus of crickets and buzz of cicadas had been quite loud through the screens, and Mike seemed to remember silence descending before he saw the Soldier at the window before.

Mike had delivered his papers on time, yawning from his hour or two of snatched sleep, and then rushed to the rectory to see Father C. before Mass.

There was no Mass said today. Mrs. McCafferty had hushed Mike and moved the conversation from the rectory kitchen to the back step; the priest was very ill; Dr. Staffney had recommended total bed rest and hospitalization if Father C. weren't better by Tuesday. In the meantime, said the housekeeper, Father Dinmen, the assistant pastor at St. Bonaventure's in Oak Hill, had agreed to come say morning Mass on Wednesday. Mike was to tell the parishioners.

Mike argued that he *had* to see Father C., that it was extremely urgent, but Mrs. McCafferty had been unrelenting. Perhaps that evening if the Father were feeling better.

So Mike had stayed around the church long enough to inform the half dozen or so elderly parishioners and to restock on holy water—he'd brought his canteen this time, and emptied one of the fonts into it—and then he was off to meet Dale and the others.

He had his doubts about going back to the McBride farm—it meant passing the cemetery for one thing—but the bright sunlight and presence of the four other boys made it hard to say no. Besides, Dale might be right: perhaps Duane had left some clue for them.

They pulled the bikes into the cornfield right at the entrance to the Mc-Bride driveway and went forward on foot, stopping at the last row of corn and peering at the McBride farm. The house was dark and silent. They couldn't see Mr. McBride's pickup in the lot anywhere, and the barn holding the combine and other equipment was shut and sealed; they could see the heavy padlock and chain on the door.

"I think he's gone," whispered Harlen. The ride out and crouching run through the corn seemed to have worn the smaller boy out; Harlen's face was pale and sheened with sweat. He scratched at his sling and cast every other minute. The heat was worse now, pressing down on the fields like a hot fist.

"Don't bet on it," whispered Mike. "Can I look through those?" he asked Kev, who'd thought to bring his binoculars.

"Let's have a drink," hissed Harlen and reached for the canteen slung over Mike's shoulder.

Mike pulled it away. "Lawrence has a water bottle. Get some of his."

"Greedy asshole," whispered Harlen and made beckoning motions toward Lawrence. Dale's brother shook his head but pulled the plastic bottle from the small Cub Scout pack he was wearing.

"I don't see anything," said Mike, handing the binoculars to Dale. "But we've got to think that he's in there."

Dale took the water bottle from Harlen. After rinsing his mouth out and spitting into the dusty soil, he peered between the cornstalks again. "I'll go in."

Mike shook his head. "We'll all go."

"No," said Dale. "It makes sense that I'd come out. And if there's trouble, I want you guys out here ready to help."

"I'll help," whispered Harlen and pulled a small pistol from the depths of his sling.

"Jesus," hissed Dale. "Is that real?"

"Wow," said Lawrence, leaning closer.

"Oh, shit," sighed Kevin. "Don't point that thing my direction."

"Put it away," ordered Mike, his voice flat.

"Eat snot and die," said Harlen. But he put the pistol away and said to Dale, "You bet your ass it's real. We should all have something like it. The other side's playing for real. I think. . . ."

"We'll talk about it later," whispered Mike. He handed the binoculars back to Kevin. "Go ahead, Dale. We'll watch."

It was a long twenty yards from the field to the house. Dale couldn't see the pickup in the lot or part of the barnyard that was now visible, but all the way across the yard and driveway he had the feeling he was being watched.

He knocked on the back door just as he had the dozens of times he'd come out to visit Duane. He half expected to hear Wittgenstein barking from the garage, then hobbling quickly forward, his tail wagging as he got Dale's scent. Then Duane would step out of the house, hitching up his corduroys and adjusting his glasses.

No one answered. The door was unlocked. Dale hesitated a second and then opened the screen, cringing at the squeak it let out.

The kitchen was dark but not cool; the heat filled the little space. There was the smell of stale air and heated garbage. Dale could see dirty dishes in the sink, spilling across the counter. The table was cluttered.

Dale moved as softly as he could across the room, walking on the toes of his sneakers. The house had a silent and abandoned feel to it, bolstering his confidence that Duane's father wasn't home. He stopped to look into the dining room before going downstairs to where Duane had slept.

A dark form was sitting in a chair near the workbench that had been the dining room table. He was holding something. Dale could see a shotgun barrel aimed in his direction.

Dale froze, still on his tiptoes, his heart stopping, then giving a thud, then stopping again.

"What do you want, boy?"

It was Mr. McBride's voice—slow, slurred, strangely without emphasis, but definitely his voice.

"I'm sorry," managed Dale, feeling his heart go thud and stop again. "I thought you were gone. I mean, I knocked . . ." He could see the man now as his eyes adapted to the dark. Mr. McBride sat in his undershirt and a dark pair of work pants. His shoulders sagged as if there were a great weight on them. There were bottles across the tabletop and on the floor. The gun was a pump shotgun and the muzzle did not waver an inch.

"What do you want, boy?"

Dale considered various lies and discarded them. "I came to see if Duane left a notebook."

"Why?"

Dale felt a great ache in his chest as his heart strained, lurched, and then began to race. He wanted to raise his hands like in the movies, but he was afraid to make any move. "I think Duane had some information that'd help us find out who . . . who killed him," he said.

"Who's us?" asked the shadow.

"Other kids. Friends of his," managed Dale. He could see Mr. Mc-Bride's face now. It looked terrible, worse even than when Dale's family had brought the food out a couple of weeks earlier. The gray stubble made Duane's dad look like an old man, and his cheeks and nose were reddened with burst capillaries. The eyes were almost invisible they were so deep in their sockets. Dale could smell the sweat-and-whiskey stink of the man.

"You think somebody killed my Duane?" It was a challenge. The shotgun remained trained on Dale's face.

"Yeah," said Dale. His knees felt funny, as if they couldn't hold him up much longer.

Mr. McBride lowered the shotgun. "Boy, you're the only one who thinks that, besides me." He took a drink from one of the bottles on the table. "I told that sonofabitch constable, told the Oak Hill police, told the State Patrol . . . told everybody'd who'd listen. Only no one would." He lifted the bottle high, emptied it, then tossed it onto the floor. He belched. "I told 'em to ask that miserable fuck Congden . . . he stole Art's car, took the *door* off so we couldn't see the paint . . ."

Dale had no idea what Mr. McBride was talking about, but he had no intention of interrupting to ask a question.

"Told 'em to ask Congden who killed my boy . . ." Duane's father fumbled through the bottles until he found one that wasn't empty. He drank deeply. "Told 'em Congden knows something about who killed my boy . . . they said my boy wasn't in his right mind 'cause of Art's death . . . Did you know my brother died, boy?"

"Yessir," breathed Dale.

"They killed him, too. Killed him first. Then they killed my boy. They killed Duane." He raised the shotgun as if he'd forgotten it was on his lap, set it back, patted it, and squinted at Dale.

"What's your name, boy?"

Dale told him.

"Oh, yeah. You've been out here before to play with Duanie, haven't you?"

"Yessir," said Dale and thought *Duanie?*

"Do *you* know who killed my boy?"

"No sir," said Dale. *Not for sure. Not until I see Duane's notebooks.*

Mr. McBride drained another bottle. "I told 'em, ask that fuck Congden, that fake justice of the peace. They say Congden's been missin' since the day after my Duanie died and what did I know about it? They think I killed *him?* Dumb sonsofbitches." He fumbled on the table, knocking over more bottles, but could not find one with anything left in it. McBride stood up, staggered to a couch against one wall, brushed some junk from it, and collapsed there, still holding the shotgun across his legs. "I should've killed him. Should've made him tell who did this to Art and my boy, then killed him. . . ." He sat up suddenly. "What'd you say you wanted, boy? Duane isn't here."

Dale felt a chill go down his back. "Yessir. I know that. I came to find a notebook Duane kept. Maybe more than one. He had something in it for me."

Mr. McBride shook his head, then grabbed the back of the couch to steady himself. "Uh-uh. He just kept his *story* ideas in his notebooks, boy. Not for you. Not for me . . ." He lowered his head to the arm of the couch and closed his eyes. "Maybe I shouldn't've kept his funeral to myself the way I did," he whispered. "It was easy to forget that he had his own friends."

"Yessir," whispered Dale.

"I wasn't sure where to spread his ashes," mumbled Mr. McBride, as if talking in his sleep. "They call 'em ashes, but there're still bits of bone in there. Did you know that, boy?"

"No, sir."

The man on the couch continued mumbling. "So I sprinkled some of them in the river where Art's went . . . Duanie'd like that, I think . . . and spread the rest out in the field where he and the dog used to play. Where the dog's buried." Mr. McBride opened his eyes and fixed them on Dale. "You think I did wrong splittin' it up like that, boy?"

Dale swallowed. His throat ached and it was difficult to speak. "No, sir," he whispered.

"Me neither," whispered Duane's father and closed his eyes again.

"Could I look at them, sir?" asked Dale.

"What, boy?" It was a sleepy, distracted voice.

"Duane's notebooks. The ones we were talking about."

"Couldn't find 'em," said Mr. McBride, his eyes still shut. "Looked downstairs . . . everywhere . . . couldn't find Duanie's notebooks. Like the fucking door of the Cadillac . . ." His voice trailed off.

Dale waited a full minute, heard the man's breathing turn into a snore, and then he took a step toward the basement stairs.

Mr. McBride pumped the action on the shotgun. "Go away, boy," he mumbled. "Go on now. Get far away from here."

Dale glanced at the stairway—*so close*—and then said, "Yessir," and went back out through the kitchen door.

The light was very bright. Dale walked a hundred feet down the driveway, feeling his t-shirt plastered to his skin, and then ducked behind the Chinese elms and into the cornfield. He didn't think that Mr. Mc-Bride had gone into the kitchen to watch him leave. He cut back through the tight rows of corn until he almost stumbled over Mike and the others still waiting there.

"Jesus," hissed Harlen, "what kept you in there?"

Dale told them.

Mike sighed and rolled over onto his back, squinting up through the cornstalks at the blazing sky. "That does it for today. He probably won't go into town until he wakes up tonight."

"Uh-uh," said Dale. "I'm going back in."

The window had been skinnier than Dale had guessed. He'd ripped his t-shirt and taken some skin off getting in.

There was another worktable under the window—the damn house seemed full of them—and Dale had placed his feet carefully and lowered himself onto it, hearing the trestles creak under him.

The basement was much cooler than outside and smelled like a base-ment: faint odors of mildew, laundry detergent, backed-up drainpipes, sawdust, cement, and ozone, probably from all the radios and electronic kits that lay around on every surface.

Dale had visited Duane's basement room before, and he knew that he'd come into the back part of the basement where the shower and laundry stuff was. Duane's "bedroom" corner was near the stairs. *Great. Where the man upstairs can hear me. And where I can't get to this window to wave.*

He tiptoed across the back room, pausing at the open door to listen. No noise from the stairway or the upper floors. Dale wished that the doorway to the stairs had been closed.

It was darker in this room; there were no windows here. *No way out.* There were various lights—a hanging cord for an overhead bulb, a lamp next to the dark mass of a bed, an artist's type of suspensor light on the big table near the bed—but Dale couldn't turn one of them on, the light would reflect up the staircase. *He won't see it if he's asleep.* A less foolhardy part of Dale's mind reminded him that the man with the shotgun *would* see it if he were awake. Even the sound might tip him off.

Dale was having trouble breathing as he crouched near the bed, waiting for his eyes to adapt to the near blackness. *What if something comes out from under the bed . . . a white arm . . . Duane! Duane's face all bloated and dead like Tubby's was, of course . . . shredded and torn the way Digger said that he . . .*

Dale forced himself to stop it. The bed was neatly made and as Dale's eyes adapted, he could see the faint furrows and ridges on the spread. Nothing came out from under the bed.

There were books everywhere. Books in homemade bookcases, stacks of books on furniture beyond the bed, rows of books on the desktop and windowsill, cartons of books under the desk, even long rows of paperbacks on the cement ledges that ran around the basement. The only thing that competed with books was the number of radios: clock radios and tabletop models, old radios in Art Deco Bakelite curves and naked radios made from kits, tiny transistor radios and one full-size Atwater Kent console job between Duane's bed and his desk that stood at least four feet tall.

Dale started looking along the shelves, in the cartons of books. He remembered what Duane's notebooks looked like: little spiral jobs, some as large as a school notebook, but most of them smaller. They must be somewhere.

The desk had yellow legal pads, cups filled with pencils and pens, even a stack of typewriter paper and an old Smith Corona typewriter, but no notebooks. Dale tiptoed to the bed, felt under the mattress, tossed the pillows. Nothing. He had moved to the makeshift closet and was patting down Duane's few flannel shirts and carefully folded corduroy pants there, feeling weirder and weirder about going through his dead friend's stuff, when his knee brushed one of the low tables by the bed and a stack of books tumbled to the floor. Dale froze.

"Who's there!" Mr. McBride's voice was filled with phlegm and confusion, but it seemed to be just up the stairs.

"Who's down there, goddamn it?" Heavy footsteps moved overhead, going from the dining room to the short hall by the kitchen where the stairway was.

Dale looked across the long room, through the open doorway, at the glint of light from the small window on the far wall. He'd never make it *to* the window, much less *through* it. Mr. McBride had just awakened from his drunken sleep—he probably didn't even remember Dale's visit—and Dale would just be a dark shape scrambling in the basement. His back itched at the thought of buckshot blowing his spine out through the front of his body.

Footsteps in the hall. "I'm comin' down, goddamn you. I've got you."

Dale heard the shotgun being pumped again. The shell Mr. McBride had chambered earlier skittered across the floor above. Then footsteps on the top stairs.

Under the bed, thought Dale. No, it'd be the first place the man looked. He had about ten seconds before McBride reached the bottom of the stairs, turned into the room itself.

Dale remembered the way they screwed around sometimes with the empty console-radio shell in Mike's chickenhouse. The bootsteps were halfway down the stairs as he bounced over the bed, pulled the Atwater Kent away from the wall, crouched behind it, and pulled it back just as the heavy footsteps reached the bottom.

"I see you, goddamn it!" It was a fierce cry. "Think you're gonna get me the way you did my brother and my boy?"

Footsteps staggered into the center of the room. There was a clothesline hanging there and Dale could hear something striking it—the barrel of the shotgun perhaps—then the sound of the line being ripped down.

"Come out of there, goddamn you!"

The radio had its working parts there, but there was just room for Dale to curl up at the bottom of the console. He covered his face with his forearms, trying not to whimper but imagining the shotgun aimed at him from eight feet away. Dale had fired his father's pump-action 12-gauge and his own .410 over-and-under. He knew the flimsy wood wouldn't shelter him for a second. He would have cried out then . . . called a surrender as if they were two kids playing hide-and-seek . . . but his voice would not work. He panted to keep from screaming.

"I see you!" cried the dead boy's father. But his footsteps receded into the other part of the basement. "Goddammit, I know somebody's down here. Come out now!"

He didn't see me. Something sharp, part of a pipe maybe, was digging into Dale's back. Electronic stuff scratched his bowed neck. There was some sort of shelf down here that cut into his shoulder. Dale was not about to move to get more comfortable.

The footsteps came back into the bedroom part of the basement. They moved slowly—stalking—to the far wall, across to the closet, back to the base of the stairs, then . . . stealthily . . . up to the desk not three feet from where Dale crouched behind the Atwater Kent.

There was a sudden noise as Mr. McBride crouched, flung back the bedspread, and scraped the shotgun barrel under the bed. He stood up then, almost leaning on the radio, Dale knew; he could smell the man. *Can he smell me?*

For a long moment there was silence so deep that Dale was sure that the half-crazy father could hear his heart beating behind the radio shell. Then Dale heard something that almost made him cry aloud.

"Duanie?" came Mr. McBride's voice, no longer fierce, no longer threatening, only cracked and broken. "Duanie, is that you, son?"

Dale held his breath.

After an eternity, the heavy footsteps, heavier now, moved back to the staircase, paused, and went up the stairs. There was the sound of breaking glass in the dining room as bottles were thrown around. Footsteps. The kitchen door banged open and shut. A moment later there came the sound of a truck engine starting up from behind the house . . . *We couldn't see it back there* . . . and tires crunching gravel, turning down the drive.

Dale waited another four or five minutes, his back and neck aching wildly now, but making sure that the silence was real. Then he shoved the radio away from the wall and crawled out, massaging his arm where it had been pinched against the shelf or something.

He paused by the bed, still on all fours, then pulled the radio cabinet farther out. There was just enough light to see by.

Duane's spiral notebooks were stacked on the shelf, at least several dozen of them. Dale could see how easy it had been to lean over from the bed or desk and set them in place.

Dale tugged off his t-shirt, ripped and sweaty as it was, wrapped the notebooks in them, and went into the other room to climb out the window. He could've gone up the stairs and out through the kitchen with less scraping to his hide, but he wasn't sure that Mr. McBride had driven off.

Dale was heading for the place he'd left the others when half a dozen arms lurched out from the first row of corn and pulled him in. He tumbled into the cornstalks. A dirty hand covered his mouth.

"God," whispered Mike. "We'd just decided he'd killed you. Let him go, Harlen."

Jim Harlen removed his hand.

Dale spat and mopped blood from a cut lip. "Why'd you do that, shithead?"

Harlen glared at him but said nothing.

"You got 'em!" cried Lawrence, holding up the bundle of notebooks. The boys started poring through them.

"Shit!" said Harlen.

"Hey," said Kevin. He looked quizzically at Dale. "Do you get this?"

Dale shook his head. The notebooks were filled with scriggles and scrawls, strange loops and dashes and curlicues. It was either some sort of impossible code or Martian.

"We're screwed," said Harlen. "Let's go home."

"Wait," said Mike. He was frowning at one of the small notebooks. Suddenly he grinned. "I know this."

"You can read it?" Lawrence's voice was awestruck.

"Uh-uh," said Mike, "I can't read it, but I *know* it."

Dale leaned closer. "You can figure out this code?"

"It isn't code," said Mike, grin still in place. "My stupid sister Peg took a course in this stuff. It's shorthand . . . you know, the sort of fast writing secretaries do?"

The boys whooped and hollered until Kevin suggested they get quiet. They set the notebooks in Lawrence's backpack as carefully as if they'd been new-gathered eggs, then ran in a commando crouch back to where they'd left their bikes.

Dale felt the sun burning his neck and arms, despite his tan, long before they got to Jubilee College Road. The distant water tower shimmered in the rising heat waves as if the entire town were an illusion, a mirage on the verge of disappearing.

They were halfway to town when the cloud of dust rose behind them, a truck closing rapidly.

Mike gestured and he and Harlen and Kev took one side, Dale and Lawrence the other. They crossed the ditch, dropped their bikes, and made ready to climb the fence into the fields.

The truck slowed, the dark cab shimmering badly in the heat from the road and its own engine. The driver stared curiously as he crept by. The truck stopped and backed up.

"What're you doing?" called Kevin's father from the high cab of the milk truck. The long trailer tank gleamed of polished steel, almost too bright to look at in the midday sun. "What are you guys up to?"

Kevin grinned, made a meaningless gesture toward town. "Just riding."

His father squinted at the boys perched on the fence wire like birds ready to take wing. "Get home quick," he said. "I need help cleaning out the tank, and your mother wanted you to weed the garden this afternoon."

"Yessir," said Kevin and gave a salute. His dad frowned and the long truck geared up, disappearing into its own dust.

They stood a minute on the road, holding their bikes awhile before remounting. Dale wondered if the others had wobbly legs.

There were no more cars or trucks before they reached the shade of town. It was dinner there, the lights filtered through a dozen layers of leaves everywhere along the streets, but the day was just as hot, summer still crushing them beneath its heel as they met briefly in the chicken-house and then fanned out for lunch and their various chores.

Mike kept the notebooks. His sister still had one of her Gregg short-hand textbooks around and he promised to find it and start decoding. Dale came over after lunch to help.

Mike checked on Memo, found Peg's book on a shelf next to her stupid diary—she'd kill him if she caught him in her room—and took the whole batch of books out to the chickenhouse.

He and Dale started looking just to confirm it was shorthand, de-cided to decode a line or two, found it tough going at first, and then fell into the rhythm of it. Duane McBride's squiggles weren't quite the same as the ones in the textbook, but they were close enough. Mike went back into the house, found a Big Chief tablet and two pencils, and went back to the chickenhouse. The boys worked in silence.

Six hours later, they were still reading when Mike's mother called him in for supper.

TWENTY-SIX

Mike volunteered to go talk to Mrs. Moon. He knew her best. The evening before, after supper and during the long, slow waning of the day's heat and light, everybody but Cordie had rendezvoused at the chickenhouse to hear what was in the note-books.

"Where's the girl?" asked Mike.

Jim Harlen shrugged. "I went out to her rattrap of a house . . ."

"Alone?" interrupted Lawrence.

Harlen squinted at the younger boy, then ignored him. "I went out there this afternoon, but nobody was home."

"Maybe they were out shopping or something," said Dale.

Harlen shook his head. He looked pale and oddly vulnerable in his cast and sling this evening. "Uh-uh, I mean it was *empty*. Crap scattered around everywhere . . . old newspapers, bits of furniture, an ax . . . like the family threw everything in the back of a truck and took off."

"Not a bad idea," whispered Mike. He had finished decoding Duane's journals.

"Huh?" said Kevin.

"Listen," said Mike O'Rourke, lifting the pertinent notebooks and beginning to read.

The four boys listened for almost an hour, Dale finishing reading when Mike's voice began to get raspy. Dale had read it all before—he and Mike had compared notes as they decoded the stuff—but just hearing it out loud, even in his own voice, made his legs feel shaky.

"Jesus Christ," whispered Harlen as they finished the stuff about the Borgia Bell and Duane's uncle. "Holy shit," he added in the same reverent tone.

Kevin crossed his arms. It was getting quite dark out and Kev's t-shirt glowed the brightest of any of them there. "That bell was hanging up there all the time we were in school . . . all those years?"

"Mr. Ashley-Montague told Duane that it'd been removed and melted down and everything," said Dale. "It's in one of the notebooks here and I heard it myself, at the Free Show last month."

"There hasn't been a Free Show for a long time," whined Lawrence.

"Shut up," said Dale. "Here . . . I'm going to skip some of this stuff . . . this is from when Duane talked to Mrs. Moon . . . it was the same day we all had dinner out at Uncle Henry's, the same day that . . ."

". . . that Duane was killed," finished Mike.

"Yeah," said Dale. "Listen." He read the notes verbatim:

JUNE 17:

Talking to Mrs. Emma Moon. Remembers the bell! Talking about a *terrible thing*. Says her Orville wasn't involved. A terrible thing about the bell. Winter of 1899–1900. Several children in town . . . one on a farm she thinks . . . disappeared. Mr. Ashley (no Montague then, before the families joined names) offered a $1,000 reward. No clues.

Then in January . . . Mrs. M's pretty sure it was January, 1900 . . . they found a body of an eleven-year-old girl who had disappeared just before Christmas. Name: Sarah Lewellyn Campbell.

CHECK IN RECORDS! WHY NO NEWSPAPER ACCOUNTS?

Mrs. Moon's sure . . . Sarah L. Campbell. Doesn't want to talk about it but I keep asking questions: girl was killed, possibly raped, decapitated, and partially eaten. Mrs. M's sure about the last part.

Caught a Negro . . . "colored man" . . . sleeping out behind the tallow factory. Posse formed. Says her husband Orville wasn't even in the county. Was on a "horse-buying trip" to Galesburg. Four day trip. (Check later what his job is . . .)

The Klan was big in Elm Haven then. Mrs. M says that her Orville went to the meetings . . . most of the men did . . . but he wasn't a night rider. Besides, he was out of town . . . buying horses.

The other men in the town, led by Mr. Ashley (the one who bought the bell) and Mr. Ashley's son—21 yrs. old—dragged the Negro to Old Central. Mrs. M. doesn't know the Negro's name. A vagrant.

They had a sort of trial. (Klan justice?) Condemned him right there. Hanged him that night.

From the bell.

Mrs. Moon remembers hearing the bell ringing, late that night. Her husband told her it was because the Negro kept swinging and kicking. (Mrs. M. forgetting that her husband was supposed to be in Galesburg!) . . . (Note: regular hangings, executions, drop the condemned to break his neck; this man swung for a long time . . .)

In the belfry? Mrs. Moon doesn't know. Thinks so. Or in the central stairwell.

She won't tell me the worst part . . . coaxing . . .

The worst part is that they left the Negro's body in the belfry. Sealed up the belfry and left it there.

Why? She doesn't know. Her Orville didn't know. Mr. Ashley insisted that they leave the Negro's body there. (GOT TO CHECK WITH ASHLEY-MONTAGUE. VISIT HIS HOUSE, SEE THE HISTORICAL SOCIETY BOOKS HE STOLE.)

Mrs. M. crying. Why? Says that there was something worse.

I wait. These cookies are awful. Waiting. She's talking to her cats now more than me.

She says that the worst part . . . worse than the hanging . . . is that two months after the Negro was lynched there, another child disappeared.

They'd hanged the wrong man.

"There's more," said Dale, "but it's just going over the same stuff. His last notes were about planning to see Mr. Dennis Ashley-Montague in person to get more details."

The five boys in the chickenhouse looked at each other.

"The Borgia Bell," whispered Kevin. "Cripes."

"Fucking aye, cripes," whispered Harlen. "Something about it's still working, still evil."

Mike crouched, touched one of the notebooks as if it were a talisman. "You think it's all centered around the bell?" he asked Dale.

Dale nodded.

"You think Roon and Van Syke and Old Double-Butt are part of it because they're with the school?" asked Mike.

"Yeah," whispered Dale. "I don't know how or why. Somehow."

"Me, too," said Mike. He turned to look at Jim Harlen. "You still got your pistol?"

Harlen reached into his sling with his right hand, came out with the snub-nosed revolver.

Mike's head moved up and down. "Dale? You have guns in the house, don't you?"

Dale looked at his little brother, then returned Mike's gaze. "Yes. Dad has a shotgun. I have the Savage."

Mike did not blink. "The thing he lets you go quail hunting with?"

"Uh-huh. It'll be my gun when I'm twelve."

"It's a shotgun, right?"

"Four-ten on the bottom," said Dale. "Twenty-two on top."

"Fires just one shell from each barrel, right?" Mike's voice sounded flat, almost distracted.

"Yeah," said Dale. "You open it to reload."

Mike nodded. "Can you get it?"

Dale was silent for a moment. "Dad'd kill me if I took it out of the house without permission, without him along." He looked out the door at the darkness there. Fireflies winked against the line of apple trees in Mike's backyard. "Yes," said Dale, "I can get it."

"Good." Mike turned toward Kevin. "Do you have something?"

Kev rubbed his cheek. "No. I mean, my dad has his forty-five service automatic . . . semiautomatic, really . . . but it's in the bottom drawer of his desk. Locked."

"Could you get it?"

Kevin paced back and forth, rubbing his cheek. "It's his *service pistol*! It's like . . . like a trophy or souvenir the guys in his platoon gave him. He was an officer in World War Two and . . ." Kevin stopped pacing. "You think *guns* will do any good against these things that killed Duane?"

Mike was a crouched and curled shape in the semidarkness, poised like some animal waiting to pounce. But all the tension was in the posture of his body, not in his voice. "I don't know," he said softly, so softly that his voice was barely discernible beneath the insect sounds from the garden beyond the chickenhouse. "But I think Roon and Van Syke were part of it, and nobody said they couldn't be hurt. Can you get the gun?"

"Yes," said Kevin after thirty seconds of silence.

"Some bullets for it?"

"Yes. My father keeps them in the same drawer."

"We'll keep the stuff here," said Mike. "If we need it we can get at it. I have an idea . . ."

"What about you?" said Dale. "Your dad doesn't hunt, does he?"

"No," said Mike, "but there's Memo's squirrel gun."

"What's that?"

Mike held his hands about eighteen inches apart. "You know that long gun that Wyatt Earp used on the show?"

"The Buntline Special?" said Harlen, his voice too loud. "Your grandma has a Buntline Special?"

"Uh-uh," said Mike, "but it looks sort of like that. My grandpa had it made in Chicago for her about forty years ago. It's a four-ten shotgun like Dale's, only it's on a pistol whatchamacallit . . ."

"Grip," said Kevin.

"Yeah. The barrel's about a foot and half long and it's got this nice wooden pistol grip. Memo always called it her squirrel gun, but I think Grampa got it for her 'cause the place they lived in . . . Cicero . . . was real tough back then."

Kevin Grumbacher whistled. "Boy, that kind of gun is as illegal as all get-out. It's a sawed-off shotgun is what it is. Was your grandpa part of Capone's mob, Mike?"

"Shut up, Grumbacher," Mike said without heat. "OK, we get the guns and as much ammunition as we can get. We don't let our folks know they're gone. And we hide them . . ." He looked around, poking the sprung couch.

"Behind the big radio," said Dale.

Mike turned slowly, his grin visible even in the poor light. "Got it. Tomorrow we've got some things to do. Who wants to go talk to Mrs. Moon?"

The boys shifted position and stayed silent. Finally Lawrence said, "I will."

"No," Mike said gently. "We're going to need you for some other important stuff."

"Like what?" said Lawrence, kicking at a can on the wooden floor. "I don't even have a gun like the rest of you."

"You're too young . . ." began Dale harshly.

Mike touched Dale's arm, spoke to Lawrence. "If you need one, you'll share Dale's over-and-under. Did you ever fire it?"

"Yeah, lots of times . . . well, a couple."

"Good," said Mike. "In the meantime, we're going to need someone who can ride really fast on his bike to try to find Roon and report back."

Lawrence nodded, obviously knowing that he was being bought off but figuring that was the best deal he was going to get.

"I'll talk to Mrs. Moon," said Mike. "I know her pretty well from mowing her yard and taking her for walks and stuff. I'll just see if she's got any information she didn't give Duane."

They sat there another few moments, knowing that the meeting was over but not wanting to go home in the dark.

"What're you gonna do if the Soldier guy comes tonight?" Harlen asked Mike.

"I'm going to find the squirrel gun," whispered Mike, "but I'll try the holy water first." He snapped his fingers as if remembering something. "I'll get some more for you guys. Get some sort of bottle to carry it in."

Kevin folded his arms. "How come only your Catholic holy water works? Wouldn't my Lutheran stuff work, or Dale's Presbyterian junk?"

"Don't call my Presbyterian stuff junk," snapped Dale.

Mike looked curious. "Do you guys *have* holy water in your churches?"

Three boys shook their heads. Harlen said, "Nobody has that weird stuff but you Catholics, dipshit."

Mike shrugged. "It worked on the Soldier. At least the holy water . . . I haven't tried the consecrated Host yet. Don't you guys have Communion?"

"Yeah," answered Dale and Kevin.

"We could get some of the Communion bread," Dale said to Lawrence.

"How?" asked his little brother.

Dale thought a moment. "You're right, it's easier to steal the over-and-under than to get the Communion stuff." He gestured toward Mike. "OK, since we know your stuff works, get some of your holy water for us."

"We could fill water balloons with it," said Harlen. "Bomb these fuckers. Make 'em hiss and shrivel like slugs getting salted."

The others didn't know if Harlen was pulling their chains or not. They decided to adjourn and think about it until morning.

Mike did his paper route in record time and was at the rectory by seven A.M. Mrs. McCafferty was already there. "He's sleeping," she whispered in the downstairs hall. "Doctor Powell gave him something."

Mike was puzzled. "Who's Doctor Powell?"

The diminutive housekeeper kept wringing her hands in her apron. "He's a doctor from Peoria that Doctor Staffney brought yesterday evening."

"It's that serious?" whispered Mike, but part of him was remembering: *the brown slugs falling from the Soldier's funnel-shaped mouth, the maggots writhing, burrowing.*

Mrs. McCafferty put one of her reddened hands over her mouth as if she were about to cry. "They don't know *what* it is. I heard Doctor

Powell tell Doctor Staffney that they'd have to move him into St. Francis today if his fever didn't go down . . ."

"St. Francis," whispered Mike, glancing up the staircase. "All the way to Peoria?"

"They have iron lungs there," whispered the old lady and then seemed unable to go on. Almost to herself, she said, "I was up all night saying the rosary, asking the Virgin to help the poor young man . . ."

"Can I just look in on him?" insisted Mike.

"Oh, no, they're afraid it's contagious. No one's allowed to go in but me and the doctors."

"I was with him when he got sick," said Mike, not pointing out to her that she'd already let him in the house, exposing him if she were a carrier. He didn't think the slugs would travel to another person . . . but the thought of it made him queasy for a moment. "Please," he asked, putting on his most angelic, altar-boy look, "I won't even go in the room, just peek in."

She relented. They tiptoed down the hall together, pushing open the dark mahogany door as carefully as they could. It did not squeak.

The smell rolled out of the room even before the blast of super-heated air made Mike stagger a step backward. The smell was like the stench from the Rendering Truck and the inside of one of those tunnels, only worse, riding on the waves of hot, stuffy air in the darkened room. Mike lifted his hand to his mouth and nose.

"We keep the windows closed," Mrs. McCafferty said a bit apologetically. "He's had the chills so bad the last two nights."

"The smell . . ." managed Mike, close to being ill now.

The housekeeper frowned at him. "The medicine, you mean? I change the linen every day. . . . Does that little bit of medicine smell bother you?"

Medicine smell? Mike thought that it was a medicine smell if you made medicine out of dead and rotting bodies. It was a medicine smell if you counted the coppery scent of blood and the stench of week-old decay as medicinal. He looked at Mrs. McM. She obviously didn't smell it. *Is it in my mind?* Mike stepped closer, hand still over his face, blinking into the darkness, fully expecting to see a rotting corpse on the bed.

Father C. looked bad, but he wasn't a rotting corpse. Not quite. But the young priest obviously was very, very sick: his eyes were closed but sunken in pools of blue-black, his lips were white and cracked as if he had been out in a desert for days, his skin glowed—not with the healthy sheen of sunburn, but with the radioactive internal glow of the most intense fever—his hair was matted and spikey, and his hands were curled on his chest like animal claws. Father C.'s mouth was open wide and a thin line of drool ran down onto his pajama collar and his breathing rattled in his throat like loose stones. He didn't look much like a priest at that moment.

"Enough," whispered Mrs. McCafferty, shooing Mike toward the stairs.

It had been enough. Mike pedaled toward Mrs. Moon's so fast that the wind brought tears to his eyes.

She was dead.

He'd expected it when he knocked on the screen door and there was no answer. He'd known it when he'd stepped into the small, dark parlor and wasn't instantly surrounded by her cats.

He knew that Miss Moon, the librarian, usually walked over from her "apartment"—actually a floor she rented in a big old house on Broad that she shared with Mrs. Grossaint, the fourth-grade teacher—to have breakfast with her mother around eight. It wasn't quite seven-thirty now.

Mike moved from room to room in the small house, feeling the same nausea he'd had at the rectory. *Quit being so weird. She went out walking early. The cats went with her.* He knew that the cats wouldn't be caught dead outside the small, white frame house. *OK, the cats ran off in the night and she went hunting for them. Or maybe Miss Moon finally took Mrs. M. to the Oak Hill Home in the past couple of days. It's past time.* That was the logical answer. Mike knew that it wasn't the right one.

He found her on the tiny landing at the head of the stairs. The second floor was small—big enough just for Mrs. Moon's bedroom and a minuscule bathroom—and the landing was barely large enough to hold the small body.

Mike crouched on the top step, his heart pounding with such ferocity that it threatened to knock him off balance and tumble him back down the stairs. Except for the funeral of his paternal grandpa years earlier, he had never seen a dead body . . . if one did not count the Soldier. Now Mike stared with a terrible mixture of sadness, horror, and curiosity.

She'd been dead long enough for her hands and arms to go rigid: the left one was crooked around the banister as if she had fallen and had been on the verge of pulling herself back up, the right hand rose vertically from the green carpet with the fingers curled as if clawing the air . . . or warding off something terrible.

Mrs. Moon's eyes were open . . . Mike realized that of all the hundreds of dead people he'd seen while watching other people's TVs, usually Dale's, none of the corpses ever had their eyes open . . . but Mrs. Moon's were so wide that they seemed to be bulging from their sockets. There was no question that she could see anything; Mike looked at the glazed and cloudy orbs and thought *This is what dead is.*

The liver marks on her face stood out almost three-dimensionally because of the blood drained away from the skin. Her neck was tense even in death, the muscles and tendons of her throat corded and stretched as if to the point of snapping from tension. She was wearing a quilted robe over some sort of pink nightgown, and her bony legs jutted straight out as if she'd fallen straight-legged and stiff, like a comic doing a pratfall in a silent film. One pink, fluffy slipper had come off. The old lady had painted her toenails the same color as the slipper, but that just made her wrinkled, warty, knotted foot look all the more bizarre, staring skyward with its old-lady toes.

Mike leaned forward, touched Mrs. Moon's left hand gingerly, and snatched his hand back. She was very cold, despite the intense heat of the house. He forced himself to look at the most terrible part of all this—her expression.

Mrs. Moon's mouth was open very, very wide, as if she had died while screaming. Her dentures had come loose and hung in the dark cavity like some bright and alien piece of plastic that had fallen in from somewhere else. The lines of her face had been molded and rearranged in a sculpture of pure terror.

Mike turned away and thumped down the carpeted stairs on his rear end, too shaky to rise to his feet. There had been only the slightest hint of decay in the air, like flowers that had died and been left in a sealed car on a hot day. Nothing as bad as the rectory.

Whoever killed her might still be in the house. Might be waiting behind the bedroom door up there.

Mike didn't stand to look or run. He had to sit there for a minute. There was a very loud noise in his ears, as if the crickets had started up again in the daylight, and he realized that small black spots were dancing in the periphery of his vision. He lowered his head between his knees, rubbed his cheeks hard.

Miss Moon'll be here in a few minutes. She'll find her mother like this.

Mike wasn't crazy about the spinsterish librarian—she'd once asked Mike why he even came by the library if he was so slow that he'd flunked fourth grade. Mike had grinned at her and said he was with friends—it had been true that day—but for some reason her comment had hurt him for many nights after that, in those seconds before drifting off to sleep.

Still, nobody deserves to find her mother like this.

Mike knew that if he were Duane, or maybe even Dale, he'd think of some clever boy-detective things to do, find some clues or something—he did not doubt for a second that the same . . . force . . . that had killed

Duane and his uncle had murdered Mrs. Moon—but all Mike could think to do was clear his throat and call, "Here kitty, kitty, kitty. Here kitty."

No movement from the upstairs bedroom or bathroom—both doors were slightly ajar—and no motion from the shadows in the kitchen or back hall.

Standing on shaky legs, Mike forced himself to go up the stairs, to stay standing this time, and to look down one final time at Mrs. Moon. She was even tinier and older looking from this angle. Mike had the powerful urge to remove the loose dentures from her gaping mouth so she wouldn't choke. Then he imagined that snapping tortoise jaw coming up, the beak of a mouth snapping down, and his hand caught in the corpse's mouth as the dead eyes blinked and fixed on him. . . .

Stop it, dipshit. When Mike cursed, he often heard Jim Harlen's voice in his mind supplying the vocabulary. Right now Harlen's mental voice was telling him to get the fuck out of the house.

Mike raised his right hand in the motion he'd watched Father Cavanaugh perform a thousand times, and blessed the old lady's body, making the sign of the cross over her. He knew that Mrs. Moon wasn't Catholic, but if he'd known the words to the ritual, Mike would have performed the Last Rites at that second.

Instead, he said a short and silent prayer and then stepped to the slightly open door to the bedroom. The door was ajar just far enough to allow him to get his head in without touching the wood of the door or frame.

The cats were there. Many of the torn and shredded little corpses were lying on the carefully made bed; some had been impaled on three of the four bedposts; the heads of several more of the cats were lined up on Mrs. Moon's dresser next to her brushes and bottles of perfume and hand lotion. One cat, a tawny one that Mike remembered as the old lady's favorite, hung from the beaded chain of the overhead light; he had one blue eye and one yellow eye, and both stared at Mike every time the surprisingly long body revolved in its slow and silent turning.

Mike slammed down the stairs and was almost to the back door when he stopped, his throat burning with the urge to vomit. *I can't let Miss Moon come in and find this.* He had only minutes, perhaps less.

The old antique against the parlor wall was some sort of writing desk. Lavender stationery lay handy; Mike lifted an old-fashioned nibbed pen, dipped it in ink, and wrote in huge, capital letters: DO NOT COME IN! CALL POLICE!

He didn't know if wiping the pen and ink lid would get fingerprints off, so he stuck them in his pocket, set the note between the frame and screen where anyone coming to the door would see it first thing, opened the door with his t-shirt around his hand, brushed the outer knob as he closed the door from the outside, and then jumped the azaleas and irises, leaped over the lower of the two birdbaths and the low hedge, and was in the alley behind the Somersets' house, running toward home at full speed and thanking heaven for the thick foliage that turned the alley into a tunnel all of its own.

He climbed into the highest level of the treehouse above Depot Street, sitting there concealed in the foliage, shaking hard, then the stem of the pen started poking into his thigh—thank God he'd had the minimal brains to stick it in with the nib pointed out or he'd have a huge ink stain on his jeans now, he could see the headline DIMWIT LOCAL MURDERER INCRIMINATES SELF WITH INKSTAIN—SO Mike stuck both pen and lid in a natural crack in the wood and hid them behind some leaves he plucked from nearby branches.

It was possible that someone could find them in the fall when the leaves turned and fell, but Mike figured that he would worry about that in the fall. *If any of us live that long.*

He sat with his back to the large bole of the tree, hearing the occasional rumble of traffic on the street thirty feet below and the soft scrape of his sister Kathleen playing hopscotch by herself on the sidewalk, and he thought.

At first Mike tried to think through things just to rid his mind of the terrible images he had seen already this hot and beautiful morning, but then he realized that he would never be rid of them—Father C.'s fevered breathing, Mrs. Moon's breathless gape of a mouth—so he put his fear and adrenaline to work trying to come up with a plan.

Mike sat in the treehouse for almost three hours. Early on, he heard cars stopping down the block, then the howl of a siren—so rare in Elm Haven—and the babble of adult voices from a block away, and he knew that the authorities had come for Mrs. M. But Mike was deep in thought by then, turning his plan over and over like a baseball being inspected for scratches or missed stitches.

It was late morning by the time Mike came down from the treehouse. His legs had cramped from sitting on the small platform for so long, there was sap on the back of his jeans and t-shirt, but he did not notice. He found his bike and rode to Dale's house.

Both the Stewart kids were wide-eyed with excitement and concern at the news of the death of Mrs. Moon. Had she merely been found dead, with the cats still alive, there would have been no thought of foul play. But the mutilation of the cats had agitated the small town as had nothing in recent months.

Mike shook his head at that. Duane McBride was dead, as was Duane's uncle, but people accepted death by accident—even the terrible death of a child—while the mutilation of a few cats would keep them whispering and locking their doors for weeks or months to come. To Mike, Mrs. Moon's death had already receded to a distant place; it was part of the terrible blackness that had been hanging over Memo and him and the other kids all summer, merely one more storm cloud in the darkening sky.

"Come on," he said to Dale and Lawrence, tugging them toward their bikes. "We'll get Kev and Harlen and go somewhere *real* private. I have something I want to talk about."

Mike couldn't help looking at Old Central as they rode past on their way west to Harlen's house. The school seemed bigger and uglier than ever, its secrets all boarded up inside, inside where it was dark all the time now, no matter how bright the sun shone out here in the world.

And Mike knew the damn place was waiting for him.

TWENTY-SEVEN

They rode to the ball diamond and hashed it out. Mike talked for about ten minutes while the others stared. They didn't ask questions while he described Mrs. Moon's body. They didn't argue when he said that it would be *them* lying around dead unless they did something soon. They didn't say a word when he outlined what they'd have to do.

"Can we get it all done by Sunday morning?" Dale finally asked. Their bikes were clustered around the low pitcher's mound. No one was visible within five hundred yards of them. The sun baked down on their short haircuts and bare arms, glinting off the chrome and old paint of their bikes and making them squint.

"Yeah," said Mike. "I think so."

"The camping part we don't do Thursday night," said Harlen.

The others looked at him. It was Tuesday morning; why was he worried about Thursday night? "Why not?" asked Kevin.

"'Cause I'm invited to Michelle Staffney's birthday party that night," said Harlen. "And I'm *going*."

Lawrence looked disgusted. The three other older boys let out a breath at almost the same moment. "Jeez," said Dale, "we're *all* invited. Half the kids in the stupid town are invited, just like every July fourteenth. What's the big deal?"

It was true. Michelle's birthday party had become a sort of Midsummer's Eve for Elm Haven kids. The party was always in the evening, always filled the Staffneys' huge yard and house with kids, and always ended with fireworks about ten P.M. Dr. Staffney always announced that they were celebrating Bastille Day as well as his daughter's birthday, and all of the kids always cheered, although none of them knew what Bastille Day was. Who cared as long as the cake and punch and fireworks held out.

"No big deal," said Harlen smugly, as if he had a secret that *was* a big deal, "but I'm going."

Dale wanted to argue but Mike said, "OK, no sweat. We do the camping part tomorrow. Wednesday. That way we'll get it over with. Then everything's cleared away for the Free Show on Saturday."

Lawrence looked dubious. His small nose was red and peeling. "How do you know there's gonna *be* a Free Show next Saturday?"

Mike sighed and crouched near the pitching rubber. The others crouched also, sealing in their conversation with their wall of backs. Mike drew idly in the dirt with his finger, as if he were outlining a play—but it was just doodling. "We make sure there's one when somebody goes to see Mr. Ashley-Montague. If we're going camping tomorrow that'll take up most of Wednesday and Thursday morning, and we've got to get ready for Sunday morning by Saturday night, that means we've got to see Mr. Ashley-Montague today or Thursday afternoon." He looked at Harlen and made a wry face. "And Thursday's *Michelle's party.*"

Dale tugged his wool ballcap out of his back pocket and put it on. The shade over his upper face was like a dark visor. "Why so soon?" he said. Mike had said that seeing Ashley-Montague was something Dale would have to do.

Mike shrugged. "Think about it. We can't go ahead with the other stuff unless we're sure. The rich guy could tell us if we're right."

Dale wasn't convinced. "And if he doesn't?"

"Then we use the camping as a test," said Mike. "But it'd be a lot better to know before we go."

Dale rubbed his sweaty neck and looked off toward the water tower and rows of corn beyond. The corn was well over his head now, a green wall that marked the end of the town and offered nothing but slow going and shadows beyond. "Are you coming?" he asked Mike. "To Ashley-Montague's house, I mean."

"Uh-uh," said Mike. "I'm going to find that other person I talked about. Try to get some of the stuff Mrs. Moon was talking about. And I think Father C. may need me."

"I'll go with you," Kevin offered to Dale.

Dale felt better immediately, but Mike said, "No. You've got to go with your dad in the milk truck, set that stuff up the way we planned."

"But I don't need to actually *do* anything with the truck till the weekend . . ." began Kev.

Mike shook his head. There was no arguing with his tone of voice. "But you've got to start doing *all* the cleanup work on the truck in the afternoon, not just helping him. If you do it all the rest of the week, he won't think about it so much on Saturday."

Kevin nodded. Dale felt miserable.

"I'll go," said Harlen.

Dale looked at the diminutive kid with his clumsy cast and sling. It didn't raise his spirits too much.

"Me, too," said Lawrence.

"Definitely not," said Dale, all big brother now. "You're the lookout, remember? How are we going to find the Rendering Truck if you don't search?"

"Aw, shit," said Lawrence. Then he glanced over his shoulder toward their house a hundred and fifty yards away under the trees, as if their mother might have heard. "Shit and hell," he added.

Jim Harlen laughed, delighted. "And heck and spit," he said in falsetto.

"I don't like the camping part," said Kevin, his voice all business. "All of us together like that."

Mike smiled. "I won't be together with you."

"You know what I mean." Kevin sounded seriously worried.

Mike did know. "That's why I think it'll work," he said softly, still doodling circles and arrows in the dirt. "We haven't been together that often when we're not around our folks and all." He glanced up. "But we may not have to do it if Dale . . . and Jim . . . get information from Ashley-Montague that says it wouldn't be worth it."

Dale was still looking toward the distant fields, his eyes filled with concern. "Problem is, I don't know how to get to Peoria today. My mom won't take me . . . the old Buick wouldn't make it even if she wanted to . . . and Dad's on the road till Sunday."

Kevin was chewing a large wad of gum. He turned and spat over his shoulder. "We don't go into Peoria very often. Thanksgiving time, to see the Santa Claus parade. I don't think you want to wait that long, right?"

Harlen grinned. "I just got my ma to stay home from Peoria. If I asked her to take us to some rich guy's mansion on Grand View Drive, she'd probably beat the shit out of me."

"Yeah," said Mike, "but would she drive you afterward?"

Harlen gave him a disgusted look. "Hey, Miko, your daddy works at the Pabst brewery, doesn't he? Couldn't Dale and me hitch a ride with him?"

"Sure, if you want to leave at eight-thirty at night to get there for the graveyard shift. And the brewery's miles south of Grand View Drive . . . you'd have to hike up that hilly road in the dark, see Mr. A. and M. at nighttime, and wait for my dad to get off at seven A.M."

Harlen shrugged. Then he brightened and snapped his fingers. "I've got transportation, Dale. How much money do you have?"

"Total?"

"I don't mean your Aunt Millie's bonds and Uncle Paul's silver dollars, dipshit. I mean money you can get your hands on right away. Like now."

"About twenty-nine dollars in my sock bank," he said. "But the bus doesn't come through till Friday, and that wouldn't get us to . . ."

Harlen shook his head, grin still in place. "I'm not talking about the fuckin' bus, amigo. I'm talking about our own personal taxi. Twenty-nine dollars should about do it . . . hell, I'll throw a buck in to make an even thirty. We can go today. Probably right now."

Dale felt his heart begin to race. He didn't really want to meet with Mr. Dennis Ashley-Montague, and Peoria seemed light-years away. "Right now? You're serious?"

"Yeah."

Dale looked at Mike, saw the seriousness in his friend's gray eyes as he nodded at him: *Do it.*

"All right," said Dale. He set a knuckle against Lawrence's chest. "You stay at home with Mom unless Mike has some scouting he wants you to do." Harlen had already started pedaling toward First Avenue. Dale looked at the others. "This is nuts," he said sincerely.

No one argued with him.

Dale got on his bike and pushed hard to catch up to Harlen.

C.J. Congden stared at them in squinting disbelief. The pimply sixteen-year-old was leaning against the front left fender of his daddy's black souped-up Chevy; there was a beer in Congden's left hand, he was wearing his usual black leather jacket, greasy jeans, and engineer boots, and a cigarette was dangling from his lower lip even as he spoke. "You fucking want me to do fucking what?"

"Drive us to Peoria," said Harlen.

"You and the pussy here," sneered C.J.

Jim looked at Dale. "Yeah," he said. "Me and the pussy here."

"An' you'll pay me how much?"

Harlen gave Dale a slightly exasperated look, as if to say *Didn't I tell you we were dealing with the walking brain-dead here?* "Fifteen bucks," he said.

"Fuck you," sneered the teenager and took a long swig of Pabst.

Harlen shrugged slightly. "We might be able to go to eighteen dollars . . ."

"Twenty-five or nothing," said Congden, flicking ash from the cigarette.

Harlen shook his head as if that were an astronomical sum. He looked at Dale and then flapped his arms as if he'd been outhaggled. "Well . . . all right."

Congden looked startled. "In *advance*," he said in a tone that showed he'd picked up the phrase from shoot-'em-up movies.

"Half now, half when the job's done," said Harlen in the same Humphrey Bogart tone.

Congden squinted hard at them through the smoke of his cigarette, but evidently the hit men in the movies always agreed to that arrangement, so he didn't have much choice. "Pay me the first half," he ordered. Dale did so, counting out twelve dollars and fifty cents from his savings.

"Get in," Congden said. He stubbed out his cigarette, spat, hitched up his pants, and squinted at the two boys as they scrambled into the backseat of the matte-black Chevy.

"This isn't a fucking taxi," snarled Congden. "One of you little fucks rides in the fucking front seat."

Dale waited for Harlen to comply, but Harlen moved his broken arm in the sling as if to say *I need room for this* and Dale unhappily got out and moved to the passenger seat in front. C.J. Congden tossed the beer can into his side yard and got into the Chevy with a solid slam of the door. He jangled keys and the huge engine roared to life.

"You sure your daddy lets you drive this?" Harlen asked from the comparative safety of the backseat.

"Shut your fucking hole before I kick the shit out of you," said Congden over the heightened roar as he revved the engine.

The teenager slammed the Hurst shifter to the left and forward and the big rear wheels threw dirt and gravel all over the front of Congden's house as he peeled out, sliding onto the blacktop of Depot Street with a wild screech of tires, spinning the steering wheel left, completing a sliding, screeching ninety-degree turn, and then roaring east on Depot until he came to Broad. That sliding turn was even wilder, using up the entire wide avenue before he got control, spinning the steering wheel lock to lock and sending a cloud of blue smoke up behind them. They were doing sixty by the time they reached Church Street and Congden had to stand on the brakes to slide to a stop on the gravel at the intersection of

Broad and Main. The skinny, pimply apparition at the wheel pulled the pack of Pall Malls from his rolled-up t-shirt sleeve, lipped one out, and lighted it with the dash lighter while pulling out in front of an eastbound semi-trailer on the Hard Road.

Dale closed his eyes as air horns blared. Congden flipped the trucker the bird in the rearview mirror and slammed up through the gears.

The sign in front of the Parkside Cafe said SPEED 25 MPH ELECTRICALLY TIMED. Congden was doing sixty and still accelerating as he roared past it. He screeched around the wide bend beyond the Texaco and the last brick house on the left, and then they were out of town and picking up speed, the roar of the Chevy's dual exhausts racketing off the walls of corn on either side of the Hard Road and bouncing back in their wake.

Dale had actually skidded his bike to a stop when Harlen had told them where they were going. "*Congden?* You've got to be kidding." He was truly and sincerely and deeply horrified. All he could remember was the bottomless black pit of the .22 muzzle the town punk had aimed at his face. "Forget it," Dale had said, spinning his bike around and ready to ride home again.

Harlen had grabbed his wrist. "Think, Dale. Nobody else is gonna drive us all the way up Grand View Drive in *Peoria* . . . your folks'd think you were nuts. The bus doesn't come through till Friday. We don't know anybody else who's got a license . . ."

"Mike's sister Peg . . ." began Dale.

"Flunked her damn driving test four times," finished Harlen. "Her folks won't let her *near* a car. Besides, the O'Rourkes just have the one junker and Mike's old man uses it to drive to work every evening. No way he's going to let it out of his sight."

"I'll find some other way," insisted Dale, pulling his wrist free.

"Yeah, right." Harlen had folded his arms, straddling the bar of the bike, and glared at Dale. "You do have a bit of pansy in you, don't you, Stewart?"

Dale had felt the heat flush of rage then and would have been quite happy to dismount his bike and beat the shit out of Harlen—he'd done it before in years past, and even though the smaller boy fought dirty, Dale knew he could take him again—but he forced himself to grip his handlebars and think.

"Think," said Harlen, echoing Dale's scurrying thoughts. "We've got to do this today. We've got nobody else. Congden's so dirt stupid that he'll do it for money without wondering why we're doing it. And it's probably the fastest way to get there except for an F-86."

Dale winced at the truth of the last part. "His old man doesn't let him drive," he said, thinking that it was only with guys like Congden that he said "old man" instead of "dad" or "father," and then remembered what Mr. McBride had said.

"His old man's been missing the last few days," said Harlen. He rocked back and forth on his bike seat. "Word's out that he and Van Syke or Mr. Daysinger or a few of those other worthless eggsuckers went up to Chicago on a weeklong binge after ripping off some schmuck tourist on 'speeding' charges. Anyway, old J.P.'s black bomber's still around, and C.J.'s been drivin' it every day and night."

Dale had felt his hip pocket where the money in the sock was folded away. It was all the money he had except for the savings bonds and Uncle Paul's silver dollars, which he knew he'd never spend. "All right," he'd said, turning back west and pedaling slowly up Depot Street, as if to his execution. "But how come an asshole like C.J. can get his license if Peg O'Rourke's too dumb to pass the test?"

Harlen had waited until they were in sight of Congden's house—with the punk lounging against the chosen vehicle out front—before he had whispered just loud enough for Dale to hear, "Who said anything about C.J. having a license?"

It was a state road that wound the eighteen miles southeast to Highway 150A, and it had never been designed for speeds like this, not even back when it was new and didn't suffer from terminal potholes and broad strips of patch tar every twenty feet. The black Chevy roared its way to the Spoon River valley and seemed to levitate as it came over the top of the hill.

Dale felt the heavy suspension dip, saw Congden squint harder through his cigarette smoke and fight the wheel, and then Dale was squinting himself, through his fingers, as they took up most of the road to sort things out before barreling down the steep incline. If there'd been a vehicle coming the other way—several trucks had just passed them headed northwest—they'd all be dead now. Dale decided that even if this all worked out, he *was* going to beat the shit out of Harlen when they got back.

Suddenly Congden began decelerating, pulling the Chevy onto the graveled side of the road just this side of the Spoon River Bridge. They were only a third of the way to Peoria.

"Get out," Congden said to Dale.

"How come I have to . . ."

Congden pushed Dale violently, slamming his head against the doorframe. "Out, fuckface."

Dale scrambled out. He looked imploringly at Harlen in the backseat, but the other boy might as well have been a stranger for all the support he gave. Harlen shrugged and inspected the upholstery of the backseat.

Congden ignored Harlen. He shoved Dale again, making him back up almost to the edge of the guardrail at the end of the bridge. The highway was built up here and they were almost at treetop level with the low scrub oaks and willows that grew along the banks below. It was at least a thirty-foot drop to the river itself.

Dale backed up, feeling the guardrail behind his legs, balling his fists in frustration. He was very afraid. "What the hell do you . . ." he began.

C.J. Congden's hand went behind his back and came out with a black-handled knife. An eight-inch blade flicked into sight and caught the brilliant sunlight. "Shut up and give me the rest of that fucking money."

"Fuck you," said Dale, bringing his fists up and feeling his whole body pounding to the wild surge of his heartbeat. *Did I really say that?*

Congden moved very fast. Long ago, Dale had learned the hard way that—at least on the subject of bullies—his father's advice was bullshit: they *weren't* cowards, at least not in any situation Dale had seen; they *didn't* back down if you faced up to them; and, most importantly, they *weren't* all huff and bluster. At least C.J. Congden and his buddy Archie Kreck weren't: they were mean-assed sonsofbitches who loved to administer pain.

Congden moved fast to do just that. He knocked aside Dale's thin arms, slammed the smaller boy against the guardrail so that Dale almost tipped over backward, and brought the blade up tight under Dale's chin. Dale felt blood flow.

"You stupid fuck," hissed Congden, his yellow teeth inches from Dale's face. "I was just gonna take your fucking little sock there and leave you here to walk home. You know what I'm gonna do now, fuckface?"

Dale couldn't shake his head; the blade would have sliced open the soft flesh under his chin. He blinked.

Congden grinned wider. "See that fucking tin thing out there?" he said, turning with his free hand toward the corrugated tower rising to a catwalk twenty-five feet or so out on the right side of the bridge. "Now, 'cause you gave me fucking *lip*, I'm gonna take you out on that walkthing there, and hang you fucking upside down, and drop you in the fucking river. Whaddya think of that, fuckface?"

Dale didn't think much of it, but the blade was cutting deeper now and he didn't really want to comment. He could smell the sweat and beer stink of Congden and he could tell from the stupid bully's tone that this was *exactly* what he was going to do. Without moving his head, Dale glanced at the silo and catwalk . . . and at the long drop to the water.

Congden lowered the blade but caught Dale by the scruff of the neck and propelled him out onto the roadbed, onto the bridge, toward the catwalk. No cars were in sight. There were no farmhouses anywhere near here. Dale's plan was simple: if he got a chance to run, he would. If, as was more likely, Congden got him out onto the catwalk, then Dale was going to jump the asshole so they'd *both* go over into the water. It was a long way down and the Spoon River wasn't very deep, even in the spring, much less the hottest part of July, but that's what Dale planned to do. Maybe he could try to land *on* the pimply asshole, driving him into the river mud . . . Congden shoved him toward the catwalk, never releasing him. Somehow he'd managed to pull out Dale's money sock and tuck it in his own front pocket. They reached the catwalk. Congden smiled and lifted the knife close to Dale's left eye.

"Let him go," said Jim Harlen. He'd gotten out of the car but hadn't come closer. His voice was as calm as ever.

"Fuck you." Congden grinned. "You're next, shithead. Don't think that I don't . . ." He'd glanced over toward Harlen and now he froze, knife still in the air.

Jim Harlen stood by the open rear door, his sling and cast making him look as vulnerable as ever. But the blue-steeled pistol in his right hand didn't look too vulnerable. "Let him go, C.J.," Harlen said again.

Congden stared for only a second. Then he slammed a forearm choke-hold on Dale, swung him around between him and the gun, and used him for a shield, the knife blade raised.

More movies, a maddeningly detached part of Dale's mind commented. *This poor asshole must think that his life is part of some dumb movie.* Then Dale just concentrated on breathing through the heavy pressure on his windpipe.

Congden was shouting, spittle landing on Dale's right cheek. "Har-len, you miserable fuck, you couldn't hit the side of a fucking barn with the thing from this distance, much less me, you fuck. Go ahead, shoot. Go ahead." He jiggled Dale like a shield.

Dale would have liked to kick Congden in the balls, or at least the shins, but the angles were wrong. The bully was tall enough that he was lifting Dale almost off his own feet in the chokehold. Dale had to dance on his toes just to keep from being strangled. And to make matters worse, he was sure at that second that Harlen *was* going to shoot . . . and hit him.

But Harlen just glanced at the gun as if he hadn't been aware that he was holding it. "You want me to shoot?" he asked, voice innocent and curious.

Congden was beside himself with rage and adrenaline. "Go ahead, you fuckin' pussy, you cocksucking little whoreson pussy, shoot the fucking gun, pussy . . ."

Harlen shrugged, lifted the short-barreled little pistol, aimed into the Chevy, and pulled the trigger. The shot was loud even out in the wide valley openness of the place.

Congden lost his mind. He shoved Dale aside—Dale teetering against the guardrail and staring at the water thirty feet below before catching a steel beam and his balance—and then Congden was running across the bridge surface, saliva and obscenities flying.

Harlen took a step forward, aimed the gun at the windshield of the Chevy, and said, "Stop."

C.J. Congden skidded to a halt, the steel kicktaps on his engineer's boots throwing sparks three feet in the air. He was still ten paces from Jim Harlen. "I'll kill you," Congden gritted through clenched teeth. "I'll fucking kill you."

"Maybe," agreed Harlen, "but your daddy's car'll have about five holes in it before you do." He moved the aiming point to the hood.

Congden flinched as if the pistol were pointed at him. "Hey, please, Jimmy, I didn't . . ." he said in a pleading tone that was far more sickening than his usual insane-bully voice.

"Shut up," said Harlen. "Dale, get your ass over here, would you?"

Dale shook himself out of his reverie and got his ass over there, making a wide detour around the frozen Congden. Then he was behind Harlen, by the open rear door.

"Throw the knife over the railing," said Harlen, adding a "Now!" when the punk started to speak.

Congden tossed his switchblade over the railing, down into the trees along the riverbank.

Harlen nodded Dale into the backseat. "Why don't we get going," Harlen suggested to Congden. "We'll ride back here. Any shit from you . . . even breaking the speed limit again . . . and I'm going to put a few holes in your dad's custom upholstery, maybe even add a new detail to that tacky dashboard." He settled in with Dale, closed the door.

Congden got in the driver's seat. He tried to light a cigarette with the same punky bravado as before, but his hand and lips were shaking. "You know this means I'm gonna kill your ass sooner or later," he said, squinting in the mirror at them, his bully voice back now and quavering only slightly. "I'm fucking gonna wait for you both and fucking get you and . . ."

Harlen sighed and lifted the pistol, aiming it precisely at the fur-lined rearview mirror with the fuzzy dice hanging from it. "Shut up and drive," he said.

The door to the rectory was open and Mrs. McCafferty wasn't around guarding the drawbridge or the moat; Mike went softly up the stairs to Father C.'s room. The sound of men's voices made him press against the wall and move silently to the open door.

"If the fever and vomiting continue," came Dr. Staffney's voice, "we'll have to transfer him to St. Francis and put him on IV just to avoid severe dehydration."

Another man's voice, unknown to Mike but one he assumed to be that of Dr. Powell, said, "I hate to move him forty miles in this state. Let's start the IV here and have the housekeeper and the nurse watch him . . . see if the fever breaks or we get any secondary symptoms before the transfer."

There was silence for a moment, then Dr. Staffney said, "Watch it, Charles."

Mike peered through the crack in the door just as the retching noises began. The doctor Mike didn't recognize was holding a bedpan—obviously a chore he was not used to—while Father C., eyes closed, face white as the pillowcase he lay against, vomited violently into the metal receptacle.

"Good God," said Dr. Powell, "has all the vomitus been of this consistency?" There was revulsion in the man's voice, but also professional curiosity.

Mike bent lower and set his eye against the crack. He could see Father C.'s head lolling against the pillow, bedpan almost against his cheek. The vomit seemed to fill his cheeks and move like molasses into the bedpan. It was less liquid than a solid brown discharge, a mass of partially digested mucousy particles. The bedpan was almost full and the priest showed no signs of stopping.

Dr. Staffney answered the other doctor's question, but Mike did not hear the comment. He had moved away from the crack and was crouching against the wall, fighting the surge of dizziness and nausea that had assailed him.

". . . where's the damn housekeeper, anyway?" Dr. Powell was saying.

"She went to drive Nurse Billings over from Oak Hill," replied Dr. Staffney's familiar voice. "Here—use this."

Mike tiptoed down the stairs and was pleased to be out in the fresh air, despite the terrible heat of the day. The sky had gone from morning blue to late-morning bleached blue to a midafternoon gunmetal glare. The fierce sunlight and high humidity lay on everything like heavy but invisible blankets.

The streets were empty as Mike pedaled downtown, avoiding line of sight to Jensen's A&P so that his mother wouldn't spy him and think of some chore he had to do. He had his own chore right now.

Mink Harper was the town drunk. Mike knew him the way every kid in town knew him: Mink was invariably polite and talkative with kids, eager to share whatever small finds he had made in his endless search for "buried treasure." Mink was a pain to the grown-ups, always asking for a handout, but he never bothered kids with his pleas. The fact that Mink had no set address—he often slept under the park bandstand during the heat of the summer days, moving to his "outdoor bed" of one of the park benches in the cool of the evening. Mink always had a reserved seat during a Free Show, and he was always willing to let kids crawl into the cool dark under the bandstand to watch the show through the broken lattice-work with him.

In the winter, Mink was less visible; some said he slept in the abandoned tallow factory or in the shed behind the tractor dealership across from the park, others said that families with a soft heart—like the Staffneys or Whittakers—allowed him to sleep in their barns and even come in for a few hot meals. But it wasn't meals that Mink worried about; his goal was knowing where the next bottle was coming from. The guys at Carl's Tavern often bought him a drink—although the owner wouldn't allow Mink on the premises to drink it—but usually their kindness quickly turned mean, with Mink at the butt of whatever joke they were pulling.

Mink didn't seem to mind, as long as he got the drink. No one in town seemed to know how old Mink Harper was, but he had served as an object lesson for mothers to hold up to their sons for at least three generations. Mike guessed that Mink was in his early seventies, at least, which would make him just the right age. And while Mink's status as town drunk and occasional handyman made him invisible to much of the population for much of the time, it was that very invisibility that Mike hoped to cash in on now.

Mike's problem was that he didn't have a bottle as currency: not even a can of beer. Despite the fact that Mike's father worked at the Pabst brewery and liked nothing better than bending an occasional elbow with the boys, Mrs. O'Rourke allowed no alcoholic beverages in the house. Ever.

Mike stopped in front of the barbershop between Fifth Avenue and the railroad tracks, looking down the heat-miraged Hard Road at the cool shade of the park and thinking hard. If he'd had any brains at all, Mike knew, he could have had Harlen cadge some booze for him before he left with Dale. Harlen's mom kept gallons of the stuff around and, according to Jim, never seemed to notice when some of it disappeared. But now Harlen was off somewhere with Dale, trying to complete the mission that Mike had sent them on, and Mike—the fearless leader himself—was left literally high and dry. Even if he found Mink, he couldn't get the agreeable old wino to talk without a bribe.

Mike let a truck roar past, not even slowing for Elm Haven's electrically timed speed limit, and then he pedaled across the Hard Road, cutting through the back of the tractor dealership, going south around the small park, and cutting back into the narrow alley behind the Parkside Cafe and Carl's.

Mike parked his bike against the brick wall and stepped to the open back door. He could hear the laughter of the half dozen or so guys in the dark front room and the slow turning of the big fan there. Most of the men in town had once signed a petition demanding that Carl's be provided with an air conditioner—it would have been the only public building in town to have one except the new post office—but according to the rumors Mike had heard, Dom Steagle had just laughed and said who the fuck did they think he was, some politician or something? He'd keep the goddamned *beer* cold and anybody who didn't want to drink there was welcome to go to the Black Tree.

Mike ducked back as a toilet flushed, a door opened a few feet down the back hallway, and someone walked heavily into the front room shouting something that caused the permanent residents there to laugh loudly. Mike peered in again: two restrooms—one saying STAGS and the other one DOES—and a third door that said STAY OUT. Mike knew that this last and closest door was the way to the cellar: he'd helped carry crates down to earn some money.

Mike slipped in, opened the door, stepped onto the top of the cellar stairs, and closed the door softly behind him. He expected to hear shouts, footsteps, but the front-room noise barely made it back here and its tone and timbre did not change. He moved down the dark stairs carefully, blinking in the darkness. There were windows along the high stone ledge, but they'd been sealed with boards decades ago and the only light was the slight amount filtering through splintered wood and the layers of dust on the outside glass.

Mike paused at the bottom of the stairs, seeing the stacks of cardboard cartons and the large metal kegs farther into the long cellar. Beyond a partial brick wall, there appeared to be tall shelves and Mike vaguely remembered that this was where Dom kept the wine. He tiptoed across the wide space.

It wasn't a wine cellar—not like the ones he'd heard Dale describe from books where the dusty old bottles were lying in their own little cradles in the shelves—this was just a bunch of shelves where Dom had dumped his cartons of wine. Mike felt his way to the right, finding the cartons as much by touch as sight, listening for the first sound of the door opening and breathing in the rich malt and hops smell of beer. A cobweb caught in his face and he batted it away. *No wonder Dale hates basements.*

Mike found an open carton on a back shelf, felt around until he had his hand around a bottle, and then paused. If he took this, it would be—quite simply—the first time in his life that he had ever knowingly stolen anything. Somehow, of all the sins that he knew of, thievery had always struck him as the worst. He'd never spoken about it, not even to his parents, but someone who stole was below Mike's contempt—the time Barry Fussner had been caught stealing other kids' crayons in second grade had meant only a few minutes in the principal's office for Barry, but Mike had never spoken to the fat kid again. Looking at him made Mike sick.

Mike thought about having to confess the theft. The back of his neck burned with embarrassment until he saw the whole scene: kneeling in the darkened confessional, the small screen having slid aside so that he could see just Father C.'s profile through the mesh, then Mike whispering, "Bless me Father, for I have sinned," telling how long it had been since his last confession and then launching into it . . . But suddenly the bent and sensitive head of Father Cavanaugh would lurch against the mesh, Mike would see the dead eyes and funneled mouth pressed against the wood, and then the maggots would begin streaming out, tumbling out, falling over Mike's prayer-cupped hands and raised arms and waiting lap, covering him with writhing brown slugs. . . .

Mike took the damn bottle and got the hell out of there.

Bandstand Park was shady but not cool. The heat and humidity lay lurking in the shadows as surely as in the sunnier patches, but at least the sun wasn't burning through Mike's crew cut into his skull here. There was someone—or something—under the large gazebo bandstand. Mike crouched at the broken opening in the trellis and peered in: the wooden support ran down only three feet or so from the raised floor to the concrete foundation rim, but the "basement" under the bandstand was dirt and for some reason it had been scooped out at least a foot below the level of the surrounding soil. It smelled of wet dirt and loam and the soft perfume of decay. Mike thought, *Dale hates basements, I hate these darn crawlspaces.*

It wasn't really a crawlspace. Mike could have stood up in there if he had hunkered over with his head lower than his shoulders usually were. He didn't; he crouched in the opening and tried to make out the slightly moving lump of darkness on the far side of the low space.

Cordie says there are other things that helped to kill Duane—things that burrow.

Mike blinked and resisted the urge to get on his bike and go. The lump on the far side of the bandstand crawlspace *looked* like an old man in a raggedy trench coat—Mink had worn that coat in winter and summer for at least six years—and, perhaps more importantly, it *smelled* like Mink. Along with the strong scent of cheap wine and urine, there came a peculiarly musky scent that was the old panhandler's alone, and may well have been the cause of his nickname so many decades earlier.

"Who's there?" came the cracked and phlegmy voice.

"It's me, Mink . . . Mike."

"Mike?" The old man's tone was that of a sleepwalker being awakened in a strange place. "Mike Gernold? I thought you was killed at Bataan . . ."

"No, Mink, Mike O'Rourke. Remember, you and I did some lawn work together up at Mrs. Duggan's place last summer? I mowed and you trimmed the bushes?" Mike slipped through the hole in the latticework. It was dark in here, but nothing like Carl's basement. Little diamonds of sunlight touched the ruffled soil on the west side of the circular pit, and Mike could see Mink's face now: the rheumy eyes and stubbled cheeks, the reddened nose and peculiarly pale neck, the old man's mouth—Mike thought of the description Dale had given of Mr. McBride the day before.

"Mike," rumbled Mink, chewing on the name as if it were another tough piece of meat he couldn't quite get through with so few teeth. "Mike . . . yeah, Johnny O'Rourke's boy."

"You got it," said Mike, moving closer but stopping about four feet from Mink. What with the old wino's wrinkled and oversized trench coat, the litter of newspapers around him, a can of Sterno, the glint of empty bottles—well, there was a territorial sense to this part of the bandstand's circle. Mike didn't want to invade the old guy's space.

"Whatcha want, kid?" Mink's voice was tired and distracted, not the usual banter he managed with children. *Maybe,* thought Mike, *I'm getting too old. Mink likes to tease the younger kids.*

"I've got something for you, Mink." He brought the stolen bottle from behind his back. He hadn't taken time to read the label out in the sunlight, and now it wasn't quite light enough. Mike hoped that he hadn't

picked up the only wine-bottle-shaped jar of cleaning fluid in Carl's basement. *Not that Mink would notice the difference too much.*

The red-rimmed eyes blinked quickly when they saw the shape of
Mike's offering. "You brung that for me?"

"Yeah," said Mike, feeling guilty as he pulled back with the offering
just a bit. It was like teasing a puppy. "Only I want to trade it for something."

The old man in the ragged coat breathed alcohol fumes and halito-
sis at Mike. "Shee-it. Always somethin'. OK, kid, whatcha want? Want
Ol' Mink to go buy some smokes for ya in the A and P? Getcha some
beer in Carl's?"

"Uh-uh," said Mike, going to his knees in the soft dirt. "I'll give you
the wine if you'll tell me about something."

Mink's neck extended a bit as he squinted at Mike. His voice was
suspicious. "Wha's that?"

"Tell me about the Negro they hung in Old Central right after New
Year's in 1900," whispered Mike.

He expected the old wino to say that he couldn't remember—God
knows the old guy had destroyed enough brain cells to support that
statement—or that he wasn't there, he would've been only ten or so at the
time—or just that he didn't want to talk about it—but instead there was
nothing but raspy breathing for a while, and then Mink held out both
arms as if ready to receive a baby. "Awright," he said.

Mike gave him the bottle. The old man wrestled with the top of it for
a minute—"What the hell is this, some sort of cork or somethin'?"—and
then there was a loud pop, something hit the roof a foot above Mike's
head, and he threw himself sideways into the soft dirt as Mink cursed
and then laughed his peculiar phlegmy, coughy laugh. "Goddamn, kid,
you know what you brung me? Champagne! Genuine Guy Lombardo
sody pop!"

Mike couldn't tell from Mink's voice whether this was good or not.
He guessed good as Mink took a tentative gulp, spluttered once, and
then began drinking it down in earnest.

Between swallows and small, polite belches, Mink told his story.

Dale and Harlen stared past C.J. Congden's greasy head and through a
tall iron gate at the mansion of Mr. Dennis Ashley-Montague. Dale realized that it was the first real mansion that he'd ever seen: set back on uncountable acres of lawn, bordered by thick green woods, perched right on
the edge of the bluff overlooking the Illinois River, the Ashley-Montague
place was a Tudorish tumble of bricks and gables and diamond-latticed
windows, all held together by the riot of ivy growing to the eaves and

beyond. Beyond the gate, the circular asphalt driveway—in much better repair than the patched concrete of Grand View Drive—curved gracefully up the slight incline to the house a hundred yards or more away. Built-in sprinklers watered different areas of the expanse of lawn with a lulling *swik-swik-swik*.

There was a speaker box and grid set onto the brick column anchoring the left side of the gate. Dale got out and went around the back of the black Chevy. The hot air rushing in during the drive had been like invisible sandpaper rasping against Dale's skin, but now that they were stopped, the dead-air heat and terrible weight of sunlight was worse. Dale felt his t-shirt soaking through. He tugged his baseball cap lower, squinting at the glare and leaf-dapple of the road behind them.

Dale had never been on Grand View Drive before. Everybody in this part of the state seemed to know about the road that wound along the bluffs north of Peoria, and about the big homes where the few millionaires around here lived, but Dale's family had never driven here. Their trips to the city tended to focus on the downtown—what there was of it—or the new Sherwood Shopping Center (all six stores of it), or Peoria's first and only McDonald's, out on Sheridan Road just off War Memorial Drive. This steep and leafy road was strange; *hills* of this size were strange to Dale. His life had been lived on the flatlands between Peoria and Chicago, and anything larger than the hills near Calvary Cemetery or out Jubilee College Road—small, wooded exceptions to a world that stretched away flat as a tabletop—were strange.

And the estates, each set back in its leafy privacy, the larger ones perched along the bluffs like Mr. Ashley-Montague's place, were like something out of a novel.

Harlen yelled something from inside the car and Dale realized that he'd been standing out here on the driveway like an idiot for half a minute or more. He also realized that he was scared. He leaned closer to the black grid of the speaker box, feeling the tension in his neck and stomach, having no idea how to activate the thing, when suddenly the speaker erupted in sound. "May I help you, young man?"

It was a man's voice, vaguely accented in the clipped way Dale associated with British actors. He remembered George Sanders in the "Falcon" movies on TV. Suddenly Dale blinked and looked around. There didn't seem to be a camera on the pillar or gate; how did they know who was here? Was somebody watching through binoculars from the big house?

"May I help you?" repeated the voice.

"Uh, yeah," said Dale, feeling how dry his mouth was, "Mr. Ashley-Montague?" As soon as he said it he wanted to kick himself.

"Mr. Ashley-Montague is busy," said the voice. "Do you gentlemen have business here, or shall I call for the police?"

Dale's heart skipped a beat at the threat, but part of his mind noted: *Wherever this guy is, he can see all of us.*

"Uh, no," said Dale, not knowing what he was saying no to. "I mean, we do have business with Mr. Ashley-Montague."

"Please state that business," said the black box. The black-iron gate was so tall and wide that it seemed impossible that it could ever be opened.

Dale looked into the car as if asking Harlen for help. Jim was sitting with the pistol in his hand but below the level of the back of the seat, presumably out of sight of the camera or periscope or whatever the voice was using. *Jesus, what if the cops do come?*

Congden leaned out of the car and shouted toward the speaker box, "Hey, tell 'em that these motherfuckers are aimin' a gun at my fuckin' car, hey? Tell 'em that!"

Dale stepped closer to the speaker, trying to put his body between Congden and the microphone. He didn't know if the box had heard; the British voice did not come again. Everything—the gate, woods, hill, lawn, gunmetal sky—everything seemed to be waiting for Dale to speak. He wondered why in hell he hadn't rehearsed this during the crazy drive down here.

"Tell Mr. . . . ah . . . tell him that I'm here because of the Borgia Bell," said Dale. "Tell him it's very urgent that I speak to him."

"Just a moment," said the voice. Dale blinked sweat out of his eyes and thought of the scene in the Wizard of Oz movie where the guy at the door to the Emerald City, the guy who was really the Wizard unless they were just using the same actor to save money . . . where the guy made Dorothy and her friends wait after all their dangerous travels to get there.

"Mr. Ashley-Montague is busy," the voice said finally. "He does not wish to be disturbed. Good day."

Dale rubbed his nose. No one had ever said "Good day" to him before. It was a day of firsts. "Hey!" he cried, banging on the speaker box to get its attention. "Tell him it's important! Tell him we've got to see him! Tell him we've come a long way and . . ."

The box remained silent. The gate remained sealed. No one and nothing moved between the gate and the mansion.

Dale stepped back and looked up and down the high brick wall that separated the estate grounds from Grand View Drive. It might be possible to get up and over it if Harlen gave him a lift, but Dale had images of fierce German shepherds and Doberman pinschers ranging the grounds,

of men in the trees with shotguns, of the cops showing up and finding
Harlen with the pistol . . .

*Jesus, Mom thinks I'm playing ball or at Mike's, and she'll get a call from
the Peoria police department saying that I'm under arrest for breaking and
entering, carrying a concealed weapon, and attempted kidnapping.* No, he
realized, Harlen would get the carrying-a-concealed-weapon charge.

Dale grabbed the speaker and put his face almost against the microphone grid, shouting, not even knowing if the thing had been switched
off or if the listener at the other end had gone about his duties in the Emerald City. "Listen to me, goddammit!" he shouted. "Tell Mr. Ashley-
Montague that I know all about the Borgia Bell, and about the colored
guy they hung from it, and about the kids that got killed . . . kids back
then and kids right now. Tell him . . . tell him that my friend's dead because of his grandfather's fucking bell and . . . oh, shit." Dale ran out of
steam and sat down on the hot pavement.

The box did not speak again, but there was an electrical humming,
a mechanical click, and the wide gate began to open.

It wasn't George Sanders who let Dale in; the silent and thin-faced little
man looked more like Mr. Taylor, Digger's dad, Elm Haven's undertaker.

Harlen stayed in the car. It was obvious that if both of the boys went
in, Congden'd be out of there like a rifle shot, probably taking the gate
with him if he had to. The promise of the other $12.50 wasn't enough to
keep him from leaving them . . . or from killing them if he got a chance.
Only the literal presence of the .38 aimed at the figurative head of his '57
Chevy kept him in line, and that was getting shakier by the moment.

"Go on in," said Harlen through thin lips. "But don't take high tea or
settle in for supper. Find out what you need to know and get the fuck out."

Dale had nodded and scrambled out of the car. Congden was threatening to go in and call the police, but Harlen said, "Go right ahead. I've
got eighteen more cartridges in my pocket. We'll see how much we can
make this heap look like a Swiss cheese before the cops get here. Then
I'll tell 'em that *you* abducted *us.* Dale and me haven't been in County
Juvenile Detention like somebody I can mention . . ."

Congden had lit another cigarette, settled against the doorframe,
and glared at Harlen as if he were imagining precisely what revenge he
was going to take. "Move it," Harlen had added unnecessarily.

Dale followed the guy he assumed was a butler through a bunch of
rooms, each of which as large as the entire first floor of the Stewart house.
Then the dark-suited guy opened a tall door and waved Dale into a room

that had to be the mansion's library or study: mahogany-paneled walls
and endless built-in shelves rose twelve feet to a mezzanine catwalk, brass
railings, then more mahogany and *more* shelves with books rising to a ceiling lost in rough wood rafters. There were slidable ladders along the base
of the lower bookcases and on the mezzanine itself. On the east side of the
room, about thirty paces from where Dale had entered, there was a giant
wall of windows spilling sunlight over the big desk where Mr. Ashley-
Montague sat. The millionaire looked very little behind that desk, and the
man's narrow shoulders, gray suit, glasses, and bow tie did nothing to
make him seem bigger.

He did not rise as Dale approached. "What do you want?"

Dale took a breath. Now that he was here, inside, he felt no fear and
very little nervousness. "I told you what I want. Something killed my
friend and I think it has to do with the bell your grandfather bought for
the school."

"That's nonsense," snapped Mr. Ashley-Montague. "That bell was
a mere curiosity—a piece of Italian junk that my grandfather was per-
suaded to believe had some historical significance. And as I told one of
your little friends, the bell was destroyed more than forty years ago."

Dale shook his head. "We know better," he said, although he knew
nothing of the kind. "It's still there. It's still affecting people the way it
did the Borgias. And that 'little friend' you're talking about was Duane
McBride, and he's dead. Just like the kids who got killed sixty years ago.
Just like the Negro your grandfather helped hang there."

Dale heard his own voice, strong, clipped, sure-sounding, and it
was as distant as a movie soundtrack. Part of his mind was enjoying the
view out the wide windows: the Illinois River gleaming wide and gray
between tree-covered bluffs, a railroad line far below, a glimpse of Highway 29 winding south toward Peoria.

"I know nothing about these things," said Dennis Ashley-Montague,
rearranging folders on his desk. "I'm sorry about your friend's accident.
I read about it in the newspapers, of course."

"It wasn't an accident," said Dale. "Some guys that've been around
that bell too long killed him. And there are other things . . . things that
come out at night . . ."

The thin man stood up behind his desk. His glasses were round,
horn-rimmed, and they reminded Dale of some silent movie comedian's.
Some guy who was always hanging from buildings.

"What things?" Mr. Ashley-Montague's voice was almost a whisper. It seemed lost in the huge room.

Dale shrugged. He knew that he shouldn't be revealing so much,
but he didn't know any other way to show this guy that they really did

know that something was going on. At that second Dale imagined a secret panel in the book-lined wall opening, Van Syke and Dr. Roon sliding softly through the opening behind him, and behind *them,* other things lurching forward in the shadows.

Dale resisted the impulse to look over his shoulder. If he didn't come out, he wondered if Harlen would leave without him. *I would.*

"Things like a dead soldier showing up," said Dale. "A guy named William Campbell Phillips, to be precise. A thing like a dead teacher coming back. And other things . . . things in the ground."

It sounded nuts even to Dale. He was glad he'd stopped before he started babbling about the shadow that had run from the closet to hide under his brother's bed. He had a sudden thought. *I haven't seen these things. I'm taking Mike's and Harlen's word for this stuff. All I've seen is some holes in the ground. Jesus Christ, this guy's going to call the local asylum and they're going to put me in a rubber room before Mom even knows I'm late for supper.* That made sense, but Dale didn't believe it for a second. He believed Mike. He believed Duane's notebooks. He believed his friends.

Mr. Ashley-Montague seemed almost to collapse into his highbacked chair. "My God, my God," he whispered and leaned forward as if he were going to bury his face in his hands. Instead, he removed his glasses and wiped them with a handkerchief from his suit pocket. "What do you want?" he asked.

Dale resisted the impulse to let out a deep breath. "I want to know what's going on," he said. "I want the books that the county historian . . . Dr. Priestmann . . . wrote. Anything that you can tell me about the bell or what it's doing. And most of all . . ." Dale did let the breath out. "Most of all I want to know how we can stop this thing."

TWENTY-EIGHT

The latticework on the west side of the bandstand carved the afternoon light into a discrete set of diamonds that crept across the dark soil toward Mike and Mink Harper as the old man alternated between long swigs of the champagne, bouts of moody silence, and longer bouts of slurred narrative.

"It was that cold winter right after the new year begun . . . new century begun, too . . . an' I was just a little shaver, no older'n you are now. How old are you? Twelve? No . . . eleven? Yeah, that's about how old I was when they hung the nigger.

"I wasn't in school no more. Most of us didn't stay in no longer than we had to . . . learn to read as much as we needed, sign our names, be able to cipher a bit . . . that's all a man needed to know in them days. My daddy, he needed all us boys on the farm to work. So's I'd already left my schoolin' behind when they hung the nigger there . . .

"Kids was disappearin' that year. The little Campbell girl got all the attention, 'cause they found her body and her family was rich and all, but there was four or five more who didn't come home from chores that winter. I remember me a little Polack kid named Strbnsky, his daddy'd worked on the railroad work gang'd come through town an' stayed, Stefan was his name . . . well, Stefan and me'd been hangin' around the saloon lookin' for our daddies a few weeks before Christmas, an' I got mine and took him home in the back of the wagon my brother Ben an' me drove in, but Stefan, he didn't get home. Nobody seen him after that. I remember the last time I seen him, trudgin' across the drifts on old Main Street in his patched knickers and haulin' that bucket he used to carry his old lady's beer home in. . . . Somethin' got Stefan, just like it got the Myers twins and whatshisname, that little spic kid who lived out where the dump is now . . . but it was the Campbell girl who got all the attention, her bein' the doctor's niece and all.

"So when the Campbell girl's cousin, little Billy Phillips, come into the saloon . . . not Carl's, Carl's wasn't built yet . . . was that big building where the goddamn dry goods is now . . . anyway, when that snotnose little Billy Phillips comes in out of the cold one evenin' saying that there was a nigger down by the tracks who had his sister's petticoat in his duffel, well, hell, that place emptied out in about thirty seconds . . . me, too, I remember runnin' to keep up with my old man's big strides . . and there was Mr. Ashley sittin' out in front in that fancy buggy of his, a shotgun acrost his lap—same gun he used to kill hisself a few years later—sittin' there just like he was waitin' for all of us.

" 'Come on, boys,' he yelled. 'Justice got to be done.'

"And that whole crowd of men sorta shouted and roared the way mobs do . . . mobs don't got any more sense than a hound after a bitch in heat, boy . . . and then we was all off, our breaths puffin' out in the late afternoon light that was all golden sort of . . . even the horses' breath, I remember that now, Mr. Ashley's team of black mares and some of the men's teams . . . and slicker'n snot on grease we was out north of town, where the old railroad cut useta be up beyond the taller' factory, and the nigger looked up once from where he was crouched over a fire cookin' fatback, and then the men was all over him. A couple of his nigger friends was there—they never went nowhere alone in those days and wasn't allowed in town after dark, of course—but his friends, they didn't put up no fight, they just slunk away like dogs that know there's a beatin' comin'.

"The nigger had this big old bedroll, and the men tore through it, and sure enough . . . there was that little Campbell girl's petticoat, all covered with dried blood and . . . and other stuff, boy. You'll know what I mean someday.

"So they dragged him down to the schoolhouse, that bein' sort of the center of everything in them days. We had our town meetin's in the schoolhouse, and the votin' come election time, and all sorts of bazaars and every sort of truck imaginable. So they dragged the nigger there . . . I remember standin' outside while the bell was being rung to tell everybody to come quick, that somethin' important was happenin'. An' I remember standin' out in the snow exchangin' snowballs with Lester Collins and Merriweather Whittaker and Coony Daysinger's daddy . . . whatever his name was . . . and a whole bunch a other boys who'd come on down with their daddies. But by and by it got dark for real . . . and cold . . . that winter was colder'n a crib full of witch's tits, the whole goddamn town was cut off, you know, sorta sealed off by the icy roads and drifts. Couldna even got to Oak Hill that winter, damn roads was so bad. Train got through, but not every day. Not for weeks that time of year, what with the drifts north of town where the cut was and the railroad havin' no snowplows up this way and all. So we was on our own.

"When we got cold we went in and the trial . . . they called it a trial . . . was almost over. Couldna took no more than an hour. There wasn't no *real* judge . . . Judge Ashley retired young and was a bit crazy . . . but they called it a trial anyhow. Mr. Ashley, he *looked* the part. I remember standin' up there with the other boys on the mezzanine where the books used to be, looking down on the center hall where all the men was crowded in, and marvelin' at how Judge Ashley looked so handsome, what with his expensive gray suit and silk cravat and that silk top hat he wore everywhere. 'Course he didn't have the top hat on when he was judgin' . . . I remember seein' the lamplight sort of glowin' on his white hair and wonderin' how a man that young could look so wise. . . .

"Anyway, Billy Phillips was just finishin' tellin' how he was walkin' home when the nigger tried to catch *him* . . . said he run after him sayin' he was goin' to kill him an' eat 'im the way he done the girl . . . and Billy, God that kid was the biggest liar I ever knowed . . . little shit useta play hooky back when I was still in school and then come creepin' in an' say he was helpin' his sick momma—Old Lady Phillips was always sick and dyin' of somethin'—said he was sick when we all knowed that he was out screwin' around or fishin' or somethin'. Anyway, Billy says he got away from the nigger, but he went back and spied on the nigger's camp and saw him take out the little Campbell girl's petticoat—she was Billy's cousin, did I tell you that?—take out her petticoat and sort of touch it there around that campfire. He says then he run into town and told the men at the saloon.

"Another guy, coulda been Clement Daysinger come to think of it . . . that was his name, Clement . . . he said that he seen the nigger hangin' around Dr. Campbell's house before Christmas, 'bout the time the little girl up and disappears. Said he hadn't remembered it before, but now it come back to him and he was sure the nigger was hangin' around real suspicious like. After Clement, some of the other folks remember the nigger lurkin' around there, too.

"So Judge Ashley banged his big old Colt pistol like a whatchama-callit . . . a gavel . . . and he says 'Do you got anything to say for your own self?' to the nigger, but the nigger just glares at everybody out of his yellowy eyes and didn't say nothing. 'Course his usual fat lips was all swole up fatter 'cause some of the men'd found cause to beat on him, but I think that nigger coulda spoke if he'd wanted to. I guess he didn't want to.

"So Judge Ashley . . . we was all thinkin' of him as a real judge again by then . . . he pounds his Colt on the table they dragged out into the hall there, and he says, 'You're guilty, by God, and I hereby sentence you to hang by the neck until you're dead and may God have mercy on your soul.' An' then that mob of men just sorta stood there for a minute until finally the Judge shouted somethin' and old Carl Doubbet, he laid hands on the nigger, and pretty soon there were a couple dozen of the men draggin' that nigger down past the little kids' classrooms, and then up the big stairway under the stain glass, and then up where us boys was watchin' . . . dragged that nigger past me so close I coulda reached out and touched those fat lips that were turnin' all purple . . . and then us kids followed as they dragged him up the stairs where the high-school level was . . . that was where Carl or Clement or one of the men stuck the black hood on him . . . and then they drug him up those last steps, the ones that aren't out in the open anymore, where they put that wall in, you know . . . and they took him out on that little catwalk that ran around the inside of the belfry.

"You can't see it no more . . . I've helped Karl Van Syke and Miller before him clean that place for forty years, so I know what I'm talkin' about . . . you can't see it no more, but it useta be that the belfry had that little catwalk around the inside and you could see down all the way to the first floor, like three rings of balconies goin' right up to that big old bell that Mr. Ashley brung back from Europe. Anyway, we was all standin' around these balconies, the first floor filled with men . . . and some wom-enfolk, too, I remember seeing Sally Moon's mommy Emma there with her weakkneed little husband Orville, both their faces just gleamin' they was so happy and excited \ . . . everyone starin' up at Judge Ashley and the few others standing around that nigger up there in the belfry.

"I remember thinkin' that they was gonna scare the nigger real bad . . . put that rope around his scrawny black neck and scare him so bad that he'd just have to start talkin', start tellin' the truth . . . but that ain't what they did. No sir, what they did was, Judge Ashley borrowed a knife from one of the men there, it coulda been Cecil Whittaker's, and he cut that damned bell rope that hung down all the way to the first floor. I remember leanin' over that high-school-level balcony and starin' down as that rope just sort of folded up and come crashin' down, folks jostlin' to get out of its way and then fillin' back in the space, their faces lookin' up past me at the nigger again. And then Judge Ashley did a strange thing.

"I shoulda figured it when he cut the rope, but I didn't. They was fiddlin' with that nigger's hood, and I figured *Now they're gonna take it off an' scare him, say they're gonna throw him over to the crowd or somethin'* . . . but they didn't. What they done was take that short end of the bell rope and tie it around the nigger's neck, the hood still on him, and Judge Ashley nods to the men up there with him and somehow they got that nigger up on that little railing that went around the inside of the belfry . . . and then, boy, there was this damn pause . . . I couldn't hear nothin' of the crowd. Musta been three hundred people there, but you couldn't hear nothin' of the usual snufflin' or scrapin' or mumblin' or even breathin' that you get from a crowd that size. Just silence. Every man, woman, and child—'cludin' me—starin' up three floors at that nigger teeterin' there on the edge of that balcony, his face hid by that damn black hood, his hands tied behind his back, nothin' holdin' him there except a couple men's hands on his arms.

"And then someone—I 'spect it was Judge Ashley, though I didn't see too clear 'cause it was dark in that belfry and I was watchin' the nigger, just like everybody else—then somebody shoved him off.

"Nigger kicked, of course. The fall wasn't far enough that it'd break his neck like a real hangin'. He kicked like a royal sonofabitch, swinging from one side of the open stairwell to t'other, kickin' his black ass off and makin' wild chokin' sounds under his hood. I could hear him real good. His feet was just a few feet from my head ever' time he swung over to our side of the high school balcony. I remember that nigger lost one shoe and the other had a hole in it that his big toe was stickin' out of, even as he was kickin'. I remember too that Coony Daysinger reached out and sorta tried to touch the nigger while he was swingin' and kickin' . . . not to stop him from swingin' or pull him in or anything like that, just touch him, sorta like you would somethin' at the sideshow if they'd let you . . . but just then we see the nigger piss his pants . . . swear to God, you could see his raggedy pants gettin' dark with the stain as it was runnin' down his leg and then the folks down on the first floor was makin' noise all right, and shovin' to get out of the way. And then the nigger quit kickin' and just swung silent-like, so Coony, he pulled back his hand an' none of the rest of us tried it neither.

"You know the strange thing, boy? When that nigger went off the ledge, the big ol' bell started ringin', which makes sense. And it kept on ringin' when the nigger was swingin' and kickin' and chokin', which nobody took no notice of 'cause all his bobbin' up and down on the end of the rope woulda made any bell ring like a sonbitch . . . but you know the strange part, boy? Some of us hung around, so to speak, 'till after they cut that nigger down and took his body out to the dump or somewhere to get rid of . . . *and that goddamn bell kept ringin'*. I think the fuckin' thing rang all that night and off an' on the next day, like that nigger was still swingin' from it. Somebody said that the hangin' musta messed up the bell's balance or somethin'. But it was a strange sound . . . I swear to you . . . ridin' outa town that night with the Old Man, smelling the cold air and the snow and the Old Man's whiskey and the sound of the horses' hooves on the ice and frozen dirt underneath, Elm Haven nothin' but dark trees and cold chimney smoke glowin' in the moonlight behind us . . . and that damn bell still ringin' its ass off.

"Say, you got another bottle of this fine champagne, boy? This one's one dead soldier."

"So you see," Mr. Dennis Ashley-Montague was saying, "your so-called legend of the Borgia Bell is as fake as the so-called authenticity certificates which caused my grandfather to buy it in the first place. There is no legend . . . only an old, poorly cast bell sold to a gullible Illinois traveler."

"Uh-huh," said Dale. Mr. Ashley-Montague had been talking for several minutes, the sunlight from the diamond-paned window behind him lying rich and heavy across the massive oak desk and creating a corona of light around his thinning hair. "Well, I guess I don't believe you," said Dale.

The millionaire scowled and folded his arms, obviously not used to being called a liar by an eleven-year-old. One pale eyebrow arched. "Oh? And what do you believe, young man? That this bell is causing all sorts of supernatural events? Aren't you a bit old for that?"

Dale ignored the question. He thought of Harlen out in the Chevy keeping a restless Congden from driving off, and knew that he didn't have much time. "You told Duane McBride that the bell was destroyed?"

Mr. Ashley-Montague frowned. "I have no recollection of such a discussion." But his voice was hollow-sounding to Dale, as if he knew that there might have been witnesses. "Very well, he may have asked me. The bell *was* destroyed, melted down for scrap iron during the Great War."

"What about the Negro?" persisted Dale.

The thin man smiled slightly. Dale knew the word "condescending" and thought it applied well to that smile. "What Negro is that, young man?"

"The Negro that got hung in Old Central," said Dale. "Hung from the bell."

Mr. Ashley-Montague shook his head slowly. "There was an unfortunate incident early in the century involving a man of color, but I assure you that no one was hung, as you put it, and certainly not hanged from the bell in Elm Haven's school."

"OK," said Dale, sitting in the high-backed chair across the desk from the man, and folding his legs as if he had all the time in the world. "Tell me what did happen."

Mr. Ashley-Montague sighed, looked as if he were considering sitting down himself, and contented himself with pacing back and forth in front of the window as he spoke. Far behind him, Dale could see a long barge working its way up the Illinois River.

"What I know is sketchy," said the man. "I was not born at the time. My father was in his late twenties but had not yet married . . . the Ashley-Montagues pride themselves in taking brides later in life. At any rate, what I know is just through family stories . . . my own father died in 1928, you know, shortly after I was born, so there is no way I can check on the accuracy of the details. Dr. Priestmann did not mention this incident in his county histories.

"At any rate, I understand there was some unpleasantness in your part of the county around the turn of the century. One or two children disappeared, I believe, although it is quite possible that they were runaways. Life on the farms was very harsh in those days, and it was not uncommon for children to run away from home rather than continue a life of hard labor with one's own family. At any rate, there was one child . . . the daughter of a local doctor, if I'm not mistaken . . . who *was* found. It seems she had been . . . ah . . . brutalized as well as murdered. Shortly thereafter, several of the more prominent townspeople—including my grandfather, who had the distinction of being a retired judge, you know— were presented with incontrovertible evidence that an itinerant Negro had carried out this crime . . ."

"What kind of evidence?" interrupted Dale.

Mr. Ashley-Montague paused in his pacing and frowned. "Incontrovertible. It is a big word, isn't it? It means . . ."

"I know what incontrovertible means," said Dale, biting his lip before adding the *dipshit*. He was beginning to think and talk like Harlen. "It means not capable of being denied. I mean what kind of *evidence*?"

The millionaire picked up a curved blade of a letter opener and tapped it irritably on the oak desk. Dale wondered if the man was going to call his butler and have him thrown out. He didn't. "Does it matter what kind of evidence?" he said and began pacing again, tapping the small knife on the desk after each circuit. "I seem to remember that it was some article of the child's clothing. And perhaps the murder weapon as well. Whatever it was, it was incontr—It was incontestable."

"And then they hanged him?" asked Dale, thinking of C.J. Congden getting antsy outside.

Mr. Ashley-Montague glared at Dale, although the effect was ruined somewhat by the millionaire's thick glasses. "I told you, no one was hanged. There was a makeshift trial . . . perhaps that was at the school, although it would have been most unusual. The townspeople present . . . all respected citizens, I might add . . . served as a sort of de facto grand jury . . . Do you also know what a grand jury is?"

"Yeah," said Dale although he couldn't have defined it. He was guessing at de facto from context.

"Well, instead of the leader of this slavering lynch mob which you seem to want to portray, young man, my grandfather was the voice of law and moderation. Perhaps there were elements which wished to punish the Negro then and there . . . I don't know, my father never said . . . but my grandfather insisted that the man be taken to Oak Hill to be turned over to the law enforcement agency there . . . the sheriff's office, if you will."

"And was he?" asked Dale.

Mr. Ashley-Montague quit pacing. "No. That was the tragedy . . . and it weighed heavily upon my grandfather's and father's consciences. It seems the Negro was being taken to Oak Hill by carriage when he bolted . . . ran . . . and although he was in manacles and leg chains, he managed to get into a swampy area just off the Oak Hill road near where the Whittaker farm is now. The men escorting him could not reach him in time because the treacherous soil would not hold their weight either. He drowned . . . asphyxiated, rather, for the swamp was essentially mud."

"I thought it was winter when this happened," said Dale. "January."

Mr. Ashley-Montague shrugged. "A warm spell," he said. "Possibly . . . quite probably . . . the accused man broke through the surface of ice. Midwinter thaws are quite common around here."

Dale had nothing to say about that. "Could we borrow the county history that Dr. Priestmann wrote?"

Mr. Ashley-Montague showed what he thought of such a presumptuous request, but he folded his arms and said, "And then will you allow me to get back to work?"

"Sure," said Dale. He wondered what Mike would say when he reported on such a fruitless conversation. *And now Congden's gonna kill me . . . for what?*

"Wait here," said the millionaire and went up the steep ladder to the library balcony. He peered through his thick glasses at the titles, moving slowly down the row.

Dale wandered under the balcony overhang, looking at the row of books at eye level closest to the millionaire's desk. Dale liked to keep his favorite books in places where he could get to them easily; maybe millionaires thought the same way.

"Where are you?" called the voice from above.

"Just lookin' out the window," replied Dale while he was scanning the rows of ancient, leatherbound volumes. Many of the titles were in Latin. Few of the English titles made any sense to him. The old book dust in the air here made him want to sneeze.

"I'm not sure I have . . . ah . . . here it is," said Mr. Ashley-Montague on the balcony above. Dale heard the sound of a heavy volume being slid out.

Dale's finger was tapping across the book spines; otherwise he wouldn't have noticed that one small book was pulled out farther than the rest. He could not read the embossed symbols on the spine, but when he pulled it out, there was an English subtitle under the same symbols on the cover: *The Book of the Law.* Under the title, in gold script, were the words—*Scire, Audere, Velle, Tacere.* Dale knew that Duane McBride had been able to read Latin easily—and some Greek—and he wished that his friend were there.

"Yes, this is it," came the voice from directly above Dale. Footsteps moved along the balcony toward the ladder.

Dale pulled the book all the way out, saw several small, white bookmarks among the pages, and—in an instant of pure bravado—stuck the small volume in the waistband of his jeans in back, tugging his t-shirt loose to hide it.

"Young man?" said Mr. Ashley-Montague, his polished black shoes and gray trousers becoming visible on the ladder three feet from Dale's head.

Dale quickly loosened the other volumes so that the gap where the book had been did not seem so visible, took three quick steps toward the window, and half-turned toward the descending man, keeping his back to the wall and staring out the wide window as if enraptured by the scenery.

Mr. Ashley-Montague was puffing slightly as he crossed the carpet and offered the historical volume. "Here. This book of notes and almost random photographs is the only thing Dr. Priestmann had sent to me. I have no idea what you think you will find in it . . . there is nothing there about the bell or the sad incident of the accused Negro . . . but you are welcome to take it home and peruse it if you promise to return it through the post . . . *in as good a condition as you find it here.*"

"Sure," said Dale, accepting the heavy book and feeling the smaller volume settle lower into the seat of his jeans. The outline of it must be visible now below the line of his t-shirt. "I'm sorry if I bothered you."

Mr. Ashley-Montague nodded curtly and returned to his desk as Dale circled slowly, trying to keep his front to the man while not making that too obvious. "You can find your way out, of course," said Mr. Ashley-Montague, already going through the notes on his desk.

"Well . . ." said Dale, thinking of how he'd have to turn to leave the room and Mr. A.-M. would look up and . . . was it grand larceny to steal an expensive book? He guessed it depended on the book. "Actually, no sir," said Dale. There was a bell on the corner of the man's desk, and Dale was sure that he would ring it and the skinny butler would come in to show him out, and then *both* men would see the suddenly square seat to his jeans. Maybe he could use the butler's entrance as a distraction to hitch up his pants without being seen, pull his shirt looser. . . .

"Come this way," said Mr. Ashley-Montague in an exasperated voice. He led the way out of the study at a fast pace. Dale hurried to keep up, glancing at the huge rooms as they passed through them, hugging the Priestmann volume to his chest and feeling the smaller book sink lower into the seat of his jeans. The top of it must be poking up at his shirt now, quite visible.

They were almost to the foyer when the sound of a television set in a small room off the main hall made both Mr. A.-M. and Dale turn. A crowd was roaring on the screen of the TV, someone was giving a speech and the echoes filled a huge hall. Mr. Ashley-Montague paused to look for an instant and Dale slipped by him, swiveling to keep his front toward the man, hanging on to the history volume with one hand while the other fumbled for the doorknob. The butler's footsteps echoed on a tile corridor.

Dale could have slipped out then, but what he saw on television made him pause and stare with Mr. Ashley-Montague. David Brinkley was saying, in his strange, clipped voice, "And so, the Democrats have chosen to give us . . . this year . . . what must certainly be . . . the strongest Civil Rights plank in the history . . . of the Democratic Party . . . wouldn't you say . . . Chet?"

Chet Huntley's woeful visage filled the small black-and-white screen. "I'd say without a doubt, David. But the interesting thing in this floor fight is . . ."

But what had compelled Dale's attention was not the newscasters speaking, nor the crowds the camera kept cutting to, but the man's picture on many of the hundreds of posters that were rising and bobbing above that red, white, and blue crowd like flotsam on a political sea. The words on the signs said ALL THE WAY WITH JFK and, simply, KENNEDY IN '60. The poster picture was of a handsome man with very white teeth and a full head of chestnut hair.

Mr. Ashley-Montague shook his head and made a snorting noise as if witnessing something or someone beneath contempt. The butler had come up to stand beside his master as the millionaire returned his attention to the boy. "I hope you have no more questions," he said as Dale backed out the door and stood on the broad stoop. Jim Harlen shouted something from the backseat of the car thirty feet away on the wide driveway.

"Just one," said Dale, almost falling down the stairs, squinting in the sunlight and using the conversation as a reason to keep backing away from the two men at the door. "What's on the Free Show this Saturday?"

Mr. Ashley-Montague rolled his eyes but glanced at his butler.

"A Vincent Price film, I believe, sir," said the man. "A motion picture called *The House of Usher.*"

"Great," shouted Dale. He had backed almost to the black Chevy now. "Thanks again!" he called as Harlen opened the door behind him and he jumped in. "Go," he said to Congden.

The teenager sneered, flicked a cigarette into the manicured grass, and floored the accelerator, half-skidding around the long turn of drive. He was doing fifty miles an hour as they approached the heavy gates.

The black iron opened in front of them.

Mike did not want to stay down there any longer. The half-gloom under the bandstand, the smell of raw earth and the heavier scent of Mink himself, even the progression of diamond-shaped nodes of light across the dark soil—all conspired to give Mike a terrible sense of claustrophobia and gloom, as if he and the old drunk were lying to-gether in a roomy coffin, waiting for the men with spades to arrive. But Mink had not finished either an extra bottle he had found under his newspapers or his story.

"That woulda been the end of it," Mink was saying, "the hanging of the nigger an' all, but it turned out that nothin' was quite the way it seemed." He drank deeply from his wine bottle, coughed, wiped his chin, and stared at Mike with great intensity. His eyes were very red. "That next summer, some more kids up and disappeared. . . ."

Mike sat up very straight. He could hear a truck passing on the Hard Road, little kids playing in the shade near the War Monument at the front of the park, and farmers chatting across the street at the John Deere dealership, but all of his attention was on Mink Harper at that moment.

Mink took a drink and smiled as if he were very aware of Mike's riv-eted attention. The smile was quick and furtive; Mink had about three teeth left and none of them were worth exhibiting for any length of time. "Yep," he said, "that next summer . . . summer of nineteen hundred . . . couple more li'l kids got disappeared. One of them was Merriweather Whittaker, my ol' pal. The grown-ups, they said that no one never found him, but a couple years later I was out by Gypsy Lane—must've been more'n a couple years 'cause I was out there with a girl, tryin' to get into her pants, if y' know what I mean. In those days, girls didn't wear no pants except their underwear so the meanin' was clear, if you get my drift." Mink took another drink, wiped his dirty brow with a dirty hand, and frowned. "Where was I?"

"You were out by Gypsy Lane," whispered Mike. He was thinking *It's weird that the kids* then *knew about Gypsy Lane.*

"Oh, yeah. Well, the young lady friend I was with didn't care none for what I had in mind—goddamned if I know why she thought I'd got her out there, sure as hell wasn't to smell the gladiolas . . . but she left in a huff to find her friend . . . we was supposed to be havin' a picnic as I remem-ber . . . and I was sorta pullin' up grass and throwin' sod at a tree, you know how it is when your John Henry's all worked up an' don't have nothin' to do with it . . . an' I pulled this hunk a grass outa the ground and there was a bone—goddamned white *bone*—rather'n a root. Bunch a god-damn bones. *Human* bones, too . . . including a little skull about Merri-weather's size. Damn thing'd been caved in an' sort a hollered out, like someone was scoopin' brains out of it for a dessert, sorta."

Mink took a final drink and flung the bottle across the dark space. He rubbed his cheeks as if he'd lost track of his story again. When he spoke it was in lower tones, in an almost confidential manner. "Sheriff told me it was cow bones . . . shee-it, as if I didn't know the difference between cow bones and human bones . . . he tried to pretend I hadn't seen me the skull and such my ownself . . . but I did, an' I know that that ol' part of Gypsy Lane ran through the back of Old Man Lewis's spread. Wouldna been hard for someone to take Merriweather out there, do whatever they done to him, and then bury his bones in a shallow grave there.

"More'n that . . . more'n Merriweather's goddamn bones . . . a few years after that, I was drinkin' with Billy Phillips before he went off to the war . . ."

"William Campbell Phillips?" said Mike.

Mink Harper blinked at him. "Sure, William Campbell Phillips . . . who'd'ya think Billy Phillips *was?* Cousin to the little Campbell girl who got herself killed. Billy was always a whinin' little toad . . . always moppin' his runny nose and figurin' out a way to get out of work or runnin' to his mommy when he got in trouble . . . I can tell you I almost dropped my teeth when he up and enlisted during the war . . . Where was I, boy?"

"You were drinking with Billy Phillips."

"Oh, yeah, me and Billy was liftin' a few right before he went overseas durin' the Great War. Normally, Billy wouldn't drink with us workin' types . . . he was a *teacher* . . . just taught those snot-nosed little kids down to the school, but to hear Billy tell he was a Harvard professor . . . anyway, him and me was in the Black Tree one night, him in his uniform an' all, and after a few drinks, snotty Billy Phillips got almost human on me. Started talkin' about what a bitch his ma was and how she'd kept him from havin' any fun . . . how she sent him away to college an' all rather'n let him marry the woman he loved . . ."

Mike interrupted. "Did he say who that woman was?"

Mink squinted and licked his lips. "Huh? No . . . I don't think . . . no, I'm sure he didn't name nobody . . . probably one of them schoolmarm types he hung around with. One little old lady 'mongst a bunch of 'em's the way we thought about Billy Phillips. Where was I?"

"Having a drink with Billy . . . he got human . . ."

"OK, yeah. Me an' Billy was hoistin' a few on the night before he was to go over to France where he got killed . . . died of pneumonia or some damn thing . . . and after he got sort of loose, he says to me, 'Mink . . . ,' they called me Mink way back then, 'Mink, you know that little girl an' her petticoat an' the alleged crime an' all?' Billy was always usin' fifty-cent words like 'alleged,' probably thinkin' that everybody in Elm Haven was too stupid to understand him . . ."

"And what did he say about the petticoat?" prompted Mike.

"Heh? Oh, he says, 'Mink, it wasn't that nigger's petticoat at all. I never went nowhere near that nigger. It was Judge Ashley who paid me a silver dollar to hide that petticoat in the nigger's bedroll.' You see, the way Billy'd figured it when he was just a little snot, was that the Judge knew who'd done it, and needed Billy's help to get him, 'cause they just didn't have no evidence an' all. But I guess when Billy got older, after goin' off to college to get smart an' all, he musta figured what the dumbest Polack in town could figure out . . . which is, namely, where in hell did the *Judge* get that little girl's underclothes?"

Mike leaned closer. "Did you ask him that?"

"Hmmm? No, don't think I did. Or if I did, I don't remember no answer. What I do remember is Billy sayin' somethin' about gettin' out of town before the Judge an' the others knew he wasn't with 'em no more."

"With who?" whispered Mike.

"How the hell do I know, boy?" growled Mink Harper. He leaned closer, squinted, and breathed wine fumes on Mike. "This was more'n forty years ago, y' know. What'ya think I am, a damn memory machine?"

Mike looked over his shoulder at the entrance to the crawlspace under the bandstand, a small rectangle of escape that seemed very far away. The sound of smaller kids playing in the park had long since faded; there was no traffic.

"Can you remember anything else about Old Central or the bell?" asked Mike, not flinching away from Mink's inspection.

Face inches from Mike's, Mink showed his three teeth again. "Never seen or heard the bell again . . . not till last month when it woke me up from a deep sleep here in my dry little home . . . but I know one thing . . ."

"What's that?" Mike found it very hard not to lean back out of the range of Mink's breath and stare.

"I know that when Old Man Ashley stuck his two-barreled Boss shotgun in his mouth and pulled the trigger 'bout a year after the war was over . . . the First War, I mean . . . that he done us all a favor. Burned down his goddamn house, too. His boy came home from Peoria where the old man's new grandbaby was just born, and he found his pappy . . . the Judge that was . . . lyin' dead with his brains blowed out. Everybody thinks it was either a accident or the ol' Judge who burned the place . . . wasn't . . . I happened to be out in the gardenin' shed with one of the servants when I seen the young Mr. Ashley's carriage comin'—he called himself Ashley-Montague after he married that fancy woman from Venice—yeah, I was in the gardenin' shed when we heard the shot and saw Mr. Ashley-Montague go in, then come out bawlin' and shoutin' at the sky and spreadin' kerosene oil everywhere on the big house. One of the servants tried to stop him . . . there'd been more of 'em at the house but they'd been laid off during that recession after the war . . . but there was no stoppin' him. He threw that oil everywhere an' lit it up and stood back to watch it burn. They never come home after that, him and his bride and the baby. Jes' to show the goddamn Free Show, that's all."

Mike nodded, thanked Mink, and scrambled for the opening, suddenly eager to get back out into the sunlight. At the exit, his body out into the fresh air, Mike asked one more question. "Mink, what did he shout?"

"Whaddya mean, boy?" the old man seemed to have forgotten what they had been talking about.

"The Judge's son. When he burned the place down. What was he shouting?"

Mink's three teeth gleamed yellowly in the dimness. "Oh, he was shoutin' that they wasn't gonna get him . . . no, by God, they wasn't gonna get him."

Mike let out a breath. "I don't suppose he said who 'they' were?"

Mink frowned, pursed his lips in a parody of deep thought, and then grinned again. "Yeah, he did, now that I 'member it. Called the guy by name."

"Guy?"

"Yeah . . . Cyrus, only pronounced like that flat cloud . . . cirrus. He kept saying 'No, O'Cyrus, you ain't gonna get me.' The way he said it, I thought maybe it was some Irishman's name. O'Cirrus."

"Thanks, Mink." Mike stood up, feeling his shirt plastered to his body, wiping a bead of perspiration from his nose. His hair was wet and his legs felt shaky for some reason. He found his bike, crossed the Hard Road, noticed how long the shadows were getting, and pedaled slowly up Broad under the canopy of arching branches. He was remembering Duane's notebooks and the slow translation he and Dale had done from the Gregg shorthand. The part where Duane had copied bits from his uncle's diary was especially tough. One word had sent them checking the squiggles and codes over and over again; Dale had recognized it from some book he'd read about Egypt: *Osiris*.

TWENTY-NINE

Dale, Lawrence, Kevin, and Harlen left on their camping trip after lunch the next day, Wednesday the thirteenth of July. Only Harlen's mother had been slow to give permission for the trip, but she relented, as Harlen put it, "when she realized she could go out on a date while I was gone."

They had a ton of stuff to carry and it was difficult piling it on their bikes and tying it down properly. Once secured, the heaps of sleeping bags, food, gear, and backpacks weighed down their already heavy bicycles so they had to pedal standing up the entire way out to Uncle Henry's, leaning over the handlebars and grunting with exertion on the hard-packed ruts between the loose gravel on Jubilee College Road and County Six.

There were patches of timber—of a sort—along the railroad tracks northwest of town, but those woods were small and too near the dump for real camping. The real woods were a mile and a half away, east of Uncle Henry's farm and north of the Billy Goat Mountains quarry behind the cemetery. Near where Mink Harper had found the bones of Merriweather Whittaker along Gypsy Lane almost fifty years earlier.

The boys had met in Mike's treehouse for almost three hours on Tuesday night, comparing notes from their trips and making plans until the sound of Kev's mother's bellowing—"Ke-VINNN!"—had echoed down Depot Street and effectively adjourned the meeting.

The leatherbound book that Dale had stolen from Mr. Ashley-Montague—an act that not even he fully believed after he had returned to Elm Haven—was a mass of foreign phrases, arcane rituals, complicated explanations of unpronounceable deities or anti-deities, and a mess of cabalistic, numerological double-talk. "Hardly worth getting your ass thrown in jail for" had been Jim Harlen's verdict.

But somewhere in the tight print, Dale was sure, there would be mention of Osiris or the Stele of Revealing that Duane's notebooks had spoken of. Dale brought the book with him on the camping trip; just another bit of weight to lug over the hills.

All four of the boys had been tense on the ride out, looking over their shoulders as every truck approached and every car passed. But the Rendering Truck did not appear, and the most aggressive act aimed at them during the slow ride out to Uncle Henry's was a little kid—possibly a boy, but it was hard to tell through the matted hair and dirty face— sticking his tongue out at them from the backseat of an overloaded '53 DeSoto.

They rested on the shady back patio at Uncle Henry's while Aunt Lena made lemonade for them and sat in the Adirondack chair awhile, discussing the best places to camp. She thought the empty pasture would be good—there was a nice view of the creek and surrounding hills from it, but the boys were insistent about camping in the woods.

"Where is Michael O'Rourke?" she asked.

"Oh, he had work to do in town. Stuff at the church or something," lied Jim Harlen. "He'll come later."

The four boys hiked east out through the barnyard at about three o'clock, leaving their bikes in the safekeeping of Aunt Lena. Their back-packs were makeshift affairs: Lawrence's inexpensive Cub Scout pack made of nylon; Kev's canvas army pack that he borrowed from his dad, the whole thing smelling of mildew; Dale's long, clumsy duffel bag, more suited to a canoe trip than this long hike; and Harlen's bulky bedroll, little more than some blankets wrapped around his junk and secured with what looked to be about a hundred yards of rope and twine. There were many halts for small adjustments and reshiftings of load.

By three-thirty they had crossed the creek near the Bootleggers' Cave and had climbed the barbed-wire fence on the south end of Uncle Henry's property. The heavy woods started almost immediately. It was cooler there out of the direct sunlight, although the canopy of leaves was not so thick as to prevent dappled areas and even broad swatches of sun on the low grass.

They slid and tumbled down the steeper part of the slope to the ra-vine north of the cemetery, Harlen's bedroll giving away completely dur-ing that maneuver so that they spent another ten minutes picking up his stuff, and then they crossed the Robin Hood Log a few hundred yards from Camp Three and headed east again, following cattle trails up the hillsides and staying within the edge of trees when there was a small glade.

Occasionally they would stop, dump their stuff, and spread out the way Mike had taught them, moving into prearranged positions and wait-ing in the best silence they could manage for several long minutes. Ex-cept for one lone cow that wandered into their area of observation on the third try—and who seemed much more startled than they were when they jumped out to scare it away—there was no sign or sound of anyone except themselves. They shouldered packs, hitched up bags and bedrolls, and plodded off deeper into the woods.

They made quite a deal about arguing over where to camp, but in truth the site had been decided on the evening before. They set up the two small pup tents—one belonging to Kevin's dad, the other a relic from Dale's father's past—on the edge of a small copse of trees in a glade about five hundred yards north of the quarry and a quarter of a mile northeast of Calvary Cemetery. Gypsy Lane ran north to south about five hundred feet west of them.

The glade was on a gradual hillside, the grass in it a little lower than knee-high and already tanned to the color of wheat by the hot summer. Grasshoppers leaped aside as they moved purposely to set up the tents, hollow out the campfire site, and set stones in a fire ring. The heavier woods started about sixty feet to the west, a little less than twenty feet to the south and east. There was a tributary to the main creek just down the hill to the north.

Normally they would have played Robin Hood or hide-and-seek to fill up the hours until dinner, but this day they just lolled around the camp or lay talking along the edge of trees behind the camp. They tried lying in the tents and talking, but the sun-heated canvas was too much for them, and the lumpy old sleeping bags were not as soft as the grass outside.

Dale tried to read his stolen book. There *was* mention of Osiris, but although the text was in English—mostly—it might as well have been a foreign language for all Dale could understand. There was talk of the god commanding legions of the undead, of predictions and punishment, but none of it made real sense.

The sky between the leaves stayed blue; no sudden storm came up to drive them back to Uncle Henry's. It was the one thing they had not had an answer to when they were planning the trip—only retreat had seemed a sane thing to do. Visibility would be too poor in a storm, their hearing too compromised.

They ate early, first devouring all the snacks that they'd packed, then getting the fire started and cooking the hot dogs they'd brought along. Finding the right sticks to hold the weenies took awhile, whittling their points to sharpened perfection took a while longer. Every time Lawrence said something about looking forward to weenies, Harlen giggled.

"What is it?" asked Dale finally. "Share the joke."

Harlen started to explain, said something about Cordie Cooke, then shook his head. "Forget it."

It was still hot by seven P.M. and Lawrence wanted to head over to the quarry and jump in. The others vetoed it, reminding him patiently of the plan. Harlen wanted to cook marshmallows over the fire by seven-thirty, but the others insisted that they wait until dark. It was proper protocol. Kevin was antsy, ready to get into their sleeping bags by eight P.M., but the evening shadows had just covered the glade by then and there was still ample light to see by, even in the woods.

Twenty minutes after that, however, the low areas north of them grew cool and dark. Shortly after that, fireflies appeared in the dark areas between the trees, winking like distant flashes of silent gunfire. The chorus of bullfrogs from the quarry and tree frogs from the marshy area down the hill started up about then, filling the encroaching twilight with sound. The crickets and cicadas in the woods behind the boys were very loud.

By eight forty-five, the sky had paled, then darkened to the level that stars were visible and at some point it was difficult to tell the masses of dark leaves from the darkening sky. The woods grew black. The last sounds of traffic from County Six half a mile to the west ceased as the last workingmen had passed north toward home and the drinking men went past south on their way to the Black Tree or town. For a while, if they strained, the boys could hear the metallic flap of the lids on the automatic pig feeders at Uncle Henry's, but it was a small and distant sound which died away with the last of the light.

Finally it was dark. For all its summer gradualness, night seemed to have suddenly descended on and around them.

Dale fed small limbs to the fire. Embers rose into the night, drifting up and out of the glade toward the stars. The boys grew closer together, their faces lighted from below. They tried to sing but found they had no will to do so. Harlen suggested that they tell ghost stories and the others scowled him into silence.

The stream down the hill made soft swallowing sounds. There was a sense of things awakening in the dark woods to hunt, the thought of many eyes opening out there, vertical irises widening to let in what little starlight there was in order to find prey.

Beneath the insect chorus and distant rumble-croak of a hundred species of frogs, there came the imagined sound of predators moving on padded feet through the night, beginning their stalk for fresh meat.

The boys tugged on sweatshirts and old sweaters, threw more wood on the fire, and sat closer until their shoulders almost touched. The fire crackled and spat, transforming their faces into demonic masks, until soon the orange glow was the only light in their world.

Mike's main problem was staying awake. He'd been up much of the night before, sitting in the old chair in Memo's room with his bottle of holy water in one hand and the consecrated Host wrapped in a handker-chief in his other hand. His mother came in to check on Memo around three A.M. and shooed him upstairs, clucking at him for his silliness. Mike had left the Host on the windowsill.

He'd checked on Father Cavanaugh after finishing his paper route; the priest was gone and Mrs. McCafferty was beside herself with worry. The doctors had decided to move Father C. to St. Francis Hospital in Peoria, but when the ambulance arrived on Tuesday evening, the priest was gone. Mrs. McCafferty swore to them that she had been working in the kitchen downstairs the entire time and would have heard him if he had come down the stairs . . . besides which, she swore, he was too ill to *come* down the stairs . . . but the doctors had shaken their heads and said that obviously the sick man did not fly away. While Mike and the other boys had been comparing notes in his treehouse and trying to decipher some of the cryptic book Dale had stolen from Mr. Ashley-Montague, there had been a search of the town by Mrs. McC. and several of the parishioners. No sign of Father Cavanaugh.

"I would swear on my rosary that the poor father was too ill to lift his head, much less wander off," Mrs. McCafferty had said to Mike while dabbing at her eyes with her apron.

"Maybe he went home," Mike had said, not believing it for a sec-ond.

"Home? To Chicago?" The housekeeper chewed on her lower lip as she considered the idea. "But how? The diocese car is still in the garage and the Galesburg-Chicago bus won't come through until tomorrow."

Mike had shrugged, promised to inform her and Dr. Staffney im-mediately if he heard of Father C.'s whereabouts, and then had gone into the sacristy to get ready to say Mass with the fill-in priest from Oak Hill. All through the service—said in a bored, droning voice by the visit-ing priest and responded to absently by the distracted altar boy—Mike had thought of the brown slugs sliding in, writhing under Father C.'s flesh. *What if he's one of* them *now?*

The thought made Mike feel sick.

He had made his mother swear she would check in on Memo that night, and then had hedged his bets by sprinkling the floor and window with holy water and placing bits of the broken Eucharist in the corners of the screen and at the foot of Memo's bed. Leaving Memo alone this night was the one part of the plan he hated.

Then Mike had packed his drugstore backpack and left before the other boys had started out. The tension of the ride out to County Six had cleared his head somewhat, but the nights without sleep still weighed on him and filled his ears with a soft buzz.

Mike hadn't gone all the way to Uncle Henry's farm, but had opened the stock gate just beyond Calvary Cemetery and ridden in along the fence on the overgrown ruts there, hiding his bike in a patch of fir trees just above the ravine and then doubling back, waiting for Dale and the others to come by. They had, almost ninety minutes later, and Mike had let out a soft grunt of relief: the chance of the Rendering Truck intercepting them had been something they couldn't plan for except to arrange a noon rendezvous back by the water tower.

Mike stayed in the woods during the boys' visit to Uncle Henry's farm, watching through the binoculars he'd borrowed from his father. The left lens of the glasses that his dad used to take out to the Chicago horse track didn't work too well—it was slightly clouded—but it worked well enough that Mike could see his friends sitting and slurping lemonade with Aunt Lena while he sat sweltering and itchy in the bushes.

Later, he followed them deeper into the woods, staying at least fifty feet away, moving parallel to their path—it helped that he knew exactly where they were headed—and trying not to be seen or heard. He'd worn a green polo shirt and old cotton slacks so as to provide some camouflage, with a change of dark clothing for the night, but he wished he had some real camouflage combat clothes.

Mike shook his head again. The difficult part was staying awake.

He had staked out an observation post at the top of the ravine less than twenty yards from where Dale and the others were camping, and it was a perfect spot; two rocks shielded him from view but allowed him a vertical viewing slit to the campsite and glade beyond; three trees grew thickly behind him, allowing no approach from his blind spot; he had taken a fallen limb and excavated a low trench so that he and his stuff were completely out of sight below the level of the rocks and shrubs, but still he had camouflaged the site further with broken branches and a fallen log pulled closer to his left.

Mike laid out his stuff: a bottle of drinking water and a bottle of holy water—marked with crayon on masking tape so as not to get them confused, his sandwiches and snacks, the binoculars, the largest section of the Host wrapped and secured in the breast pocket of his polo shirt, and finally—removed from the pack with great care—Memo's squirrel gun.

He realized now why the thing must be illegal—eighteen inches of shotgun barrel and the walnut pistol grip, it *looked* like something a Chicago mobster would use back in the thirties to blast a rival mobster. Mike opened the breech with a soft click of the securing lever on top, smelling oil as he held the barrel up to catch the last light of evening down the smooth bore. There had been shells in the box with Memo's gun, but they looked very old so Mike had worked up his nerve and gone down to

Meyers' Hardware to buy a new box of .410 longs. Mr. Meyers had raised one eyebrow and said, "I didn't know your daddy went hunting, Michael."

"He doesn't," Mike had said truthfully. "He's just real tired of the crows getting into the garden."

Now, as the last vestiges of twilight faded, Mike set the new box of shells in front of him, inserted one into the breech, clicked the squirrel gun shut, and stared down the long barrel at the boys around their campfire fifty feet away. It was too far away for the short-barreled shotgun; Mike knew that. Even Dale's over-and-under couldn't hit much at this range, and the sawed-off thing Mike was aiming was useless beyond a few yards. But within that closer radius, he knew the pattern of shot would be a terrible thing. Mike had bought Number Six shot—suitable for quail or larger things.

The thicket to the south of where Dale, Kev, Lawrence, and Harlen had set up camp would make silent approach impossible and *any* approach almost impossible. Mike was perched on the edge of the ravine to the north; it would be very difficult for anyone to cross the stream and climb that bluff without making a lot of noise. That left an approach through the thinning woods to the east or across the glade to the west. Mike could see both approaches clearly from his vantage point, although the fading light made it difficult to see much detail now. The voices of his friends chatting around the fire seemed soft and muted as the sound drifted across the cooling air to him.

The squirrel gun had a notched rear sight and a small bead sight on the end of the barrel, although both were more for ornamentation than use. One pointed the thing and pulled the trigger, allowing the widening cloud of birdshot to do the aiming. As darkness fell, Mike realized that his hand was slippery on the walnut pistol-grip. He fumbled in the box of shells, set two extra cartridges in his shirt pocket, several more in his pockets, and then put the box back in his pack. He clicked on the safety and set the weapon on pine needles beside the rock, forcing his breathing into a more steady rhythm and chewing on a peanut butter and jelly sandwich he'd packed in a hurry that morning. The smell of hot dogs across the glade had got his appetite going.

His friends turned in shortly after dark. Mike had tugged on his black sweater and changed into a dark pair of pants, and now sat forward expectantly, peering into the dimness, trying to ignore the background insect and frog sounds to pick out any noise, to look past the shifting leaf-shadows and firefly blinks to find any hint of movement. There was none.

He watched as Dale and Lawrence settled into the open pup tent nearest the fire, their feet visible as lumps in two sleeping bags illuminated by the flickering light. Kevin and Harlen crawled into Kev's tent a few yards to the left and farther from the fire. Mike could see where Kev's ballcap was just visible at the opening of his sleeping bag. Harlen had obviously settled in the opposite direction, and the soles of his sneakers stuck out of his bedroll. Mike rubbed his eyes, stared harder into the gloom while trying not to look directly at the fire, and hoped that they had all listened carefully to him.

Who made me boss and king? He shook his head tiredly.

Staying awake was the hard part. Several times Mike started to drift off, only to snap awake when his chin touched his chest. He rearranged himself so that he was leaning uncomfortably into the crack between the rocks, his arm beneath him, so that if he drifted off, the weight of his body would come down heavily on his arm and wake him.

Despite the awkwardness of the position, he was half dozing when he realized that someone was coming across the glade.

Two forms were moving slowly from the west—from the direction of County Six—moving with the deliberation of hunters with branches underfoot. They were tall forms, clearly adults. They took a step, paused. Took another step. They set their feet deliberately, their motion a ballet of silent stalking.

Mike felt his heart begin to pound so wildly that it hurt his chest and made him dizzy. He gripped the squirrel gun in both hands in front of him, remembered the safety, and clicked it off. His fingers were sweaty and felt oddly numb.

The two tall figures were twenty feet from the boys' camp now and pausing, almost invisible in the blackness. Only starlight on their eyes and hands gave them away when they were not moving. Mike leaned forward, straining to see. The men were carrying something—walking sticks? Then Mike caught the glint of starlight on steel and realized that both men carried axes.

Mike's breathing hitched, stopped, then staggered on. He forced himself not to fixate on the two men—they were clearly men, tall, long-legged, wearing dark clothes—but to extend his senses around him. All this secrecy and planning and waiting would be for nothing if someone were sneaking up behind Mike.

There wasn't anyone behind him. At least not as far as he could tell. But there was movement in the trees *behind* the tents. Mike could see motion there now. At least one more man, approaching as slowly as the two in the glade, but not as silently. This one was shorter and was less successful in avoiding dry sticks underfoot. Still, if Mike had not known which way they had to come from, he would not have seen or heard them.

A wind came up, stirring leaves overhead. The two figures in the glade took advantage of the covering sound to move five steps closer to the camp. The axes were raised across their chests in a port-arms position. Mike tried to swallow, found his mouth dry, and forced spit into it.

Mike shook his head violently, trying to separate this reality from his dreamscape. He was so *tired*.

The three men had converged on the camp now. They stood just beyond the glow of the fire, long-legged shadows within shadows. Mike saw starlight gleam and realized that the third figure, the one farthest away from him, was also carrying an ax or something long and metallic. Mike literally prayed that it was not a rifle or shotgun.

It won't be. They *don't want the noise.*

Mike's hand was shaking as he extended both arms across the top of the flat rock, aiming the shotgun at the two figures but keeping the sights high enough that the buckshot wouldn't rip into the low pup tents.

Fire. Fire now. No. He had to be sure. That was the whole idea . . . to be sure. *What if these guys are farmers out clearing some timber? At midnight?* Mike didn't believe it for a second. But he did not fire. The idea of firing a weapon at a human being made his arms shake all the more wildly. He braced them against the top of the rock and gritted his teeth.

The two men on this side of the fire moved silently around the dying campfire now. The embers illuminated only dark clothing, high boots. The men's faces were hidden under caps pulled low. There was no sound or motion from the pup tents. Mike could still see the bulges where Dale and Lawrence's feet would be in the sleeping bags, Kev's ballcap, Harlen's sneakers. The man on the far side of the campsite moved in amongst the trees there, stepped closer to Kevin's tent.

Mike had the urge to scream a warning, to rise up and shout, to fire the squirrel gun in the air. He did nothing. He had to *know*. He wished he'd chosen an observation post closer to the campsite. He wished he had a rifle or pistol with greater range. Everything seemed wrong, miscalculated. . . .

Mike forced himself to concentrate. The three men were standing there, two near Dale and Lawrence's tent, one near Kev and Harlen's. They did not speak. It seemed as if they were waiting for the boys inside the tents to awaken and join them. Mike had a dizzying instant where he imagined that this tableau would remain the same all night—the silent figures, the silent tents, the fire growing dimmer and dimmer until he could see nothing at all.

Suddenly the two closer men stepped forward and swung their axes in a silent blur, slamming through the tent canvas, ripping into the sleeping bags beneath. A split second later the third man swung his ax into Kevin's cap.

The ferocity of the attack was so sudden, so unannounced, that Mike was taken totally by surprise. He gasped aloud as the wind was knocked out of him by the reality of events.

The two closer men raised their axes again, slammed them down again. Mike heard the blades cutting through collapsed canvas, through the sleeping bags and the contents of the bags, and chunking into the soil beneath. They raised the axes a third time. Behind them, the shorter man was swinging wildly, grunting loudly as he did so. Mike watched as one of Harlen's sneakers flew free, landing near the fire. A shredded bit of red sock—or something else red—still clung to it.

The men were gasping and panting now, grunting at each other in nonsense syllables, making animal noises. The axes rose again.

Mike pulled the hammer back, cocked it, squeezed the trigger. The flare of the shotgun blast blinded him; the recoil threw his locked hands and arms back high, made him almost drop the gun.

He gasped for breath, saw both men still standing but turning now, eyes gleaming in the last light, and then Mike was fumbling for another shell. They were in his breast pocket, under the black sweater he'd tugged on.

Mike got to his knees, feeling in his jeans pocket for a shell. He opened the breech, tried to shake the spent cartridge out. It stuck. His fingernails found purchase on the brass rim. It burned his fingers as he tugged it out, slammed home a second shell, clicked the breech shut.

One of the men had jumped the fire and was moving in his direction. The second had frozen, ax still high. The third grunted something and continued to hack away at what was left of Kevin and Harlen's collapsed tent, slashed bags.

The first man landed on this side of the fire and rushed toward Mike with a great pounding of boots. Mike raised the squirrel gun, thumbed the hammer back, and fired. The blast was tremendous.

He ducked down, flung out the empty cartridge, loaded another. When he rolled back up, the man was gone—down in the weeds or gone. The other two seemed frozen in firelight.

Then the noise and madness began.

Flames erupted from the thick timber less than ten yards south of the campsite. Another shotgun roared. The third man seemed yanked backward by invisible wires, ax flying and turning in the air to land directly in the flames, the man himself rolling into the high weeds of the glade. A pistol fired—Mike could tell it was a .45 caliber semiautomatic by the rapid, heavy coughs—three shots, pause, three more shots. Another pistol joined the mad moment, firing as rapidly as the unseen shooter could pull the trigger. There was a high slap of a .22 being fired, then a shotgun again.

The third man ran. Right toward Mike.

Mike stood up, waited until the pounding figure was twenty feet from him, and fired Memo's squirrel gun at the gleam of the man's eyes.

The man's cap or part of his skull flew high behind him. The figure threw the ax in Mike's direction and went down, scrabbling and moaning through high weeds, sliding down the ravine to the northeast with a crashing of vines and saplings. Some large insect buzzed right past Mike's ear and he ducked down just as the ax struck the rock with a shower of sparks and spanged away to his left.

Mike reloaded, raised the squirrel gun, swiveling with both hands on the pistol grip, arms straight, breathing through his mouth, and had the hammer cocked and pressure on the trigger before he realized that the glade and campsite area was empty except for the slashed and silent tents and the dying fire. He remembered the plan.

"Go!" he shouted and ducked down, sweeping up his pack and running northwest between the glade and the edge of the ravine. He felt branches snapping off as he smashed them with his shoulders and head, felt something gouge a long scratch along one cheek, and then he was at the first checkpoint—the fallen log where the cow path ran along the steepest part of the ravine.

He dropped behind it, raised the weapon.

Footsteps pounded from his right.

Mike squinted, whistled once. The running figure whistled twice in return and ran past without slowing. Mike tapped him on the shoulder.

Two more forms, two return whistles. Backpack snaps jingled as they hurried past. Mike tapped them on the shoulder. Another form approached in the darkness. Mike whistled, heard no response, aimed Memo's squirrel gun at the midsection of the hurtling figure.

"It's me!" gasped Jim Harlen.

Mike felt the sling under his hand as he tapped Harlen on the shoulder as the smaller boy hustled past, Keds pounding on the bare dirt path under the low trees.

Mike crouched behind the wide log and waited another minute, counting seconds by Boy Scouts, squirrel gun raised. It was a very long minute. Then he was moving along the trail, hunkered low, backpack over his left shoulder and the gun in his right hand, head always moving, trusting his peripheral vision. He felt like he'd been running for miles but realized that it had been only a few hundred yards.

There was a low whistle ahead of him and to his left. He returned three whistles. A hand tapped his shoulder as he moved past and Mike caught a glimpse of Kevin's dad's .45 automatic. Then Mike found the cutoff, the slight bend in the trail, and he rolled into the high weeds there, feeling brambles but ignoring them, whistling once, letting Kevin move past, and covering the trail both north and south for another forty-five Boy Scouts before he allowed himself to slide down the hillside himself, trying to keep as silent as possible on the soft loam and thick carpet of old leaves.

For a second Mike couldn't find the opening in the solid mass of brambles and bushes, but then his hand found the secret entrance and he was squirming in on his belly, sliding into the solid circle of Camp Three.

A penlight winked in his face, went out. The other four were whispering urgently, their voices high on adrenaline and euphoria and terror.

"Shut up," hissed Mike. He took the penlight from Kevin's hand and went around the circle of faces, almost whispering in each boy's ear—"All right?"—"You OK?" Everyone was all right. All five of them, including Mike, were present and accounted for. There were no extra bodies.

"Fan out," whispered Mike and they moved to the edges of the circle, listening, Kevin to the left of the only entrance with his automatic reloaded and ready.

Mike sprinkled holy water on the ground and branches. He hadn't seen the things that left the holes, but the night was far from over.

They listened. Somewhere an owl called. The chorus of crickets and frogs—stilled for a while by the explosions of gunfire—had started up again, but was slightly muffled here halfway down the hillside. Far away, a car or small truck passed over the hills on County Six.

After thirty minutes of silent listening, the boys huddled together near the entrance. The urge to babble had passed, but they took turns whispering, their heads almost together so the sound couldn't be heard outside of Camp Three.

"I couldn't believe they really *did* it," Lawrence was gasping.

"Didja see my fucking sneaker!" Harlen kept hissing at them. "Chopped it right off the edge of the sweatshirt I'd stuffed in 'em."

"All our stuff's chopped to bits," whispered Kev. "My hat. All the stuff I'd put in the sleeping bag."

Gradually, Mike got them off their soft exclamations and wild-eyed descriptions, and had them report. They'd done what the plan had called for. Dale thought the waiting for dark was the hardest, cooking hot dogs and roasting marshmallows as if they were just camping. Then they'd settled into their tents, stuffing their bedrolls and bags, slipping out one by one to the prearranged positions in the deadfall behind the campsite.

"I was layin' on a fuckin' *anthill*," whispered Harlen and the others stifled laughter until Mike ordered them to shut up.

Mike had set out the ambush positions so that they wouldn't be firing across the campsite at each other—they'd all be firing northeast or northwest—but Kevin confessed that in his excitement after the men had chopped up the tent, he'd fired toward Mike's position. Mike shrugged, although now he seemed to remember something humming past his ear just after the second man had thrown the ax at him.

"OK," he whispered, drawing the others closer with an arm across their backs, "so now we know. But it's not over. We can't leave until morning . . . that's hours away. They could be getting reinforcements . . . and not all the reinforcements are human."

He let that sink in. He didn't want to scare them to the point they couldn't function, just keep them alert. "But I don't think that'll be the way it happens," he whispered, his head touching Kevin's and Dale's. They were like a football team in a huddle. "I think we hurt 'em. I think they're gone for the night. In the morning, we'll check the campsite, get whatever stuff we can, and get the hell out of here. Who brought some blankets?"

They'd planned on keeping five for Camp Three, but somehow they'd only hung on to three. Mike pulled out an extra jacket, assigned two people to watch for the first hour—Kev had a glow-in-the-dark wristwatch dial—assigned himself first watch with Dale, and told the others to turn in. No more whispering.

But he and Dale whispered a bit as they crouched by the opening in the solid wall of high bushes.

"They really did it," Dale whispered, echoing his little brother's statement twenty minutes earlier. "They really tried to kill us."

Mike nodded, not sure if the other boy could see him even from two feet away. "Yeah. Now we know they're trying to do to us what they did to Duane."

"Because they figure that we know?"

"Maybe not," Mike whispered back. "Maybe they're just going to get all of us on general principles. But now we know. And we can go ahead."

"But what if they use . . . the other things?" whispered Dale. Harlen or somebody was snoring very softly, his white socks glowing from where they stuck out from under the blanket.

Mike still clutched the bottle of holy water. The squirrel gun was in his other hand, loaded, needing only the click of the safety and the pull of a hammer. "Then we get them, too," he said. He wasn't as confident as he sounded.

"God," whispered Dale. It sounded more like a prayer than a curse. Mike nodded, huddled closer, and waited for dawn.

THIRTY

Just after first light they went back to search for bodies.

It was one of the longest nights Dale Stewart could ever remember. At first there was the terror, excitement, and adrenaline rush to ride on, but after the first watch with Mike, when it was Dale's turn to sleep with several hours left until dawn, there remained only the terror. It was a deep, sick-making terror, a fear of the dark combined with the startle-awake sound of someone breathing under your bed. It was the terror of embalming tools and the blade at the eye, the terror of the cold hand on the back of your neck in a dark room. Dale had known fear before, the fear of the coal bin and the basement, the fear of the all-enveloping black circle of C.J. Congden's rifle aimed at him, the testicle-raising fear of the corpse in the water in his basement . . . but this terror went beyond fear. Dale felt as if nothing was to be trusted. The ground might open and swallow him up . . . literally . . . there were *things* under the soil, other things of the night just beyond the flimsy circle of branches that was their only protection. The men with axes might be waiting just beyond the leaves and branches, their eyes dead but bright, with no breath rising and falling in their chests but with a rattle of anticipation in their throats.

It was a long night.

Everybody was awake at the first hint of gray through the thick branches overhead. By five-thirty A.M.—according to Kevin's watch— they were packed up and moving back along the trail, Mike thirty paces in the lead, calling the others forward with hand signals, freezing them into immobility with a motion.

A hundred yards from the campsite they fanned out, moving apart and abreast, each keeping two others in sight while they slowly advanced from tree to tree, shrub to shrub, staying low in the high grass there. Finally they could see the tents, still collapsed—Dale had half expected to find everything unharmed, the violence of the night before only a shared nightmare—but even from a distance they could see the smashed tents, hacked canvas, and scattered clothing. An ax lay blackened and half-buried in the ashes of the fire. Harlen's left sneaker lay near it.

They advanced slowly, allowing Mike on the north wing and Dale on the south wing to almost encircle the campsite. Dale was sure that he would see the bodies first . . . one in the glade where Mike had shot the first man, another on the edge of the ravine . . . but they found no bodies.

Their first temptation was to paw through the wreckage of their camp, making jokes and laughing with the release of tension, but Mike made them fan out again, sweeping southeast all the way to the quarry, north to the fence bordering Uncle Henry's property, east back almost to the road. There were no bodies.

But they found blood. Spatters of blood in the glade, about where the man Mike shot at would have gone down. Blood on rocks and shrubs in the ravine. More blood on the opposite side of the little valley, near the fence.

"Got one of the bastards," said Harlen, but his bravado sounded hollow in the sunlight, with the blood already drying to brown patches on weeds and fallen logs. There were great amounts of the stuff. The thought that they had actually shot someone—a human being—made Dale's knees go weak. Then he remembered the axes rising and falling on the tent where he would have been sleeping.

They returned to the camp, eager to salvage what they could and be gone. A single ax lay charred and blackened in the campfire ashes.

"My dad will be upset," said Kev, folding the remains of his tent.

"My old lady'll shit bricks and kittens," said Harlen, holding up the remains of his blanket and peering through one of the rents in it. He looked at Kevin through the hole. "You can say the tent blew over into a barbed-wire fence, but what can I say about my best blanket? That I was having a wild wet dream and humped it to death?"

"What's a wet dr—" began Lawrence.

"Never mind," Dale said quickly. "Let's get this stuff loaded, bury what we don't want to haul back, and then get out of here."

They carried their shotguns and pistols and squirrel guns openly until they crossed the fence and were almost in sight of Uncle Henry's. Then they broke them down or put them in packs and duffel bags. Dale had let Lawrence carry the Savage over-and-under once they were out of the woods, literally, but he'd kept the .410 and .22 shells in his pocket. The gun seemed heavy after an hour of toting it, but it was shorter and lighter than most shotguns. The night before, during the shooting, Dale had wished that he'd brought his dad's pump shotgun, despite its weight and size. Firing one shell from each barrel of the over-and-under and then opening the breech to reload had been maddening. Dale remembered glancing past the rock where Lawrence had been crouching, staring with wide eyes, at Kevin and Harlen on their knees in the thicket, firing their pistols—the heavy cough of Kevin's .45 and the impressive flash and blare of Jim's snub-nosed .38 making Dale want to cover his ears. *Did we really do that?*

They had. They'd just spent thirty minutes picking up all the spent brass and hunting for all the discarded shotgun shells, burying them fifty feet from their former campsite with the blankets, sleeping bags, and tents too torn to carry home. Mike had retrieved his bike.

Aunt Lena offered them breakfast, but the boys didn't have time for it. Uncle Henry was going into town and they scrambled to throw their bikes in the back of his pickup and clamber in themselves.

The long ride home was the part of this that Dale and the others had been dreading. Now the long bike ride became a few minutes of clatter and dust, gravel flying behind the truck as they roared down the steep hill past the cemetery into the shadow of the glen. There was still dew on the corn and weeds by the road.

"Look!" Lawrence said as they passed the Black Tree.

They looked. The place was closed and dark under the big trees at the edge of the ravine, even the owner's car gone. The horizontal light lay low and heavy across the gravel driveway.

But something sat far back in the low trees at the west side of the lot. A truck. Dale caught a glimpse of scabrous red paint, foliage reflected on a windshield half-hidden by branches, the sense of a high-sided truck-bed deeper in the shadows.

"The Rendering Truck?" called Kevin over the noise in the back of the pickup. They were already to the junction of Jubilee College Road, and the truck had not emerged from the parking area.

Mike shrugged. "Could be."

Dale felt himself beginning to shake and he gripped the side of the pickup to stop it. His forearms strained with the effort. He imagined them coming up that long grade, panting and bent over their handlebars, tired from the long night and the hill, and suddenly that red nightmare coming to life with a roar of its V-8 engine, squeaking and weaving and throwing gravel behind it as it leaped out of hiding, sweeping across the driveway in two seconds, the stench of decomposing livestock corpses coming in front of it like a shock wave.

The ditch was deep on the west side of the road there, the fence between them and the woods high. Could they have gotten off their bikes and into the trees in time?

And what if Van Syke had had a gun? Or what if he had wanted them to flee east into the woods, toward Gypsy Lane?

At that second, with the rows of corn tall on either side, the sun already high in the sky and the water tower approaching and the cloud of dust broiling behind the pickup, Dale was totally and absolutely certain that something *had been* waiting in those woods for them.

They still would be there. Only Uncle Henry's offhand offer to drive them into town had turned their plan from a total nightmare into the limited success it was. Dale looked across the truckbed at Mike, his friend's gray eyes clouded with fatigue, and knew that Mike knew. Dale wanted to touch him on the shoulder, tell him that it was all right, that he couldn't have planned for everything . . . but his arms were shaking too badly to let go of the side of the truck just yet. And, more than that, Dale knew at that second that it *wasn't* all right, that Mike's miscalculation could have cost them their lives on this beautiful July morning.

What *was* waiting in the darkness of the woods back there?

Dale closed his eyes and thought of Mrs. Duggan, eight months dead . . . of Tubby Cooke the way Dale had seen him, white and bloated, the skin beginning to come off like white rubber that's rotted from the inside out . . . of long, moist things tunneling underfoot, jaws waiting under the thin blanket of loam and leaves . . . of the Soldier the way Mike had described it, face rippling and flowing into a lamprey's funnel ringed with teeth. . . .

They rode into town without speaking, waving tiredly as Uncle Henry dropped each of them off.

Evening fell a bit earlier this night than the last, almost imperceptibly so but enough to remind the careful observer that the solstice had passed and that the days were getting shorter rather than longer. The sunset was that long, achingly beautiful balance of stillness in which the sun seemed to hover like a red balloon above the western horizon, the entire sky catching fire from the death of day, a sunset unique to the American Midwest and ignored by most of its inhabitants. The twilight brought the promise of coolness and the certain threat of night.

Mike had meant to nap during the day—he was so tired that his eyelids felt gritty and his throat was sore from fatigue—but there was too much to do. "Vandals" had torn the screen off Memo's window during the night; Mike's mother had heard the noise and gone rushing in to see the breeze blowing papers and old sepia photographs off Memo's table, the curtains billowing out wildly into the yard as if someone had just passed through them.

Memo was all right, although agitated to the point that her blinking made no sense and she would not wait for questions to answer. Mike's mother was upset—at the vandalism, at the fact of her son's obsession coming true. She had called her husband at work and then called Barney, who had come over in the middle of the night, scratched his head, and said that vandals had been a problem that summer and asked Mrs. O'Rourke if Michael or any of the girls had had a run-in with C.J. Congden or Archie Kreck. Mike's mom had said that her girls were not allowed to *talk* to trash like Congden or Kreck and that Mike didn't have anything to do with them; then she asked if this vandalism and the Peeping Tom Mike had seen might be related to the killing of Mrs. Moon's cats—a crime the entire town was talking about. Barney had scratched his head again, promised that he'd patrol by their house more often, and gone about his business. Mike's dad had called back from the brewery and said that he'd been able to change shifts with someone and that after Saturday night, he'd be off nights for the entire summer rather than just three weeks.

Mike had repaired the screen—his mom had retrieved it and locked it in place, but the latch had been torn out of the sill and the frame had been broken in two places—and while doing so he noticed the slime. It was dried to the color and texture of old mucus and wasn't immediately visible because of the torn filaments of the screen itself. But it was there. Mike had touched it and shuddered.

Once, a couple of years earlier when Mike was eight or nine, he and his dad had been fishing on some dark tributary of the Spoon when Mike had hooked an eel. Freshwater eels were rare even on the broader Illinois River, and Mike had never seen one before. As soon as the long, yellow-green, snakelike body broke the surface, Mike had thought *water moccasin* and turned to run, forgetting for a second that he was in a rowboat. His dad caught him by a belt loop just as Mike was leaving the boat at high speed, and—intrigued by the writhing thing on the end of the boy's line—had reeled in first his son and then the eel, ordering Mike to use the net on it.

Mike remembered his revulsion and fascination at the thing. The eel's body was thicker than that of a snake, more reptilian and *ancient* somehow, and it rippled and flowed like something not spawned on this world. The body was coated with a layer of ooze, as if the thing secreted mucus. The long jaws were lined with needle-sharp teeth.

Mike's dad had tied off the net and lashed it to the side of the boat to keep the thing alive in the water until they returned to the bridge where they'd parked, and they slowly trolled back that way, Mike aware of the writhing thing just below the waterline. But when they beached the small boat, the eel was gone. It had somehow slithered through a gap in the net one-fifth the diameter of its body. All that was left was a coating of slime, as if the thing's skin and flesh had been mostly liquid and not too important to leave behind.

Just like the goop on the screen.

Mike cleaned the remaining windowscreen with kerosene, as if to kill any germs left behind, re-glued and stapled the frame as best he could, replaced the broken part of the screen, and set it back in place, adding two more latches—one on the lower sill and one on the upper.

He found the bit of consecrated Host in the dirt below the window. He imagined the Soldier sliding upward to that window in the dead of night, its fingers flowing between the grille of the screen, its long snout questing toward Memo like a lamprey closing on a particularly juicy fish. . . .

Had the Host and the holy water stopped it? Or was it the Soldier at all? Possibly some other thing had come for his grandmother last night. . . .

Mike felt like crying. His clever scheme had ended in confusion and near disaster. Mike had seen the Rendering Truck set back in the trees behind the Black Tree. He had *smelled* it. And that stench of death could have been from the rotting bodies of his friends if they had chosen to ride home on their bikes the way he had planned.

Mike knew that they were in a war as certainly as his father had known during World War II. Only there were no fronts or places of safety in this war, and the enemy owned the night.

He pedaled over to St. Malachy's after lunch, but there was no word on Father Cavanaugh. The Highway Patrol and the Oak Hill police had been notified by the archdiocese of the priest's disappearance, but Mrs. McCafferty told him that everyone seemed to believe that Father C. had been discouraged by his illness and had gone home to Chicago. The thought of the young priest on the road somewhere, sick and feverish in a bus station, made her start crying again.

Mike reassured her that Father Cavanaugh hadn't gone home.

He dropped by Harlen's long enough to borrow a bottle of wine—Harlen said his mother would never miss it, it was Ripple, some "moose piss" that a cousin had given her—and Mike put it in a brown bag and rode his bike down to Bandstand Park. He didn't really think that he'd get any more useful information from Mink, but he felt like he still owed him something. Plus, it reassured him that someone had actually *seen* some of the events that were clouding Mike's life these days.

Mink was gone. His bottles and newspapers and even the rags of his flappy coat—the coat he wore summer and winter—were strewn about the dirt-floored crawlspace as if a localized hurricane had struck. There were five holes—each red-rimmed and perfectly round, each about eigh-

teen inches across—riddling the dirt floor as if someone had been drill-
ing for oil.

You're imagining the worst Mike told himself. *Mink's probably off doing an odd job somewhere, having a drink with his buddies somewhere.*

Except that Mike was sure he wasn't. He imagined those mad
moments—during the night?—with Mink awakening from his wino
dreams to the buckling of earth, the smell of decay and something worse
rising into his hideout of almost seven decades. Mike imagined the old
man hopping around that dark space as something large and white and
terrible crashed up through the earth the way Mike's eel had broken the
surface of the water, long jaws snapping, blind eyes searching.

The last hole was less than three feet from the crawlspace exit. Mike
could see the cartilage-and-tendon gut-red walls of the thing. The space
under the bandstand still smelled somewhat of Mink, but more of the
charnel-house stench of the holes.

Mike tossed the bottle in—it landed upright near the rags of Mink's
coat like some diminutive headstone—and then he left, pedaling wildly
across Main close enough to a semi that the driver blasted his airhorn at
him, skidding around Second Avenue past the bushes of Dr. Viskes's
house, then up toward Old Central and home.

He wasn't going to Michelle Staffney's birthday party—the idea
seemed absurd to him after the past few days—but Dale came by and suggested that it would be a good idea for them to stick together that night.

"The party's over by ten when they shoot off the fireworks," said
Dale. "We can get home earlier if you want to."

Mike nodded. His mother and sisters would be up until at least ten—
Peg had the duty of watching over Memo tonight—and Mike didn't think
that anything would happen that close to sunset. So far nothing had.
Whether it was the Soldier or something else out there, it liked the late
hours of the night.

"Why don't you come," said Dale. "There'll be lots of light and
people . . . we need the fun."

"What about Lawrence?" asked Mike.

"He doesn't want to go to some girl's stupid party . . . plus he wasn't
invited . . . but Mom's going to let him stay up and play Monopoly with
her until I get home."

"We won't be able to take our guns to the party," said Mike, realizing even through the fog of fatigue how weird that sounded.

Dale smiled. "Harlen's going to have his. We'll borrow it if we need
it. We've got to do *something* other than wait between now and Sunday
morning."

Mike grunted.

"So you're coming?" said Dale.

"We'll see."

Michelle Staffney's party started at seven P.M., but parents were still dropping kids off from station wagons and pickup trucks at dusk ninety minutes later. As always, the big old home and yard on Broad Avenue had been transformed into a multicolored fairyland, part carnival, part used-car lot, and part pure chaos: colored electric lights and Japanese lanterns were strung from the long front porch to the trees, through the trees to poles above the tables bedecked with food and punch, from the poles to the trees at the rear of the house, and from there to the huge barn at the back of the property. Kids ran to and fro despite the best efforts of several adults to corral them, and there were clusters of shouting children in the backyard playing Jarts, a lawn game with steel-tipped darts heavy enough and sharp enough to split the skull of a water buffalo, much less a kid. Other kids gathered in the side yard where the Staffneys had dug out a dozen Hula-Hoops of various colors, reviving—if only for this night—the hysteria that had claimed the town and nation two years earlier. Still more groups gravitated to critical mass near the barbecue pit, where Dr. Staffney and two male helpers cooked and handed out hot dogs and hamburgers to a seemingly inexhaustible supply of hands and mouths, where tables with red-checked vinyl tablecloths held chips and dips and drinks and pre-dessert desserts, and from where some of the chubbier and/or hungrier kids never strayed.

A record player was working on the front porch and many of the girls clustered there, rocking on the porch swing, dangling legs from the porch railing, and generally giggling their way through the evening. Boys played tag and chased each other through the crowds, occasionally being shouted at by Dr. or Mrs. Staffney or one of the helpers, more frequently growing tired of tag and distilling the game down to its essence of seek-out-and-shove.

The first dozen or so children to arrive had dutifully shown their invitations, but after fifty or sixty kids had shown up, Michelle's party had turned into a sort of kids-only countywide party that was drawing siblings of Michelle's classmates', farm kids she had never spoken to, and a few older, junior-high-age boys who had to be shooed away by adults to the chorus of moans from the girls on the porch. Even C.J. Congden and Archie Kreck cruised by, the '57 Chevy's engine growling and rumbling, but they didn't stop. Two years earlier, Dr. Staffney had called the Highway Patrol to evict C.J. and his friends.

By nightfall, the party was really getting going, with the girls dancing—trying to do the jitterbug steps their older siblings and parents had shown them, some gyrating to rock and roll, a few imitating Elvis until the adults ordered them to stop—and even a few of the bolder boys had joined the porch group, laughing at the girls, shoving, poking, and generally getting their hands on the opposite sex as much as possible without actually *dancing* with them.

Dale and Mike had come together, had been early in line to grab their hot dogs—Dale eating one while twirling a yellow Hula-Hoop, and now they were wandering through the yard, blinking at the laughter and motion. Both were tired. Mike's eyes looked bruised and hollowed out.

Harlen and Kevin came over to join them. Kev had to shout to be heard over the screams of the Jarts crowd where someone had just accidentally speared a chunk of watermelon. "I just saw something we should've had last night!" he called.

Mike and Dale bent closer. "What's that?" They'd warned each other not to talk about things where others could hear, but with the current commotion, they could barely hear themselves.

"Come on," said Kev, beckoning them toward the side yard.

Chuck Sperling and Digger Taylor were putting on a demonstration of walkie-talkies to two small but rapt crowds of younger children. The little kids clamored for the privilege of speaking to one another across sixty feet of lawn and noise.

"Are they real?" asked Mike.

"What?"

Mike leaned closer to Kevin's large left ear. "Are . . . they . . . *real*?"

Kevin nodded while slurping Coke through a straw. His parents never allowed him to have soft drinks at home. "Yeah, they're real. Chuck's dad got them wholesale."

"What's their range?" asked Dale. He had to repeat the question.

"About a mile, according to Digger," said Kevin. "They're short-range enough that they don't need an FCC license or anything. Strong enough to be real walkie-talkies."

"Yeah," Mike said, "we could've used that. And we still could. I wonder if we could get two of those before Sunday."

Harlen stepped forward. He was grinning lopsidedly and looked strange. It took Mike a minute before he realized that Jim Harlen was wearing his finest clothes—wool pants much too warm for such a night, a blue shirt and bow tie, a fresh sling. "Hey," grinned Harlen, "you want 'em? I'll get 'em for you."

Mike leaned closer, sniffed. "Jesus, Jim, you been drinking whiskey or something?"

Harlen pulled himself upright, looking affronted but still grinning. "Just a little pick-me-up," he said, speaking slowly and distinctly. "You gave me the idea, Mike old pal. What with borrowing the Ripple an' all."

Mike shook his head. "Did you bring . . . the other thing?"

Harlen looked puzzled. "Other thing? What other thing? You mean flowers for our hostess? My pack of little rubber things . . . those things? . . . for my meeting with Miss S. later?"

Dale reached past Mike and tapped Harlen's sling and cast hard enough to hear the rap on plaster. "*That* thing, dipstick."

The smaller boy looked wide-eyed and innocent. "Oh, *this* thing?" He started to pull the .38 caliber pistol into the light.

Mike shoved it back between cast and sling. "You're drunk. Show that thing around, and Dr. S. will throw your ass out of this party before you *see* your heart's delight."

Harlen bowed and made a graceful *salaam*. "As you wish, mon Capitan." He stood too suddenly and had to brace his feet apart to stabilize himself. "Well, do you want 'em or not?"

"Want what?" Mike had his arms folded and was looking toward the street.

"The radios," said Harlen, exasperated. "You want 'em, I'll have 'em for you by tomorrow. Just say the word."

"Word," said Mike.

Harlen bent low, salaamed again, and backed into the crowd, almost knocking over a seven-year-old preparing to launch a Jart.

It was late, after nine, and Mike was ready to head home by himself if Dale and Kev weren't ready to leave, when Michelle Staffney came up to him while he was finishing his third hot dog.

"Hi, Mike."

Mike said something with his mouth full, pushed the last of the bun in, and tried again. It wasn't much more successful the second time.

"I haven't seen you much lately," said the redhead. "You know . . . since we changed grades and all."

"You mean since I flunked," managed Mike. He'd gotten most of the mouthful down without choking, but he wasn't going to smile for fear of stray bits of bun flying out.

"Well, yes," Michelle said demurely. "I guess I miss our talks."

"Yeah," said Mike, not having the faintest idea what talks she was talking about. They'd been in the same class from first grade through fourth—Mike's folks had kept him out of kindergarten—but he didn't remember talking to Michelle Staffney more than once or twice in all those years, and those "talks" were on the order of a shouted "Hey,

Michelle, throw the ball back, wouldja?" on the playground. "Yeah," he said again.

"You know," she said, leaning closer and almost whispering, "those talks we used to have about religion."

"Oh, *yeah*," said Mike, getting the last of the hot dog down and wishing desperately for a soft drink, a glass of water . . . anything liquid. He did remember talking to Michelle once in second grade—they'd been waiting for a turn on adjacent teeter-totters—and saying something about how weird it was being Catholic when most of the kids weren't. "Yeah," he said a fourth time, realizing that this particular bit of repartee might be getting a bit worn.

Michelle looked beautiful tonight, although *ravishing* was the word that came to Mike's mind. She was wearing a green chiffon dress, sort of pooched out like a ballerina's whatchamacallit although not as short, and her long red hair was held back by a green hairband and one green ribbon. Her eyes were green. Her legs were very long. Mike noticed that she'd . . . well, *changed* . . . in the past few months, possibly during the six weeks since school let out. The upper part of her dress was . . . well, *fuller* . . . and her legs were different, and her hips were different, and when she lifted her bare arm to adjust the hairband just so, Mike noticed the tenderest stipple in the gentle curve of her armpit. *Does she shave there? Like Peg and Mary? Does she shave her* legs?

Mike realized that Michelle had said something to him. "I'm sorry . . . what?"

"I said, I'd like to talk to you a little later. Talk to you about something important."

"Sure," said Mike. "When?" He figured perhaps August.

"How about in thirty minutes. In the barn?" Michelle gestured toward the large structure with a graceful sweep of her hand.

Mike turned, stared, blinked, and nodded as if he had never noticed the huge barn before. "Yeah," he said, mystified, but Michelle was already gone, moving gracefully away to mix with more of her guests. *Maybe she's inviting everybody to the barn.* Somehow, Mike didn't think so.

He wandered back toward the barbecue pit, all thoughts of leaving early banished from his mind. His mom and the girls were up tonight, taking care of Memo. He wished Harlen had brought his bottle of whiskey or wine or whatever to the party rather than his dumb gun.

"How about in thirty minutes? In the barn?" echoed through his skull as he tasted and tested the precise intonation, connected it with the exact motions. Like most of the boys in Elm Haven, Mike had had a crush on Michelle Staffney for . . . well, forever. But unlike most of the other boys, possibly because he'd flunked out of her grade and therefore, in his mind, out of her thoughts, he hadn't been fixated on the crush. It was easier ignoring Michelle when you only saw her on the playground or once in a while in church or at school when she was eating a baloney sandwich for lunch.

Mike doubted if he would ignore her again soon. *Poor Harlen,* he thought with a pang of sympathy for his friend and his bow tie. Then he thought, *Screw Harlen.*

Mike had no watch so he stayed near Kevin for the next thirty minutes, sometimes lifting his friend's wrist to check the time without asking. Once Mike noticed Donna Lou Perry and her friend Sandy in one of the clusters of kids on the front lawn and he had the impulse to go over and talk to her—give her the apology for the skins-and-shirts thing on the ball diamond last month—but Donna Lou was laughing and talking with her friends and Mike had only eight minutes left.

The barn was beyond the limits of the party, and although the wide main doors were padlocked, there was a smaller door in the shadows under the large oak that towered over the driveway. Mike clicked open the latch and stepped in. "Michelle?" The place smelled of old wood and straw that had been heated by the warm day. Mike was about to call again when he realized that he was being teased: Michelle had no thought of talking to him in private—it was just another put-on like the way she must have tantalized poor dumb Harlen.

And now poor dumb Mike, thought Mike, turning back to the door.

"Up here," came Michelle Staffney's soft voice.

At first Mike couldn't locate the source of that voice, but then the light from the strung bulbs outside, diffused as it was through dusty panes, illuminated a ladder rising between empty stalls to what must be a loft. The roof of the barn was lost in shadows thirty feet above.

"Come on up, silly," called Michelle.

Mike climbed, feeling the small vial of holy water in his pocket—a last-minute attempt to prepare for all eventualities before leaving home. *Hi, is that a vial of holy water in your pocket or are you just happy to see me?*

The loft was a dark litter of straw, but a soft light shone through a door in the north wall that partitioned the old barn from the newer addition of garage. Mike realized that the Staffneys had added a little room over the garage.

Michelle leaned on the doorframe, smiling at him. The colored light through two little windows on the east and west side of the little room backlighted her and created a corona around her red hair. "Come on in," she said shyly, stepping back to let him through. "This is my secret place."

"Hmmm," said Mike, stepping past her and feeling more aware of her warm presence there than of the little room under the eaves with its desk, dark lamp, and assortment of undersized chairs. An old sofa ran close under the bare boards of the eaves. "Sort of like a clubhouse, huh?" he said and mentally kicked himself. *Idiot.*

Michelle smiled. She stepped close to him. "Do you know why this month is special, Mikey?"

Mikey? "Uh, because it's your birthday?"

"Well, yes," said Michelle, taking another step closer. Mike could smell the soap-and-shampoo cleanness of her. The pale skin of her arms looked slightly rose-colored from the glow of colored bulbs in the high branches outside. "A girl's twelfth birthday is important," she said, almost whispering, "but there are things that happen to a girl that are *more* important, if you know what I mean."

"Sure," said Mike, almost whispering because she was so close. He had not the foggiest idea in the world what she was talking about.

Michelle stepped back and put one finger to her lips, smiling slightly as if debating whether to tell him a secret. "Do you know that I've always liked you, Mikey?"

"Uh . . . no," Mike said truthfully.

"It's true. Ever since we used to play together in first grade. Remember when we used to play house out on the playground . . . you'd be the daddy and I'd be the mommy?"

Mike vaguely remembered playing girls' games during part of first grade. He'd soon learned to stick on the boys' side of the playground. "Sure," he said with much more enthusiasm than he felt.

Michelle half turned, pirouetting like a ballerina or something. "Do you like me, Mikey?"

"Sure." What was he supposed to say—Uh-uh, you look like a toad? And truth be told, he liked her very much at that moment. He liked the way she looked and smelled and the soft sound of her voice and he liked the warm tension of being with her—so different than the cold, stomach-tensing nervousness of the rest of this mad summer. . . . "Yeah," he said, "I like you."

Michelle nodded as if he had said some magic word. She took two steps back, stopping near the window, and said, "Close your eyes."

Mike hesitated only a second. With his eyes closed, he could smell the straw from the loft next door, a soft mixture of oil and concrete and fresh-cut pine from the garage below, and still—elusive but present—the scent of her shampoo and warm flesh.

There was a soft rustling and Michelle whispered, "All right."

Mike opened his eyes and felt as if someone had hit him solidly in the solar plexus.

Michelle Staffney had slipped out of her party dress and stood before him only in a small white brassiere and simple white underpants. Mike felt as if he had never seen anything so clearly—her pale white shoulders with gold freckles on her arms and upper chest, the white curve of her small breasts above the line of elastic of her bra, her long hair flowing behind her, a corona of red light with the light flowing through it, the soft black curve of her eyelashes on her cheek as she blinked—Mike tried not to let his jaw drop as he took in the curve of her hip and the fullness of white thigh, the slender ankles with her short white socks still on. . . .

Michelle stepped closer and he could see the blush on her cheeks now and the flush of red on her neck. Her whisper was barely audible. "Mikey . . . I thought we could just . . . you know . . . look at each other." She moved closer, so close that he could have put his arms around her if his arms had been able to function. She touched his warm cheek with a cool hand.

The warmth of her face came closer and Mike realized that she had whispered something to him.

"What?" His voice was too loud.

"I just said," she whispered, "that if you take off your shirt, I'll take off something else."

Mike felt as if he were somewhere else, watching himself on television or on a movie screen as he tugged his shirt over his head, dropped it on the couch behind him. His arms did go around Michelle now as they turned slightly so that the light was behind him, the panes of the rear window six feet from his face. People were singing out on the lawn.

"My turn," whispered Michelle. He was sure that she would take off her socks, but instead she put one hand behind her back and—in a motion that took Mike's breath away with its feminine alienness—somehow unhooked the brassiere. It fell to the floor between them.

Mike could not stop himself from looking down, noticing as he did so that Michelle's eyes were either closed or almost so, the long coppery lashes fluttering against her cheek. Her breasts were pale, soft, the nipples not yet risen from the pink areolae that tipped them.

Michelle put one forearm across her small breasts as if suddenly shy and leaned closer, raising her face to Mike's. With a rush of feeling so strong that Mike felt dizzy, he realized that she was going to kiss him, that he must kiss her back, and that his mouth and lips had gone as dry as sticks.

She touched her lips to his, pulled her face back slightly as if to look at him quizzically, and kissed him again, sharing her moisture.

Mike put his arms around her, felt his excitement growing, knew that she must feel it, too, but did not move back. He thought of confession, of the darkness of the confessional with the priest's soft, interrogative voice. It was the same excitement he had known on his own, known as a solitary sin, but it was not the same at all—this warmth between them as they held each other, the kiss going on and on and on—the excitement he felt, his erection chafing against his Jockey shorts and jeans, the excitement Michelle returned to him through the softest motion of her hips and lower body—all this belonged in a different universe from the solitary imaginings and sins that Mike had confessed in the darkness. This was a new world of experience, and part of Mike's consciousness realized it even as that consciousness was submerged in sensation, even as they broke from the kiss for a second to gasp unromantically for air, then pressed their lips together again, Michelle's right hand on his chest now, palm sliding across him, and Mike's fingers pressing on the perfect curve of the small of her back, moving to feel her tiny shoulder blades.

They dropped to their knees, somehow moved to their right to lie upon the sofa cushions, never breaking contact for a moment. When the kiss ended for a second, Mike felt Michelle's soft gasps in his right ear, and he marveled at how perfectly the curve of her cheek fit into the line between his jaw and neck. He could feel her pressing against him and he realized that nothing in his life had prepared him for the swirling thrill of that second.

Mike tasted her hair on his lips, moved it aside with a gentle hand, and opened his eyes for a second.

Less than six feet in front of him, staring in through the small paned windows set in the wall a sheer twenty feet above the alley behind the garage, Father Cavanaugh stared in with dead, white eyes.

Mike gasped and pulled back, striking the arm of the sofa.

Father Cavanaugh's pale face and black shoulders seemed to float outside the window. His mouth was open wide, hanging slack like a corpse's jaw which no one has thought to shut. Gibbets of brown drool trailed from his lips and chin. The priest's cheeks and forehead were pitted with what Mike first thought were scars or scabs, but then realized were perfectly round holes in the flesh, each at least an inch wide. The apparition's hair seemed to float around it in an electrified tangle. Black lips were pulled back from long teeth.

Father Cavanaugh's eyes were open but blind, milky white, the eyelids fluttering as if in an epileptic fit.

For a second Mike was sure that he was looking at the priest's corpse, that someone had tugged it into the trees with a wire around the neck, but then the jaw moved up and down, there came a sound like stones clacking in a small container, and then curled fingers clawed at the windowpane.

Michelle heard the sound and pulled away, her arms going across her chest even as she looked over her shoulder.

She must have caught a glimpse of something even as the dead face and black shoulders whisked out of sight as if being lowered on a hydraulic lift. Mike clamped his hand over the girl's mouth as she started to scream.

"What?" she managed when he released the pressure on her.

"Get dressed," whispered Mike, feeling a pulse pounding against his side but not knowing if it was hers or his. "Hurry."

There was a second scraping against the rear window thirty seconds later, but they were both scrambling down the ladder from the loft, Mike going first into the darkness below, feeling the surge of sexual excitement fading even as the chemicals of terror replaced whatever hormones had controlled him a moment earlier.

"What?" whispered Michelle as they paused by the door. She was straightening the straps of her party dress and crying softly.

"Somebody was spying on us," whispered Mike. He looked around the barn walls for a weapon—a pitchfork, a shovel, anything—but the walls were bare except for some rotting leather tack.

Impulsively, Mike leaned forward, kissed Michelle Staffney quickly but firmly, and then opened the door.

No one noticed them returning from the shadows under the oak.

THIRTY-ONE

Dale was growing tired of the party and was about ready to leave on his own when he saw Mike and Michelle Staffney coming around the side of the house.

Michelle's dad had been moving through the crowd for several minutes, asking kids if they'd seen his daughter. The doctor had a new Polaroid camera and wanted to take some pictures before the fireworks began.

At one point Dale had gone through the kitchen and down the hall to use the bathroom—the one part of the interior of the house open to kids on this night of nights—and he passed a book-lined little room where a television set was flickering unattended. The TV set showed a mob of people under red, white, and blue banners. Dale had paid just enough attention to world events since visiting Ashley-Montague's place on Tuesday to know that tonight was the next-to-last night of the Democratic Convention. Dale stepped into the room long enough to get the gist of what Huntley and Brinkley were saying: Senator Kennedy was on the verge of being nominated as the Democrats' candidate for president. As Dale watched, a sweating man in a crowd shouted into the microphone: "Wyoming casts all fifteen votes for the next President of the United States!"

The camera showed the number 763 superimposed. The crowd went insane. David Brinkley said, "Wyoming's put him over the top."

Dale had just gone back outside when Mike and Michelle came out of the shadows of the backyard, Michelle picking up a flotilla of her girl-friends and running into the house, Mike looking around wildly.

Dale went over to him. "Hey, you OK?" Mike didn't look OK. He was pale—even his lips were white—and there was a film of sweat on his brow and upper lip. His right hand was clenched in a fist and was shaking slightly.

"Where's Harlen?" was all that Mike replied.

Dale pointed to the cluster of kids where Harlen was holding forth on his terrible accident, telling all about how he'd been climbing on Old Central's roof on a dare when a gust of wind had sent him on a fifty-foot fall.

Mike strode over and roughly pulled Harlen from the group.

"Hey, what the shit . . ."

"Give it to me," snapped Mike, using a tone that Dale had never heard from his friend before. He snapped his fingers in front of Harlen. "Hurry."

"Give what . . ." began Jim, obviously ready to argue.

Mike slapped Harlen's sling hard enough to make the smaller boy wince. He snapped his fingers again. *"Give it to me. Now."*

Neither Dale nor anyone Dale knew—much less Jim Harlen—would have disobeyed Mike O'Rourke at that moment. Dale imagined an *adult* giving Mike whatever he wanted right then.

Harlen glanced around, slipped the small .38 revolver out of his sling, and handed it to Mike.

Mike glanced at it once to make sure that it was loaded, then he held it down at his side—almost casually, Dale thought, so that no one would look twice at his right hand and the pistol in it unless you knew that it was there. Then he left, moving toward the barn with long, quick strides.

Dale glanced at Harlen, who raised one eyebrow, then both boys hurried to catch up, moving through the throngs of kids running toward the front yard where Dr. Staffney was taking pictures with his magic camera while some friends were setting up the aerial display rockets.

Mike moved around the south side of the barn, into the shadows there. He stayed close to the wall, his right hand raised now, the short barrel catching the last bit of light from the overhead bulbs. He whirled when Dale and Harlen stepped into the shadows, then waved them back against the wall.

Mike reached the end of the barn, stepped around some bushes there, crouching to look under them, then spun around—raising the pistol toward the black alley. Dale glanced at Harlen, remembered Jim's story about fleeing down this very alley from the Rendering Truck. *What had Mike seen?*

They came around the back of the barn. A single pole light half a block away down the alley only seemed to accentuate the darkness here, the black masses of foliage, the black-against-black outlines of other sheds, garages, and outbuildings. Mike had the pistol raised, his body sideways as if ready to aim north down the alley, but his head was turned and he was looking at the wood on the back of the Staffneys' garage. Dale and Harlen moved closer to look with him.

It took a minute for Dale to see the irregular rows of splinters going to the small window twenty-some feet above. It looked as if a telephone lineman had used his spiked climbing boots to gouge footholds on the vertical wooden wall. Dale looked back at Mike. "Did you see someth—"

"Shhh." Mike waved him into silence and moved across the alley, closing on a tall raspberry bush on the opposite side.

Dale could smell raspberries in the darkness, as the fruit was crushed underfoot. Suddenly he smelled something else . . . a rank animal smell.

Mike waved them back again and then raised the pistol, the muzzle aimed head-high at the dark bush, his right arm straight and steady now. Dale clearly heard the click as the hammer was pulled back.

There was a hint of white there—a pale sketch of a face between black branches—then a low growling, a rumbling deep in some large creature's chest.

"Jesus," Harlen whispered frantically, "shoot! *Shoot!*"

Mike held the aim, thumb still on the hammer, arm never wavering as the white face and a dark mass too large and too strangely shaped to be a human being separated itself from the raspberry bush and moved toward him.

Dale backed against the barn wood, his heart filling his throat, feeling Harlen scrabbling to run. Mike still did not shoot.

The growling rose to a crescendo; there was a dark scrabbling of claws on the cinders and gravel of the alley; teeth glinted in what faint light there was.

Mike planted his feet wide and waited while the thing advanced.

"Down, goddamn you dogs!" came a whiney voice from that pale circle of a face. The last word had been pronounced "dawgs."

"Cordie," said Mike. He lowered the weapon.

Dale could see now that the teeth and dark bodies on either side of Cordie belonged to two very large dogs—one a Doberman pinscher, the other some sort of variation on a German shepherd. Cordie held them on short leashes that looked like rawhide thongs.

"What are you doing here?" asked Mike, still looking up and down the alley rather than at her.

"Could ask you the same thing," snapped Cordie Cooke. Dale heard the last word as "thang."

Mike ignored the question, if it was a question. "You see somebody back here? Somebody . . . strange?"

Cordie snorted what might have been a laugh and the two dogs looked up at her quickly, licking their chops, waiting to know if they should be happy with her. "Lotsa strange somebodies around here at night these days. Got anybody in particular in mind?"

Mike turned so he was speaking to Dale and Harlen as much as to the girl. "I was upstairs there." He gestured with the pistol toward the window above them. "I saw something outside the window. Somebody. Somebody very strange . . . strange."

Dale looked up at the black glass and thought *with Michelle?* He knew the priority of that thought was stupid, but it hurt him somehow to think it just the same. Harlen just frowned at the window and then back at Mike, not comprehending; Dale realized that Harlen hadn't seen Mike and Michelle come out of the shadows together.

"I jes got here," said Cordie. "Me an' Belzybub an' Lucifer come down to see who's at the snot's party this year."

Harlen moved closer and stared at the dogs. "Belzybub and Lucifer?" They growled him back several hasty steps.

"I thought you'd moved away," said Dale. "Thought your family'd moved." He'd almost said *up and moved*. Listening to Cordie talk was contagious.

The shapeless gunnysack of a dress moved up and down with what might have been a shrug. The huge dogs returned their attention from Jim back to their master . . . mistress . . . whatever. "Pa's run off," she said tonelessly. "Couldn't stand the damn night things. He always was no good in a pinch. Ma an' the twins and my sister Maureen an' that no-good boyfriend of hers, Berk, all took off for Cousin Sook's up at Oak Hill."

"Where are you staying?" asked Mike.

Cordie stared at him as if in wonderment that anyone could think she was stupid enough to answer that question. "Somewheres safe," she said shortly. "Why was you aimin' little Jimmy's popshooter at me? You think I was one of the night things?"

"Night things," repeated Mike. "You've seen them?"

Cordie snorted again. "Why the hell you think Pa'd run off an' Ma an' the others had to give up the house, huh? Goddamn things was comin' around most nights and sometimes in the day."

"Tubby?" said Dale, his insides tense. *The pale mass under black water, the eyes clicking open like a doll's.*

"Tubby 'n' that soldier fellow, and the dead ol' woman, and some others. Kids to look at 'em, only not much left but bones an' rags."

Dale shook his head. There was something about Cordie's matter-of-fact acceptance of the insane curve of events that made him want to laugh and giggle and keep on giggling.

Mike lifted his left hand, slowed it as the dogs growled, and touched her shoulder. Cordie seemed to jump at the touch.

"I'm sorry we haven't been out to see you," he said. "We've been trying to figure out what's going on ourselves, spending our time running or fighting. We should've thought of you."

Cordie cocked her head in an almost canine motion. "Thought of me?" Her voice was strange. "What the hell you talkin' about, O'Rourke?"

"Where's your shotgun?" asked Harlen.

Cordie snorted again. "The dogs is better'n that ol' gun. I got it, but I turn the dogs loose on 'em if those things make for me again." *A'gin.*

Mike had been walking north down the alley and now the others followed. Their shoes and the dogs' claws made soft sounds on cinders. There was a cheer from the Staffney front yard, but the noise seemed very distant.

"So they've tried to get you too, huh?" said Mike.

Cordie spat into the dark weeds. "Two nights ago, Belzybub pulled mosta the left hand off the thing that useta be Tubby. It was clawin' to get in at me."

"In where?" asked Harlen. He was looking over his shoulder at the dark shrubs and shadowy lawns on either side, his head moving like a metronome.

Cordie didn't answer. "You boys wanta see somethin' that's stranger than your guy at the window?" she asked.

Dale could hear the words his mind framed—*Not really, thanks anyway*—but he said nothing. Harlen was too busy glancing at shadows to speak. Mike said, "Where?"

"It ain't far. 'Course if you gotta get back to Miss Silkypants' party, I understand."

Dale thought *What if it's not Cordie? What if they got her?* But it looked like Cordie . . . spoke like Cordie . . . *smelled* like Cordie.

"How far?" persisted Mike. He'd stopped walking. They were about thirty yards away from the Staffneys' barn, not quite to the single pole light along the entire stretch of alley. Dogs were barking in many of the yards, but Belzybub and Lucifer ignored them with almost princely disdain.

"The old grain co-op," Cordie said after a silence.

Dale winced. The abandoned grain elevators were less than a quarter of a mile from where they were: up the alley to Catton Road and then west across the tracks, down the old overgrown lane that used to connect the town with the road to the dump. The elevators had been abandoned since the Monon Railroad discontinued service to Elm Haven in the early 1950s.

"I'm not going there," said Harlen. "Forget it. No way." He looked over his shoulder toward a sudden sound as some dog the size of Belzybub's head strained at his rope to get free in one of the backyards.

"What's there?" said Mike. He put the pistol in the waistband of his jeans.

Cordie started to speak but stopped. She took a breath. "You gotta see it," she said at last. "I don't understand what it means, but I know you ain't gonna believe me unless you see it."

Mike looked back toward the noise of the Staffney party. "We'll need a light."

Cordie pulled a heavy metal four-cell flashlight from some deep pocket of her shapeless dress. She clicked it on and a powerful beam illuminated branches forty feet above them. She turned it off.

"Let's go," said Mike.

Dale followed them through the pool of yellow glow from the pole light but Harlen held back. "I'm not going out there," he said.

Mike shrugged. "OK, go on back. I'll get your pistol back to you later." He walked on with Dale, Cordie, and the two dogs.

Harlen scurried to catch up. "Fuck that. I want that back tonight." Dale guessed that he didn't want to walk the half block back to the party by himself.

There were no streetlights on Catton Road as they reached the end of the alley and stepped out onto the gravel there. Cornfields to the north rustled in a faint breeze which carried the night-scent of growing to them. The stars were very bright.

With Cordie and the dogs leading the way, they turned west toward the railroad tracks and the dark line of trees ahead.

The dead bodies were hanging from hooks.

From the outside, the door of the old grain elevator storehouse had looked secure with a heavy padlock and chain in place. But Cordie had shown them that the metal bar holding the lock could be pulled out of the rotten wooden frame with little effort.

The dogs would not go in. They whined, pulled at the rawhide thongs, and showed the whites of their eyes.

"They'll go after the movin' dead ones all right," said Cordie, tying them to a stanchion just outside the door. "It's what's in here they don't like. Don't like the smell."

Dale didn't like the smell either. The main warehouse space was twenty-five or thirty yards long and three stories high, the ceiling criss-crossed with wooden and iron crossbraces. It was from a row of those beams that the carcasses hung.

Cordie played her flashlight beam across the flayed things hanging there while the boys pulled their shirts over their noses and mouths and advanced slowly, blinking at the stench. The air was filled with the swarm-sound of flies.

When Dale first saw the carcasses—the ragged flesh and raw bone of them—he'd thought they were human. Then he recognized a sheep . . . then a calf, strung by the hind legs and hanging head down, the neck impossibly arched and gaping in an obscene smile . . . then another sheep . . . then a large dog . . . a larger calf . . . there were at least twenty carcasses hanging over the long trough made of split fifty-gallon oil drums.

Cordie stepped close to the calf, set her hand on the nearly severed neck. "See what they done? I think they hung 'em up here *before* they cut their throats." She pointed. "Blood goes downhill here . . . through that pipe . . . out through that gutter over there so they can load up without havin' to carry buckets of the stuff outside."

"Load up?" said Dale, then realized what she meant. Someone had used the trough to transport the blood outside to the loading dock . . . *to what? Where did they take it?*

Suddenly the stench of decomposing flesh, the overpowering smell of blood, and the high hum of a million flies made Dale dizzy and sick. He staggered to a window, forced the old latch, lifted a movable pane there, and gasped in fresh air. The trees closed in darkly outside. Starlight reflected on rusted rails.

"You've known about this place?" Mike said to Cordie. There was an odd, flat note in his voice.

The girl shrugged, moved the light along the beams. "A few days. One of the things got one of my dogs t'other night. Followed the blood here."

Harlen was trying to use the top of his sling as a mask. His face above the black silk was very pale. "You've known about this and haven't *told* anyone?"

Cordie turned the flashlight on Harlen. "Who's I supposed to tell?" she said flatly. "Our ol' school principal maybe? That dipshit Barney? Maybe our justice of the peace, heh?"

Harlen turned his face away from the light. "That'd be better than telling nobody, for Chrissakes."

Cordie began walking down the row of carcasses, shining the powerful flashlight first on ribs and flesh, then on the rusted and blood-coated trough beneath. The blood looked black and thick as molasses in the flashlight beam. The trough was so coated with flies that it looked as if the metal were moving. "I told you, didn't I?" said Cordie. "It's what I found here today made up my mind to tell somebody."

She had come to the end of the line of carcasses, far in the rear of the warehouse space. She moved the flashlight up.

"Jesus fuck!" said Harlen, jumping back.

Mike had been carrying the pistol at his side since coming through the door. Now he lifted it and moved forward.

The man hanging there had been strung up like the animals—legs tied together by a wire looped over an old iron hook—and at first glance his body was very similar to the sheep and calves: naked, ribs outlined against white flesh, throat cut so thoroughly that the head had come close to being severed. Dale thought that the neck looked like the mouth of some great white shark with ragged bits of flesh and cartilage in place of teeth. The underside of the man's chin was so streaked that it looked like someone had upended bucket after bucket of thick red paint on him.

Cordie walked up to the trough and, while still keeping the light steady on the corpse, grabbed it by the hair and pulled the dangling head forward.

"Jesus," gasped Dale. He felt his right leg begin to vibrate of its own accord and he set a hand on his thigh to steady it.

"J.P. Congden," whispered Mike. "I see why you couldn't tell the justice of the peace."

Cordie grunted and let the head hang free again. "He's new," she said. "Wasn't here yesterday. Come here an' look at somethin' though."

The boys shuffled forward, Harlen holding the sling to his face, Mike still keeping the gun high, and Dale feeling as if his legs were going to fold under him. They lined up along the trough like thirsty men at a bar.

"See here?" said Cordie, grabbing J.P. Congden by the hair again and pulling forward until the corpse was leaning out into the light and the wire creaked above them. "See?"

The man's mouth was open wide, as if frozen in a shout. One eye stared blindly at them but the other was almost closed. The face was streaked with caked blood from the throat wound, but there was something else. It took Dale a minute to see it.

The former justice of the peace's temples were flecked with wounds and his scalp was half-dangling, as if Indians had started to scalp him and then thought better of it.

"Shoulders, too," said Cordie, still speaking in flat but vaguely interested tones, sort of the way Dale imagined Digger's dad or a pathologist talking during an autopsy or embalming. "See on the shoulders there?"

Dale saw. Holes. Cuts. It looked like someone had poked him a few dozen times with a sharp, perfectly round blade—certainly not enough to kill him, but terrible all the same.

Mike understood first. "A shotgun," he said, looking at the other two boys. "He just caught the edge of the pattern."

It took Dale a minute. Then he remembered. *One of the men running from the campsite directly at the spot where Mike had been hidden. Then the blast of Mike's squirrel gun. The man's cap flying off and him going down in the grass.*

Dale felt sick again and he walked back to the window, hanging on to the dusty sill to steady himself. Flies whizzed by . . . more on their way inside.

Cordie let the corpse hang free again. "I just wondered if his own people done that, or if someone else is fightin' these things."

"Let's go outside," said Mike, his voice suddenly shaky. "We'll talk."

Dale had been staring outside at the dark trees, taking long, deep breaths and letting his eyes adapt to the darkness there, when suddenly the night exploded with light and noise. He threw himself away from the window, landing on the rough boards and rolling.

Mike grabbed the flashlight from Cordie, killed the light, and dropped to one knee, pistol raised. Harlen started to run, hit the trough, and almost fell into it, his good arm going deep into the caked blood. A million flies took wing.

The room was suddenly illuminated by the flare-bright bursts of light from outside—first phosphorous white, then bright red, then a green that made the dangling carcasses look covered with a brilliant mold. The burst of light would come through the dusty panes and then the sound of the aerial explosion, forcing its way through the pane Dale had opened. Only Cordie Cooke remained precisely where she had been—her round face scrunched up as she squinted at the light. Outside, her dogs were going crazy.

"Aw, shit," breathed Harlen, rubbing his hand on his jeans. The blood came off in brown smears. The explosions outside redoubled in number and intensity. "It's only Michelle Staffney's goddamn fireworks."

There was a general sighing and slumping. Dale got to all fours, turning to look into the shadows and watch the carcasses as they came into existence and then disappeared with the vagaries of light from the skyrockets—green and red, pure red, the naked flesh and protruding ribs and slit throats, blue, blue and red, white, red, red, red . . . Dale knew that he was seeing something that he would never forget as long as he lived. And something that he would want to forget as long as he lived.

Saying nothing to each other, resetting the metal bar and padlock behind them, they went back out into the night and took the road back to town.

THIRTY-TWO

Friday the fifteenth of July had no dawn. The overcast was low and heavy and the cloudy sky merely paled to a lighter shade of gray as night turned to morning. While the clouds stayed low and threatening all day, the promised storm did not arrive. The moist heat lay over everything.

By ten A.M. all the boys were congregated on the low slope of Kevin Grumbacher's front lawn, staring at Old Central through Mike's binoculars and talking in low tones.

"I'd like to see it myself," Kevin was saying. His expression was dubious.

"Go ahead," said Jim Harlen. "I'm not going. There may be more corpses there by now. Maybe yours'll be added to the lineup."

"No one's going," Mike said softly. He was staring at the boarded windows and doors of the old school.

"I wonder what they use the blood for," said Lawrence. He lay on his stomach, head down the slope. He was chewing on a piece of clover.

No one ventured a guess.

"It doesn't matter what they use it for," said Mike. "We know that thing in there . . . the thing disguised as a bell . . . needs sacrifice. It feeds on pain and fear. Read them that part in the book you got from Ashley-Montague, Dale."

Harlen snorted. "*Stole* from Ashley-Montague is more like it."

"Read it, Dale." Mike did not lower the binoculars.

Dale thumbed through the book. "Death is the crown of all," read Dale, "so sayeth the *Book of the Law. Agape* equals ninety-three, seven one eight equals Stele six six six, sayeth the Apocalypse of the Cabbala. . . ."

"Read the other stuff," said Mike. He lowered the glasses. His eyes were very tired. "The stuff about the Stele of Revealing."

"It's sort of a poem," said Dale. He tugged his baseball cap lower to shade his eyes.

Mike nodded. "Read it."

Dale read, his voice falling into a faint singsong rhythm:

"The Stele is the Mother and Father of the Magus,
The Stele is the Mouth and Anus of the Abyss,
The Stele is the Heart and Liver of Osiris;
At the Final Equinox
The Throne of Osiris in the East
Shall look to the throne of Horus in the West
And the days shall be so numbered.
The Stele shall demand the Sacrifice,
Of cakes, perfumes, beetles, and
Blood of the innocent;
The Stele shall render unto those
Who serve it.
And in the Awakening of the Final Days,
The Stele shall be created of two
Of the Elementals—earth and air,
And may be destroyed only by the
Final two.
For the Stele is the Mother and Father of the Magus;
For the Stele is the Mouth and Anus of the Abyss."

The kids sat in a circle. Finally Lawrence said, "What's an anus?"

"You are," said Harlen.

"It's a planet," said Dale. "You know, like Uranus?"

Lawrence nodded his understanding.

"What are the other two whatchamacallems?" said Harlen. "The other two elementals. The ones that could destroy the Stele?"

Kevin folded his arms. "Earth, air, fire, and water," said Kevin. "The Greeks and the guys before them thought that these were the basis of everything. Earth and air creates the thing . . . fire and water could destroy it."

Mike took the book and held it in his hand, as if trying to pull something else from it. "As far as Dale and I can tell, that's the only mention of the Stele of Revealing in this book."

"And we only have Duane's notes to suggest the Stele has anything to do with anything," said Harlen.

Mike set the book down. "Duane and his Uncle Art. And both of them are dead."

Kevin glanced at his watch. "OK, so what good does this do us?"

Mike sat back. "Tell us about your dad's milk truck again."

Kevin's voice took on some of the same lilt of litany that Dale's had held. "It's a two-thousand-gallon bulk tanker," he said. "The shiny tank is all stainless steel. My father takes the truck out every morning . . . except Sunday . . . and picks up the milk at the bulk tanks on the dairy farms. He leaves early . . . usually about four-thirty in the morning . . . and has two routes. He does one every other day. Besides transferring the milk to the plant, he samples it, weighs it, does a quality check, and actually handles the pumping.

"Our truck's got a centrifugal pump that works at eighteen hundred rpm—it's a lot faster than a positive-feed pump that uses an electric motor. They only get about four hundred rpm. Dad can transfer about seventy-five gallons a minute from the bulk tank on the dairy farm to his tanker. He needs a two-hundred-thirty-volt outlet to do it, but all the dairy farms have one.

"He's got a sample tray and liquid coolant in the compartment at the rear of the truck. That's where the pump is, too. The hose fits on those red compartments on the side . . . the ones that look sort of like the side of a firetruck.

"Sometimes I ride with him, but he usually doesn't get home until about two in the afternoon and I have chores to do, so I get my allowance by scrubbing out the tank, cleaning the truck, and gassing it up." Kevin paused for a breath.

"Show us the gas pump again," said Mike.

The five boys walked to the north end of the house. Mr. Grumbacher had built a large tin shed there to house the truck, and between the huge double doors and the house were the gravel turnaround and the gas pump. Dale had always thought it sort of neat that his neighbor had his own gas pump.

"The milk plant helped pay to put it in," said Kevin. "Ernie's Texaco isn't open early or on weekends, and they didn't want Dad going all the way to Oak Hill to gas up."

"Tell us again," said Mike. "How much does the underground tank hold?"

"Twelve hundred gallons," said Kev.

Mike rubbed his lower lip. "Less than the tanker."

"Yeah."

"There's a lock on the pump," said Mike.

Kevin tapped it. "Yeah, but Dad keeps the key in the right-hand drawer of his desk. The drawer's not locked."

Mike nodded, waited.

"The filler cap's set in the ground there," said Kevin, pointing. "It's got a lock, too, but the key's on the same ring as the pump key."

The boys were silent for a moment. Mike paced back and forth, his sneakers making soft noises on the gravel drive. "I guess we're set then." He did not sound convinced.

"Why Sunday morning?" asked Dale. "Why not tomorrow . . . Saturday morning? Or today?"

Mike rubbed his hand through his hair. "Sunday's the only day that Kevin's dad stays home. It's too busy around here in the afternoons . . . we need it to be early. Just after sunrise is best. Unless some of you want to do this at night."

Dale, Kev, Lawrence, and Harlen looked at each other and said nothing.

"Besides," continued Mike, "Sunday seems . . . well, *right*." He glanced around, a sergeant assembling his troops. "In the meantime, we get ready."

Harlen snapped his fingers. "That reminds me, I've got a surprise for you guys." He led them around front to where his bike was sprawled on the lawn. There was a shopping bag hanging from the handlebars; Harlen removed two walkie-talkies from it. "You said this might come in handy," he said to Mike.

"Wow," said Mike, taking one of them. He touched a button and static rasped. "How'd you get them away from Sperling?"

Harlen shrugged. "I went back to the party for a minute last night. Everyone was out back eating cake. Sperling'd left these sitting on one of the tables. I figured that anybody who doesn't watch after his stuff better than that doesn't really want to keep it. Besides, it's just on loan."

"Uh-uh," said Mike. He opened a panel and checked the batteries.

"I put new ones in this morning," said Harlen. "These things work pretty well up to a mile. I tested it out with my mom this morning."

Kevin cocked an eyebrow. "Where did she think you got these?"

Harlen smiled. "Door prize at the Staffney party. You know rich folks . . . big parties, big prizes."

"Let's try it out," said Lawrence, taking one of the walkie-talkies and jumping on his bike. A minute later he was out of sight down Second Avenue.

The boys lay on the grass. "Home Base to Red Rover," Mike said into the radio. "Where are you? Over."

Lawrence's voice was tinny and static-lashed, but quite audible. "I'm just goin' past the A and P. I can see your mom working in there, Mike."

Harlen grabbed the walkie-talkie. "Say 'over.' Over."

"Over-over?" came Lawrence's voice.

"No," growled Harlen. "Just *over*."

"Why?"

"Just say it when you're finished talking so we know you're finished. Over."

"Over," said Lawrence between gasps. He was obviously pedaling hard.

"No, you dope," said Harlen. "Say something else and *then* say 'over.'"

"Hey, drop dead, Harlen. Over."

Mike took the radio back. "Where are you?"

Lawrence's voice was getting fainter. "Just gone past the park, goin' south down Broad." After a moment's silence. "Over."

"That's almost a mile," said Mike. "Pretty good. You can come on home now, Red Rover." He looked at Harlen. "Ten-four."

"God *damn* it!" came the boy's small voice.

Dale grabbed the walkie-talkie. "Don't you swear, damn it. What's wrong?"

Lawrence's voice was very tiny, more like he was whispering than the signal was being affected by distance. "Hey . . . I just found out where the Rendering Truck is."

It took less than thirty minutes to finish filling the Coke bottles with gasoline. Dale had brought the rags.

"What about the gauge on the pump?" said Mike. "Doesn't your dad keep track of the gallons used?"

Kevin nodded. "But since I do most of the fueling for him, I keep the log. He won't notice these few gallons." Kevin did not look happy at the deception.

"All right," said Mike. He crouched to draw in the dirt behind the Grumbacher shed as Dale and Lawrence carefully set the Coke bottles in a partitioned milk crate Kev had provided. "Here's the deal," said Mike. He drew Main Street, then Broad going south past the park. He used the twig he was holding to sketch in the circular drive of the old Ashley-Montague place. "You're sure the truck was back there?" he asked Lawrence. "And that it was the Rendering Truck?"

Lawrence looked indignant. "Sure I'm sure."

"It's in the trees there? The old orchard behind the ruins?"

"Yeah, and it's all covered over with twigs and a net and junk. Like the whatchamacallit the soldiers use."

"Camouflage," supplied Dale.

Lawrence nodded vigorously.

"OK," said Mike. "Now we know where it's been. It makes sense, too, in a weird sort of way. The question is, are we all agreed that we do something about it today?"

"We already voted," snapped Harlen.

"Yes," said Mike, "but you know how risky it is."

Kevin squatted and picked up a handful of gravel and dirt, letting the dust filter through his fingers. "I think it'd be riskier to leave the truck alone until Sunday. If we go ahead with our plans, the truck can always intervene."

"So can the underground things," said Mike. "Whatever they are."

Kevin looked thoughtful. "Yeah, but we can't do anything about them. If the truck's gone, that's an important variable eliminated."

"Besides," whispered Dale, his voice as flat as flint on steel, "Van Syke and that goddamn truck tried to kill Duane. It probably *was* there when he died."

Mike used the drawing twig to scratch his forehead. "All right, we voted. We agreed. Now we do it. The question is where and who. Where the rest of us wait and who are the decoys."

The four boys leaned closer to look at the crude map of the town that Mike had drawn.

Harlen's good hand came down on the spot representing the Ashley-Montague mansion. "What about just getting it where it is? The house there's already burned to shit."

Mike used the twig to deepen the hole in the dust. "Yeah, that's OK if the truck's empty. What about if it does what we think it might?"

"We can take it there," said Harlen.

"Can we?" Mike's gray eyes locked with his friend's. "There are trees in the front and the orchard in back, but could we get set in time? How do we get in . . . down the tracks? We've got a lot of junk to carry. Plus, the ruins are right on the edge of town, just a block or so from the firehouse. There're always a couple of volunteers out front, chewing the fat."

"Well, then, where?" said Dale. "We've got to think of the decoys."

Mike chewed on his thumbnail a moment. "Yeah. It's got to be a private enough place that Van Syke will make his move. But close enough to town that we can get back easy if things go wrong."

"The Black Tree?" said Kevin.

Dale and Mike emphatically shook their heads at the same second.

"Too far," said Mike. The memory of the previous morning's close call was obviously still sharp and clear to him.

Lawrence used his finger to extend the line of First Avenue north. He sketched in a lump on the west side of the street just where Jubilee County Road came in. "What about the water tower?" he said. "We could go out across the ballfield and move up through this line of trees here. It'd be easy to get back."

Mike nodded, thought a minute, then shook his head. "Not enough cover," he said. "We'd have to cross the open playing field to get back and the truck could cross it easily . . . and a lot faster."

The boys frowned and studied the squiggles in the dirt. The clouds were low above them, the humidity worse than ever.

"What about out west of town," said Harlen. "Toward the Grange Hall?"

"Uh-uh," said Mike. "The decoys'd have to go out the Hard Road to get there and it doesn't have a shoulder or anything. The truck'd get them for sure. Plus we couldn't get back on our bikes, we'd have to cut across fields behind the Protestant Cemetery."

"I don't want to have anything to do with cemeteries," said Dale.

Harlen sighed and mopped his face. "Well, hell, that leaves my idea of doing it right at the mansion. It seems to be the only place."

"Wait," said Mike. He drew Broad Avenue north all the way to Catton Road, then sketched that road west two blocks, did some crosshatching to show the railroad tracks. "What about the grain elevator? It's out of sight . . . but close enough that the decoys might make it."

"It's *theirs*," said Dale, horrified at the thought of going back there.

Mike nodded. His gray eyes were almost luminous now, the way they often looked when he had an idea he liked. "Yeah, but that'll just help them be more confident about going for us . . . going for the decoys. Plus, we've got a couple of ways to retreat . . ." He sketched quickly with the short stick. "The dirt road along the east side of the tracks here . . . Catton Road here . . . the old dump road here . . . even the woods or the railroad tracks if we have to leave the bikes."

"The truck can come down the railroad line," Kevin said flatly. "Its wheels are far enough apart that it can straddle the rails . . ."

"The ties would make that a bumpy ride," said Harlen.

Kevin shrugged. "It chased Duane right through a fence and into a cornfield."

Mike stared at the map as if sheer intensity could force a better plan. "Anybody got any better ideas?"

Nobody did.

Mike brushed out the map. "OK, four of us get set there while one person is the decoy. That's me."

Lawrence shook his head. "Uh-uh," the eight-year-old said defiantly. "I found 'em. I get to be decoy."

"Don't be stupid," snapped Mike. "You've got that little seventeen-inch bike. You couldn't outrun a guy in a wheelchair."

Lawrence balled his hands into fists. "I could outrun that old rusty junker of yours any day of the week, O'Rourke. I can do *wheelies*."

Mike sighed and shook his head.

"He's right," Dale said, amazing himself even as he spoke. "Your bike's not fast enough, Mike. Only it shouldn't be him . . ." He poked his brother with a finger. "It should be me. My bike's the newest, plus we need you to be waiting there. Your throwing arm's a thousand times better than mine."

Mike thought a long moment. "All right," he said at last. "But if there's nobody there when you get to the mansion, just tell us over the walkie-talkie and we come there. Got it? We'll do it there and not worry about the fire department being so close."

Harlen held up his hand as if he were in class. "I think I should do it." His voice was almost but not quite steady, his lips pale. "You guys have two arms to throw. Decoying may be what I could do best here."

Kevin made a derisive noise. "Whoever's decoy needs two hands," he said. "You're better off waiting with the rest of us."

Mike looked amused. "Don't you want to volunteer to be the hero, Kev?"

Kevin Grumbacher shook his head without smiling. "I'll be doing enough on Sunday."

"If we ever get to Sunday," muttered Dale.

"Wait," said Harlen. "Do we bring the guns?"

Mike thought. "Yes. But we don't use them unless we have to. The elevator's not that far from town. Somebody might hear and call Barney."

"People along Fifth or Catton Road'd just think it was somebody shooting rats at the dump," suggested Dale.

"Which is about right," said Mike. He looked around at them. "Shall we do it?"

It was Lawrence who spoke. "Yeah, but I *am* going to be decoy. Dale can come along if he wants, but I found it and I'm going to check it out. No argument."

Harlen sneered. "Whaddya going to do, halfpint? Tell your mommy if we don't let you do it? Hold your breath until you turn blue?"

Lawrence crossed his arms over his chest, squinted at all of them, and smiled a slow and lazy smile.

THIRTY-THREE

Dale and Lawrence pedaled across Main and skidded to a stop in the gravel of the parking strip along the west side of the park. Dale pulled the walkie-talkie strap over his head and keyed the transmit button; they'd given Mike and Kev and Harlen fifteen minutes to get in position.

"Red Rover to Dresden Base. We're at the park. Over." It had been Kev's idea to name the other team Dresden Base—Kev's dad had served as a navigator in the Army Air Forces in World War II.

"Roger, Red Rover." Mike's voice was faint and static-lashed. "We're all set here."

Lawrence was all ready to go, leaning over his handlebars and grinning like a dope, but Dale didn't want to move just yet. "Mike," he said, already abandoning the radio codes, "they're going to see the radio."

"Yeah, but we can't do anything about that. Just don't let Chuck Sperling or Digger see it."

Dale looked over his shoulder before he realized that Mike was making a joke. Ha ha.

"Red Rover?"

"Yeah?"

"Try to talk into the radio when you're out of sight of the truck. The rest of the time, keep it strung over your back. They probably won't notice it."

"Roger," said Dale. He wished he had one of the pistols. They'd decided to leave Dale's Savage over-and-under behind, but Dresden Base had brought Harlen's .38, Kev's dad's big .45, and Mike's grandmother's squirrel gun with them in a canvas duffel bag. Dale and Lawrence had the radio and their bikes.

"Moving out," said Dale. He reslung the radio and pedaled south down Broad, Lawrence right at his side on the smaller bike. Approaching the intersection with the street where Sperling lived, Dale looked at Lawrence. "Would you really have told Mom?"

Lawrence grinned. "Sure . . . I found it. It's *my* truck, in a way. No way I was gonna be left behind."

"You're going to end up in the back of the Rendering Truck with all the other carcasses if you don't do exactly as I say. Got it?"

His brother shrugged.

They paused at the entrance to the circular drive at the old Ashley place. "You can't see it from here," whispered Lawrence. "You've got to get around by the house."

"Just a second." Dale pulled the walkie-talkie around. His bladder was sending urgent signals and he wished he'd gone into the house before leaving. "Dresden Base, come in. Over." Three calls and Mike responded.

"We're heading down the drive." They pedaled slowly, moving in the center of the driveway to keep the branches and brambles off them. Suddenly Dale stopped and pulled behind a tree, Lawrence following. "Dresden Base, Dresden Base . . . Red Rover here."

"Go ahead, Red Rover."

"I see it. It's right where punko said it'd be."

Lawrence bashed his older brother on the upper arm.

"Leave the transmit button open," said Mike. "Let the thing dangle. Let me see if I can hear you."

Dale let the radio hang. "Testing," he said, feeling how dry his mouth was and how full his bladder felt. "One, two, three . . ." He lifted the gray plastic case.

"Yeah, Red Rover, I can hear you. Just talk loud when you want us to hear. We're ready here, Dale. You guys set?"

"Yeah." Dale felt the tension in his body as he straddled the center bar of the bike, left hand clenching and unclenching on the handlebar.

"Remember," came Mike's raspy voice, "no chances. I don't think they'll do anything in town, in broad daylight. He cuts you off, just go into a store or something. Got it?"

"Yeah."

"Don't go right up to the truck even if it doesn't respond," said Mike. They'd gone over all this already. "We'll meet at the park. Don't hang around there."

"Roger," said Dale. He lowered the radio. "We're going," he said loudly.

Lawrence was slightly ahead as they pedaled up the last part of the drive to the house, took the narrower lane along the north side of the ruins. The Rendering Truck was almost invisible, covered as it was with what looked like an old net and cut branches. It was tucked in behind a long rusted shed and the greenhouse with its broken panes and rusted metal lattice. A casual passerby would think the truck was just another abandoned relic of the Ashley estate.

Dale sincerely hoped it was.

They stopped just beyond the carbon-smirched tower of bricks that had been the fireplace. The mansion itself was almost lost to weeds and brambles, charred rafters poking from the dark space of the basement. An ornate pump stood on what had once been a back patio: local kid-myth had it that people drowned dogs in the well here.

The Rendering Truck looked hot and dead in the flat, gray glare of day. The windows reflected gray sky.

Lawrence dismounted, stood by his bike, and looked at his brother. Dale glanced over his shoulder, made sure the way down the driveway was clear, and said, "Do it."

There were plenty of loose rocks here; the lane had once been paved with cobblestones. Lawrence's first throw was accurate enough to bounce a fist-sized rock off the hood of the truck forty feet away. The second throw caught a fender.

"Nothing yet," Dale said loudly enough for the radio to hear. His first throw missed. The second rock landed on the camouflage net and branches. The smell of decomposing animals was very strong now.

Lawrence's third throw hit the metal strip between the panes of wind-shield glass. His fourth was flat and hard and broke the right headlight. The truck was silent and nothing around it stirred.

Dale was winding up and Lawrence was saying "I don't think there's anyone . . ." when the Rendering Truck's starter ground, the engine roared, a differential whined, and the whole thing came rattling and bouncing out of the space between buildings, the net and branches flying aside as the boards of the trailer section tore through the flimsy camou-flage.

"Go!" screamed Dale, dropping his rock and leaping onto his bike. His left foot missed the pedal and he almost fell onto the crossbar—the type of ball-breaking drop that made you just want to curl up on the grass for an hour—but he caught himself, almost tipped the bike over, got his head down and his ass high, and was pedaling furiously, Lawrence three yards ahead and not looking back, both boys barreling down the long drive between the arching brambles and the Rendering Truck less than fifty feet behind them, its roar and its stench curling like a tidal wave at their heels.

"Give me the lighters," Mike said to Harlen. They were lying prone be-hind the faded co-op sign on the tin roof of the grain elevator, about fifteen feet above the loading dock. Kevin was across the narrow drive, lying flat on the warehouse roof. It had been Harlen's job to bring the cigarette lighters, and he had checked his pocket and said he had them before they rendezvoused on Catton Road.

Now Harlen patted his pockets and looked wide-eyed. "I guess I forgot them . . ."

Mike grabbed Harlen's shirt and half-lifted him from the hot tin roof. "Don't fuck around, Jim."

Harlen produced five lighters, all topped off with fluid. Harlen's dad had collected the things and they'd been lying in the bottom of a drawer for three years.

Mike tossed two across to Kevin, put one in his pocket, and dropped back down behind the sign. Suddenly the radio squawked and Dale's voice shouted, "It's coming after us!"

The Rendering Truck was faster than they thought it would be, grinding gears as it roared out of the driveway after them. Even with their half-block lead, the thing was going to catch them before they got to Main Street. Wide yards led to nothing but the railroad embankment and cornfields on their left; the street to Sperling's house on their right was a cul-de-sac.

Dale caught up to Lawrence, got a bit ahead, glanced back and saw the red cab and rusted grille of the Rendering Truck closing the gap, and then leaned right, cutting across Bandstand Park, the rear fender of his bike clattering. The two boys went on either side of the War Memorial, cut between the park benches and the Parkside Cafe, and skidded out on the sidewalk in front of the cafe and Carl's Tavern.

Dale frowned, head low over the handlebars, elbows high. This wasn't going as planned—they had to get the truck up Broad, headed north. Now the thing had squealed to a halt to let a semi go past heading east and pulled onto Main—chasing them *east.*

"Come on!" Dale called to Lawrence and launched his bike out over the eighteen-inch curb. Lawrence jumped his at the same instant. A west-bound station wagon blared its horn at them as they cut in front of it, and then they were on the north side of the street, still headed east but closing on the intersection with Third Avenue.

The Rendering Truck was half a block behind them and cruising at thirty miles per hour. Dale saw a hint of movement through the windshield glare and the truck swerved to straddle the center line. *Van Syke or whoever's driving doesn't give a damn who's watching,* thought Dale. *He's going to run us down right here.*

Dale shouted something at his brother and they leaned left, their left arms brushing across the top of the low hedge in front of Dr. Viskes's house, their bike tires laying down rubber on the uneven sidewalk pavement. There was a drainage ditch between the sidewalk and Third Avenue here, and if either one of them skidded into it, the Rendering Truck would be on them.

They didn't. Dale let Lawrence pull past as they flashed up the sidewalk on the west side of Third, heading north now. An old man with a cane—Cyrus Whittaker, Dale thought—shouted at them as they whizzed by on the sidewalk.

The Rendering Truck turned north on Third.

Another block and they'd be passing the house where Dr. Roon rented a room, then coming into view of Old Central. Dale didn't want to see either one of those places, as much as he was tempted to reach the schoolyard and just cut across it to Depot Street and home. His mother would see the madman chasing them in the truck and call Barney or the sheriff . . .

Dale shouted at Lawrence, and his brother cut left on Church Street, heading back toward Broad. The truck came to the intersection sixty feet back, slowing to let a pickup go past.

Dale took the lead again and skidded onto the sidewalk, heading north along Broad past the library and the boarded-up stucco building that had been Ewalts Recreation Palace. They were almost to Mrs. Doubbet's house when Dale glanced over his shoulder and realized that the truck was no longer following. He hadn't seen it turn west on Church Street after them.

"Shit!" yelled Dale, pulling out onto Broad and skidding almost completely around. Lawrence slid to a stop next to him and they looked south along the wide avenue, waiting for the scabrous red cab of the truck to appear on Church.

The Rendering Truck pulled out of the alley twenty-five feet behind them, sliding from behind the forsythia bushes along the north side of Old Double-Butt's property as stealthily as a cat.

Lawrence got moving first, leaping his little bike onto the curb on the west side of the street and careening down the alley north of the post office. Dale was right on his tail, shouting their location at the walkie-talkie dangling from its strap. If Mike or anyone said anything back, Dale didn't hear it.

The Rendering Truck crossed Broad and accelerated down the alley after them, its bumper less than thirty feet behind Dale's back tire. Lawrence's bike was wobbling far right as the boy's body leaned left, then rocked left as Lawrence came down on the right pedal. He whooped and cut left across Mrs. Andyll's backyard, ducking under a clothesline, leaving tire tracks in the corner of her vegetable garden, and throwing cinders into the air as he led the way down her drive toward Church Street.

We'll lose the truck, thought Dale, *but we're going south again. The wrong way.*

They didn't lose the truck. It swung left after them, the double rear tires throwing great divots from Mrs. Andyll's lawn and garden. The cab of the truck ripped four clotheslines right out of their uprights and came down the drive dragging sheets and print dresses.

Dale and Lawrence went west on Church Street, standing to pedal, their rumps higher than their heads. The Rendering Truck gunned its engine and came up the street after them. Dale looked back and saw that one headlight was burning.

Just before they reached St. Malachy's, Dale led the way left and they cut between a house and a garage separated by less than four feet, roared past a lady and her infant sitting in a wading pool, and actually rode across a Doberman's chain before the dog realized that trespassers were in the yard. He and Lawrence came out into the alley and turned east again, Dale catching a glimpse of the truck barreling down the narrow street that ran along the railroad embankment half a block to the west.

The two boys headed up Fifth toward Depot Street, both of them panting hard now, Dale feeling the fading of energy that the first rush of terror had given him. His legs felt very tired. *We're less than halfway there.*

The Rendering Truck almost beat them to the intersection at Depot Street and Fifth.

Dale saw the red cab screeching around the corner near the depot, and then he cut right across the street and into the alley that ran north and south behind the Staffneys' place. *Where Mike saw his priest friend Thursday night. What if that guy steps out in front of us, grabs our handlebars?*

Dale fought down the sudden weakness and turned to check on Lawrence. His brother's face was beet-red, his crew cut as wet as if he had been swimming, but he looked up and grinned at Dale.

The Rendering Truck pulled into the alley behind them and shifted up through gears, the sides of the high-sided bed behind the cab shearing off branches and bushes as it came. The dogs along the alley went nuts.

Dale shouted their position at the walkie-talkie as they cut across the backyard of the last house before Catton Road. It was going to be close.

They went across the railroad crossing at thirty miles per hour, their bikes flying fifteen feet until the rear tires crashed down on hard-packed dirt on the narrow lane beyond. The Rendering Truck came on as if emboldened by the trees and isolation here.

Dale had a sudden image of the Soldier or one of the other things stepping out of the trees onto the narrow lane ahead of them, of the thing's mouth pulsating and extending the way Mike had described it. . . . He pedaled harder, shouting at Lawrence to move, move, *move.*

They circled around south to the clearing where the abandoned grain elevator and warehouse rose from the weeds. Dale glanced back just as the Rendering Truck stopped at the entrance to the drive . . . Dale imagined that it looked like a huge, wild, red dog at that moment, sniffing, knowing that its prey was cornered but cautious just the same.

Lawrence rode ahead just as they planned, barreling between the elevator proper with its faded sign on the roof and the long warehouse extension. It was a narrow lane where the trucks had pulled in to be weighed and to load or unload their grain, but it was wide enough for the Rendering Truck. Barely.

But the truck did not come on.

Dale had skidded to a halt just at the opening of the weighing lane, and now he stood on one leg, the other bent over the bike's crossbar, gasping and staring at the truck twenty yards away. *What if Van Syke has a gun?*

The engine roared. Dale could smell the cargo and see the stiffened legs of what looked like a couple of cows and a horse, sticking up above the off-white boards siding the truckbed, could even make out the reddened and hairy arm of the driver of the truck . . . but it did not come on.

Waiting for reinforcements? Does that goddamn thing have a radio? Can Van Syke call Roon and the others?

Dale dismounted and stood holding his bike. He could feel rather than hear the silent shouts of his friends behind him. *If they're there. Maybe something's already got them . . . got Lawrence when he went through . . . and has me trapped.*

He stood there facing the truck, seeing it rock as if the driver were popping the clutch in with the brakes still engaged.

Dale lifted his right arm and gave the unseen driver the finger.

The Rendering Truck came on, gravel flying and dust rising in a cloud.

Dale didn't have time to get back on his bike. He shoved it aside and turned and ran, cutting between the elevator and the warehouse, his Keds pounding on the rotted boards of the truck scales. He hadn't reached the end of the building when the Rendering Truck roared in behind him.

The lighter flared on the first try, the soaked rags ignited, and Mike stood to toss the twelve-ounce Coke bottle of Shell Premium onto the roof of the truck cab. What he saw as the truck roared by underneath made him pause for the split second it took to miss the cab and hit the truckbed: the rear of the Rendering Truck held not only dead livestock but other things—*human* things—that looked as if they had just been disinterred from old graves: brown soil, brown rags, brown flesh, and the bright white of bone.

Mike threw, Harlen tossed a second later, and both of them watched Kevin stand and fling his bottle from the warehouse rooftop.

Mike's Molotov cocktail exploded in the rear of the truck, igniting the bloated corpse of a cow, the dried flesh of a horse, and the rags of several of the human corpses. Harlen's bottle struck the back of the cab and splattered it with gasoline, somehow without igniting. Kev's struck the left front fender of the cab and exploded in a ball of flame.

Dale leaped to the left as he came around the building, almost colliding with Lawrence on his bike. His brother looked as if he were ready to drive back out through the narrow drive just as the Rendering Truck exploded through the gap, its cargo bed on fire and its left front wheel throwing gobbets of flame and melted rubber at them.

Mike and Harlen grabbed the next bottle from the duffel bag and ran to the edge of the tin rooftop, not worrying about being seen now, holding the lighter next to the rags.

The Rendering Truck skidded in the gravel and dirt of the co-op's back drive, turning in a frenzied circle. It was trapped. To the west lay a seven-foot-high barrier of abandoned railroad ties and iron rails, stacked for fifty feet along the edge of a small creek. Straight ahead, to the south, the woods closed in like a solid wall. To the east, running tight against the warehouse, was a six-foot-deep concrete drainage ditch separating the compound yard from the railroad embankment.

For a second Mike thought that the truck was going to try to jump that paved moat, but at the last second the driver slammed on the brakes and swung the vehicle left, completing his turn. The two right-rear wheels spun out over nothing for a moment and then the truck was screaming back toward Dale and Lawrence.

"Get out of there! Move!" Mike and Harlen and Kevin were screaming, but the boys below did not need the advice. Lawrence's bike rattled up a ramp onto the loading dock of the warehouse and Dale came pounding along a second later. They disappeared under the roof where Kevin stood, bottle and lighter still in hand, and then the truck was back, the flames diminishing on the fender and wheel.

Mike saw what Van Syke was going to do a second before the still-smoldering left front fender smashed into the first column supporting the roof where he and Harlen stood. The loading dock on the other side was too high for the truck to mount it, but this roof was held up just by the three columns running parallel to the truck scales.

Harlen screamed something, he and Mike lit their rags and threw, and then the roof was going down with them on it, the sign ripping free and falling onto the scales, Mike's duffel bag and the radio going flying as the south end of the roof folded first, dumping the boys and everything else in a cloud of dust.

Harlen's Molotov cocktail exploded on the hood of the truck; a second later, Kevin's second throw struck the back of the cab and ignited the spilled gasoline already there. Kevin ran to the front of the warehouse porch, readying a third bottle.

The Rendering Truck revved its engine and charged back through the narrow drive, seemingly intent on running down Harlen and Mike, both of whom lay stunned in the dust and rubble and tin of the collapsed roof. The truck rammed tin and wood, folded great sections of the shattered roof in front of it—Mike stared dully at it and thought of a bulldozer pushing its way toward them—but several of the broken support posts were set deep in cement and hindered the truck's advance.

The rubble of the roof was blocking the drive.

Mike staggered to his feet, lifted Harlen under one arm and the duffel bag with the other, and stumbled toward the loading dock as the truck backed off into the front driveway.

The left section of the truck's windshield had shattered and Mike caught a glimpse of the gun rack and muscled arm reaching just as Dale and Lawrence came into sight at the front of the warehouse dock. "Get down!" screamed Mike.

Dale pulled his brother off the bike and leaped behind a pile of wooden skids just as the rifle fired twice . . . a third time. A dusty windowpane above the skids shattered and dropped glass on the crouching boys.

Mike had dropped the lighter, but he pulled the spare from his pocket, ignited the soaked rags, and threw the Coke bottle at the grille of the truck thirty feet away. It dropped early, rolled under the cab, and exploded, sending flame blossoming up around the engine and both front wheels. He pulled Harlen out of sight just as the rifle came through the broken windshield and fired twice. Wood splintered from the corner molding of the warehouse.

Kevin dropped another bottle on the right running board, still another into the mass of burning bodies behind the cab.

The Rendering Truck backed up, turned around, and roared down the drive, trailing flames, turning left rather than right toward town.

"We got it! We got it!" Harlen was screaming as he jumped up and down.

"Not yet," said Mike, carrying the heavy duffel and running for his bike where it was hidden behind the grain elevator. For the first time he realized that the truck had ignited the wooden side of the elevator and bits of the collapsed roof. The fire was already spreading to the ware-house wall, where a hundred years of sawdust and old wood was catch-ing faster than the gasoline that had started it.

Dale ran out into the front drive and retrieved his bike—which the Rendering Truck miraculously had missed each time it had backed past it—straightened its handlebars, and leaped on while running. Lawrence sped past, in hot pursuit of the truck despite the fact that the boy had no weapon. Mike and Harlen got on their bikes and pedaled out past an el-evator already burning to the second story.

"Cut through the woods!" shouted Mike, bouncing left between the trees, taking a shortcut to the overgrown lane that ran from the grain elevator to the Dump Road. He assumed that the truck would turn left on the Dump Road, heading back along the railroad tracks toward the depot and town, but when they came crashing out of the weeds and un-dergrowth onto the narrow gravel drive, the truck was visible a hundred yards ahead, going north toward the dump. Flame and black smoke still rose from the jouncing vehicle.

The boys put their heads down and concentrated on riding faster than they ever had before, their bikes jostling and bouncing over ruts and stones in the twin lanes.

Mike was out in front, and he caught up to the Rendering Truck just as they reached the widened area where the Cookes and another poor family had lived. Both shacks looked abandoned.

Somehow Mike managed to get a bottle out, hold it in his left hand against the handlebar, and fumble out his lighter as he pulled alongside the truck.

The rifle barrel came out the driver's window.

Mike braked, skidded, pumped hard to get behind the truck, and pulled up on the right side as they both entered the last hundred yards of road to the dump. Dale, Lawrence, Kevin, and Harlen pumped along in single file behind.

Mike caught a second's glimpse of Karl Van Syke's long face—he was grinning maniacally through the flames and smoke curling back from the hood—then the rifle came up again and Mike lobbed the already-flaming Coke bottle through the passenger-side window.

The explosion blew out the remaining windshield glass. The heat forced Mike to drop back behind the truck, and what he saw there al-most made him dump his Schwinn into the ditch alongside the road.

The carcass of the cow, or the horse, or both, bloated with methane and the other gasses of decomposition, exploded . . . showering flames and bits of flaming decayed flesh into the woods on either side.

But that wasn't what made Mike's jaw sag open.

The brown, rotting, once-human things seemed to be writhing and tugging at one another as the flames enclosed them . . . the denizens of some evacuated cemetery trying to pull themselves to their knees, to their feet, but finding no muscles or tendons or bone with which to do so. The brown things struggled and writhed, falling back into each other's embrace as the entire heap of carcasses began to burn.

The flaming truck did not slow for the wooden gates at the dump entrance. Boards splintered with a sound like more rifle shots and then the large truck was through, bouncing across the ruts and heaps of landfill with five bicycles in pursuit.

The Rendering Truck got as far into the mounds of refuse, old tires, sprung sofas, rusted Model-T's, and moldering organic garbage as it could before it slewed left and slid to a stop on the edge of a forty-foot drop into the part of the ravine here that had not been filled. The boys slid to a stop thirty feet back, waiting for the truck to turn on them.

It did not. The flames had enveloped cab and truckbed now; the wooden slats at the rear were parallel strips of fire.

"Nothing could live through that," whispered Kevin, his mouth open as he stared.

As if the driver had heard, the flaming door on this side slammed open and Karl Van Syke slid out, his one-piece jumpsuit charred and smoking, his face streaked with soot and sweat, arms reddened. He was grinning almost from ear to ear. A scoped rifle was in his huge hands.

All the boys looked around and raised their feet to the bike pedals, but it was sixty or seventy feet to the nearest cover—a cornfield to their left. It was almost a hundred yards to the dump entrance and the line of woods behind them.

"Get down!" shouted Mike, dropping his bike in front of him and scrabbling at the heaped landfill to find cover.

The other four boys threw themselves flat, inching toward any rotted tire or rusted drum that might offer cover. Harlen had his .38 in his hand but did not fire . . . it was too much distance for the short-barreled gun.

Van Syke took two steps from the flaming vehicle and raised the rifle, taking careful aim at Mike O'Rourke's face.

During the turmoil, a small figure with two dogs had come over the top of the highest heap of garbage. Now she released the thongs and said, "Git 'im!" in a surprisingly soft voice.

Van Syke looked to his left just as the first dog, the Doberman named Belzybub, covered the last twenty feet of ground. He swiveled his rifle and fired, but the huge brown animal had already leaped, striking his chest and driving both of them back into the flaming cab of the truck.

The big dog named Lucifer was next, growling and leaping at Van Syke's kicking legs.

Mike dug Memo's squirrel gun out of the duffel, saw Kevin pull his dad's .45 from his belt, and all five boys rushed forward even as Cordie slid her way down the garbage slope.

One of Van Syke's flailing legs caught in the half-open window of the door and swung it shut on him and the dog. Cordie and Mike rushed forward, but at that second the gas tank beneath the truck ignited, sending a perfect mushroom of flame eighty feet into the air. Mike and the girl were both lifted off their feet and thrown across the rough ground, the German shepherd-mix named Lucifer landing scorched and howling at their feet. Belzybub was still in the cab; Dale and Lawrence grabbed Mike and Cordie and dragged them back, watching the two dark shapes still struggling in the curling vortex of orange flame.

Then the motion stopped and the truck burned, filling the world with the stench of melting rubber and something far worse.

The six kids stood there, almost a hundred feet away now—driven back by the terrible heat—shielding their watering eyes and staring. A siren sounded back through the woods, somewhere around the grain elevator. Another siren whooped along the Dump Road.

Cordie was weeping and cradling her other dog. The shepherd-mix had lost most of his hair. "Foun' my hideout, didn't you?" said Cordie between sobs. "Couldn't leave me alone, could you?"

Harlen started to protest that they hadn't known she was living in the goddamn *dump,* for Chrissakes, but Mike hushed him with a hand on his chest and said, "Is there another way out of here? We've got to get going before the fire trucks arrive."

Cordie gestured toward the corn. "They'd see ya if you took the railroad tracks back, but cut across the Meehans' field there for about half a mile, an' you'll get to Oak Hill Road about a quarter of a mile above the Grange Hall. You can take it to the Hard Road."

Mike nodded, seeing the map in his mind. They rushed to the barbed-wire fence, tossed their bikes across, and started to climb. "Aren't you coming with us?" Dale called to Cordie.

The sirens were closer now. The girl in her dumpy, soiled dress had climbed the hill of garbage, still carrying the large dog. "Uh-uh. Y'all go on." She turned and spat in the direction of the huge pyre that had been the Rendering Truck. "At least that fuck's dead." She disappeared over the mound of refuse and old tires.

The boys pulled their bikes into the corn just as the first fire truck and its retinue of rushing pickups came through the shattered gate.

It wasn't easy pushing their bikes through half a mile of soft soil between seven-foot-high rows of corn only nine inches apart, but they did it.

When they reached Oak Hill Road and turned south, pedaling past the Old Grange Hall, where Mike and Dale had gone to Boy Scout meetings in another lifetime, the cloud of black smoke was still rising thick and heavy from the dump far to the northeast.

THIRTY-FOUR

It was just after sunset on Friday evening and Mike was half-dozing in the chair in Memo's room when his sister Margaret came in to tell him that Father Cavanaugh was at the door.

The boys had spent the better part of an hour taking the long way home from the dump. They'd stopped at Harlen's to wet each other down with a garden hose, soaking their clothes to get the stench of burned rubber and flesh off them. Mike's eyebrows had been all but burned off by the last explosion, and he'd shrugged and said he couldn't do anything about that, but Harlen had taken him in the empty house and drawn eyebrows back on with his mother's eyebrow pencil. Kevin had tried making a joke about Jim's skill with the makeup, but none of them were in the mood to laugh.

After the first few minutes of euphoria over their triumph at the dump, the reality of the morning's events had hit the boys hard. All of them had had the shakes—even Lawrence—and Kevin had walked into the weeds to vomit twice on the way into town.

The cars and trucks still rushing out toward the grain co-op and the dump did nothing to relieve their tension. But mostly it was the shock of the images that continued to shake them up through the long afternoon: *the man and dog still wrestling, still moving in the flaming pyre that was the cab of the truck; the sounds of man and animal screaming in pain, their cries intermingled and indistinguishable, the smell of burning flesh. . . .*

"Let's not wait," said Harlen, his lips pale. "Let's burn the fucking school this afternoon."

"We can't," said Kevin. His freckles were very clear against the sudden pallor of his face. "Dad's got the milk truck at the bulk plant until after six on Fridays. They do inventory."

"Burn it this evening then," insisted Harlen.

Mike was looking into the mirror above the sink in Jim's kitchen, trying to wiggle his painted-on eyebrows. "You guys really want to do this when it's getting dark?" he said.

The thought silenced them.

"Tomorrow then," said Harlen. "During the day."

Kevin had his father's .45 service automatic spread out on the kitchen table as he cleaned and oiled it. Now he looked up, holding the empty magazine clip in one hand and a small spring in the other. "Dad will be out on his route until about four. But I have to wash it and gas it afterwards."

Harlen had pounded the table. "Fuck the milk truck then. Let's use these Whatchamacallem cocktails."

"Molotov cocktails," Mike said from the sink. He turned back toward the others. "You guys know how thick those stone walls of Old Central are?"

"At least a foot," said Dale. He sat limply at the table, too tired to raise his glass of Squirt. His wet sneakers made squeegee sounds as he wiggled his toes.

"Try two feet thick," said Mike. "The damned place is like a fort, more brick and stone than wood. With the windows boarded, we'd have to go inside to throw the Molotov cocktails. You want to do that . . . go inside . . . even in the daytime?"

No one said anything.

"We do it Sunday morning," said Mike, sitting on the edge of Harlen's counter. "After first light but before people start coming in to town for church. We use the tanker and the hoses, just as we planned."

"That's two nights away," Lawrence had whispered, speaking to himself but speaking for all of them.

The gray day had faded to a pale twilight, the air thick with humidity unleavened by breezes, when Mike had dozed off in Memo's room. His father was working his last night on the graveyard shift and his mother was in bed with one of her migraines. Kathleen and Bonnie had bathed in the copper tub in the kitchen and were upstairs getting ready for bed. Mary had gone out on a date and Peggy was in the front room reading a magazine when the knock on the door made Mike stir in his sleep.

Peg leaned on the doorframe, frowning. "Mike . . . Father Cavanaugh's here. He said that he had to talk to you . . . that it's important."

Mike lurched awake, grabbing the sides of the armchair to keep from falling. Memo's eyes were closed. He could barely make out the soft pulse at the base of her throat. "Father Cavanaugh?" For a second he was so disoriented that he was ready to believe that everything had been a dream. "Father C.?" he repeated, coming awake now with a shock. "Did he . . . did he *talk* to you?"

Peg made a face. "I told you what he said."

Mike looked around in a sudden panic. The squirrel gun was in the duffel bag at his feet along with a water pistol, two of the remaining Molotov cocktails, and pieces of the Host carefully wrapped in clean linen. A vial of holy water sat on the windowsill next to one of Memo's small jewel cases, which held another segment of the Eucharist.

"You didn't invite him in . . ." began Mike.

"He said he'd wait on the porch," said his sister. "What's *wrong* with you?"

"Father C.'s been sick," said Mike, glancing out at the yard and field across the road. It was dark, the last of the twilight having bled away while he slept.

"And you're afraid of catching it?" Peg's voice sounded scornful.

"How'd he look?" asked Mike, moving to the doorway of the bedroom. He could see the living room from here, one lamp burning there, but not the front-porch screen door. No one came to the front door except salesmen.

"Look?" Peggy chewed a nail. "Sort of pale, I guess. The porch light's out and it was sort of dark. Look, shall I go tell him that Mother has one of her headaches?"

"No," said Mike, pulling her into Memo's room with a rough jerk. "Stay here. Watch Memo. Don't come out no matter what you hear."

"Michael . . ." began his sister, voice rising.

"I *mean* it," said Mike in tones that even an older sister could not argue with. He pushed her into the chair. "Don't leave until I come back. Got it?"

Peg was rubbing her arm. Her voice was shaky. "Yeah, but . . ."

But Mike had scooped up the squirt gun, tucked it into his waistband under his shirt, set the linen-wrapped Host on Memo's bed, and was out the door.

"Hello, Michael," said Father Cavanaugh. He was sitting on the wicker chair at the end of the porch. He extended an arm toward the porch swing. "Come . . . be seated."

Mike let the screen door close behind him, but he did not move to the swing. That would put Father Cavanaugh between him and the house.

It's not Father Cavanaugh!

It looked like Father C. He was wearing his black coat and Roman collar. The only light out here was the lamplight coming through curtains, but while Father C.'s face was pale—almost haggard—there was no sign of the scars Mike had seen the night before. *He was hanging outside Michelle's garage window. Hanging by what?*

"I thought you were sick," Mike said. His voice was very tight.

"No longer, Michael," said the priest, smiling slightly. "I have never been so well."

Mike felt the hair rising on the back of his neck and he realized that it was the priest's voice. It sounded something like the real Father C., but at the same time, the voice was *wrong*—as if someone had buried a tape recording of the priest's voice in the man's stomach and was playing it through a speaker deep in his throat.

"Go away," whispered Mike. He wished by all the saints and the Virgin that he hadn't told Dale to take the second walkie-talkie when Harlen wanted the other one. It had made sense at the time.

Father Cavanaugh shook his head. "No, not until we talk, Michael . . . come to some agreement."

Mike set his lips and said nothing. He glanced over his shoulder at the front lawn near Memo's window; the rectangle of yellow light fell on an empty lawn there.

Father Cavanaugh sighed and moved to the porch swing, patting the now-empty wicker chair. "Come, sit down, Michael my lad. We must talk."

"Talk," said Mike, moving so that his back was against the wall of the house near the lighted window. The cornfield was like a black wall across the road. A few fireflies were visible in the garden behind the porch swing and trellis.

Father C.—*it isn't Father C.!*—made a gesture with pale hands. Mike had never noticed how long the priest's fingers were. "Very well, Michael . . . I come to offer you and your little friends a . . . what shall we call it? A truce."

"What kind of truce?" said Mike. He felt as if his tongue had been given a shot of Novocaine.

It was dark enough now that the priest's black garb blended with the night, allowing only his hands, face, and the white circle of his collar to reflect the light. "A truce that will allow you to live," he said flatly. "Perhaps."

Mike made a noise that he'd meant as a laugh. "Why should we make a truce? You saw what happened to your buddy Van Syke today."

The face above the swing opened its mouth and laughter emerged . . . if one could call a sound like the rattling of stones in an old gourd *laughter*. "Michael, Michael," he said softly, "your actions today had no significance whatsoever. Our buddy, as you call him, was scheduled to be . . . ah . . . retired tonight anyway."

Mike's fists clenched. "Like you retired C.J. Congden's old man?"

"Precisely," came the voice from deep inside the thing in priest's garb. "His usefulness was effectively at an end. He had other . . . ah . . . services to offer."

Mike leaned forward. "Who in hell *are* you?"

Again the rattle of stones. "Michael, Michael . . . all the explanations in the world could not begin to make you understand the complexity of the situation you have stumbled into. Trying to explain would be like teaching catechism to a cat or dog."

"Go ahead," whispered Mike. "Try me."

"No," snapped the white face. There was no illusion of small talk in the dead voice now. "Suffice it to say that if you and your friends accept our offer of a truce, you may live to see the autumn."

Mike felt his heart lurch in his chest. His legs were suddenly weak as he leaned against the wall in what he thought was a relaxed, almost casual manner. Once, during a High Mass with Father Harrison years before, just after he'd become an altar boy, Mike had fainted after twenty-five minutes of kneeling. He felt a similar rushing in his ears now. *No, no, hold on, pay attention.*

"Who's this 'we' you keep talking about," said Mike, amazed to hear his own voice sounding so strong, "a bunch of corpses and a bell?"

The white face moved back and forth. "Michael, Michael . . ." The priest stood, took a step toward him.

Mike glanced furtively to his left, saw something the size of the Soldier step out of the field across the road and begin gliding toward the lawn near Memo's window.

"Call him off!" cried Mike. He pulled out the water pistol.

The face of Father Cavanaugh smiled. He snapped his fingers and the Soldier glided to a stop under the linden tree thirty feet away. Father C.'s smile continued to broaden, pulling back to show his back teeth, broadening further until it seemed the man's face would snap in half as if on a hinge. That impossible mouth opened wide and Mike saw more teeth—rows and rows of teeth, endless lines of white that seemed to recede down the thing's gullet.

The Cavanaugh-thing made no pretense of moving its mouth or jaw as the voice came up from its belly. "You surrender now, you motherfucking little worm, or we shall rip your fucking heart from your chest . . . we shall chew your balls off and serve them to our minions . . . tear your fucking eyes out of their sockets the way we did that putrid friend's of yours. . . ."

"Duane," whispered Mike, feeling his breathing stop, lurch, and start again, although reluctantly. His neck and belly ached from tension.

In the shadows of the lawn, the Soldier began gliding toward Memo's window once again.

"Ah, yesssssss," hissed Father Cavanaugh, taking another step toward Mike. His long fingers were rising. His face was . . . melting, it looked to Mike . . . flesh flowing under skin, cartilage and bone rearranging itself, the long nose and chin moving together to form the snout that Mike had seen on the Soldier in the cemetery. *When they killed Father C.*

He could not see the slugs yet, but the priest's face was becoming more of a funnel than a face. The thing took another step closer, hands coming up.

"Fuck you!" shouted Mike, pulling the squirt gun from his waistband and squeezing the trigger.

The Father Cavanaugh–thing seemed startled a second, then stepped back, then laughed, making a sound like teeth biting into slate. Behind Mike, the Soldier glided out of sight beyond the edge of the house.

Mike raised the squirt gun with a steady arm and fired another stream of holy water into the thing's face. *It doesn't work . . . he doesn't believe.*

Once their fifth-grade teacher, Mrs. Shrives, had meant to do an experiment where she took a few drops of hydrochloric acid from a beaker and used an eyedropper to drip it onto a fresh orange. Instead, the old lady had accidentally overturned the beaker, drenching the orange and the thick felt cloth the beaker had been on.

That same sizzling, hissing noise now emanated from Father Cavanaugh's face and clothing. Mike saw the white flesh of the snout shrivel and curl, as if the skin itself were being eaten away by the holy water. The man's left eyelid hissed and was gone, the eyeball sizzling as it stared at Mike through raised fingers. Great holes were appearing in the black coat and Roman collar, allowing a stench of dead flesh to escape from the interior.

Father Cavanaugh screamed like Cordie's dog had several hours earlier, lowered its misshapen head, and rushed the boy.

Mike jumped aside, squirting more holy water on the thing and seeing fumes rise thicker from its hissing, burning back. Peg, Bonnie and Kathleen were shouting from inside the house. His mother's voice came weakly from her back bedroom.

"Stay in your rooms!" he screamed and jumped onto the lawn.

The Soldier had wrestled the screen out of its frame and was leaning into the lighted window, his fingers scrabbling on wood.

Mike ran forward and squirted the last of the holy water onto the back of its neck.

The thing did not scream. A smell worse than the burning Rendering Truck rose from it and it flung itself into the loose soil of the flower bed under the window, scrabbling and kicking its way through the shrubbery into the darkness.

Mike turned just as the Father Cavanaugh figure leapt from the porch and reached for him. Mike ducked under the long arms, dropped the empty squirt gun into the bushes, and reached for Memo's small jewel case on the sill.

Peg was visible through the billowing curtains, standing by the doorway of Memo's room, hands to her mouth. "Mike, what . . ."

Father Cavanaugh's long fingers closed on Mike's shoulders and jerked him back out of the light, into the darkness under the linden tree. The tall priest-form hugged Mike closer.

Mike smelled the stench in his face, saw the face cracked now with acid-chewed scars, sensed things writhing under that flesh and in the long tunnel of the proboscis, and then Father C. leaned forward, the cartilage of its snout pulsating above Mike's face.

He had no time to look. Mike opened the case, lifted the large piece of consecrated Host out, and thrust it against the obscene opening in the thing's face just as the pressure of the slugs inside it threatened to burst forth.

Mike had watched once as C.J. Congden had fired a 12-gauge shotgun at a full watermelon on a post only eight feet away.

This was worse.

The Father Cavanaugh–thing's snout and face seemed to explode sideways with chunks of pasty white flesh bouncing off the house and pattering on the linden leaves. There was a scream, audibly from the figure's belly this time, and Mike dropped the Host as the thing staggered backward, fingers to what was left of its face now.

Mike jumped back as he saw six-inch brown slugs curling and writhing in the grass as the Host seemed to glow from some blue-green radiance of its own. Fragments of Father Cavanaugh's flesh hissed and deliquesced like snails caught out of their shells in a rain of salt.

Peg was screaming from the bedroom. Mike staggered to the porch, saw his mother come to the door—her eyes racked with the pain of the migraine and the washcloth still raised to her temples—and both of them watched as the shadow of Father Cavanaugh staggered onto First Avenue, hands still over its ruined face, a terrible noise like a boiler rushing toward explosion rising out of it.

"Mike, what . . ." his mother said through her pain, blinking to see clearly, just as the headlights caught the figure staggering out from under the linden tree.

The cars barely slowed when they came into town on First Avenue, despite the sign a hundred feet up the road that posted the speed limit at thirty-five. Most of the cars continued at forty-five or fifty miles per hour until they reached the Hard Road three blocks south. This pickup must have been doing sixty, perhaps more.

Father C. staggered directly into its path, the tall figure bent almost double in pain, hands over its face. It removed its hands in the last second of squealing brakes.

The grille of the pickup caught the priest full in the face, the body disappeared under the truck but was dragged another hundred and thirty feet, Peg screamed from inside the house, and Mike's mother put her arms around her son as if protecting him from the sight.

By the time he and his mother walked out to see what had happened, the Somersets and Millers and Meyerses had already come out of their homes, Barney's rarely used siren was screaming a block or two away and rapidly approaching, and the driver of the pickup was on his knees on the pavement, covering his own face with his hands as he stared under the truck at what was left of the priest and muttering over and over, "I didn't see him . . . he just rushed out."

Through the cloud of shock and terror that had dulled Mike's senses, he slowly recognized the driver. It was Mr. McBride, Duane's dad. The man was sobbing and leaning on the running board of his pickup.

Mike turned away from the murmuring crowd, walking back toward the house as he bit hard on the fleshy part of his hand below the thumb. He was afraid that if he let up on the pressure he would start to laugh or cry, and he was not sure if he would be able to stop.

THIRTY-FIVE

Saturday the sixteenth of July was as dark a day as there can be in Illinois in midsummer. In Oak Hill, where the streetlights were controlled by photoelectric sensors, the lights went off at five-thirty A.M. and flickered back on at seven-fifteen A.M. The dark clouds seemed to move in above the treetops and hang there. In Elm Haven, the few streetlights were switched on and off by an old electrical timer in the annex next to the bank, and no one thought to turn them back on when the day grew darker rather than lighter.

Mr. Meyers opened his dry goods store on Main Street at precisely nine A.M. and was surprised to find four boys—the Stewart kids, Ken Grumbacher's boy Kevin, and another boy in a sling—waiting to buy squirt guns. Three apiece. The boys deliberated for several minutes, taking care to choose the most reliable guns and the ones with the largest water reservoirs. Mr. Meyers thought it odd . . . but he thought most things in this brave new world of 1960 odd. Things made more sense when he had opened the store back in the twenties, when trains came through every day and people knew how to behave like civilized human beings.

The boys were gone by nine-thirty, keeping their newly purchased squirt guns in sacks and riding off with not a word of good-bye. Mr. Meyers shouted at them not to park their bikes on the sidewalk, that it was a hazard to pedestrians and against the city ordinances to boot, but the boys were gone, out of sight up Broad Avenue.

Mr. Meyers went back to taking inventory of dusty things on the high old shelves, occasionally looking out across the street and above the park to frown at the dark clouds. When he took his coffee break at the Parkside an hour later, old-timers in the back booth were talking about tornadoes.

Mike was questioned several times on Saturday: by Barney, by the county sheriff, and even by the Highway Patrol, who sent two troopers in a long brown car.

The sixth grader tried to imagine the puzzle that the sheriff and Barney were trying to assemble—Duane McBride and his uncle dying under mysterious circumstances, Mrs. Moon dying of natural causes but her precious cats being slaughtered, the body of the justice of the peace being found charred almost—but not quite—beyond recognition in the grain elevator, his throat cut according to the county coroner, while the body of Congden's friend Karl Van Syke—charred beyond immediate recognition but identified by his front gold tooth—was pulled out of the cab of the scorched Rendering Truck owned by Van Syke and Congden. The body of an unidentified dog was also discovered in the truck.

Town gossips were already piecing together motives for the murder; Congden and Van Syke sharing ill-gained profits from the justice of the peace's various scams, a falling-out between partners in crime, a brutal murder, then an accident with the gasoline that Van Syke had obviously used to douse the elevator before torching it, the fleeing man too frightened to abandon his burning truck for fear of being caught at the scene, the exploding gas tank . . .

By noon on Saturday, the locals had explained everything but the dead dog . . . Van Syke hated dogs, and no one had ever seen him allow one near him, much less in his truck. Then Mrs. Whittaker at Betty's

Beauty Salon on Church Street came up with the obvious deduction—
J.P. Congden's large watchdog had disappeared some weeks earlier. Obviously that no-good Karl Van Syke had stolen it, or dognapped it, and
the ownership of the dog was part of the dispute that led to the grisly
murder.

Elm Haven had not had a real murder for decades. The townsfolk
were shocked and delighted—especially delighted now that the obvious
culprit behind the slaughter of Mrs. Moon's cats had been found.

How Father Cavanaugh's accidental death figured into this was not
quite as certain. Mrs. McCafferty told Mrs. Somerset who called Mrs.
Sperling with the information that the priest always had been a bit un-
stable, making fun of his own vocation, even calling the diocese vehicle
on loan from Oak Hill Lincoln-Mercury the "Popemobile," according to
Mrs. Meehan, who helped with all the church functions. Mrs. Maher at
the Lutheran Ladies' Auxiliary told Mrs. Meehan at the Methodist Bazaar that Father Cavanaugh had a history of insanity in his family—he
was Scotch-Irish and everyone knew what *that* meant, and it had been
common knowledge that the young priest had been transferred from a
large diocese in Chicago as punishment for some bizarre act there.

Now everyone knew what the bizarre acts included: being a Peeping
Tom, trying to break into people's houses, and probably killing cats as
some sort of dark Catholic ritual. Mrs. Whittaker told Mrs. Staffney,
who confirmed it with Mrs. Taylor that Catholics used dead cats in certain secret rituals. Mrs. Taylor said that her husband had told her that
the young priest's face had been "crushed and peeled," his words, by the
sharp grille of Mr. McBride's pickup truck. Mr. Taylor had pronounced
Father Cavanaugh as "perhaps the deadest on arrival dead-on-arrival"
that he had had the solemn duty to prepare. The archdiocese bishop
called early Saturday morning from St. Mary's in Peoria and told Mr.
Taylor not to prepare the body for anything except shipment on Monday
to Chicago, where the family would claim it. Mr. Taylor agreed, but
added cosmetology to his bill at any rate, since "the family can't see him
like this . . . it's as if something had exploded *outward* from his face."
Again, Mr. Taylor's words, to quote Mrs. Taylor to Mrs. Whittaker.

One way or the other, however, the people were sure that the mystery
had been solved. Mr. Van Syke, whom, it turned out, no one in town had
trusted very much, murdering poor old Justice of the Peace Congden
over money or a dog. Poor Father Cavanaugh, whom, it turned out, all of
the Protestants and not a few of the older Catholics had never considered that stable, had gone out of his mind with a congenital fever and had
tried to attack his altar boy Michael O'Rourke before running in front of
a truck.

The townspeople clucked and the phone lines hummed—Jenny at the county switchboard hadn't counted so many calls coming out of Elm Haven since the flood in '49—and everyone had a good time solving things while they kept one eye on the dark clouds that continued to build over the cornfields to the south and west.

The sheriff wasn't so easily convinced that things were solved. After lunch he came back for the third interview with Mike since the night before.

"And Father Cavanaugh spoke to your sister?"

"Yessir. She told me that Father C. wanted to talk to me . . . that it was important." Mike knew that the tall sheriff had spoken to Peg twice before also.

"Did he tell her what he wanted to speak to you about?"

"No, sir. I don't think so. You'll have to ask her."

"Mmmm," said the sheriff, looking at a small spiral notebook that made Mike think of Duane's notebooks. "Tell me again what he *did* talk to you about."

"Well, sir, as I said before, I couldn't really understand him. It was like when a person's talking in a fever. There were words and phrases that seemed to make sense, but it didn't all go together."

"Tell me some of the words, son."

Mike chewed his lip. Duane McBride had once told him and Dale that most criminals screw up their lies and alibis because they talk too much, feel too much need to embroider facts. Innocent people, said Duane, are usually a lot less articulate. Mike had had to go home and look up the word "articulate" after that conversation.

"Well, sir," said Mike slowly, "I know he used the word sin several times. He said we'd all sinned and had to be punished. But I had the feeling he wasn't really talking about us . . . just people in general."

The sheriff nodded and made a note. "And that's when he started shouting?"

"Yessir. About then."

"But your sister says that he heard both of your voices. If you didn't understand what the father was saying, why were you talking?"

Mike resisted the impulse to rub sweat off his upper lip. "I guess I was asking him if he was OK. I mean, the last time I saw Father C. was when Mrs. McCafferty let me in to see him on Tuesday. He was really sick then."

"And did he say he was all right?"

"No, sir, he just started shouting that the Judgment Day was nigh . . . that was his word, sir, nigh."

"And then he ran off the porch and started attacking your grandmother's window," said the sheriff, checking his notes. "Is that right?"

"Yessir."

The sheriff scratched his cheek slowly, obviously not satisfied with something. "And what about his face, son?"

"His face, sir?" This was a new question.

"Yes. Was it . . . strange? Lacerated or distorted in any way?"

Not if you don't call turning itself into a sort of lamprey snout distorted, thought Mike. He said, "No, sir. I don't think so. He was pale. But it was pretty dark."

"But you didn't see any scars or lesions?"

"What are lesions, sir?"

"Like deep scratches? Or open sores?"

"No, sir."

The sheriff sighed and reached into a small gym bag. "Is this yours, son?" He held the water pistol.

Mike's first inclination was to deny it. "Yessir," he said.

The sheriff nodded. "Your sister said it was. Aren't you a little old to be playing with squirt guns?"

Mike shrugged and allowed himself to look embarrassed.

"Did you have this out on the porch last night? When Father Cavanaugh was visiting?"

"No," said Mike.

"You're sure?"

"Yessir."

"We found it below the window," said the sheriff. He pushed his hat back on his head and smiled for the first time during the interview. "It shows how paranoid I'm getting in my old age . . . I had the police lab up at Oak Hill actually analyze the contents. Water. Just water."

Mike returned the big man's smile.

"Here, son. Here's your toy back. Is there anything else you can tell me that could help? Where this came from, for instance?" He held up the Soldier's campaign hat.

"No, sir. Maybe it was in the bushes. Father C. had it on when he pulled the screen off."

"And it's the same hat you saw when you reported a soldier as a Peeping Tom a few weeks ago?"

"I guess so, sir. I don't know."

"But it's the same style of hat?"

"Yessir."

"But you didn't recognize this soldier as your priest the other times you saw him out on the lawn?" The sheriff watched Mike very carefully.

Mike thought a minute, just as he had the last couple of times he'd been asked this. "No, sir," he said at last. "Before I would've said it wasn't

Father Cavanaugh . . . he seemed smaller the first time I saw him . . . but it was dark, and I was looking through the curtains." Mike made a confused gesture with his hands. "Sorry, sir."

The tall man unlimbered from where he sat on the couch, touched Mike's shoulder with one large hand, and said, "That's all right, son. Thank you for your help. I'm sorry you had to see that last night. We may never know what was wrong with that gentleman . . . your Father Cavanaugh, I mean . . . but I doubt that he meant to do what he did. Whether it was the fever his doctors were talking about or whatever, I don't think the gentleman was in his right mind."

"I don't either, sir," said Mike, walking the sheriff to the door. Mike's father and mother were waiting on the porch. All three of them waved as the sheriff's car moved away slowly down First.

"Let's do it this afternoon," Harlen said in the treehouse an hour later. All of them were there . . . all except Cordie Cooke. Harlen and Dale had gone out to the dump just after breakfast to find her, but there was no sign except for some ratty blankets in a shattered lean-to near the railroad embankment.

Mike sighed, too tired to argue. Dale said, "We've been over this, Jim."

Kevin was thumbing through a Scrooge McDuck comic—something about finding Viking gold to judge from the cover—but he put it down to say, "We're waiting till morning. I'm not going to steal Dad's truck right in front of him. We have to convince him that somebody else took it and sprayed Old Central with gas."

Harlen snorted. "Who? All the suspects are ending up dead. This'll be the goddamnedist week in the history of Elm Haven, and somebody's gonna figure out that we had something to do with it sooner or later . . ."

"Not if you keep your big trap shut," said Dale.

"Who's going to make me, Stewart?" sneered Harlen.

The two boys leaned toward each other until Mike pushed them apart. "Cool it." His voice was very tired. "One thing's for sure, we're not going to sleep apart tonight and let those things pick us off one by one."

"Right," said Harlen, settling back against a huge limb, "let's all get together so they can pick us off in one big gulp."

Mike shook his head. "Two teams. My folks've already said I could stay with Dale and Lawrence tonight. They think I just want to get out of the house because of last night."

The boys said nothing.

"Harlen, you got it cleared to spend the night at Kev's?"

"Yeah."

"Good. That way we can keep in touch all night with the walkie-talkies."

Dale tore a leaf from a branch and began stripping it into smaller and smaller pieces. "Sounds good. Then we load the tanker with gas in the morning and spray the school. Just after first light, right?"

"Right," said Mike. He turned toward Kevin. "Grumbacher, you sure you can drive it?"

Kev raised an eyebrow. "I told you I could, didn't I?"

"Yeah, but we don't want any surprises come tomorrow morning."

"No surprises," said Kevin. "My father lets me drive it on back roads every once in a while. I can do the gears. I can reach the pedals. I can get it to the schoolyard."

"Coast it out quietly," said Dale. "We don't want your folks waking up."

Kevin moved his chin up and down slowly. "Their bedroom's in the basement, and they've got the air conditioning going. That'll help."

Lawrence had been silent but now he leaned into the group. "You guys really think that whatever's in that school's just going to sit and wait for us to do something? That it's not going to fight back?"

Mike snapped a twig. "It's been fighting back. I think it's running out of allies to fight with."

"Nobody can find Dr. Roon," said Harlen. He scratched at his cast. It was scheduled to come off in a few days and the itching was driving him nuts.

"The lady that rents his room says he's on vacation in Minnesota," said Kevin.

"Uh-*huh*," said the other four in sarcastic unison.

"And the Soldier's still out there somewhere," said Mike.

No one made a joke this time.

"And old Double-Butt and her partner," said Harlen. "And the burrowing things. And Tubby."

"Minus his hand," said Dale. "He can't give us the finger." No one laughed.

"That's seven of 'em right there," said Lawrence, who'd been counting on his fingers. "There's only five of us."

"Plus Cordie," said Dale. "Sometimes."

Lawrence made a face. "I don't count girls. Seven of them . . . not counting the bell thing itself . . . and only five of us."

"Yeah," said Mike, "but we've got a secret weapon." He took his squirt gun out of his belt and shot Lawrence in the face.

The eight-year-old spluttered. Dale shouted, "Hey, don't waste it!"

"Don't worry," said Mike, setting it back in his belt. "That's not holy water. I'm saving it for later."

"Did you get the other thing?" said Harlen. "The bread stuff?"

"The Eucharist," said Mike. He chewed his lip. "Uh-uh, I wasn't able to. Father Dinmen came over from Oak Hill this morning to say Mass, but he locked the church afterward. I can't get in. I was lucky to grab the last of the holy water after the service."

"You've got that half you kept with your grandmother," Dale reminded him.

Mike's head moved slowly back and forth. "Nope, that stays with Memo. Dad's home tonight, but I'm not taking any chances."

Dale started to say something but at that minute they heard the cry "Kev-INNNN," echoing down Depot Street. They all scrambled down out of the oak.

"See you after dinner!" Dale called to Mike as he and his brother ran for home.

Mike nodded and walked back to the house, pausing by the outhouse to watch the black clouds that were moving low over the fields. Despite the apparent motion of the clouds, there was no breeze. The light had a yellowish tinge.

Mike went in to wash up and to pack his bedroll and pajamas for the sleepover.

THIRTY-SIX

Mr. Dennis Ashley-Montague sat in the back of his black limousine and stared at the passing cornfields and crossroads towns during the hour drive to Elm Haven. Tyler, his head butler, chauffeur, and bodyguard, did not speak, and Mr. Ashley-Montague saw no reason to break the silence. The limousine's tinted windows always imparted a certain element of storm light to the view, so Mr. Ashley-Montague did not take undue notice of the dark skies and sickly light that lay over the forests and fields and rivers like a rotting curtain on the verge of opening.

Elm Haven's Main Street was emptier than usual, even for a Saturday night, and when Mr. Ashley-Montague stepped out of the limousine at Bandstand Park, the darkness overhead was immediately perceptible. Instead of the usual scores of families waiting patiently on the grass, only a few faces watched Tyler carry the massive projector from the limousine's trunk to the bandstand. A handful of other trucks and cars pulled in to park diagonally while Tyler was arranging the speakers and other equipment, but overall the turnout was one of the lowest in the nineteen years that the Ashley-Montagues had been providing this free Saturday-evening entertainment for the dying little town.

Dennis Ashley-Montague returned to the backseat of the limousine, locked the doors, and poured a tall glass of Glenlivet unblended Scotch from the bar set into the soundproofed partition behind the driver. He had considered not coming tonight—not allowing any more Free Shows—but the tradition ran deep and his sense of being the village squire to this assortment of inbred bumpkins and rednecks served a certain perverse purpose in his life.

And he wanted to speak to the boys.

He had seen them at previous Free Shows over the years; their grimy little faces watching the movie as if it were some bright miracle, their cheeks protruding with gum and popcorn . . . but he had never really *looked* at one until that fat boy—the one whose friend said he had been killed—had questioned him on the bandstand over a month earlier. Then that amazing little fellow who had shown up at Mr. Ashley-Montague's front door . . . he had actually had the temerity to *steal* a leatherbound copy of Crowley's translation of *The Book of the Law*. Mr. Ashley-Montague saw nothing in that book that could help the boys if his grandfather's Stele of Revealing were actually awakening from its long slumber. Mr. Ashley-Montague knew of nothing that could help any of them if that were the case, himself included.

The millionaire finished his drink and strolled back to the bandstand, where Tyler had finished his final arrangements. It was not yet eight-thirty in the evening . . . usually the twilight would linger another thirty minutes in these latitudes . . . but the clouds had brought night early.

Mr. Ashley-Montague felt a great sense of claustrophobia seize him: from where he stood the town seemed sealed in by eight-foot-tall corn—to the south beyond the ruins of his ancestral mansion, to the north four long blocks up the dark tunnel of Broad Avenue, west only a few hundred yards to where the Hard Road doglegged to the north, and east down the silent gauntlet of Main Street with its dark shops. The timer had not yet turned on the streetlights.

Mr. Ashley-Montague did not see the boys he was looking for. He saw Charles Sperling, the bratty son of that Sperling man who had had the sheer temerity to approach Mr. Ashley-Montague for a loan for some business venture, and next to him the flat-faced, overly muscled Taylor boy—*his* grandfather had received capital injections from Dennis Ashley-

Montague's grandfather in exchange for some favors of forgetfulness at
the time of the Scandal.

But few other children, and not many families tonight. Perhaps they
were worried that a tornado was coming.

Mr. Ashley-Montague checked the darkening yellow sky and realized that no birds were making a racket as they usually did in the tall
trees here at sunset. There was no insect noise whatsoever. No breeze
moved the branches, and even the darkness had a yellowish tinge to it.

The millionaire lighted a cigarette, rested on the railing of the
bandstand, and considered where he would take cover if the sirens suddenly warned of an approaching tornado. There were no homes open to
him here and he would not go to the ruins of the mansion, despite the
wine cellar still intact there, since the workmen clearing the place had
found the suspicious tunnels burrowed through solid rock there last fall.

No, Mr. Ashley-Montague decided, if there were solid warning of a
tornado or serious storm, he would simply get back in the limousine and
have Tyler drive him home. Tornadoes might smash little towns like Elm
Haven, but they did not bother with luxury vehicles on the highway, and
there was no record of one ever touching down along Grand View Drive.

He nodded to Tyler and the other man cued up the first cartoon and
switched on the projector lamp. There was a smattering of halfhearted
applause from the few people on their benches and blankets. Tom and
Jerry began chasing each other around a primary-colored house while
Mr. Ashley-Montague smoked another cigarette and watched the skies
south of town.

"Tornado, do you think?" said Dale as they stood on the porch of his
house and looked down Second Avenue. Few cars passed on the Hard
Road and those that did had their lights on and were going slowly.

"I don't know," said Mike. They'd all seen tornado weather before—it was the bane of the Midwest and the one form of weather most of
their parents feared—but those bruise-black clouds to the south had
seemed to be building for days now. The sky there seemed like a negative
emulsion of daytime, the trees and rooftops illuminated by the last of a
yellow light while the sky was like the opening to a black abyss. A faint
ripple of greenish light along the horizon of cornstalks suggested lightning, but there were no actual flashes as such, no visible lightning strokes,
only an occasional surge of green-white phosphoresence that got the old-
timers at the store talking about chain lightning and ball lightning and
other phenomena that they knew nothing about.

Mike lifted the walkie-talkie and keyed transmit. Two clicks came
back, showing that Kevin was listening.

"Can you talk?" Mike said softly into the radio, not playing around with codes or call signs.

"Yeah," responded Kevin's voice. Even though the other boy was less than a hundred feet away in the ranch house next door, the transmission was broken up by static and hissing. It was as if the atmosphere was boiling on some plane they couldn't see.

"We're going to go inside and turn in," said Mike. "Unless you guys want to go down to the Free Show."

"Ha ha," came Harlen's voice. Mike could just imagine the smaller boy grabbing the radio.

"You guys all tucked in over there?" asked Dale, leaning close to Mike's walkie-talkie.

"Very funny," said Harlen. "We're watching Grumbelly's TV in the basement. The bad guys just kidnapped Miss Kitty."

Dale grinned. "They kidnap Miss Kitty every week. I think Matt should just let them have her."

Kevin's voice came back, low and tense. "I have the key for the morning."

Mike sighed. "Roger that. You guys have pleasant dreams tonight . . . but make sure you've got fresh batteries and leave the line open."

"Roger" was Kev's laconic reply. The static crackled and popped.

The three boys went upstairs to Dale and Lawrence's bedroom. Mrs. Stewart had set up an extra cot under the south window; she had been very understanding that Mike was upset after the previous day's terrible accident with Father Cavanaugh. She didn't mind a bit if Mike slept over. Mr. Stewart was going to be home early Sunday afternoon and perhaps all of them could go on a picnic down along the Spoon or Illinois rivers.

They got into their pajamas. They would have preferred staying dressed this night, but Dale's mom would surely check in on them and they didn't want any problems. They kept their clothes laid out, and Dale set the small alarm clock for four forty-five. He noticed that his hand was shaking slightly as he wound the clock.

They lay on their beds, Mike on his cot, reading comics and talking about everything except what they were thinking about.

"I wish we could've gone to the Free Show," Lawrence said during a lull in the talk about the Chicago Cubs. "That new Vincent Price movie's playing—*The House of Usser*."

"House of *Usher*," said Dale. "It's from an Edgar Allan Poe story. Remember when I read you the 'Masque of the Red Death' last Halloween?" Dale felt a strange pang of sorrow and it took him a moment to realize that it had been Duane who had told him about the wonderful Poe stories and poems. He looked at his nightstand, where Duane's note-books were carefully banded together. Downstairs, the phone rang twice. They could hear the muffled tones of Dale's mom answering it.

"Whatever," said Lawrence, putting his hands behind his head on the pillow. His pajamas showed little cowboys on rearing Palominos. "I just wish we could see the movie."

Mike set down his Batman comic. He was wearing nondescript blue pajama bottoms with his t-shirt. "You don't want to walk home in the dark, do you? Your mom didn't want to go because of the storm, and I don't think it's a great night to be wandering the streets."

There came the sound of footsteps on the stairs and Mike glanced toward his duffel bag, but Dale said, "It's mom."

She stood in the doorway, attractive in her soft white summer dress. "That was Aunt Lena. Uncle Henry's hurt his back again . . . trying to move some stumps out of that back pasture . . . and now he can't unbend at all. Dr. Viskes has prescribed some painkillers, but you know how Lena hates to drive. She wonders if I could bring the pills out."

Dale sat up in bed. "The pharmacy's closed."

"I called Mr. Aikins. He'll go down and open it up to fill the pre-scription." She glanced out the window at the ripple of lightning still outlining trees and homes to the south. "I'm not sure I want to leave you guys here with a storm coming. Do you want to come along?"

Dale started to speak, then looked at Mike, who nodded at the walkie-talkie on the floor next to him. Dale understood: if they went out to Uncle Henry's, they'd be out of touch with Kevin and Harlen. They'd promised.

"Uh-uh," said Dale. "We'll be OK here."

His mother looked out at the storm-tinged darkness. "You're sure?"

Dale grinned and waved a comic. "Sure . . . we've got snacks and pop and comics . . . what more could we want?"

She smiled. "All right. I'll just be gone twenty minutes or so. Call the farm if you need me." She glanced at her watch. "It's almost eleven. Be thinking about putting out the lights in a few minutes."

They listened to her bustle around downstairs, the back door slam-ming, and the old car starting up. Dale stood at the window to watch it go down Second toward the downtown.

"I don't like this too much," said Mike.

Dale shrugged. "You think the bell or whatever it is disguised itself as a stump to hurt Uncle Henry's back? You think it's all part of a plan?"

"I just don't like it." Mike stood and got into his sneakers. "I think we'd better lock the doors downstairs."

Dale paused. It was an odd thought—they only locked the doors when they were going away on vacation or something. "Yeah," he said at last. "I'll go down and do it."

"You stay here," said Mike, nodding toward Lawrence, who was too engrossed in his comic book to notice. "I'll be right back." He lifted his duffel bag and padded across the landing and down the stairs. Dale strained to hear the front-door bolt being slid shut, the footsteps down the hall to the kitchen. They'd have to watch for their mom's return so they could get downstairs to unlock everything before she got to the back door.

Dale lay back in bed, seeing the silent lightning out the south window and the shadows of leaves in the big elm out the north window to his right.

"Hey, look at this!" laughed Lawrence. He was reading the Uncle Scrooge comic—his favorite reading matter in all the world—and something in the tale of Viking gold had tickled him. He held the page out toward Dale.

Dale was actually sleepy; he reached for the comic and missed. It fluttered to the floor.

"I've got it," said Lawrence, reaching down between the beds.

The white hand and arm shot from beneath the bed and grabbed Lawrence's wrist.

"Hey!" said Lawrence and was instantly jerked off the bed, bedclothes flying. He landed on the floor with a thump. The white arm began dragging him under the bed.

Dale didn't have time to shout. He grabbed his brother's legs and tried to hold on. The pull was inexorable; Dale was coming off his own bed, sheets and spread bunching around his knees.

Lawrence screamed just as his head went under his bed; then his shoulders were pulled in. Dale tried to hang on, tried to pull his brother back up, but it was as if there were four or five adults pulling from under the bed and there was no letup on the pressure. He was afraid that if he didn't quit pulling so hard, Lawrence would be torn in half.

Taking a deep breath, Dale jumped down between the beds, kicking his own bed away, lifting the dust cover that their mom had insisted on sticking on Lawrence's bed over the boy's protests that it was sissy.

There was a darkness under there . . . not a normal darkness, but a blackness deeper than the impenetrable storm clouds along the southern horizon. It was an ink-spilled-on-black-velvet blackness under there, covering the floorboards and broiling like a black fog. Two massive white arms came out of that blackness and stuffed Lawrence into the hole like a lumberjack feeding a small log to the sawblade. Lawrence screamed again, but the cry was cut off abruptly as his head disappeared into the round blackness within blackness. His shoulders followed.

Dale grabbed at his brother's ankles again, but the white hands were relentless. Slowly, kicking and writhing but silent, Lawrence was pulled under the bed.

"Mike!" screamed Dale, his voice shrill. "Get up here! Hurry!" He was cursing himself for not grabbing his own duffel bag on the other side of the bed . . . the shotgun, the squirt guns . . . no, there wouldn't have been time. Lawrence would be gone.

He was almost gone as it was. Only his legs protruded from the blackness.

Jesus, Jesus, he's being pulled into the floor! Maybe it's just eating him up as he goes! But the legs were still kicking; his brother was still alive.

"Mike!"

Dale felt the blackness begin to curl around him then, tendrils and tentacles of darkness thicker and colder than a winter fog. Where the tendrils touched, Dale's legs and ankles prickled as if they had been touched by dry ice. "Mike!"

One of the white hands released itself from the chore of feeding Lawrence to the darkness and grabbed at Dale's face. The fingers were at least ten inches long.

Dale lurched backward, lost his grip on Lawrence's ankles, and watched as the last of his brother was fed to the darkness. Then there was nothing under the bed but the black fog, receding on itself now, the impossibly long fingers sliding backward and down like the hands of a sewer worker lowering himself into a manhole.

Dale threw himself under the bed, reaching into the darkness, groping for his brother even as he felt his hands and forearms go numb in the terrible chill, even as the blackness folded on itself, tendrils pulling in like a movie of some ebony blossom folding up for night, run at high speed . . . and then there was only the perfect circle of darkness—*a hole! Dale could feel emptiness where the solid floor should be!*—and then he tugged his hands back as that circle contracted all too quickly, snapping shut like a steel trap that would have taken Dale's fingers off in an instant. . . .

"What?" cried Mike, exploding into the room with his bag in one hand and the long-barreled squirrel gun in the other.

Dale was on his feet, sobbing but trying not to, pointing and babbling.

Mike dropped to his knees, rattled the barrel of the small shotgun across the solid floorboards. Dale dropped to his knees and elbows and pounded that floor with his fists. "Fuck, fuck, fuck, fuck, fuck!" There was nothing down there but boards and dust bunnies and Lawrence's dropped Uncle Scrooge comic.

A scream echoed up from the basement.

"Lawrence!" shouted Dale, running for the landing.

"Just a second! Just a second!" shouted Mike, holding him back until he could retrieve Dale's duffel bag and the radio. "Put the damn Savage together."

"We can't wait . . . Lawrence . . ." gasped Dale between sobs, tugging to get free. Another scream echoed from the basement, farther away this time.

Mike dropped the squirrel gun on the bed and shook Dale with both hands. "Assemble . . . the . . . Savage! They *want* you to go down there with no weapon. They *want* you to panic. *Think!*"

Dale was shaking as he put the shotgun together, locking the barrel in the stock. Mike stuck two loaded squirt guns in his belt, tossed the box of .410 shells to Dale, slung the walkie-talkie over his shoulder, and said, "OK, let's go down there."

The screams had stopped.

They pounded down the stairs, through the dark hall, across the kitchen, and through the inner door to the basement stairs.

THIRTY-SEVEN

You want us over there?" asked Kevin over the walkie-talkie. Both he and Harlen were dressed and ready in Kev's bedroom.

"No, stay where you are unless we call you," radioed Mike from the top of the stairs. "We'll push the transmit button twice if we need you."

"Gotcha."

Just as Mike signed off, the lights in the Stewart house went off. He pulled his flashlight from his duffel bag and left the bag on the step to the kitchen. Dale reached for the flashlight his dad kept on a two-by-four cross brace near the head of the stairs. The kitchen and house beyond through the open door to the inside were dark; the basement was beyond darkness.

There was a scrabbling, slipping sound.

Dale slid the .410 shell in, left the .22 barrel empty, and clicked the gun shut. He slid the barrel-select to shotgun. His flashlight beam played on the cinderblocks at the curve of the steps near the bottom. More scrabbling sounds came from around the corner.

"Let's go," he said, holding the flashlight with one hand and the shotgun steady with the other. Mike followed with the squirrel gun and his own flashlight.

They jumped down the last two giant steps, smelling the moist after-flood stink of the place. Ahead of them, the furnace and the hopper sent out pipes like a gorgon's hair. The slipping, rock-sliding noise came from their right, through the small doorway in the cinderblock wall.

In the coal bin.

Dale went in fast, the flashlight beam swinging left to right and then back again: the hopper, walls, the small heap of coal left from the winter, the north wall with its panel to the outside and the coal chute shoved in one corner, cobwebs along the near wall, back to the open space.

There was a faint glow in the crawlspace under the front of the house and the porch: not a light, not that bright, but a pale, phosphorescent gleam rather like the radium dials on Kevin's watch. Dale stepped closer and played his flashlight into the low, cobwebby space.

Twenty-five feet in, where the crawlspace normally ended in rough stone and cinderblock at the south end of the porch, the flashlight glinted on the ribbed walls of a hole eighteen inches across, perfectly round, and still emitting the putrid green glow they had seen from the coal bin.

Dale shoved his stuff on the ledge and wriggled into the crawlspace, ignoring the cobwebs in his face as he began moving across the moist soil toward the tunnel.

Mike grabbed his ankles.

"Let me go. I'm going after him."

Mike didn't argue, he pulled Dale forcibly backward until his pajama tops scraped over the cinderblock ledge.

"Lemme go!" shouted Dale, trying to free himself. "I'm going after him."

Mike grabbed his friend's face and silenced him, pressing him back against cold stone. "We'll all go after him. But that's what they expect you to do . . . go down this tunnel. Or go straight to where they're taking him."

"Where's that?" gasped Dale, shaking his head, still feeling the imprint of Mike's strong fingers on his jaw.

"Draw a line," said Mike, pointing in the direction of the tunnel.

Dale turned dull eyes toward the darkness there. Southwest. Across the schoolyard . . . "Old Central," he said. He shook his head again. "Lawrence might still be alive."

"Maybe. They haven't taken anyone before that we know of . . . just killed them. Maybe they do want him alive. Probably to get us to go after him." He keyed the transmit button. "Kev, Harlen, get all your stuff and

meet us outside at the gas pump in about three minutes. We're going to
get dressed and we'll be right there."

Dale flung himself around so that the flashlight beam illuminated the
tunnel again. "OK, OK, but I'm going after him. We'll go to the school."

"Yeah," said Mike, leading the jog up the stairs, illuminating the dark
hall and stairway with his flashlight, "you and Harlen find a way into the
school while Kevin does his thing. I'm going to follow the tunnel."

They reached the bedroom and Dale tugged on jeans and sneakers
and a sweatshirt, forgoing niceties such as underwear and socks. "You
said they'd expect us to go to the school or follow down the tunnel."

"One or the other," answered Mike. "Maybe not both."

"Why should you go in the tunnel? He's my brother."

"Yeah," said Mike. He took a tired breath. "But I've got more experience with these things."

Mr. Ashley-Montague had a couple of more drinks in the back of the
limousine while the cartoons and short subject were on the screen, but
he came out when the motion picture started. It was a new release, quite
popular in his Peoria theaters: Roger Corman's *House of Usher.* It starred
the inevitably hammy Vincent Price as Roderick Usher, but the horror
film was much better than most of its kind. Mr. Ashley-Montague especially liked the predominant use of reds and blacks and the ominous
lighting that seemed to throw each stone of the old Usher mansion into
sharp relief.

The first reel was over when the storm came up. Mr. Ashley-
Montague was leaning against the rail of the bandstand when the branches
far above began to whip back and forth, loose papers blew across the park
grass, and the few spectators either huddled under blankets or began leaving for the shelter of cars and homes. The millionaire looked over the roof
of the Parkside Cafe and was alarmed at how low and fast-moving the
black clouds seemed when they were silhouetted by the silent lightning. It
was what his mother always called "a witch's storm," the kind more often
seen in early spring and late autumn than in the belly of summer.

On the screen, Vincent Price as Roderick Usher and the young gentleman caller carried the massive coffin holding Usher's sister into the
cobwebbed vaults of the family crypt. Mr. Ashley-Montague knew that
the girl was only suffering from the family catalepsy, the *audience* knew,
Poe had known it . . . why didn't Usher know it? *Perhaps he does,* thought
Mr. Ashley-Montague. *Perhaps he is a willing participant in the act of burying his sister alive.*

The first peal of thunder cracked across the endless fields to the south of town, rumbling from the subsonic up through the teeth-rattling and ending on a shrill note.

"Shall we call it a night, sir?" called Tyler from the projector. The butler/chauffeur was holding his cloth cap in place against the wind. Only four or five people remained in their cars or under trees in the park to watch the film.

Mr. Ashley-Montague looked up at the screen. The coffin was vibrating; fingernails clawed against the interior of the bronze casket. Four floors above, Roderick Usher's almost supernatural hearing picked up every sound. Vincent Price shuddered and put his hands over his ears, shouting something that was lost under another peal of thunder. "No," said Mr. Ashley-Montague. "It's almost over. Let's allow it to run a bit."

Tyler nodded, visibly displeased, and held his suit tight around his throat as the wind rose again.

"Denissssss." The whisper was coming from the shrubbery under the front of the bandstand. "Deniiiisssssss . . ."

Mr. Ashley-Montague frowned and walked to the railing there. He could see no one in the bushes below, although the wild commotion caused by the wind and the relative darkness there made it hard to tell who might be crouching in the tall shrubs. "Who is it?" he snapped. No one in Elm Haven took the liberty of calling him by his Christian name . . . and few people elsewhere were granted that right either.

"Deniiiiisssssssss." It was as if the wind in the bushes were whispering.

Mr. Ashley-Montague had no intention of going down there. He turned and snapped his fingers at Tyler. "Someone is playing a prank. Go and see who it is. Remove them." Tyler nodded and moved gracefully down the steps. Tyler was older than he looked—he had, in fact, been a British commando in World War II, heading a small unit which specialized in dropping behind Japanese lines in Burma and elsewhere to create havoc and fear. Tyler's family had fallen on hard times since the war, but the man's experience was the primary factor in Mr. Dennis Ashley-Montague hiring him as body servant and bodyguard.

On the screen, the broad white canvas rippling wildly as the wind got between it and the wall of the Parkside Cafe, Vincent Price was screaming that his sister was alive, alive, *alive!* The young man grabbed a lantern and rushed toward the crypt.

Overhead, the first bolt of lightning exploded, illuminating the entire town in a moment of stroboscopic clarity, and making Mr. Ashley-Montague blink blindly for several seconds. The thunderclap was staggering. The last of the movie-watchers ran for home or drove off to beat the storm. Only the millionaire's limousine remained on the strip of gravel parking behind the bandstand.

Mr. Ashley-Montague walked to the front of the bandstand, feeling the first cold drops of rain touching his cheeks like icy tears. "Tyler . . . never mind! Let's load up the equipment and . . ."

It was the wristwatch that he saw first, Tyler's gold Rolex catching the flare of light from the next stroke of lightning. It was on Tyler's wrist, which was on the ground between the bushes and the bandstand. The wrist was not attached to an arm. A large hole had been kicked . . . *or chewed* . . . in the wooden latticework at the base of the bandstand. Noises came from that hole.

Mr. Ashley-Montague backed up to the rear railing of the bandstand. He opened his mouth to shout but realized that he was alone—Main Street was as empty as if it were three A.M., not even a solitary car moved down the Hard Road—he tried to shout anyway but the thunder was almost continuous now, one clap overlapping the next. The sky was insane with backlit black clouds and the winds of a full-fledged witch's storm.

Mr. Ashley-Montague looked at his limousine parked less than fifty feet away. Branches whipped overhead, one tearing free and falling across a park bench.

It wants me to run for the car.

Mr. Ashley-Montague shook his head and remained right where he was. So he would get a little wet. The storm would stop eventually. Sooner or later the town constable or the county sheriff or someone would stop by on their nightly inspection, curious why the movie was still running in the rain.

On the screen, a woman with a white face, bloodied fingernails, and a tattered burial gown moved through a secret passage. Vincent Price screamed.

Beneath Mr. Ashley-Montague, the wooden floor of the seventy-two-year-old bandstand suddenly bowed upward and splintered with a sound rivaling the crash of thunder overhead.

Mr. Dennis Ashley-Montague had time to scream once before the lamprey mouth and six-inch teeth closed on his calves and legs to the knee and dragged him down through the splintered hole.

On the screen, a long shot of the House of Usher was backlighted with lightning much less dramatic than the real explosions above the Parkside Cafe.

"Here's the plan," said Mike. They were all by the pump next to Kevin's truck shed. The doors were open to the shed and the pump was unlocked. Dale was filling Coke bottles but looked up now.

"Dale and Harlen go to the school. You know a way in?"

Dale shook his head.

"I do," said Harlen.

"OK," said Mike. "Start in the basement. I'll try to meet you there. If I'm somewhere else in the place, I'll *eeawkee*. If I can't, search the place on your own."

"Who has the radios?" asked Harlen. He had taken his sling off so both arms were free, although the light cast still made his left arm clumsy.

Mike handed his radio to Harlen. "You and Kev. Kev, you know what you're supposed to do?"

The thin boy nodded but then shook his head. "But instead of a couple of hundred gallons like we'd planned, you want it *all* pumped?"

Mike nodded. He was tucking squirt guns in the waistband on his back, filling his pockets with .410 shells.

Kev made a fist. "Why? You just wanted a bit of it pumped onto the doors and windows."

"That plan's not going to work," said Mike. He clicked open his grandmother's squirrel gun, checked the cartridge, slammed it shut. "I want that thing *full*. If we have to, we'll drive it right through the north door there." He pointed across the schoolyard. The wind had come up, the lightning was ripping the sky, and the sentinel elms were waving yard-thick limbs like palsied arms.

Kevin stared at Mike. "How the *heck* do we do that? There are four or five steps on that front porch. Even if the thing is wide enough for the truck, it'd never get up those steps."

Mike pointed at Dale and Harlen. "You guys know those thick old boards they stacked up by the dumpster when they ripped the old porch off the west end of the school last year?"

Harlen nodded. "I know 'em. I almost fell onto them a few weeks ago."

"OK—we'll stick those on the front porch of the school before you go in. Like a ramp, sort of."

"Like a ramp . . . sort of," mimicked Kevin, looking in at his father's four-ton bulk tanker. Every time the lightning rippled across the sky— which was almost constant now—the huge stainless-steel tank reflected the flash. "You've got to be shitting me," he said to no one in particular.

"Let's go," said Dale. He was already starting down the hill toward the school, leaving the others behind. "Let's go!" There was no sign of his mother's car. All the lights were out in this part of town. Only Old Central seemed to glow with the same sick light that illuminated the interior of the clouds.

Mike clapped Harlen on the back, did the same with Kevin, and jogged down the slope toward Dale's house. Dale had paused across the street, looking back at his friend. Mike heard the edge of a shout but the words were drowned by the next roll of thunder from the storm. It might have been "Good luck." Or possibly "Good-bye."

Mike waved and went down into the Stewarts' basement.

Dale waited an impatient thirty seconds for Jim Harlen and then ran back up the gravel drive. "Are you coming or not?"

Harlen was poking around in the Grumbacher truck shed. "Kev said that there's some rope in here . . . ah, here." He pulled two thick coils of rope from nails on the rafters. "I bet this's twenty-five feet each, easy." He fitted the bulky coils over his shoulders and chest like bandoliers.

Dale turned around, disgusted. He started to jog across the dark playground, not worrying if Harlen could keep up. Lawrence was in there somewhere. Like Duane. . . . "What the hell do you want *rope* for anyhow?" snapped Dale as Harlen caught up, already panting from the short run.

"If we're going in that fucking school, I'm going to have a way to get out that's softer than the last time."

Dale shook his head.

Branches were tearing off and falling around them as they passed under the sentinel elms. The short grass of the playing field was rippling and flattening under the wind, as if a huge, invisible hand were stroking it.

"Look," whispered Harlen.

The ridges of the burrowing things were everywhere now, humps of raw soil that curved and wound and intersected, carving the six acres of playground into a wild geometry of wakes.

Dale reached into his belt and pulled out a squirt gun, feeling how foolish that was even as he did so. But he clipped the Boy Scout flashlight onto his belt and kept the squirt gun in his left hand, the Savage over-and-under in his right.

"You got some of Mike's magic water?" whispered Harlen.

"Holy water."

"Whatever."

"Come on," Dale whispered. They leaned into the rising wind. The sky was a mass of boiling black clouds silhouetted by the greenish lightning. Thunder rolled like cannon fire.

"If it rains, that'll really fuck up what Kevin's planning to do."

Dale said nothing. They passed the north porch, went under the boarded windows . . . Dale noticed that the wind had torn the boards off the stained-glass window above the entrance, but that was far too high to reach . . . and they jogged around the northwest corner, past the dumpster where Jim had lain unconscious for ten hours, into the shadow on the north side of the immense building.

"Here are the boards," gasped Harlen. "Grab one and we'll dump it on the front steps like Mike said."

"Screw that," said Dale. "Show me that entrance you said you knew about."

Harlen stopped cold. "Look, it may be important . . ."

"*Show* me!" Without planning to, Dale had raised the shotgun so that the barrel was pointing in Jim Harlen's general direction.

Harlen's small pistol was tucked in his belt, under the absurd coils of rope. "Listen, Dale . . . I know you're half nuts about your brother . . . and I usually don't give a shit about orders from somebody else, but Mike probably had a reason. Now help me with a couple of these boards and I'll show you the way in."

Dale wanted to scream with frustration. Instead, he lowered the shotgun, set it against the wall, and lifted one end of the long, heavy plank. They'd stacked several dozen of these old boards here when they had demolished the west porch of the school last fall; now they still lay there, waterlogged and rotting.

It took the boys five minutes to carry eight of the damn things around to the north porch and to dump them on the stairs. "These things wouldn't even hold up a bicycle if they're supposed to be a ramp," said Dale. "Mike's crazy."

Harlen shrugged. "We said we'd do it. Now we've done it. Let's get going."

Dale hadn't liked leaving the shotgun and he was pleased to find it still leaning against the wall when he got back. Except when the lightning illuminated everything in its flashbulb explosion of glare, it was quite dark along this wall of the school. All of the schoolyard pole lamps and streetlights were off, but the upper floors of the building itself appeared to be wreathed by a greenish glow.

"This way," whispered Harlen. All of the basement windows had wire-mesh coverings as well as the plywood boards. Harlen stopped at the window closest to the southwest corner of the school, ripped back the long, loose board, and kicked at the rusty mesh. It swung free. "Gerry Daysinger and me kicked the shit out of this thing one dull recess last April," said Harlen. "Give me a hand."

Dale propped the shotgun against the wall and helped to pry the mesh away from the wall. Rusted metal and brick dust sifted into the window well below the sidewalk level.

"Hold it," said Harlen, the words almost drowned by the rising wind and a roll of thunder. He sat on the ground, leaned into the well, pulled the mesh loose, and kicked the pane of glass out with his right sneaker, smashing the wooden muntin while he was at it. He kicked a second pane out, then a third. Half the small window lay open into darkness, the shards of glass reflecting the mad sky.

Harlen scooted back on his rump, extended an arm, palm up. "After you, my dear Gaston."

Dale grabbed the shotgun and lowered himself in, legs scrabbling in the darkness, his left foot finding a pipe, setting the gun in to use both hands to keep himself away from the broken glass. He jumped from the pipe to the floor five feet below, found the shotgun and held it across his chest.

Harlen clambered in behind him. Lightning revealed a riot of iron pipes, massive elbow joints where pipes connected, the red legs of a big worktable, and lots of darkness. Dale unclipped the flashlight from his belt, fumbled the squirt gun back into his waistband.

"Turn it on, for Chrissakes," whispered Harlen, his voice taut.

Dale clicked on the light. They were in the boiler room; pipes littered the darkness overhead, and huge metal tanks rose like crematoria on either side. There were shadows between the gigantic furnaces, shadows beneath the pipes, shadows in the rafters, and a darkness deeper than shadows outside the door to the basement hallway.

"Let's go," whispered Dale, holding the flashlight directly over the Savage's barrel. He wished he'd brought .22 shells as well as the .410s.

Dale led the way into the darkness.

"Son of a bitch," whispered Kevin Grumbacher. He almost never cursed, but nothing was going right here.

The others had all left him, and Kevin was doing his best to ruin his dad's truck and livelihood. It made him sick: breaking into the pump and buried gas tank, using the milk hose to pump gasoline up into the stainless-steel bulk tank. No matter how much they cleaned the rubber hose, there'd always be some gasoline left to contaminate the milk. These hoses cost a small fortune. Kevin didn't even want to think about what he was doing to the tanker itself.

The problem was, with the electricity off, the air conditioner in their house would be off and that would wake his mother and father up fairly soon . . . sooner if the storm got any louder. His dad was famous for being a sound sleeper, but his mother often wandered the house during storms. It was just lucky that their bedroom was downstairs next to the TV room.

Still, Kevin had had to get the tanker truck out of the garage without starting the engine; he had the key, but was sure the noise would wake his father up without the air conditioner to shield it. The storm was getting louder, but Kevin couldn't count on the truck engine not being heard.

Luckily the driveway was on the hill, so Kevin had set the truck in neutral and allowed it to coast the ten feet or so necessary to get close enough to the gas pump. He'd run the centrifugal pump cord into the 230-volt outlet in the garage and then remembered that there was no power. *Great. Just fucking great.*

His father had a Coleman gasoline-powered generator in the back of the truck shed, but that would make more noise than the truck itself.

There was nothing to do but try. Kevin set the proper switches, threw the proper levers, primed the generator's carburetor once with gas from the jerry can in the truck, and jerked hard with the pull-starter. The generator popped twice, coughed once, and started right up.

It's not so loud. No louder than about ten Go-Karts in a big aluminum barrel.

But the back door to the house did not fly open, his father did not rash out with his robe flapping around him and his eyes wide with fury. Not yet.

Kevin plugged the power cord into the proper outlet, pulled the shed doors closed against the wind that tried to rip them out of his grasp, and fumbled with the keys to get the lid off the underground-tank access panel. He used the nine-foot stick his dad kept by the side of the shed to check the fuel depth: it seemed almost topped off. Kevin fumbled with the rear doors of the tanker, got the bulky hose out, attached, and snaked across the drive to the filler cap. The hose uncoiling into the darkness of the tank made him think of things he did not want to think about.

The storm was getting wilder. The birch and poplars in front of the Grumbacher ranch house were doing their best to rip themselves apart while the aerial display was lighting the world below in false Kodachrome colors.

Kevin threw the switch and saw the transfer hose stiffen and ripple as the vacuum pump began the transfer. He closed his eyes as he heard the first of the high-test gasoline start to gurgle and splash into the well-scrubbed and nearly sterile stainless-steel milk tank. *Sorry, kiddies, your milk's gonna have a little bit of Shell undertaste for a while.*

His dad was going to kill him, no matter what happened. Kevin's father rarely showed his anger, but when he did it was with a red-eyed Teutonic fury that frightened Kevin's mother and everyone else within a lethal radius.

Kevin opened his eyes, blinking as the wind hurled grit and gravel at him. Dale and Lawrence weren't in sight on the schoolyard anymore, and Mike had disappeared into the Stewarts' basement. Kevin suddenly

felt very alone. *Seventy-five gallons a minute. There must be at least a thousand gallons in the tank below—half the bulk tanker's capacity. What . . .
fifteen minutes pumping time? Dad'll never sleep through all of that.*

Kevin was six minutes into the transfer, the pump gurgling and
bucking in his hands, the generator making its hot-rod noises in the echoing shed, and the storm building to some insane crescendo, when he
looked out from his hill and saw the ripples in the earth of Old Central's
playground.

It was like the wake of two sharks in the ocean, fins parting water
like ripples in a wind tunnel. Only that was not ocean or wind—whatever
was coming was carving its way under the solid soil of the playing field,
headed straight for the road and then for the milk truck.

Two wakes. Two ridges being churned into existence like two giant
moles were digging their way straight for him.

And they were coming fast.

THIRTY-EIGHT

After the first ten yards or so, Mike found the tunnel easier going.
It was wider now, closer to twenty-eight or thirty inches across
rather than the tight squeeze he'd forced his shoulders into at the
beginning. The ribbed sides of the tunnel were hard, made of packed
earth and some gray material with the consistency of dried airplane glue,
and they reminded him of the track a Caterpillar tractor or bulldozer left
in the soil after the mud had dried for days in the sun. Mike thought that
crawling through the tunnel was no more difficult than forcing one's way
through one of the smaller corrugated steel culverts they laid under a
road.

Only this one went on for hundreds of yards—or miles—rather than
a few yards.

The smell was bad, but Mike ignored it. The light from his flashlight
reflected red off the ribs of the hole, making Mike think again of a long
gut, an intestine to hell, but he tried not to think about that. The pain in
his elbows and knees grew worse by the minute, but he put that out of his
mind, reciting Hail Marys interspersed with the occasional Our Father.
He wished he'd brought the remaining bit of Eucharist he'd left on Memo's
bed.

Mike crawled farther, feeling the tunnel twist to the left and right,
sometimes descending, sometimes rising to the point he guessed there
was less than a yard of dirt over his head. At the moment he felt deep.

Twice he'd come to a junction with other tunnels, one burrowing off the left almost straight down, and Mike had shone his flashlight, waited, listened, and then crawled on, keeping to what he thought was the most recently excavated burrow. At least this tunnel *smelled* the strongest.

At every turn, Mike expected to come across the corpse of Lawrence Stewart, clogging the way ahead. Perhaps there would be just bones and tatters of flesh left . . . perhaps it would be worse. But if Mike found the eight-year-old, at least he could leave the warren of tunnels with honor and tell Dale and the others that there was no reason for them to go into the school at night.

Only Mike could never find his way back now. There had been too many twists, more than enough turns to lose him permanently. He stayed with the main tunnel—he *thought* it was the main tunnel—and kept moving ahead, his jeans torn at the knee now, the flesh underneath bleeding. It was like crawling on ridged concrete. The flashlight wavered on red soil, now illuminating twenty yards of shaft, now twenty inches as the tunnel dipped or turned again. Mike expected a visitor at every bend.

The squirt guns in his waistband were leaking, making him feel like a damned fool. It was one thing to fight monsters, he thought. Quite another to fight them with wet underwear. He pulled the worst offender from his belt and clamped it in his teeth; better a dribbly chin than to look like you needed diapers.

The tunnel turned right again, began dropping steeply. Mike inched ahead, using his elbows as brakes, the flashlight beam bobbing against the red roof. Mike kept crawling.

He felt it coming before he saw it.

The earth began to tremble slightly. Mike remembered one long-ago summer night when he and Dale had been watching a ballgame over at Oak Hill and had gone for a moonlit walk along the railroad tracks. They'd felt a vibration in the soles of their sneakers and then put their ears against the rails, *feeling* the distant coming of the daily express between Galesburg and Peoria.

This was like that. Only much stronger, the vibration coming up through the bones of Mike's hands and knees and shaking his spine, rattling his teeth. And with the tremors came the stench.

Mike deliberated about turning the light off and then decided to hell with it—these things could certainly see *him*, why not return the favor. He lay prone, the flashlight under his chin now, Memo's squirrel gun in his right hand, the squirt gun in his left. Then he remembered that he'd have to reload and he hurried to fumble out four more cartridges, wrapping them in the short sleeve of his t-shirt where he could get them in a hurry.

For a second the vibration seemed all around him, above him, *behind* him, and he had a moment of pure panic as he thought of the thing exploding on him from behind, seizing him from the rear before he managed to squirm around, get the gun aimed behind him. Mike felt the panic rise like dark bile, but then the vibrations localized and intensified. *It's ahead of me.*

He lay flat, waiting.

The thing came around a bend in the tunnel perhaps twelve feet ahead of him. It was worse than Mike could have imagined.

For a second he almost let his bladder go, but controlling that helped him to control his thinking. *It's not so bad, it's not so bad.*

It was.

It was the eel that Mike had caught and run from in a small boat, and a lamprey with its all-devouring mouth and endless rows of teeth disappearing into the gut that was its body, and it was a worm the size of a large sewer pipe, with quivering appendages that might have been a thousand tiny fingers ringing the mouth, or perhaps waving tendrils, or perhaps serrated lips . . . Mike didn't give too much of a damn at that second.

The flashlight illuminated gray and pink flesh, pulsing blood vessels visible through the skin. No eyes. Teeth. More teeth. Pink gut not so dissimilar from the tunnel itself.

The thing paused, tendril lips writhed, the lamprey mouth pulsated, and it came on at a terrific speed.

Mike fired the squirt gun first—*Holy Mary, Mother of God*—saw the water arch the ten feet, saw the pink flesh hiss, realized that the thing was too big to be destroyed or seriously inconvenienced by holy water or acid, saw it still rushing on, knew that he could never back away in time, and he fired the squirrel gun.

The blast deafened and blinded him.

He broke the breech, flipped out the empty, took a shell from his sleeve, slammed it home, clicked the breech shut.

He fired again, blinking away retinal echoes.

The thing had stopped . . . it had to have stopped . . . he'd have been in its gut already if it hadn't stopped. The flashlight was askew. Mike reloaded, aimed, steadied the flashlight with his left hand.

It *had* stopped. Less than eight feet away. The circular jaw of the thing had been shattered in several places. Pieces of the tunnel dribbled onto it. Greenish-gray fluid leaked from the giant worm body.

It seemed more bemused than hurt, more curious than frightened.

"Fuck you!" screamed Mike between Hail Marys. He fired again.

Reloaded. Thrust the squirrel gun another yard closer by wiggling forward and fired again. He had at least ten shells left. He wiggled and
flopped to get some out of his right side pocket.

The lamprey thing withdrew around the bend in the tunnel.

Still screaming, only partially coherent, flailing on raw elbows and
knees, Mike followed it as quickly as he could.

"Where are we?" whispered Dale.

They had come out of the boiler room into a narrow hall, followed it
left around several corners, come into a wider corridor, and now were in
a narrow one again. Giant pipes ran overhead. The basement hallways
were littered with stacked school desks, empty cardboard drums, shattered chalkboards. And cobwebs. Many, many cobwebs.

"I don't know where we are," Harlen whispered back. Both boys
had their flashlights on. The beams flickered from surface to surface like
demented insects. "This west end of the basement was Van Syke's area.
None of us came in here."

That was true enough. The hallway was narrow, the ceiling low,
there were many small doors and access panels on the slanted concrete
and stone walls. The pipes dripped moisture. Dale thought that the place
was a maze, that they'd never find their way to the halls he knew from
years of going to the basement restrooms. The stairway to the basement
was below the central stairways.

They came around another turn. Dale's thumb had been tense on
the hammer of the over-and-under for long minutes, even though it had
been locked back. He was sure he was going to blow his own leg off any
second. Both of Harlen's arms were straight out—the flashlight in the
hand below the cast, the .38 revolver in the other hand. Harlen was moving like a jerky weathervane in a strong wind.

The basement of Old Central was not silent. Dale heard creakings,
slidings, raspings—the pipes carried hollow echoes and reverberating
moans, as if some huge mouth was breathing into them from above—
while the thick stone walls seemed to be expanding and contracting
slightly, as if something large was pressing and relaxing pressure from the
opposite side.

Dale came around another corner, swinging the light in fast arcs, the
Savage raised to his shoulder despite the ache in his right arm.

"Holy shit," Harlen whispered reverently as he came around behind
him.

They were in the main basement corridor now. Dale recognized it
from years of coming down to the restroom, marching down to the music

and art rooms at the far end of this long hall. The stairways—one for coming down, one for going up—were another twenty yards along this corridor. Maybe.

The pipes dripped moist gray stalactites now. The walls were covered with what looked like a thin film of greenish oil. There were mounds of gray matter in the hall—like unformed stalagmites or giant, melted candles.

But that wasn't what had caused Harlen's comment: the walls were perforated with holes—some a foot and a half or so across, others opening from floor to ceiling. Tunnels ran off from the central corridor and disappeared into the soil and rock of the playground. A faint phosphorescence came from these tunnels; Dale and Harlen could have switched off their flashlights and still seen quite clearly in this windowless place.

They did not switch off their flashlights.

"Look," said Harlen. He pushed back a door that had the single word BOY'S stenciled on it. Inside what had been their restroom, the metal stalls had been ripped out of their mountings and twisted like thin tin. The toilets and urinals had been torn from their mountings and pushed almost to the ceiling, trailing torn pipes and dangling fittings.

The long room was almost filled with the gray stalactites, mounds of softly pulsating greenish wax, strands of something that looked like a spiderweb made of hairless flesh. The round hole in the wall to their left was at least eight feet across. Dale smelled the odor of wet earth and decay wafting out of it. There were a dozen other tunnels, some in the floor and ceiling.

"Let's go," whispered Harlen.

"Mike said he'd meet us down here."

"Mike may not be coming," hissed Harlen. "Let's find your brother and get our asses *out*."

Dale hesitated only a second.

The stairways had been shut off by swinging doors. One of them on the north side had been torn off its top hinges and hung askew. Dale leaned on it, shone his light up the stairway.

A dark fluid pulsed down the steps between gray mounds and the glazed, waxy icing on the walls. It came under the doors and pooled around Dale and Harlen's sneakers.

Dale took three deep breaths, wrenched the door aside, and led the way up the stairs, toward the first landing, feeling and hearing his tennis shoes squish on each step. The liquid was a dull brownish-red, but it felt too thick for water, possibly too thick for blood. More like motor oil or transmission fluid. It smelled a bit like cat urine.

Dale imagined a giant, three-story cat crouched above them, and he almost giggled. Harlen gave him a warning glance.

"Mike'll come up looking for us," he whispered to Harlen, not caring who heard. But at that second he did not believe that Mike was still alive.

Two long blocks south, across the abandoned and darkened Main Street, Bandstand Park was empty except for the limousine parked on the strip of gravel on the west side. The projector was still running because it had been plugged in to the volunteer fire department's circuit. The bandstand was silent, the large hole in the floor visible only from a certain angle. A large branch had fallen on the speakers, smashing both of them and silencing the film.

The screen had partially ripped loose from its moorings on the side of the Parkside Cafe, the fifteen-by-twenty-foot canvas slapping and snapping against siding like a fast-firing cannon. On the screen, a man and woman struggled in what looked to be a dungeon. The camera cut to a room above them where a tumbled candelabrum ignited a red velvet curtain. The fire spread, rising to the ceiling.

A woman opened her mouth to scream, but there was no noise except the crack of canvas and the louder crack of lightning.

A long semi went by on the Hard Road, its metal sides buffeted by the gale-force winds, its wipers flashing despite the fact that it was not raining here. It did not slow as it passed through the SPEED 25 MPH ELECTRICALLY TIMED ZONE.

Lightning to the south revealed a solid wall of black moving across the fields toward Elm Haven at the speed a horse could run at full gallop, but there was no one to see it.

On the whipping screen and the white siding of the cafe, flames seemed three dimensional as they devoured the House of Usher.

Kevin jumped onto the high fender of the bulk tanker, grabbed the walkie-talkie, and clicked the transmit button five times. There was no answering click.

"Hey, Dale . . . hey, something's coming here!" he shouted into the radio. The speaker returned only static and a crackling that echoed the lightning overhead.

Something was indeed coming. The twin wakes of fresh soil being plowed across the schoolyard disappeared beneath the asphalt of Depot Street.

Like sharks diving deep, thought Kevin. He had his father's Colt Government Model .45 in both hands now and he racked a round into the chamber, holding the semiautomatic's grip steady in his left hand, finger on the trigger guard, while he pulled the slide back. The first round chambered, the automatic "cocked and locked" as his father called it, Kevin set his thumb on the hammer as he waited for the lamprey-things to emerge on this side of the street.

Nothing happened for a minute or more. There was no noise—or at least no noise audible over the crash of storm and continuing gurgle of the centrifugal pump. Kevin held the automatic in both hands and gently lowered the hammer before he shot his foot off. He looked down at the pump and hose, decided that it was still feeding properly, and stayed on the truck rather than jump down.

One of the lamprey-worms surfaced six feet to the right of the truck, the other threw gravel into the air as it arched out of the driveway. Their bodies were long and segmented. Kevin saw the working mouth as the first one passed, saw the quivering tendrils and pulsating gut lined with teeth.

He raised the pistol as the thing surfaced and dove again, but he did not fire. *Mein Gott!* His arms were shaking.

The one in the driveway dove to the right as it submerged again, displacing more gravel and passing under the hose as its endless back disappeared. *What if it hits the underground tank?*

Kevin climbed higher onto the truck, looking down into the open filler cap on top now, calling desperately into the walkie-talkie. "Dale . . . Harlen! Anybody! Help. Come in, over!"

Static-lashed silence.

Kevin clambered forward to the cab, leaned down and swung the passenger-side door open, thinking of getting in out of the wind.

The lamprey-thing surfaced five feet to the right of the cab and lunged, the mouth opening wider than the width of the body itself, flaps and tendrils pulsing as it smashed into the door with a *thud* that rocked the three-and-a-half-ton vehicle.

Kevin had released the door and rolled across the roof of the cab, away from the thing, his mouth open and ready to scream but with no sound emerging but rapid gasps. He teetered on the driver's side of the cab, fingernails clawing at the smooth metal of the roof. He went over but managed to grab the upper frame of the open window and land heavily, his feet clanging on the running board, the radio flying out onto the grass of the yard.

The second lamprey surfaced fifteen feet out and cut through the grass in an arching rush that left sod flying ten feet into the air. Kevin saw it coming, saw the radio knocked farther away by the thing's wake, and then he swung himself up onto the hood of the truck, his long legs scrabbling for purchase there.

The second lamprey-thing smashed into the driver's door with the same blind fury that the first had shown. It backed away, arching its quivering feeding-mouth six feet into the air, like a cobra weaving before striking. Kevin spread-eagled himself on the rocking hood and looked to his left; the first thing had backed off, had dived into the gravel again, and now rose in full force to crash into the right door again. Glass broke and the heavy door warped inward.

The instant the first lamprey backed off, before the second one attacked again, Kevin scrambled over the hood and roof of the cab, leaping onto the higher steel tank, feet sliding out from under him, but not before he threw himself forward and grasped the cylindrical filler cap in the center of the tank, his legs sliding off to the right.

Nine feet of lamprey unwound from the soil and went for his legs, tendrils quivering. Kevin got the full benefit of the death-stench rising from the thing's pulsing interior, and then he swung his legs up like a trick horse-rider, hanging completely by the force of his arms, his blue jeans skidding against the curved steel tank.

"Go git 'em!" came a voice over the wind.

Kevin looked over the tank to see Cordie Cooke standing by the truck shed. The wind plastered her shapeless dress against her and flapped it like a manic brown flag behind her. Her short, crudely chopped hair stood straight back from her face.

Cordie released the large dog she was holding back by a leather thong. It threw itself across the ten yards to the worm-thing on the far side of the truck. Kevin swung his legs up and over as the segmented thing rose and struck again on the lawn side.

It fell back, leaving a trail of slime on the side of his father's steel tanker. There was a dent in the steel not ten inches from Kevin's raised sneaker.

The dog growled and leapt on the first lamprey, its massive forelegs spread as it landed on the thing's segmented back. The lamprey arched and then dove, the dog chewing and growling, leaping from its back to run six paces before leaping on it again as the lamprey surfaced farther down the driveway.

"Come on!" screamed Kevin.

Cordie ran down the hill and jumped for the fender. She would have fallen back if Kevin's hand hadn't caught her wrist and pulled her up. The first lamprey surfaced and slammed its mouth into the tank a foot below her bare legs; it slid off the rear fender and began circling again, the growling and chewing dog going crazy on its back. The second lamprey was circling on the lawn as if it were building up speed.

"Up here," gasped Kevin, pulling her to the top of the tank. They stood, balancing in the high wind with their arms out, legs straddling the raised filler cap.

The first lamprey suddenly arched back on itself, its open end coming around faster than a snake could strike. The dog had time to howl once before most of it disappeared into the wide feeding orifice. The body pulsed, the mouth widened, the dog became a lump near the front of the giant worm, and it dove again, disappearing beyond the gravel into the yard near the street.

"Lucifer!" said Cordie. She was sobbing without noise.

"Look out!" cried Kevin. They swung off the right side of the truck as the second lamprey charged in from the yard again, its pulsing mouth rising eight feet into the air and slamming into the top of the tank near the filler cap this time.

Kevin and Cordie looked over their shoulders as the first thing circled and came back.

The centrifugal pump continued to chug and the gasoline continued to pump into the bulk tank as both lamprey creatures rose and converged.

THIRTY-NINE

Dale led the way up the stairs to the first floor, pausing at the landing to shine his light around the corner. More dark fluid trickled down the steps. The banisters, railings, and the lower section of the green walls were streaked with the waxy, chitinous material he had seen in the basement. The two boys stayed near the center of the steps, weapons raised.

There had been swinging doors at the top of the north stairwell, but both had been broken off their hinges. Dale paused there, watched the thick fluid seeping under the smashed wood, and then he leaned forward and shone his flashlight into the main hall of Old Central.

The light bounced off a confusing mass of dripping pillars and walls that Dale did not remember being there. Harlen had whispered something. Dale turned his head back. "What?"

"I said," repeated the smaller boy with careful enunciation, "that there's something moving in the basement."

"Maybe it's Mike."

"I don't think so," whispered Harlen. He swung the flashlight beam behind him. "Listen."

Dale listened. It was a scraping, sliding, rasping noise, as if something large and soft had filled the entire hallway below them and was pushing desks, chalkboards, and all the other detritus down there ahead of itself.

"Let's go," whispered Dale and stepped out over the stained and hanging door.

He felt Harlen step into the great space behind him, come up next to him, but Dale did not turn to look. He was too busy staring.

The interior of Old Central looked nothing like the building Dale had left for the last time seven weeks earlier. His neck first pivoted as he took in the scene, then arched as he looked up through the center stairwell.

The floor was awash with thick, almost-dried brown fluid that rose to the top of Dale's sneakers like some great molasses spill. The walls had been covered with a thin layer of pinkish, vaguely translucent material that reminded Dale of the naked and quivering flesh in a nest of newborn rats he had uncovered once. The organic-looking stuff dripped from railings and banisters, hung in great cobwebby strands from portraits of George Washington and Abraham Lincoln, dribbled in even thicker webs from the hooks in the cloakrooms, dangled from the doorknobs and transoms, hung from the corners of the boarded windows like huge, irregular picture frames made of pulsing flesh, and rose toward the mezzanine and dark stairs above in a great cheesy mass of strands and rivulets.

But it was above them that the nightmare grew obscene.

Dale arched farther back, seeing Harlen's flashlight beam join his own.

The second- and third-floor balconies were almost covered with gray and pink strands, the filaments growing more substantial as they rose toward the central belfry, arching and crisscrossing the dark space up there like flesh-colored flying buttresses in a cathedral designed by a lunatic. Stalactites and stalagmites of graying epoxy were everywhere, dripping from darkened light fixtures, rising from railings and balustrades, hanging across the great central space like clotheslines made of torn flesh and ribbed cartilage.

And from those "clotheslines" hung a foul wash of what looked like pulsing red egg sacs. Dale's flashlight beam stopped on one and he saw dark shadows inside, scores of them. They were moving. The entire sac pulsed and throbbed like a human heart hung on a bloody thread. There were dozens more.

Shadows moved on the mezzanines. Liquid dripped from the dark stained-glass window. But Dale had eyes for none of this. He was looking at the belfry.

Above the third-floor landing, the "high-school level" that had been closed off for so many years, someone had torn out the broad-planked floor of the belfry. And that is where the glow was coming from.

"Glow" was not the right word, Dale realized, as he stared at the bluish-green throbbing, stared open-mouthed at the radioactive false light of the thick, fleshy web tendrils that filled the belfry, and at the redly glowing thing centered there.

He might have called it a spider, for there was a sense of many legs and more eyes; he might have described it as an egg sac itself, for Dale had seen the half-formed heart and reddish eye of such a thing in the yolk of fertilized eggs on Uncle Henry's farm; he might have said it was a face or giant heart, for it resembled both in a sick way . . . but even from forty feet beneath the thing, staring upward with a growing sense of despair and sickness, Dale knew that it was none of these things.

Harlen tugged at his arm. Reluctantly, almost unwillingly, Dale Stewart tore his eyes away from the center of the flesh-web far above.

The first floor here, so far from the sick glow in the belfry, was very dark, a complex fold of shadows on shadows. Now one of those shadows moved, separated itself from the web-spun tunnel of a first-grade cloak-room and stepped softly toward the boys.

Arms shaking, Dale raised his shotgun as the pale face floated into focus above the shadow of a body.

Dr. Roon stopped ten feet from them. His black suit blended with the darkness; his face and hands shimmered softly as Harlen's flashlight beam danced there. There were other sounds behind him, softer sounds in the basement behind the boys.

Dr. Roon smiled more broadly than Dale had ever seen him smile.

"Welcome," he whispered, blinking against the light. His teeth looked slick and moist. "Look up again, why don't you?"

Dale flicked a glance upward, not taking his eyes off the man in black for more than a second. What he saw made him ignore Dr. Roon and look up again, lowering the shotgun so as to hold the flashlight beam more steady.

Lawrence was up there.

Mike decided that taking the tunnel had not been among the smartest choices he had ever made. His hands and knees were bleeding openly now, his back was killing him, he was lost, he felt like several hours had passed, he was sure that he had almost certainly missed anything that was happening in the school, the lamprey-things were coming back, he was almost out of shotgun shells, his flashlight was giving out, and he'd just discovered that he suffered from claustrophobia.

Other than that, he thought, *I'm doing just fine.*

There were so many branchings and twists in the tunnel now that he was sure that he had gotten lost. At first it had been easy identifying the main branch from the tributaries since the primary tunnel had been harder packed and still redolent from the huge worm-thing's passage, but now *all* the tunnels were like that. He'd had to decide between multiple branches a dozen times in the last fifteen minutes, and he was sure that he had chosen wrong. He was probably somewhere out beyond the burned hulk of the grain elevator and still heading north.

Fuck it, thought Mike, and then added an Act of Contrition to his mental rosary of Hail Marys and Our Fathers.

Twice the lamprey-things had almost had him. The first time he had heard and felt the approach from behind and struggled in the narrow tunnel to get the fading flashlight and Memo's squirrel gun aimed the right direction without blowing his foot and ankle off. He had seen the mouth tendrils waving like pulpy white seaweed before firing the first time, not taking time to flinch from the sound before reloading and firing again. The thing had burrowed down through the floor of the tunnel, allowing Mike to get off one final shot at its back. It was like throwing gravel at armor plating.

A minute or so later, that lamprey or its twin had burst through the roof of the tunnel not five feet in front of his face as he crawled along, the open face pulsing and writhing blindly as it sought him. Mike had forgotten that the things didn't have to stay in their old tunnels, and that oversight had almost killed him.

He had thrown the useless squirt gun into the maw of the thing, seeing the teeth-lined gut clearly as it swung his way, and then he had fired, reloaded, fired, reloaded.

It was gone when he blinked away the retinal echoes.

He had clambered forward wildly, panicked now, glancing up at the roof of the tunnel and down between his hands, waiting for the mouth to emerge and take him.

It had emerged a moment later, several yards ahead of him, but had continued burrowing straight down as if panicked itself by something on the surface. The tunnel had filled with the reek of gasoline.

Mike had stopped crawling for a moment, stunned with the implications of that smell. *God, God, it's gotten to Kev's tanker truck.* He wished he had one of the radios. *Do radios work underground?* Kev or Duane would know. Then he remembered: Duane was dead; Kevin might be, too.

Mike crawled forward, his body reduced to a simple organ designed to transmit pain from various extremities to his exhausted brain. It was cool down here. It would be nice just to curl up in a nice warm ball and go to sleep here, let the last of the batteries drain away and the light fade . . . just sleep and dream of nothing.

Mike crawled forward, the squirrel gun loaded but tucked in his waistband along his right leg, his palms leaving bloody prints on the corrugated tunnel floor.

The noise when he heard it was louder than the lamprey sounds he'd heard before previous attacks. It was as if both creatures were coming down the tunnel after him. From behind. Very quickly judging from the rapid buildup in vibration and sound.

Mike crawled faster, the flashlight in his teeth, his head banging stones and the tunnel roof as he hobbled along as fast as he could.

The burrowing sounds increased in intensity behind him. He could smell the things now . . . the rotted garbage and dead-flesh stench of them, and above that another smell . . . sharp and terrible. He glanced back and saw a fierce light approaching around the bend in the tunnel behind him.

Mike flung himself forward, losing one of the squirt guns and not noticing it. The flashlight flickered out and he threw it away; the widening tunnel was illuminated fully by the flare of the lamprey's passage behind him.

Something large and loud and bright filled the space behind him. He felt heat from it, as if the lamprey mouth and gut had become a furnace.

Suddenly the tunnel floor dropped out from underneath him and Mike tumbled downward, sliding and scrabbling on loose rock and cold, flat stone. It was some sort of wider cave here, dark as the tunnel but much wider, and Mike pawed out Memo's squirrel gun and cocked back the hammer even as he continued kicking himself sideways, finally slamming up against a vertical slab of stone.

The light from the tunnel opening grew brighter, the earth shook, and the lamprey suddenly appeared, tendrils and maw pulsing wildly. It rumbled past Mike like an express freight train not deigning to pause for such an unimportant stop, its glowing and blazing flesh passing not two feet from Mike's sneakers as he tried in vain to push himself into the solid wall behind him.

The thing had passed, crashing through more stone and continuing on into darkness, leaving a trail of slime and smoldering flesh, before Mike realized two things: the lamprey had been on *fire* and Mike was no longer in the tunnel.

He was in the Boy's restroom in the basement of Old Central.

Kevin went one direction and Cordie the other, each of them teetering on the slick curve of the steel tank. The lampreys smashed into the center where Cordie and Kevin had been, pounding against the stainless steel and sliding back to earth with a scraping of teeth on metal. One of the things brushed against the hose as it surged past, pulling it from the filler tube in the ground. Gasoline sloshed back downhill and splashed the grass.

"Shit," whispered Kevin. He teetered forward and glanced down into the open filler cap of the bulk tank: more than half full, not full enough.

The lamprey-things were both circling in the soft soil of the lawn, their gray-and-pink backs arching like some caricature of the Loch Ness Monster. Kevin heard a door slam and wondered if it were his father or mother, looking out the door at the southeast corner of the house, staring above the whipping treetops at the wall of storm. He hoped not. Two steps onto the lawn would show them the lamprey-things circling; another two steps and they would see the truck pulled onto the north drive.

"Stay here," he shouted and let himself slide down the curved side of the tank, bouncing off the metal ledge above the left rear fender with the longest leap he could manage.

He hit and rolled near the open end of the hose. It was sucking air now, the centrifugal pump still working. Kevin started to lower it back into the underground fuel tank.

"Look out!"

He swung to his right and saw both of the lampreys rushing toward him, tearing through the sod as fast as a man could run.

Kevin dodged behind the truck, sweeping the hose around instinctively. But the movement of his right hand on the switches was not instinctive, merely an act that seemed to precede the mental command.

The first lamprey was six feet from Kevin's feet when the pump reversed and the gasoline sprayed from the tanker onto the open maw of the thing. It dove into gravel. Kevin sprayed its back as it curled beneath the ground, pouring more gasoline into the hole when it had passed.

The second one had veered right and circled, and now it swept in. Cordie screamed just as Kevin raised the arc of gas fifteen feet out onto the lawn, soaking the front of the thing.

A stench of gasoline warned him that the first lamprey had surfaced behind him. Kevin jumped to the rear fender as the thing swept blindly past, mouth chewing at the left rear tires. He soaked it down, poured more gas into the hole it left.

With gas fumes rising all around, Kevin swung himself onto the back compartment of the truck, reached down to reverse the suction again, and took the chance of running to the underground tank opening and dropping the hose into it again. Fuel began to feed. *Another three or four minutes. Maybe less.*

He jumped for the fender from five feet out, knowing it was too far away but seeing the hump of the lamprey's back rushing under the truck. His feet hit metal, slipped, his knees struck hard, and Kevin's fingers clawed on the almost frictionless curve of the tank. He was falling backward to the broiling mass of flesh beneath him.

Cordie leaned far over, her right hand still on the filler cap above, and grabbed him by the wrist. His weight almost pulled her off. She grunted. "Come on, Grumbelly, *climb,* goddamn you."

Kevin kicked, found a foothold on the chewed-up tire, and clambered up just as the lamprey-thing surged against the wheel again.

He lay gasping and wheezing on the top of the tank. If they rose and struck this high again, they'd have him. He was too tired and shaky to move for a moment. "They're soaked," he gasped. "All we've got to do is light them."

Cordie sat cross-legged, watching the things circle under the lawn. "Great," she said. "Y'all got a match?"

Kevin slapped his pockets for his father's gold lighter. He sagged, still clinging to the filler cap. "It's in my gym bag," he said, pointing to the small canvas satchel he'd carefully set on top of the gas pump ten feet away.

Harlen's flashlight beam joined Dale's.

Almost forty feet above them, perched on the railing of the third-floor level, Lawrence sat in a wooden chair that had two of its legs dangling over the long drop. Dale's brother looked tied into the chair, but the "ropes" appeared to be thick strands of the fleshlike material that hung like torn tendons everywhere. A strand of the material ran around Lawrence's mouth and disappeared behind his head.

Another strand, a thicker strand, formed a noose around his neck and ran up into the belfry . . . into the pulsing red egg-sac there.

The chair teetered on the overgrown railing. An adult figure was standing there, white arms holding the chair in place but none too steadily.

"Put your weapons down," ordered Dr. Roon, his voice as imperative as a whiplash. *"Now."*

"You'll kill us," Dale said through lips gone numb. He forced himself to lower the flashlight beam to Dr. Roon. There were other man-sized shadows moving in the cloakroom and dripping first-grade room behind the principal.

Dr. Roon smiled again. "Perhaps. But if you do not put the weapons down *now*, we will hang him this second. The Master would welcome another offering."

Dale glanced up. The third-floor landing seemed miles away. Lawrence was wiggling as if trying to free himself, his eyes wide. In the red-and-green glow from the belfry, Dale could see his brother's cowboy pajama tops. He wanted to shout at him not to move.

"Don't do it," whispered Harlen, leveling the .38 at Roon's long face. "Kill the motherfucker."

Dale's heart was pounding so loudly in his ears that he barely heard his friend. "He'll kill him, Jim. He really will."

"He'll kill *us*," hissed Harlen. "No!"

But Dale had already laid the Savage on the floor.

Roon stepped closer, almost within arm's length. "Your weapon," he said to Harlen. "Now."

Harlen paused, cursed, glanced upward, and laid his pistol on the sticky floor.

"The toys," said Roon, gesturing impatiently toward the squirt guns in their belts.

Dale started to lower the plastic weapon, turned the muzzle upward at the last second, and squeezed a long burst of holy water directly into Dr. Roon's face.

The ex-principal shook his head slowly, removed a handkerchief from his suitcoat's breast pocket, mopped his face, and calmly removed his glasses to wipe them. "You silly, silly boy. Just because the Master spent a thousand years in the center of such belief and still reacts to old habits, not all of us grew up in the land of Popery." He set his glasses back in place. "After all, *you* don't believe in this miraculously altered water, now do you?" He smiled and, without warning, slapped Dale viciously across the face. A ring on the principal's hand ripped a furrow from Dale's cheek to jaw.

Harlen shouted something and lunged for his pistol, but the man in the black suit was quicker, cuffing the boy on the side of the head with such force that the sound echoed up the open stairwell. Roon bent and picked up the pistol as Harlen fell to his knees.

Dale wiped blood from his cheek and saw the Soldier gliding through the dark beneath the stained-glass window. Something else, something taller and blacker, was moving on the library mezzanine above. Thunder was just audible through the thick walls and boarded-up windows.

Dr. Roon set his large hand on Dale's face, fingers and thumb digging deep into the boy's cheeks just below the eyes. "Set the radio toy down . . . slowly . . . that's good." He moved his grip to the back of Dale's neck and catapulted him forward, over the shotgun, squirt gun, and walkie-talkie lying in the thick syrup that had been a floor. Roon dragged Harlen with them and smashed the squirt gun as he passed, kicking the radio back toward the basement.

Stumbling to keep up, Roon's hands like vises on their necks, Dale and Harlen were shoved and pushed up the stairs to the second floor.

FORTY

I'll never get to it in time," Kevin shouted over the sound of the storm. It was only fifteen feet from the back of the truck to the gas pump and gym bag, but the lampreys were circling closer with each pass. He had seen how fast they could move.

Cordie's pale face was illuminated with every flash of lightning. She was smiling, her small mouth pursed. "Unless you got a whatchama-callit," she said. "A distraction."

Before Kevin could say anything, she had slid down the far side of the tank and jumped to the gravel drive, running downhill toward the street for all she was worth.

The lampreys swung left and accelerated after her like sharks sensing blood in the water.

Kevin slid down the tank and leapt off the left rear fender, grabbing the satchel and heading back toward the truck just as the hose started sucking air in the empty underground tank. Instead of clambering onto the back of the truck, Kevin swept around in a circle, picked up the walkie-talkie, and jumped for the cab.

Downhill, Cordie had reached the asphalt of Depot Street two yards ahead of the first lamprey. It drove deep as she staggered into the center of the street and stopped, jumping up and down and waving her arms at Kevin. He couldn't hear her shouts for the thunder.

Smart, he thought, but at that second one of the lamprey-things broke surface on the far side of the street and used its momentum to slide across the asphalt surface like a trained porpoise sliding out of a pool onto wet cement.

Cordie threw herself aside, the mouth missing her by inches, and went down hard, kicking and scraping her heels to crawl away from the writhing thing. At least twenty feet of the lamprey's body was out of its hole now.

Kevin pawed through the gym bag, removing the lighter he'd told her about and the truck keys he hadn't. The engine started on the first try. Kevin had a fleeting thought of all the gasoline he'd been spraying around, of the eleven or twelve hundred gallons sloshing in the uncapped tank behind him and the stuff still dribbling from the hose . . . thinking of the ignition spark he was putting into the middle of this vaporous mixture. *To hell with it,* he thought, feeling the adrenaline filling his body like some wild elixir, *if it goes I won't know about it.*

Cordie was pulling herself backward by her elbows and heels on dark pavement, kicking at the thrashing thing that still twisted to find her, its mouth expanding to twice the size of the body.

Kevin slammed the truck in gear and roared down the gravel drive, rolling right over the body of the thing, feeling the vibration coming up through the truck frame as if he had hit a massive telephone cable or something. Then he was out the door and pulling Cordie in while the lamprey began to unwind back into its hole like a hose on a tension reel, spraying fluid as it backed off the pavement.

Kevin stood in the open doorway, lighter in his hand, watching the thing slide past four feet away but knowing that the lighter flame would never last long enough in the wind to ignite the lamprey.

Cordie tore a three-foot swatch of her dress off and handed it to Kevin.

He crouched, wadding the old fabric into a ball, using the truck door as a windbreak. The dress had been half-soaked in gasoline itself and flared on the second strike of the lighter.

Stepping quickly away from the tanker, Kevin threw the mass of flaming material at the lamprey just as the maw of the thing slid off the asphalt.

It somehow sensed the wadded dress coming at it and made the mistake of catching it in its multi-flapped jaws. The front of the lamprey ignited with a geyser of flame, the gasoline catching in the folds of its ridges, blue flame running back along its segmented body seemingly at the speed of light.

Gasoline spilled on the street ignited with a *whoosh,* creating a long fuse that curled around toward the back of the tanker truck.

Cordie hadn't waited for it to catch up. She had scooted over behind the steering wheel as soon as Kevin was out the door and now she floored it, driving north along Depot and getting the rear of the truck out of the circle of spilled gasoline a second before it ignited.

Kevin shouted and ran alongside, pulling himself up onto the passenger side, finding the door bashed in and stuck there, and pulling himself in through the window, headfirst, legs flailing.

"Turn left," he gasped.

Cordie was just barely tall enough to reach the pedals and steer at the same time; as it was, she was half-standing behind the wheel, stretching her toe to the accelerator, elbows bobbing up and down as she managed the large steering wheel. The truck was roaring and surging in first gear.

The walkie-talkie squawked on the seat between them. The voice was Mike O'Rourke's.

"Mike," gasped Kevin, lifting the thing, "what are you doing with the . . ."

"Kev!" came the urgent voice of Mike O'Rourke. The sounds of screams and shots could be heard above the static crackling from the speaker. "Blow it! Now! Blow the goddamned place!"

"You have to get out!" Kevin shouted into the walkie-talkie as Cordie manhauled the wheel left, sending them screeching down the long sidewalk toward the north door of Old Central. They bounced over stones and tilted sidewalk slabs. Fifty feet out, the second lamprey broke the surface and rushed to intercept them.

"Blow it, Kev!" screamed Mike over the walkie-talkie. His voice was wilder than Kevin had ever heard it. "Blow it *now!*"

The radio went dead, as if the other walkie-talkie had been destroyed.

Cordie looked at him, glanced left at the thing in the ground arching ahead of them, nodded once, showed gray teeth in a grin, and floored the accelerator.

Dr. Roon dragged Dale and Harlen up stairs that looked like a waterfall of melted wax, beneath the stained-glass window, which seemed to have grown a tapestry of fungus, under huge webs apparently made of sinew, past stalagmites of bone, below stalactites of what appeared to be fingernail material, up past the library mezzanine, onto the second-floor landing and into their regular classroom. The door was half its regular size and almost concealed by thin filaments of black hair that spouted from nodes in the walls. Roon shoved the boys through just before they would have blacked out from the terrible pressure of his grip.

The rows of old-fashioned desks were in the same place. The teacher's desk was where Mrs. Doubbet had left it. The portrait of George Washington was just as Dale remembered it.

Nothing else was the same.

A thick carpet of fungus had grown up from the bare-board floor and covered the desks in undulating folds of blue-green. There were bumps rising from most of the desks—soft curves like the heads of children hiding under blankets, the sharp angles of shoulders, the gleam of bare bones where fingers emerged from the carpet of algae and mold.

Dale choked as the foul air filled his lungs; he tried not to breathe, but finally he had to gasp in the miasma of decay or pass out.

He could barely see across the room for the hanging webs of tissue that covered the windows, filled most of the space between the desks and the twelve-foot-high ceiling, and clung to the walls in great, bulbous clusters. It looked like living muscle tissue; Dale could see veins and arteries through the moist, translucent surface. Occasionally something soft and fibrous shifted in the broader strips of tendon-web and eyes seemed to blink at the visitors.

Mrs. Doubbet and Mrs. Duggan sat behind the teachers' desk in front of the room. Both were erect, alert, and dead. Mrs. Duggan showed the effects of months in the grave. Something small and furtive moved in the socket of her left eye. Mrs. Doubbet looked as if she had entered the room alive quite recently, but her eyes were now filmed over with the thin cataracts of death, and the ligamentlike material grew from her body at a dozen places, connecting her to the chair and desk and walls and web. Her fingers twitched as Dale and Harlen stumbled in.

The class was assembled.

Harlen made a sound in his throat and turned as if to throw himself out the door.

Karl Van Syke came through the strands of hairlike filament where the door had been. For a second Dale thought that the Negro from Mrs. Moon's story had returned: Van Syke was totally black except for the pure white marbles of his eyes, but the blackness was from skin and flesh charred to a scaly caricature of a man. His chin and lower jaw were gone, most of the muscle of the arms and legs burned away, the fingers transformed to curled claws of bone that looked like some semiabstract sculpture of a man made from carbon. Pale liquids oozed from the interior of the thing. It turned its head toward the two boys and seemed to sniff the air like a hunting dog on a scent.

Dale grabbed Harlen and backed away until they were touching the first row of desks. Something shifted in the mound of fungus at their backs.

Tubby Cooke rose from a desk at the back of the room and stood standing there. The bloated fingers on his remaining hand were twitching like white worms.

Dr. Roon came through the door. "Take your seats, children."

Staring, consciousness skidding like a car on unseen ice, Dale moved to his regular seat and lowered himself into it. Harlen took his desk near the front . . . where the teachers could watch him.

"You see," whispered Dr. Roon, "the Master rewards those who do His bidding." He opened a pale hand toward the figure of Karl Van Syke.

The thing appeared still to be sniffing, feeling the air with bent fingers. "There is no death for those who serve the Master," said Dr. Roon, moving to stand next to the teachers' desk.

The Soldier and what once might have been Mink Harper came into the room, carrying the chair in which Lawrence sat still enmeshed in fleshy strands. His head was back and his eyelids were fluttering.

Dale started forward but stopped when the Van Syke thing circled in his direction, sniffing, feeling the air like a blind man. The white form that had been Tubby moved through the shadows behind Dale.

"Now, we're all ready to commence," said Dr. Roon, glancing at a gold watch he pulled from his vest. He looked up at Dale and Harlen and smiled one last time. "I suppose I could explain . . . tell you all about the wonderful Age which now begins . . . talk to you about what small inconvenience your little escapades have caused us . . . go into great detail of how you shall serve the Master in your new forms. . . ." He clicked the watch shut and set it back in his vest. "But why bother? The game is over and it is time for your part in it to end. Good-bye."

He nodded and the Soldier began gliding forward, legs not moving, arms coming up slowly.

Dale had tried not to look at the face of the Soldier and the other things in the room, but now he stared. The face was no longer even a simulacrum of humanity: the long snout looked as if it were the crater remaining after something had erupted from the elongated skull. There were other, deeper rents in the white flesh of the face. Smaller things moved in the orifices there.

The Soldier glided toward Jim Harlen while the black Van Syke felt its way toward Dale. Dr. Roon and the shredded thing that wore part of Mink Harper's face moved to block the doorway. Dale heard a creaking and soft groaning that seemed to come from the walls and floors, and the web of ligaments and nodes seemed to flush a deeper pink. Liquid dripped from the ceiling in viscous strands.

"Fuck this," said Harlen, getting out of his desk and backing up until he reached Dale. His lips were trembling almost uncontrollably as he whispered to Dale, "I knew I never liked school."

Together they leapt the first row of desks, wading through mounds of fungus toward the back of the room. The Soldier glided effortlessly to their right. The corpse of Tubby Cooke lowered its face to the algae and disappeared under it like a child crawling under its favorite blanket.

Dale and Harlen leapt to the top of adjacent desks, ducking their heads to avoid the pale egg-sacs above them. Mold clung to their jeans and sneakers in long strands.

Dr. Roon looked impatient and snapped his fingers. The entire building seemed to hold its breath as Van Syke and the Soldier crawled over the first row of desks.

Downstairs, there was the sound of a gunshot.

Mike had come into the central hall of the basement assessing his losses: the flashlight was broken, he had lost one of the squirt guns filled with holy water and smashed the second one when he had rolled on it coming out of the tunnel, his pants were ripped at the knees and soaked in the front and back—the squirt guns—and the only advantage of that, he thought, was that no vampire-thing was going to bite him in a crotch damp with holy water.

Despite the windowless basement, he found that he could see once his eyes adapted to the glow—both from the phosphorescence that seemed to be seeping from the walls and the brighter glow of the burning lamprey-thing in the central hallway.

Mike presumed it was dead. Its flesh was charred in a thousand places, embers burned where its entrails should be, and the maw had quit opening and closing. He presumed it was dead but he gave it a wide berth, creeping past against the wall, staring in some awe at the mass of debris the dying thing had shoved in front of it for the length of the base-ment hallway. Heavy clouds of smoke and the smell of burning fish rose from the carcass.

Mike decided to assess his resources as he climbed the sticky stairs to the first floor. He had Memo's loaded squirrel gun and four extra shells left; the rest had been fired or lost in the hasty exit from the tun-nels. He was bruised and bleeding and shaking from head to foot, but otherwise fine. Mike stepped over the shattered door into the main hall on the first floor of Old Central.

Mike had only a few seconds to stand blinking, taking in the changes that a few weeks of summer had wrought in the old school, staring up at the pulsing red sac of legs and eyes forty feet above him in the now-open belfry. He had taken a step and put his foot down on Dale Stewart's Sav-age over-and-under when a motion in the shadows froze him in the act of crouching.

Something was moving toward him from Mrs. Gessler's second-grade room, moving and making soft mewling noises. The sound had almost been lost in the sudden creaking and groaning of the building as the storm outside rumbled and whined.

Mike dropped to one knee, quickly raised the Savage, and tucked it under his left arm as he held the squirrel gun ready, barrel up.

Father Cavanaugh came out of the shadows, making soft noises that might have been attempts to speak. Its lips were gone and even in the faint light Mike could see the crude stitches where Mr. Taylor, the undertaker, had sewn the gums together. It might have been trying to say, "Michael."

Mike waited until it was seven or eight feet away and then lowered the squirrel gun and shot it in the face.

The blast and echoes of the blast were incredible.

The priest's remains were knocked backward across the resinous floor, the body rolling against the overgrown banister of the stairway while parts of the skull went elsewhere. Essentially headless, it rolled to its hands and knees and began crawling back toward Mike.

In a state of perfect calm, his body handling the motions while his mind dealt with other things, Mike shifted the squirrel-gun grip to his other hand, broke the breech of the Savage over-and-under, checked that the cartridge in it had not been fired, set the barrel of Dale's shotgun against the back of the priest-thing just as its fingers reached his sneakers, and pulled the trigger.

The obscenity that resembled his friend writhed on the sticky floor, its spine visibly severed, as Mike backed away, pulled two of his four remaining cartridges from his pocket, and loaded one in Memo's gun and one in Dale's. His foot touched plastic and he looked down to find the radio under his toe. He raised it, brushed the strands of goo from it, keyed the transmit button, heard the welcome static, and shouted into it.

Kevin answered after his third call.

Thank you, Sweet Jesus, prayed Mike. He said into the radio, "Kev! Blow it! Now! Blow the goddamned place!" He repeated the orders and then dropped the radio as he heard Dale's voice screaming from the second floor. Choosing the guns over the walkie-talkie, Mike bounded up the stairs as fast as he could climb.

The webs and node clusters and very walls were shaking and trembling around him, as if the school were a living thing on the verge of awakening.

Mike almost lost his footing and went down on the cluttered, sticky stairway, found his balance, and jumped onto the second-floor landing. The red light from above was growing stronger by the second.

"Mike! In here!" screamed Dale's voice from beyond a screen of black fibers where the door to Mrs. Doubbet's room once had been. There was a sudden growling as if a pack of starved dogs had been let loose.

Mike knew that if he hesitated two seconds he would never have the nerve to go in there. Cocking both weapons, he went through the opening low and rolling.

FORTY-ONE

The lamprey was going to beat them to the front door.

Cordie Cooke was doing her damnedest to steer the tanker in a straight line down the forty yards or so of sidewalk to the front door. One of the left rear tires sounded like it was shredding rubber and was making the rear end of the heavily laden truck veer and fishtail. Kevin alternated among pounding the dashboard, trying to raise Mike again on the walkie-talkie, and urging Cordie on.

The remaining lamprey reached the graveled spot near the north door, dove deep one last time, and reared up as the truck came bouncing down the last fifty feet of sidewalk toward it.

Kevin saw the flimsy boards on the stairs where Dale and Harlen must have thrown them, knew immediately that they couldn't hold the weight of the truck for a second, and then realized that they had to get the hell out of here. Impact was seconds away.

His door was jammed stuck.

Kevin spent only a second wrestling with it before sliding across the seat into Cordie, shoving her against the driver's door while fumbling across her lap for the door handle.

"What the fuck you think you're . . ."

"Jump! Jump! *Jump!*" Kevin was screaming, pounding against her. The truck slewed left but both Cordie and he grabbed the wheel and realigned it just as the lamprey came up out of the ground at them like some giant jack-in-the-box.

Cordie slammed the door handle and they both went out, hitting gravel hard enough to knock one of Kevin's side teeth out and break his wrist. The girl grunted once and rolled onto the grass unconscious as the truck and lamprey collided at forty-five miles per hour and the maw of the thing went through the windshield like a javelin.

Kevin sat up on gravel, arched his neck in pain as his right wrist gave way, hobbled on knees and his other hand to Cordie, and started dragging her backward just as the truck and unreeling lamprey struck the front porch.

It was not a straight shot after all. The truck's left front fender hit the concrete railing and smashed the cab sideways just as the first two steps stopped the front axle cold, collapsing what was left of the cab onto the lamprey as four tons of steel tank jackknifed vertically over the porch and speared through the boarded-up front doors.

The bulk tank was too wide. It crumpled like a giant beer can as it smashed wall and doorframe inward, throwing plywood splinters and eighty-four-year-old lathing sixty feet into the air. The body of the lamprey was jerked out of its hole like a snake in a coyote's teeth, and Kevin caught a brief glimpse of the segmented body being squashed flat against the door and frame.

The reek of gasoline filled the air as Kevin staggered another thirty or forty feet toward the line of elms with Cordie under his right arm. He had no idea where his dad's .45 or the gold lighter were.

The lighter.

Kevin stopped, turned, collapsed on the lawn, beyond worrying about the second lamprey.

The gasoline hadn't exploded. He could see the rivulets running from the shattered tank, could see the gas that had splashed the walls and was seeping into the interior, could hear the gurgling and smell the fumes. *It hasn't exploded.*

Damn, it wasn't fair. In the movies that Kevin watched, a car went off a cliff and exploded in air for no reason except the director's need for pyrotechnics. Here he'd just destroyed almost fifty thousand dollars of his father's livelihood, smashed four tons and a thousand gallons of gasoline into a tinderbox of a school . . . and nothing! Not a goddamned spark.

Kevin dragged Cordie another sixty feet from the wreck, propped the unconscious and possibly dead girl against an elm, ripped a long strip of cloth from the rags dangling from her, and headed back . . . staggering like a drunk, with no idea where the lighter was or how he'd find a flame or how he would get away alive if he did.

He'd think of something.

Dale and Harlen screamed warnings as they heard Mike on the stairs. The two boys were leaping from desk to desk, trying to stay a row away from the Soldier and Van Syke. The fungal growth and old corpses in the seats made it hard for the things to move between the desks. But the white lump that was Tubby emerged as a white hand groping for them, a white face rising from the mold at their feet.

Dr. Roon and Mink Harper moved to either side of the door, waiting for Mike. They were on him the second he rolled in the opening. Roon was too fast; he slapped the barrel of the over-and-under aside just as Mike pulled the trigger. Instead of taking the principal's face off, the blast severed a bit of web near the ceiling, bursting an egg sac and sending the entire mass of tendons and filaments writhing.

Mink Harper was not so fast. The thing used what fingers it still had to grasp Mike's right wrist, the remnants of the Mink-face began to elongate into a funnel, but Mike had time to cock the hammer, thrust the eighteen-inch barrel of the squirrel gun into Mink's belly, and squeeze the trigger. The body seemed to levitate, draping itself across one of the strands hanging between the light fixture and the Gilbert Stuart portrait of Washington. Immediately, the tendon-web began to flow over and into Mink's flesh. Mike fumbled in his pocket, felt the two remaining shotgun shells, tugged one out, dumped the used shell from the breech of the Savage, and slammed in the new shell.

Dr. Roon made a noise and wrestled the shotgun away with almost no effort. He kicked Mike in the head, the boy rolling away from the blow but not quite quickly enough, and lowered the Savage's sights toward Mike's unconscious face.

"No!" shouted Dale. He and Harlen were only a few steps away from Van Syke, leaping from desk to desk toward the waiting Soldier, but now he flung himself into space, over the Soldier's reaching arms. He hit Roon's shoulder and then the doorframe, rolling away as the shotgun deflected and fired. The blast struck the corpse of Mrs. Duggan square in the chest, shredding the last remnants of her burial dress and throwing her against the chalkboard. Slowly the twitching arms pulled the thing back toward its desk.

The body of Mrs. Doubbet began to stand, strands of the fleshy web parting with soft sounds. Its eyelids were flickering wildly over white orbs. Lawrence had come to in his chair and began pulling and tugging at his bonds as the teacher came closer.

Dr. Roon lifted Dale by the shirtfront and shook him. *"Damn you,"* breathed the man in Dale's face. He threw him headfirst through the door and stepped out after him.

The black form of Karl Van Syke bent low over Mike.

Jim Harlen had jumped to the first row of desks, trying to come to his friends' aid, but the bulky coils of rope still slung over his shoulders caused him to lose his balance for a second and he went down, grabbing at a thin web but merely succeeding in pulling it down with him as he fell into the fungus between the rows. The web was warm to the touch and it leaked.

Harlen shouted in defiance as the Soldier leaned over the row toward him.

Outside on the landing, Dale caught a last glimpse of his brother trying to shake free of the strands that bound him to the chair and then Dr. Roon was on him again, lifting him by the throat and carrying him toward the railing.

Dale felt his heels bang against the banister as Roon lifted him higher, holding him out over the twenty-five-foot drop, his fingers deep in the flesh of Dale's throat. Dale kicked and clawed and scratched at the man's face, but Roon seemed to be beyond pain. The man blinked blood out of his eyes and doubled the pressure on the boy's throat. Dale felt darkness closing in, his field of vision narrowing to a receding tunnel, and then he felt the entire building shake, Roon staggered backward with him as the entire landing vibrated like a raft on rough seas, and they were both rolling across old boards as the stink of gasoline filled the air.

Although dazed and suffering from a concussion, Kevin was trying to be scientific as he stumbled toward the wreck. One item of curiosity was why great crowds had not arrived after the incredible noise of the collision between truck and school. Kevin blinked up at the lightning, paused to listen to the overlapping peals of thunder, and nodded wisely. *Ah-hah.*

He went back to thinking scientifically. He needed a flame, a spark . . . what could ignite the gasoline? His dad's lighter would, but that was lost somewhere. Flint and steel would give him a spark. Kevin patted his pockets dully, but found no flint and steel. *What if I pound a rock against the steel tank until I get a spark?* Something about the idea did not seem quite right. Kevin set it aside as a contingency plan.

He staggered another twenty feet closer, bare feet splashing through puddles of gas now. *Bare feet.* He stared down bemusedly. Somehow he'd lost his shoes in the bailout. The gasoline was cold against his skin and it burned where he was scratched. His right wrist was beginning to swell now, and the hand hung limply and *wrong* beneath it.

Be scientific, thought Kevin Grumbacher. He stumbled back a few steps and sat down on a relatively dry patch of sidewalk to think about this. He needed a spark or a flame. What could give him those?

He squinted up at the storm, but the lightning did not take the cue to strike the tanker truck at that moment, although the jagged bolts of light seemed fierce enough. *Maybe later.*

How about electricity? He could crawl back into the cab and turn the key in the ignition, see if the battery would give a spark. From the smell, it would only take a spark.

No, that wasn't any good. Even from where Kevin sat sixty feet from the rig, he could clearly see the cab crushed and twisted under the weight of tank itself. And the cab compartment was probably full of smashed lamprey-thing.

Kevin frowned. Perhaps if he lay down and got a few minutes rest, the answer would come to him. The sidewalk looked very soft and inviting.

He moved a shiny stone aside and lowered his head to the cement. Something about the stone had not felt right.

Kevin sat up, waited for the next lightning flash to illuminate the night, and lifted his father's Colt .45 semiautomatic from the gravel. The grip was broken. There were scratches on the steel finish and the small front sight did not look right.

Kevin rubbed away the blood that was trickling into his eyes and squinted at the leaking bulk tanker twenty yards away. *Why did I do that to Dad's truck?* It didn't seem terribly important to answer that right now, perhaps later. First he had to create a spark or flame.

He turned the .45 over and over in his hands, making sure the barrel wasn't plugged with dirt and brushing away as much of the dust from the steel finish as he could. There was no way he was going to slide this back into his father's trophy box without him noticing that something had happened to it.

Kevin raised the pistol and then lowered it again. Had he racked the first round in already? He didn't think so; his father didn't like carrying around a "cocked and locked" weapon when they went target shooting together out by Hartley's pond.

Kevin set the pistol between his knees and racked the slide with his left hand. A cartridge ejected and rolled on the sidewalk, the lead slug clearly visible. *Damn.* He *had* loaded one. How many did that leave? Let's see, a seven-round magazine minus this one . . . the math was too difficult for Kevin right at the moment. Perhaps later.

He lifted the pistol in his left hand and aimed at the tanker. The lightning made the aim sort of tricky. *If you can't hit something literally bigger than a barn door, you'd better not even try.* Still, he was pretty far away.

Kevin tried to stand but found that it made him too dizzy. He sat down heavily. OK, he'd do it from here.

He remembered to push the safety slide off and then he aimed, frowning through the low rear sight. Did a striking bullet make a spark or open flame? He couldn't remember. Well, one way to find out.

The recoil hurt his good wrist. He lowered the automatic and stared at the tanker. No flame. No spark. Had he missed the damn thing? He lifted a shaking arm and fired twice more. Nothing.

How many bullets did he have left? Two or three. At least.

He sighted carefully at the circle of stainless steel and slowly squeezed the trigger just as his father had taught him. There was a sound like a ballpeen hammer striking boilerplate and Kevin grinned triumphantly. The grin changed to a frown.

No fire. No flame. No big boom.

How many more bullets did he have in here? Perhaps he should take the magazine out, remove the slugs, and count them. No, better yet, count the brass that had ejected onto the sidewalk. He saw two or three reflecting the wild light, but hadn't he fired more than that?

Well, he had at least one slug left. Maybe two.

Kevin raised a wildly shaking arm and fired again, knowing as soon as he squeezed the round off that he probably had shot so high that he'd missed the front of the school, much less the steel tank.

He tried to remember why he was doing this. It eluded him, but he knew that it was important. Something about his friends.

Kevin rolled onto his stomach, lay prone with the automatic braced on his damaged wrist, and squeezed the trigger, half expecting the hammer to fall on an empty chamber.

There was a recoil, the glimpse of a flash just below the shattered filler cap on top of the tank, and eight hundred gallons of the remaining gasoline ignited.

Dr. Roon had just gotten to his feet when the explosion blew the railing into a thousand pieces and sent a solid mushroom of flame billowing up the open stairwell. Roon stepped back against the wall almost calmly, glancing down with what appeared to be almost academic interest at the two-foot shaft of splintered balustrade that had pierced his chest like a stake. He set a tentative hand on the end of it but did not tug at it. Instead, he leaned against the wall and sat down slowly.

Dale had rolled up against the wall and covered his head with his arms. What was left of the railing was on fire, the bookshelves on the lower mezzanine had erupted into flames, the stained glass had melted and was running down the north wall, and every inch of the second-floor landing was smoking and charring beneath him.

Six feet away, Dr. Roon's pantlegs began smoldering and the soles of his shoes grew soft and shapeless.

In the open stairwell ten feet to Dale's left, the webs of pink flesh were flaming and melting like clotheslines in a burning tenement complex. The hissing of the soft material sounded like screams.

Dale stumbled through the smoldering doorway.

The classroom was on fire. The explosion had knocked everyone off their feet—living and dead alike—but Harlen had helped Mike to his feet and both boys were ripping at the bonds on Lawrence. Dale took time to sweep up Mike's squirrel gun from the floor and then joined them, pulling away the hardened strands from his brother's arms and throat.

Dale pulled Lawrence to his feet while Harlen tugged the chair away. Strands still remained, but Lawrence was able to stand and speak. He threw one arm around Dale, the other around Mike. He was crying and laughing at the same time.

"Later," shouted Dale, pointing toward the burning mass of desks and darkness where the Soldier and Van Syke had struggled to their feet. Tubby was in there somewhere.

Mike rubbed blood and sweat out of his eyes and fumbled the last shotgun shell from his pocket. He took the squirrel gun from Dale and loaded it. "Go on," he shouted through the smoke. "Get going. I'll cover you."

Dale half-led, half-carried his brother out onto the landing. Roon was gone. The edge of the landing was a wall of flame with bits of the web and egg sac falling in molten spheres from above.

Dale and Harlen staggered to the stairs with Lawrence between them. The library mezzanine and stairway below them was gone, replaced by a thirty-foot pyre of flames. It looked as if the stairway had collapsed all the way into the basement. The bricks glowed white hot.

"Up," said Dale. Mike backed out of the classroom and joined them as they moved quickly up the stairs to the next landing, then kept on going to the third floor that had been closed off for so many years.

There were hisses and screams from the "empty" high school classrooms up there . . . rooms that had lain in darkness and cobwebs for decades. The boys did not wait around to investigate.

"Up." It was Mike speaking this time, pointing toward the narrow stairs to the belfry. The boards smoked and charred underfoot as they climbed. Dale heard noises below which might have been the central stairway collapsing into the inferno below.

They came out onto the narrow catwalk that ran around the inside of the belfry. The boards were narrow and rotten and Dale looked down once, saw the flames licking up toward him from the floor fifty feet below, and he did not look down again.

Instead he looked straight out at the thing hanging from its web in the center of the belfry.

The bulbous, translucent sac may have been bell-shaped at one time. Dale thought he saw the mountings and fixtures for a bell where the thing had anchored itself with the most tendrils and web attachments. It did not matter.

What he saw now looked back at him . . . at all of them . . . with a thousand eyes and a hundred pulsing mouths. Dale sensed the thing's outrage, the total disbelief that ten thousand years of quiet dominance could end in such farce . . . but mostly he sensed its rage and power.

You can still serve me. The Dark Age can still begin.

Dale and Lawrence and Harlen were staring right at the thing. They felt the tremendous warmth touch them . . . not just the heat from the flames, but the deeper warmth at knowing that they could serve the Master, possibly even save Him through their service.

Together, legs moving as a creature with one mind, the three of them took two steps toward the edge of the catwalk and the Master.

Mike raised Memo's squirrel gun and fired into the egg sac from a distance of six feet. The sac ruptured and dribbled its contents, hissing, into the rising flames.

Mike tugged them back and used the gun as a hammer to bash out the rotted slats on the side of the belfry.

Cordie woke up in time to drag the unconscious Grumbacher back from the conflagration. The front of his clothes was blackened, his eyebrows were gone, and it looked as if the explosion had knocked him back some distance.

She pulled him back to the elms and slapped his face until his eyes flickered open. Together they watched the small figures crawl onto the roof of the burning school.

"Shit," said Harlen, sliding down a steep pitch of gable to the edge of the roof, "I think I saw this scene in *Mighty Joe Young.*"

They all stood at the south edge of the school roof, hanging on to whatever handholds they could find. It was at least four stories to the hard-packed gravel and cement walks of the playground straight below.

"Look at it this way," gasped Dale, hanging on to Lawrence while Lawrence clung to a fist-sized hole in the shingled roof. "At least you'll get to use your ropes."

Harlen had unwound the first of two twenty-five-foot lengths of rope. Parts of it were charred and it looked anything but safe. "Yeah," he said to himself, "but how?"

"Uh-oh," said Mike. He had been gripping the corner of a chimney and staring back the way they had come across the gable tops.

Behind them, a tall figure fought its way through the smoking belfry slats.

Dale couldn't make out anything except a black silhouette. "Is it the Soldier? Van Syke?"

"I don't think so," said Mike. "It must be Roon. I don't think the other things can move or act with their Master dead. They were like parts of a bigger thing." The boys watched as the dark figure disappeared behind a gable, moving toward them quickly. Mike turned and said quietly to Harlen, "If you're going to use that rope, I'd suggest you hurry."

Harlen had tied a slip knot and now made a lasso. "I could rope that branch out there, we could swing out and down."

Dale and Lawrence and Mike stared at the high branches of the elm. They were at least thirty feet away and much too thin to hold even one of the boys.

Behind them, the figure reappeared along the central roofline and followed the same path to the south gable that they had. Smoke billowed from between the old shingles, half-obscuring the form, but Dale thought that he could make out Dr. Roon's black suit and bloodied features.

The heat from the burning north end of the building was terrible. The boys had to turn their faces away as the entire belfry went up.

"Hey," said Lawrence. "Look."

Two or three miles away, illuminated by the wild strobes of lightning, a tornado had lowered itself from the black clouds whirling out of the southwest, the funnel rising and falling. For a long second the boys simply stared. Dale found himself silently urging the twister on, inviting it to come their way and finish everything here in a final maelstrom of destruction.

The tornado rose, dipped behind trees and fields far to the east, touched down somewhere beyond the town, and whipped away into the darkness toward the north. The wind suddenly rose as the storm front passed, pelting the boys with leaves and branches and threatening to pry them loose from their perch on the eave of the roof.

"Give me that," Mike said to Harlen. He took the rope, retied the knot, looped it over the four-foot chimney, and slid down to the edge to link the two lengths of rope together with quick, sure knots. He finished, tugged to test the rope, tossed the end over the eaves, and said, "You first," to Dale.

They could hear the dark figure scrabbling across shingles on the other side of the gable behind them.

Dale did not argue or hesitate. He swung onto the edge of the gutter, saw nothing but air beneath him, got his legs around the rope, and lowered himself over. He swung slightly at the overhang, feeling how flimsy the rope was.

Harlen helped lower Lawrence onto the rope and the two brothers started shinnying down, Dale acting as a brake for the smaller boy. He felt his hands beginning to tear and chafe.

"Go," said Mike. He was looking up the steep roof toward the gable, but Roon had not yet appeared.

"My arm," Harlen said softly.

Mike nodded and stepped to the edge. Dale and his brother were

twenty feet down and still descending slowly. The rope did not go all the
way to the ground but Mike couldn't tell how close it came.

"We'll go together," said Mike. He stood and pulled Harlen's arms
around him from behind. "Hang on to me. I'll worry about the rope."

Dr. Roon came over the smoldering gable, moving on all fours like a
spider with missing legs. A piece of shattered railing still protruded from
his chest. He was gasping and growling, mouth open very wide.

"Hang on," said Mike, swinging Harlen and himself over the edge.
The entire rooftop was smoldering and smoking; the fire had reached the
attic. The chimney itself must be very hot against the rope, Mike knew.

"We'll never make it," Harlen gasped in his ear.

"We'll make it," said Mike, knowing that they wouldn't have time to
lower themselves far before Roon reached the overhang above them. *All
he has to do is cut the rope.*

Below them, Dale and Lawrence reached the end. They were still at
the top level of the first-story window, at least fifteen feet from the ground.

"It's nothing," whispered Lawrence. "Do it."

They both let go at the same second, hitting and rolling in the loose
sand of the playground near the slide. It was nothing.

They stood on shaky legs and ran back from the flames erupting
from windows and the south door. Dale shielded his eyes and looked up
at the outline of the two boys against the bright brick. They were halfway
down, still thirty feet from the ground, with Harlen clinging to Mike's
shoulders for all he was worth.

"Go! Go!" the brothers screamed at Mike as a dark figure appeared
at the edge of the roof.

Mike glanced up, wrapped his arms and legs around the rope so
that it wound around the inside of his arm and between his ankles, whispered "Hang on" again to Harlen, and let himself slide, the rope whining between his palms.

Dale and Lawrence watched in horror as Roon seemed to hesitate at
the edge of the roof, glanced back up at the flame rising from the gable
itself now, and then quickly looped a coil of rope around his wrist. Moving like a black spider, Roon lowered himself over the eaves above Mike
and Harlen. He began to descend quickly.

"Oh, shit," whispered Lawrence.

Dale pointed and began to scream at Mike. Above the overhang,
where neither Mike nor the rapidly descending Roon could see, the roof
suddenly burst into a thousand discrete points of flame—like a piece of
film acetate suddenly browning, melting, and burning through, Dale
thought—and the long south gable collapsed inward with a shower of

sparks that filled the sky. The old chimney stood by itself for a second, a brick tower in a geyser of fire, but then toppled inward.

"Jump!" screamed Dale and Lawrence in unison.

Mike and Harlen fell free the last six or eight yards, landing hard and rolling in the deep sand.

Above them, the descending form of Dr. Roon was suddenly tugged upward as the rope jerked tight around its wrist. He threw his free arm out in the last second before he struck the overhang of the burning eave, was dragged above it, and disappeared into the firestorm, looking for an instant like a thrashing insect on a string being tossed into the flames of a campfire.

Dale and Lawrence rushed forward, arms raised against the heat, and dragged Mike and Harlen out past the playground equipment, into the ditch on the edge of School Street. The four of them watched as Kevin and Cordie made a wide circle of the burning, collapsing school to join them there.

Without warning, the streetlights and houselights of Elm Haven snapped on. The children huddled together, Cordie ripping the last of her dress into strips and wrapping them around Mike's bleeding hands. None of them thought it odd that she stood there in her gray slip, nor that Kevin was barefoot and bleeding, nor that the other four boys looked like chimney sweeps in sooty rags. Suddenly Lawrence started giggling and they all laughed until they cried, holding each other and pounding each other on the back.

Then, as the laughter died away before it turned to tears, Mike was whispering something, tugging Kevin close. "You heard somebody stealing your dad's truck," he gasped between coughs. He had inhaled too much smoke. "You called us on our toy walkie-talkies, we tried to catch up to it. We thought we saw Dr. Roon driving. Then it hit the school and the fire started."

"No," said Kevin dully, rubbing his temple, "that's not the way it happened . . ."

"*Kevin!*" said Mike, grabbing the boy's sooty t-shirt with a bloody hand and shaking him.

Kevin's eyes cleared. "Yesss," he said slowly. "Someone was stealing dad's truck. I went out to chase him."

"We couldn't catch up," said Dale.

"Then the fire started," said Lawrence. He squinted at the blaze. The roof had fallen in completely now, the belfry was gone, the windows had burned away and the walls were falling in. "And boy did it start."

"We don't know who or why," coughed Mike, sagging back onto the grass. "We tried to get the guy out of the truck and we got all messed up like this. But we don't know anything else."

Two distinct sirens began to wail—the civil defense siren on the bank warning of a tornado that had already passed, and the higher, shriller siren on the volunteer fire department half a block south. Headlights appeared on Second Avenue and Depot Street and they heard the sound of heavy trucks approaching. People appeared on the sidewalks and street-corners.

Supporting one another in clusters of twos and threes, their shadows thrown far across the playing fields by the rising flames of the burning building, the six children walked back toward the welcoming lights of the houses where some of their parents waited.

FORTY-TWO

On Friday, August 12, 1960, the *Echo* communications satellite balloon was successfully launched from Cape Canaveral.

That afternoon, Dale and Lawrence and Kevin and Harlen and Mike rode their bikes out to Uncle Henry's and Aunt Lena's where they hiked the back pastures and spent hours digging for the lost Bootleggers' Cave back along the creek. It was very hot.

Cordie Cooke appeared shortly before dinner and watched them dig. Her family had moved back to their home along the Dump Road, and kids in town had commented on how much time she spent with Mike and the others these days.

The digging was slow. Harlen's new cast had come off almost two weeks earlier, Kevin's smaller cast a week after that, but both boys favored those arms and all of the boys except Harlen had healing scabs on their palms. They handled the shovels and spades carefully.

Amazingly, just before dinnertime—Dale's and Lawrence's folks' station wagon had just pulled in the drive a quarter of a mile away and honked at them—Mike's shovel broke through into darkness.

Old, cool air swept out of the ten-inch hole they had opened into the hillside. Always optimistic, Lawrence had brought a flashlight along. They widened the hole a bit and played the flashlight beam inside.

It was no mere gopher hole. An entrance shaft littered with dusty bottles and other hasty filler material appeared to open to a wider, deeper space beyond. The boys could see dark wood that might have been a crate or the edge of a bar. A dark curve was certainly an old tire, possibly a wheel still on a Model A entombed there just as Uncle Henry had always said.

The boys started digging away at the hole, enlarging it, tossing clods and stones downhill toward the creek, when suddenly they stopped as by silent consensus. Cordie looked up from where she was sitting in the shade across the creek. Her new jeans from Meyers' Dry Goods looked crisp and stiff on her. She brushed dust off her saddle shoes.

Mike pulled the shovel back and looked at the other four boys. "It's real," he whispered. He set the shovel down and rubbed his lower lip. "But there's no hurry, is there?"

Kevin leaned on his short spade and ran a hand through his crew cut. The scar on his temple near the hairline was small and white and almost invisible. "I don't see why there should be any hurry," he said. "It's been there thirty-some years. It can keep."

Dale nodded. "Uncle Henry really wouldn't want all those people and reporters and tourists and stuff swarming around here. Not now. Not with his back still healing and all."

Harlen folded his arms. "I don't know," he said, looking from face to face. "There might be something valuable in there."

Lawrence shrugged and grinned. He had been clawing wildly at the dirt, working hard to open the entrance tunnel wider. Now he pushed some of the dirt back in place. "Don't you get it, Jim? It'll always be there. It's not going anywhere. If the stuff is worth something now, think of how much it'll be worth if we come back in a few years and dig it up." He started pushing more earth back over the foot-wide opening. "It'll be our secret," he said, grinning at them and setting his glasses higher on his small nose. "Just ours."

They worked to conceal the tunnel with as much effort and enthusiasm as they had shown in finding it. They filled it in, tapped the dirt down, returned heavy stones to their original places by dragging them back uphill, set sod and bushes back in place, and even moved a root back that they had laboriously pulled aside. They stood back to admire their handiwork for a moment—it looked raw now, but in a week or two it would be grown over again—by autumn no one could tell that they had ever dug here.

Then they started up to the house for dinner.

Mike paused on the cow path up the hill and looked at Cordie, still sitting on the opposite hillside and stripping leaves from a branch. "Coming?" he said.

"Boys," she said, shaking her head. "When God didn't have no more parts for smart, he made dumb."

They waited in the long shadows of the hillside while she crossed a log across the creek and climbed to catch up.

The investigation into the strange events of the week of July 10–16 had gone on visibly for weeks and were still going on, although elsewhere and out of sight and at a much less urgent level now.

The central event turned out to be the disappearance of Mr. Dennis Ashley-Montague and his servant. When the limousine was found at Bandstand Park long after midnight on the night of the fire, abandoned, the Free Show projector still throwing a blank rectangle of white light onto the side of the Parkside Cafe, the Sheriff's Department, the Oak Hill police, and eventually the FBI had become involved in the manhunt. For weeks, FBI men in tight black suits, skinny black ties, and polished black Florsheims had been seen walking the streets of Elm Haven, hanging around the cafe, and even drinking Pepsis in Carl's and the Black Tree—"blending in" and picking up local gossip.

There was enough local gossip.

There were a million theories to explain the theft of Ken Grumbacher's truck, almost certainly stolen by Dr. Roon, the former principal, the fire, the grave-robbing of several bodies from Mr. Taylor's funeral home, and the disappearance of Elm Haven's patron millionaire. Rumor had it that forensic experts had found not just the bones of Dr. Roon and the missing corpses in the collapsed ruins of Old Central, but had found the shards of enough bones to make one think the school had been in session when the building burned. Some days later, word in the barbershops and beauty salons was that tests had shown that many of the bones were old, quite old, and more theories centered around the strange behavior of Calvary Cemetery's former groundskeeper and the school's custodian, Karl Van Skye. Mrs. Whittaker had it on good authority from her cousin in the Oak Hill police department that Mr. Van Syke's gold tooth had been found in a charred skull amidst the ruins.

Ten days after the fire, on the same day that wrecking cranes came to knock in the last of the charred brick walls, and bulldozers arrived to load the bricks into dump trucks and fill in the surprisingly deep basement of Old Central, word in the Parkside Cafe and on the party lines was that the FBI had made a breakthrough in the case. It seems that the 1957 black Chevrolet belonging to Justice of the Peace Congden had been seen on Grand View Drive, near Mr. Ashley-Montague's mansion, on the day J.P. was reportedly killed, four days before the fire in the grain elevator and five days before the Old Central fire and the disappearance of the millionaire. Mr. Caspar Jonathan ("C.J.") Congden was wanted for questioning by the FBI.

Jim Harlen may have been the last person to see C.J. in Elm Haven—
Harlen saw the sixteen-year-old peeling rubber toward the Hard Road
in his Chevy just after ten A.M. on the morning that the rumor of his being wanted for questioning came up. He did not return.

Kevin told the police, the Sheriff's Office, the FBI, and his father the
story about he and Harlen awakening to the sound of the generator running and coming out just in time to see the truck being driven away. Neither boy knew for sure what made the driver swerve toward Old Central.

Several days after the fire, it was the sheriff who found pieces of
metal in the wreckage with .45 caliber slugs in them. Kevin subsequently
confessed that when he saw the truck being stolen, he had run in and
grabbed his father's .45 and fired several shots after it. He didn't think
that was what caused the driver to lose control, but he wasn't sure.

Ken Grumbacher shouted at his son for such irresponsibility and
grounded him for a week, but seemed quietly proud of his boy's actions
when discussing them with the other men over morning coffee or while
transferring milk to the new bulk tanker. The truck had been adequately
insured.

All of the other kids—except perhaps Cordie Cooke, who blended
into the darkness later that night while the town was watching the fire
department lose to the fire, and who was not seen again for more than a
week—were questioned by parents and police. Mike's and Dale's and
Lawrence's parents were shocked that their children had received burns
and scratches in trying to pull open the jammed door of the truck before
it exploded, trying to rescue the driver, whose identity they were not
certain of. Jim Harlen stayed with the sheriff that Saturday night, and
his mother was properly shocked and impressed by the report of her
son's actions when she arrived home from Peoria the next morning.

Mike's grandmother, Memo, did not die. Instead she began showing marked improvement, and could whisper a few words and move her
right arm by the second week in August. "Some old people, they put up
good fight," was the prognosis of Dr. Viskes. Mr. and Mrs. O'Rourke
spoke to Dr. Staffney about finding specialists to oversee therapy needed
for her full recovery.

The week after the fire, the boys started playing a lot of baseball
again—sometimes ten and twelve hours at a stretch—and it was Mike
who went to Donna Lou Perry's house to apologize and ask her to join
them again as pitcher. She slammed the door in his face, but her friend
Sandy Whittaker began playing with them the next day, and soon after
several of the more athletic girls showed up for the morning choosing of
sides. Michelle Staffney turned out to be a fairly decent third baseman.

Cordie Cook did not play baseball, but she went for hikes with the boys and often sat silently with them while they played Monopoly on rainy days or just hung around the chickenhouse. Her brother Terence was officially listed as a runaway by the County Sheriff's Office and the State Highway Patrol. Mrs. Grumbacher took an interest in helping the Cooke family after it was determined that Mr. Cooke was gone for good, and several other ladies in the Lutheran Care Society made visits to the Cooke house with food and other items.

Father Dinmen came down from Oak Hill to say Mass only on Wednesdays and Sundays at St. Malachy's, and Mike continued as altar boy, although he thought he might quit in October when the new priest was scheduled to be assigned to the diocese.

The days passed. The corn grew. The boys' nightmares did not disappear altogether, but they became less troublesome things.

The nights grew slightly longer each day, but seemed much shorter.

Mr. and Mrs. Stewart had come out to Uncle Henry's for steak dinner, and they had brought the O'Rourkes and the Grumbachers. Harlen's mother arrived later with a gentleman friend whom she was "seeing regularly" now. The man, named Cooper, was tall and quiet and actually looked a bit like the actor Gary Cooper, except that his front teeth were a bit crooked. It might have been why he rarely smiled. He gave Harlen a Mickey Mantle glove during the last weekend's visit and had smiled his shy smile when they shook hands. Harlen still wasn't sure about him.

The kids ate on the deck over Uncle Henry's garage, eating their steak on paper plates and drinking fresh milk and lemonade. After dinner, while the grown-ups talked on the patio out back, the kids made for the hammocks on the south end of the deck and stared at the stars.

During a lull in their conversation about extraterrestrial life and whether kids on planets around other stars would have teachers or not, Dale said, "I went out to see Mr. McBride yesterday."

Mike put his hands behind his head and rocked his hammock out over the railing. "I thought he was moving to Chicago or somewhere."

"He is," said Dale. "To be with his sister. He's already gone. I caught him Tuesday, right before he left. The house is empty now."

The five boys and a girl were quiet for a moment. Near the horizon, a meteorite streaked silently. "What'd you talk about?" Mike said after a while.

Dale looked at him. "Everything."

Harlen was tying his shoe and still rocking in his hammock. "Did he believe you?"

"Yeah," said Dale. "He gave me all of Duane's notebooks. All the old ones with the stuff he'd been writing about."

They were silent for another period. The soft conversation from the adults somehow blended with the cricket sounds and noise from the bullfrogs down by Uncle Henry's pond. "I know one thing," said Mike. "I'm never going to be a farmer when I grow up. Too much work. Construction maybe, working outside's OK, but never a farmer."

"Me neither," said Kevin. He was still chewing on a radish. "Engineering school for me. Nuclear engineering. Maybe I'll serve on a sub."

Harlen swung his legs out over the railing and rocked his hammock. "I'm gonna do something that makes me a lot of money. Real estate maybe. Or banking. Bill's a banker."

"Bill?" said Mike.

"Bill Cooper," said Harlen. "Or maybe I'll be a bootlegger."

"Whiskey's legal," said Kevin.

Harlen grinned. "Yeah, but there are other things that aren't. People always pay a lot of money for things that make them stupid."

"I'm gonna be a big-league ballplayer," said Lawrence from where he sat on the railing. "Probably a catcher. Like Yogi Berra."

"Uh-*huh*," four of the boys said in unison. *"Sure."*

Cordie was also on the railing. She had been looking at the sky, but now she stared at Dale. "What y'all gonna be?"

"A writer," Dale said softly.

The others stared. Dale had never suggested anything of the kind before. Embarrassed, he brought out one of Duane's notebooks that he'd been carrying in his pocket. "You should read this stuff. Really. Duane spent hours . . . *years* . . . writing down this stuff about how people look and what they say and how they walk . . ." He paused, hearing how silly he sounded but not caring. "Well, it's like he knew exactly what he was going to be and how long it'd take him to get ready to be it . . . years of work and practice before he could even *try* something as hard as a story . . ." Mike touched the notebook. "It's all in here. In all his books."

Harlen squinted at him, dubious. "And you're going to write Duane's books? The books he would've written?"

"No," said Dale softly, shaking his head. "I'll write my own stories. But I'm going to remember Duane. And try to learn from what he was doing . . . what he was teaching himself . . ."

Lawrence seemed excited. "You gonna write about all the real stuff? The stuff that's happened?"

Dale was embarrassed, ready to end this part of the conversation. "If I do, twitto, I'm going to describe just how big and flappy your ears are. And how tiny your brain . . ."

"Look!" interrupted Cordie, pointing to the sky.

They all raised their eyes to watch Echo move silently across the sky.

Even the adults stopped in their conversation to watch the small ember of the satellite move between the stars.

"Gosh," whispered Lawrence.

"It's way up there, ain't it?" whispered Cordie, her face strangely soft and glowing in the starlight.

"Just where and when Duane said it'd be," whispered Mike.

Dale quietly lowered his head, knowing that the satellite—like the Bootleggers' Cave, like so many things—would be there tomorrow night and the day after, but that this moment, with his friends around and the night soft with summer sounds and breezes, and the voices of his parents and their friends just beyond the house, and the sense of endless summer days that August brought—that this moment was only for now and must be saved.

And while Mike and Lawrence and Kevin and Harlen and Cordie watched the satellite pass over, their faces raised in wonder at the bright new age now beginning, Dale watched them, thinking of his friend Duane and seeing things through the words that Duane might have used to describe them.

And then, knowing instinctively that such moments must be observed but not destroyed by observation, Dale joined his friends in watching as Echo reached the zenith and began to fade. A minute later they were arguing baseball and shouting at each other about whether the Cubs would ever win another pennant, and Dale was only slightly aware of it as a warm breeze blew across the endless fields, rustling the silk tassels on a million stalks of corn as if promising many more weeks of summer and another hot, bright day after the short interlude of night.